MW01269120

The Justice Tapes

A Novel

Herbert Beigel

LP

Lightsway Publishing
Tucson, Arizona

Published in the United States by Lightsway Publishing
38327 S. Arroyo Way
Tucson, AZ 85739

Print ISBN: 978-0-9851308-2-4

E-Book ISBN: 978-0-9851308-0-0

Library of Congress Control Number: 2015942725

Printed in U.S.A.

First Edition

19 18 17 16 15   10 9 8 7 6 5 4 3 2 1

Cover design by Kim Marie Webb
Interior design and production by Dovetail Publishing Services

The Justice Tapes is a work of fiction. All of the incidents and characters, except for a few public figures incidental to the story, are figments of the author's imagination, and any resemblance to persons living or dead is purely coincidental.

For Kim Marie,
My Wife, Lover, Friend
And Muse.

"We have been happily borne—or perhaps have unhappily dragged our weary way—down the long and crooked streets of our lives, past all kinds of walls and fences made of rotting wood, rammed earth, brick, concrete, iron railings. We have never given a thought to what lies behind them. We have never tried to penetrate them with our vision or our understanding."
—Alexander I. Solzhenitsyn

"Laws are not made for the good."
—Socrates

"I say that you cannot administer a wicked law impartially."
—Nathan Douglas; Harold Jacob Smith

"Whose law? We're on our own here. We can make our own law."
—Talbot Jennings, Jules Furthman, Carey Wilson

"Distrust all in whom the impulse to punish is powerful."
—Friedrich Nietsche

DRAMATIS PERSONAE

The World of the Lawyer

???, Lawyer	name and current residence unknown
Rachel???	daughter of lawyer
Samuel ("Sam") Brandt	Boston lawyer
Molly Marie Brandt	Sam's wife
Erin Brandt	Sam's daughter
McKinley Washington	stock clerk
Patrick	a bartender at Murphy's
Arthur Conklin	lawyer
Peter Varick	Boston federal prosecutor
Susan Gold	Boston federal prosecutor

The World of Cornelius Michael Sullivan

Cornelius Michael Sullivan	Belfast, Northern Ireland historian
Mary Catherine Sullivan	Cornelius's wife
Lucy Sullivan	Cornelius and Mary's daughter
Da	Cornelius Sullivan's father
Tommy Glynn	IRA activist
Bridget Glynn	Tommy's wife

The World of the Mafia

Salvatore Marinelli	New York restaurateur
Peter Marinelli	Salvatore's son
James Crosetti	Salvatore's driver and bodyguard
Vincente Marinelli	Salvatore's cousin
Danny Marinelli	Vincente's son
Carlito Gavencci	Boston
Whitey Delaney	Boston
Uncle	Boston
Kurt Hauer	Uncle's nephew
Eudie Lufman	bookmaker
Gene Lufman	lawyer and Eudie's son
Smith Corcoran	FBI agent

Others

Dr. Stephen Bamberger	psychiatrist
Arthur Conklin	lawyer
Albert	the lawyer's father
Sarah	the lawyer's mother
Jonathan	the lawyer's brother

A Note to the Reader

The most remarkable aspect of life is its uncertain course toward a certain end.

There was a time not too long ago, however, when I thought my future was set. A Dublin publisher had given me an advance to write a book on Irish Americans. This enabled me to take a sabbatical from teaching at Queens University, Belfast and to pay for a month long trip to New York City. There, I intended to interview recent Irish immigrants. Perhaps I would travel a bit.

During the weeks before my departure I vacillated about taking the trip. Mary and I had been apart only once in our twelve years of marriage and that for just two days when I joined a study group in Paris. Moreover, my father's condition had worsened. Were it not for Mary, who was a great believer in my work, I would have stayed in Belfast.

I arrived in New York on a late Sunday afternoon and took a cab to the apartment, a first floor studio on 51st Street near Second Avenue. I fell asleep on the couch and did not awaken until dusk. While unpacking I considered how to spend the evening. Then I saw the recorder at the bottom of the suitcase.

At the first Irish tavern I entered, the cacophony of boisterous patrons and metal rock music sent my teeth vibrating as if invaded by a dentist's drill. The bartender was flirting with several young women at the bar. I saw little hope of getting his attention and left.

I crossed Second Avenue to a tavern named Murphy's. The residue of cigarette smoke had all but darkened the windows. Though a sign beckoned the passersby with an offer of two drinks for the price of one, the tavern was nearly empty.

I sat on a stool in the middle of the bar. The bartender, about thirty, stood under a television fastened to the wall by a brass rack. He was dressed in a white shirt, bow tie, and black slacks; overdressed, it seemed, for the drab surroundings. He was picking at the oak counter, which had a long crack running along its length. A few stools to my left, a man lifted his empty glass. The bartender grabbed a bottle and brought it to him. I thought the man must be a regular, for the bartender smiled at him as he filled his glass.

I judged the man to be in his early fifties. His unruly white hair called to mind a university professor. But his expensive dark Italian suit, silk tie, onyx cufflinks, and gold watch were the attire of a businessman or professional.

The man slid his glass toward me. In a moment he was sitting on the stool at my side and speaking. His words, delivered in the rat-a-tat of a carnival barker, cascaded over me. As if by reflex, I reached in my pocket and turned on the recorder. And so my adventure began.

I have removed from the transcripts my comments and questions, although there should be no difficulty understanding what I said from his remarks. In my words—appearing in Italics—I have set down the other key events of my story, relating to the best of my ability what I was thinking at the time. I learned about the meeting described in the Prologue from a letter I received.

A final note: I never attempted to verify his stories. I know some will believe it is important to determine whether the cases he described are true, and they may of course investigate the public record. I do not share this view. As I later came to understand, the truth lies as much in what could be true as in what is true.

The court that hears all the evidence, without fear or favor and with justice as its watchword, is the court of history. In this court I, Cornelius Michael Sullivan, swear to tell the truth, the whole truth, and nothing but the truth, so help me God.

Cornelius Michael Sullivan
22 June 2000

PROLOGUE

*T*HREE MEN SIT AROUND A SMALL TABLE *in the rear of a Lower Manhattan restaurant. Another man leans against a wall covered by photographs of American cultural, political, and business icons: Frank Sinatra, Tony Bennett, Ella Fitzgerald, Marilyn Monroe, and Marlon Brando with bongo drums; former mayors of New York Fiorello LaGuardia, Robert Wagner, Edward Koch, and David Dinkins; real estate magnate Donald Trump, corporate raider Carl Icahn, and junk bond trader Michael Milken; sports figures Joe DiMaggio, Mickey Mantle, Muhammad Ali, and Dorothy Hamill. These photographs are not studio portraits; they are snapshots, capturing the owner as he greets his guests. Time, though it has changed them all, has had little effect on this gracious host. His white hair, craggy face, and wiry body have been a constant, and his easygoing manner has endeared him to friends and strangers alike.*

The owner looks around the dining room, proud of his restaurant's long history. Although less than an hour has passed since closing, the dining room is pristine. Tomorrow morning at eleven, his dedicated staff will set the tables with white linen, Haviland china, and Christofle flatware. At noon, another day of dining will begin.

They wait for the owner to speak first, an encomium due a man of respect. His diminutive stature and hunched shoulders belie his strength of will. His kind eyes and warm smile mask a life filled with violence and betrayal, from the murder of his mother, father, and three brothers to his present leadership of the New York Mafia. He remembers, as if it were yesterday, hiding beneath a cracked floorboard in the kitchen of his childhood home; listening to the agonizing death cries of his family; walking around the bloody bodies into the bedroom and retrieving his father's pistol from inside the lining of the mattress. He remembers shooting two of the murderers while they sat in the dining room of the third assassin's home, and how he raced into the bedroom where he encountered the last traitor fumbling with his jammed gun. The doomed man, only nineteen, cried out that the boy's uncle ordered the executions. His plea earned him a bullet through each eye.

As the owner surveys his domain, he sees a glass case on the wall near the entrance. The pistol is mounted next to a knife. He remembers his thirteenth

1

birthday—Easter Sunday—when, during the celebration in the town square, he sought out his uncle and, in front of his wife and children, garroted him with the knife while firing three bullets into his mouth with the pistol. Afterwards, he stood with his bloody hands raised in the air, defiantly displaying his uncle's intestines.

No wonder the owner believes in family. Before his wife became ill, she rarely left his side. In the early years she worked with him in the kitchen of the restaurant. Later, she served as hostess to the rich and famous who have graced the dining room for more than four decades. His grief at her passing was relieved by the honor his three sons have bestowed on him through their distinguished careers in medicine, engineering, and education. Yet, all is not as it should be. A fourth son languishes in a tiny cell at the Riker's Island Jail. He awaits word on his request for a new trial. The owner and the other men harbor no illusions about the outcome.

One of the men is a lawyer. He wears the professional's clothes: dark suit, white shirt, and lightly patterned red tie. Though a frequent patron for many years, his visits have declined since he gave up his law practice. He spends the day at home reading and basking in the love and devotion of his wife and daughter, a young woman the owner has met and would be proud to call his own.

The other man at the table is the same age as the lawyer, but his full head of dark brown hair and tanned face suggest someone ten years younger. He carries a gun beneath a Brooks Brothers black suit jacket with frayed lapels. The jacket is unbuttoned, the blue shirt and gray tie are stained with mustard, and the end of the oversized belt sways back and forth like a pendulum. The owner does not respect this man, but for the time being will tolerate him. He has worked with the devil's agents before; he will do so again.

The man leaning against the wall is tall with broad shoulders and a barrel chest. His eyes are alert and watchful. He too carries a gun. Since dropping out of Hunter College twenty years earlier to support his invalid mother, he has worked as driver and bodyguard for the owner. He will be forever grateful to the owner for all that he has done.

The owner begins the meeting by reviewing the plan. All save the man in the Brooks Brothers suit agree on the course of action.

"What is your objection?" the owner asks.

"We never agreed to murder," the man in the Brooks Brothers suit says.

The driver grunts. "What's this we shit?"

"He likes to refer to himself in the plural," the lawyer says.

The owner lights an unfiltered cigarette. "The traitor's fate is our business. You need only make sure that your colleagues will believe he is a fugitive."

"Not a problem."

"You must also make sure that the Boston police suspect nothing."

"Also not a problem. Those Mick cops won't investigate. They never do."

The owner notices the lawyer rubbing his chin. "You are not satisfied?"

"Lawyers are never satisfied."

The man looks at the driver but addresses the owner. "How do we know he'll testify?"

"You have my word," the driver says.

"No disrespect, but we're not worried about your word."

The driver takes a step forward, his shoulders pulled back. He is ready to act.

"Meaningless insults accomplish nothing," the owner says. *"It is enough you have my assurance."*

The lawyer continues rubbing his chin. "This fellow I'm supposed to meet. Sullivan. Are you sure he won't suspect anything?"

"He has no reason to suspect anything."

"I want your promise," the lawyer says to the man. *"You won't detain him."*

"Why do you care?"

"Because you don't."

The man's arms are twitching. "I can't make promises for the U.S. Attorney."

"You've been reassigned to the domestic terrorism unit."

"It's where the Bureau sends agents they don't trust."

"You'll be in charge of the investigation."

"Do not be concerned," the owner says to the lawyer. *"As long as you say nothing to this man Sullivan, he'll be no use to the authorities."*

The lawyer lights a cigarette.

What is the matter?" the owner asks.

"Suppose he figures out what's going on?"

3

The driver laughs. "Your job is to make sure he doesn't."

"You're giving too much credit to my gift of gab."

"You're a lawyer, aren't you?"

"It's risky. Two weeks of talking. I don't know."

The owner smiles. "Then we will execute our plan sooner."

"We can't. They won't change Patrick's shift until the morning of the twenty-second."

The man at the table pushes his chair away and rises. He pats the bulge in his jacket, as if to check for his wallet. The driver reaches for his gun. The owner grabs the driver's arm.

"Sorry," the man says. "It's a nervous habit."

"A habit you should break," the owner says.

"He's not the only one who has nervous habits," the lawyer says after the man has left. He paces around the dining room.

"Yours are not as dangerous," the owner says.

"I don't blame you for worrying," the driver says to the lawyer.

"I've known him for many years," the lawyer says.

"Then you know he's double crossed everybody he ever dealt with."

"He won't this time. Without your testimony, he's sunk."

"He also values his life," the owner says.

They walk through the dining room and out the door into the night air. A few buds on the Maple trees are ready to show their leaves, earlier than usual because of the record setting heat wave. The lawyer and the owner stand off to the side, while the driver gets into a limousine.

"Everything will be all right," the owner says to the lawyer.

"I guess I'm not supposed to care about a murder."

"You are not responsible."

"Is it really so simple?"

"Are your complicated legal rules better?"

"I'm done with the law."

"I have a question. The answer may be none of my business."

"Everything is your business."

"You are a successful man, but not one for whom success came quickly or easily. The lines on your face are too deep. Had you agreed, I would have put

your photograph on the wall. Yet, you have decided to leave the law forever. Why?"

"What I want to do for justice, the law won't tolerate."

"Ah, I could understand if he were your son. But he is my son."

"You know he's not the reason."

"The other one does not have your blood."

"Close enough."

"It is not too late to change your mind."

The lawyer shakes his head. He pulls from his pocket an empty cigarette pack, which he crumbles and tosses into a garbage bag on the sidewalk. "Let me have a cigarette," he says.

"You should carry a spare pack."

"It's a problem I have. I never keep anything in reserve."

The owner hands the lawyer a cigarette.

"What if Sullivan thinks I'm crazy and walks out on me?"

"There are other ways."

The lawyer's right eyelid flutters. "Damn," he says and presses his hand against the eye.

"Let me tell you a story," the owner says. "When I was a young boy, my father took me to Mount Aetna. He told me a monster lives inside the mountain. He said the steam rising into the sky means the monster is asleep. He said the monster had been sleeping for many years. It awakes only when angry, spitting fire and hot lava. I wanted to know what makes the monster angry. What makes anyone angry, my father said. Injustice. Then he told me the monster used to live inside another mountain, not far from the ancient city of Pompeii. Even in its sleep the monster observed the people of Pompeii treating each other with disrespect and worshiping wealth instead of love and friendship. One morning, the monster awoke from a long sleep. Its anger blew the mountaintop into the sky, burying Pompeii under ten feet of ash and dust. Only the animals survived. They had stampeded into the distant hills an hour before the eruption. Their sensitive ears had heard the monster stirring. I was shaking in terror, afraid when my father said we would walk to the summit and see if the monster was angry. I knew the monster would not be angry with my father; he was a good man who loved his wife and children.

But as we walked up the path, I thought of everything I had done in my short life and became very afraid. I clutched my father's hand. When we reached the mouth, the steam singed my skin. Sweat poured down my face and soaked my clothes. I cried the whole way down the mountain."

"Have you gone back?" the lawyer asks.

"Once."

"And?"

The owner laughs. "The monster slept like a baby."

"I should go there."

"No. There are other monsters and they live inside us, ready to awake when angered. Do not fear. The monster's fire is the fire of justice."

Book One

Samuel Brandt

CHAPTER ONE

May 10, 1998

DOES JUSTICE NEED A DEFENSE? You bet it does. The law and its army of lawyers have launched a devastating attack. Lawyers have made the law, not justice, their God. Yes, law is the enemy of justice. And like a jealous God, the law expects us to follow it without question. I spent twenty-nine years following the law. It's time for a change.

Have you read the novel *Remains of the Day*? An old butler devoted his life to serving a wealthy Englishman. The butler believes a life of service is an honorable life. After his master dies and the house is sold, the new owner encourages the butler to take a vacation. As the butler tours the country-side he learns that his master was an unprincipled and feckless man lacking morals and values, guided only by narrow-minded self-interest. Near the end of his trip the butler stops at a roadside park. He sits on a bench and reviews his wasted life. Not even a spectacular fireworks display lightens his mood. A stranger sits next to him. He sees that the butler is distressed. Enjoy what remains of the day, the stranger says. So here we are. I'll be the butler and you'll be the kind stranger. Together, we'll enjoy what remains of the day.

I convinced myself that I could discuss justice with other lawyers. I was wrong. If you try to discuss justice with a lawyer, you'll likely be met with the blank stare usually reserved for the fuzzy minded idealist. Lawyers pretend they're deep thinkers. In reality, they're masters of deception, hiding behind long forgotten Latin words, archaic phrases, and mangled English: res ipsa loquitor, assumpsit, pleading fraud with particularity, scienter, breaking the close, mutual mistake of fact or law, res, mens rea, motion for a more definite statement, interrogatories, requests for admissions, offer of proof, offer of judgment—the list is endless. These fancy words and phrases do serve a purpose: they give the law panache—the panache of a charlatan.

I know you didn't volunteer to be my sounding board, but I hope you'll lend me some of your valuable time. Why are you looking at me like that? There are stranger places to have an intelligent conversation, you know. Where am I anyway? Somewhere on Second Avenue in the Fifties? I wasn't paying attention. What's the name of this place? Mclennahan's, McInerney's, or Murphy's . . . oh, what's the difference? I'll tell you one thing; we don't have to worry about running into many lawyers. They prefer drinking at tonier locations. No, I'm not a bigot. I love the Irish.

The bartender gave me a dirty look when I ordered an Amaretto on the rocks. He was unhappy about having to open a bottle so covered with grime and dust the booze looked brown instead of maroon. I doubt he's ever served anyone Amaretto, because he charged me the same price he charged that other fellow in the suit for a glass of cheap bottled beer.

Today is my birthday. I'm fifty-four. You might be wondering why I'm alone on my birthday. Whatever guess you make would be wrong. Guesses should only be allowed on multiple-choice exams, and life is an essay question. But if you want to help celebrate my birthday, you'll listen to me.

Damn! No cigarettes. Excuse me. As Arnold Schwarzenegger said: "I'll be back." I'm in trouble. Obviously, you're satisfied with your dreams and don't need the movies. Arnold is a movie star, and . . . forget it.

I had heard that Americans are not only gregarious in pubs, but they also tend to wallow in self-pity. Nevertheless, I decided to stay. When he had reached for a cigarette, a black and white photograph fell out of his shirt pocket. A handsome young man with wavy black hair and a chiseled face is standing in front of a blackboard.

Handsome fellow, don't you agree. Albert was twenty-six. I inherited his eyes, a negligible amount of his intelligence, and none of his élan. I'm glad his picture interests you. I miss him. No, I don't know what the writing says. He studied at Oxford under John Galsworthy and became an English professor at the University of Vienna. He certainly looks grand. He was unaware the Anschluss was approaching. I like looking into the past. For any given moment, you know the future as well. Try it. Think back; then look forward from there. It gives you a rush.

If I'd known we would be talking, I'd have prepared an outline. But I should be able to manage without one. If you have to consult an outline before you can explain your life, you're in serious trouble. As a lawyer, I'm used to summarizing other people's lives. With you, I have an opportunity to do the same for myself. I don't expect you to judge me, but it would be nice if you'd raise your hand in approval whenever I make a good point. Lawyers are human. They appreciate a pat on the back.

You have an interesting face, long, lean, and unlined. No traumas in your life, I guess. Your mouth is straight. Each corner is the same distance from the center of your chin.

Recently, I was cleaning out my office and found my high school graduation picture. (Sarah, my mother, framed it along with every other physical representation of my childhood: letters I wrote from camp, report cards, bar-mitzvah photographs and pictures I drew in kindergarten. She was proud of me for what I did, prouder still for what I didn't do.) You can see the lines crossing my forehead like dried creek beds. My mouth is straight, though. Unfortunately, as I practiced law and talked from both sides of my mouth, it turned crooked.

I hope it's OK to start slowly. You'll learn the law as I did, in fits and starts, and understand how it has stampeded across the country, flattening justice everywhere.

I started my legal career in 1970. I was a Special Attorney for the Department of Justice, Organized Crime Section. Before you get too excited, you should know that every lawyer who worked for the Justice Department was a Special Attorney. There were no *general* attorneys. The same was true at the FBI. Every agent was a Special Agent.

"Organized crime" is a euphemism for the Mafia, a phrase invented to avoid offending Italians. The section consisted of eighteen field offices called "strike forces." I was assigned to the Boston—whoops, I mean the Chicago Strike Force—where I joined three other prosecutors and my boss, Assistant Chief Pete Varick, a farm boy from Bedford, Pennsylvania.

Pete believed in the law like others believe in love. He would do anything for the law. I felt the same way. Though I grew up watching TV shows about idealistic lawyers, like *Perry Mason* and the father and son team on *The Defenders,* I never believed that most defendants were falsely accused and didn't think it was a mistake to become a prosecutor. I changed my mind after the debacle called *United States vs. Eudie Lufman.*

At age fifty-five Eudie was enjoying the good life. He was jovial and carefree, confident his petty criminal activity fell well beneath the radar of federal law enforcement. And there was no need for him to worry about the Chicago vice squad, whose members he kept happy with generous monthly payoffs.

His sunny disposition matched his roly-poly frame, round face, and thick lips, as well as Santa Claus's tummy matches his laugh. But he was no Santa Claus, unless you think Santa Claus is more interested in receiving than in giving. He was the master of the spread, knowing with seemingly clairvoyant precision when to lay off bets and when to take them for his own account. And except for his stomach, he looked no more like Santa Claus than you or me. He hated the ever-present stubble of hair on his double-layered jowls, which he shaved twice, sometimes three times a day.

Eudie and his wife Esther had lived for thirty years in a small bungalow in Rogers Park, on Chicago's northside. They raised two sons, an aeronautical engineer and a lawyer. He had been an excellent provider for his family, early on establishing separate accounts to hold money he put away for his sons' education.

Eudie had run afoul of the law before. In 1937, he was a twenty-one-year-old high school dropout working at the Mafia controlled dry cleaners on Chicago's Mob infested Touhy Avenue. He quit and became a dealer in discounted alcohol tax stamps on the black market. He got away with it for a time and saved enough money for a dowry he planned to give Esther's parents. (The sincere but unsophisticated Eudie didn't realize a dowry runs from bride to groom.) His luck ran out in 1938 and he was arrested.

Eudie had given the dowry money to Lenny Patrick for safekeeping. Patrick controlled gambling on the north side and served as a tutor and mentor for whoever wanted to get into the gambling business.

It was still the Dark Ages of constitutional law and Eudie, not wanting to use the money he had given Patrick, stood trial without a lawyer. He was convicted and sentenced to a year in prison.

After his release, he married the patient Esther and they rented a base-ment studio near Patrick's office. He couldn't find a job but was too proud to let Esther ask her parents to return the dowry. While she worked in a bakery he hung around Patrick's office, earning a few dollars a week making deliv-eries. Then Esther got pregnant. She worked until her fifth month, when a series of infections forced her to bed. He went to Patrick for help. Pat-rick hired him to manage a numbers game in the hillbilly section of Chicago and later gave him the capital to start a bookmaking business. Eudie got along well with his customers and quickly increased his monthly take. Two months after the baby was born, they moved into a new home. Except for how he made a living, his was the model American family.

Eudie wasn't surprised when the cops raided his house. The head of the vice squad had tipped him off, explaining that "downtown" was under political pressure to clean up gambling on the north side. Eudie stored his gambling records in the hollowed out base of the old lawnmower he hadn't used in ten years and assured Esther the cops would wipe their shoes on the door-mat before entering.

In the front foyer a rookie cop grabbed a white pad lying on a tele-phone table. He noticed a series of numbers on the top sheet and assumed they represented bets Eudie had taken on the telephone. It was Betty Gor-don's telephone number, however. Betty was Esther's mahjong partner.

I hate the idea of searches. Who wants a law that allows the govern-ment to invade our homes at the stroke of a judge's pen, a judge who lacks either the means or the inclination to question the information in the appli-cation? We wouldn't need constitutional rights if the government stopped passing laws that sanction invasions of our privacy. We wouldn't fear the police if we gave them no laws to enforce. If I had the power, I would abolish all laws.

Was I in the presence of an anarchist, or a man who would say anything because he took nothing he said seriously? He lifted his glass with one hand and pushed forward my glass with the other. As the bartender poured me a Guinness and refilled his glass, I again had the feeling they were well acquainted. But why would the man mislead me? I did not care whether he was a long-term patron of Murphy's.

The vice squad cops searched the living room and den while the downtown cop went into the bedroom. He saw a small-caliber gun on a shelf in the headboard. Eudie produced a registration in his wife's name; he said he had bought the gun for her protection. The cop seized the gun anyway.

At headquarters, the senior vice squad officer submitted his report and gave the evidence clerk a plastic bag containing the note from the pad. The downtown cop filed his report together with a photograph of the gun and the registration. He gave the gun to the vice cop and instructed him to put it in the evidence bag.

The downtown cop was an informant for various federal agencies, including the Alcohol, Tobacco, & Firearms Division of the Treasury Department. As was his practice, he sent a copy of the report to Johnny Berger, his contact at the agency.

Johnny checked the registration; it seemed to be in order. He then ordered a copy of Eudie's criminal record. On it was Eudie's tax stamp conviction.

When Johnny walked into my office, I knew I was in trouble. I had heard that he was a "numbers man," office lingo for an agent who would press for an indictment no matter how trivial the crime. His idea for prosecuting Eudie was even less than trivial. He said Eudie had violated a recently enacted federal statute, which prohibited possession of a firearm by a convicted felon.

I went to see Pete. Although he agreed that on the scale of criminal behavior Eudie's crime ranked somewhere below a parking ticket, he said my duty was clear. I asked him what duty required me to prosecute Eudie for a crime that shouldn't be a crime. He said I had a duty to the law. He also said I had a duty to him. If we refused to bring a case a strike force agent developed, we'd have trouble obtaining cooperation on investigations we wanted pursued. I thought his logic was a bit strained; it smacked of extortion, with Eudie playing the victim. Then Pete came up with the argument that usually succeeds, particularly with someone insecure like me. "If you don't do it," he said, "I'll have to find someone else."

Not that indicting Eudie would be more embarrassing than other strike force cases. We indicted Harry the "hit man" Levine for making a false statement on a home mortgage application. He said that he was earning $100,000 a year managing a Laundromat owned by his wife's cousin. He waived his right to a jury trial and argued that his privilege against self-incrimination entitled him to hide what he did for a living. The judge agreed he had a constitutional right not to answer the question but also ruled that, once he answered, the law required him to tell the truth. Then the judge castigated Pete for wasting his time. He gave Harry probation and fined him a dollar.

We indicted a small-time thug for extorting one hundred dollars a month from the owner of an adult bookstore. The defendant had so little credibility in gangland he was unable to protect anyone from anybody. When the bookstore owner complained to the FBI, he was paying protection to six different extortionists.

At the insistence of veteran postal inspector Seymour Gubowitz, a renaissance man who was a Rhodes scholar with a law degree and doctorate in economics, we started a mail fraud investigation of three former used car salesmen who had formed a company called Inspectors and Officials of Illinois. The name gave the impression that the salesmen were working for the state and could insulate customers from citations for building code violations. The salesmen sold ads in the company magazine, which included nothing *but* ads bought by other duped businessmen—except for a three-page photo layout of the organization's annual convention in Palm Beach Florida. The photographs were taken at a Ramada Inn in Chicago; actors posed as state officials. The conventioneers were friends of the salesmen. Since we were unable to prove the salesmen ever said they were state employees, we dropped the investigation.

The most shameful case had the pathetic Anthony Corelli—dying from cirrhosis of the liver and unemployed in his chosen profession as a collector of "juice" loans—defending an indictment charging him with failure to file tax returns. Anthony wrongly assumed he had to file only if he made money. He pled guilty and asked the court for mercy. The court was represented by Abraham Lincoln Kaye, real last name Kalmanovitch, a first generation American of Russian descent whose parents' hero was—you guessed it—Abraham Lincoln. The walls of Abe's office were plastered with portraits of Lincoln. At the sentencing hearing, Abe summarized Anthony's work habits, which ranged from mildly beating tardy but financially strapped borrowers to breaking the thumbs of deadbeats. Then he asked Anthony if he loved his wife. Anthony was no fool. With as much feigned emotion as he could muster, he said she was the love of his life. Abe, who believed that undying marital love redeemed even the worst sinners, gave Anthony a suspended sentence, conditioned on his wife signing an affidavit swearing she loved him too. She signed the affidavit, but for a price: the $2,000 balance in Anthony's savings account.

He paused to finish his drink. I said I needed to use the washroom, though my real intention was to leave. The tavern had filled while he was talking and I was able to hide behind the crowd in the dining area. When I got to the other side I started toward the front along the wall opposite the bar. As I neared the door a man stepped in my way.

"That fellow is a character," he said.

"What do you mean?"

"He says crazy things."

"How do you know?"

"He comes every night, always sits at the same spot, drinking and trying to get people to listen to him. He made a run at us."

"Us?"

"Me."

"I had the impression this was his first time here."

"Your impression is wrong."

"Do you know who he is?"

"Ask him."

I did not care for his threatening tone.

"Stick around," he said.

He moved his hand under my elbow. "Let go of me," I said.

He inserted his other hand into his suit jacket and pulled out a thin wallet the size of a passport. He flashed it open and closed like an expert card shark shuffling a deck with one hand.

"FBI," he said. "We've been watching him."

"Watching him?" I whispered. "Why?"

"Confidential."

"What difference does it make whether I stay or go?"

"You've talked to him for a while. He'll suspect something if you disappear."

"How long do you want me to stay?"

"We'll let you know." His use of the plural confused me, but I said nothing as he jerked his head toward the bar. "He's starting to look around. You'd better go back." He let go of my arm.

I returned to the bar.

I thought you'd deserted me. I saw him follow you to the bathroom. I hope he didn't hassle you. He's as crazy as they come. He once tried to convince me he was an FBI agent. He showed me phony identification. Did he pull that stunt with you? He barely opens his wallet so you won't get a good look at it. When I asked to see it again, he panicked and left. What's funny is he wanted me to talk to another man at the bar, so *he* wouldn't leave. He said he was under surveillance. Of course, he didn't explain why he was watching him. What's the matter? I know I told you this is my first time here. You misunderstood. He was pestering me at the bar across the street. He's an itch I can't scratch. Maybe we should buy him a drink and tell him to leave us alone. Where did he go? I don't see him.

I did not know what to think, though I should have noticed that the man was inebriated. How absurd to believe he was a government agent. I drank the rest of my Guinness. Then I laughed.

What's so funny? Oh, you're laughing at yourself. I know how you feel. When I was a kid, Albert—my father's name, did I tell you?—used to talk about his friend, a government agent. He told me his phone number and let me dial it. I called the number at least a dozen times. No one ever answered. He said the agent was rarely home, traveling from city to city on the most sensitive assignments. I believed him. You always believe your father, don't you? Hey, look at me. Don't you always believe your father?

The last thing I intended to do was to tell this stranger about my father.

Where was I? After the meeting with Pete I decided to check the legislative history. You're a historian? You don't say. I was so wrapped up in my story I neglected to ask what you do. Would I know your books? Working on your first book. May I ask the subject? You came to the right place. How long have you been married? You're wearing a wedding ring. Any children? Lucy. Nice name. Me? Sure I do. A wife and daughter.

I wanted to know what caused Congress to worry about convicted felons with guns when most states have their own elaborate registration schemes. The bill's opponents asked the same question. The supporters answered by saying possession might affect interstate commerce and was therefore an appropriate subject for federal regulation. But Eudie's gun had nothing to do with interstate commerce. It was to be used, if at all, for protection against intruders. The law is the law, as they say. It wasn't up to me to decide whether it made sense. It was my job to win. Don't tell me you thought lawyers had loftier concerns, like justice and fair play? Then you'll be happy to hear it was hardly a foregone conclusion I would secure a conviction. We didn't have the gun.

Without the gun, I'd be forced to rely on the photograph and police testimony. According to Johnny, I couldn't count on the senior vice cop who had conspired with the evidence custodian to destroy the gun. The last thing they wanted to see was Eudie convicted when the raid had been conducted for show. That left me with the downtown cop's testimony. I hoped it would be enough.

On Patrick's recommendation, Eudie hired Frank Mallin as his lawyer. Frank had spent his career representing the underworld's bookmakers, car thieves, chop shop operators, juice loan collectors, hijackers, and counterfeiters. He quoted Eudie a $30,000 fee. Eudie raised the money by pawning the amethyst ring he'd given his girlfriend, taking out a home equity loan, and borrowing the rest from Lenny.

For a young lawyer, having the chance to battle a premier defense attorney should have produced ripples of excitement and anticipation. But what little enthusiasm I felt was tempered by the knowledge that Judge Julius J. Hoffman would preside at trial.

Even today, twenty-eight years later, I experience heart palpitations remembering my dread of looking at Hoffman's owl-like face, with its beady eyes and hairs sticking out of flaring nostrils. He was so short that when you stood in front of the bench you could only see his face. His tiny head would bob and weave, like a puppet without a body. When he left the bench, his head seemed to glide along the top as if it were on rollers.

His reputation for sadism scared me the most. Although he liked giving lawyers a hard time, he took special pleasure in picking on novices. He hadn't always been a curmudgeon. In earlier times he had been patient and judicious. The Chicago Seven trial changed him.

The Chicago Seven were young radicals who the government charged had unlawfully disrupted the 1968 Democratic Convention. At the trial, they decided to test Judge Hoffman's mettle by using the courtroom as a platform for their political views. The trial deteriorated into a circus like atmosphere in which lion tamer Hoffman was unable to control the lions. When pounding his gavel—his whip, if you will—failed to quiet the defendants, he ordered the marshal to put Bobby Seale, the most ornery defendant, in chains. Liberals were horrified while conservatives praised Hoffman's dedication to order and discipline. I thought it was funny. Who goes to the circus to see a lion in chains?

The Seven were convicted. One theory was that the older middle-class jury felt sorry for Hoffman and thought an acquittal would push the country into anarchy. Most knowledgeable lawyers believed that the Court of Appeals would reverse the conviction and chastise Hoffman for violating the defendants' rights to a fair trial. In addition to manacling Seale, he told the jury he thought all the defendants were guilty.

He also disliked the government lawyers. He was convinced they laughed at him behind his back and deliberately failed to give him moral support when he tried to bring order to his courtroom. Someone gave him the moniker "Julius the Just," an ironic reference to his reputation for meting out harsh sentences. With the appeal still pending as the Lufman trial began, I knew I'd be dealing with a judge not in the best of moods.

There I was on the first day of trial, standing unsteadily before the jury, ready to deliver my opening statement. I knew explaining what I intended to prove was much easier than convincing twelve jurors to convict Eudie for violating a law they never heard of or if they had cared about. One thing was for sure. I had no idea how the jury might be leaning.

A fast-growing cottage industry of self-anointed gurus of jury selection had become the new rage for trial lawyers. In the old days, wily prosecutors and defense attorneys often hired investigators to interview prospective jurors (most common in small towns where the jury pool was small), but contact with jurors was soon prohibited as jury bribery and tampering became popular extralegal tactics. In federal court, most judges, including Hoffman, didn't allow lawyers to ask questions before deciding whether to accept a prospective juror. The new jury science was supposed to have made questioning jurors unnecessary, presuming it was possible to predict how they would decide by analyzing scanty information on their job, family, and the magazines and newspapers they read. Hogwash. Predicting how a juror will decide a case from a few background facts smacks of determinism, last in vogue in the early 1900s when alienists saw a new way to make money by claiming to be soothsayers.

Opening statements are boring. The lawyers are supposed to summarize what evidence they intend to offer. It's not the time for argument. I delivered my statement in a monotone. My hope was not so much that the jury would be swayed by the appeal of the case—nonexistent, I thought—but what Hoffman would later tell the jurors about the law and their obligation to follow it. I was counting on what I've come to despise: blind faith in the law.

Mallin's opening statement wasn't more dynamic. He introduced himself and thanked the jurors for giving him the privilege to address them. Then he commiserated with them for having to waste a glorious spring day cloistered in a windowless courtroom. For his finale, however, he raised his voice and with oratorical fervor reminded them of their duty to acquit unless the evidence established Eudie's guilt beyond a reasonable doubt.

Reasonable doubt, the touchstone of our faith in law and the most recognizable phrase in its lexicon, is a concept so fixed in the firmament of American jurisprudence no one bothers to understand what it means, if it means anything. Judges tell us reasonable doubt is doubt based on reason or doubt that would cause one to hesitate before making an important decision, like doubt whether to make an offer on a house, buy a Cadillac or Lincoln, go through with the wedding, agree to have gum surgery, or the other crucial decisions that vex us throughout our lives. But defining reasonable doubt is only part of the problem. People never doubt the reasonableness of their beliefs and they never think their doubts are unreasonable. When judging the credibility of a witness, should you be reasonably sure or absolutely sure the witness is telling the truth? Is there a difference? What if you have nothing except the witness's sincerity to help you decide whether he's telling the truth? Shouldn't the judge tell a witness to doubt his memory when recalling events of long ago or doubt what he saw even on a bright day? By far, juries convict more innocent defendants because of mistaken eyewitness testimony than any other reason. What about our feelings, our intuition, our gut reactions, whatever you call the part of you that makes wise decisions without conscious evaluation of reasonableness? If you're a person constitutionally racked with doubt, are you disqualified from being a competent juror? If so, we should exclude from the jury agnostics and philosophers. What about an atheist? Atheists are free from doubt, reasonable or unreasonable. The old doubt everything and everyone; the young doubt nothing. Politicians and the religious never admit having doubts. Scientists are trained to be skeptical; for them, doubt is by definition reasonable. Since lawyers believe in nothing, they would have to admit they consider doubt irrelevant.

I'm a skeptic. The law treats the skeptic's doubt as unreasonable, since the standard for determining guilt assumes that with sufficient evidence certainty is possible. The law is so cocksure it blithely disregards how many innocent defendants spend years in prison for crimes they didn't commit.

The law is like a general who claims to care about human life. Let's try to limit casualties and avoid killing noncombatants, but not at the expense of losing the war. And like the law, most wars have nothing to do with individual freedom or justice and everything to do with, power, religion, money, and territory. Lincoln started the Civil War to preserve the Union. No one's liberty was at issue—Lincoln didn't free the slaves until two years into the war—and the South didn't violate the law when it seceded. Lincoln used the war as an excuse to suspend important constitutional rights like the writ of habeas corpus. In World War II, we used the law to put Japanese Americans in concentration camps and to seize their assets and personal possessions. Laws have kept people from getting jobs, voting, going to the school of their choice, drinking, smoking, striking, and proving their innocence —once you're executed, you can't prove a thing. The people are forever persuading their representatives or the courts to repeal or nullify a law that current consciousness has decided was ill advised. Everybody is operating under the theory we'll be more enlightened tomorrow than we are today. But if that's true, how can you have confidence today's laws are just? I'm telling you, we'd be better off if . . .

Why are you agitated? Did I say something wrong? Do you know an innocent man rotting away in jail? Of course, you don't. If you did, you wouldn't be sitting here passing time. If you were interested in justice, you'd want to be spending your time promoting it. Have an Amaretto. I know it tastes sweet, but it soothes the nerves.

You want to say something? Sure, go right ahead. Because I'm doing all the talking doesn't mean I don't care to listen. You grew up in a country whose history has been riddled with subjugation of a politically powerless minority, often in the name of the law. You thought America is the beacon of light for individual rights. And now you're depressed because I'm telling you that the law has driven justice into hiding.

I told you justice needs a defense. Although I admit law has justice by the throat, we don't have to sit by and watch it suffocate. I'm not so foolish to presume you and I can save justice, but we might loosen the noose. Please be careful to understand me. I'm not proposing a revolution, for God's sake.

What do you mean you have to call it a night? Aren't you having a good time? Are we on for tomorrow? You want to hear the rest of Eudie's story, don't you?

I'd hate for you to think I'm a bitter man, given to desperate rants. I'm not as cynical as was Oliver Wendell Holmes, our greatest jurist. Responding to a lawyer's complaint that a decision was unjust, he said, "I must remind you that this is a court of law, not a court of justice." I agree with Holmes; unlike him, I take no pleasure in his terrible truth.

You might suppose I hold lawyers in contempt. Lawyers are human and I would never want to be contemptuous of who we are. Lawyers weren't born wanting to work in the fields of injustice. They didn't come out of the womb ready to fight words with words and manipulate the truth. They learned how to use these weapons in law school.

May 10, 1998

The profession isn't for everyone, even for everyone who thought it was for them. Less than half of law school graduates practice law. Still, they are lawyers and, what's more, they think like lawyers. Infiltrating every corner of American life, they spread their gospel of obfuscation while pretending they have cornered the market on clear thinking. Lawyers are everywhere: they are soldiers and politicians, presidents of corporations, and heads of labor unions. Isn't it strange that the most hated profession supplies many of society's leaders?

You want to know why I went into law? I don't remember why. No, it wasn't because of TV. My favorite show was a western and I never wanted to be a cowboy.

I do admit that law school was fun: three years of picking apart what judges say to justify their decisions. And you learn never to agree with anything. If by graduation you haven't had your moral center permanently dislodged, at least you're able to move it around at will. Lawyers love to play the devil's advocate, which says a lot about whose side the law is on.

I guess it's time to call it quits for the evening. I can't tell you how much I appreciated your company. I'll see you tomorrow? You promise? Incidentally, I don't believe I got your name. Cornelius Michael Sullivan. A fine name. It has the soul of the Irish in it. My name? My name is not important. But thanks for asking. I'll take care of the check. The least I can do is buy the drinks. Cornelius, wait. I want to say a proper goodbye. Enjoy what remains of the day.

Chapter Two

May 11, 1998

I ATE BREAKFAST THE NEXT MORNING *at a coffee shop near Murphy's. The conversation of the night before seemed like a dream. Although I found what he said fascinating, the experience made me uncomfortable. Perhaps it was my encounter with the man who claimed to be an FBI agent; perhaps it was the gnawing sense that our meeting was more than happenstance. More likely, I was allowing demons to steal reason from my brain. No explanation was needed for the lawyer's desire to engage me in conversation. Who, after all, is a better confidant than a stranger?*

As I sipped from a cup of espresso I reviewed my plan for the day. After leaving the coffee shop, I would walk to the New York Public Library on 42nd Street, which boasted a marvelous collection of original documents on the great nineteenth century Irish immigration. Following a few hours of study, I would find a quiet café to review my notes. If I was not tired, I might explore a new neighborhood in the evening and interview some residents. And before the hour grew too late, I would call Mary.

I unfolded the New York Times I had purchased at the corner news-stand. I skimmed the front page and turned to the second page. The lead story caught my eye.

The story dealt with Tommy Glynn's deportation case, once a topic of considerable conversation in my family. Misery and bad luck had stalked Tommy for much of his life. His father died in prison in 1975 while serving a twenty-five-year sentence for his part in terrorist attacks against the British; a few months later, his mother died of asthma. In May 1979 he was arrested for a car bombing. A fifteen-year-old boy was driving along Bedford Street toward the Oxford Street bus station when the bomb went off without warning. He died instantly. Four pedestrians also perished. The teenager was a student at the school I had attended. My father knew the boy's family and we went to the funeral. The mourners' overwhelming grief, almost too much to bear, started me down the road to disengagement from the "cause" and all things violent.

More memories washed over me. Soon after Tommy's arrest my father was released from jail. He had spent a month in custody on false charges that he permitted his automobile repair shop to be used for outfitting cars with bombs. While our family thanked the Lord for his safe return, Tommy was tried, convicted, and sentenced to thirty years at Long Kesh prison. There, he joined more than two thousand other prisoners, many of whom were incarcerated simply because they were suspected members of the Irish Republican Army ("IRA"). But the British were not satisfied with the wholesale detention of IRA members and sympathizers. Lord Gardiner objected to treating these so-called Special Category prisoners as prisoners of war. They had been previously permitted to use their own money and wear normal work clothes; visiting hours were flexible. No longer. In 1980 Tommy participated in several demonstrations, and prison authorities took punitive action. In H Block 3, where Tommy and one hundred other prisoners were kept, all the furniture was removed; prisoners slept on mattresses, dank with the smell of urine and excrement. They were not allowed books or newspapers and prevented from exercising. Tommy spent three years living this way.

In 1983 Tommy and thirty-eight other prisoners staged the largest prison escape in British history. Seventeen were caught; Tommy was not among them. The British arrested his wife Bridget and shipped her to Armagh prison. They announced that she would remain in prison until he was apprehended. Their three young children went to live with Tommy's older brother in Crossmaglen, a few miles from the Irish border.

In 1985 Tommy was arrested at a meatpacking facility near New York's Hudson River piers. How the authorities learned of his whereabouts was never disclosed. I had heard rumors that whoever provided him shelter in New York betrayed him, but after a time they stopped. Tommy had become old news.

The article said that Tommy had spent the last thirteen years in American prisons. The courts had repeatedly denied his requests for bail, saying he was dangerous and might flee the country. For the past several months he had been housed at Riker's Island jail in New York while his lawyer, Samuel Brandt, submitted final arguments to the courts. (The story noted that Brandt was married to Tommy's sister and lived in Boston.) Earlier, the judge rejected his argument that Tommy was a political prisoner and therefore exempt from extradition. Brandt then presented a confidential affidavit to the court, said to contain new evidence. At a hearing on 8 May, the judge ruled that the affidavit was not competent evidence and ordered Tommy's deportation for 22 May, the same day my countrymen would vote whether to approve the peace agreement.

I spent the afternoon at the New York Public Library, though I did not do my intended research. Instead, I attempted to corroborate what my anonymous companion had told me. Judge Julius Hoffman, the Chicago mobster Lenny Patrick, and the strike forces were real enough, but I could find nothing on Eudie Lufman. If he had existed, he was not important enough to have left his mark on history.

It did not surprise me when curiosity took me back to Murphy's that evening.

Great to see you again. Have a seat and a Guinness. I've been looking forward to our meeting. You have a question? Tommy Glynn? Who is he? Riker's Island. It's the largest prison in the world, a terrible place. It looks like a concentration camp. No, we should not return him to Northern Ireland. Once you leave a country, you should be free of its laws.

Another question? What comment about Boston? Oh, that one. A slip of the tongue. Boston didn't have a strike force. I guess I was getting ahead of myself when I said that. You went to the library to look up his case? If his story were in the books, you wouldn't need me to tell you about it.

Where was I? Thank you. My first witness was the downtown officer who took the photograph of Eudie's gun. I marked the photograph Government Exhibit 1 and handed it to the witness. That's when my trouble started.

To introduce the photograph into evidence, I had to establish its relevance. To be relevant, evidence must have probative value. Probative is lawyer-speak for evidence that tends to establish a fact. If the photograph tended to prove that the gun was in Eudie's possession, it's probative and therefore relevant. If something is located in your vicinity, do you possess it? Not necessarily. Possession is a function of access or control, not geography. If the gun were locked in a safe in the bedroom closet but only Esther knew the combination, she would be the possessor.

I asked the officer to describe the photograph. Mallin jumped to his feet and objected. Before I could respond—though I had nothing to say, having no idea why he objected—Judge Hoffman sustained the objection. Since I didn't know what was wrong with my question, I asked him for an explanation. Sticking his head forward like a crane and bearing down on me with his beady eyes, he said, "Why, Mr. Prosecutor, before you can have the witness testify about the contents of the photograph, it must be admitted into evidence." I offered the photograph. Mallin objected again. "Sustained," Hoffman said with obvious glee. "Mr. Prosecutor, I will not admit the exhibit until you establish its relevance."

Like an actor in his first play who forgets his lines, I wanted to get off the stage. I asked for a recess. Hoffman lurched forward, as if he was going to throw himself on top of the bench. He was enjoying my distress. "Counselor," he squealed, "Need I repeat that this court has established a fixed time for the morning recess." It was then I learned my first important lesson as a lawyer. If a lie will extricate you from an uncomfortable situation, go right ahead and tell it. "I'm indisposed," I said. His head swiveled like a gun on a turret and faced the jury. "Counsel for the government complains he's indisposed." He picked up a dictionary and opened it. "According to Mr. Webster, indisposed means slightly ill." He looked at me. "Are you slightly ill?" The twelve jurors were staring at me. "Yes," I whispered. "Very well," he said. "You have five minutes to effect a cure."

I took the elevator to the strike force offices three floors below. Panting like a sick dog, I raced into Pete's office and explained my dilemma. He gave me a solution so obvious I wanted to quit on the spot.

When court resumed, I asked the downtown officer to describe *only* the physical area shown in the photograph. Presto, I had established the relevancy of the photograph and avoided asking the witness to mention the gun in the headboard. Hoffman guffawed. "Well, well," he said to the jury. "Counsel for the government has recovered his wits as well as his health." The jurors laughed. Would they acquit Eudie because of my incompetence or convict him because they felt sorry for me?

Now, it was Mallin's turn. Esther testified Eudie had bought the gun because she was afraid to be alone on the many nights he worked late—not identifying his job of course. On cross-examination I got her to admit Eudie had access to the gun, though she added that he never touched it. Eudie took the stand and parroted her testimony. When I pressed him on whether he had ever touched the gun, he claimed he was terrified of guns. He also said he had asked the storeowner to deliver the gun by messenger so he wouldn't have to carry it. During the next recess Johnny asked me if he should find the storeowner. I said no. Whether Eudie had actually handled the gun was irrelevant.

Mallin moved to dismiss the case. The appellate court had reversed the 1938 conviction because Eudie didn't have a lawyer at trial. (It hadn't done Eudie any good; he was already out of prison when the court announced its decision.) No matter, I argued. The conviction had been merely voidable, not void. Since it was still a matter of record, it satisfied the felony requirement of the gun possession statute. Orwellian doublespeak, you say? Why of course. In our world the law occupies Room 101, and in this case Hoffman was the guard. He denied Mallin's motion.

I had told Pete I couldn't imagine a jury convicting Eudie. He told me not to worry; I should simply remind the jury of its duty to follow the law. "But what will happen if the jury believes the law is unjust?" I asked. Pete echoed Justice Holmes when he replied, "The law is the only justice that counts."

I took Pete's advice and asked the jury to put sympathy aside and follow the law. I wanted to believe in what I was saying. But it was no use. I wanted the jury to acquit Eudie.

The jury deliberated for a little less than two hours. When they returned to the courtroom they looked at me rather than Eudie. Pete had said jurors never make eye contact with the party against whom they have decided. He was right. The jury returned a guilty verdict.

Hoffman sentenced Eudie to two years in prison. I was shocked. At worst, I thought Hoffman would give him a suspended sentence. What depressed me the most, however, was Hoffman's reference to what I had said in closing argument: "An orderly society cannot afford to countenance violations of the law, even if we believe the law is bad." It wasn't even my line. I read it in the transcript of another trial.

Six months later, the court of appeals reversed Eudie's conviction and ordered his acquittal. Although it rejected Mallin's argument that the 1938 conviction was void, it ruled that Congress had improperly based the statute on the theory that possession of a gun affected interstate commerce. Therefore, it said, the statute violated the constitutional limits on federal power.

Not only was I happy for Eudie, I was happy for myself. My faith in the law was restored—temporarily, that is. Very temporarily. Two days later, Richard Conners, an Assistant United States Attorney, marched into my office and demanded the Lufman file. I asked him if he needed bedtime reading. Displaying the lack of humor that is a prosecutor's most defining characteristic, he said the strike force had fallen asleep at the switch. (Prosecutors love to turn clichés into platitudes.) What he was planning, however, was no laughing matter.

I gave Connors the file and went to see Pete. "How can we permit this?" I asked.

"Our favorite FBI agent wants Eudie to be his informant," he said.

"Smith Corcoran?"

"Yes."

"What did Eudie say?"

"The wrong thing."

"Good for him."

"Not for long. Smitty figures an indictment will change his mind."

"Indictment for what?"

"Perjury."

"That's insane. He was testifying in his own defense. What's the—"

"Why do you think I told him I wanted no part of it? With my luck, the case would be assigned to Abe Kaye and he'd dump on me again. It doesn't matter, though. We're just soldiers. If one soldier doesn't want to charge, there's another one who will."

"What about the law? What about fairness?"

He laughed.

"Did I say something funny?"

"No. It's just easier to laugh than to cry."

Smith Corcoran joined the FBI after graduation from Notre Dame Law School. From the beginning he had his own agenda. He liked to say that an agent could "make it big" by courting higher-ups in the Mafia. When I asked him how cavorting with mobsters could advance his career, he smiled and said I had a lot to learn.

Smitty looked like an FBI agent was supposed to look. He was tall, but not too tall, stocky but not too stocky, had short hair cropped above the ears, a straight nose, and thin lips. In other respects he was a renegade. He hated the squeaky-clean image J. Edgar Hoover required of his agents and seemed to go out of his way to antagonize his superiors. His best friend was an ex-Chicago cop rumored to be a bagman for a corrupt city alderman. This prompted the FBI to monitor Smitty's every move, assigning five agents to tail him around the clock. He loved to joke about it. He said the FBI was no more competent investigating its own than it was investigating the Mafia.

Smitty was also something of a rogue when it came to his view of cops and robbers. He believed the pursuer and the pursued shared a special bond; good and evil, he said, were the two sides of the same coin. "We know where we stand," he said. At first I was confused; I didn't know who he was talking about. But then I realized he always referred to himself in the plural—the royal we—as if he were the government instead of just another faceless government operative.

Was it possible? Was it other than impossible? I had never met anyone who said "we" when he meant "I." Yet just the previous night, the strange man who claimed to be an agent, who I concluded was merely a mentally unbalanced stalker, had used the "royal we." And now to have heard about an agent from nearly three decades before, in a distant city, was too much to . . . But I had no time to speculate. He continued speaking, unaware or unaffected by what must have been my startled reaction.

Before the Lufman fiasco, Smitty and I worked together investigating a Boston betting ring run by two Italians and an Irishman. They established a nationwide network of bookmakers; in Chicago they did business with Lenny Patrick—Eudie's boss. Since Boston didn't have a strike force, we were assigned the case. The whole investigation consisted of a wiretap. Why bother with surveillance or witnesses when you can sit in a room wearing earphones and drinking coffee?

"He's tight with Lenny Patrick," Smitty said. We were eating lunch in the building cafeteria. Smitty was working on his third hotdog; mustard dribbled down his chin. I was eating chicken noodle soup, though I couldn't find any noodles in the broth.

"We can indict Patrick from the evidence on the wiretap," I said.

"We're after something else."

"What?"

"Think big for a change." That was another thing about Smitty. He never missed a chance to be cryptic.

"Help me out," I said.

"Boston."

"What about Boston?"

'The land of opportunity."

"Opportunity for what?"

He leaned across the table and looked in my bowl. "Fucking government," he said. "Too goddamn cheap."

That was the answer to my question, though I didn't know it at the time.

Smitty's basis for charging Eudie with perjury was as clever as it was cockeyed. Eudie had testified that he bought the gun for his wife and registered it in her name; testimony I assumed was truthful. Smitty, who never believed anything anyone ever said, checked the records at the Illinois Firearm Registration Bureau. He discovered that Eudie had originally registered the gun in his own name, changing it to show Esther as the owner after he was indicted.

I told Smitty that the constitutional prohibition of double jeopardy precluded an indictment for perjury. Eudie shouldn't be prosecuted twice, when the facts were the same. Smitty, however, knew the protection wasn't all it seemed. By using different statutes, the government may bring a series of indictments charging crimes that arise from the same factual circumstances.

"Even so," I said, "Eudie wasn't asked about the original registration. So where's the lie?"

"The first registration shows Eudie lied when he claimed he bought the gun for his wife."

"A jury won't convict. They'll see we're persecuting him."

"Don't be so sure. Remember your closing argument. 'An orderly society cannot afford to countenance . . . '"

"It was somebody else's closing argument."

"It worked, didn't it?"

"To convict a defendant for perjury, you have to show the false testimony was material to the subject of the proceeding in which it was given. Since we prosecuted Eudie for possession, not ownership, it makes no difference why or for whom he bought the gun."

"Where did you go to law school, Harvard?"

"You know I didn't go to Harvard."

"Some other Ivy League joint. Are we right?"

"This is about being fair to Eudie, not where I went to law school."

"We'll be fair to Eudie, if Eudie is fair to us."

I'm amazed how long a person will sit in a dark room before he realizes it's easy to turn on the lights. For Smitty, the issue wasn't whether the law was good or bad, it wasn't whether Eudie violated the law, and it wasn't about fairness. The issue was how to force Eudie to become an informant. I once represented a businessman who the government was intent on squeezing for information about his father, a Mafia godfather. He wouldn't cooperate. So they trumped up a fraud case using a group of informants. At the trial . . . I don't want to talk about it. I'll get upset. Let's stick with what happened to Eudie.

Although I'd given up on persuading Smitty to leave Eudie alone, I got to thinking about perjury. The law places a high premium on the truth, an irony really, because no quality better defines what it is to be human than lying. "Lying is man's only privilege over all other organisms. Lying is what makes me a man." Who tells the truth? Who knows the truth? But plenty of people claim to tell the truth: the holier-than-thou, goody-goodies, journalists, pseudo savants, evangelists, born-again Christians, psychics . . .

The best of us find it difficult to be truthful with ourselves, let alone others. I'm baffled why we insist on punishing each other for what we all do. If you can't lie to protect yourself or twist the truth to vanquish your enemies, you're defenseless. Should taking an oath before God force one to tell the truth against his self-interest?

Maybe religion is to blame. For some reason, we're not supposed to lie to God. But God knows everything, so what's the difference? A Catholic confesses to a priest, who at least promises to keep his mouth shut. A Jew confesses to himself because he can't trust his rabbi to keep a secret. (Recently, a woman sued her rabbi for telling her husband she was having an affair.) A Protestant never confesses, which makes sense, because Protestants never do anything wrong.

The trial was delayed for five months while Mallin filed a series of motions challenging the government's right to proceed. Hoffman denied them all. As Smitty predicted, he ruled that the double jeopardy rule didn't protect Eudie from the perjury charge. Then Eudie got a lucky break. A week before the trial was to begin, Hoffman broke his hip when he fell trying to get out of a bathtub. James Harding, a black judge, got the case.

In those days, it was OK to be politically incorrect, even OK to tell racist jokes. Lawyers were no exception. They joked that Harding was lazy and shiftless. He did work hard in the morning, but the lunch hour stole his energy. There was a time when I could have two martinis at lunch and be able to sit through an afternoon deposition without falling asleep, but Harding regularly pushed the limits of consciousness with three aperitifs, four glasses of red wine, and two cognacs. He spent the afternoon dozing on the bench, and his snoring often drowned out the testimony. Drink also confiscated his ability to make a decision. In a case in which the defendant waived his right to a jury trial, he deliberated for two days and then announced he couldn't make up his mind. Everyone joked this was the first hung bench in legal history.

Fortunately, Eudie's case was called in the morning. Smitty and I entered the courtroom and sat in the last row as Harding was saying he had been thinking about Mallin's motions to dismiss. Ignoring Judge Hoffman's analysis of double jeopardy, he dismissed the indictment. If the Founding Fathers were alive, he said, they would redraft the Constitution to ensure that all Eudie Lufmans could live their lives free of persecution. He liked what he said so much he repeated it three times.

I gave Eudie a thumbs up from my lap, which annoyed the heck out of Smitty. His arms were folded across his chest and his lips were screwed shut. He was breathing heavily through his nose. He sounded like a gas leak in a mine.

"Lighten up," I said.

"We're not through with Eudie," he said without moving his lips.

"What do you mean by that?"

But Smitty didn't answer; he just continued glaring at Eudie, who was smothering Mallin in a bear hug.

A block from the federal building was Berghof's, Chicago's version of a German beer hall. In homage to Teutonic fortitude, there were no seats or stools. I stopped in for a sandwich. Eudie and Mallin were standing at the bar, drinking steins of beer. "Join us," Eudie said. Not wanting to be seen with a defendant—now former defendant—I turned to leave. "Don't worry," Eudie said. "I'm harmless." I ordered a beer—I hate beer.

"I know you were doing your job on the gun charge," Eudie said. "But you have to admit, the case was bullshit. And the perjury rap was more bullshit."

"I agree," I said under my breath in case I was being recorded.

In the mirror behind the bar I saw Smitty walking purposively toward us. Eudie slapped him on the back, like they were old friends.

"Did you hear that?" Eudie said, pointing at me. "He's glad I got off. There's hope."

Smitty grunted and stepped between Eudie and me. "Our offer is still open," he said.

Mallin curled around Eudie and stuck out his chin. "You guys never give up, do you?"

"We always get our man."

I took a sip of the warm beer and stepped away from the bar. The less I knew the better. Smitty and Eudie were laughing. They were right to laugh. I was a young prosecutor who didn't know a damn thing about anything.

Outside, I stood by the window and watched them. They had stopped laughing and were deep in conversation. I wondered whether Eudie, who had withstood two prosecutions, had changed his mind about becoming an informant. I never asked Smitty about it. I thought I could practice law and skip the intrigue.

I'll tell you what I did learn. Eudie moved to Boston a few months later. A scrod fisherman caught the betting ring's former bookkeeper—or what was left of him—in his fishing net. The bookkeeper had been keeping two sets of books, one for the organization and the other for himself. One of the bosses, the Irishman I think, found out and, as they said in *The Godfather*, it wasn't personal. You never saw *The Godfather?* You need to catch up.

We never made a case from the wiretap. The wire broke and we missed two weeks of conversations. It prevented us from proving that the business had operated for thirty consecutive days, a requirement of the federal anti-gambling statute. It also requires at least $2,000 a day in bets. If the ring handles a million bucks a day for twenty-nine days, takes a day off and starts again, there's no violation. But if the ring does $2,000 a day for thirty days you can go to prison. Why didn't we obtain a warrant for a second wiretap? Smitty closed the investigation. He also moved to Boston. Pete said the FBI wanted him out of Chicago but he could choose where he wanted to go. For a while I wondered why he chose Boston but then I forgot about it. Smitty and Eudie were out of my life and I had other cases to prosecute.

There he is again.

The man in the suit. He was sitting at the end of the bar staring at us. Had he been listening?

He's a dybbuk, Connie. Do you mind if I call you Connie? Thanks. It's our second night together. That makes us friends, right? Don't let him bother you. What can he do to us? I'll give him the lawyer's evil eye. Maybe he'll dematerialize. Nope. He keeps staring. Do you want to go somewhere else? One place is as good as the other. You sure?

What should I talk about now? You want to know more about me? The topic on the table is law and justice; my life story is nothing but a sidebar. You disagree, I see. You think if I tell you my childhood you'll better understand the pathology of the legal mind. I had no idea the Irish were into psychology. I do know what I'm saying. My wife is Irish! She's my second wife. I wasn't smart the first time around. I married the first person who fell in love with me. She was Jewish. That made Sarah happy. Sarah is my mother. What's that? I can't remember if I was in love with my first wife. You can't remember love any better than you can remember pain.

I have one child. Her name is Rachel. I love biblical names. My present wife was a flight attendant who gave up fending off flirtatious salesmen to help me set up my law practice. Just the one child. She isn't able . . . Mind you, I knew from the beginning. I'm satisfied. How much love does a person need? You only have one child? As soon as your book is finished? You're a planner. I never planned anything until . . . no, that's a boring subject. What's interesting is when I was in law school and had no plans at all. As Sarah said, I had my whole life ahead of me. Who needed a plan?

When I went to law school you couldn't expect to get a summer job in a law firm until after the second year. It's different now. Law firms realize that knowledge and experience are unnecessary for most of what passes as the practice of law. So I spent the first summer at home, hanging out at the neighborhood pool and working nights at the post office.

When I returned to school for the fall semester, I signed up for interviews. Representatives of law firms visited the school throughout the fall. They would talk to each applicant for fifteen minutes and then decide whom to invite for a second round. Since law firms usually hired new lawyers from the ranks of their summer interns, there was a sense of urgency in landing a summer job. A sign-up sheet for each firm was posted on the wall outside the school library. I remember how the students jostled for places on as many sheets as possible, pushing and shoving like they were fighting to get into a rock concert.

If you weren't in the top third of the class, it was pointless to sign up for an interview. The firms were interested in the best students. For reasons no one has ever explained to me, the conventional wisdom is that good students make good lawyers. I'm not sure what makes a good lawyer. Accomplishing what a client wants? Convincing a client not to do what he wants? Manipulating a judge or jury? Lying? Conniving? Take your pick. In law school, a good student was someone who did well on exams, which consisted of hypothetical cases in which you were supposed to identify the issues. The more issues you identified the better your grade. The professors didn't care whether you knew the law—anyone can look up the law. The trick was to list as many ways as possible to avoid, undermine, or circumvent the law. That's what lawyers mean when they talk about identifying issues.

I was in the top third of the class and signed up for thirty interviews. But only Goodman & Greenman, a midsize Philadelphia firm of no particular distinction, invited me for a second interview. In my case, I guess, being a good student didn't mean I would be a good lawyer.

Goodman & Greenman's offices were on the twentieth floor of a downtown building with a view of the William Penn statue atop City Hall in one direction and the polluted Delaware River in the other. The receptionist, a matronly woman with a carnation in the lapel of her blue suit, was guarding a box of chocolates when I entered. As I approached she squeezed the box against her chest. She told me to have a seat and look through the firm brochure, a heavy gold-leafed portfolio that looked like a wedding album.

The name of the law firm was embossed on the cover. Inside were glossy photographs of the partners with brief biographies and a description of the practice areas. On the back cover was the firm's "vision statement," signed by the founding partner, Henry M. Goodman, and dated in 1918. (His biography said he founded the firm after returning from the Great War.) It was hard to read, written in some kind of calligraphy that reminded me of the Magna Carta. I spent ten minutes sounding out each syllable, like a dimwitted game show contestant. Halfway through the first line I realized what it was: "The law is my shepherd, I shall not want." I looked past the receptionist down a long hall—lawyers dashing in and out of offices—and closed my eyes. I saw green pastures.

I started at the top: an interview with Mr. Goodman. Tall and lanky, ninety years old—if I was to believe the biography—he had me sit next to him on a wooden bench in his office. He said he sat on that very bench while reading law with his grandfather in '98. Then he asked me how the Samuelsons were doing. I said I didn't know the Samuelsons.

Spittle trickled from his lips, down his chin, and onto his black bow tie. He tilted his head forward and wiped his chin with the end of the bow tie. He took an embroidered handkerchief from the pocket of his beige and white seersucker suit jacket and gently patted his lips, as if he were tending to a wound. After he put the handkerchief away, he said, "False modesty is unbecoming in a lawyer."

I was thinking of modifying my approach and saying I knew the Samuelsons when he grabbed my face and yanked it close to his. "Aren't you Jeremy Katz?"

His eyes weren't six inches from mine but they might as well have been a mile away. The whites were streaked with purple veins and a milky film reached over the pupils. It was apparent that he was nearly blind.

"No," I said. "I'm not Jeremy Katz."

He slumped against the back of the bench. His narrow shoulders sagged and seemed to disappear into his bony elbows. Mr. Goodman was little more than a skeleton in a suit of clothes.

"I'm sorry." I said.

"No matter, you'll do."

"I hope so."

Suddenly he slammed his hands against his knees. "Do you play bridge?"

"Yes, but I'm not very good."

He put his palms on the bench and pushed off. His knees cracked; it sounded like dead branches snapping. Breathing heavily, he lumbered to his desk and opened the top drawer. He returned with a book.

"Charles Goren's masterpiece on bridge. Study this and we will have a match at summer's end."

Bernie Mazur, the head of litigation, was my next interview. He was short and fat, with bushy black hair and a square face marked by a hooknose and protruding chin, the bottom of which I could see through his wiry beard. He looked like a pirate. He didn't offer me a seat. For five minutes I stood in front of his desk while he drew lines through a brief he was reading, saying with each turn of the page, "No, no, no, wrong, wrong, so very wrong." When he finished reading, he threw the brief in a can that was overflowing with other briefs.

"Do you want the job?" he bellowed.

"Yes, sir."

"Do you have any questions?"

"No, sir."

"Good. You'll go far."

I didn't know whether to stay or leave. "Don't just stand there," he said. "In this business you have to think fast and you have to act fast. Moving fast also helps."

As I started out of the office, I noticed a photograph on the wall.

"My wife," he said unhappily.

"She's beautiful."

"She's the old codger's daughter."

"Mr. Goodman?"

"There's only one codger in this firm, thank God."

"You met her after you joined the firm?"

"Before. How do you think I got the job? Why do you think I have this big office?" He put his feet on the desk. There was gum sticking to the sole of one shoe. "If you're smart, you'll do the same."

"Does he have another daughter?"

"You're quick," he said. "I like that. She just turned sixty-five and is available. Her husband died last month. Naturally, the firm is handling the estate."

"I do have a question," I said.

"Make it a good one."

"Who is Jeremy Katz?"

He swung his feet off the desk and lifted the foot with the gum on the shoe. While picking at the gum, he said, "There is no Jeremy Katz."

"There isn't?"

"The coot has asked each prospect in the last twenty years if he's Jeremy Katz. You may be surprised to hear this, but almost half the prospects claimed to be Jeremy Katz. They didn't get offers."

"You mean—"

"He probably also asked you if you knew the Samuelsons."

"Yes."

"That's always his opening gambit. They don't exist either. Twenty percent never make it to the Katz part of the interview because they said they were friends of the Samuelsons. And since you're holding Goren's book, you obviously didn't tell him you were a champion player with thousands of points in duplicate bridge. Another fifteen percent fell off the bike on that one."

"I told Mr. Goodman I knew how to play bridge. I don't know how to play bridge."

"Don't sweat it. If complete honesty were the standard, we'd never hire anyone."

On my first day of work, Ralph Greenman, the other named partner, sent for me. He said he'd heard that I was honest, though not too honest. He said that meant he could count on me to discreetly handle a sensitive assignment. At his suggestion I sat on an oversized velvet couch under what he claimed was an original Monet. I sank so far into the cushion that my arms were forced skyward into the position of a drowning man struggling to reach the surface. Mr. Greenman took a cigar from a leather-covered humidor and lit it with a table lighter that had a miniature twenty-eight carat gold golfer on top. When he flicked the lighter, the golfer took a swing, and flame shot out from the end of the club.

Mr. Greenman matched my ideal of how a successful lawyer should look and dress (I like to believe that my opinion has changed over the years): tanned face, wet lips, prominent chest and moderate paunch, custom-made shirt with French cuffs bearing his initials, black suspenders, and wing-tipped shoes.

"Our esteemed client Mr. A," he began, "is the President of the X Company. A has heard about an offer to buy Z Incorporated, a business that will help expand the market for X's products. Indeed, Z will be a moneymaker for anyone who buys it, a fact of which A is well aware. A came to see me for advice. He'd like to resign from X and purchase Z for his own account. Your job, young man, is to research the law and tell me whether Mr. A may legally take advantage of this opportunity." (I don't know why he didn't use Y.) It could have been an assignment on *Mission Impossible*, though of course this conversation occurred before that show was on the air. Maybe the creators stole the idea from Mr. Greenman.

I struggled unsuccessfully to stand. "It's best to slide off," he said. I took his advice and slithered down the cushion to the floor. "One other thing," he said. "Time is of the essence. I need your answer tomorrow morning at seven."

I found the answer in a couple of hours. But it didn't make me happy; I knew it would make him mad. Did you ever hear of the *corporate opportunity* doctrine? No surprise. You don't look like the corporate type. You have honest eyes.

The corporate opportunity doctrine is one of the law's commandments. The law has millions of commandments. *Thou shalt not take advantage of a business opportunity that would be good for your company* is a commandment—I forgot the number, but it's near the top.

At twelve single-spaced pages my memo could pass for a model of circumlocution, replete with footnotes and citations that populate the nirvana of the lawyer. The only case that I found which gave a glimmer of hope to Mr. A came out of Reno, Nevada. The owner of a brothel sued his former manager for stealing prostitutes to staff his new operation down the street. Before the manager gave notice, he offered a job in his new business to the next six women seeking employment. The owner claimed the former manager had seized a corporate opportunity by hiring the women. The jury awarded the owner $200,000. The appellate court reduced the verdict to a dollar. Citing a hundred-year-old case dealing with stolen cattle, the court ruled that hookers were fungible. A dissenting judge objected to comparing prostitutes with cattle.

I got to the office the next morning at 6:45 with the precious memo tucked under my arm. The front door was locked and I didn't have a key. I settled on the floor and waited.

Mr. Greenman arrived at seven. He looked at me like I was a bum who had snuck past the security guard. I scrambled to my feet and held out the memo. He shot me a *what's-this* glance and took the memo. As I followed him through the door and down the hall toward his office, he thumbed through the pages. When we reached the oak paneled doors to his office he said, "You'll be a great success someday, if you learn how to be goal oriented." My face collapsed in despair.

He wrapped one arm around me and said I shouldn't be discouraged. "If a client comes to you and asks how to get something done, you don't tell him he can't do it. No, you tell him how to do it. And if his scheme is against the law, you figure out how to beat the law at its own game. J.P. Morgan, a dream client if there ever was one, said something like that."

Mr. Greenman pushed open the doors to his office and invited me to join him for a screwdriver. He opened a cabinet I assumed contained law books or files, but it was a fully stocked wet bar. As he took a bottle of orange juice from the refrigerator and vodka from the shelf, he asked me if I had copies of the memo. I told him I had run out of carbon paper and all the stores were closed when I typed the memo, which was well past midnight. "Perfect," he said. He finished making the drinks, pouring at least three shots of vodka in each glass. As he watched me take a tentative sip he drank his glass dry in a series of satisfied gulps. He made another drink, this time vodka with no orange juice, and carried my memo to what I thought was a copier. He inserted the memo in a slot and pressed a large red button that looked like an emergency stop button on an elevator. I heard a grating noise, the same sound a car makes when you try to switch from drive to park while the car is moving. Before I could tell him the copier was jammed, thin strips of paper were coming out the other end. They reminded me of white streamers, the kind you see at a parade. He tossed the remnants of my memo in a cardboard box. The box was stuffed with the sliced-up remains of memos, briefs, and letters: voices of principle, silenced forever.

Two days later I read a story in the Philadelphia Inquirer about a prominent Philadelphian who had resigned as president of his company to start a new business, one that would compete with his former company. The Board of Directors was said to be preparing a lawsuit. I showed the article to Bernie Mazur and told him of my memo's fate. "I hope you don't think you wasted your time on the memo," he said. I admitted that the thought had crossed my mind. "What Greenman didn't tell you," he said, "was that we represent the company not the President. And we'll be representing the company in the lawsuit. Your memo was very helpful."

"Why did he destroy it?"

"It wouldn't do to leave evidence that we knew what the president was planning."

In the Fall I signed up for more interviews. I picked firms I hadn't interviewed before. I wasn't optimistic. I didn't know what I had done wrong the previous year and a complete reworking of my persona—if that was the problem—was beyond my ability. If necessary, I could work for Goodman & Greenman. Mazur gave me the news on my last day of work. He said Goodman was very impressed with me—two weeks earlier I had joined him and his two granddaughters for a bridge game in his office—and Greenman considered me a *comer* from the moment he read my memo.

It was dispiriting to sit through interviews knowing there was something keeping me from breaking through but not knowing what it was. I used different hairstyles: brushed back, brushed across, a part, no part, curly. I wore different colored suits, some with a vest, and tried various shoe styles. I experimented with different combinations of shirts and ties: blue shirts, white shirts, striped shirts, shirts with and without French cuffs, and ties with and without tie clips. I alternated between seriousness and casualness, sometimes shifting from one to the other during the same interview. I spoke of my love for the law and my interest in business. I said I didn't plan to marry for a decade so I'd be able to work around the clock. I said I planned to marry upon graduation so I would need to be successful to support a family. I said I was a first generation American and wanted to prove myself. I said my parents were wealthy German Jews who had made a fortune in banking. Nothing worked.

While I was walking out of each interview with a verbal rejection slip, classmate Ellis Coze was receiving offers. I was amazed. He was in the bottom half of the class and hadn't bothered with interviews the previous year. Instead, using the profits he had made on his bar mitzvah money—he had invested in profitable gold mining stocks that had tripled in value—he chartered a thirty-foot sailboat and cruised around the Caribbean with his girlfriend, a fetching combination of brains and beauty. She was a Phi Beta Kappa in anthropology and the homecoming queen.

Ellis interviewed thirty-seven law firms and received thirty-seven offers, all the more remarkable because he was the worst dresser in the law school. He favored sheer cotton shirts he bought on sale at Wannamaker's through which you could see his flabby breasts. His baggy slacks were unpressed and his dull-white penny loafers were smudged with salt stains. His ties were different shades of red, decorated with clowns and circus freaks.

One morning toward the end of interviewing season, I saw Ellis and his girlfriend eating breakfast in the school cafeteria. She was nibbling on a slice of dry toast. He was studying the sports section while swallowing whole a gigantic stuffed donut. As I walked over to their table, he was trying to snare a gob of jelly that had squeezed out of the donut. He missed and it hit the newspaper with a splat. I knew it was then or never. "Excuse me," I said. "I have to know." He dabbed the jelly off the newspaper with his index finger and stuck it in his girlfriend's mouth. As she licked the jelly and sucked his finger he said, "Can you fuckin' believe it? The Yankees lost. Two outs in the bottom of the ninth and they give up a grand slam." His girlfriend whimpered like he had just read the obituary of his best friend. She wrapped her arms around him and puckered her lips. Then she blew in his ear. "Oh baby, I'm so sorry." Out of disgust or failure of nerve—I'm not sure which—I walked away without getting the answer to my question.

Several years later, a client took me to a Yankees game. During the seventh inning stretch, I went into the bathroom. Guess who was there? I hadn't seen Ellis since law school, but I knew from alumni bulletins that he wasn't practicing law. After working a year for an old-line New York firm he resigned to start a headhunting business. He'd gotten divorced after his wife, formerly the girlfriend, ran off to Kenya with a fellow anthropologist to search for Adam's Eve.

He slapped me on the back and asked me how I was doing. This time, I said to myself, I'm not going to blow it. "How did you do it?" I asked. "How did you convince all those firms to offer you a job?"

"Look around," he said.

The large bathroom was full of men standing at urinals, staring at the walls, either daydreaming or trying to coax their uncooperative prostate glands into action.

"This bathroom is humongous," he said. "Even between innings when everyone is taking a leak, it's easy to find a urinal where you won't have anyone standing on either side of you. That's important to most people. Pissing is one of those activities we want to do in private and if we can't do it in private we want a certain amount of room. I never thought about it until the reception for my Bar Mitzvah. My grandfather took me aside and said now that I'm a man I need to concentrate on developing charisma. It reminded me of that scene in *The Graduate*. He seemed to be making sense, so I listened. He said next time I go to a game I should observe whether anyone voluntarily stands next to me in the bathroom. I thought he was crazy. What does that have to do with charisma? But at the next ballgame, I figured what the hell, I'll do what he said, I'll go to the bathroom at some point and test his theory. Between the fifth and the sixth inning I had to take a leak. I walked into this bathroom and headed straight to that urinal over there, the one in the middle. No one was on either side of me. Then this man—he had no teeth and hair was growing out of his forehead——took the urinal to my left, saw me, and changed his mind. He moved two urinals away. I was crazed. I must have gone to twenty-five games that year. It was always the same. No one stood next to me. At the last game of the season a fat guy walked right up to the urinal next to me. And he smiled at me. It was fantastic. I didn't even care if he was gay. Something magical had happened. During the offseason I scoped out public bathrooms all over the city. By the start of college I had a ninety-percent success rate. My record was forty-two straight with a guy standing on one side and twenty-three on both sides."

"I'm not sure I understand."

"Think about it," he said smiling.

I did think about it. What Ellis had said was nonsense, but it was nonsense with a point. I had never realized how important it was to make people feel safe with you. If a prospective client will stand next to you at the urinal, he'll hire you; he may even pay your fee. Jurors will believe what you tell them. Judges will give you the benefit of the doubt.

Why did Ellis quit the practice? You've asked the sixty-four dollar question. Maybe his technique was fool's good. Once you've seduced the other guy and he stands close to you, then what? Don't you have to do something besides piss with him? For all I know, Ellis woke up one day and realized he had never left the bathroom, if you know what I mean. Maybe his knack for intimacy was only good for a few seconds, roughly the time it takes to empty your bladder. Still, he had something, a quality you can't define. I don't have it, Connie. Never did. The other day I stopped in the men's room at LaGuardia. Out of twenty urinals only two were unoccupied: the one to my left and the one to my right.

Excuse me. I need a glass of water. No, I'm OK. Maybe I've been talking too much. Where's the water? Thanks. Where was I? Oh, look. Our crazy friend is leaving. God, I need another glass of water. Hey, Patrick, bring me a refill. How do I know his name is Patrick? He's Irish, isn't he? Aren't all Irish bartenders named Patrick?

My eyes are burning. Is it the smoke? You're fine? I guess it's me. Shit! God, they're really burning, like somebody poured salt in my eyes. I know I'm a bit worked up, but don't worry. I'll be fine. Where are you going? You're tired? Already? I hope we're on for tomorrow. I hate to act like a charter member of the lonely guy's club, but it's been a long time since I've had a friend to talk to. No, I'll stay for a while longer. I want to finish my water. Oh, Connie, be careful walking home. Excuse me? I guess I assumed you live close by.

His parting salvo bothered me. Did he know where I lived? And why was he so intent on having my company? If he had some purpose other than casual barroom talk, what was it?

I was so deep in thought I nearly collided with a garbage collector. He was lifting large black bags into the back of a truck, going about his menial task with grim determination as if he were single-handedly responsible for a clean city. I laughed. I was in no position to judge my new friend or anyone else.

As I turned the corner at 51st Street I saw the man in the suit standing on the other side of the street. The man who used the royal we. He was smoking a cigarette and watching me. I quickened my pace. He stayed where he was.

CHAPTER THREE

May 12, 1998

I COULD NOT BLAME MARY *for being upset. Not only had I failed to call since arriving in New York, I started the conversation by talking of my nights at Murphy's. She interrupted to inform me of my father's declining health. On the morning following my departure he had a severe attack and slipped into unconsciousness for several hours. Emergency paramedics enclosed him in an oxygen tent. The doctor arrived and gave the family the bad news. At most, my father might linger for a few weeks. Why had she not called me? I had given her the telephone number of the studio before leaving. She said, "Sometimes, my dear, it is for you to take the first step." It was a much-deserved reproach.*

I asked her whether I should come home. She reminded me how excited I had been about the trip; I reminded her she had encouraged me to go. As our conversation wore on in an unhappy tete-a-tete I resisted accepting responsibility for the present state of affairs. Yet it was I who decided five years before to break off relations with my father, and I had ignored my mother's entreaties to resolve my differences with him. I clung to my belief that sins should not be forgiven or forgotten, while at the same time I considered myself to have lived a life of innocence.

At last I was able to change the subject and tell her more about the man I had met at Murphy's.

"Is he Irish?" she asked.

"He is not Irish."

"Then why would you interview him?"

"I do not know."

"Whatever are you saying?"

"I suppose I . . . I don't know."

"Are you all right?"

"Yes."

Mary knew me well enough to select a happier topic. She reported on Lucy's activities, proudly describing her sterling performance in a school production of "H.M.S. Pinafore." I wanted to speak to her, but she had gone to a friend's house after school.

"This man you've been talking to," Mary said.

"Yes."

"What does he do?"

"He is a lawyer."

Silence. Then: "You should ask him about Tommy Glynn."

I was stunned. "Why would I do that?"

"It popped into my head, because I saw a thing on the TV."

"Concerning his case?"

"Yes. How did you know?"

"A newspaper story."

"What did it say?"

"He's going back to Long Kesh."

"That's what the man said."

I was quite confused. "What man?"

"The man interviewed on TV."

"Who was he?"

"His lawyer. I don't remember the name."

"What else did he say?"

"You quiz me so."

"I am sorry."

"Something about the American court refusing to hear evidence that would prove Tommy's innocence."

So this was the nature of the affidavit mentioned in the New York Times. For some reason, the possibility Tommy might be innocent disturbed me.

"On the day I left you said something odd," I said.

Mary laughed. "You always tell me I say odd things, Connie."

"No, hear me. You said my father was happy I was going to America."

"Indeed he was."

"What did he say?"

"I didn't memorize it."

"Please try."

I could hear her fingers tapping. In my mind's eye I saw her standing in our kitchen, telephone in hand, looking through the window into our back yard, perhaps recalling, as I was, the tranquil times we sat in the small gazebo, holding hands, happy to be together.

The tapping stopped. "Your father said he wanted you to find your heart."

"What does that mean?"

"I don't have a clue, dearest. But it was a wonderful thing for him to say."

The rest of the call, no more than a minute, consisted of awkward stabs at intimacy, mostly on my part. Talking on the telephone with a loved one is difficult. The inflections, body language, and nuances of eye movement are lost. And when the call has been completed and the phone is back in its cradle, it is as though the other person has disappeared, like a wispy cloud dissolving in the wind.

I sat at the desk and opened my notebook. I thought I would list the coincidences that had occurred during the past two days. But I stared at the blank page and wrote nothing. My father's comment had smothered all other thoughts. His arrogance was unbounded. I was not the one who had lost his heart.

I wondered what I could do to make the environment cheerier. I wanted the studio to be like my study at home. A colorful knickknack might help. A few potted plants. Perhaps some flowers. I wished I had the funds to rent or purchase a good chair for reading. The furniture was functional at best: a sofa bed against one wall, two rickety end tables with lamps on each (one missing a shade), a small desk (barely large enough to accommodate my notebook), a three-drawer pecan bureau with several holes where the knobs had been, a round tweed rug, a seventeen-inch television (which I had yet to turn on), a telephone, and one stool in the kitchenette. On the wall across from the sofa and above the television hung three metal shelves, on which I had placed a four-volume History of Ideas, the collected plays of Sean O'Casey, and a photograph of Mary and Lucy playing by the gazebo. A window in the front of the studio provided a view of 51st Street. Another window in the rear overlooked a small courtyard that looked as if it had been unattended for some time. Scattered among patches of dead grass and weeds were empty cans, broken bottles, two ripped suitcases, and an old gas stove.

I opened the front window. The air was damp from a light shower. The gray sky gave the city the look of dawn. I moved away from the window.

I took a shower and shaved. I dressed in brown corduroy pants, plaid flannel shirt, and the cashmere sweater Mary had given me on my thirty-sixth birthday. To complete the outfit I put on a blue blazer. Standing in front of the mirror that covered the length of the bathroom door, I saw a man of quiet confidence and poise, a most welcome fiction. I tugged at my jacket to smooth the single wrinkle on the left pocket. Then to the closet to get an umbrella. Now, I was ready to face the day.

As I walked along 51st Street I rhythmically tapped the umbrella on the sidewalk, keeping silent time to the taps of Mary's fingers during our telephone conversation. I replayed in my mind what she had said, juxtaposing what I knew about Tommy with my father's comment. What did Tommy and finding my heart have in common? "Nothing," I said out loud. Several pedestrians looked at me. I dropped my head in embarrassment.

At the corner newsstand I bought a New York Times, but resolved not to read it until I completed a satisfactory day of research. I reached the library as a light rain grew into a downpour. After ordering several monographs from the librarian in the main reading room, I took a seat at a long wooden table and waited. I looked at the folded newspaper on the table but did not open it. Work must come first.

After a half-hour I returned to the information desk. The librarian showed me a stack of requests and suggested I practice being patient. I found a seat and opened the newspaper. The front page was dominated by articles on the various investigations of President Clinton—in which I had no interest—but the lead line of a story at the bottom of the page was on another matter: "FBI ON TRIAL IN BOSTON," it announced, as if it might be possible to bring a government agency to justice.

Three defendants, leaders of the infamous Savin Hill gang, were seeking dismissal of the racketeering charges against them. They had accused an FBI agent of sanctioning their criminal activities for the past twenty years. The judge had scheduled a hearing for 15 May. I read about the history of the gang, named in honor of an area in Dorchester, once a solidly Irish Boston neighborhood that produced John "Whitey" Delaney, the gang's founder. The other two defendants were Italian: Carlito Gavencci and Vincente Marinelli, the latter a cousin of Salvatore Marinelli, the head of the New York Mafia. Salvatore and Vincente had feuded for years over territorial prerogatives in the Northeast. Delaney was not participating in the current proceedings. On the day the grand jury voted to approve the indictment he left his harbor-front condominium to meet Gavencci and Marinelli for lunch at Jimmy's Harborside, a popular Boston restaurant. He never arrived and had not been seen since. The story closed with a brief biography of Smith Corcoran, the FBI agent who had been the contact for the gang and whom Gavencci and Marinelli alleged had shared in their profits. Known to friends as "Smitty," he was fifty-three and a twenty-eight-year veteran of law enforcement. He had begun his career in Chicago.

Smitty. The coincidences were piling up like the scrapbooks of a long life. I tore the article from the newspaper. I walked over to the desk and cancelled my request for the monographs.

Outside, the rain had stopped and a hazy sun was playing peekaboo behind thick clouds. I purchased a hot pretzel at a corner food stand and sat on a bench, ignoring the soaked wood. I reread the article. When I finished I left the pretzel for the pigeons that had gathered at my feet.

I started walking with no destination in mind. At Times Square I came to a cinema. I could not remember the last time I had seen a movie. On the wall next to the ticket booth was a large poster. The faces of father and son overlaying a silhouetted New York suggested a family in transition. I spent the afternoon inside the dark theater, watching the film twice. It was called "The Godfather."

Goodness, Connie. You look like you came from the Harvard or Yale Club. Very Ivy League. No, I'm not making fun of you. I like your outfit. All you're missing is a bow tie.

I told you Smitty moved to Boston. Put the article away. I've read it. I was as surprised as you were. Do I believe the allegations against him are true? I wouldn't be surprised if they were. I told you he had an agenda. No, I haven't tried to contact him. Why would I? The past stays in the past where it belongs. Yes, I could have picked a different case to tell you about. But I thought you'd get a kick out of hearing how the government was served its comeuppance in the vendetta against Eudie. So it turns out to have an interesting connection to the present. What are you going to do? *Sue me, sue me, shoot bullets through me . . .* It's a song, Connie. What's the matter? Haven't you seen *Guys and Dolls?* Is Belfast a cultural wasteland? Where else would you be from? You don't look French. Connie, lighten up. It was a guess. I'm not psychic. What became of Eudie? Beats me. If he isn't dead, he's in his eighties. He's probably running a bingo game somewhere in Florida. You're right. I did say Eudie moved to Boston and went to work for a gambling business. Was it the Savin Hill gang? Could have been. Why are you pulling out the article again? I told you I read it. Oh, right. It did say two Italians and an Irishman ran the gang. Yes. Yes. You've convinced me. It must be the same gang. How many gangs are run by two Italians and an Irishman? I'll tell you what. Why don't I leave and let you commit the article to memory? Oh, you already have. You're not joking, are you? Will you stop being so goddamned serious? We're supposed to be having a good time. I understand. I'd miss my wife, if I were across the Atlantic from her. Is it any of your business? She's home, if you must know. She's a writer. No, she no longer works at the law firm. She worked there for ten years. Now what? You don't say. The nutcase was standing on the corner last night when you left. You should have come back. I would have walked you home.

Are you certain? Interesting. I know a lot of people who use the royal we. Doctors, for instance. You know how they say: "Are *we* feeling better?"

Was I satisfied with his explanation? I was not sure. It was as if two sides of me—the cynical son of an angry Irish Catholic and the mild mannered student of history—were locked in a debate, with one or the other side gaining the advantage at different times.

Come on. Let me buy you a Guinness. We're not here to review Smitty's career, Eudie's retirement, or the Savin Hill gang's criminal enterprise. I've been thinking about last night's discussion. All that nonsense on interviewing and the secret of success. I'm supposed to be focusing on the war between law and justice, not my fragile psyche. Pathetic.

You look distracted. It's not the article again, is it? Tommy Glynn? I told you I . . . Interesting. The lawyer was on TV in Belfast? I wish I'd seen it. I don't know. Curiosity, nothing more.

I was anxious to find my place in the world of law, but Uncle Sam had other plans. I turned twenty-five a month before graduation and had a year left of eligibility for the draft. In response to criticism that white, upper-middle class men were ending up at the bottom of the draft list, the government set up a lottery system. I drew number sixty-two, which guaranteed I'd be drafted.

My only out—other than fleeing to Canada, an option I had neither the guts nor a sufficiently rebellious spirit to seriously consider—was to find a job that would give me a deferment until I was twenty-six. Bertha, the head of the placement office, was a peacenik and offered to help. She gave me a list of the sixty federal judges who were willing to certify that their law clerks' services were necessary for the effective administration of justice. In other words, helping judges was more important than serving our country in Vietnam.

As you might have suspected, these judges were flooded with applications and I received one rejection after another. To get the feel of the military I window shopped at army surplus stores and took a tour of a munitions factory. I went to see the movie, *The Green Berets*, but left the theater thinking John Wayne hadn't been any nicer to the Vietnamese than he had been to the Indians. I asked about joining the Judge Advocate Corp and was told I would have to make a five-year commitment. I ran into a veteran who had lost an arm and three toes when he fell on a grenade. He said I'd be lucky to come home in the same shape.

I was getting ready to call Sarah and Albert and tell them to stock up on stamps when I received a letter from the Honorable Thor W. Gunderson, a federal judge in Washington, D.C. The letter said I could come in for an interview. Bertha told me not to get my hopes up. All of Gunderson's clerks during his twenty years on the bench had been graduates of Georgetown, his alma mater.

Gunderson occupied a spacious suite with a view of the Capitol building. On the walls of the anteroom were numerous citations and photographs, a kind of graphic biography of his distinguished career: pictures of Senator Hubert Humphrey—who had recommended his appointment to President Truman—Eisenhower, and Supreme Court Justice Earl Warren; a letter from the American Civil Liberties Union, congratulating him for having the courage to rule in favor of a government researcher who'd been fired because of past membership in a Communist front organization; various awards and honors from organizations in Minnesota where he had been Governor for four terms.

When the secretary ushered me into his office I was taken aback by his casual dress. He looked like he'd been Governor of Montana rather than Minnesota. In his denim pants and brown leather sports jacket that reached a little below the brass buckle on his western style belt he could have passed for a retired cowboy or the star of a Marlboro commercial.

I sat in a comfortable leather chair to the side of his shiny mahogany desk. From a metal ashtray that was shaped like an arrowhead he took an unlit pipe and stuck it between his yellow teeth.

"As you may have heard," he said in a high-pitched nasal voice with a Swedish accent, "I've always hired my clerks from Georgetown. But I like to see who else is out there. I hope you won't be offended that I put the resumes in a pile and selected one at random."

"No, sir."

"Naturally, your chances would be better if you were a member of a minority group."

"I'm Jewish."

"I don't consider the Jewish people to be a minority. In numbers, perhaps, but they're . . . well, let me say it this way . . . they make their presence known."

"Yes, sir."

"I've wanted to hire a Negro clerk, but Georgetown has so few. I do support affirmative action. We must see to it that every school is integrated. But sometimes the Negro doesn't want integration."

"Yes, sir."

He took the pipe out of his mouth and tapped it on the desk. "If you intend to practice law, young man, you will have to learn to say more than 'yes, sir.'"

"Yes, sir."

He grinned. Maybe I have a chance, I thought.

"I would consider it a great honor to serve as your clerk," I said.

He put his chin to hand as if to strike the pose of Rodin's *The Thinker.* "Everyone wants to clerk for a judge in this court. I'm sure you're aware we're the most important federal district in the land. On any given day, we may be called upon to decide a seminal legal issue, a question that would have presented a challenge to Holmes or Frankfurter. At any moment we may stand at the intersection of history, where to turn right would take us back to the past, and a turn left forward to the future." He let out a booming laugh that quickly segued into a coughing spasm. He removed a handkerchief from his jacket pocket and spit into it.

"Alas," he continued as he examined what he deposited into the handkerchief, "three years ago, on my sixty-fifth birthday, I became a Senior Judge. Now I preside over the law's junkyard: fender benders, slips and falls, petty larceny, car theft, trespass . . . " He opened the top drawer of the desk and pulled out a sheet of paper. "And now this!" he shouted.

"What is it?"

'They want to send me to Malta.'

"There's a court in Malta?"

"My dear boy, there's a court everywhere."

I imagined spending mornings on white sandy beaches, drafting his opinions, enjoying frozen Daiquiris at lunch, slumbering blissfully every afternoon at the private pool next to my villa, drinking fine wine from the vineyards of Polynesia—are there vineyards in Polynesia?—and learning the indigenous dances in the embrace of a young woman of unfathomable beauty . . .

"Don't you want to know what I told them?" he asked.

Reluctantly, I pulled away from my imagined enchantress. "Yes, of course."

"I told them to fuck off."

Her image faded. She was gone forever. "Yes, sir," I said.

"Then you agree I was right to reject the assignment?"

. "I don't think Malta is at the intersection of history."

He thrust a hand across the desk. "Welcome to the fight. This time I know our side will win."

"Isn't that—?"

"*Casablanca.* You do love the movies, I trust. Like Daedalus, a lawyer must escape the labyrinth of the law. He must don wings and fly to other worlds."

Though I didn't know what he was talking about, I was happy to get the job.

$$⚖$$

I couldn't wait to tell Bertha the good news. As I described the interview her smile grew wider and her pink cheeks puffed up like pink balloons. "Isn't it great," I said. "He picked me instead of a Georgetown student."

"I knew you would get it."

"How? You said he only hires clerks from Georgetown."

"That was before he became a Senior Judge. Didn't you have your eyes open? Didn't you notice there wasn't a law clerk around? No one wants to work for a judge who rejects the interesting cases."

"He turns cases down? I thought—"

"He decides what cases he wants to hear. A fringe benefit of being a senior judge. And the cases he wants are the ones requiring the least amount of work."

Still, my year with Gunderson had its rewards. Most clerks have so much work they can't afford the time to watch trials. Gunderson gave me little work and, in any case, wanted me to see lawyers in action. He said they were models of what *not* to emulate. Sometimes it seemed as if he were representing one side or the other. He'd interrupt lawyers and take over questioning the witnesses; he'd tell jurors what he thought of the case; he'd advise litigants to speak up if they thought their lawyers were doing a poor job. When he ruled on motions he would always tell the lawyers that they missed the most important issue.

As he had warned, the cases were indeed from the law's junkyard. Junk can be interesting, though. There's nothing quite like watching a welfare recipient, her personal injury lawyer in tow, fighting the great fight against the department store that neglected to shovel the snow off the sidewalk. Or watching the prosecutor pursue petty thieves as if they had committed war crimes. Or listening to a husband testify that he should be awarded damages because his wife refused to have sex with him.

As the end of the term neared, Gunderson took on a string of cases in which the defendants were charged with possession of a stolen car. In each case the defendant waived his right to a jury. In each case the defendant said his uncle had lent him the car and he didn't know it was stolen. In each case Gunderson acquitted the defendant.

"How could you believe the defendants?" I asked him on the last day of my term.

"Why shouldn't I have believed them?"

"They all said the same thing."

"I don't know that."

"You don't?"

"I'm a different jury in each case. One jury doesn't know what the other one has heard."

"But you do know," I insisted.

He retired a month later to care for his sick wife. They bought a small piece of land in the Minnesota woods. She died the following year. A month later he was found on the floor of his cabin, dead from a self-inflicted gunshot wound. By his side was a book of Greek myths. The first story was about Daedalus, the architect of the Cretan labyrinth and the inventor of wings.

Telling that story reminds me of the first and only time I represented a defendant in a criminal case. No, I'm not being honest. Not too long ago I did have another criminal case, but what was criminal in that case wasn't what the defendant did. Besides, by that time I was already who I am now and I prefer to talk about who I was. You see, Connie—and this may seem odd—I have an overwhelming desire to explain myself to you. I want you to understand me. Is that OK? Because if it isn't, I'll finish my drink and leave.

What was the reason for his outburst? This was our third night together and I had not said much, nor had I evidenced lack of interest in his stories. And it was more than odd that he wanted to explain himself. What was there to explain? He sounded almost as if he was apologizing to me. Or was he apologizing for his life? The only way to find out was to listen.

Thanks, Connie. Patrick! Get this man another Guinness. He's a saint! No? You're hungry. I am too. Let's go to dinner. My treat. They serve food here? I'm used to . . . The truth is I'm spoiled. I know a terrific Italian restaurant. The owner always gives me a good table, toward the rear where you can watch wise guys from Staten Island, old men fawning over their young mistresses, and the occasional tourist who wants to see how a mobster behaves in public. The name? Marinelli's. What is it? Your pink face has turned white.

I took out the article and showed him the reference to Vincente and Salvatore Marinelli.

You're too clever, Connie. Marinelli is a common Italian name. If I read in the paper that a man named Sullivan was the head of the Irish Mafia, am I to assume he's your relative? Are you related to the Sullivan brothers who died in World War II? Maybe you're the great-great grandson of the boxer, John L. Sullivan. OK, you win. I won't play games. In fact, the owner of Marinelli's is a Mafioso. Is he the Marinelli mentioned in the article? Yes. So what? It's not a crime to eat in a restaurant owned by a mobster. You're being silly. Life is full of coincidences.

    I'm not protesting too much. I told you a story about Eudie Lufman and Smitty's efforts to make him an informant. Now, Smitty is stuck in a controversy involving gangsters in Boston, including a man named Marinelli who happens to be the owner of a restaurant I frequent. Leave if you're so suspicious. You're not my prisoner.

*   And just a few moments ago I had decided to stay. I was a fool. I had not come to America to spend evenings in taverns listening to a stranger tell stories from his life. Find your heart, my father had said. How was I to find my heart talking to someone who was by turn open and secretive, friendly and hostile, who needled me every time I asked a question? I played with the empty glass of Guinness. He waited for my decision. I stopped playing with the glass and looked at him. He was the picture of serenity. "Let us eat," I said.*

I'm glad we decided to stay. We can eat at the Italian restaurant some other time. Let's see what on the agenda here. Oh, right. Chicken potpie. Great. No? Why would I want to insult you? Chicken potpie is a standard Irish dish, isn't it? Don't be so sensitive. Lighten up. I'll tell you another story, this one about my client, Leonard Stone, and our journey through what we illogically call our criminal justice system; we should just call it our criminal system, and guess what, often, the criminal is as much the system as the defendant.

Leonard was a sad sack of a man. He weighed no more than a hundred and thirty pounds. Since he was approximately your height—close to six feet—he looked like a long distance runner, except he was out of shape and constantly wheezing from a four-pack-a-day cigarette habit. But thin doesn't begin to describe him. It was how the weight was distributed: his fat face, bulging cheeks, and potbelly left few pounds for his arms and legs.

"The mass of men lead lives of quiet desperation," and Leonard was a quiet and desperate man. His father died when he was six and his mother left home when he was twelve. He and his sister lived with his aunt until he was sixteen, when he dropped out of high school. He lived alone and flitted from job to job: grocery store clerk, gas station attendant, janitor, that sort of thing. He got older and lonelier.

I met Leonard when he was thirty-six and living in a one-bedroom apartment in Oak Forest, a suburb southwest of Chicago populated largely by lower middle class workers and retirees. He was employed as a warehouseman at a scrap metal company located across from a trailer park. On a steamy August night in 1974 he attacked Linda Cox in her trailer while her two-year-old daughter cowered in fear under a wobbly trundle bed.

Leonard's sister was married to Joe Markowitz's next-door neighbor. Joe was the head of litigation at Litowitz, Smith, Cohen & Whitmore, where I worked after leaving the strike force. She called Joe for help. Joe had never handled a criminal case and asked me to represent Leonard.

What did I know about defending a criminal case? I had been a prosecutor. You put on your witnesses, cross-examine the defense witnesses, and give a well-reasoned closing argument. You don't need skill, passion, or imagination. To defend you need every trick of the best courtroom performers and a theory that will overcome your biggest obstacle: the guilt of your client.

The evidence against Leonard was overwhelming. Linda knew who he was from the numerous times she'd seen him sitting on the grass outside the trailer park. If you believed her account, Leonard had been a miserable failure as a rapist. After he broke into the trailer, he brandished a knife and forced her onto the bed. As he held her throat with one hand, he put down the knife and massaged his limp cock. She grabbed the knife and stabbed him several times in the back. He ran out and drove home, where he took off his bloody tee shirt and threw it in the bathtub. In the morning he went to the grocery store to buy a bagel, two hard-boiled eggs, and bacon. The cops were waiting for him when he returned. He acted surprised that he was being arrested. The cops asked if he wanted a lawyer. He said he didn't know any lawyers and would like to call his sister. After the call, they asked him to remove his shirt. They saw the wounds. Later that day, armed with a search warrant, they went back to his apartment. They found a bloody tee shirt with six jagged holes in the back.

What defense could I manufacture from these facts? Linda had identified him and the physical evidence tied him to the crime. Conviction for attempted rape carried a maximum sentence of thirty-five years, an astonishing amount of time when you consider all he did was grab her throat. I realize he was intent on doing more, but he couldn't. No, I'm not being callous. OK, you win. Maybe I am—but only a little. He may have had rape in his heart and mind, but his cock wanted nothing to do with Linda Cox. Think about it. Thirty-five years is a long time to spend in a cage. That's longer than the sentences most murderers receive. In fact, didn't you tell me Tommy Glynn was sentenced to thirty years for a car bombing? Sure you did. You forgot.

I had not forgotten. And why had he suddenly mentioned Tommy Glynn? When I first referred to Tommy, he said he had never heard of him.

Ah, here we are. Shepherd's pie for you and Chicken potpie for me. Excuse me? The point? The point is that the law is interested in punishment, and the punishment never fits the crime. Punishment is mischief. Smart fellow, Jeremy Bentham. He also said punishment is evil. You don't have to be in favor of rape to question the justice of putting people in prison, which after all is just a bunch of cages. What does punishment accomplish? Retribution?

Deterrence? Lately, the law has been moving more in the direction of individual retribution. We have what's called a *victim impact statement,* which the judge considers when imposing sentence. Why should the impact on a victim, whatever that means, affect the length of the sentence? If a rape victim doesn't suffer lasting psychological injury, should the defendant receive a lighter sentence than in a case where she's emotionally ruined for life? If I steal a hundred dollars from a millionaire, should I be treated lightly because the victim isn't a pauper? What if I didn't know the victim's wealth? What if I intended to be Robin Hood and stole from the poor by mistake?

I'm not trying to defend Leonard. He wasn't a model citizen. He contributed nothing of value to society. He frittered away his days in dead-end work and drank away his nights. He squandered whatever potential he possessed. And lest you think his attack on Linda Cox was nothing more than a glitch in an otherwise law-abiding life, he had assaulted a woman once before. Fifteen years earlier he accosted a sixty-two-year-old woman on the platform of a train station. He snuck up behind her and placed his hands under her coat and between her legs. The judge sentenced him to two years at the state penitentiary in Joliet. Loss of freedom represented only part of his punishment. He was raped a dozen times at Joliet.

Leonard's sister posted a bond and he was released. When I met him he said he didn't remember trying to rape Linda. In fact, he said he didn't remember what happened between his fourth bottle of beer at a local bar and restaurant called the White Horse Inn and waking up the next morning with a hangover and dull ache in his back. He said he was incapable of rape. What about the old woman at the railroad station? I asked. As if another lawyer had prepared him for his talk with me, he nonchalantly said the attack happened during a difficult time in his life. A girlfriend had broken up with him, he was having trouble paying his bills, and his future was bleak. I said he wasn't the only one who had suffered the trifecta of contemporary life's most common problems. He continued his apologia, extolling the virtues of the prison psychiatrist who had helped him deal with his abandonment issues. He sounded as if he'd taken an adult education course on current trends in psychology.

I was left to ponder whether he should plead guilty and hope for leniency. It would be difficult to negotiate a deal in light of his previous conviction. Even so, I called the prosecutor, Gil Rose, who I didn't know, so I couldn't expect much. Still, as Sarah never grew tired of saying: It never hurts to ask, to which I add, if you can handle rejection.

The telephone conversation didn't last long. Rose asked for an offer. I suggested four years, the minimum sentence for attempted rape. He laughed and asked me to make another proposal. "OK, I said, "ten years, five in prison and five on probation." This time he didn't laugh, but what he said was worse: "I spend my days prosecuting all kinds of scumbags, but rapists are a special type of scumbag. Twenty years, not a day less. Take it or leave it." I hung up the phone and waited for cocktail hour.

You were right about the food. It's excellent. You want to stay here or go back to the bar? I'll take the check. I told you it was my treat. I'll put it on my credit card. Wait a second. You might see my name. No, it's not because you've heard of me. My name wouldn't mean a thing to you. Why won't I tell you? Because you're inquisitive. You'll run to the library tomorrow and look me up. You'll find out everything you can and won't want to hear my other stories. I know you've told me your name, but you're not famous like me. I haven't contradicted myself. I can be famous without being known to you. How many American lawyers have you heard of? Who? Samuel Brandt? Who is he? Tommy Glynn's lawyer? You're teasing me, Connie. He's not famous.

I said the name Samuel Brandt to test him. Ridiculous. Did I expect him to tell me he was Samuel Brandt? If he was Samuel Brandt, why not tell me?

When I got home I made a martini and retreated to the den. I couldn't sit still and started walking around the room. If you're going to represent a guilty defendant, you need imagination. On top of the TV was *The Terminal Man*, a book I had read a couple of months before. I took the book and thumbed through the pages. There was Leonard's defense.

The plot centers on an everyman who experiences uncontrollable and unpredictable bursts of violence. He has a rare form of brain damage called psychomotor epilepsy. And he can't remember his violent acts.

Leonard's claimed loss of memory didn't mean he suffered from psychomotor epilepsy. But the possibility intrigued me. If he did have brain damage, I could use the insanity defense.

The insanity defense is a legal concoction with no scientific basis. Insanity is not a disease or medical condition. It's a shorthand description for the state of mind that society believes should absolve a defendant of responsibility for criminal conduct. Traditionally, a defendant could use the defense only if he didn't know right from wrong. This principle, called the McNaughten rule, remained the prevailing standard until the 1950s. Few could take advantage of it. Unless mental illness caused the accused to lose his cognitive functions, chances were he knew the difference between right and wrong. On the other hand, the defendant who met the test was, more often than not, too mentally disabled to cooperate with his lawyer and thus not competent to stand trial. He might spend his life in an institution and never be tried. For this defendant, the insanity defense was a life sentence.

In 1954, federal appeals court judge Richard Bazelon decided it was time to broaden the defense. In a case in which a defendant was convicted because he knew right from wrong, Bazelon ordered a new trial. He ruled that the insanity defense would now include any mental disease or defect, which rendered the defendant unable to either appreciate the nature of his act or conform his conduct to the requirements of the law. A little later, Illinois adopted the new standard.

I sent Leonard to a neurologist who took an electroencephalogram ("EEG"). An EEG records the patient's brain waves on a graph. In theory, the neurologist can look at the graph and see whether the patient is having a seizure. Imagine my astonishment when the neurologist called and said he had detected evidence of seizure activity in Leonard's anterior temporal lobe, the part of the brain where psychomotor epilepsy supposedly originates.

I saw the neurologist at the hospital. He didn't have his own office, the ones that are used by whoever is on duty. It was befittingly sterile: blank walls except for an eye chart, an examining cot covered with paper sheets, and a shelf of sample medications. He was a young man, not long out of medical school. I had picked him because he didn't charge much.

He wasn't as encouraging in person as on the phone. He said he wasn't sure what the EEG meant. He also refused to say whether Leonard had brain damage. And regardless of what the EEG showed, he said it wasn't possible to know whether Leonard actually had seizures; his psychomotor epilepsy might by asymptomatic. In short, an EEG could not reveal whether Leonard had a seizure when he attacked Linda Cox. Then he made the most damaging point, one I should have seen if I hadn't fallen so much in love with my own cleverness. Despite the characteristic spikes of psychomotor epilepsy during the EEG, Leonard had remained calm and aware. He hadn't jumped off the examining table and attacked the nurse.

It was clear the young doctor wasn't going to risk his reputation for Leonard Stone. He said he'd testify the EEG graph was consistent with psychomotor epilepsy, but nothing more. If asked, he would say he didn't have an opinion whether Leonard had ever experienced a seizure. He did offer that Leonard's lack of memory supported the seizure hypothesis. But Leonard's lack of memory was a significant disadvantage. He wouldn't be able to testify what he was thinking during the attack. He couldn't say he had a seizure.

I obviously needed help and asked him if he knew anyone who might offer a more aggressive opinion. He suggested I call Dr. William Gruenberg, a well-known psychiatrist.

Excuse me. I have to make a call. We'll continue at the bar. Order me a drink, please.

He headed toward the payphone, leaving his cigarettes on the table. A matchbook had slipped out of the cellophane wrapper. On the cover were the words, Jimmy's Harborside. The name was familiar. But I could not remember where I had seen it.

Where is my drink? You forgot! Connie! How could you forget? You look distracted. Oh, thanks. What would I do without cigarettes? Jimmy's Harborside? It's a restaurant in Boston. I haven't been there in years. Matchbooks spread through the population like a contagion. Not too long ago I asked a guy for a light and he gave me a matchbook from a restaurant that closed twenty years ago. I could have gotten these anywhere.

Thanks, Patrick. Isn't Patrick the best? He's always ready with our drinks.

When I got to the office there was an envelope on my desk from Gil Rose. It contained the test results on Leonard's tee shirt. The report said the blood tested as type B. Leonard was type O.

I went next door to Joe's office. Joe was a fount of knowledge in areas having nothing to do with business litigation. I showed him the lab report.

"As crazy as it seems," I said, "this suggests Leonard is innocent."

"Not innocent," he said. "But almost as good. A corrupted blood sample often comes up as type B. But it's still a problem for Rose. The lab technician can't say for sure that the blood was tainted."

I returned to my office and thought about Joe's comment. What problem could Rose have? The other evidence against Leonard was more than enough to convict. His tee shirt was riddled with holes and Linda had identified him. One thing, however, could be in my favor. No prosecutor wants to be embarrassed.

I called Rose. I didn't have to say a word. "If you read the report, you know you got me," he said. "I'll take a plea to aggravated assault and recommend six months in county jail. Tell your client he lucked out."

I was looking forward to delivering the good news to Leonard. But when I called him, he didn't want to discuss Rose's offer. He had talked to the neurologist. And he knew about Gruenberg. I tried to steer the conversation back to what Rose had said, but he would have none of it. He said he wanted to come to the office to discuss the insanity defense. After the call, I realized I hadn't said anything about an insanity defense.

He didn't arrive until the end of the day. "Where were you?" I asked.

"The library." He lit a cigarette and paced nervously back and forth in front of my desk.

"Doing what?"

"Reading up on the insanity defense."

"Forget about it," I said.

"The neurologist said this Gruenberg fellow is an expert."

"The offer I got from Rose is better. You'll be out in six months."

He sat on the couch under the college and law degrees Sarah had framed.

"I don't think so," he said.

"The judge will go along with what Rose recommends."

He flicked ashes on the floor. I brought him an ashtray. He put it on the floor next to the ashes and looked at the degrees. "You're a smart guy," he said.

"We're not talking intelligence here, Leonard. We're talking what's practical."

"I get headaches all the time."

"Take aspirin."

"I have brain damage."

"It's bullshit. Forget it."

"The neurologist said I have psychomotor epilepsy. Doesn't that beat all. It explains everything."

"Leonard, pay attention. The prosecutor knows you jumped Linda, Linda knows you jumped Linda, and I know you jumped Linda. If we try an insanity defense and it doesn't work, you'll go to prison until you're an old man. Do yourself a favor and take the deal. Do me a favor and take the deal."

He pulled out a sheet of paper from his back pocket. "Got this in the library. It says here that drinking can start a seizure. It also says—"

"Let me see that." Leonard handed me the paper. It was a copy of an article written by Gruenberg.

"I want you to call Dr. Gruenberg," he said. "I don't want to plead guilty to something I didn't do."

"But you did it."

"If I did, and I'm not saying I did, I didn't know what I was doing."

On it went for the next hour. He wouldn't budge. He even parried my argument that a jury would have no sympathy for him, whatever doctors might say. "Then forget the jury," he said. "We'll leave it up to the judge."

I called Rose and told him Leonard had rejected his offer. "He's insane," Rose said.

Dr. William Gruenberg. In 1966, Richard Speck, a twenty-four-year-old drifter who had served time in prison for theft and forgery, murdered eight student nurses in their Chicago dormitory. Gruenberg examined Speck for 100 hours. He concluded that drugs and alcohol combined with brain damage had triggered a seizure and was the cause of his rampage. The jury was unconvinced and convicted Speck.

I left a message for Gruenberg at his office. He called me back from his country club. He said he no longer practiced medicine. He ran a counseling service for overstressed corporate managers. After I described the case he said Leonard would have to take a series of psychological tests. Depending on the results, he might agree to testify.

Leonard took three tests: the Wechsler Adult Intelligence Scale, the Rorschach Inkblot Test, and the Thematic Apperception Test. The Wechsler is a conventional intelligence test. The other two plumb the mind by eliciting stories and images from the patient. The responses are then compared with the results from other patients.

At the interview with the psychologist Leonard added a fact to his account of the night he attacked Linda. He said he remembered smelling a strange but familiar odor while drinking at the White Horse Inn. Strange because the odor was noxious, familiar because he had smelled the same odor when he attacked the old woman on the railroad platform. Gruenberg's office was a large room on the ninth floor of a dilapidated office building with a view of Grant Park and Lake Michigan. The office, however, was grungy: dust everywhere, paint peeling off the walls, flies buzzing around like they owned the place. A small picture of Jung hung at an angle behind a leather-covered desk. Afternoon light came through the dust-covered window, unassisted by an overhead gold plated fixture with a burnt out bulb and a pole lamp with empty sockets. In the dim light I tripped over the corner of an Oriental rug.

Gruenberg was sitting behind his desk. His face was very round, almost swollen. His eyes were close together, with pupils grotesquely magnified by thick tortoise shell glasses that sat crookedly on his broad pudgy nose. His face looked like it had been constructed from spare parts. If you painted a portrait of him in the realistic style you would be judged deficient in perspective and proportion.

He asked me to sit, apparently oblivious that there were no other chairs in the office, no furniture at all in fact. "It's clear," he said. "A classic case of psychomotor epilepsy. It's a wonder your client hasn't raped more women."

"He didn't rape her. He couldn't get an erection and she stabbed him."

"It was the alcohol," he said. "Alcohol is poison for the epileptic."

'That's why he couldn't get an erection?"

"No, the alcohol set off the seizure. His failure to have an erection arose from deep-rooted psychological problems."

I asked the penultimate question, which he would have to answer at trial. "Are you convinced to a reasonable degree of medical certainty that the combination of alcohol and his damaged brain produced a seizure, thus making it impossible for him to conform his conduct to the requirements of the law?"

"Yes."

I tested him with the counterfacts. "Assume Stone was planning to break into Linda's trailer when he left his apartment, but first stopped at the White Horse for a few drinks."

"Is that true?"

"The knife Linda used on Leonard came from his kitchen."

"Have you discussed this with him?"

"He says he doesn't remember taking the knife."

"Ah, just as I suspected. The seizure began before he left home."

"He wasn't drinking at his apartment."

Gruenberg took off his glasses and put them on the desk. His eyes shrunk to peepholes. "I never said that alcohol is the exclusive triggering agent."

"What else, then?"

"Any kind of stress. Bad day at work, worry, depression. A seizure may last for hours, even days. He could have had two seizures, or three, each increasing his vulnerability."

"Aren't you speculating?"

"Thinking out loud is a better way of putting it. Seizures of the anterior temporal lobe are sneak attacks. They can come at any time. No warning, no advance symptoms. Leonard could have been experiencing seizures— minor attacks—without noticing them, and all the while his resistance was weakening."

"How can you be so sure?"

He was on his feet. "Come." I followed him to the window. "Look at the Buckingham fountain. Beautiful." It was indeed beautiful, its ornate brown bowl and tower tending toward burgundy in the light of the setting sun. "See the pattern of the water, rising and falling. Imagine they're brain waves. Look closely. See the needle of water shoot above the dome. A seizure. It doesn't happen in discrete intervals. It's not like Old Faithful. But suddenly—look, two in a row. Wait! There. Another one."

We stood in front of the window for another minute or so. No more needles appeared. "See," he said. "All is calm again." He moved away from the window. "Random acts of violence years apart happen for a reason. Your client attacked the woman for a reason. The reason was a seizure. I'll stake my reputation on it."

On the way to my car I stopped by the fountain. I watched the thirty-foot spout for an hour. Not a single needle shot up from the cone of water. A stiff breeze came up and distorted the cone, spraying a fine mist through the air. I wondered what my EEG would look like. Could human action be so easily identified from spikes on a graph? What about the heart? Silly romantic metaphor. The heart pumps blood. Does nothing else. Don't you agree, Connie?

For God's sake, Connie, what is it now? Will you hold on? Patrick, get this man a glass of water. Last night, I was upset. Now it's you. Here, drink slowly. You don't want to choke on water, do you?

Look what time it is. I've got to go. Are you all right? Sit here for a few minutes and relax. Patrick won't throw you out. I'm counting on seeing you tomorrow night, you know.

He threw a few bills on the bar and hurried away. Patrick brought me another glass of water and waited while I drank it. He watched me as if he expected that I would want to speak with him. But I could think only of what my father had said: find your heart.

I handed Patrick the glass and got off the stool. The matchbook, the one with Jimmy's Harborside on it, was in front of me on the counter. I put it in my pocket.

When I got home I undressed and went to bed. I quickly fell into a deep, dreamless sleep.

CHAPTER FOUR

May 13, 1998

I N ALL THE YEARS *I lived in a city and country where fear and danger are an unwelcome constant I never experienced such palpable anxiety as when I rose the next morning. At first, I was confused. I did not know where I was. Then, as my eyes focused on the room around me, I knew.*

I wiped the sleep from my eyes and picked up my clothes from the floor. A matchbook fell out of the pile. An anchor on the front, small lettering at the bottom: "Jimmy's Harborside." So familiar, but I could not place it. Then, as my mind gradually came to life, I remembered. The newspaper story. Of course.

The article was still in my pants pocket and I hurried to retrieve it. There, in the second paragraph was the reference to the restaurant where Savin Hill gang leader Whitey Delaney was to meet his colleagues the day he disappeared. Another coincidence?

In the shower, I turned the nozzle to the hardest spray. I knew I could not continue as I had. I decided that this night I would confront him and demand answers. The showerhead sputtered, the water stopped flowing and then resumed, scalding my skin, just as suddenly turning as cold as ice. I nearly fell as I stepped over the side of the bathtub. I raised a fist toward the ceiling. Cursed New York, I said out loud. Why had I come here?

Once dressed, I was pleased to see that I had recovered some of my equanimity. I would walk to the Irish Tourist Bureau and see if they might assist me in what was, after all, the original purpose of my trip. I had not come this far to wend away my days worrying and my nights in idle chatter.

At the corner of 53rd and Lexington I stopped at an outdoor café for an espresso. I took a seat at a rickety table and watched the stream of people

coming from the underground tube, so many thousands of strangers rushing to work. One man was standing still as the people swirled by him as they would around a statue. He was tall and holding a newspaper up high in front of his face. A few yards ahead, a black limousine pulled alongside the curb. The driver stuck his head out the window, looking this way and that. Suddenly, the world went as black as the limousine.

Light returned in a blur of colors. A man in a brown and white checked sport jacket was cradling my head. "Are you all right, sir?" he asked.

"What happened? I was—"

"I was sitting in my limo waiting for a customer and I saw you keel over. You must have fainted."

He helped me to my feet and held me around my back while I regained my equilibrium.

He handed me my wallet. "It fell out when you fainted."

"Thank you."

"You look pale. Can I take you to a doctor?"

"No, thank you. I am all right."

He brushed my jacket with his hands. "Are you sure?"

"Yes."

He led me back to the table. I touched the back of my head and felt a large knot. I wanted to offer him additional thanks but he had already walked away and was getting into the limousine.

I did not continue to the Tourist Board. Instead, I returned to the studio and got into bed. I woke up late in the afternoon with the oddest thought. The driver had left in his limousine without a passenger.

My apologies if I ran out in a huff last night. I was pooped. And I think I upset you. Nothing compared to today? What about today? What happened? Let me feel that. It's a whopper. Did you go to the doctor? I can give you the name and number of my doctor. I am paying attention. Go ahead. Maybe his customer got in the limo when you were unconscious. Honestly, Connie, I don't know what to say. It doesn't sound so odd to me. There could be any number of reasons. Maybe he got a call on his cell phone canceling the pickup.

What else is troubling you? The matchbook? For goodness sake, Connie, we've been through this. Jimmy's is a very popular Boston restaurant.

When did you last speak to your wife? No wonder. You need a little sweet-talking from home. Here, I'll write down my credit card number and you can call her from the payphone. She'll be thrilled to hear from you.

He wrote the number on a bar napkin. As I went to the telephone I saw the strange man, the faux government agent, sitting alone at a table. He was reading a newspaper, holding it high in the air. I felt nauseous again. The walls and tables shifted and twisted. A sconce light flickered. I teetered and crashed into a chair.

He was beside me. While Patrick gave me a glass of water, he rubbed my neck.

"You're hot as an iron," he said.

"I am fine."

"You might have a concussion."

"That man. He is in the back."

"What man?"

"The man who said he was an agent."

"Connie, please. See for yourself. He's not here."

I looked. Indeed, he was gone. "He was here a moment ago."

"Connie, I didn't see him come in and I didn't see him leave. What else can I say?"

What he could say was that the agent—or whoever he was—had been standing in the plaza when I fainted. A gesture or a quirk can be as certain a means of identification as a fingerprint. Holding the newspaper up high was his fingerprint.

Was it fair for me to think that he had something to do with the earlier incident? I would bide my time, listening and watching for more clues to this mystery.

I put the recorder on the bar and pressed the play button. "Tell me what happened to Leonard Stone."

I told Joe about the meeting with Gruenberg. He said it was fine that Gruenberg was so definite in his opinion, but I would need another psychiatrist. Gruenberg's reputation had been tarnished by his involvement in the Speck case. Joe suggested I call Dr. Stephen Bamberger, a lawyer who had given up the law for medicine. He had also written extensively on the insanity defense. If he agreed with Gruenberg's diagnosis, it would add considerable strength to Leonard's defense.

Where Gruenberg's office made psychiatry seem one step away from sorcery, Bamberger's office made psychiatry seem the province of the hip and urbane. The chrome bookshelves behind the chrome desk were stuffed with medical texts and books of poetry, philosophy, and history. It's as if Bamberger wanted his guests to appreciate the breadth of his learning.

Bamberger looked and dressed the part of psychiatrist as dapper scholar: tall and lean with the angular face of a male model, matching Calvin Klein navy blue blazer and gray slacks, and Bally shoes. The scent of his Jovan cologne found every corner of the office.

As I described the case and the meeting with Gruenberg, Bamberger sat with his feet propped on his desk, like an indulgent father listening to his young and innocent son's tale of a first trip abroad. And he was only a couple of years older than I was, which intimidated me even more.

"There's a foolproof method for determining if Mr. Stone is suffering from psychomotor epilepsy," he said.

"What's that?"

"Sodium Amytal."

"Is it like Sodium Pentothol? Truth serum?"

"Yes, but calling it truth serum implies that concretized truth has value."

"I'm afraid you've lost me, Doctor."

"The drug is like a two-way periscope. The subconscious is submerged, trapped and blinded by the murky depths. Amytal thrusts the mind above the surface into the light, where it can see and be seen."

"I understand."

"Do you? With light comes exposure. With exposure comes danger."

"The drug has side effects?"

"Just one. The patient may experience a psychotic break."

"How long does it last?"

"It varies. A few minutes, a few hours. The patient recovers—most of the time."

"And when he doesn't recover?"

He reached in his desk drawer and removed a loose-leaf binder. "Would you care to review the current studies?"

"No thanks. Will he remember what happened on the night of the attack?"

"What makes you think he's forgotten?"

"You think he's lying?"

"Malingering is the appropriate term. Lying is a word for lawyers."

"You're a lawyer."

"Was a lawyer."

"Do you have something against the law?"

He returned the notebook to the drawer and slammed it closed, a little too emphatically I thought. "The law declaims, psychiatry explains," he said.

"Very well put," I said. "Especially since I need you to explain my client."

He slid a sheet of paper across the desk. "This is a consent form. Have Mr. Stone sign on the dotted line. We'll conduct the experiment, I mean test, tomorrow at nine." He smiled, a sly mischievous smile. "If we're lucky, he'll flip out. We'll know if he has brain damage."

"What if he doesn't agree to the test?"

"Oh, he'll agree. He doesn't want to go to prison, does he?"

He catches me as I am about to fall off the stool. Arms carry me along. I am floating.

Lying on a cot in a hot room, slipping in and out of consciousness, cold and wet cloth around my head. A man in a white apron is throwing slices of chicken on a grill. He and Patrick are standing next to him.

"It didn't have to happen," he says.

"Don't look at me," Patrick says. "It wasn't my idea."

"We had time."

"The sooner the better."

The room spins and I fall into unconsciousness.

He was removing the cloth.

"What did not have to happen?" I asked.

"Falling off the stool. I should have seen you were in bad shape."

"It was something else."

"It was nothing else."

"Who did not want to wait?"

He wiped his brow with the cloth. "It's hot in here."

"Patrick said they did not want to wait. Wait for what?"

"Wait for you to come to," he said, sounding exasperated and impatient. "We called a doctor. He examined you while you were unconscious. He said you had a mild concussion and would be fine."

"Why do I not believe you?"

"Let me take you home."

"No. I want to continue our talk."

"Why?"

"I want to hear about the truth serum. Perhaps it will give me an idea how to get the truth from you."

He laughed and helped me off the cot. "At least you've been paying attention."

I stayed in the waiting room while Leonard took the Amytal. Bamberger appeared two hours later, beaming. You would have thought he had just performed the first successful heart transplant. He said Leonard had the hoped-for psychotic break. He was barely under the drug when he started babbling incoherently. He flailed his arms and hit a nurse in the ribs, breaking two of them. Two other nurses rushed into the room with a straitjacket. He quieted down an hour later. He was sobbing, a good sign, Bamberger said. Crying was another sign of brain damage, which was news to me.

More surprises awaited me. Bamberger played a tape recording of Leonard's ranting. In between moans and groans he described what happened that night, but it sounded more like a wish-fulfillment fantasy than a faithful account.

Leonard said he had met an Oak Forest cop at the White Horse Inn—he didn't say when—who bought him a drink. During their conversation, the cop said Linda liked to invite men to her trailer for sex and that he had been a frequent visitor. He said he had heard she was attracted to Leonard: sexually charged by the way he walked, the graceful way he crouched when he lowered himself to the grass outside the trailer park, and the sensuous way he licked drops of beer from the rim of the can.

Leonard talked about his mother and in almost the same breath said he could see a train jump the tracks at a station, plowing over dozens of people standing on the platform. Then he switched to the scene inside Linda's trailer. She was entreating him with open arms, welcoming him to her bed. He saw her white skin, torn panties, and bra with a broken strap. He sat up and screamed that the cop was stabbing him. The cop cackled as he stabbed him, insane cackles that wouldn't stop.

I waited for three hours until Leonard was well enough to leave the office. His eyes were puffy and swollen. We said nothing to each other as we got into a cab. He sat with his hands clasped between his legs, chanting as if in prayer. When I got out of the cab and told the driver to take him home, Leonard said, "I hope you believe me now."

I wasn't sure whether he was referring to his brain damage or what he had said while in the grip of the Amytal. It didn't matter. "I believe you," I said.

Our judge was Major K. Stinson, an ex-Chicago cop. He'd been on the bench for twenty years and, despite his law enforcement background, had a reputation as "soft on crime." As Leonard had directed, I waived his right to a jury. At the same time, I gave Stinson a letter signed by Bamberger, which suggested that Leonard should sit outside the courtroom during the medical testimony. If he heard what the doctors said, he might have another seizure. The letter was a clever, albeit transparent, device for us to tell Stinson that Leonard was sick.

Linda was the first witness. She was not what I expected. She was barely five feet tall. If she was a sexy siren that had driven Leonard to distraction, she had done her best to conceal it. Her brunette hair was tied in a bun with a rubber band and she wore a baggy wool sweater and long skirt. Her small-boned face was pasty white and her eyes were hollow and colorless. It was difficult to see her as Leonard had described: wearing cut-off shorts and V-neck tee shirt. Even Leonard was fooled. When she entered the courtroom he whispered, "Is that her?"

Did you ever know you've forgotten something important but can't remember what it is? That's how I felt as I rose to cross-examine Linda. Something was bothering me. I bided my time, asking mundane questions, methodically reviewing her life. I was putting Rose and Stinson to sleep, but I was hoping I'd remember what I knew was there.

In the middle of asking her why she dropped out of high school in the ninth grade I realized what I had missed. On direct examination she had described the attempted rape, breaking down in tears with every answer to Rose's soft-spoken solicitous questions. Because Leonard could not remember what happened in the trailer, she could have said anything without fear of contradiction. Yet, she had given few details. What was she afraid of? I asked Stinson for a recess.

Outside the courtroom, I said to Leonard: "What happened that night?"

"You know I don't remember."

"Bullshit. You remember what happened. You just don't want to tell me."

He was wearing a wrinkled suit at least three sizes too large for his emaciated body. He looked so bereft.

When he didn't answer, I continued: "Listen to me carefully. I know we have a team of doctors to testify you have psychomotor epilepsy, but that doesn't mean a goddamn thing. Stinson can decide the case however he pleases. I think I know what happened, and I think what happened is your passport out of here. But I can't do it without you."

"I'll say what I said when I took the drug."

"That's a bigger lie than your lack of memory."

"How do you know?"

"A cop didn't stab you. Linda did. The only fingerprints on the knife are yours and hers."

He was weaving back and forth, as if he were dancing with an imaginary partner.

"I'm brain damaged," he said. "If what I said isn't what happened, then I don't know what happened. You'll convince the judge to acquit me because I'm sick."

The clerk opened the door and signaled that we had two minutes left in the recess.

"Have it your way," I said. "But answer one question."

He eyed me suspiciously. "What?"

"Why did you take a kitchen knife when you left the apartment?"

"I don't remember."

"You remember going to the White Horse Inn."

"Yes."

"Had you gone there before?"

"I go every other Friday. On pay day."

"You took the knife for a reason. What was it?"

He looked away from me. He was hiding something.

"Turn around," I said.

He turned around and I ran my hand across his back. He flinched when I touched the wounds, rough from newly formed scar tissue.

"They're scattered," I said.

"What of it?"

"You were moving when you were stabbed."

"Maybe I was trying to get off the bed."

"Maybe." He could see I didn't believe him.

"I know why I took the knife."

"Why?"

"I'll tell you. But you still have to use the doctors. You still have to convince the judge I'm sick."

"Why did you take the knife?"

Leonard said he started taking the knife with him to the White Horse Inn after he'd been mugged two months before. He was jumped immediately upon getting out of his car in front of the restaurant, in full view of an off-duty Oak Forest cop who did nothing to stop the robbery. He said he never really intended to use the knife. It wasn't any sharper than a butter knife; he carried it because it made him feel safer.

"So, what was the big secret?" I asked. "Why didn't you want to tell me?

"I didn't think you would believe me."

As we walked back into the courtroom I again had that peculiar feeling of missing something.

I asked Linda about her sexual history. I couldn't do that today. To encourage victims to come forward, most states have passed laws preventing the defense from bringing up the victim's past sexual relationships. Even in the anything-goes environment of the old days Stinson could have stopped me. Our defense was insanity, not consent. Perhaps Stinson was as interested in Linda as I was.

It didn't take long to show that Linda in the courtroom wasn't the same as Linda in the world. She admitted that her ex-husband had walked out after he discovered her in bed with another man. Since then—two years—she had had sex with more than twenty men. She couldn't or wouldn't give me the exact number. I got her to acknowledge that her outfit was Rose's idea.

I turned to her encounters with Leonard. On direct she had testified he did more than sit on the grass and watch her play with her baby. On numerous occasions he had come on to her at the gas station; she rejected his advances every time. Leonard had told me none of this. I was asking questions blind without knowing the answers—or at least the truth—a dangerous stratagem. She could submarine me at will. I thought there might be fragmentary truth in Leonard's drug induced ramblings and asked her if she invited men into her trailer during the day. She hesitated and glanced at Leonard. I had guessed right. She was afraid he had told me about the parade of men who came to her trailer. She grimaced and said she had entertained men from time to time, quickly adding that they were friends from the neighborhood.

I led her through her account of the attempted rape. "How do you know he wasn't erect?" I asked.

"A woman knows," she said, as if she were referring to some bodily function of her own.

"Do you lock your door at night?"

"Yes."

"Was it locked that night?"

"I think so."

"How did Mr. Stone get in the trailer?"

"I wouldn't know. Broke in, I guess."

"Was the door damaged?"

"I don't know."

"There's nothing in the police report indicating damage."

"I don't know what's in the police report."

"You told the police your daughter was on the floor, crying during the attack."

"Yes."

"I assume she doesn't sleep on the floor."

"Of course she doesn't."

"Where does she sleep?"

"In her crib."

"Where was the crib located?"

"Next to my bed."

Rose was on his feet. "I don't see the relevance of this line of questioning."

Stinson looked over the top of his glasses at Rose. "Is that an objection?"

"It is," Rose said.

"Overruled." He smiled at Linda, as if he had done her a favor. She didn't return the smile.

"I think the baby was in bed with me," she said.

"You think?"

"Yes." Her voice was tremulous. "No, I'm sure. She was crying. I took her into bed with me."

"What time was it?"

"I don't know."

"Before Mr. Stone entered your trailer?"

She glared. "Yes."

"When was it, Miss Cox, that your daughter went from the bed to the floor?"

A quiet courtroom becoming even quieter is a special moment, a state beyond silence. The air hangs still, everyone stops breathing, and motion ceases: the absolute zero of human interaction.

"Did you hear my question, Miss Cox?"

"Would you please repeat the question?" Now her voice was steady but sorrowful.

"When did your daughter move from the bed to the floor?"

"I don't know how she got on the floor."

"Was she on the floor when you got into bed with Mr. Stone?"

She put her head down and sobbed. Tears flowed down the sides of her nose to her lips. I could taste the salt in her tears. I could smell her cheap perfume. Trial lawyers are predators; their vision converts sight into taste and smell.

"Miss Cox, you invited Mr. Stone to your trailer that night, didn't you?"

She wiped her nose with the back of her hand. "No," she said. "I didn't."

"You told him to come after your daughter was asleep, didn't you?"

"No."

"Because you had an engagement with someone earlier in the evening. A cop."

Like a cornered prey, she parted her teeth and bared her teeth, several of which were chipped. "He was a friend!" she shouted.

Snarling, no longer human, I said, "And you told Mr. Stone to stop at the White Horse Inn for a few drinks to give you time to finish your first assignation, isn't that true?"

"I don't know where he was before he broke into my home."

I possessed the confidence of a blind man crossing a street with a trusted seeing-eye dog. "You went to the gas station earlier in the day for cigarettes, didn't you?"

"Yes."

"You met Mr. Stone there, didn't you?"

"Maybe."

"He asked you out."

"Yes."

I approached the witness box. She had stopped crying and her eyes were challenging me.

"And this time you said yes, you said he could come over." I stared unblinkingly at her, a trick of cross-examination. A frozen gaze silences the witness, takes away her voice and allows a second question before she can answer the first. "You figured what the heck I'll give the guy a try. Maybe he can satisfy me. You liked having new men in your bed, Miss Cox, didn't you—"

I had crossed the invisible line that divides aggressive questioning and badgering. Stinson sustained Rose's objection.

As I continued, her story flew apart, like a vibrating fan that loses its blades one at a time. She couldn't remember when she first saw the knife. She couldn't remember whether she had cried out. She admitted she might have been mistaken when she told the police her daughter was on the floor. She admitted her neck had shown no signs of strangulation.

"Where was Mr. Stone when you stabbed him?"

"I don't understand."

"It's not a difficult question, Miss Cox."

"He was on top of me."

"What was he doing?"

"Raping me."

"You said he couldn't perform. You said, 'A woman knows.'"

"He was trying to rape me."

"You reached for his knife."

"Yes."

"You stabbed him."

"Yes."

"Many times."

"Yes."

"Six times?"

"I wasn't counting."

I locked on her eyes again; this time she looked away. "I suggest that things didn't happen as you've said. You didn't knife him while you were lying on the bed."

"I stabbed him in the back."

"Yes, Miss Cox, you did stab Mr. Stone in the back. But not when he was on top of you. You wouldn't have been able to reach his back."

"You weren't there."

"You're right, Miss Cox. I wasn't. And neither was Mr. Rose or Judge Stinson. That's why we need the truth from you."

"I am telling the truth."

85

"Are you? I think you let Mr. Stone into your trailer. He took off his jacket. He was nervous. Excited. You too. Or maybe you just wanted to get it over with so he'd stop hanging around your trailer. Either way, he couldn't perform. You pushed him off in disgust. He got mad. You fought. You grabbed his jacket and threw it at him. His money and knife fell out. You took the knife—"

Rose was on his feet. "I've heard enough," he shouted.

Stinson looked amused.

"Defense counsel has an overactive imagination," Rose said.

"It's not how it happened," Linda said to no one in particular as she looked at her hands, folded in her lap.

"There's no question pending, Miss Cox," Stinson said. Turning to me: "Ask a question."

"I have no further questions."

My seeing-eye dog had gotten me safely across the street, but I couldn't chance another intersection. My theory of what had happened was rank guesswork.

Stinson adjourned for lunch. I begged Leonard to let me withdraw the insanity defense and seek an acquittal. I thought I could convince Stinson to go my way on the issue of consent. But Leonard stubbornly shook his head.

"Why?" I asked. "The judge is convinced she's a nympho and he probably thinks, at worst, you were overanxious and forced the situation. Continuing with the insanity defense is tantamount to admitting you tried to rape her."

"Why can't you say I didn't do it, but if I did, I was sick?"

"Sometimes the law lets you call heads and tails on a single flip of the coin. This isn't one of them."

Leonard looked past me. Rose was helping Linda off the stand and leading her out of the courtroom.

"She's an oversexed bitch," Leonard said.

"Good. Then we can drop the insanity plea."

"No. I did it."

"What?"

"I did it to the old woman at the train station and I did it to Linda."

"Christ, Leonard!"

"I'll take my chances with the doctors," he said, his teeth clenched, his forehead tight with rage.

I bought a hot pastrami sandwich and sat by the Picasso sculpture in the courthouse plaza. I played out the possibilities. Maybe the facts weren't as I thought. Maybe Leonard was guilty. Maybe his guilt depended on your perspective.

A woman who will sleep with anyone has slept with everyone but you. You come from a world where rejection is the worst insult. You've never been invited to life's round-the-clock parties. You've been lonely and depressed for too long. Your life is governed by your paycheck; it allows you one night a week to go out and get drunk. You've got your knife with you. Dull though the knife is, it gives you power, power your cock doesn't have.

Sitting alone at the White Horse Inn, you drink and think of your mother, the old lady on the train platform, and your empty life. You're angry and the drinks make you angrier. You puzzle over Linda's conflicting messages: the yes of her tight tee shirt and shorts, the no of her cold words and the insults she hurls at you with her empty eyes. That day, at the gas station, you said you had your paycheck in your pocket, your way of offering to pay her, to treat her as the prostitute you know she is. But she said nothing and laughed, a rejection as searing as the knife wounds you would later receive.

When you leave the White Horse Inn you're primed. You drive to the trailer park, no specific plan in mind, just feel propelled into action. It's been a long time since you've acted. You're sick of being a coward. You're disgusted with never being able to get it up. You hadn't gotten it up with the old woman at the train station, even when you put your hands under her dress and felt her soft skin. As you park the car, you see the cop come out of her trailer, the asshole cop that stood by and did nothing when you were mugged. He got his, why shouldn't you get yours? You're at the front door, ready to break in. Before you can crash your shoulder against the door, it opens. She's wearing the tight tee shirt. You can see her nipples, still aroused from her time with the cop. She's holding her daughter like she's a duffel bag, but you don't care. You push her inside. She puts the baby on the floor. You grab her throat and pull out the knife. Your money falls out of the jacket. You're on top of her. She's afraid, but she isn't stupid. She says she wants you. And she is excited. Rough sex is exciting. She helps you take off your jacket. She unbuckles your belt and pulls down your pants. You're soft. You want her to give you time, but she pushes you off the bed, laughing as you hit the floor. Tears sting your eyes. You crawl on the floor, anxious to retrieve your money and get out of there. But she won't let you off so easily. She takes the knife and goes for you. You're too drunk to defend yourself. You don't know how you escaped, but you somehow manage to get outside and stumble to your car. You can still hear her laughing.

You wake up in the morning wanting to forget what happened. But the pain and the bloody tee shirt in the bathtub won't let you forget. You decide to forget anyway. If you can't remember, then the world will never know the truth. She won't admit that she wanted you and you couldn't respond. If you're arrested, you'll say nothing. You'll never tell anyone, not even your lawyer.

Then the miracle comes, like in those Bible stories your mother read to you as a kid, before she walked out. Your lawyer says you have brain damage. It explains everything, not just what happened at the trailer, but also the old woman at the train station, the rejections, the inability to make love. You're not responsible for what has gone wrong with your life.

What was that, Connie? Is that what happened? How should I know? As Linda said, I wasn't at the trailer. A trial isn't a crystal ball in which you can see the past. It's the kind of mirror you find in a funhouse, sending you a distorted reflection of reality. And we judge others using this perversion of reality. "Ne'er of the living can the living judge—too blind the affection, or too fresh the grudge." Who said it? Somebody named Anonymous. Anyway, Connie, try not to interrupt. I'm on a roll with this story.

Gil Rose came up to me. "Can I bum a cigarette?" he asked.

I gave him one.

"You're doing a great job," he said.

"I wonder."

"Question. Why are you fooling with an insanity defense? Seems to me you have a chance to get the sleaze bag off on consent. With this judge anyway."

"I have to do what my client wants."

"He's already made one mistake."

"Tell me about it. I told him to take your deal."

He sat next to me on the concrete wall. He looked up at the Picasso. "Big mother, isn't it. Never have been able to figure out what it's supposed to be."

"Some kind of bird, I think."

"It looks like a vampire, or the flying dinosaur, what do you call it?"

"Pterodactyl," I said, sounding more confident than I felt.

"Yeah, that's it." He sounded less confident than he should have.

I might as well show off a bit, I figured. "Scientists say birds and dinosaurs are related."

"You didn't learn that shit in law school."

"You're right."

"Dinosaurs were wiped out by meteors. Am I right?"

"Yes. The law of nature."

Rose smiled ruefully. "I've got my hands full trying to enforce the laws of Illinois."

"Maybe that's what will happen to us."

"You mean extinct like the dinosaurs? No way. We'll still be around when everyone else is dead."

"First thing, kill all the lawyers. Somebody said that one. Guess no one took the advice."

He took a long drag on his cigarette. "You're a cynical son-of-a-bitch."

"Aren't you? We don't do anything for anyone."

"Sure we do. We fight other people's battles. Mercenaries. Except my side doesn't pay shit."

We sat there for a little while, not speaking, two warriors from enemy camps meeting on neutral ground, our personal demilitarized zone.

"The offer is still open," he said. "Six months."

"He won't take it."

He flicked an ash against the base of the sculpture. It landed intact. "Does he really believe Stinson will decide he was insane?"

I shrugged.

"That's what I like about being a prosecutor. My client doesn't believe in anything. We just follow a bunch of rules."

"What if he's innocent? What if he didn't try to rape her?"

"I don't think about what if. I don't decide guilt or innocence. Like I said, I follow a bunch of rules. It's easier."

I didn't try to push Leonard into the deal. What would have been the point? He was convinced of his mental infirmity. And the neurologist set the tone of our patchwork defense, readily conceding to Rose that the EEG should not be taken as an indicator of acute seizure activity. "It could very well be asymptomatic," he volunteered, causing me to disguise my groan with a cough.

What, now, Connie? I'm sweating, you say? Guess I am. Don't know why. Lately, I get tired, then I break out in a sweat. Or is it the other way around? I never used to get tired. Or sweat, for that matter, certainly not when I'm sitting still and just talking. Should we quit early tonight? Dinner? Are you sure? Why don't you turn off the tape machine? We'll chat about nothing. We'll return to Leonard's case after dinner, if you're up for it. If I'm up to it.

Was he prepared to tell me the truth behind our original chance encounter, which I was becoming convinced, was not chance at all? And no longer could I accept as coincidences the relevance of his stories to what had occurred in my life.

As we ordered—the same entrees as the night before—he talked of ordinary matters, a welcome change. He spoke of baseball, basketball, movies, golf, and science fiction novels. When dinner arrived he lapsed into silence, staring at his food as he ate. I did not wish to interrupt what seemed to be meditation and focused my attention on each spoonful as if I were a food critic.

After the waitress cleared the table he suggested we resume our talk at the bar. First, however, I wanted to draw him out. With the recorder off, perhaps he would reveal more of himself.

"Tell me more about your parents." I said.

"What's to tell?"

"What was it like growing up with them?"

"*The freedom. I remember the freedom. Not freedom to do what I wanted, but freedom to think. In my family, it was not possible to have an unacceptable thought.*"

"*I wish to express a thought.*"

"*Go for it, Connie.*"

"*Why am I here?*"

"*Like in the old joke, everybody has to be somewhere.*"

"*I do not know the joke.*"

"*Lover hiding in closet, husband comes home, opens closet, and says 'what are you doing here . . . ' You get it, don't you?*"

"*I do not find a story of an illicit affair to be humorous.*"

"*Relax, Connie. It's a joke.*"

"*Please. Why am I here?*"

"*To listen to me.*"

"*What else?*"

"*Stay with me until I finish.*"

"*How long?*"

"*A few days, a week, maybe longer.*"

"*A week! It has already been four days.*"

"*Four nights, Connie. The days are yours.*"

He looked toward the front. I followed his eye line.

"*That man again,*" *I said.*

"*He doesn't give up.*"

"*You know who he is.*"

"*No.*"

"*I don't believe you. Who is he?*"

"*I can't say.*"

"*You can't say or you won't say.*"

"*Come off it, Connie. What do you want from me? Maybe he's your guardian angel. No, I'm your guardian angel.*"

"*I demand to know what is happening.*"

He leaned forward, a gesture not of intimacy but of warning. "*Sometimes it's better not to know everything.*"

"*I should leave.*"

"*If you like.*"

I looked at the man. He had taken a seat at the far end of the bar.

"Tell me this," I said. "I saw a man in the plaza when I fainted this morning. He was holding a newspaper strangely, the way that man at the bar was holding a newspaper earlier in the evening. Is he the same man?"

"There you go again, Connie."

"He is the same man. I am sure of it."

"Excuse me," he said. He got up from the table and walked straight to the man, who, caught off guard, pushed his stool backwards. He said something to the man and pointed at the door. The man shook his head in disgust, but got off the stool and hurriedly left the tavern.

"All taken care of," he said when he returned.

"What did you say to him?"

"I told him to leave us alone."

"What did he say?"

"First he said he was minding his own business. Then he said he had a right to be here. Then he said have it your way."

"You know him. I can see it in your eyes."

"It's a myth, Connie. It's a myth that you can see through the eyes into the mind."

As suspicious as I wnard as of Dr. Gruenberg's intellectual integrity, I assumed he would acquit himself well on the stand. The neurologist had testified about the EEG and had even done me a favor by suggesting that it was increasingly common to diagnose epilepsy from test results alone. So, all that Gruenberg had to say was that Leonard's brain damage had set off a seizure. He would then conclude by saying that Leonard met the standard for legal insanity.

Ah, Connie, the best laid plans . . . I saw it from the outset. He was too sure of himself. He answered too quickly, sometimes before I finished the question, giving his testimony the appearance of being rehearsed, canned like a movie script. Troubling also was Rose's inattention; throughout my direct he ignored Gruenberg, reading what looked like a transcript.

When I finished, I returned to my chair and waited for the onslaught.

"Good morning, Dr. Gruenberg," Rose said.

"Good morning, Mr. District Attorney," Gruenberg said. He couldn't even issue a greeting without sounding haughty.

"If I correctly understand your testimony, Leonard Stone had a seizure, a rather lengthy seizure, during which he took a knife from his apartment, went to the White Horse Inn for several drinks, then sauntered over to Miss Cox's trailer, brutally assaulted her, all while in the throes of a seizure that stripped him of the ability to control himself." Rose finished the question with a great intake of air, as if he had just stopped holding his breath after a very long time.

"A reasonably accurate paraphrasing of my testimony," Gruenberg said.

"And you are confident of your opinion to a reasonable degree of medical certainty."

"Yes."

"You reached this opinion because of the medical and psychological tests, is that right?"

"In part."

"What else did you consider?"

"What happened that night."

"You weren't there, were you?"

"Of course not."

"So your opinion is based on hearsay."

I objected: "Your Honor, Mr. Rose knows very well that an expert opinion is always based on assumed facts."

"Quite correct," Stinson said. "But I know the law. No need to worry."

I was worried. I knew what Rose was up to. He would change a fact here or there to test Gruenberg's resolve.

Rose continued: "Counsel asked you to assume that the defendant doesn't recall what happened after he arrived at the White Horse Inn, is that correct?"

"After a few drinks, yes."

"When you interviewed the defendant, he told you of his lack of memory."

"Yes."

"You believed him?"

"It wasn't an issue."

"Not an issue? Then, even if Mr. Stone did remember and lied to you, your opinion would remain the same."

"Yes."

"His lack of memory was not a factor in your opinion?"

"It was not a factor."

"I'm confused, Dr. Gruenberg. I thought you testified that a lapse of memory is a fundamental consequence of psychomotor epilepsy?"

"Among others."

"So, if the defendant was lying, you'd have to consider it."

Gruenberg bristled. I didn't like to see him bristle. A witness who bristles is a witness who is losing control. He was also measuring his words, another worrisome sign.

"I told you the issue of Mr. Stone's veracity has no effect on my diagnosis."

I objected again. "Your Honor, there is no evidence Mr. Stone remembers the assault."

"At the appropriate time," Rose said, "I will introduce evidence that the defendant remembers what happened."

"Objection overruled," Stinson said.

Rose approached the witness box, as I had done when Linda testified. "There's a reason why what the defendant remembers is immaterial to your opinion, isn't that correct, Dr. Gruenberg?"

"I don't know what you mean."

"I think you do."

"I'm sorry. You'll have to enlighten me."

"If I can."

Rose returned to his table and picked up the volume he had been reading during direct examination.

"Are you a religious man, Dr. Gruenberg?" Rose asked.

"It depends on your definition of religious."

"Subscribing to the tenets of a church, organized religion, if you will."

"A narrow definition of religious, Mr. District Attorney."

"Humor me."

"You haven't said anything funny."

Stinson was peering over his glasses again. "We can do without the by-play, gentlemen."

"Let's be serious, then," Rose said. "Is it fair to say you subscribe to a specific value system?"

"I have values."

"Tell me about them?"

"We don't have the time."

"I'll be the judge of that."

"I'm the judge, Mr. Rose," Stinson said.

"Yes, your Honor, I was—"

"Give us a brief summary, Dr. Gruenberg," Stinson said, a tinge of annoyance creeping into his voice.

"A summary wouldn't do them justice," Gruenberg said.

"Your Honor," I said from my seat, "I don't see—"

"Neither do I," Stinson said. "Help us out, Doctor. Give us an example of your values. One will do."

"Life is precious."

"So glad I limited you to one," Stinson said.

"Let's attack the problem from a different angle," Rose said.

"Be my guest," Gruenberg said.

"Are you familiar with determinism?"

I wanted to put my head on the table. No, I wanted to knock it on the table.

"I am familiar with determinism," he said, unfazed.

"Define it please."

"Determinism holds that one's behavior is determined by what has come before, by the panoply of his genes, life history, outside events and forces that act upon him."

"You're a determinist, aren't you?"

"I believe in determinism, if that's what you mean."

"You believe a person's behavior is preordained, determined by factors beyond his control."

"That's an oversimplification, Mr. Rose."

"How would you put it?"

Again, Gruenberg bristled, but this time he half-closed his eyes, as if to mock his own anger. "I'm not here to debate philosophy, Mr. Rose."

Rose was a good enough lawyer to continue with his questions regardless of Gruenberg's answers.

"As such," Rose said, "your opinion about the defendant's actions is a function of your belief in determinism, your belief that his actions were the inevitable consequence of everything preceding it."

"My philosophy and my medical opinion are entirely different matters."

"When I asked you to assume that the defendant hadn't lost his memory, you said your medical opinion would not change."

"Yes," Gruenberg said, elevating his voice a few notes and making it sound like a question. A sign of uncertainty.

"And if I changed another fact, your opinion would still not change, isn't that correct?"

"I can only tell you if you give me the change."

"In fact, no change in the assumed facts would cause you to modify your opinion."

"I can't agree to such a broad generalization."

"Indeed, you believe the defendant couldn't control his actions because he had no free will."

"A philosophical issue."

"Do you or do you not believe in free will, Dr. Gruenberg?"

"If you are speaking in philosophical terms, then I—" Gruenberg stopped himself as he looked at what I was now certain was a transcript, though Rose was holding the book as if it were the Ten Commandments.

"You testified on behalf of Richard Speck," Rose said.

"I did."

"You were asked questions about determinism, weren't you?"

"I testified for several days. I was asked many questions on a variety of subjects."

"Should I read from your testimony?"

Gruenberg looked at me. He was no longer bristling.

"It won't be necessary," Gruenberg said.

"Why won't it be necessary?" Rose asked, rotating his back away from Gruenberg.

"I recall the gist of my testimony."

Still with his back turned and looking at me, Rose said sarcastically, "Give us the gist, Dr. Gruenberg."

"Speck couldn't help himself."

Rose was smiling victoriously. He dropped the transcript on the table. It landed with a thud. "Why couldn't Speck help himself?"

"Brain damage."

"What else?"

"Nothing else."

Rose wheeled around on his toes, his version of a pirouette: "At the Speck trial, you were asked whether your opinion of the defendant's ability to conform his conduct to the requirements of the law would change if your medical diagnosis of brain damage proved erroneous?"

"The prosecutor put that question somewhat more elegantly, Mr. Rose."

"Pardon my inelegance, Dr. Gruenberg. Were you asked that question at the Speck trial?"

"Yes."

"Do you remember what you said?"

"Yes."

"What did you say?"

"I said Mr. Speck was a monster."

"Were you speaking medically or philosophically?"

"No, I . . . I . . . "

"Yes, Dr. Gruenberg. I'm listening."

That familiar, complete silence permeated the courtroom, the state of absolute zero that occurred during my cross-examination of Linda.

"He was a monster from the day he was born," Gruenberg said. "He could not change who he was."

Dr. Gruenberg, what would you say about Leonard Stone if it came to pass that he was not suffering from brain damage and remembered everything, remembered planning to attack Linda Cox, was suffering from no mental defect or disease. What would you say then?"

Stinson took off his glasses and set them on the bench.

"I would say . . . " Gruenberg said softly. "I would say Mr. Stone could not control his actions."

97

"Because . . . ?"

"Because self-control is a conceit we use to lend meaning to our lives."

"Thank you, Dr. Gruenberg," Rose said, as if Gruenberg had conferred an honor upon him, which in a way he had.

I could have asked Gruenberg more questions, tried to rehabilitate him. But trying to restore the credibility of a witness who has been so thoroughly discredited is like trying to breathe life into a corpse.

I couldn't blame Gruenberg. I knew he had testified at the Speck trial. I could have gotten the transcript and read it. Later, Joe would say I shouldn't be too hard on myself. The problem, he said, lay with Leonard, who hadn't let me drop the insanity defense. But if he had heard what Stinson said after Gruenberg got off the stand, he would have thought differently.

"You have another witness?" Stinson asked.

"Yes. Dr. Bamberger."

"Not another determinist, I presume."

"I hope not."

"Good. I don't need another philosophy lesson."

"Neither do I."

"After Dr. Bamberger?"

"He's my last witness."

"You don't intend to pursue the line of defense you hinted at in your cross of Miss Cox?"

"I don't intend to call witnesses, but in my summation I will argue that—"

"A waste of time."

"I don't understand, your Honor."

"It's clear to me your client attacked her."

"I appreciate your candor, but I don't—"

"Don't misunderstand me, counsel. I judge, but I don't prejudge. Your cross-examination was quite effective; you did a marvelous job of putting your words into her mouth."

"I don't think—"

"It's your case and you can do whatever you like. I have been known to change my mind."

"If my cross-examination was so effective, why do you believe my client attacked her?"

"Come now counsel, I have heard two-dozen rape cases during the last year. In nearly all of them the defendant claimed the woman consented. In half the cases the defendant went further and said he was seduced. Standard defense. Standard nonsense."

I remembered the conversation with Judge Gunderson, how he thought of himself as a different jury in each case. Stinson was no Gunderson. What happened in the first case affected his judgment in the one-thousandth case. He was as much of a determinist as Gruenberg.

"But your Honor," I said, "you should decide this case on its own merits."

Stinson looked at the court reporter. "We're off the record."

He knew his comments could give me an issue on appeal. He is supposed to wait for the conclusion of the evidence to form an opinion of the case. Unrealistic, perhaps, but whoever said the law was realistic about human nature.

"I appreciate having the benefit of your remarks," I said.

He neatly parried my sarcasm. "I thought you would," he said.

The next morning Dr. Bamberger did a yeoman's job of injecting a much-needed dose of scientific objectivity into our defense. For all of his post-modern office décor and dilettantish savoir-faire, he charmed the old Victorian Stinson. On several occasions, Stinson interrupted my questioning to ask about the EEG and the psychological tests. He liked the business about the weird smell and the effect on Leonard when he took the Sodium Amytal. Bamberger also explained why Leonard hadn't become violent during the session. He said, absent the influence of alcohol, seizure activity would not result in violent action.

Bamberger was more adroit than Gruenberg had been in handling cross-examination. He was ready for Rose's main line of attack: despite twice monthly drinking-benders, Leonard hadn't gone on a rampage of assault and rape until the night he attacked Linda. Bamberger said it took years of drinking before the brain lesion sparked a violent seizure. What about the two-decade old attack at the train station? Rose asked. Did

Bamberger believe a seizure had produced that attack? A trick question, for an affirmative response would have undermined what he'd said about the need for years of alcohol abuse. No, Bamberger replied, he saw no connection between the two incidents. Leonard had deep-seated emotional problems, but those problems hadn't caused the attempted rape. Bamberger wasn't satisfied, however; he wanted to stick it to Rose. "Mr. Rose, you should not forget that the old woman was a surrogate mother, not a young slut like Linda." Rose objected, but Stinson laughed and said, "Cheer up, Mr. Rose. You win some, you lose some."

Though Bamberger's performance had gone far in compensating for Gruenberg's testimony, I couldn't be sanguine about Leonard's prospects for acquittal. Rose's comment that Leonard had lied about his amnesia worried me. Rose knew something I didn't.

Jack Kramer, the State's expert, was a thirty-five-year courtroom veteran. He had testified in more than one hundred cases. Fortunately, like Gruenberg, he was an easy mark, though for a different reason. Whereas Gruenberg believed that free will was a humanistic fiction, Kramer believed there was no malady, physical or psychological, which could deprive a person of the ability to control his actions. So wedded was he to individual responsibility that he called drug addiction a misnomer, said it should be called a habit—a habit everyone could break, and yet ... Sorry, Connie, I'm in a funny mood. *My Fair Lady.* You have seen *My Fair Lady*, haven't you? And I've grown accustomed to your face.

Kramer scoffed at Bamberger's diagnosis that the Amytal-produced ravings confirmed the presence of psychomotor epilepsy. He said any severely neurotic individual would react the same way. "The subject's impulse to rape was entirely resistible," he said. "Besides," he added. "I saw no evidence of brain damage. He was able to repeat a series of seven numbers backwards, which proves his brain functions nominally." The amused Stinson interjected, "Then I must have brain damage, because I can't remember a telephone number in forward order, let alone backwards."

As arranged, Leonard heard none of this testimony. He stayed out in the hall. Through the door windows I could see him pacing the hall, cigarette glued to his lip with saliva. In the middle of my cross-examination I heard a crash. The sheriff, who was standing near the door, rushed out,

Rose and I close behind. Leonard was writhing on the floor. A dark-haired young woman was kneeling over him, trying to hold down his arms. Bamberger, who'd been watching Kramer's testimony, squatted on the floor with us. While the sheriff held Leonard's kicking legs in place, Bamberger forced open his mouth to make sure he hadn't swallowed his tongue. In a minute or so he stopped convulsing. His eyes were closed, but he was breathing normally.

Someone called an ambulance. Stinson let me put Bamberger on the stand to testify that the episode in the hall was another psychotic break. Bamberger said the Sodium Amytal had a lingering effect, to be expected in a brain damaged patient.

In the hullabaloo, I had forgotten about the young woman. She was Rose's next witness. She was stunning: tall and strong-boned, with striking feminine features. Her sensuous lips seemed permanently fixed in a semi-pout. Luminous turquoise eyes captivated whoever looked into them. She would cock her head and flash an elfin twinkle of her eyes, as if she knew she could control you at her whim. Her flowing jet-black hair descended passed a long, elegantly sculpted neck to the top of a tight suit.

I was smitten from the moment she walked across the courtroom to the witness stand. She swiveled her hips like a runway model. As I watched the clerk administer the oath I was too dazzled by her beauty to worry about what she would say. Meanwhile, Leonard—released from the hospital after an hour with no apparent ill effects—was scribbling on a pad. "Don't ask her any questions," he wrote.

Her name was Carla Smith. She lived in Park Forest South, a newer middle class community of garden apartments and townhouses, not far from Oak Forest. She was thirty-two and single, an assistant systems analyst for the Illinois Central Railroad. She testified that she met Leonard a week after his arrest at the White Horse Inn. She had gone there with friends. No one at her table smoked and she skipped the appetizer to withdraw to the bar where she could have a cigarette. Leonard was having his first drink of the evening. He introduced himself, but said little else. She liked that he was quiet. Most men were too pushy. As she was leaving to return to her friends, he shyly asked if he could see her again.

She hadn't gotten to the important part of her testimony and I was already dumbfounded. What could she have seen in Leonard? Why hadn't he told me about her? As the questioning continued I learned she had dated Leonard for three months. They would go to dinner—when he could afford it— or bowling. On her birthday they went to a professional wrestling match. The wrestling match was her idea, she said. He would have preferred a candlelight dinner at the Palmer House Hotel. So that was it, I thought. Leonard was a closet Casanova, a blue-collar bon vivant. Never judge a book by its cover, never judge a man . . . good advice, Connie. Don't judge.

Rose directed her attention to a Wednesday night, not long after his arrest. She and Leonard were having drinks at the White Horse Inn.

"What did he say about the charges against him?" Rose asked.

"He said he had great news. He said he was as good as acquitted."

"Did he say why?"

"He said his lawyer was convinced he was suffering from brain damage. He used a medical term; epilepsy I think is what he said. He also said he told his lawyer he couldn't remember what happened in the trailer."

"What did you say?"

"Nothing at first. I laughed."

"Why?"

"Leonard never forgets anything."

"Please continue."

"He said that after his lawyer sent him to a doctor for a brain test he went to the library and did research. He said that's when he knew he could fool everybody."

"What did you say?"

"To be honest, I was upset. I didn't think he had to lie. He had told me about the arrest. He said he didn't try to rape her. I believed him. Otherwise, I never would have gone out with him. He said she asked him over for a drink to thank him for watching her daughter one afternoon when she had to run some errands. He told me she tried to come on to him and he said he'd better leave. He said he carried a knife for protection because he was mugged once. Then she had his knife; he didn't know how she had gotten it. She was cutting him. He said she was a crazy woman with a repu-tation around town for picking up men."

She looked at Leonard and cocked her head, not flirtatiously but in silent disapproval. He did not return her look.

"So I guess it was all a lie," she said. "If he was innocent, he wouldn't have to say he was sick."

I asked Stinson to strike her answer. Her opinion of Leonard's guilt wasn't relevant.

Not that it mattered, but Stinson agreed.

Rose smiled and continued. "Miss Smith, please tell us what you said to the defendant."

"I said I didn't want to see him anymore."

"What did he say?" Rose asked.

"He begged me not to leave him. He said he needed me." Her soft, enchanting turquoise eyes turned cold and metallic. This was a woman to be reckoned with!

"How did you respond?"

"I told him he had never needed me. I said if he needed me, he would have been honest."

What does a trial lawyer do when he doesn't know what to do? He concentrates on the unspoken; he probes for a vulnerable spot; he darts in and out of the witness's life, looking for an opportunity to catch her in a lie; he searches for a reason to lie. In the courtroom, where truth is a stranger, establishing a motive to lie is as effective as proving the lie.

I had forgotten about Leonard's note. As I stood, he grabbed my elbow. "I told you not to question her," he said.

"I have to."

"No."

"She's killing us."

"Counsel," Stinson said. "We don't have all day."

I yanked my elbow away and took a couple of steps toward Carla. "Did you and Leonard enjoy a loving relationship?"

"Yes."

"But you're no longer seeing each other."

"No, we're not." She sounded regretful.

"Because you thought he was guilty."

"No. He lied to me, you know, about what happened between the woman and him. He should have told me he had sex with her. Even if he was drunk and raped her, he should have told me."

"Leonard is not charged with raping Linda Cox."

"I thought he was."

"Attempted rape."

"Oh." Her eyes widened, as if, for the first time, she understood something that had bewildered her.

"Was there anything you wanted to add, Miss Smith?"

"No," she said, though she seemed to want to say more.

"You said you had a loving relationship."

"Yes."

"In a relationship there are squabbles and disagreements, large and small. Your relationship with Leonard was no exception. Correct?"

"I guess."

"What did you argue about?"

"I don't know. I hated his drinking."

"Why?"

"He drank too much."

"Was he ever drunk with you?"

"Yes, but not falling down drunk."

"What's the most you saw him drink?"

"He would have a few beers, two cocktails..."

"Do you drink?"

"Occasionally."

"What is drinking too much to you might not be too much to someone else."

"I wouldn't know."

"What else did you argue about?"

"Nothing else."

"Was money an issue?"

"No."

"Sex?"

She hesitated before answering. "No."

"Have you ever been married?"

"No."

I angled to the side where I could see her legs. They were thin, too thin for the rest of her body. She had put on weight. And her suit was even tighter than I had thought, the jacket stretched tight around her back.

"Do you have children?" I asked.

"Two."

"Do they live with you?"

"In Florida. With my mother."

"Where is their father?"

She looked down. "There are two fathers."

"I see," I said slowly. "How many times did you have sexual intercourse with Leonard?"

The question surprised her. She looked at Rose, beseeching him for help. I longed to have her look at me that way.

"I don't know," she said. "We dated for quite a while."

"Keep your voice up, please," Stinson said, hand under his chin, mesmerized by either her beauty or her testimony—or both.

"More than six?" I asked.

She stiffened. She did not care to be challenged. "I didn't keep track."

"Not every time you saw him."

"Of course not."

"When did you and he first make love?"

"I don't understand."

"On the first date, the second date—"

"Third I think."

"Did you initiate it or did he?"

"I don't remember."

"Where did you make love?"

"In my apartment."

"Did he spend the night?"

"I think so."

"You don't remember?

"I don't remember."

I was stalling. I thought I knew the truth—or rather the part of the truth that brought her to the courtroom to help the state put Leonard in prison—but I wasn't sure.

Stinson was impatiently rocking back and forth. I couldn't stall any longer.

"When you met Leonard at the White Horse Inn and told him you were breaking up, was it a regular date?"

"I don't know what you mean."

"What day was it?"

"A Wednesday, I think."

"Your dates with Leonard were usually on the weekends, isn't that correct?" I was guessing.

"Every other weekend," she said ruefully. "When he got paid."

I would continue guessing until I guessed incorrectly. "This particular date was your idea, wasn't it?"

"Yes."

"You had something you wanted to tell him, didn't you?"

"Not wanted to."

"Something you felt you should tell him?"

"Yes."

"You wanted to tell him before he found out."

"Yes."

"You could only hide it for so long."

"Yes."

I knew. And in that moment I was not the hardboiled attorney for the defense, but just a guy who wanted to understand.

"You hide it well, Miss Smith."

Rose was on the march, charging to the front like a commuter trying to catch the train before it leaves the station. "I protest," he shouted.

Ever the unflappable jurist, Stinson said, "I don't know how to rule on a protest, Mr. Rose."

"I mean object." Rose said, panting—lawyers are miserably out of shape.

"Overruled."

Carla's shoulders were shaking. She was crying. I wanted to kiss her tears away.

"When you told Leonard you were pregnant, what did he say?"

She composed herself and cocked her head. Was she angry or flirting? "I don't remember," she said.

"Did he say congratulations, wonderful, terrific, let's celebrate?"

"I don't remember." She had withdrawn to a place that I was not permitted to enter.

"Did you tell him you were pregnant before or after he told you about his new defense?"

"After."

"Why?" A question a lawyer should never ask during cross-examination.

But instead of using the question as an opportunity to say whatever she wanted, she meekly responded: "I'm not sure."

"Were you afraid he would be upset?"

"I might have been."

"He had a right to be upset, didn't he?"

"I don't know."

"He was upset, wasn't he?"

"No. He was calm."

I feigned surprise. "He was calm?"

"I told him I wanted to get married."

"Oh, so you were proposing to him. That must have made him happy."

"No."

"No? He wasn't happy?"

"I couldn't marry him."

"But you said you wanted to get married."

"Yes."

"Didn't you love him?"

"I wanted to love him."

Now she was using my trick, staring me into silence. She was hypnotizing me with her eyes, as green as a perfect emerald.

"You didn't love him, did you?" Though I was sad, my voice was sharp.

She didn't answer.

"Miss Smith?"

Still no answer.

"The baby wasn't his, was it? You weren't pregnant by Leonard Stone. Another man made you pregnant, isn't that correct?"

"Yes," she said, her voice cracking.

"You told him the baby wasn't his."

"I didn't have to."

"You didn't have to?"

"He knew it wasn't his."

"How did he know, Miss Smith? How did he know the baby wasn't his?" I moved close to her, not to intimidate, but to be close. I wanted her to know my questions had nothing to do with what I was feeling. I could smell her perfume. It sent me memories of sitting on the front step to my house on an early spring day, tulips and daffodils in bloom. I wished I, not Leonard, had met her at the White Horse Inn.

"Would you like to change your previous testimony, Miss Smith?"

She averted her eyes. Stinson removed his glasses and shifted sideways. He wanted to show Carla his best profile. I pictured us fighting for her love.

"Miss Smith," he said. "If there is anything you would like to amend, anything at all, please do so." He couldn't have been more unctuous.

She smiled gratefully. "Thank you, your Honor. I would like to make a change."

"Go ahead, my dear."

"Leonard and I never made love. He wanted to. I wanted to. But he couldn't."

"May I continue?" I asked Stinson. I was jealous. I wanted her back with me.

"Let's give Miss Smith a moment to compose herself," Stinson said.

"I'm all right," she said. She was looking at me again. She knew what I wanted. And I knew she would give it to me.

"Miss Smith," I said. "It was you, not Leonard, who had been less than forthright."

"Yes."

"You had been seeing another man."

"Yes."

"And you decided to tell Leonard. That's why you asked to see him."

"Yes."

"Your meeting with Leonard had nothing to do with what happened with Linda Cox."

"I knew he didn't have sex with her."

"How did you know, Miss Smith?"

"Because it was impossible."

Her shoulders were rising and falling. She was making a heaving sound, all in a fast series the way a locomotive chugs as it's getting up to speed. "He told me the first time . . . the first time I invited him to my home. He said he couldn't . . . then, at the White Horse Inn when he told me he had to say he was crazy because no one would believe him, and even if they did believe him, he didn't want anybody to know . . . he was too ashamed . . . and when I told him I was pregnant, he was calm . . . and he said, see, I have to show them I'm sick, so they'll help—"

I was so enthralled with Carla I had forgotten about Leonard. I heard his feet clumping on the parquet floor, a wild beast loose on the pampas. He grabbed my neck, throttling me. "She's lying," he screamed. "She's carrying my baby."

The sheriff flew into his back, knocking us both to the floor. Leonard's hands were still locked on my throat. I was choking and close to blacking out. Then, as if nothing had happened, I was breathing and the weight was off me. The sheriff had Leonard standing with his arms twisted tightly behind his back. He was putting on the cuffs. I grabbed the rail of the empty jury box and pulled myself up. Rose was next to Carla, comforting her. No one was comforting me.

Stinson was banging his gavel. "I want to see the lawyers in chambers."

"I want to ask another question," I said, one finger pointing in the air, a meek protest against nothing.

"You can't be serious," Stinson said.

The sheriff was dragging Leonard by the handcuffs. It must have hurt, but Leonard didn't utter a sound. Bamberger was in close pursuit as they pushed open the swinging doors and disappeared into the hall.

"Please, your honor," I said.

"This is highly irregular."

Rose was standing with Carla, holding her hand. I wanted to hold her hand. Steadying my nerves, I said, "Why did you tell Leonard you didn't want to see him anymore?" Gone was any semblance of formal interrogation. I just wanted to know.

"I didn't tell him."

"But you didn't see him again."

"No." Rose was squeezing her hand. She took it away. She was mine again.

"Why?" I asked.

"He said he never wanted to see me again. He said he hated me. He said I was wrong to cheat on him."

"What did you say?"

"I said it wasn't cheating. I said I wasn't cheating because he had never made love to me."

Stinson was half out of his seat.

"Please, your honor."

"Make it quick."

"Miss Smith, why did you agree to appear in court today?"

She moved away from Rose. "He asked me."

"How did he find you?"

"I found him."

"When?"

"The day after that night at the White Horse Inn."

"You called Mr. Rose because you were angry?"

"Yes."

"You wanted to hurt Leonard?"

"Yes."

"Do you still want to hurt him?"

She lowered her head as tears fell like a gentle spring shower. Her crying made me love her more.

"Carla."

"Yes."

"Do you still want to hurt Leonard?"

"No."

"Is there anything else you want to tell us?"

"Leonard would never hurt anyone. He's the kindest man I ever met."

"Thank you, Carla."

Stinson was off the bench. Rose was running after him. "I want to ask this witness more questions."

He stopped but didn't turn around. "Want all you want, Mr. Rose. I'm taking fifteen minutes. Then I'll see you two in chambers."

Rose and I sat next to the Picasso sharing my last cigarette. We both looked like we'd come out of a sauna, though I was in worse shape than he was. My white shirt was gray from sweat and my curly hair had gone straight.

"The judge is going to want us to make a deal," he said, handing me the cigarette. We could have been sharing a joint.

"What's the deal?"

"Same as before."

"I thought the offer expired."

"I've renewed it."

"Leonard is innocent. Drop the case."

"I can't."

"Why not?"

"He is not innocent."

"You said having an opinion about guilt or innocence gets in the way."

"It does, but I can still have an opinion."

"He can't get it up."

"He wanted to get it up. He tried to get it up. That's attempted rape." He took the cigarette from me and dragged out a last puff.

I didn't have a retort. "I need another cigarette," I said.

"You don't have time. I'll see you in Stinson's chambers."

I took my time anyway. I bummed a cigarette from an art student who was sketching the Picasso on a large piece of poster board. I asked him what he thought it looked like. "An angel," he said.

After the meeting with Stinson, I went to see Leonard in the lockup. He turned his back on me. I told him what the judge had said. "Take the deal," I said. "Get it over with. Get on with your life."

"You fucked me," he said.

"I'm sorry."

"I told you not to question her. No one would have ever known."

"I was trying to win the case."

"Don't give me that. I saw how you were looking at her. You want her. You'll call her after I'm sent away."

"For God's sake, Leonard."

"I tried to rape her."

"Carla?"

"Not Carla. Linda."

"I don't believe you."

"Remember when she said a woman knows. She didn't know jack shit. I was inside her. If she hadn't grabbed my knife, I would have gotten—forget it. It doesn't matter."

"I wanted to fight for you."

"You're so goddamn clever with those fucking degrees on the wall. They don't mean shit. The law doesn't mean shit."

"Leonard—"

"You wanted to be a big shot. It was funny when you decided I might have psychomotor epilepsy. I thought of the idea before you did; you were too stupid to realize it. The judge was going my way. I could see it after Bamberger testified. Then I had the seizure. Pretty good, don't you think? Bamberger was afraid I would swallow my tongue. Bullshit. Didn't have to. The smell. I read about that in the library. Flipping out in Bamberger's office? Also pretty good, huh? He believed that shit about the cop. You should have been there. The drug could have been fucking aspirin. A glass of beer gives me more of a hit. You wanted to be the hero. You couldn't leave her alone."

"What should I tell the judge?" I asked, too defeated to argue with him.

"Tell him whatever you want."

Leonard pled guilty. Carla was sitting in the last row. Leonard never looked at her. I wanted to talk to her, but I didn't. Our relationship had ended with her testimony.

Stinson sentenced Leonard to a year, six months more than Rose recommended. Leonard was taken out of the courtroom, put in a van, and driven to county jail. I bought a pack of cigarettes and smoked them all while I sat by the Picasso. It no longer looked like a bird, or a pterodactyl, or an angel. It didn't look like anything other than what it was—a clump of metal fashioned by the mind of a stranger.

I never saw Leonard again.

He touched my shoulder, squeezing it lightly. "Tomorrow," he said and was out the door before I could speak. I did not know what to think. Leonard's story was careening around the walls of my head like billiard balls. Had Leonard tried to rape Linda Cox? Or had he invented facts to give himself a sense of completeness, at least fill a corner of the vacuum that had been his life?

I walked to the studio without incident: no man on the corner watching me, no haunting suspicions terrifying me, anxiety shadowing me no more.

I switched on the light and sat at my desk. I could not write. Then I saw it, the television I had yet to watch. I pressed the remote control until I found the news. A blurry videotape carried a shaky image of an old, rusted bridge, towers piercing the night sky. The camera swept down to three men on the shore who were dragging something out of the water. The camera zoomed in closer as the voiceover of a newscaster described the scene: "The body pulled from the chilly waters beneath the Mystic River Bridge has been identified as Samuel Brandt of Boston, recently in the news as the attorney for soon to be deported IRA terrorist Tommy Glynn. Samuel Brandt, dead of an apparent suicide at age fifty-four."

An answer to one question, but another question raised. If he was not Samuel Brandt, who was he?

BOOK TWO
FISCHEL SCHAECHTER

CHAPTER FIVE

May 14, 1998

I SAT IN THE COFFEE SHOP on *Second Avenue, sipping espresso and hoping to have a day free from mishap. My head continued to throb from the previous day's fall; any sudden move immediately made me dizzy.*

I could not stop thinking of Samuel Brandt's death. I had wanted my new friend—was he a friend?—to be Samuel Brandt, as if that would have explained the strange goings on. Of course, it would have explained nothing. His death had done nothing more than remove the critical connection to Tommy Glynn. On the other hand, there suddenly occurred to me that I was connected to Tommy. I remembered an incident, which I had previously thought of as inconsequential but now struck me as having a ghostly, premonitory nature.

In 1990, while working as a reporter for the Andersontown News, I was dispatched to Greysteel County, Derry, to investigate a Unionist shooting. One of the victims had worked for the newspaper as a typesetter and had been on holiday visiting family. I interviewed several witnesses, but learned nothing of interest. Such attacks were as unsolvable as a century-old mystery. I was sitting in my car putting away my notes when a policeman opened the door and told me to get out. I showed him my identification and he demanded to see my notes. I refused and he took me to the police station.

I was put in a windowless room with a table and two chairs. Buzzing fluorescent lights had patches of black in the tubes, and I feared the room would soon be plunged into darkness. After what seemed like a long time but was probably less than an hour (the police had seized my watch along with the notes), two detectives entered. One, an older man with a sharp jaw, pushed me into a chair and slapped me across the face. The other sat next to me and began the interrogation. The ordeal continued for the next two hours as they alternated questions with blows, so severe they split the skin of my cheeks and neck. Their questions had nothing to do with the murder; rather, they were interested in whether the IRA planned to retaliate.

I could not tell them what they wanted to know and thus had no choice but to suffer the pain of their blows. After a few hours they left the room. I think they had gotten tired of pummeling me without reward.

I was released in the morning. The authorities had decided it would be politically embarrassing to keep me in custody. My boss, the deputy editor, had threatened to send a new reporter every day, an empty threat, as there was only one other reporter at the paper.

My story ran in two parts, one about the shooting and the other about my night in jail. The story led to a groundswell of protest, though without effect. My photograph appeared next to the articles. For a short while I was a local hero of sorts, my father leading the way with daily plaudits. He thought I had reinvested in the "cause." Then I started receiving numerous solicitations to become active in the IRA—instigated by my father no doubt—which soon caused me to resign from the newspaper and take refuge in the haven of university life.

After the articles appeared friends took me out to celebrate. We went to McInaney's, an Andersontown pub across from the police station. Since Mary and I had gotten married I was happy to stay home and rarely went to pubs. It felt like my first time there. I recognized none of the help; turnover had been high, as an increasing number of young people had moved to America to find better opportunities.

We had just finished watching a darts match on the second floor and had gone downstairs for a last round of Guinness. The bartender—rumored to be an IRA operative—refused to take my order until I accepted his congratulations. As he was energetically pumping my hand he said, "You should be careful, Tommy. If I recognized you, others will."

I took my hand away and said he was mistaken. He nodded knowingly, as if he and I shared an important secret, and went to pour the Guinness. A patron sidled up to me. "In case you might be wondering," he said, "he was thinking you're Tommy Glynn."

"Why would he think that?"

"He saw the photograph of you in the paper. Don't you know? You could pass for Tommy or his twin, that's for sure."

The confusion was absurd. Tommy was incarcerated in America. Had the bartender thought he escaped and taken a new name and job as a reporter? I thanked him and rejoined my friends. I told them of the mix-up and we laughed. But then one of my friends said, "Good thing the Gardai' [police] didn't make the same mistake. You would be at Long Kesh Maze drinking piss."

When I told Mary, she said, "Jesus, Mary, and Joseph. It's a good thing Tommy is in jail."

That night I dreamed that Tommy was free, leaving me to convince the authorities that I was Cornelius Michael Sullivan. I was called to the dock to answer the charges. I was startled to see no witnesses who would swear who I was, just the crowd shouting, "Tommy, Tommy." As the judge was about to pronounce sentence, I woke up sweating. What a terrible curse, I remembered thinking, to sacrifice one's identity and freedom for another.

In another day or two, I put the incident out of my mind.

I thought about listing everyone that the lawyer had mentioned in my notebook. Perhaps that would help me make sense of everything. But as I opened the notebook and stared at a blank page, I realized that no matter what I committed to writing, I would not find the answers notes, charts, or diagrams. My search must take me out into the world. I would travel to Boston and attend the court hearing to learn about the Savin Hill gang. And I would investigate Samuel Brandt and discover, if I could, the connection with Tommy Glynn, the lawyer, and me. One thing was certain. The encounter in Murphy's on my first night in America had not been an accident.

I returned to the studio where I rested and played the tapes. I telephoned Mary and we enjoyed a pleasant conversation. She did not bring up Tommy Glynn and I mentioned neither the suicide nor my accident. I had called early enough to speak to my darling Lucy. She filled me with joy when she said she missed me.

I called the Boston Globe and asked to be connected to the obituary department. A pleasant sounding woman said the funeral was scheduled for noon on the morrow, in Brookline, a nearby suburb of Boston. To my inquiry when a biographical obituary would appear, she said the newspaper did not plan to run one. She said Brandt was not a prominent Bostonian, having moved to Boston within the past year. She did not know from where he had come.

She did have a death notice in her files, which Mrs. Molly Marie Brandt had sent to the newspaper. Samuel had left a daughter: Erin, age 25. It also said that contributions should be made to an organization working to stop the extradition of Irish nationals imprisoned in the United States. I asked about parents or siblings. She said the notice did not mention other family members. "We don't investigate the submissions," she said. "We print what we receive."

Suddenly, my dizziness returned. I lay on the bed and was asleep within a few moments.

It was just before six when I woke. I hurried out of the studio and was around the corner when I realized I had forgotten my tape recorder. Not wanting to be late, I continued on to Murphy's.

I was startled that he was not at the bar. While I was settling on a stool to wait, Patrick came over to me, though it was not to take my order. He was carrying a slip of paper. "This is for you," he said.

The paper bore the letterhead of the Park Lane Hotel on 59th Street. It read: "Meet me under the Hans Christian Anderson statue in Central Park. Patrick will give you directions."

"What does this mean?" I asked Patrick.

"What it says, I guess."

"Why there?"

"You'll have to ask him."

Patrick gave me the directions. After returning home to retrieve my tape recorder, I hailed a taxi. Ten minutes later I was standing at the corner of 72nd Street and Fifth Avenue, near an entrance to the park. The directions said the statue was a short walk away.

From the moment I stepped into the park it enchanted and captivated me. I did not realize heaven could be found in the midst of grime. The stately trees watched over the landscape like angels. I walked down a long, sloping tree-lined path, which ended at an oval-shaped pond, perhaps as much as a quarter mile in circumference. A wide sidewalk circled the pond and was crowded with adults and children. Many of the children were watching toy sailboats floating in the water. Some of the children were holding a box with what looked like an antenna protruding from the top.

In the distance, on the other side of the pond, I saw a statue in the shadow of an oak tree. I also saw the familiar curly hair blowing in the breeze. He was sitting on his knees at the edge of the pond, a few yards from the statue. He was holding a box and looking across the water.

In a few moments I was at his side.

Hi. I was beginning to think you weren't going to show up. I wouldn't have blamed you. Not knowing whether to believe my stories, funny things happening . . . . But you came, that's what counts.

I love it here—peaceful, even with all the people. If you look in certain directions, you can imagine that you've gone back to the nineteenth century, to that fin de siècle moment when despair was fashionable. Behind you, for instance, past the statue through the trees, are the apartment buildings along Central Park West, some of them dating back to the turn of the century. I like to pretend that I live in one. Maybe the Dakota: fifteen rooms with a library, several sitting rooms, formal dining room with a button on the floor to buzz the cook, a living room facing the park. On a day like this, I would open the windows and smell the fresh spring air, hear the sounds of horse drawn carriages and the occasional toot from a newfangled motorcar.

Do you want to try your hand at the controls? It's easy. My boat is the large one with the blue hull and red sails. I bought it a couple of months ago. It was time I learned the rudiments of sailing. You never know when experience at the helm will come in handy. The round knob—the radio— controls the rudder; the smaller button moves the sails. The main sail and jib work together. It doesn't permit sophisticated maneuvers—there's no motor—but what the heck, you're still the captain. The wind does the work and you do the steering. In a few minutes, we'll bring in the boat on the other side. I keep it in that big shed. See the hot dog stand next to it. Fantastic hot dogs. You've never had one? You're in for a treat. Have two hot dogs because we're not going to be able to have dinner tonight. I have to leave in an hour. I'll be back tomorrow in time for our regular get together.

This was the moment when I knew I had to say something.

Yes, I know what happened. I knew yesterday. I haven't been entirely honest with you, Connie. I did know Sam Brandt. I saw no reason to tell you earlier. You just would have gone into a paranoid funk. But now . . . well . . . you see, I'm going to Boston. My plane is at nine. The funeral is tomorrow.

Move the sail around. Turn the knob. Good, it's on the way to the other shore. Come, I want to show you something.

He started to lead me past the statue, but I stopped for a better look. It stood in the center of a cul-de-sac. Eight or nine feet in height, the burnished bronze figure of Anderson was an imposing sight. It was seated on a large high-backed chair, a book of tales in its lap opened to "The Ugly Duckling." A top hat sat at its side, as if the real life Anderson had been on his way to a formal dinner party when he stopped at the pond to read to a group of children who had gathered around him. As I looked at the face, so carefully sculpted to convey kindness and gentleness, I imagined myself in another place and time, at Anderson's feet with the other children, listening to stories that would delight generations to come.

A deep melancholy tarnished the romance of it all. My father had never put me on his knee or tucked me in bed. He had never read me a story. I realized how much I hated my world: a violent world, a world leaving no room for innocence or aesthetics, a world where it was so much easier to hate than to love.

A curved row of green benches bordered the cul-de-sac. He pointed to a small metal plaque on the top slat of the bench on the end. On it was an inscription:

> "Out of the mouths of babes and sucklings hast thou ordained strength."
> —Psalms 8:2
>
> **Gift of Molly Marie and Samuel Brandt (1994)**

Sam loved children. He used to say that a child's innocence represented the only purity in the world. Sometime I try to remember when I lost my innocence. Was it the first time I lied to my mother Sarah, telling her I had finished my homework when I hadn't, or said I had brushed my teeth for a minute when it was thirty seconds? Or was it at Benny's shoeshine shop, where I used to stop on the way home from Hebrew school? I stole a magazine there; it had pictures of naked women lounging by a swimming pool at a nudist camp. When Sarah found it in the back of the closet, I said my brother Jonathan had brought it home. She believed me, though Jonathan said I was lying. I was more convincing than he was. You can't be both innocent and convincing. Or was it in the sixth grade when I told Peggy Hammerschlag I loved her, though I actually hated her, but knew she would kiss me if I said what she wanted to hear? Maybe I lost my innocence in stages, the innocence withering away in a society that treats innocence as a sign of weakness. Do you realize that the concept of innocence is nowhere found in the law? At best, you may be found not guilty. "Had laws not been, we never had been blamed, for not to know we sinned is innocence." Who? William Davenant. You're right, Connie. Impressive. You're a scholar and a gentleman.

I know what you're thinking. You're thinking I'm naive to believe in innocence. As naïve as I am to believe in justice. Innocence and justice are blood brothers. Guilt and the law are brothers in blood.

Enough said. I guess it's the news about Sam that's got me talking like this. Speaking of Sam, I suppose you want to hear how I know him. Let's walk. I don't want my boat to crash on the rocky shore. I know it isn't rocky. My boat isn't a real schooner either. Don't be so literal.

I met Sam in law school. But our friendship came later. We practiced in different cities. He stayed in Philadelphia while I went to Washington and then to Chicago. We became reacquainted when I happened to represent a woman who owned a brownie store. She wanted to sue his client, a Philadelphia company she hired to manufacture her batter. The manufacturer was using her recipe to make its own batter for use in company owned stores in the south. None of these stores competed with my client—her business was restricted to the Chicago area—making problematical the amount I could recover. We settled the case for $50,000 and his client's agreement not to use her formula.

Sam and I hit it off. It was just one of those things. We saw life the same way, with a mixture of idealism and cynicism. So we kept in touch. We'd see each other at bar association conventions and occasionally have dinner or drinks here in New York. I attended his wedding and he attended mine.

Here we are. Wait while I put my boat away.

I made a mental note to telephone a Philadelphia paper. I wondered why Brandt had moved to Boston. But I had no time to think about this, for he quickly returned. I followed him to the food stand. As he ordered, I decided to ask his name.

Why do you want to spoil such a beautiful evening? I don't want to tell you my name. Sure, I have something to hide. Otherwise, why wouldn't I tell you who I am? But what I have to hide is my business. I haven't asked you to do anything against your will. You should respect my privacy. Maybe if things turn out, I'll tell you. But rest assured, Connie, my name would mean nothing to you.

Let's order. Over there are the condiments. I recommend mustard, sauerkraut, and a sampling of the other goodies. What do you want to drink? Sorry, no beer or alcohol. Blame the law, a stupid law.

Come on. We'll sit by the pond. Look at the beautiful sky. New York has the finest pollution sunsets in the country. The smoke from the factories in New Jersey refracts the light.

I'm sorry again. God, I'm doing a lot of apologizing tonight. I haven't finished telling you about Sam. The truth is I'm feeling guilty about what happened, as if I should have noticed something was wrong. About a week before you and I hooked up, Sam and I met for drinks. He wasn't his usual energetic self. The Tommy Glynn case was bothering him. He'd been working on it for years and done an incredible job avoiding a deportation order. He knew time was running short. He said he had one last chance, an affidavit from someone in Belfast. I don't know who it is. He wouldn't tell me. He led me to believe that this person was responsible for the car bombing and ready to own up to it. Still, he wasn't hopeful. Whoever signed the affidavit couldn't or wouldn't come to the U.S. He thought the court would probably refuse to consider it, which as you know from the story in the Times is exactly what happened. Molly was taking it hard. She and her brother are very close.

The next night I joined Sam and Molly for dinner at Jimmy's Harborside. Jimmy's is a seafood restaurant in Boston—really? No, Connie, that can't be. I said I hadn't been there in years? You listened to the tapes again, so you're sure. What can I say? I did go there. Shame on me. You caught me in another lie, this time a big one. Be real! Why would I lie about having gone to a Boston restaurant you never heard of?

May I continue? Thank you. You're testy this evening. At dinner we talked about Tommy, but not in a morbid or defeatist way. After all, there was some hope in the new treaty, you know, the one scheduled for the referendum on the twenty-second. It has an amnesty provision, which might cover Tommy's situation. And if it doesn't, Sam planned to petition the Northern Ireland court to consider the affidavit. I remember we drank several toasts to the future and justice for Tommy. He seemed happy. Obviously, I was wrong.

Remember when I made a telephone call last night? Going to the bathroom. I checked my voice mail; there was a message from Molly. She had telephoned from Jimmy's, where she was having dinner with Erin, Sam's daughter. I called her back. She said Sam had gone to Dallas on a case, but was supposed to have flown in to meet them for dinner. She was worried. He hadn't arrived or called; unusual, she said, because Sam always let her know if he was going to be late. What could I say? I thought she was making a big deal about nothing.

When I got back to the hotel, another message was waiting for me. I called her right away. Horrible. She was being brave and stolid on the phone, but I could see the nightmare: a cop waiting for her at the house when she and Erin drove up, his blank look conveying the bad news, then his report that Sam's death was not an accident, not even the crime of another. I said I'd go to Boston this morning, but she said it wasn't necessary and would see me at the funeral.

That's the whole story. I hope you're satisfied. What? You have questions. What are they?

I had so many questions I hardly knew where to begin. The clerk at the Boston Globe told me Brandt had moved to Boston within the last year. Why? What happened to his law practice in Philadelphia? Was he practicing law in Boston? Did he have an office and where was it? Who would represent Tommy Glynn? I started with the last question.I

I have no idea who's going to represent Tommy. I should think he'd hire a British lawyer, since his fight here is over. If you're so interested, I can put you in touch with Molly. I'm sure she'd be happy to talk to you. Do you want to come to the funeral with me? It might not be the ideal time—

A piece of the hot dog had gone down my windpipe and I was choking. He raised my right arm and slapped me on the back. I could not breathe. His strong arms encircled my torso and squeezed. I gagged and spit out the offending piece.

For goodness sake, Connie. I never saw anybody turn so blue. Have you ever done that before? You should eat more slowly. Look. There was a toothpick stuck in the hot dog. Do you think it caused you to swallow the wrong way? If you had died, I could have sued for damages—on your wife's behalf, that is. What are her damages? The money you would have made, the value of your love and affection, and lost sexual satisfaction.

Which reminds me. If you want to see the law at its silliest, you should study tort law. Like the criminal law, it's based on fault and blame. Instead of sending the defendant to prison, however, we punish him by assessing damages. Every kind of injury is worth a certain amount. If you lose an arm, it's worth "x," if you lose a leg, it's worth "y," and so on. And tort law isn't confined to personal injury. It covers that big world of controversy in business relationships when there isn't a contract to rely on.

You want another drink? Sure, wait here and I'll get it for you. Another lemonade? You got it.

I rubbed my throat. It was sore. I would be happy when I returned to the studio. At least, I was safe there.

He had sounded detached when speaking of his dead friend. His reaction to the suicide seemed too casual, spoken as a newscaster might express sadness at the death of a celebrity. And then he quickly had returned to discussing the law, almost flippantly, as if nothing at all untoward had happened.

The area around the pond had emptied; the food stand was closing as he paid for the lemonade. The air had cooled and I shivered.

Here you are. Drink slowly.

Damn, look at the time. We'll have to wait until tomorrow evening to discuss the law of torts. What are your plans for the rest of the evening? Read and watch TV? Don't watch the lawyer shows. You'll get a good impression of lawyers, which, I'm sorry to say will be the wrong impression.

Enough foolishness. I know I've told you how much I appreciate our time together, but it means even more now. With Sam dead, we have to begin a new life. I have to begin a new life. Did you ever have that feeling? Whenever you lose a loved one, it's as if your own life has ended. Your life goes on, but it's not the same life. Most people don't see it that way. They just fall through the emptiness into their own black hole, expecting to come out on the other side of the universe without so much as a scratch. I know I can't be the same person after this loss and will have to treat his death as a new beginning, a new beginning for me; I have no choice. Having this opportunity to speak to you, to review my life in the law, is part of the new beginning.

Rest well tonight. Be careful what you eat. Don't faint and don't see gremlins on every street corner.

His departure left me disturbed. Though I had thought he was unfeeling about Sam Brandt's death, he had become nearly overcome with emotion in the moments before he left. It was as if I had been listening to two different people.

Though the skyline was gleaming with light and the promise of excitement, I felt alone, as if wandering through a home with an infinite number of rooms, all brightly lit but empty, silent like the courtroom at the moment of truth. Sitting by the pond, I could believe I was the only inhabitant of New York.

A police officer on a horse rode by. He suggested I leave the park, saying it was unsafe at night. I told him I felt safer in the park than on the streets. He gave me what I was certain was his special smile for fools and rode on.

The stars and city lights cast long shadows across the pond. Then, to my right, a few yards away, I saw a man walking toward me. He looked familiar, but in the darkness I was not certain. I nervously pulled at the bottom of my jacket and rose to greet him.

"Hello," I said.

He did not acknowledge my greeting.

"Were you watching me?" I asked, trying to keep my voice smooth and assured.

He would not answer.

"Do you not speak?"

"Be careful," he said.

"Of what?"

"Be careful not to learn more than you should."

He abruptly took a step closer. I backed away, moving my arms up to my chest, ready to defend myself. He smiled and gently swiped my shoulder as if I were an old friend and walked away. I stood stock still, staring across the pond, watching the city lights shimmering in the air. When I finally turned, he was already halfway up the path to Fifth Avenue.

When I reached the top of the hill, I saw him across the street, standing next to a black limousine, clearly visible in the light cast by a shop window. He was the driver who had helped me when I fainted.

A man was sitting in the back seat of the limousine. The street side window was rolled down. There it was, his signature, the unruly white hair.

I ran into the street. Car horns blared and a taxi swerved to avoid hitting me. I zigzagged crazily, as if I were dodging bullets, all to no avail, for when I reached the other sidewalk the limousine was gone.

"Are you all right, buddy?" the taxi driver yelled.

"Yes, thank you," I said breathlessly.

"Damn drunken fool," he mumbled, as he sped away.

The Lord blessed me with an uneventful walk home.

CHAPTER SIX

May 15, 1998

B Y THE TIME THE TAXI STOPPED *at the gates to the cemetery I had been traveling for six hours: five hours on the bus, a half-hour waiting in a taxi line outside the Greyhound station, and another half-hour in the cab, most of which was spent crawling along narrow streets overflowing with cars.*

As I looked out at the cemetery I was reminded of the funeral for Bobby Sands, the first of the hunger strikers to die at Long Kesh prison in 1981. The funeral was a remarkable sight. I had not wanted to attend, having just quit working at my father's car repair shop and wanting nothing further to do with political matters. My mother, however, advised me that my father would be offended if I did not accompany the family to the funeral. So I joined them and one hundred thousand other citizens in the four-mile procession from St. Luke's Church to Milltown cemetery.

Bobby had been an on again off again prisoner for many years. On his last go around, he was sentenced to fourteen years at Long Kesh. He had been in the wrong place at the wrong time: a passenger in a car in which the police had found a gun under the floorboard. He was convicted though the prosecution had no evidence that he was aware the gun was in the car.

I asked the driver to wait and got out of the taxi. The cemetery looked more like parkland than burial ground. Clumps of oak and maple trees sprinkled the landscape. The tombstones were small and unimposing, ranging from plates in the ground to markers a few feet high. A gravel walkway led to the chapel, a square red-bricked building with Hebrew lettering across the façade. A few cars were parked in the adjoining lot.

I knew this would not be a hero's funeral: no multitude holding hands, no honor guard to carry the coffin to the grave, no impassioned speeches and eulogies from friends and dignitaries. The morning Globe had confined the news of Brandt's death to a small squib buried in the second section. Shame and embarrassment are the pallbearers for a suicide.

Yet, surely he must have had many friends, I thought, as I walked to the chapel. Where were they?

A burly middle-aged man stood next to the door. His arm shot out, blocking my way.

"Are you a family member?" he asked.

"No."

"You can't go in."

"Why?"

"The service is restricted to family members."

I could see past his arm into the chapel. A rabbi stood behind a lectern, speaking in a low voice to two men and two women in the first row, the only persons present. The one I expected to be there, however, was not.

"Mrs. Brandt invited me," I said.

He looked at me skeptically, not surprising since I am a terrible liar. "Friend of hers, is that what you're saying?"

"Mr. Brandt, actually."

"What's your name?"

"Sullivan."

"You've got an accent," he said accusingly.

"I am from Belfast."

"Are you a terrorist?"

I searched his face for evidence of good humor. Finding none, I said simply, "I am a writer."

"A reporter?"

"Of history."

"Wait here." He went inside and slid into the second row, where he bent over the shoulder of the older woman. She turned and looked at me. I smiled and waved, as if we were old friends. She said a few words to him and he nodded.

When he came back he said, "OK, Sullivan, Mrs. Brandt said you can go inside, but sit in the last row and don't interfere."

I was puzzled. Why would she consent to my admission? Did she know about me? Who told her and when?

I took a seat and tried to hear what the rabbi was saying. But he was too far away. And he was whispering, making me feel I had intruded on a private audience.

When the service concluded, the group walked single file up the aisle. An old black man, walking with a cane, was the first. The second man was about the same age: small but sturdily built, deep lines in forehead and cheeks, and prominent eyes flashing at me for longer than curiosity required. The younger woman was most attractive: tall, slim, with long blonde hair tied behind her head, accentuating her smooth, high forehead, prominent cheekbones, and full lips. This must be Erin, Samuel's daughter. Last was Molly Marie Brandt. She was of modest height, but carried herself regally, with a face that reflected pride and intelligence. Her flaming red hair fell loosely to her shoulders and she wore a black suit that did little to conceal her slim but strongly constituted frame. There was no denying her Irish womanhood. I could see the resemblance to her brother Tommy, which naturally affected my opinion of her looks; a likeness to Tommy was a likeness to me. I put a hand to my mouth to cover my smile, lest she think I was disrespectful.

I waited a few moments and went outside. The group was walking across the grass to a row of folding chairs under a makeshift canopy. The burly man was still by the door.

"I thought only relatives were permitted inside," I said.

He was watching the others. "I know what I said."

"Who is the black man?

"Who do you think?"

What I had first thought was a harmless gruffness I now took to be something more sinister. His question was not politely put, and struck me as a threat. Foolishly, I chose to treat it as a joke. "His father, I would presume."

"Are you trying to be funny?"

I hastily retreated. "Not successfully, I am sure."

"He's a friend . . . as you claim to be."

"Is the other older man the father?"

He had looked away from me and in the direction of the others, but now he returned to me with renewed antagonism. "For someone claiming to be a friend, you know very little about his family."

"I was a business friend."

"You said you're a historian."

"I have business interests as well."

I doubted he believed me, but he was willing to continue our conversation. "His father is dead. So are his mother and brother."

"I did know that."

"Sure you did."

"Since you asked me my name, do you mind if I ask yours?"

"Gene."

"Are you a friend or relative?"

"I'm a lawyer."

"One of his partners, then."

"I'm going down there," he said, avoiding my question. "Do you want to come with me?"

"No, thank you. I will watch from here."

"Suit yourself," he said.

"I was expecting to see another friend of Samuel."

"What's his name?"

"I do not know."

He laughed. "You don't know very much about anything, do you."

"I met him in New York. He is a lawyer from Chicago."

"I can't help you."

I looked at the gathering by the gravesite and realized that there was something odd. "Where is he?"

I could see his patience was at an end. "How should I know?"

"Not the friend from Chicago. Where is Brandt? Where are his remains?"

"Arizona."

"Arizona?"

"His parents and brother are buried in Tucson."

He pushed by me and entered the chapel. In a few moments he returned with several men I had not seen before. They went on to the canopy.

"Who are they?" I asked.

"They work for the cemetery. We need a minion."

"Minion?"

"Catholics," he said with a sneer. "They only know their own rituals. We need ten men to start the service."

"Oh, I see. A quorum."

He snickered. "I said a minion. This isn't an Elks club meeting."

He walked away before I could ask more questions. I wanted to know the old white man's name, why Brandt left Philadelphia (in my rush to catch an early morning bus, I had forgotten to telephone a Philadelphia newspaper), and why so few came to the funeral.

I waited until he was with the others before going to the parking lot. Among the late model cars was an older one, rusted and pitted, with a New York license plate. A fragment from a sticker was on the front windshield bearing the letters "cin." I assumed the letters must be part of a word. The front windows were open. On the front seat was a paperback book, "The Fire Next Time,'" by James Baldwin. I reached inside and opened it. At the top of the inside cover was the inscription: "A gift from one revolutionary to another, Your friend always, Sam."

I moved on to a powder blue, late model Cadillac. The windows were closed and the doors locked, but I could see a manila folder and a law book on the front seat. This must be Gene's car, I thought. The license plate both confirmed my guess and startled me: L-U-F-M-A-N. I thought back to the first night at Murphy's. Eudie Lufman raised two sons, one of whom became a lawyer.

Now I was truly frightened. Too much had been planned, orchestrated for my benefit. Even what had seemed to be a trivial story about a long forgotten case connected with the present in a disturbing way, a foreshadowing, but of what?

Lufman was at my side. "You like to snoop, don't you, Sullivan."

"You should have told me your last name. You see I knew your—I should say I knew of your father. He—"

"You're either a reporter or a cop."

"Really, I am who I said."

"I think you should leave."

133

His look was menacing. "By all means," I said quickly.

"Mrs. Brandt wanted me to give you a message."

"What kind of message?"

"She said, 'You shouldn't have come.'"

Brave though I may have been, determined though I may have become, passionate in seeking the truth though I was, I had not lost my ingenuousness. "Think nothing of it," I said. "It was only proper—" I stopped when I saw his self-satisfied grin. The message was his warning, and I had been too naïve to see the troubles that lie ahead.

I toyed with the idea of having the taxi driver take me to the parking lot where we would wait for the mourners, then to follow them to their destination. But when I saw that the fare was now more than sixty dollars and considered how much money was in my wallet, I decided to proceed directly to the courthouse.

The nausea had returned and I was tired. "Please wake me when we arrive at the courthouse," I said.

"Whatever you say."

"Thank you." I closed my eyes.

"If you don't mind me asking, who was the funeral for?"

I stretched and moved forward in my seat to get a better look at him. He was a young man with a ruddy complexion and a neatly trimmed handlebar mustache. His arms were covered with tattoos: multicolored snakes on one arm and a partially clad woman on the other.

"A lawyer," I replied. "By the name of Samuel Brandt."

"Is he the guy who jumped off the bridge?"

"Yes. You read it in the newspaper?"

"Nope. Heard it on the radio."

"What did you hear?"

"Something about a legal case he was hooked up with."

"What case?"

"You know, the one with the mobsters. It's been in the papers."

"The Savin Hill gang?"

"That's the one."

"Did you hear how Brandt was involved?"

He reached into an ashtray under the meter and pulled off a wad of gum. He stuck it in his mouth and started chewing furiously. "You a reporter?"

"Indeed, I am," I said, smiling.

"You don't say. Yeah, well, I don't remember exactly what it said on the radio. I wasn't paying too much attention."

"Try to remember."

"Are you sure you're a reporter?"

"Yes. Why do you ask?"

"You don't look like one."

"What do I look like?"

"Well, not look like. Sound like. Your accent and everything."

"I am from Belfast."

"One of them foreign correspondents. Cool."

"Thank you."

"Now I remember," he said as he pulled over to the side of the road. He put his arm over the seat and faced me. He was chewing so fast he had to swallow every few seconds. "The radio said the Irish guy who's on the lam . . . let me see . . . oh, yeah . . . Delaney, Whitey Delaney. He ran the gang, you know, and they can't find him, nobody knows where he disappeared to, so you see this—darn, I lost my train of thought."

"You were telling me about the case."

"Yeah, right. See, this Brandt fellow was supposed to testify—hey, I'm taking you to federal court. Is that where . . . ?"

"Yes, but please, go on."

"Sure. Anyhow, and don't quote me, 'cause I really ain't positive."

"Do not be concerned. You are just repeating what you heard on the radio."

"Yeah, well, sure, you make a lot of sense. Brandt's daughter, I guess it was, she was congregating with the mobsters, and the Feds must have figured—oh, yeah, she said she didn't know nothing. I guess they decided maybe her father does, but now he's in the ground, so they're shit out of luck."

"I see."

He took the gum out of his mouth, examined it for a moment, and then threw it out the window. "We better get going. It's not fair to keep the meter running while I'm jawing."

I leaned back in the seat as he pulled out into the traffic.

I was sitting on a piano chair in a large white room at the Belfast Repertory Theater. The director, playwright, and theater manager were seated behind a table. The director asked me if I was ready for the audition. I said I had not been provided a copy of the play. The playwright, who I was shocked to see was the lawyer, said it was unnecessary for me to read the play; he said I could perform adequately, knowing only the scene in which I was to appear. Then the director, who now had my father's face, spoke: "Deliver the lines with your heart." I nodded. I felt a strange, paralyzing sensation flow down my face, starting with my eyes. I reached up with my hand. My eyes were gone! Then slowly downward: no nose, no mouth. Yet, I could still see. The theater manager handed me a sheet of paper. "Here," he said. "Read it." The paper was blank. His face was blank. I looked at the other two men. Their faces were blank. Another man, the taxi driver, entered the room. "Are you OK?" he asked. I did not answer. He came to me and shook my shoulders. "Are you OK?" he repeated.

I opened my eyes. The driver was shaking me. "Are you OK?" he said.

"Where are we?"

"The courthouse, where else?"

I ran my hand across my face and was relieved to find my features intact. "I was dreaming."

He handed me my notebook. "You didn't write down what I said."

"I will do it later."

"My name is George Crone, with a 'C'. In case you decide to mention me in your article."

I gave him an extra twenty dollars. "I'll be here when you come out," he said. "Won't charge you for waiting, neither."

The large courtroom included ten rows for spectators, all full. I squeezed in at the end of the second row. A lectern with a microphone was positioned in

the front center of the courtroom, ten feet or so from the witness stand and the judge's bench. Directly behind the lectern were two long tables, one in front of the other. Two men sat at the forward table. The man on the left was reviewing papers while the other man, short and thin, sat quietly with veined, gnarled hands folded in front of him. At the other table sat a young woman. Before her were two large boxes of documents containing folders with colored tabs.

The judge appeared to be waiting for the younger man at the forward table to approach the lectern. The man in the witness box slouched comfortably against the back of the seat. Seemingly indifferent to the proceedings, he patted his mouth to suppress a yawn. He was wearing a black and white jogging suit with the top two buttons open and a heavy gold necklace around his neck. His thick black hair looked windblown, as if he had taken a break from exercising to testify.

"Is he dressed properly?" I asked the gentleman sitting next to me.

"You mean Gavencci? He always dresses the same. I understand he even makes love to his mistress in those clothes."

Gavencci certainly had the countenance of a gangster. Rough-hewn dark skin, a boxer's nose—broken too many times I suspected—and a snarling mouth combined to portray a brutal, violent man. More terrifying than his look was the way he peered around the courtroom, as if he were seeking out his next victim.

"Mr. Gavencci," the lawyer said from behind the lectern, "before lunch we had touched on your connection to the Jones Printing Company."

"You mean what I had to do with it?" he said in a light Italian accent.

"Yes, Mr. Gavencci."

"What about it?"

"How were you associated with the company?"

"Cousin Kurt."

"Would that be Kurt Hauer?"

"You got it."

The judge, whose cherubic face made him look more like an altar boy than a judge, said with a smile, "Mr. Hauer is not of Italian extraction, I assume."

"Not hardly," Gavencci said. "He ain't a cousin either. We call him Cousin Kurt because we like it better than Herr Kurt, if you get my meaning."

"I'm not sure I do."

"He belongs to one of them Hitler groups."

The judge sighed. "Let's get back to the subject du jour," he said to the lawyer.

Just then, the courtroom door opened and Gene Lufman appeared. The judge, the lawyers, and Gavencci looked at him.

"Your Honor," the woman lawyer said. "The record should note that Eugene Lufman has entered the courtroom. We will be calling him as a witness on behalf of the government."

"In that case," the judge said, "Mr. Lufman will have to step outside."

"Just as well," Lufman said affably. "I don't see any empty seats."

He left and the lawyer resumed his examination. "Mr. Gavencci, please describe your dealings with Jones Printing Company."

"I wouldn't call them dealings. Cousin Kurt, I mean Mr. Hauer, called me to say that a million bucks was coming into the pension fund and he was looking for an investment."

"Why did he come to you?"

"I'm an investment banker." Spectators, including the gentleman next to me, chuckled. Gavencci made a sound like a bear's growl. "Would anyone in the peanut gallery like to meet me outside to discuss my credentials?" The chuckling stopped.

"That won't be necessary," the judge said with decided Weltschmerz.

"What was Mr. Hauer's position at Jones Printing?" the lawyer asked.

"Beats me. I don't care for titles."

"I'm curious, Mr. Gavencci," the judge said. "What is your objection to titles?"

"Well, your Honor, it's like this, and please don't take no offense, since you got a title and it probably means a lot to you, but the way I see it we live in a democracy and we shouldn't be bothering with no titles. I even feel the same about the . . . ."

"Yes, Mr. Gavencci?"

"Never mind."

A few spectators tittered. "I don't understand," I said to my neighbor.

"Gavencci was going to criticize the Mafia's penchant for titles like 'Godfather,' 'Capo,' and 'Consigliere.'"

"Thank you," I said, grateful to be sitting next to such a knowledgeable observer.

"Who was the president of Jones Printing Company?" the lawyer asked.

"Peter Marinelli."

The lawyer pointed at the older man at the table. "Vincente Marinelli's nephew."

"Yeah, brother Salvatore's son. Right."

"Please continue."

"Well, see, I happened to know this magazine company which was in the shit can because it couldn't get money to expand its business, you know, like from conventional bank financing."

"Why?"

"The suits didn't want to be associated with the magazines it published."

"What kind of magazines?"

"Girlie stuff."

"Then what happened?"

"I told Mr. Hauer we could purchase the company for a million bucks, give or take."

"What did Hauer say?"

"He said let's go for it."

"You had previously dealt with Peter Marinelli?"

"I lent him a couple of bucks for a down payment on three hotels in South Beach."

"Near Miami, Florida?"

"That's the place."

"Did Marinelli pay you back?"

"Yes."

"With money he borrowed from a bank to renovate the hotels."

"Something like that."

"How did you know the source of the money Marinelli used to repay you?"

"He told me."

"Were you wearing anything when he told you?"

"Yeah, I hope so." Nervous laughter filled the courtroom.

"Something other than clothes, Mr. Gavencci," the lawyer said.

"Oh, yeah, right. I was wearing a wire."

"A recording device?"

"Right."

"At whose request were you wearing it?"

"Smitty."

"His full name, please."

"Smith Corcoran."

"The FBI agent?"

"The one and only." He said this as if there were no other agents in the FBI.

"What was your arrangement with Corcoran?"

"I give the Feds what they want; they give me what we want."

"Which is?"

"Leave us alone."

"Who was us?"

"Me, Vinny, and Whitey."

"Whitey Delaney?"

"Yes."

"Were there any other terms in your arrangement with agent Corcoran?"

"Money."

"How so?"

"No free lunches in this world. Smitty was looking for dough."

"How much?

"In the beginning, it was a couple of grand a month, then later ten percent of our take."

"When did this arrangement begin?"

"It started around 1985, I think."

The lawyer took a few steps forward. *"Mr. Gavencci, you said that Corcoran wanted information. What kind of information?"*

"He wanted evidence against certain people."

"Who?"

"People."

"Mr. Gavencci, please. Who?"

Gavencci fingered his gold necklace. Clearly, he was a man who did not like to divulge secrets.

The lawyer took another step forward. "Who?"

Gavencci pulled at the necklace and said, "Peter Marinelli, for one."

"Why did agent Corcoran want information on Peter Marinelli?"

"He never said, but I had a pretty good idea."

"What was your idea?"

"Objection," the woman lawyer said. "Calls for speculation."

"Sustained," the judge said.

Gavencci went on to describe his relationship with Corcoran. I was astounded by the corruption he so casually outlined. In addition to receiving a share of profits from the gang's illegal operations, Corcoran would alert the Savin Hill gang to planned wiretaps and police raids.

"When did your relationship with Corcoran terminate?" the lawyer asked.

"Last year, in November. Monday the seventeenth."

"How can you be so precise about the date?"

"Monday night football. Lost a ton on the game, I should have . . . well, anyway, that's how I can be so . . . precise."

More laughter from the spectators. I did not laugh; I was too busy writing in my notebook.

"What happened?" the lawyer asked.

"Smitty said we needed to meet."

"Where?"

"Gene Lufman's house."

"Who is Gene Lufman?"

"He's a lawyer. The son of my former bookkeeper."

"He's no longer your bookkeeper?"

"Retired."

"Where?"

"Jupiter Island. On the fourteenth hole, lucky son-of-a . . . . Excuse me, your Honor."

"I wouldn't mind retiring to Jupiter Island," the judge said.

"Was Mr. Lufman at the meeting?"

"He certainly was. Gotta have your lawyer at important meetings."

"Anyone else at the meeting?"

"No."

"Are you certain?"

"Yeah, unless the Feds were listening in."

"Who said what at the meeting?"

"Smitty told us our deal was off. He said he wanted to be straight with us; he couldn't protect us no more."

"Why not?"

Gavencci winked at the government lawyer. She smiled wanly, though with a coquettish twist of her mouth, which caused Gavencci to smile lecherously. Her mouth instantly dropped and she returned her eyes to the pad in front of her.

"He said the strike force had a new lawyer assigned to investigate my businesses, a looker with a tight ass, literally and figuratively." He looked at her again and said, "No offense ma'am, but I'm under oath. I wouldn't want you to charge me with perjury."

She turned away in disgust. She obviously regretted her brief flirtation with such an obviously dangerous man.

The lawyer stepped in between Gavencci and the prosecutor, blocking his view. "Please, Mr. Gavencci," he said.

"Have it your way. Smitty said she was a real tiger and gung-ho on putting my compatriots and me out of business. I didn't give a . . . no skin off my back. I was looking to retire anyway. Everybody, including me, has got a right to retire."

"You weren't angry?"

"Me?" He spread his arms in mock surprise. "I never get angry."

The lawyer coughed and the judge said, "An admirable quality."

Gavencci turned to the judge. "Well, Judge, you gotta be cool to . . . "

"I withdraw the compliment, Mr. Gavencci."

"Mr. Gavencci," the lawyer said. "Do you know Samuel Brandt?"

Gavencci shifted in his seat. For the first time during his testimony he appeared nervous. "What about him?"

"How do you know him?"

"I think I met him at a restaurant. Lufman introduced me."

"Are you aware that Mr. Brandt passed away recently?"

"Jumped off a bridge is what I heard."

"Did you know he was scheduled to testify for the government in this matter?"

"Yeah. You told me."

The lawyer coughed again. "Indeed, I did. But you should never say what we discussed—"

"Right. Attorney-client privilege."

"Do you know why the government subpoenaed Mr. Brandt?"

"Haven't got a clue. Also haven't got a clue what Lufman is going to say, but he better tell the truth or—

"No further questions," the lawyer said abruptly. Gavencci looked displeased that he had not been able to finish his answer. For all his lighthearted glibness, he was clearly a man who enjoyed making a threat and backing it up.

The government lawyer stood to cross-examine but stopped when the judge raised his hand. "We'll adjourn for the day," he said. "This hearing will resume at ten on the twenty-second."

The courtroom quickly cleared, though the government lawyer remained, gathering papers and stuffing them in her briefcase. I had not realized until she stood how petite she was, at least a head shorter than I, but looking even smaller because of her tiny and delicate face. She could easily pass for a teenager.

I walked up to her. "Excuse me," I said.

"Yes?" she said with the air of impatience that usually means a "no."

"I was an acquaintance of Sam Brandt."

She pulled out a briefcase from under the table and began stuffing papers inside it. She was acting as if she had not heard me.

"I am interested in what Mr. Brandt was going to say, had he been able to testify."

I had gotten her attention. "Are you a reporter?"

"Yes, from Belfast. We are interested in Samuel Brandt because he was representing Thomas Glynn."

"The IRA bomber?"

"Yes."

"His testimony would have had nothing to do with the Glynn case."

"Indubitably. I am interested in this hearing for background."

"Not for publication?"

"No."

"He was going to corroborate Lufman's testimony."

"Which is?"

"You're not much of a reporter, Mr. . . . "

"Sullivan."

"It's been in the news, Mr. Sullivan. Leaks. I do my job in a foot of water. The government is a leaky faucet that can't be repaired."

"Pardon my ignorance, Miss . . . "

"Gold. Susan Gold."

"Ms. Gold, I arrived from Belfast only yesterday."

"Mr. Lufman will testify that the meeting at his house never occurred."

"How would Mr. Brandt confirm that?"

"He was having dinner with Mr. Lufman."

"Why would Mr. Lufman betray his client Gavencci?"

"It's not betrayal to tell the truth, Mr. Sullivan."

"Mr. Gavencci seems . . . well, he seems dangerous. Is not Mr. Lufman afraid?"

"Gavencci wouldn't have the nerve to try anything. It would be too obvious."

"Nonetheless, I would imagine—"

"Look, Mr. Sullivan, I'm not in the psychology business. If you want to know Lufman's reason for coming forward, you'll have to ask him."

"Of course."

"And Lufman isn't our sole corroborating witness. We have someone else who will testify Corcoran never made a deal with the Savin Hill gang."

"Who?"

"You are in the dark, aren't you, Mr. Sullivan. James Crosetti is the other witness." Seeing that the name meant nothing to me, she continued: *"Crosetti works for Salvatore Marinelli."*

"The New York restaurateur?"

"The restaurant business is not his principal occupation."

"What does he look like, this man Crosetti?"

She furrowed her brow.

"I am sorry to ask so many questions," I said.

"It's what reporters do," she said. "You are a reporter, aren't you?"

"Yes."

"Do you have identification?"

"My passport." I started to reach in my pocket, but stopped when I saw a man enter the courtroom. He was signaling to her. She frowned, displeased about something.

"I have to go," she said.

"If I may ask, who is he?"

"My boss."

He hurriedly came to the table, rubbing his neck like he had a rash. He was an ordinary looking man of perhaps fifty or a few years older, the sort of man one might see a dozen times and still be unable to describe.

"This is Mr. Sullivan," Gold said. "He's a reporter from Belfast."

"Long way to travel."

"I am gathering background for a story about Tommy Glynn."

"Pretty deep background. This is a Mafia case."

"Peter," Gold said. "You remember that Brandt—"

Clearly, they had a relationship that went beyond business. "Tell me about the other Irishman," I said, "this Whitey Delaney."

"You should know. He's from Ireland."

"He grew up in Belfast," Gold said. "Came here in '69 and started the Savin Hill gang with Gavencci and Marinelli."

"Didn't you know that?" he asked.

"No, I . . . as I said, I am here only to gather background. My assignment is to write about Tommy Glynn."

"Then you would know that Delaney is Glynn's father-in-law."

Would know? I asked myself. There was much I should know, but did not. She placed her hand on my elbow. "Are you all right?" she asked.

"Quite, Ms. Gold." I said.

"You look pale."

"It was a long flight."

"Susan, please," he said.

"If you'll excuse me," she said, "I have work to do."

He took her arm, but did not offer to help carry the heavy briefcase. They were at the door when I thought of something else.

"*Excuse me,*" *I said, running up to them. "Would it be appropriate if I called you, that is, if I have additional questions?*"

She put her case on the floor and took a business card from her suit jacket. "You can call me, but I can't promise anything."

"*Thank you so much,*" *I said. I reached out to shake her hand, which she graciously accepted.*

"*Come on, Susan,*" *he said. "We have a lot to do.*"

I did not want him to leave in bad humor. "It was a pleasure to meet you as well," *I said.*

"*Sure,*" *he said.*

"*I did not get your name.*"

He sighed as if I were an annoying gnat that refused to fly away. He handed me his card.

They were already out the door when I looked at the card. At the top was the emblem of the United States Department of Justice. Underneath was his name: Peter Varick.

I nearly tripped over my own feet dashing into the hall. I caught up to them at the elevator, its doors opening.

"*What is it now?*" *he asked, now clearly irritated.*

"*Were you once in charge of the Chicago Strike Force?*"

The elevator door started to close and he put a hand out to stop it. "Who told you that?"

"*Well, I . . . I must have read it in the Boston Globe, in one of the stories about the case.*"

"*The stories only mentioned me,*" *Gold said. "This is my case.*"

"*No . . . no, I am certain . . .* "

He removed his hand from the door and they stepped into the elevator. The last thing I saw before the doors closed were their suspicious eyes.

Crone was standing next to his taxi. What a wonderful person he was to have waited. And then I noted the hour and what I had not taken into account when planning my journey. Even if I caught the five o'clock bus, I would not be back in New York until ten.

May 15, 1998

A few feet away Gavencci and Marinelli were talking. I wanted to move closer so I could overhear what they were saying, but it was not possible to do so discreetly.

A black sedan approached the curb. I thought it might be their car. Though I do not remember, the car window must have been open. From what other location could have come the hail of bullets that struck the two men and shredded their bodies? One bullet missed them and caught the step beneath me, slicing off a shard of concrete that splintered in the air, grazing my scalp. Blood dripped into my eyes and I fell to the ground. People were scrambling helter-skelter like a startled bunch of chickens while several police officers were skipping up the steps, two at a time.

Arms were around my back, lifting me by the armpits. "Quick, let's get out of here," Crone said.

I don't know what to ask you first. You leave a message with Patrick saying you'll be hours late, and then you show up with a nasty cut on your head. Did you faint again? You know I'm staying at the Park Lane. You should have called me. Oh, I guess you couldn't, because you don't know my name.

What did you say? Did you say Sam? Sam Brandt? Your head wound has discombobulated you. Sam Brandt is dead. All right, Connie, I'll tell you my name. But I warned you; it won't mean a thing to you.

He reached in his suit jacket and took out a passport. He placed it on the bar and lit a cigarette while I opened it. I looked at the photograph and then the name.

Fischel Schaechter. I know, Connie, it's not what you expected and it is a bit tricky to pronounce. You say the *ae* like the *e* in bed.

Patrick came over with drinks and whispered to him.

A call for me. Be right back.

Fischel Schaechter. What a wonderful name. But knowing his name answered none of my questions and meant nothing to me, just as he had warned.

He was standing at the other end of the bar, telephone in his ear, listening and watching me at the same time. He put another cigarette in his mouth and Patrick rushed to him with a light. I sipped my Guinness and wondered.

That was Molly on the telephone. I called her this afternoon to apologize for not making it up to Boston. She told me what happened. I don't know which is the bigger surprise: you're going to the funeral or standing in the killing field outside the courthouse.

Don't you want to know how Molly recognized your name? Really? You've decided not to ask me questions? That's a switch. I'll tell you anyway. When I told her I'd see her at the funeral, I mentioned we'd met. I thought you would go with me. But you said nothing when I offered, and then you got the piece of hot dog stuck in your windpipe. When she saw you at the service she assumed I would be walking into the chapel at any moment. That's why you were able to go inside. As you must have noticed, it was a small funeral. Such a pity, because Sam had a lot of friends.

How do I know you were present at the shooting? Educated guess. Tell me why you survived. No, I'm not making light of it. Well, maybe I am. Sorry. You want to talk about it? Later? OK, what should we discuss? Law stories. You want to hear more law stories? I'm flattered.

I had been honest. I did want him to resume telling his stories of law. I wanted to lose myself in his world of law. I wanted to understand this unusual man. And I was beginning to believe that the answers to my questions were embedded in his past.

Morris Cohen—the Cohen of Litowitz Smith, Cohen & Whitmore—rued the day he became a lawyer; he would have preferred to be an aesthete. Whenever we spoke, he chose a different subject for each lecture: Pre-Columbian architecture, abstract expressionism, Scottish folk music, the classical antecedents of rock and roll, and the Stanislavsky school of acting were a few areas he would cover before agreeing to discuss a legal problem.

Client files, law books, and legal pads had no place in the life of Morris Cohen and were nowhere to be found in his office. You could believe you were in the musty library of an English professor: cracked leather recliner with matching ottoman; small antique birch desk; cabinet equipped with record player, FM tuner, classical music albums (the Berlin Philharmonic was his favorite orchestra); several bottles of French Margaux in an oak wine rack; books without dust covers to give the place the feel of a nineteenth century reading room. If he wasn't reading, he was cleaning his pipes and listening to *The 1812 Overture*.

He ignored the lawyer's dress code, shunning suits and ties. Not having to dress for court was his stated excuse for becoming a corporate lawyer, though he was known to have stage fright—he refused to propose a toast at his son's Bar Mitzvah. He always wore one of two outfits: off-white turtleneck sweater and black pleated pants, or black turtleneck sweater and off-white pleated pants. He had a goatee, blonde as the hair on his head, though the goatee had the texture of steel wool. Unhappy with the look—with his slim yet flaccid body, he had the mien of a tennis pro gone to seed—he dyed his blonde hair and beard black and every month assiduously added flecks of white. When I joined the firm, he had just turned fifty and his hair was the color of soot; he soon began using Clairol to restore the blonde.

I had been with the firm a month when I received my first invitation to his office. I wished I'd brought a candle. A thick fog enveloped the room, which I knew from the smell of cherry was produced by his pipe smoking. The only light came from an antique lamp that was supposed to simulate gaslight but just flickered and crackled like any dying light bulb. Purple velvet drapes covered the length of the exterior wall, obscuring what I imagined was a spectacular view of downtown Chicago. I thought I'd somehow stumbled into Count Dracula's study, an impression that was reinforced when I peeked behind the drapes and saw nothing but plaster. A lawyer in the office said Morris had the windows sealed over before he installed the drapes. We started calling his office *The Cask of the Amontillado*.

His largest client was Movies Unlimited, which distributed films to non-theatrical markets: colleges, prisons, hospitals, and film societies. In the days before consumer videotape machines, this was the only real market for older films other than TV. A major supplier to Movies was RKO, which had ceased making films and derived its revenue from the rental of its library. Movies Unlimited was RKO's exclusive licensee for the non-theatrical markets.

The most prestigious film on RKO's list and consistent moneymaker was *Citizen Kane.* Though released in 1941, it was still under copyright and its renewal term wouldn't expire until 1997. Movies had learned that Classic Films, a small New York company, had included *Citizen Kane* in its catalogue. The president of Movies told Morris the only way Classic could have obtained prints was to have engaged in illegal copying in violation of RKO's copyright. I should be honored to represent his best client in a case, which Morris said was a "laydown." He expressed the same opinion to the executives at RKO, whose permission he needed to sue.

Morris failed to tell me his client would not be an ideal plaintiff in a copyright infringement suit. For years it had been using its control of *Citizen Kane* to force customers into renting its less desirable films, a marketing practice known as "tying," illegal under the antitrust laws. Customers hadn't complained, but it was inevitable that a competitor, particularly if provoked, would take action. And Morris, who sat on the Board of Directors and knew of Movies' sales tactics, never advised his client to change its approach.

When I questioned the wisdom of proceeding with the lawsuit, Morris was furious. "Classic can't raise our business practices as a defense to its thievery," he said. I reminded him of the doctrine of *unclean hands,* under which a court might refuse to enforce RKO's copyright if its licensee was violating the law, but he wasn't going to change his mind anymore than he would restore the windows to the sealed-up wall in his office. Moreover, he had already told RKO and Movies we would win the case, and if there is one act a lawyer will acknowledge as a sin, it's confessing error.

As I expected, Classic raised the tying defense in response to our complaint. It also asserted an even more dangerous claim: RKO's copyright was invalid.

The claim was based on information uncovered by film critic Pauline Kael who argued in a recent book that Herman Mankiewicz was the sole author of the script and only he was entitled to renew the copyright for a second term. Of course, I had to tell Morris of this potentially disastrous development. I found him in his office—no surprise, he only left it to go home—lying in the recliner and sucking on a pipe. The imitation gas lamp was bathing his face in a yellow glow, giving him the pallor of a gout-ridden nobleman. I told him the bad news.

"Why didn't you warn me?" he said.

"The Kael book was just published."

"Rubbish," he said.

"What do you want me to do?"

"What any good lawyer does."

"Fold a bad hand?"

He pressed a button on the side of the recliner and returned to the seated position. He took the pipe out of his mouth and pointed it at me. "Your hand is irrelevant," he said. "A good player bluffs by raising the bet."

"How do I bluff?" I asked.

"Is Mankiewicz alive?"

"He died a few years ago."

"There you go. The book is hearsay."

"The drafts of the screenplay clearly show Mankiewicz was the author."

Morris pressed the button again. A scratching noise accompanied a violent vibration. His chair looked like it was in the midst of jet-stream turbulence. His pipe flew through the air, narrowly missing my head. He fell out of his chair and was on the floor at my feet. "You figure it out," he shouted, kicking the recliner. The vibrating stopped.

I retrieved the pipe from the middle of the hall. When I turned to go back inside, the door was shut. He had put on *The 1812 Overture* and I thought it best not to disturb him. I took the pipe to my office and sat in my chair, pretending to be smoking and thinking. Eventually, I got tired of waiting for a brilliant idea; I had also bitten through the stem of the pipe. I went to three different shops before I found a replacement. It cost me seventy-five bucks.

⚖️

I called the General Counsel of RKO and asked if he could schedule a meeting with Orson Welles. I assumed Orson would be anxious to defend his authorship of *Citizen Kane,* and I could then use his affidavit to respond to Classic's allegations.

The General Counsel, sounding on the phone as if I had interrupted his afternoon nap, already knew why I was calling. "You realize that if you jeopardize our copyright in *Citizen Kane,* we'll hold your firm responsible for our lost profits."

"Do you want us to drop the case?"

"I want you to win it."

"Then I need to talk to Welles."

"Need and gratification are two different things."

"I don't understand."

"Welles won't talk to us and I doubt he'll talk to you."

"Why?"

"He hates RKO for ruining his second film, *The Magnificent Ambersons*, but he hates lawyers more."

"What do you suggest?"

"You can talk to John Houseman."

Houseman is best known for his portrayal of the irascible law professor in *The Paper Chase*, though he had a long career in the theater. With Welles, he was co-founder of The Mercury Theater, which was famous for its radio play of *War of the Worlds* that convinced a gullible segment of the country we were being invaded by Martians.

He lived in a beach house in a gated enclave in Malibu called the Colony, a cluster of small, overpriced homes along the Pacific Ocean thirty miles from Los Angeles. The Colony counted among its residents film and television celebrities, but you wouldn't know you were in a neighborhood of nabobs and parvenus from what you could see as you drove on the main thoroughfare. The houses were dull gray, wood-framed—many in disrepair—and sat on postage-stamp lots. The general drab was exacerbated by how the houses were situated: front facing the ocean and back to the street, giving the passerby a string of garage doors and garbage cans to look at.

He greeted me at the door, wearing a green terry cloth robe. His oversized slippers made a flipper-like sound as he walked. He led me into a large room with a cathedral ceiling, country kitchen, and view of the ocean. He sat on the futon couch and I sat in the futon chair. Turning right to business, I handed him a short affidavit I had prepared for his signature. It stated that Welles had written the final script.

He read the affidavit and put it on the glass table between us. Then he took a half-smoked cigar from a metal ashtray and chewed on the end like a man who has something important to say.

"I want to tell you a story," he said.

"I would love to hear it."

"Back in '41, when we were still in the planning stages for the film, Orson and I had dinner every night. One evening, I suggested we pick a different project for his first film. I knew William Randolph Hearst would be livid at what would no doubt be an unflattering portrayal, and I didn't think Orson—or I for that matter—needed the aggravation. Now, the only way to get anywhere with Orson was with threats or bribery and I didn't have enough money for a bribe. So I threatened to quit on the spot. You know what he said?"

"No."

"He said, 'At least stay and finish your dinner.'"

"Did you quit?"

"I should have. What did I ever gain by being associated with history's most revered movie? I doubt anyone other than the film connoisseur is even aware of the driving force I lent to the enterprise."

I had learned to be obsequious when the occasion required. "I'm aware of your contribution, Mr. Houseman."

He put the cigar in the ashtray and picked up the affidavit. "The problem with affidavits is that even when they state the truth, it's a watered-down truth, like a scotch and water at a cheap bar: too little scotch and too much water. Young man, I'm afraid this affidavit is not even a watered-down version of the truth; it's a straight-up lie."

"I guess cheap liquor is cheap liquor, with or without the water."

"I commend you. It's a rare lawyer who appreciates a metaphor."

"Then Mankiewicz did write the script?"

"Orson couldn't stomach a Hollywood hack getting credit for his movie. And he considered me just another meddling producer. Orson's ego would never have allowed him to give Herman the credit he deserved. He also knew Hearst would blame him for the film. That's how he justified taking out the copyright in his name. He was a brilliant rationalist, who could justify any fiction when it came to himself."

I drove along the Pacific Coast Highway, the worthless affidavit on the seat next to me. Now what? I was on the verge of causing my clients to lose the rights in the best movie ever made. It would not just be a blot on my resume; it would be the whole resume!

I stopped the car in a parking lot and walked down to the crowded beach. Two kids were fighting over a pail, screaming: "It's mine. No, it's mine." A woman grabbed the pail from them. She said, "If you boys can't share, then I'll keep the pail."

When I got back to Chicago, I called Classic's lawyer. I proposed that his client could continue to distribute the prints it had but that it must agree to make no others. Also, I said Movies would change its marketing practices if Classic withdrew its claim that the film's copyright was invalid. The court records of the case would be sealed. No one would ever know of the claims.

Classic's lawyer immediately agreed. Even Morris liked the deal. Classic's exploitation of a limited number of prints would not significantly reduce RKO or Movie's profits. And, as far as the world knew, RKO held a valid copyright.

⚖️

What's your question, Connie? What does this story have to do with justice? Hey, I just tell the tales. You're supposed to interpret them. It's the listener's job.

Look at the time. I wish you had gotten here sooner. So much to say, you know. Oh well, there's always tomorrow. Except, that's not true is it? Someday, one day, will be our last and tomorrow won't come for us.

I was nearly asleep when I heard scratching against the rear window. I crawled to the foot of the bed. A black cat was clawing the window. I opened it and the cat jumped in my lap, meowing plaintively.

I filled a small bowl with water and put it on the floor. The cat circled the bowl and then began drinking, finishing in no time. I refilled it and got back into bed. The slurping continued for a while and was followed by the mellow sound of purring.

I thought of an Irish fable I had read as a child. An old man, Hero, was so convinced of his own righteousness he believed he could trust everyone. Who would harm a righteous man? One day, the Devil's agent paid him a visit, and the egotistical Hero assumed he was one of God's angels. The agent instructed him to jump into a dark well, assuring him that because of his virtue no harm would come to him. Hero believed that this presented an excellent opportunity to prove he was the most righteous of men. Without a moment's deliberation, he leaped into the well, perishing in the fall. The townspeople concluded he had committed suicide, a sin in the eyes of God and man. He had wasted a life of righteousness with one foolish act of trust.

Was Fischel Schaechter the Devil's agent? Would he ask me to commit a foolish act of trust?

CHAPTER SEVEN

May 16, 1998

I N THE MORNING *I FOUND a nearby pet store where I bought supplies for my new roommate: cat food, bowls, box and litter, toy mouse and scratching post, and a ball that jingled as it rolled on the floor. I also bought a copy of the New York Times.*

The cat appreciated my efforts. After ravenously eating a bowl of food, it climbed on my lap to have its head scratched as I dialed the telephone number of the Philadelphia Inquirer.

The obituary editor said she had never heard of Samuel Brandt. When I suggested that it was her business to be aware of the death of a prominent citizen, she said she knew all of Philadelphia's luminaries and abruptly hung up the telephone.

Next, I obtained Fischel Schaechter's business number from Chicago directory assistance. (No residence phone number was listed.) I dialed the number and after several rings a recording came on the line: "You have reached the law offices of Fischel Schaechter; please leave your name and telephone number." I did neither.

I called the Park Lane and asked to be connected to Fischel Schaechter's room. The operator said she could find no record of a Schaechter. Perhaps he had checked out, I said; she replied that he was not on file as a guest at any time during the previous month.

I tore the chart off the wall and put it in my notebook. The cat jumped to the floor and grabbed the toy mouse by the neck, violently swinging it back and forth. Somewhere I had read that cats enjoyed torturing their prey. As between the cat and the mouse, I identified with the mouse.

It took a while but I found a store that sold out of town newspapers. I had already read The New York Times story about the shooting. There, the reporter speculated that the perpetrators were members of a rival gang and that Whitey Delaney might be dead. But the reporter freely conceded these were hunches without facts to support them.

I left the store with two Boston newspapers. The morning was warm and sunny and I decided to walk. For the first time since I fainted my head was clear. Perhaps I could finally enjoy a day in New York.

Though I had no destination in mind, I soon found myself on 59th Street, across from the southernmost entrance to Central Park. Like a sentimental thief who returns to the scene of his crimes, I continued walking until I came to the pond and the Hans Christian Anderson statue.

The beautiful day had brought out scores of parents and children. They were milling around the pond and in the plaza in front of the boat shed and food stand. The cul-de-sac, however, was unoccupied.

I sat on the Brandt bench and opened the Boston Herald. A front-page story said that authorities had not identified any suspects, but were planning to interview Gene Lufman, Salvatore Marinelli, and James Crosetti. It also provided further information about some of the people mentioned during the hearing.

Evidently, severe tensions existed between the two wings of the Marinelli family, originating fifty years before in Sicily. Despite the long-standing feud, Salvatore Marinelli forged a business alliance with his cousin Vincente. Gene Lufman was Gavencci's corporate attorney, though it was rumored that he had acted as a spy for Salvatore. The story also mentioned Peter Marinelli, currently incarcerated at Riker's Island jail and awaiting word on his appeal from convictions in two cases: bank fraud associated with the purchase of hotels and embezzlement of funds from the Jones Printing Company Pension Plan.

I opened my notebook and took out the chart. I knew more than I did before, but the additional information had enlarged the mystery of Schaechter's relationship with these people. And of my role, I knew nothing. In frustration, I ripped the chart into tiny pieces and threw them in the ashcan next to the bench.

Across the pond, a man and woman were leisurely strolling my way. There was no mistaking Fischel, and in a few seconds I recognized the woman as Erin Brandt. *The face of the other man, trailing a step or two behind, was blocked by Fischel's stocky frame.*

Suddenly, Fischel stopped and turned slightly to the side, at the same time pointing in my direction. I thought perhaps he had seen me, but he soon dropped his arm and resumed walking. He must have been showing the other man where they were headed and I was fortunate to be standing in shadow. In any case, they would soon be upon me.

I could have gone around the other side of the pond, but instead I climbed onto the ledge and hid behind the oak tree. My little foray into sur-reptitiousness reminded me of when I was a child, playing hide and seek with friends among the small houses in Divismore Park, a poor Catholic section of West Belfast. Back then, of course, the point was to be caught after a reason-able amount of time.

The trunk of the tree was quite wide; as long as I kept my arms close to my side, I was confident I would not be seen.

"A most pleasant spot." The man's voice was hoarse and thickly Italian, like Vito Corleone in *The Godfather*.

"Nice idea, don't you think," Fischel said.

"My father always loved children, but he had to be satisfied with me." Erin sounded wistful, which did not surprise me in view of her father's demise.

"Yes," the Italian said. "I enjoy a quiet place to talk. Nowadays, that is not so easy to find."

"I wish you had told me what you were planning," Fischel said.

"What makes you think it was my plan?"

"I just assumed that you wanted to get rid—"

"Do not be so quick to assume; it is not a good practice, causes one to often miss the truth."

"If not you, then who?"

"It could have been one of many. We cultivate enemies like corn. Every-where you look heads rear." His laugher came in short raspy bursts.

Though Fischel also laughed, Erin did not. "What about that man, Sul-livan?" she asked. "Is he in danger?"

At the mention of my name, I nearly gasped.

"He will be safe. Jimmy watches."

"What if he checks and sees that it's missing?" Fischel asked. What could be missing? I wondered.

"You will think of something," the Italian said. Another raspy laugh.

"I told you we shouldn't have done it so soon," Fischel said. Despite the Italian's relaxed manner, Fischel sounded quite agitated.

"Do you think they will find him?" the Italian said.

"His photograph," Fischel said. I did not understand what photograph they could be referring to.

"He cannot tell them what he does not know."

"He can tell them about me."

"I'm scared," Erin said.

"Do not fear my dear," the Italian said. "In a few days you will be together." I was hopelessly confused. Who was Erin joining?

I heard a clang followed by the rustling of papers.

"What are you doing?" Erin asked.

"Look at this," Fischel said. "Someone must have been pretty disgusted. Did you ever see a piece of paper torn in such tiny pieces?"

I put a hand to my mouth. How stupid I had been.

"Is it your practice to search garbage?" the Italian sounded as lighthearted as ever.

""I should take this home and use it as a jigsaw puzzle," Fischel said. I had become faint and slowly knelt to my haunches. It was becoming harder to breathe.

"But then I've never been very good at puzzles," he added.

"Now what are you looking at?" the Italian asked.

"I love old trees," Fischel said. "Their trunks are so thick. Even I, fat stomach and all, could hide behind it."

"Why would you want to hide behind a tree?" Erin said, laughing.

"Watch me," Fischel said.

I heard his footsteps. He was climbing onto the ledge. I wished I had brought a rosary.

"We have no time for foolishness," the Italian said.

The footsteps stopped. I allowed myself the slightest of breaths as he stepped off the ledge.

"*We should have another meeting,*" *Fischel said. Just like that the merriment was gone, replaced my oppressive solemnity.*

"*I agree,*" *the Italian said.* "*Tonight. I'll inform the others.*" *A few seconds of silence and then:* "*You worry too much, my friend. You must have faith.*"

"*It's hard to have confidence in the unknown.*"

"*Ah, I said faith, not confidence.*"

When I came out from behind the tree, Erin and Fischel were already a considerable distance away, near the top of the hill. The Italian had gone around the other side of the pond where he met a tall man, whom I instantly recognized as the limousine driver. And the Italian was none other than the old man at Brandt's funeral.

I hurried along the path. Upon reaching the crest of the hill, I saw Erin and Fischel walking south. I followed them, keeping a safe distance. We passed by a zoo where a crowd had gathered to watch a zookeeper serve a bucket of fish to three seals. When Erin and Fischel joined the onlookers, I hid behind a vendor selling balloons. He shoved several balloons in my face, telling me to get out of the way if I was not a serious customer.

In twenty minutes we reached the 59th Street exit. Erin and Fischel were proceeding west on the opposite sidewalk. They disappeared through the entrance of the Park Lane Hotel.

I crossed the street and looked through the revolving doors into the lobby. They were standing at the registration desk, talking with the clerk. Beyond them, the lobby narrowed to a bank of elevators, which at the other end opened to another seating area.

I walked around the block and entered the hotel from 58th Street. In the meantime, Erin and Fischel had left the front desk, though they could be elsewhere in the front lobby, a large section of which was concealed from view by the elevators. I was nearing the elevators when Erin emerged from the lobby. Fortunately, she was not looking in my direction, and I hastily retreated to an alcove of pay telephones. She pushed a button for the elevator and waited. Shortly, one arrived and she got on. I moved to a chair near the exit, from where I could see the elevators. I took the Boston Herald and held it in front of my face—a technique which, of course, I had only recently learned—and reread the article about the shooting. Periodically, I took a quick peek to see if my quarry reappeared.

When my arms got weary, I lowered the paper and turned sideways with a hand over my face. After a few minutes I returned to my original position. I repeated this process for an hour. This business of surveillance, I learned, was wearisome.

I was about to abandon my spying when Erin appeared, carrying a suitcase. She walked quickly through the front lobby and out onto the sidewalk. A black limousine pulled up to the curb. The driver was the man from the plaza and the park, and of course I was not surprised to see that Fischel was in the back seat. He leaned forward and opened the door. She kissed him on the cheek and climbed inside.

The house phone was on a small table by the front window. I dialed the operator as I watched the limousine drive away. I asked her to connect me to Erin Brandt's room, but she said no one by that name was registered. Slamming down the telephone, I cursed in too loud a voice, producing stares from a number of people, including a passing bellman.

"Is there a problem, sir?" he asked.

"I was expecting to meet a friend, but the operator says she is not registered."

"What is the name?"

"Erin Brandt."

"I'll check for you."

He walked over to the front desk and spoke to the registration clerk. She flipped through a box of file cards and pulled one out. He took the card and returned.

"What was the name again?" the bellman asked.

"Brandt," I said.

"We do have a Brandt on file."

"I knew I was right."

"You said you were looking for a woman."

"Yes."

"It says here, Samuel Brandt."

I was beginning to learn that this world was a place without sense or meaning, as mysterious and formless as before the eve of creation. "That is impossible," I said.

"I don't see why, sir. Our records are very exact. A Mr. Samuel Brandt checked out three days ago, on the thirteenth."

I thanked him and left the hotel. With my own eyes I had seen Erin Brandt take the elevator to what must have been her room, for she had returned with her suitcase. Moreover, I recalled that Fischel had said Samuel Brandt was in Dallas on business before returning to Boston to commit suicide on the thirteenth, while Erin and Molly waited for him in vain at Jimmy's Harborside.

Nausea returned and I hardly could stay on my feet. I stumbled through a door into a restaurant. The maitre' de said, "Welcome to the Oyster Bar" and asked me if I wanted a table. I pointed dumbly at a counter in the shape of a horseshoe and walked unsteadily to an empty stool without saying a word.

The room was noisy with patrons speaking different languages, one on top of the other, a chorus of gibberish sounding like mad citizens clamoring around the Tower of Babel. A man next to me was sipping broth from an enormous bowl. He saw me staring and said, "Turtle soup." I merely raised my hand and a like-sized bowl appeared before me. I took a sip and scalded my tongue.

As I slowly sipped the steamy soup, I reviewed each fact I had learned that day, hoping to find what I was missing. With the last spoonful, I had an idea.

The pay telephone was located by the bathrooms. It swallowed three of my coins before I realized it was broken. A man in an apron came out of the men's room and saw my frustration. He hit the coin box a few times with his fist, and my coins clunked into the change box. He took a coin and held it up to the light, then pressed it in the slot, giving it a twist with his thumb. "You can make your call, now," he said. Though I wanted to express my gratitude, all I could think of was how helpless I had become.

"Excuse me," I said to the hotel operator. "Do you have a Glynn registered?"

"We did. Checked out an hour ago."

So simple and so obvious, though prompting even more questions. Why would Erin Brandt register in the maiden name of her stepmother, Molly

Marie Brandt? From whom was she hiding? Why had Fischel lied about where he was staying? Why was it necessary for him to play these games with me? And, indeed, was it only a game?

For the remainder of the day I rested and played with Cuchulainn, the name I gave the cat in honor of the legendary Ulster folk-hero, renowned for his strength and courageous deeds in defeating enemy armies only to eventually fall to the enemy Queen Maeve through trickery.

As I readied to depart for Murphy's, I noticed the newspapers on my desk and remembered I had not read the Boston Globe article about the shooting. The front-page story, however, simply rehashed the report in the Herald. I tossed the newspaper on the bed, and the second section fell away. There in front of me was a photograph, taken within moments of the attack, showing me sprawled on the steps. To the right of the photograph was a headline: "FBI Looks For Witness Wounded in Shooting." (So this was the photograph Fischel and the others discussed in the park.) I picked up the section and read the accompanying story. Only one sentence interested me, a quote from prosecutor Peter Varick: "We hope the wounded witness will read this story and come forward. Make no mistake, however, we will find him."

I have a special surprise tonight. You look more scared than thrilled. Believe me, it's an excellent treat, a welcome change of pace, I promise you.

I told you, I'm staying at the Parker Meridian. You're kidding; I guess I misspoke. Why? Did you try to call me there? I hope it was nothing urgent. The notepad? What notepad? Oh, the one with the directions to good old Hans Christian. I've had that for years. I probably have three-dozen pads at home from hotels across the country. Hey, so I'm a petty thief. You should have seen my mother, Sarah. She took towels, ashtrays, bars of soap . . . our house was a museum of hotel logos.

I did not know whether to cry or laugh at the sly inventions he used to throw me off course.

Connie, I hate to say this, but you look like someone Satan has taken hold of. Your face is red, bent out of shape, contorted like ... well, forget it. Please. Calm yourself. If I said the Park Lane, I'm sorry. It's the Parker Meridian. My favorite hotel.

Lunch tomorrow? I'd love to have lunch with you, but my daytime schedule is a bit hectic. I have a brief due on the twenty-second. Tough case. Complicated. I might have alluded to it. The first criminal case I've handled in years, the first one since Leonard Stone. They threw the cliché-riddled book at my client, what we lawyers call the federal criminal code: embezzlement, money laundering, racketeering, conspiracy, mail fraud ... that's it, I think. It's enough, don't you agree?

No, Connie, I can't bring myself to talk about it. Sometime soon, perhaps. I'm not trying to keep it a secret; it's just that ... . Hey, I know. Secrets. The law of secrets. I'm not kidding. We have laws to cover everything, including secrets. I'll tell you this little ditty and then we will attend to your treat.

You would never know Barry Leavitt was a rising young entrepreneur from his appearance. At twenty-one he was the owner and operator of Chicago's hottest new pizza restaurant, but he looked and dressed like a pre-pubescent adolescent. His regular outfit consisted of torn jeans, cut off at the calves—before cutoffs were in—and a paint-stained University of Illinois sweatshirt.

He dropped out of college in the middle of his sophomore year, after a professor asked him why he was so intent on making academics his mortal enemy. He returned home and was spending his time organizing his record collection when his frantic parents turned to Uncle Lowell for help.

Lowell Sonnenschein was the family millionaire, owner of twenty-seven McDonald's franchises. He was a dedicated bachelor, taking on new girlfriends nearly as often as he acquired franchises. He was always on the lookout for new business opportunities. The day after he got the call from Barry's parents, he saw an ad for a new *ma and pa* stuffed pizza restaurant on the south side of Chicago. He and his new girlfriend went to check it out.

The restaurant was located in a lower middle class neighborhood, a melting pot of blacks, Irish, and Italians. It was hardly a culinary palace. The pizza came on a paper plate with one napkin smaller than a dollar bill. You got a knife and fork out of a plastic cup, but the knife was useless, breaking in half if you tried to slice the pizza with it.

When Lowell and his girlfriend arrived, they were stunned to see that the place was packed; they had to wait in line for a half-hour. What distinguished Marinelli's—no joke, that's the name... The owner is Danny Marinelli, Vincente Marinelli's son. I don't know how Danny landed in Chicago. Believe me, I don't. I swear it's another coincidence. For Christ's sake, Connie, let's not go off on a tangent. I'm trying to tell you about an interesting case.

What distinguished Marinelli's was its stuffed pizza: thick dough shaped to hold generous amounts of cheese, pepperoni, anchovies, bacon, or whatever ingredients you order.

Lowell and his girlfriend went gaga over the pizza. They sat outside on the curb and, as Sarah used to say, stuffed their face before going back for seconds. After they finished eating, Lowell left his girlfriend outside to fend off the neighborhood Casanovas, while he marched directly into the kitchen as if he owned the joint. He introduced himself to Danny and his wife and offered to buy them dinner at Arnie's, a swank Chicago restaurant in the nightclub district.

Danny and his wife had never been to downtown Chicago and eagerly accepted the invitation. They loved the ride in Lowell's white Mercedes and were riveted by Arnie's art deco interior, live band, and tuxedo-clad waiters.

During dinner, Lowell told Danny the story of how he got started in the business, how he revived an under-performing McDonald's in Kenosha, Wisconsin, which led to awards of other locations. As his girlfriend explained the art of high fashion to Danny's wife Rosalie—she unabashedly admitted she made her own clothes—he showered Danny with advice on how he could turn his small store into a million-dollar business. What they really needed, he said, was a sage to advise them, organize the books, design flyers, and show them how to increase their prices without driving away business. He would charge nothing for his services, he added. He just wanted a small favor: hire nephew Barry, who needed a career and was willing to work cheap. Danny was a trusting soul and accepted Lowell's offer. To celebrate their arrangement, Lowell ordered an expensive bottle of wine, which Danny insisted on paying for. Lowell graciously accepted the gesture, because he knew that a victim is happier when he participates in his own euchring.

Barry quit after three months. He had gotten what he needed out of the job: he had stolen what Uncle Lowell had sent him to steal. Uncle Lowell signed a lease for a store on the north side, which would accommodate ten times the number of customers as Marinelli's south side hole in the wall. They named it Baretti's and it specialized in—you guessed it—stuffed pizza.

Danny thought he'd been conned. He donned a fake mustache and beard and stopped in Baretti's a few days after it opened. One taste of the combination pizza gave him fits; the sauce tasted the same as his. And his was not just any tomato sauce. Great-Grandma Francesca had given it to her daughter, Grandma Isabella, who passed it on to Angelina (Vincente's wife), who handed it down to Danny. Grandma Isabella had stood in the town square and watched her husband, Vittorio, get stabbed to death by . . . and I'm sorry, I have to whisper . . . Salvatore when he was only twelve and Vincente was eleven. The way Salvatore tells the story—if you can get him to talk about it—Vincente's father encouraged a bunch of young toughs who were up and coming Mafiosi to murder Salvatore's father and his family in retribution for unspecified offenses during the long-running Mafia war. During the attack, Salvatore hid under the floor in the kitchen. He was the only survivor. After he took his revenge on the killers, he went after the uncle, on Easter Sunday no less. The truth, I swear it. So Isabella raised Vincente without a father . . . anyway, Danny came from a violent heritage.

Here again he had taken a slice of the past and wedged it into the cracks of the present.

It was obvious to Danny that Barry had stolen the recipe. As Danny reflected on the first time he met Uncle Lowell and the wining and dining at Arnie's, he got so angry he scalded his hand on the metal grill of his new oven. Rosalie's caresses and loving care could take away the pain in his hand but not in his head. His head was scalding with a different kind of heat—the heat of rage.

I was six months out of the Litowitz firm and in partnership with Gordon Lazarus—I'll tell you about that later—when Barry and Uncle Lowell came to see me. Lowell had gotten my name from his brother-in-law Morris Cohen, who thought representing a relative was nepotism. Morris's judgment hadn't improved since the *Citizen Kane* case.

As you might suspect from my brief history of the Marinelli family, Barry and Lowell were fortunate to have to defend only their wallets. Danny had telephoned Vincente to ask for the name of an experienced arsonist who would torch Baretti's, preferably when both Barry and Lowell would be in the building. Vincente said Danny should call a hit man and gave him Harry Levine's telephone number—the strike force never did prosecute Harry for anything serious. When Danny called, Harry refused the assignment, saying it was against his principles to kill a fellow Jew. Instead, he told Danny to contact his lawyer, the same one who helped him escape with the dollar fine in the mortgage loan application case.

The lawyer filed a lawsuit for Danny. He claimed that great-grandma's recipe was a trade secret and therefore entitled to legal protection. If the judge decided in favor of Danny, he could order Barry to stop using the tomato sauce. He also could order Barry to close the restaurant.

Barry and Lowell were not about to admit they were thieves. They brought me several cookbooks containing dozens of recipes for tomato sauce, which showed how each of them used essentially the same ingredients with modest variations in the proportions. "Sure, I learned how Danny made the tomato sauce," Barry said. "But if you add a little basil here and subtract a little oregano there, you get a different result." No wonder he dropped out of college. He didn't understand that the law dislikes a thief, even if what he steals has no value.

That night my wife and I went to dinner at Gordon's house, a sprawling five-bedroom ranch in a nouveau riche suburb of Chicago. My wife and Gordon's wife, Jackie, hated each other. Jackie, a pencil-thin blonde who spent her time filing her nails and yelling at their two daughters to clean their rooms, had antagonized my wife by committing the three most serious crimes possible when businessmen's wives meet. She talked about how wonderful Gordon was, an implicit criticism of me; she said how wonderful *she* was, an implicit criticism of my wife; she insisted their country club was better than ours. We didn't belong to a country club, but the comment still angered my wife.

I hadn't had the pleasure of meeting their daughters. On our previous visit, they were at a pajama party whose chaperones were soon thereafter exposed as the organizers of a wife-swapping club. They were identical twins who not only looked alike; they also talked and dressed alike. In personality, however, they were different species. One was a bitch like mother Jackie; the other a sweetheart like . . . well, not like father Gordon, who was whatever you call the male version of a bitch, asshole I guess. It was as if at birth they had been assigned personalities from the extremes of behavior so you could tell them apart when they got older.

Their surface sameness concealing vast differences inspired me to consider whether the tomato sauces might be different, even if the physical elements were the same. The twins had obviously responded to their shared genes and childhood experiences differently; perhaps the twin sauces had their own reactions to the ovens, the temperature, and the length of the cooking process. And then there was perception. I might think the evil twin was a bitch, but someone else might think she was a sweetheart. The world is full of things that are the same, but are viewed as different: bottled water, aspirin, high-end stereo receivers, and cheap vodka, to name a few.

On Saturday, I ordered a pizza from each of Chicago's five best-known stuffed pizza restaurants. I made up bottles for the sauces, including ones for Marinelli's and Baretti's. I labeled them "A" through "G" and asked my wife to taste each sauce. She was no help, saying they all tasted equally lousy. I mixed her an Apricot Sour—just the way she liked it—and repeated the test. She still couldn't tell one from the other. I took the test and concluded—no surprise—that each one had its own special taste. My objectivity, however, was open to question, since I knew which bottles contained what sauces.

I looked through the cookbooks Barry and Lowell had given me. One was written by a Professor Nagel from the University of Cincinnati—what's the matter? Why did you cut me off? Why do you have to think? This isn't nuclear physics. OK, OK. I'll spell it for you.

C-i-n-c-i-n . . . I recited those letters until they were like a canticle. Those letters held special meaning for me, but what was it? "Of course," I said out loud.

Of course what? Yes. I'm listening. Oh, Connie, you have lost it. Did his car have Ohio plates? Who is he? I haven't a clue. I told you Sam was good at making friends. Maybe he was a friend of Molly. If it's so important to you, I'll find out. Do you want me to call right now? Good decision, Connie. I don't relish troubling Molly with something so trivial. What else could "cin" stand for? You say it was part of a sticker on the windshield? Let me see . . . I know. Sam used to talk about an old clerk who worked at his firm in Philadelphia. He said he was the most dedicated employee he ever had. When the clerk's wife died he moved to New York to live with his sister. I had no idea that Sam kept in touch with him

What has that got to do with "cin"? See, Connie, there is an answer to every question. Sam was active in the Practi-cin-g Law Institute. It sponsors law seminars, continuing legal education for lawyers, and the like. I attended one of their conferences at Penn law school. You get a parking sticker for the windshield. The clerk probably drove Sam to the conference and scratched it off when he moved to New York. No, Connie, I don't know for sure. And neither do you. So let's drop it.

Speaking of old black men, I have an interesting story to tell you, but I'll save it for later. May we please return to the law of trade secrets?

If you will believe that, Cornelius Michael Sullivan, you will believe anything, I said to myself. But what was the alternative? If the old black man was from Cincinnati, what could that mean? Samuel Brandt was from Philadelphia.

Connie, wake up. Are you with me; are you ready to rejoin my world?

I called the professor and he agreed to see me the next day. He said it was about time the real world found a use for him. I should have taken his comment as a warning, but I smelled victory. Or did I smell the sauce?

I stunk up the Delta 727. It seemed that the sauce's principal ingredient was garlic. The passengers must have thought I had a terminal case of halitosis. Several passengers stared longingly at the oxygen mask compartments. The old lady sitting next to me didn't mind, however. Her mouth was wide open and she was taking deep breaths; I doubt she had breathed through her nose in a decade.

Did you ever wonder what kind of person teaches cooking? This professor looked like a terrorist. Whoops. Have I struck a nerve? You don't believe that terrorists look a certain way. Are you a terrorist? If you are, then I have to agree with you. Do I look like a terrorist? I'm glad to hear I don't, though I couldn't complain if I did, considering how I used the law to terrorize. How does Webster define terrorism? "The use of force or threats to demoralize, intimidate, and subjugate, especially such use as a political weapon or policy." Sounds like a good definition of the law.

I'll amend my description of the professor. He looked like a specific type of terrorist—say the Unabomber—reclusive, with a pale face, scraggly beard, blotchy neck, and bony arms. He was so gaunt I thought he might be on a starvation diet; maybe he didn't enjoy eating.

After I showed Professor Nagel the bottles and told him my idea, he said he needed five minutes of meditation. He wanted to expunge all taste from his mind and body. He said he had eaten a student's final exam before I arrived. I started to retch, but recovered when he said the exam was a Western omelet.

He went into the bathroom and closed the door. I could hear him chanting in a foreign language. He sounded like a Gregorian monk in a medieval monastery. I arranged the bottles on the table and waited.

When he reappeared he was holding a gallon-sized pitcher of water, which he drank in large gulps, paying no attention to the water dribbling down his neck. He rubbed his tongue over his lips and inside his mouth and said he was satisfied that his palate was clean.

He sat on the floor cross-legged and opened each jar. He put his nose a few inches from the top and smelled of the sauce with deep breaths, like a mountain climber starved for oxygen. He repeated the routine three times. Then he stuck his nose in each bottle and inhaled the sauce like it was a line of cocaine, pausing to explain how his technique would allow the sauce to more efficiently reach the most sensitive taste buds at the rear of his tongue.

He tasted the sauces from different spoons and in varying order. Had I brought with me an infinite supply of sauce, the test would have lasted forever. When the bottles were empty, I looked at him expectantly. His cheeks had swelled to twice their normal size and had changed from bleached white to ruddy, the same color as the sauce. His stomach was straining against his shirt, and his chest had shrunk to a thin strip between his armpits. If you placed an apple on top of an upside down soup bowl, you would have the general idea how he looked.

He said he needed an hour to digest the evidence—literally or figuratively, I wasn't sure. I said I would come back later. I stopped at a pizza shop downtown, from where I had an excellent view of the Ohio River and the hills of northern Kentucky. I was wicked hungry; I ordered the deluxe combination pizza, ziti, two orders of garlic bread, minestrone soup, the special salad—the dressing was included for no extra charge—and, for dessert, an extra-large vanilla ice cream cone.

What are you writing, Connie? You don't want to tell me? Have it your way.

I wrote a single world on a bar napkin: "wicked." For the most part, Fischel had used little slang. I wanted a reminder to investigate whether the word was specific to a particular region. I had come to doubt everything he said, including where he lived.

Nagel greeted me with a report in one hand and a bill for his services in the other. The report was one sentence: "All seven sauces are identical in taste, texture, and aroma."

"How can that be?" I asked.

"Oh, I admit the ingredients might be mixed in different ways or in different proportions. But tomato sauce is tomato sauce."

I looked at the bill. "Twenty-five hundred seems a trifle high."

"You should be happy I didn't charge you for the Maalox," he said and belched.

I moved away, trying to avoid the waves of garlic. "I'll send you a check," I said.

"Don't you want your bottles back?"

"You keep them."

I had gone in search of a defense and left empty-handed. But wait, I said to myself as I boarded the plane, if the sauces tasted the same . . .

"What do you mean I should stop using my sauce?" Barry and Lowell were standing with me at the door to my office. Court would begin in a half-hour.

"We don't have time to debate. We will not object to the entry of a permanent injunction."

"But I'll have to close my store." Barry squeezed a blackhead on his chin until the puss stained his fingertips yellow.

"You were going to hire a cooking expert," Lowell said.

"I did. He thought your sauce tasted the same as Marinelli's."

"Oh," Barry said, dejected. "Then we'll lose the case."

"The settlement is the same as victory," I said.

"I'm confused," Barry said.

"I get it," Lowell said. He smiled mischievously like a little boy who has figured out how to get away with stealing his playmate's blocks.

"I'm glad somebody understands me," I said.

"I sure don't," Barry said.

Lowell turned to Barry. "It's like this, my poor *schlep* of a nephew. Our attorney, being such an ethical person, prefers not to say what we should know without him having to say it."

I put them in the conference room and stopped in to see my partner Gordon. He didn't like what I said. He wanted me to go ahead with the hearing. Since Lowell had agreed to pay us by the hour, we would have made more money if the case continued. If we lost, we could charge extra for the appeal. I said I didn't like making money by losing cases. Gordon accused me of being "unlawyer like."

I fetched Barry and Lowell from the conference room. Barry was happy now. "I can't thank you enough," he said. "You're so intelligent."

Behind me, I heard Gordon muttering. "Real smart."

After the judge entered the injunction, Danny put on his disguise and went to Baretti's. He took one bite of the pizza and smiled. No doubt about it, he thought, Barry had changed the sauce.

Barry and Lowell were also happy. The critics unanimously agreed: Baretti's sauce was tastier and tangier than Marinelli's. Within a year, Barry and Lowell would open another five stores, one of which was two blocks away from Marinelli's. That store drew the half of Marinelli's customers that preferred not to dine on the curb.

Danny was content. He had no interest in making a lot of money, no desire to return to Arnie's or anywhere else downtown. He would not follow Barry's lead by leasing a truck for home deliveries, and he rejected Rosalie's advice to expand his menu. No submarine sandwiches, onion rings, fried clams, fried zucchini, fried calamari, or soft ice cream would be served in his store. Pizza was meal enough for the true connoisseur. Great-grandma's recipe had satisfied generations before him and would survive Baretti's or any other pretender. Danny had his injunction, which, to his thinking, was all the justice he needed.

I met Danny once. The case had been over for a year. I was returning from a White Sox game when a detour took me by his restaurant. He was shorter and thinner than I expected. I don't know why, but I think of Italian men as big—fleshy and swarthy. He was nice enough, giving me a tour of his small establishment and proudly showing me his new oven. On the wall above the counter was a picture of his mother, Angelina. She was walking with a goat at the foot of Mount Aetna. It reminded me of a story about a monster that lives inside the volcano, asleep until awakened by injustice.

He treated me to a pizza, which he personally prepared. I was the only one in the restaurant. He asked me what I thought of the sauce. I said the critics didn't know what they were talking about. Great-Grandma Francesca 's secret was a secret for the ages. I didn't have the heart to tell him the truth. What difference would it have made? "All the knowledge I possess everyone else can acquire, but my heart is all my own."

Heart. The word stung, and I took a long drink of Guinness. Did he have some special knack for tormenting me?

He excused himself to use the bathroom, saying I should be prepared to leave upon his return. Evidently, I was to receive my treat at another location, though I was beginning to wonder whether he ascribed the usual meaning to the word.

As I was waiting, I overheard two gentlemen talking at the bar. One man spoke with the same accent as taxi driver Crone in Boston. He said to his drinking partner, "Man, it was wicked funny."

And there was the bar napkin in front of me, on which I had written "wicked."

I looked up from the napkin and saw a man at the front entrance. It was the limousine driver.

Do you need to use the facilities before we go? Oh, I see you noticed my buddy, Jimmy. He's going to drive us.

Should I say that I recognized him from the park? Should I ask why he had warned me? No, I would not. Instead, I followed them out the door where Fischel introduced me to Jimmy.

Jimmy. During the conversation at the Hans Christian Anderson statue the Italian referred to a Jimmy.

My friend and I got in the back seat of the limousine while Jimmy settled behind the wheel and started the car. "Are you comfortable, gentlemen?" Jimmy said with mock English formality.

"Drive on Mr. Crosetti," Fischel said. In the dark, he could not see that my mouth was open and my eyebrows twitching. James Crosetti, witness for the government in the Boston case against the Savin Hill gang, employee of Salvatore Marinelli.

We rode in silence for several minutes.

"Would you like to know where we're going?" Fischel said.

"I like surprises," I said, making sure my voice was thick with irony.

"You're the surprise."

"How am I the surprise?"

"Half the time you act like you're afraid of your own shadow, and the other half you go with the flow."

"Go with the flow?"

"Move with instead of against the current."

"Like Fitzgerald."

"But that boat was moving against the current."

We lapsed into silence again, like two old friends who are so comfortable together they speak only when necessary.

"May I ask you a question?" I asked.

"You can always ask," he said.

"Earlier, when you were telling me about the pizza case, you used the word, wicked."

"Did I? Damn!"

"It bothers you?"

"I hate Boston slang. It's distressing that it may have rubbed off on me."

"You've never lived in Boston?"

"No, Connie. Once a Chicagoan, always a Chicagoan."

"I see."

He reached behind the seat and pushed a square piece of glass, which burst into light. He looked at me closely, like a doctor examining a patient for telltale moles.

"My wife is from Boston," he said.

"Oh."

"I thought I told you."

"No."

"Are you sure? The former flight attendant. She quit to help in my firm."

"You did not say where she was from."

"Then I probably didn't mention that Molly Brandt introduced us."

"You did not."

"At Jimmy's Harborside."

"My oh my," I said, making no effort to hide the sarcasm.

"Connie, you're being peevish. I have been sharing my innermost thoughts with you."

"Then why do I not feel more appreciative?"

"Your head wound?"

"You are not funny. I could have been killed."

We were driving through narrow side streets. I was growing increasingly anxious. "Where are we?" I asked.

"We're almost there."

"One more question," I said.

"Only one?"

"You said Brandt was to arrive in Boston to meet Erin and Molly at Jimmy's Harborside."

"Right."

"You said he was coming from Dallas."

"Right again."

"Might you have been mistaken?"

He switched off the light. "I only know what Molly said."

"What if I were to tell you Brandt checked out of the Park Lane Hotel on the thirteenth? That he did not go to Dallas but was here in New York."

"I would say either Molly misunderstood or Sam went to New York instead of Dallas without telling her. And I'd ask you where you got your information."

"Why would he lie about his destination?"

"I don't know the answer to that question any more than I know why he committed suicide."

The car stopped. We were on a quiet tree-lined street. Old-fashioned street lamps were evenly spaced on both sides.

"Maple trees," I said.

"This is my favorite street in New York."

"What is the name of it?"

"Maple Street, of course."

"What are we doing here?"

"Your treat, Connie. We're dining at Marinelli's."

I did not know what I expected, but Marinelli's was a welcome change of pace from the dark and dreary Murphy's. The large room was light and airy with perhaps two-dozen tables and booths. Photographs covered every inch of the walls, each featuring Salvatore Marinelli with one or more guests, many of whom were celebrities. But there was something more interesting about the photographs. Salvatore Marinelli was the Italian I had seen in Central Park.

"I see you are admiring my mementos," Salvatore said.

I was standing at the front of the restaurant looking at a glass case in which a pistol and knife were mounted. The gun was an old-style pistol and the knife an ordinary carving type with a serrated blade.

"What do they signify?" I asked.

"As in the prayers of Mass, one for the living and one for the dead."

"I do not understand."

"They are a reminder of what happened long ago in the country of my birth."

"Sicily," Fischel said.

"Weapons frighten me," I said.

"Then we will speak no more of them. You are here for the luxury of food and drink. My establishment provides a respite from the world of cares."

Salvatore led us to a large round table, set in a small alcove. A booth with soft, velutinous cushions was fastened to the wall, and on the shelf above it sat an antique pewter vase filled with white roses. We had a view of the entire room: to the picture window looking out onto the street, and in the opposite direction to the kitchen and a small door with a metal sign that read, "Office."

I sat in the booth and Fischel sat across from me with his back to the room. Salvatore lifted his hand and a waiter instantly appeared. Salvatore left to stroll around the restaurant, stopping at each table to have a few words with the diners.

"Would you care for a drink, sir?" the waiter asked.

I was undecided. This fine restaurant was worthy of more than a Guinness.

"A glass of wine, please," I said.

"Good idea," Fischel said. "Red or white?"

"You decide, please." I was more nervous than when I had hidden behind the oak tree.

He slowly turned the pages, naming one wine after the other.

"It is all the same to me," I said. "I do not know one wine from another."

"You shouldn't be so critical of yourself. For most of my life I thought the only wine was Manischewitz."

"Is that an expensive brand?"

He laughed. "Never mind."

"I do not come from a well-to-do family."

"It's cheap wine, Connie. Anyway, money doesn't make one sophisticated."

"Only more comfortable."

He turned more pages and then said a number.

"St. Julien, 1982," the waiter said. "Excellent." He took the wine list and left.

"Has he tasted all the wines?" I asked.

"Oh, my dear Connie."

"I obviously do not know fine wines or the restaurants that serve them."

He laughed heartily. "Irish wit rears its sardonic head."

"I was being perfectly serious."

"Were you now?"

"Now you sound like me."

"Impossible. We're so different. Tell me about your family."

I was more than a little surprised at the question. He had spent all of our time together talking about himself. "I would prefer not to at the moment," I said.

"Why?"

The waiter returned with the wine. "Should we let it breathe?" he asked.

"No," Fischel said. "Mr. Sullivan could use a drink now."

The waiter poured a few drops in my glass, and I tasted it. It was mellow and smooth.

"Raise the glass if you're satisfied," Fischel said.

I did so and the waiter filled our glasses, Fischel's first.

"May I propose a toast?" he said.

"Please do."

"I am he, as you are me, and we are all together."

He clicked my glass and we drank. "Interesting," I said.

"The wine or the toast?"

"The toast."

"The Beatles."

"Pardon me?"

"It's from a Beatles song."

*I put down my glass. I did not intend to be distracted. "Why am I here?"
I asked.*

"Here we go again. I told you. For a treat."

"What is it you want from me?"

*"We've been through that. I want you to spend time with me. A few more
days."*

"Why?"

"Did you ever hear the phrase, 'Take the law into your own hands?'"

"Yes."

"Sometimes you have to act outside the legal process."

"Vigilantism."

"Exactly."

"So you and your cohorts are vigilantes."

"In a way."

"What way?"

"I made a decision."

"What decision?"

*"So far, I've told you about four cases. Four cases out of hundreds during
twenty-seven years as a lawyer. Look at what you've learned. If the law isn't
used to persecute, it's beside the point. And the criminal law is so wedded to
punishment . . . . Oh well, we're here to have a good time."*

"You have not told me your decision."

"I decided to take justice into my own hands."

The waiter returned with a plate of salami and assorted cheeses.

Fischel pushed the plate in front of me. "Help yourself," he said.

"Is this your way of telling me you have violated the law?"

"I haven't violated any laws."

*"Then you're planning to violate the law. And you have enlisted me in
your enterprise in a manner you refuse to disclose."*

*"Think what you're saying, Connie. Since coming to New York, have you
broken the law? Have I asked you to break the law?"*

I took a slice of cheese.

*"I haven't, have I," he said. "It's not a crime to talk to me. It's not even a
crime to follow me around."*

"I have not been following you!"

"Oh come on, Connie. Don't lie. You're not a lawyer, for Pete's sake."

"Why did your driver or Mr. Marinelli's driver or whoever he works for . . . ?" I was sputtering, my words coming in fits and starts. "Why did he tell me to be careful what I learn?"

"He was trying to protect you."

"From what?"

"If you knew from what, you wouldn't be protected."

I had difficulty keeping my voice low. "You are speaking in circles. Once again, you have cleverly shifted the conversation to me, when it is you who are refusing to answer my question."

"I am so sorry, Connie. What was the question?"

"Are you intending to violate the law?"

"No, I am not intending to violate the law."

"I do not believe you."

"If you weren't going to believe the answer you shouldn't have asked the question."

"What I should do is leave."

"Do as you please."

"You have not been honest with me. You have not been honest since the first night we met."

"I have done my best to be honest about what matters." He looked genuinely sad.

"To you, perhaps. Not to me."

"You owe it to yourself to stay."

"I do not. And who are you to tell me—"

"Then you owe it to your father."

"What are you saying? I owe my father nothing! And what do you know of my father?"

"It's not important what I know, except that I know you haven't spoken to him in years."

"How do you know—?"

"It's written across your face."

"I do not have to accept this."

"It's true, isn't it?"

"Do not speak—"

"Why haven't you spoken to your father?"

"It is none of your affair."

He shrugged and ate a piece of salami. *"Are you staying or leaving?"* he asked calmly.

I would not let him get the better of me. *"I am staying. For now."*

"Good, let's order," he said, as if we had just finished a pointless lovers' spat. *"The fish is excellent, but if you're in the mood for pasta, Salvatore prepares a special sauce that's known throughout the city. He probably stole the recipe from his grandmother, the same grandmother . . . wow, wouldn't that be funny . . . I wonder if the tomato sauce here—"*

"My father betrayed his partner," I blurted out.

"I'm listening."

"I was seventeen. I was working at his auto repair shop. It was a bad time. You could not walk down the street and be certain you would reach your destination alive. Everywhere buildings had been blackened from fire or torn apart by explosions. One day, the police came to the shop and arrested my father. They said he had rigged a car with a bomb. The driver, a young boy whose family we knew, several innocent bystanders . . . so tragic. I thought they had arrested the wrong man. After they took my father away, another group of policemen came to search. I stood outside and waited. They came out with a leather bag. They asked me if I had seen it before. I had not."

"What was in it?"

"I assumed it contained paraphernalia for making a bomb. I thought they planted the evidence."

"Why?"

"They were determined to charge my father with whatever they could contrive. He was a member of the Provisionals, an aggressively violent wing of the IRA. And he had a history. A year or so earlier, a hotel in Comber was firebombed and a dozen people were killed. Later, he was overheard at a tavern talking about the vandalized telephone boxes, which prevented the IRA's warning from going through so that the hotel could be cleared. The police took him in for questioning, but let him go home after a couple of hours. From then on, I thought they were waiting to charge him with anything they could think up. Sure enough, they did."

"Go on."

"They let him go after a few weeks."

"Why?"

"He said they arrested the real perpetrator."

"But if they were anxious to pin something on your father—and it sounds like they were—why let him go?"

"We did not think about it. We were happy to have him home."

"You were close to your father."

"Yes, but only because my two brothers were closer to my mother. They never felt a need to communicate with my father, which is typical in an Irish family. And my three sisters were equally unquestioning."

"You questioned?"

"No, not questioned. I learned the truth."

"What truth?"

"Five years ago. I was in the midst of my university studies. I thought I had left the past behind me. Our family gatherings were once a week, on Sundays at my parents' house. My father was not well. The emphysema was beginning to take its toll. One of my brothers quit bartending to help him at the shop and . . . "

"What is it, Connie?"

I took the bottle of wine and filled my glass. My hands were shaking. He helped me raise the glass.

"Tell me," he urged.

"He left the dinner table to go to the bathroom. When he did not return, Mum asked me to check on him. I found him on the bathroom floor, doubled over and gasping for breath. I tried to help him, but he pushed me away. He got to his feet and leaned against the basin. He said he had something to say."

"What about?"

"The car bombing. He said he had rigged the car with the bomb."

"What did you say?"

"I asked him why the police set him free."

"And?"

"He said he gave them the name of his partner."

"Who?"

"He refused to say. He said it was unimportant. He said I would not know him. He said the name would mean nothing to me. Just as you said of your name."

"You believed him?"

"What did it matter? I was angry, angrier than I could have conceived possible. It was the kind of anger that threatens to consume you, that robs you of breath, and freezes your thoughts. He had no right to burden me with his sins. I was not his priest."

"No, just his son."

"A son is entitled to live. I was interested in the future, not the past."

"Did he tell your brothers and sisters? Your mother?"

"He said he told only me."

"Why you?"

"I do not know, unless . . . "

"Unless what?"

I had been ready to say something but, unaccountably, the thought disappeared.

"Did you tell anyone?"

"My wife."

"What did she say?"

"She said I should do as I saw fit."

"What's happening with his health?"

"He cannot leave his bed. He is in constant need of oxygen."

"Let me get this straight, Connie. You stopped speaking to your father because he ratted on his partner."

"Yes."

"You're as bad as the law when it comes to excessive punishment."

"He was a coward. And he was responsible for the deaths of innocent citizens and that poor boy that drove the car. He was only fifteen years old. Da should have been the one who died, not the boy."

"Oh, so now you are his executioner; you kill him with your silence."

"His years of smoking are killing him, not I."

"Aren't you forgetting something?"

"What do you mean?"

"Who your father turned in."

I did not understand what point he was trying to make. "I told you. He said I would not know him."

"Oh, yes," he said. "You did tell me."

Throughout dinner I could not stop thinking about what he had said. Then, as the waiter was clearing our table, I remembered something too horrible to contemplate, because it had been there for me to know from the day after my father was released.

"Tommy Glynn," I shouted.

"Shh, Connie, keep your voice down."

"Yes, that's it. Tommy was Da's partner. Da betrayed him. The day after Da was released they arrested Tommy. The newspaper said an informant had given the police the evidence they needed. Oh, my God, the informant was Da."

Quite a shock, I'm sure. Your father betrayed Tommy Glynn. I wish I could say I know how you feel. But you're kidding yourself, Connie, if you think you abandoned your father for what he did. You abandoned your father because of who you are. The trouble is you don't know who you are.

You look insulted. I can understand that. Who wants to be on the receiving end of a sermon? It's tough to discover you've betrayed yourself, that you've lived a life paying no attention to what goes on. Listen to my life, calm and uncluttered but just as deceiving as yours. We each learn who we are in different ways; yet, somehow our journeys are so similar.

Don't get me wrong. I've tried not to take life too seriously. Life is a comedy, not a tragedy. We'll order after dinner drinks. In honor of the occasion, I'll forego the Amaretto. We'll sample the brandy and enjoy a couple of cigars. This time of night, Salvatore allows smoking. I know it's against the law. It's the same old story. Yesterday, today, and tomorrow. Yesterday, you could smoke wherever you want; today there's hardly anywhere you can smoke; tomorrow, we'll be allowed to smoke again. It's like wide ties and pleated pants. They always come back, only to disappear again, or vice versa. Anyway, who's going to issue a citation to the Godfather of New York?

Picture the sight. In my despair, I could not resist holding a goblet of brandy in one hand and a Cuban cigar in the other.

I was born on May 10, 1944 at the Jewish Hospital in Cincinnati, Ohio, fifty-four years before the day we met. Sarah, Albert, and four-year-old brother Jonathan took me home to a two-flat brick building on Prospect Place, in the middle of Cincinnati's Jewish neighborhood, one block from a Hebrew school and two blocks from the Orthodox *shul* where Jonathan and I would celebrate our Bar Mitzvahs. Our apartment was on the second floor, remodeled when Sarah was pregnant with me: hardwood replaced the plank floor and shag carpeting; the walls got a new coat of glossy white paint; an Amana double-door refrigerator and freezer with room for three ice cube trays and speckled Formica counters brightened the new kitchen. The living room was big enough to fit a sofa, two chairs, and an old chest of drawers with a radio on top. A door led to a foyer and two small bedrooms of equal size with a connecting bathroom. There was a tub, no shower, and a sink with separate faucets for hot and cold water, which automatically shut off after a few seconds.

After I started sleeping through the night, my crib was moved into Jonathan's bedroom. His bed was next to a window that opened to an alley. When I outgrew the crib, the landlord, reeking from coal, brought up a trundle bed with drawers under the box spring where we could keep our toys. I cried for a day after Jonathan told me there would only be room for his toys; I'd have to be satisfied with putting mine on the floor under my bed. When Jonathan went to Harvard, I found the drawers in the basement of our house. I took them to my room and put comic books in them.

You already know what Albert looks like from the photograph I showed you. You could ask why I don't carry a picture of Sarah, and I could answer that I don't have one that would fit in my wallet. My mental picture of her, however, is more real than a two-dimensional representation could ever be. I hesitate even to describe her. Would it tell you the way she smelled when she held me to her chest? Would a description of her hands convey what it was like to watch them fluff my pillow and tuck me under the covers? How do you photograph the comfort of a mother's kiss? Would it show her infectious laugh? Make no mistake, she was a beauty: lustrous brunette hair, bright hazel eyes, small nose, and full lips. Short and compact, a couple of inches shy of five feet. I towered over her before I was eleven. She was somewhat of a coquette, flirting with every one, including her enemies: the salespeople she accused of giving her a raw deal, foolish neighbors she despised for watching soap operas all day, and the few who deigned to criticize her husband and two sons. Her exuberance, endless energy, and devilish smile disarmed friend and foe alike. She was a dynamo that couldn't be shut off.

Albert wasn't much of a talker. When he did speak, it was always about something intellectual. It fell upon Sarah to recount their history, but she told me little. The past was not as important to her as the present and future. She was born in a small town in Poland, whose name she couldn't remember and which she claimed no longer existed. Sometime before she was ten, her family—parents, younger sister, and older brother—moved to Vienna, where her father opened a bakery. She dated Albert for six years. Shortly before Hitler swept Austria into his Third Reich, they left for the United States and settled in Hamilton, Ohio. He was a salesman for a tool manufacturer and traveled around Indiana and Kentucky selling his company's wares, always fastidiously dressed, and charming.

Albert was unhappy with the life of a traveling salesman. He took a position in Cincinnati with a wallpaper and paint company and managed one of its stores for twice what he had been making. He brought Sarah and little Jonathan to Cincinnati and they rented the apartment on Prospect. Sarah got pregnant. A nice simple beginning.

Before my beginning was their past, less detailed than a dream because I knew so little. I knew nothing of what their lives were like in Vienna, what happened to their friends when the Nazis turned their world upside down. If they ever looked backwards, they did so privately. And I never asked. Near the end of his life, Albert spent time with a graduate student who was writing a book about life in Vienna in the years before World War II. She met with him once a week for three months and tape-recorded their conversations. I've got the tapes now. I've never listened to them. They're in the bottom drawer of my desk. One of the ironies that divides generations. Sarah and Albert never wanted to speak of the past, and I never wanted to know about it.

Albert worked long hours at the store and rarely got home before I went to bed. On Sunday, his one day off, he would sit at the small table in the kitchen reading books in German. When he took a break, it was to play catch with Jonathan on the sidewalk, while I watched from a high chair on the porch.

My favorite activity was accompanying Sarah to the supermarket. I loved to ride on top of the grocery cart. I could see the shelves where the goodies were stocked: candy, chocolate chip cookies, Jell-O, and Devil's Food bars. A different kind of excursion, however, is coded in my brain. To this day, my heart races at the memory of it.

I don't remember exactly how old I was, but my walking had improved and I no longer needed a stroller. I thought we were headed for the supermarket. At the corner Sarah told me to wait while she went to the Laundromat. She leaned over and kissed my cheek, admonishing me to stand perfectly still until she returned.

The light turned green and she was gone. I couldn't believe she had abandoned me. I couldn't summon the strength to scream, just stood there, more terrorized than before or since. Smiling people walked by, amused at my plight, a few bending down to ask my name, one jostling my hair as if I were a friendly dog. I followed Sarah's instructions and stood like a statue, not blinking, not swatting away a fly that landed on my nose, not rubbing my eyes when they got wet. My insides, though, were moving in every direction: lungs wheezing, stomach growling, leg muscles contracting. The tears came, first a trickle, then a stream.

She returned in a few minutes. She wiped the tears from my face and kissed me. "I did not leave you," she said in her thick Austrian accent. "I am always with you."

When I was four, we moved into a new house in a recently constructed subdivision of St Bernard, a tiny municipality surrounded by Cincinnati. St. Bernard was an old company town. Ninety percent of the adult population worked at Proctor & Gamble, makers of Ivory soap and other necessities of life. Our street sported the first new houses built in the town since before the war.

Life in St. Bernard was pretty much the same as it had been on Prospect Place. Albert continued to work and read, and Jonathan, already on his way to becoming an energetic social butterfly, made friends with the other boys in the neighborhood. I remember sitting on the curb and watching them play baseball in the street, a version called Association: three players to a team with hits determined by whether the ball is hit past or over the fielders. Jonathan never invited me to play; he wouldn't even let me keep score. He did make me retrieve the ball when it was hit in someone's front yard, usually Mr. Guthrie's, the resident curmudgeon. Then I, not Jonathan or his friends, had the privilege of enduring Mr. Guthrie's threats to send me where bad little boys are kept, a place he never described, though I knew it was not a place I wanted to go. Fortunately, Mr. Guthrie never made good on his threats.

When the summer was over I had my revenge. On the first day of school, Sarah appointed Jonathan as my escort. I didn't mind walking with him to school, but my kindergarten class would be over at noon and I'd have to wait until he finished his classes. Because my teacher, Miss Fletcher, thought it was dangerous for me to sit outside alone, she deposited me in front of the principal's office where everyone could see me when they walked by. It was the street corner across from the Laundromat all over again.

Sarah was waiting on the porch when we arrived home. She took one look at Jonathan and screeched. His face was a mess: caked blood on cracked lips, a deep gash in his cheek, and a purple walnut-sized bump on his forehead. I was unmarked, as neat and clean as when Sarah had dressed me that morning. After she was satisfied that Jonathan's bones were in place, she asked what happened. On the way home, he said, a group of high school boys had accosted us. They called us various names, like "yid kid" and "four-eyes." Jonathan pushed me to the side and put his hands up. Unfortunately, intention and result are often galaxies apart. They wrestled him to the ground and took turns hitting him.

I was looking at the floor during Jonathan's recitation, not out of shame but to hide my pleasure, as if I had hired the toughs to beat up Jonathan for his failure to let me play Association. Sarah put her hand under my chin and asked, "What did you do to help your brother?"

"I held his cap," I said.

After dinner, Sarah sat at Albert's desk and wrote the story. She sent it to Reader's Digest. Albert said she was wasting her time, because no one could read her handwriting. She couldn't read it either. Every letter looked the same and the words ran into one another like a row of slanted hills. But a couple of weeks later, an official looking envelope came in the mail with a gold star on it, like the kind I used to get from my piano teacher whenever I completed an assignment. We all sat at the kitchen table while she nervously opened the envelope. A cigarette dangled from her mouth, smoke streaming out of her nostrils. Ashes dropped on the letter and a corner caught fire. Albert grabbed the letter and poured coffee on it. Holding up the charred document, he read it as if he were giving Sarah an award. The editors had selected her story for publication. Enclosed with the letter was a check for ten dollars and a certificate "suitable for framing."

Sarah bought a brisket and hung the certificate above her sewing machine. Twenty-one years later, I came across it sandwiched between old literary magazines Albert sent me to keep. (He was afraid Sarah would throw them away.) I framed it in brass behind non-glare glass and presented it to her on her sixtieth birthday. She put it back above her sewing machine where it remained until she died.

Most kids want to be famous when they grow up. I wanted to be famous as a kid. In a world that paid no attention to kids, I knew that you could survive only by rejecting authority. That meant becoming a revolutionary. I would fight to overthrow the established order, which for me was the elementary school, run by the detestable Mr. Grunthal.

Grunthal looked like Adolph Hitler, down to the rectangular mustache and thin strands of black hair falling over on one side of his brow. With every step he shook his head, throwing the loose hairs back on his skull. He watched over his school children like a commandant. He once caught two first graders, a boy and a girl, under the bleachers at the baseball field, where they were studiously inspecting each other's anatomy. He made them cut out the letter "N" from their spelling books and pin them to their shirts. The "N" stood for naughty, his version of *The Scarlet Letter.*

My idea of revolution was playing marbles. I loved feeling them in the palm of my hand and the power when I sent them rolling with a flick of the thumb; I loved the clicking sound when they collided. The colors dazzled me, especially when they were in wavy patterns like an impressionistic watercolor. In the sixth grade, I organized a cadre of marble-playing kids; we called ourselves the Marbleists. At lunch we'd take our pails—we hid the marbles under the sandwiches—and go to our playing ground, the tennis court on the far side of the high school. The court had a new blacktop surface and smelled of tar. I knew every wrinkle, slope, and bubble. My marble collection grew with the spoils of victory.

Playing marbles was the stuff of revolution because Grunthal believed square dancing was the only acceptable form of recreation. He required everyone to participate during the lunch hour. Over the objection of Mr. Anderson, the sixth-grade teacher and basketball coach, the dances were held in the gym. Every night Mr. Anderson could be found on his hands and knees rubbing out the scuffmarks on the floor.

For most of the school year Grunthal didn't know that the Marbleists existed. We had instituted a rotation system, which assured that none of us would miss two dances in a row. But then Corey Gunnison, our worst marble player, betrayed us. On Corey's day at the dance, Grunthal noticed I was absent and asked him where I was. He confessed on the spot and volunteered to show Grunthal our hideaway.

When Grunthal came around the corner of the high school, everyone ran off in different directions. I wasn't a coward and stood there, proudly straddling my marbles.

He took me to his office and demanded the names of the gang members. I refused. He opened a metal cabinet behind his desk and removed a wooden paddle with a line of holes down the center of the blade, designed to give the swats the aerodynamic efficiency necessary to inflict maximum pain. He said if I named the others, he would put the paddle away, forget he had seen me on the tennis court, and return my marbles. If I declined his offer, he would pronounce sentence and immediately carry it out: ten swats with "Marie Antoinette." I asked him who Marie was and he waved the paddle.

Did I beg or grovel? I'm proud to say I did not. Did I tell Sarah, Albert, or Jonathan? No. But I told my cowardly fellow marbleists, informing them that I was disbanding the group because I could no longer bear to associate with them. They quickly took up square dancing.

Did I give up marbles? I certainly did not, though I had no one to play with. Jonathan said marbles was a child's game, Sarah said she couldn't take time away from her sewing, and Albert played only with Jonathan. So I

made up imaginary opponents and played in competitions every bit as scin-
tillating as the ones on the tennis court. I also became an excellent square
dancer, which made Grunthal think the swats had softened my heart as well
as my ass. But I was still a revolutionary, if only in my mind.

*He crushed out his cigar. He said he had to leave for a moment and I should
order more brandy. He went out the front door. I could see him through the
window talking to Jimmy.*

    *The waiter came over. "Excuse me," I said. "Does Mr. Schaechter dine
here often?"*

    "I'm sorry," he said. "Will you point him out to me?"

    *I began to raise my hand and then dropped it. He shrugged and walked
away. I lowered my head and closed my eyes. I looked inside my mind and
saw nothing.*

Connie, you are too much. Much too much. I stepped outside to make sure
Jimmy would wait for us and you make trouble. If you must know, I never
use the name Schaechter at restaurants. I started using aliases a few years
ago when a restaurant in Denver screwed up my reservation. The numskull
of a host thought my name was too difficult to spell or pronounce; he wrote
down Schick or Schock, I forget. They refused to seat me when I couldn't
produce identification in whatever name it was. I'll prove it to you. "Salvatore, Salvatore . . ." What? You believe me? A miracle, even if it's the brandy
talking. I don't mind how drunk you are. I want you to stay here and listen
to the autobiography of my childhood. I should give it a name. I know; I'll
call it, *Young Fischel.*

    Here's our brandy. And bring us two more cigars. Thanks, waiter.

What did the waiter say? "My pleasure, Mr. Samson."

In the sixth grade I broke the speed record for reciting the multiplication
tables. I set a new record for every table, one through twelve. Mr. Anderson
kept a chart of the records on a bulletin board.

    Forty years later, I went back to the old neighborhood. I parked my car
in front of the house. It needed a paint job and new awnings. Otherwise, it

was just as Sarah and Albert left it when they retired to a warmer climate. I followed my old route to school: past the dead end street with the metal fence on which I had almost severed my thumb, the barber shop, the drug store with the ice cream and soda fountain, all still there as if Disney had taken over the neighborhood and named it Nostalgialand. When I got to the school, I was disappointed to see that it was empty, except for an old janitor who told me it was Easter recess. I liked that, so retrograde. Everywhere else it was called spring break.

The door to Mr. Anderson's classroom was open. Though it was now a faculty lounge, I could see the ghosts of my past chewing on the ends of pencils, as they watched Mr. Anderson pull down a map of the United States with the names of the states scratched off so he could test us. The bulletin board was still there, right where I remembered it, under an oil painting of Stonewall Jackson, from whom Mr. Anderson claimed he was directly descended. In the columns for the "2" and "4" tables were stickers with the name Jones and a date in 1988. My name in blue ink, smudged and faded but unwounded by time's arrow, was there for the others.

As I was standing in front of the bulletin board, awed by my enduring childhood victories, I heard a woman's voice. "I know you," she said.

I turned to see an old woman, though there was something familiar in the thickly wrinkled face. "Miss Fletcher?"

"You're not in kindergarten any more. You may call me Marjorie."

"You're looking good, Marjorie," I said, though I was remembering her long, strawberry blonde hair that had swept to-and-fro as she lovingly printed words on the blackboard.

"If you like white hair, wrinkled skin, and red-veined eyes with falling eyelids."

"I could say the same for myself."

"Your eyes are still bright."

"It's the contact lenses."

"So you've come back to reclaim your past."

"The good part, anyway. Look, most of my records withstood the test of time. I'm the Jesse Owens of multiplication tables."

I followed her to a couch in the back of the room. As she sat, she primly tugged at the hem of her flower-print dress like a shy young girl. She patted the cushion and I sat next to her.

"You don't remember, do you?" she said.

What could I say but no?

"It was this time of year, Easter. I was telling the class the story of the resurrection. You raised your hand before I finished. I told you to put your hand down; the bathroom would have to wait. I don't have to go to the bathroom, you said. Well, this is a switch, I said to myself. I was unaccustomed to my students interrupting my stories with a question, particularly my religious stories. You were different. You wouldn't accept anything on faith."

I laughed. "That's because I'm Jewish."

"No. Something else. You didn't believe in miracles, any miracle. At Christmas you had wanted to know what a virgin was and when I told you—in a "G" rated way, naturally—you folded your arms, like you're doing now. You said that Joseph would have had to put his thing in Mary in order to make Jesus. I said you were correct in principle but this was a special case. You said, 'Even God has to follow the rules.'"

"I've changed. Now I don't believe in rules."

She looked at me skeptically. "I should have been prepared for your Easter question. Not a question, really, but a statement, your personal article of faith. You said I was fibbing to the class. You said, 'When you're dead, you're dead.'"

"What did you say?"

"What could I say? The resurrection was another miracle? I decided religion did not belong in the classroom. I never told a Christmas or Easter story again."

"I hope it's not too late to apologize."

"Why in heaven's name would you apologize? At five years old, you were an intellectual challenge. You spoke your mind. You made me think."

"I apologize for not remembering what a wonderful teacher you were."

She took a tissue from a pitted, red vinyl clutch bag and dabbed her eyes.

"You're an angel."

I kissed her hand and got up to leave. "By the way," I said. "I don't believe in angels."

"Now there," she said, her voice rising with the command only teachers possess, "you would get an argument from me."

The first woman I fell in love with was Jonathan's girlfriend. He was in the twelfth grade, she was in the tenth, and I was in the seventh. Her name was Carol. She was tall with a large frame—substantial was how Sarah described her. She had a bobbed nose and lips that were always puckered. She liked wearing dresses—alternating between blues and greens—and she was proud of her belts in every style and color. My favorite belt was black with a white clasp in the shape of a clover, which fit tightly around her waist and accentuated her hips and breasts. Her one defect—dare I say the word—was masculine hands. She briefly experimented with fake fingernails, her idea of making her fingers look longer and thinner, but I was glad when she stopped using them. A slight imperfection enhances beauty, a flaw that enables you to appreciate what is otherwise perfect.

When I saw her in the hallway between classes, I died for a nod, a hello, a smile, anything. Sometimes she did more, asked me how I was, and I was in my own personal heaven for days. Her intoxicating smell, like from a fresh peach, stayed with me for hours. When Jonathan had a date with her, I'd ask him if I could go along—he refused to take me, no surprise. When he called her on the telephone, I would run downstairs to the other phone and listen to their conversation. For her fifteenth birthday I bought a card with a heart and arrow through it and stuck it behind between the screen and front door of her house. On the card I wrote with my left hand—in case she was a handwriting expert: "If you let me, I'll give you more love than he ever could." I wallowed in paroxysmal ecstasy when he called to wish her a happy birthday and she said a secret admirer had asked her to run off with him, an offer she intended to accept unless he treated her better. When he got off the phone, he said he was going to break up with the ungrateful slut. Unfortunately, he changed his mind.

It was all I could do to wait until he graduated and left for Harvard. I hoped it would be "out of sight, out of mind." One evening I jimmied the lock of the school office and found her class schedule. I drew a map of the high school, complete with intersection points for what I hoped would be regular rendezvous.

What I should have remembered was an aphorism more powerful than out of sight, out of mind: absence makes the heart grown fonder. My accidentally-on-purpose encounters in the hallways no longer produced even a nod, let alone a smile or greeting. If she acknowledged me, it was with a frosty smile, as if I had been the one to tell Jonathan to leave Cincinnati. After two weeks of suffering I threw away the map—not that I needed it, I knew her movements by heart—and vowed to forget she was alive. But she was fastened to my brain like a metal plate. I started pinning notes on her locker containing what I thought were irresistible teasers: "Here's looking at you, kid," and "Just say you love me. You don't have to mean it." I even used my right hand, hoping she *would* recognize my handwriting. Verbal masturbation. After the third such note I walked by her table in the cafeteria. She treated me like a stalker, refusing me even a glance.

In November, I was coming out of Social Studies and on my way to Gym when I saw her leaning against a locker. She ordered me over with a curled-up index finger.

"Do you ever talk to your jerky brother?" she asked.

"Only when he asks me to send him the sports section from the Cincinnati Post."

"He hasn't called me in two weeks."

"Maybe he's short of money."

"He's seeing someone else, isn't he?"

I saw my opening. "Now that you mention it, the last time he called he asked my mother to suggest a nice birthday present."

She pushed off the cabinet. I wanted to kiss her. But she was six inches taller than I was, and I would have needed a footstool. "My birthday is in June," she said.

"He was talking about someone he knows at Radcliff."

"Radcliff is a girl's school."

"Right."

She fell back against the cabinet. She looked so sad. It would have broken my heart had revenge not already taken it.

"Would you like to go to the movies on Saturday?" I asked.

At first I thought she was going to laugh at me, but her puckered mouth and sad eyes were saying something else.

"A matinee," I said.

Whatever she had been thinking was gone. "Aren't you too young for me?"

"You're not too old for me."

"But you're Jonathan's brother."

My young soul knew that when all is nearly lost, confession is your last chance, especially if you confess to desperate acts. "I put the birthday card behind the screen door of your house. I pinned the notes to your locker."

The bell started ringing. "Class," she said.

"I know."

We stood there until the bell stopped ringing. The hall was deserted. She kissed me on the forehead. "You're sweet," she said.

"I don't want to be sweet."

"It's good to be sweet. You'll have the girls falling all over you."

"Jonathan isn't sweet and he's got you."

The corners of her mouth dropped. I was losing her.

"Anyway," I said. "I'm sorry about those notes."

She had that thinking look again. "So, you were my secret admirer."

"Now that I've confessed," I said, "it's not a secret."

Her face brightened. "You said a matinee?"

"At the Forest Theater. It's a good theater: refrigerated air, buttered popcorn, pretty good candy selection—"

"What's playing?"

"A double feature, two westerns: *The Man from Laramie* with Jimmy Stewart, and *Wichita* with Joel McCrae."

"I hate westerns."

"Oh."

"I'll make a deal with you."

"OK." I hoped that whatever she had in mind would require me to stay close to her: carry her books, run her errands, let her tie me in chains, and any other duties she could dream up.

"If you keep leaving me notes, I'll go to the movies with you," she said.

A secret of life, she was telling me.

"There's more." She put her lips to my ear. I was so excited I grabbed my crotch, praying that she didn't notice. "I want . . . " Her breath whooshed into my ear, sending a shiver down my spine. "I want you to never, ever tell Jonathan."

I took my hand off myself. "That's it?"

"Our secret," she said, her lips thin and resolute.

For the rest of the month we went to the movies every Saturday, except for the Saturday after Thanksgiving. Jonathan had come home to spend the weekend. He took her to dinner, dancing, even to the movies—the rat. But after he returned to Harvard, Carol and I resumed our routine, as if there had never been an interruption. If anything, we were closer. She would hold my hand in the theater and afterwards we'd sit in the park and share a basket of fries I bought at Frisch's Big Boy. When over Christmas break Jonathan went to Ft. Lauderdale with his buddies, she said she was finished with him.

Romance is like an unfinished railroad line. The money has run out and the tracks end in the middle of nowhere. When you reach the end of the line, you can get out and walk or stay on the train and hope someone will pick you up. Either way, the ride does not reach your destination. Shortly after New Year's Carol told me how far our train would take us. We were at Frisch's and she was feeding me fries, putting them into my mouth one at a time. She said we would never be lovers. She didn't say why.

We continued to act like lovers. We stood and sat closer together than ordinary friendship would allow, our breath intermingling and soft-spoken words gently caressing our ear lobes. We shared our dreams: those given to us while asleep, those created while awake. We put the world behind an opaque soundproof glass. "Lovers alone wear sunlight," and we wore that yellow glow for a time.

During the summer we saw the Reds play at Crosley Field, where she spent half her paycheck from her job at Shillitos—Cincinnati's largest department store—on tickets, hot dogs, chips, and soft drinks. We took a Sunday afternoon cruise on the Ohio River in an old-time riverboat, spent another Sunday at Coney Island, moving from ride to ride, ending on the Ferris wheel. When the Ferris wheel stopped at the top, I pretended to be scared. She held my hand and kissed me on the lips.

Sarah suspected something, I'm sure. Midway through the following school year, she asked me why I paid no attention to Dorothy Block. Dorothy was the daughter of one of Sarah's customers—Sarah supplemented Albert's income by hemming dresses for rich Jewish ladies—and often came with her mother to the house. Dorothy was a knockout: slim but busty, long legs, and a face that would put Marilyn Monroe to shame. But my heart belonged to Carol. Even so much as a glance at another woman was adultery. When I told Sarah I wasn't going to call Dorothy, she said, "I'm not asking you to fall in love with her." Then she added knowingly, "Or anyone else." Yet, she never said another word and never asked me why I wouldn't play baseball on Saturdays with my friend Stevie Jonas.

When Carol left for the University of Miami there were no tearful good-byes, promises to write, or plans for a future together. It was as if we each had taken our own trip and stopped for a few days in a small town where no one knew us. We would have talked for a while, told each other about our pasts, and speculated what the future might bring. And then we would part, moving on to our different destinations, like two strangers who meet in a bar, spend a few nights together, and go their separate ways. Sort of like us, Connie.

I did see her again, years later. She had married a rabbi and was living in Cleveland with their two children. He had been indicted for pilfering the funds of his synagogue. They were broke and it looked like he would land in jail. She had heard I was in Chicago and called me. I guess she wanted someone from the past to talk to, someone uncorrupted by her present life. I left the office as soon as we ended the telephone call and flew to Cleveland. She met me at the airport. She was on her way to meet her husband at his lawyer's office. There was too little time to go somewhere else; we had coffee at the Starbucks in the terminal. She looked the same, but the life in her eyes was gone and she no longer stood tall like I remembered. Although she knew I was a lawyer, she didn't ask my advice about her husband's case and we didn't talk about our current lives. Instead, we traveled together to the past, to the Forest Theater, the float down the Ohio River, the magical moments when we sat swaying in the gondola on the Ferris wheel.

Before we knew it, our time was over. We looked at each other the way people do at the end of a journey: wistfulness tinged with sadness, but with the joy of having made the trip. We couldn't decide whether to shake hands, kiss, or just say good-bye. We started laughing. And we kept laughing. Some of the dozen or so travelers in the other booths and at the counter started to laugh. Soon, everyone was laughing. No one knew what was funny, including us. We turned to wave like we were honeymooners standing on the deck of a cruise ship acknowledging the well-wishers below on the dock. Our makeshift retinue lifted their coffee cups in salute. "Bon voyage," they called out.

The restaurant had emptied and Salvatore was locking the front door. The waiter reappeared with more brandy.

"Have you had enough?" Fischel asked.

"I could drink another glass."

"I wasn't referring to the brandy."

"Oh."

"Do you want to hear more or should I save it for another night?"

"The restaurant is closed."

"It's closed for those who want to come in, not for those already here."

"If I want to leave, can I?"

"You're not a prisoner."

Salvatore was walking back toward the office. "Salvatore," Fischel said. "My friend is worried we won't let him leave when he wants."

"Why would he want to leave?" Salvatore said.

"Yes, Connie, why would you want to leave?"

I took a sip of brandy. "I do not want to leave. Tell me more."

When I'm asked what I remember best about childhood, I say the sounds: books slamming shut when the school bell rings out the day, Albert starting the car on a cold winter morning so it will be warm when he drives me to school, the crack of the baseball bat when I slug the ball over the outfield fence at the playground, Sarah humming a German folk melody while she alters a customer's dress, at my bar mitzvah service the old men in the congregation murmur when I sing the prayers just right, the crackling on the trolley wires, the splat when my high-dive ends with a belly flop, Albert's laugh when Sid Caesar plays the hero in a takeoff of *High Noon* in which all the characters have Yiddish names like *Shmatte, Shlemiel,* and *Ganze Mishpocha.* Most of all, I remember the sound of crickets on a summer night, chirping like an audience cheering.

I'm not sure, but I suppose crickets sleep during the day. Still, I wished they had made some noise, if only to bid me good-bye as I boarded the bus for the first day of my first summer job at Steiner's Wholesale Dry Goods Company. I got the job because Benjamin Steiner's wife was one of Sarah's customers. I had seen him once when he brought her to the house to have her sack dresses hemmed. After she went inside he got out of the black Cadillac and lit a cigar. He paced back and forth for a few minutes and then came up to the porch, where I was reading a Captain Marvel comic book. He yanked it from my hand and yelled, "Filth, this is filth," spitting tobacco juice on the cover. I spent the evening wiping the grime off Captain Marvel's face.

Steiner assigned me to the shoe department. It was on the third floor of an eight story building with no air-conditioning and windows that hadn't been washed in so long they looked like someone had boarded them up. Huge cockroaches, like those giant insects in a sci-fi movie, kept me company as they darted through the shadows in the narrow canyons of cartons stacked floor to ceiling.

Steiner paid his workers as little as possible and allowed only the minimum that the law required in working conditions: a ten-minute cigarette break every two and a half hours and a lunch break after six hours. He spent his day visiting each floor in sequence. If he caught you resting, he fired you on the spot. The employees were as expendable as the defective stock he couldn't give away to the owners of discount stores who came shopping from depressed towns in the hills of Kentucky and Indiana.

I worked under McKinley Washington, the stock boy in the shoe department. McKinley had moved to Cincinnati in the early fifties after the Louisiana factory he worked for went out of business. His ailing sister needed taking care of, and McKinley, without wife or children, was happy to help. She was sicker than anyone knew and died a month after he moved in with her. She left him her house, a ramshackle two-flat on Vine Street, a couple of miles from downtown in the poorest section of the city. There was no money in her estate. McKinley, an elementary school drop out, could secure nothing better than the lowest position at Steiner's, a position from which he had not been promoted in the seven years before my arrival. He had never received a raise, earning minimum wage: a dollar per hour, take-home pay $33.40 for a forty-hour week.

He was a strapping man with skin as black as coal. He had a regal bearing, always trying to maintain an erect posture. Even when reaching for a box of shoes on the floor, he wouldn't bend over. He kept his back straight while he squatted like a gymnast doing a deep knee bend. His voice was deep and mellifluous—the voice of an opera singer. He spoke slowly, carefully enunciating each word, as if he wanted to hide the poverty of his education as well as his wallet.

He became my only friend at Steiner's and taught me the tricks of the trade. He showed me how to remove a carton of shoes from the bottom of a twelve-carton stack without bringing the tower crashing down on my head. It was akin to pulling a tablecloth off a table, leaving undisturbed the dishes, silverware, and glasses; an acquired skill, perfected only after much practice and a quick and steady hand. It was also a trick that was virtually a job requirement, since Steiner would wax apoplectic if we took more than a few seconds to retrieve a shoe in a specific size for a customer— not enough time to remove one box at a time if the requested shoe was at the bottom. I suggested we reorganize the contents so each carton would contain every size of a particular style and then stack the rows by styles. McKinley grinned at my naiveté and informed me in his precisely worded if somewhat ungrammatical way how this method of organization would create a different problem. "The folks who come shopping at Steiner's," he said, "likes most times to buy one size, maybe sevens, because the feets of them who buy from them are the same size." I waited for him to tell me he was joking, but he wasn't joking. The size of people's feet, when charted on a graph, cluster around set points; there aren't as many who wear size thirteen as who wear size seven, for example.

In my third week on the job Steiner distributed an announcement, which reported that Congress had increased the minimum wage twenty-five cents per hour. McKinley asked me to read it to him. When I finished he laughed so hard tears trickled down his cheeks. He asked me to read it again, stopping me where it said that thereafter employees could no longer work overtime. McKinley, who had averaged twenty hours of over-time a week, thus adding another $25 to his paycheck, would now see his salary effectively cut. Worse, Steiner expected him to complete the same amount of work as before; he was forced to eat his daily ham and cheese sandwich on a makeshift table fashioned from shoe cartons in the basement storage area where he spent most of his time.

A few days later, McKinley took me aside and said he needed a favor. He was fed up with the law's failure to protect the working man. At first, I thought he wanted me to conspire to blow up the building or assassinate Steiner, but what he wanted was more daring and challeng-ing. He wanted me to teach him to read and write so he could find a bet-ter job. Nearly one hundred years after the Emancipation Proclamation McKinley had grown tired of being a slave.

Every evening after work I rode the bus to his house. The tenant upstairs, a middle-aged woman who worked in a factory across the river, was our chef. She cooked a variety of delectable dishes from the cookbook of recipes in her mind, all with chicken. We sat at a small table in the living room, ate our dinner, and then began the lesson; I often stayed two hours or more. Though I wanted to ask questions about his life—his growing up poor and black, his mother and father, his dreams and regrets—his look said he had let me in his life for one purpose only.

I brought the books of my childhood: thrillers like the *Buddy* series, where in each volume the author took the reader on an adventure with Buddy; baseball books—McKinley's favorite sport; a collection of sci-ence-fiction short stories—he took a special interest in stories about the apocalypse. I made a chart of the alphabet and a list of seven hundred basic words. He was a fast learner; in just a few weeks he was able to read the eas-ier books.

Although Sarah viewed my teaching as a reflection of an admirable, hitherto unknown, noble streak, she fretted about my being out at night where I was vulnerable to the city's less than noble denizens. She always waited for me, assuming her post on the front steps of our house, a dress in her lap to work on, pin between her lips. For hours she peered down the dark street, anxious to see me round the bend on the way home to safety.

At summer's end, I told McKinley I was willing to continue the lessons, perhaps on weekends—Sarah would never allow me to see him during the week once school started—but he said I had done enough; I had "set him on the road to paradise" and he could go the rest of the way on his own. He said we would have a last evening together, a final lesson I thought.

We got off the bus a block before our regular stop. He took me into a tavern called "Big Al's." It was an otherworldly place. The late afternoon sunlight filtered through the checkerboard windows, shooting long slices of light across the four booths in front and the pool table in the back. Three men were busy playing Stripes and Solids, but when they saw McKinley they raised their bottles in salute. "My best friends," he said.

We sat in a booth. He ordered two glasses of Schoenling beer; he said it was the poor man's champagne. He summoned his friends and introduced us. "This is teacher," he said, as if that were my name. As they shook my hand, he reached inside his work shirt and pulled out a paperback book: *Native Son*, by Richard Wright. The cover was shiny and the price sticker was still on the back cover. He opened it to the first page, cleared his throat, and began to read, carefully pronouncing each word as he did when he spoke. Occasionally, he paused to study a word or to sound it out phonetically. He read for an hour; his friends never moved. Other patrons at the bar came over and joined in the listening. McKinley didn't notice them; his eyes were fixed on the pages. He was living in the world of words.

After he read several pages, he looked up and saw the people who had gathered around his booth, more than a dozen. "Read us some more," a pool player said. And he did. It was after midnight when I got off the bus. There was lightness in my step, though it was due as much to the several beers as it was to my ebullient mood. As I rounded the bend I saw Sarah sitting on the front porch, dress in her lap, staring into the darkness. She saw me and there was a sudden rush of air. The crickets were making a racket, louder than usual. Sarah opened her mouth, no doubt ready to berate me for putting her through a fearful hell all those hours. I wanted to cry, not because I was scared or had allowed the beer to play havoc with my feelings. I wanted to cry because I knew I had done something worth remembering. And Sarah saw that I knew and didn't say a word. She held open her arms and hugged me close, rocking me back and forth, as she had when I was a little boy.

I never again heard crickets make so much noise.

Salvatore was gesturing from the door next to the kitchen.

"Damn," Fischel said. "I'm guilty of bad timing."

"Why?"

"I didn't think it would take so long to tell you the story of my youth."

"I am not tired."

"Salvatore is. We'll have to continue some other time."

"We could go to Murphy's."

"It's after two. Murphy's is closed."

We walked outside where Jimmy was leaning against the side of the limousine.

"I hope you enjoyed my stories," Fischel said.

"You say that as if I will not see you again."

He opened his jacket. "Look at the label: Giorgio Armani. This suit cost twenty-five hundred bucks. Absurd! I have more than thirty suits like this one. Think of what you could buy with $75,000. And I haven't given you the totals for my shirts, pants, sport jackets, shoes, cuff links, ties, designer underwear, socks, exercise outfits, golf clothes, swimming suits, and assorted beachwear."

"You did not answer me," I said.

"Oh, Connie, do you think you could get rid of me so easily?"

Jimmy opened the back door of the car and I got in.

"Take him home," Fischel said.

"You are not coming?" I asked.

"I want to walk for a while."

Before I could protest, the car pulled away from the curb. I looked out the back window. Fischel had lit a cigarette and was looking down the street, as if he was waiting for someone.

"Let me out here," I said, as we rounded the corner.

The car screeched to a stop. "Why?" *Jimmy asked.*

"I want to walk home."

"It's too far."

"I will hail a taxi if I get tired."

"I promised I would take you home." He seemed more suspicious than concerned.

"I will be all right, I assure you."

He opened the door for me. *"Just remember this. What you think you know, you don't. And what you don't know should stay that way."*

"I must say, Jimmy, I am quite tired of the intrigue."

He slapped me on the back. *"You and me both."*

"Do you have a cigarette?"

"You don't smoke."

"It is time I started."

As I walked, I heard the door shut behind me and the limousine move away in the opposite direction. I turned at the corner. I knew where I was headed, but was unsure what I would do when I got there. I sat on a stoop and watched part of a newspaper float through the air like a paper airplane. I remembered the last time I had smoked. It was that night at McInaney's when my friends and I celebrated the newspaper article about my brief stay in custody. I felt a prickle at the back of my head. I scratched the spot, as if to peel away a layer of memory. Though the incident—the bartender claiming I was Tommy Glynn—was trifling, it had troubled me so much that I had taken a cigarette from one of my friends.

Again, my head prickled. Another scratch, another memory.

I was nineteen. A crisp March day at the time of the hunger strike. I was getting off a bus, two blocks from my father's shop. I was jittery about telling him that I had decided to work for the Andersontown News. We had had a terrible tiff the night before, precipitated by a debate on whether martyrdom ever achieves its intended purpose. I hated our debates, which invariably deteriorated to the point where we did not hear each other's diatribe. This one was not much different, though this time we at least responded to each other.

As was the usual case, we ignored the rest of the family, who were happy to devote their attention to our traditional Sunday dinner of Irish stew with boiled potatoes and cabbage. I said a hunger strike by Bobby Sands or anyone *else would do no good. What could it accomplish? A few modest improve-ments in prison conditions? Gaining unification with the Republic would be as remote as it had ever been. My father became agitated, but instead of repeating his typically trite monologue on freedom and independence, he asked me a simple question: "Do you think one man's actions can ever have a real effect?" It depends, I answered, citing the great men and women in history whose actions changed the course of events. He laughed at me, his way of saying I did not know what I was talking about. He picked at his food for a few moments and then lifted his fork in the air, as if to get God's atten-tion. "What about God's army?" he said. "His loyal servants. The ordinary people. Me." He lowered the fork and shook it. "Me," he shouted. "Can I have an effect?" I wanted to tell him his question was absurd; if he performed an act that had great impact on people and events, he would no longer be ordi-nary. But this would have continued the debate, and I had grown tired of his posturing. I stared into the teeth of his fork. "Of course, Da, you can have no effect," I said. "You fix cars." He stopped shaking the fork and looked around the table. Everyone's head was bowed, as if they were praying. He threw the fork at me. I ducked and it whizzed by my ear. It stuck in the wall. Other than Mum looking up and saying, "Now see what you've gone and done," we finished the dinner in silence.*

I was still thinking about the argument when I saw him standing in the side lot to his shop. He was talking to a man and jabbing at a piece of paper. Then they saw me. The man took the paper from my father's hand and put it in his pocket. He walked quickly across the street and disappeared into a crowd.

When I asked Da about the man, he said it was none of my business. I did not pursue the matter, because I was more interested in the decision I had made. He listened to what I had to say, which surprised me. Although I had not thought so at the time, his meeting with the man must have had a profound effect on him. "So this is how you punish your Da," he said.

Such an inconsequential event in life, I thought, as I rose from the stoop and threw the cigarette in a gutter. Memories were random, fragmentary, unreliable.

I reached Maple at the other end from where Jimmy had dropped me off. Fischel was still standing in front of the restaurant. He was talking to Jimmy and another man, whom I could not see clearly. Fearful of being discovered, I slipped behind a boarded-up newsstand.

When next I looked they were gone. Since the limousine was still parked in front of the restaurant, I assumed they had gone inside. This, I believed, must be the meeting they discussed in the park.

Near the restaurant was a narrow causeway cut between two buildings, ending at an alley that ran parallel to the street. I hurried through the causeway into the alley. Bits of light streaked through cracks of a shuttered window. I heard voices, indistinct, muffled.

At first, I thought I had stepped on a piece of rope, but an earsplitting squeal and dark shadow informed me otherwise. I had disturbed the alley's principal resident. I pressed my back against the wall next to the window, not knowing whether I was more terrified of the rodent or someone coming to investigate. The shutters rattled.

"They are cemented shut," I heard Salvatore say.

"He should check it out." The voice had that threatening tone I knew so well from so little contact: the voice of the man who held the newspaper high.

"It's probably Connie," Fischel said. He chuckled in a way I had not heard before, like someone who regrets the humor of what he says.

"He insisted on walking home," Jimmy said.

"I was kidding," Fischel said.

"We should see who's out there," the man said.

"I'll go have a look," Jimmy said.

If I attempted to return the way I had come, I would surely run into him. But I could not see more than a few feet past the window. A glass shattered. Was it Jimmy or the rodent? I fell to my knees and crawled away from the window. I could still hear them.

"So we are agreed on the second location," Salvatore said.

"You're sure it's abandoned," my friend said.

"Yes."

"I hope you know what you're doing," the man said.

"It is not your concern," Salvatore said.

I was on the far side of the alley. My knee scraped against a hard object. I lowered my hands to the ground and touched metal, round and open at one end.

Jimmy stepped into the light and whispered through the shutters. Fortunately, his face was facing the light, which blinded him even more effectively than the dark. He slowly turned his head. His eyes were open wide, pupils dilated like Cuchulainn's in the dark. Unlike Cuchulainn, however, he could see nothing.

I put my hand on the ground for support. It was not the ground! The rodent darted across the alley, knocking a bottle into Jimmy's leg. "Fucking rat," he screamed. I was grateful for the creature's diversionary sortie and put my legs in the pipe, using the ground to push myself inside.

Jimmy resumed his search just as I disappeared into the pipe. I heard his breathing and stopped my own. His leg hit the pipe. I was inside a tuning fork. He sat on the edge of the cylinder. I could have touched his feet. He struck a match and the opening filled with flickering light. As his feet moved, the match fell to the ground. He struck another one. I lifted my jacket and buried my head inside. Using my hands, I spread it across the diameter of the pipe. The light from the match cut across the fabric and cast his face in silhouette. As his head moved inside the pipe, the shadow grew large and distorted. Then the image of a hand joined the face. He was pulling at my jacket. I held tightly to the inside lining. He was breathing heavily. "Fucking thing is stuck," he mumbled. He gave one more yank and withdrew his grip. His face and hand receded like a ghost returning to the night. I took my first breath in what felt like an eternity, barely able to suppress a cough that would have brought him back into the cylinder.

When I was sure he was gone I crawled out of the pipe. My hair, damp from muck and grease, was stuck to my scalp; my knees ached. I collapsed against the wall and waited.

I heard Jimmy's voice inside the restaurant.

"The only rat out there is a rat," Jimmy said.

"Connie is not a rat," Fischel said.

"If he knew, would he tell?" Salvatore said.

"He doesn't hate his father that much," Fischel said.

"I am not so sure. The hate one feels toward a loved one is always more intense than for a stranger."

"So is love."

"Well said."

"And he still doesn't know he is missing—"

"Say no more. The walls may have ears."

"As well as sight," the man said. "The Bureau has a new camera that they can put behind the screw of a light switch."

"Very well," Salvatore said. "Let us conclude. Each of us is clear what must be done."

"We're not," the man said.

"Meaning what?" Jimmy said.

"Meaning the Boston case is dead like the defendants. We're off the hook."

"That hook, perhaps," Salvatore said.

"You've gotten what you want. The Boston cops suspect nothing."

"We need you for one other matter."

"And what would that be?"

"When the time comes you will make certain no one knows two are missing."

"We're not magicians."

"It should not be difficult. You will be in charge."

"That wasn't part of our deal."

"It is now," Fischel said.

"And if we don't agree?" the man said.

"Oh, but Mr. Corcoran," Salvatore said, "you must agree."

So, the man was Smith Corcoran, the man who persecuted Eudie Lufman, moved to Boston, formed an unholy alliance with the Savin Hill gang, held the newspaper before his eyes when I fainted in the plaza. My God, I thought, what were they planning?

Corcoran sighed. "How will we account for two who are missing? Who can promise that?"

I heard the sound of a chair tipping over. "Christ, put your gun away," Corcoran said.

"Salvatore warned you about that habit," Jimmy said.

"We were just going to give you the fucking map," Corcoran said.

"Let me see that," Fischel said. "*Buddy and the Secret of the Lost Cave.*"

"What are you talking about?" Corcoran said.

"A book I read when I was a kid. There was a picture of a map; it showed the way to a cave full of treasure."

"There's no treasure on our island."

"Oh, Mr. Corcoran, you are wrong." Salvatore said.

I walked home. Somewhere in the alley I had lost my wallet. Feeling like a soldier wounded in battle, I wandered aimlessly. I looked like just another homeless person, an anonymous waste product of the city's digestive tract. After what seemed like several hours, I found myself on Second Avenue.

The dawn light was creeping up the sky when I reached the studio. Cuchulainn welcomed me with an affectionate swipe of his tail and an arched back.

"So my dear Cuchulainn, a friend I can trust, will you consider some questions that are plaguing me?"

He brushed against my leg. I took him in my arms and listened to his purring.

"Very good, Cuchulainn. I am glad you want to help. What am I missing? I came to this city with few possessions but many hopes. Now, look at me. Still few possessions, but questions instead of hopes."

Cuchulainn wiggled out of my arms and jumped to the floor. He circled the room, sniffing in every corner. I watched him until he found a moth, which he tormented until it lay lifeless on the floor.

Before I fell asleep, I pretended I was studying a map that would lead me to the lost cave.

CHAPTER EIGHT

May 17, 1998

I WOKE TO THE SOUND OF TAPPING. *Cuchulainn was sitting on the radiator, staring at Gold and Varick through the window. They were approaching the front door.*

Tail flapping, Cuchulainn paced back and forth like a lion in a cage. I wrapped the blanket around my waist and went to the window. "Please allow me to dress," I mouthed. They nodded and stopped short of the door.

I took my time dressing while I mulled over what I would say to them. Fischel had been right. The less I knew the better.

"You sleep late," Gold said, when I opened the front door. She walked through the vestibule into the studio with Varick close behind. He avoided my eyes.

I glanced at the clock on the desk. It was after two.

"We had a bit of trouble finding you," Varick said, as if I had been deliberately hiding.

"I did not know you were looking for me."

"Your wife knew," Varick said.

"You have been in touch with Mary?"

"Yesterday," Gold said. "Only one Cornelius Sullivan has come to the U.S. in the last month."

"Why did you lie to me about your employment, Mr. Sullivan?" Varick asked.

I looked at Gold. "I was afraid you would not speak to me."

She laughed. "Then you shouldn't have said you were a reporter."

"It worked," I said with more jocularity than I felt.

"What else did you lie about?" Varick asked. Obviously, he was not inclined to banter.

"Nothing. I . . . "

"Let me help you. Why did you say I had been on the Chicago Strike Force?"

The question seemed harmless. "As I told you, I read it in the Boston Globe."

"And, as I told you, the Boston Globe didn't mention my name."

"Then I read it somewhere else."

"Those are nasty scratches on your face, Mr. Sullivan," Gold said.

I touched my cheek and felt two prominent abrasions, gotten from my time inside the pipe. "From when I fell to the ground," I said. "In front of the courthouse."

"They look fresh," Gold said. "And dirty." She pinched my cheek and a pebble fell into her hand. She twisted it in her fingers, as if she were examining a diamond. She smiled and handed the pebble to me. She knew I was lying.

"Do you mind if we sit?" Varick asked.

"I only have the one chair."

Varick sat in the chair. Gold, still smiling, sat on the bed. I thought she must be used to his caddish ways.

"We've taken the opportunity to look into your background, Mr. Sullivan," she said.

She removed a notebook from her briefcase and began reading: "Born 1961, the second of six children to Noel and Margaret Sullivan. Noel was active in the Provisional wing of the IRA, which he had joined in 1971 when your family was evicted and moved in with relatives. In 1973, the family moved to a house in Clonard Gardens in the heart of the conflict area. In 1979, Noel bought the car shop where he worked. He paid in cash."

"Is this necessary?" I asked.

"We want to make sure we have our facts straight," Varick said.

"In that case, you should note that my father was not active in the Provisionals. He attended a few meetings, as I recall. And he had done well at the shop. It was not unusual—"

I thought I might be saying too much and stopped.

"If I may continue," Gold said. "While the business may have been doing well, Noel had problems. He was arrested in 1979 for a car bombing near *the Oxford Street bus station. The driver, a teenager, and several pedestrians died in the blast. He was released a few weeks later and Thomas Glynn, a fellow member of the Provisionals, was charged."*

"I do not see the relevance—"

"You came to the Boston hearing because of your interest in Glynn, didn't you?" Varick said.

"Yes."

"In 1983," Gold said, "Glynn escaped from prison. In 1985 he was apprehended in New York."

Cuchulainn was nibbling at my feet. "May I feed the cat?" I asked.

"Be my guest," she said brightly, as if she were on a social call. Varick, on the other hand, could not have looked dourer. Both buttons on his suit jacket were fastened and his shirt collar was tight around his neck. His Adam's apple protruded unnaturally as he kept raising his chin to stretch his neck. He reminded me of a fish.

The cat food was in a bag in the closet. My clothes hung above it and I remembered that I had lost my wallet. I took a moment to search the pockets of my jacket and pants. Nothing. Then I realized my passport was also gone.

"Is something wrong, Mr. Sullivan?" Gold asked. She was bouncing on the bed as if she were trying out a new mattress.

"No," I said firmly.

I filled Cuchulainn's bowl with food.

"The hearing," Varick said. "Why did you go to the hearing?"

"I already told Ms. Gold. I was interested in Tommy Glynn and when I read that his lawyer had committed suicide—"

"That's funny," Gold said.

"Pardon me?" I returned the bag to the closet and checked once more for my passport.

"I distinctly remember your telling me that you and Mr. Brandt were acquainted."

"Yes."

I walked over to the desk and pretended to organize my notebooks. A little nonchalance might enhance my credibility, I thought.

"How did you know Brandt?" Varick asked.

"I met him in connection with the Glynn case."

"Here in New York?"

"Yes."

"Your wife said you came to New York to write a history book."

I held up one of my empty notebooks. "True enough, but I also was interested in Mr. Glynn."

"When did you meet Mr. Brandt?" Gold asked.

Each lie was like a shovel digging a larger hole, one in which I would be buried if I was not careful. "The day after my arrival in New York, I believe."

Gold opened her briefcase and took out a pad. Her eyes darted up and down as she flipped through the pages. "You arrived on the tenth."

"Yes."

"So you met Brandt on the eleventh," Varick said. "Monday the eleventh."

"That sounds right."

"Where did you meet him?"

I hesitated and they noticed. "You should be honest with us, Mr. Sullivan," Gold said.

"Marinelli's Restaurant."

"How did you know to meet him there?" Varick asked.

"I called his office."

"You mean his home," Gold said.

Was she laying a trap? "Yes," I said.

"Try and be precise, Mr. Sullivan," she said solicitously, more as if she was interested in helping me rather than finding out whether I was telling the truth.

"I explained to Mrs. Brandt that I wanted to interview her husband. She said he was in New York and I called his hotel to arrange for the meeting."

Varick questioned me about the fictional meeting at the restaurant. I related invented conversations, largely based on information from the newspaper stories I had read. At first they took notes, but soon stopped. I had worn them out. But I could not stop talking.

"You did not ask me about the shooting."

"Should we have?" Varick said.

"Is that not why you wanted to see me, to ask if I could identify who was in the black sedan."

"Can you?"

"No."

Varick smiled.

"I saw nothing. If I had, I would have called you."

"Of course," Varick said cryptically.

Gold leaned down to pet Cuchulainn. Varick followed suit; the cat scampered away and crawled under the bed. "Cats don't like me," he said. I was tempted to ask if humans felt the same, but it hardly behooved me to turn him against me even more.

I accompanied them to their car. While Gold put her briefcase inside, Varick stayed by my side. "I have two things to say to you."

"Yes?"

I was never on the Chicago Strike Force. I was in private practice before deciding to dedicate myself to government service. Boston is my first assignment."

His face started to move in a circle, and his rapidly bobbing Adam's apple dissolved into a blur. "Vertigo," I said, leaning on the car for support.

"Have you been to a doctor?" Gold asked.

"It will go away of its own accord." The spinning slowed and then stopped. "What else did you want to tell me?" I said to Varick.

"Your interest in Mr. Glynn is more than academic, isn't it?"

"Well, I suppose, if you mean he is a countryman . . . ."

"He's referring to your father," Gold said.

"My father?"

"Yes, the affidavit."

"Affidavit?"

"The one Brandt submitted in his last ditch effort to stop the extradition, signed by your father. He confessed to the bombing. You came here to help with the case. Brandt did ask your help, didn't he?"

I was determined not to allow what they were saying to be reflected on my face. "No. What help could I provide?"

"Who are you protecting?" Varick demanded. "What are you hiding?"

"No one and nothing," I said, letting the shock of the revelation be expressed in anger at Varick.

"I hope not, since no one is protecting you. When you're ready to tell us the truth, call me."

"I have told you the truth."

"Have you? You didn't meet Brandt on the eleventh at Marinelli's Restaurant."

"Yes I did."

"The eleventh was on a Monday," Gold said. "Marinelli's is closed on Mondays."

I prayed for the vertigo to return, anything to distract them, but their faces, the street, the sky, held steady.

"I must have confused the dates. Perhaps it was the twelfth."

They got in the car. "Consider this, Mr. Sullivan. Whoever killed Gavencci and Marinelli might also have intended to kill you. Next time they won't miss."

"For God's sake, Peter," Gold said. "Don't scare the man."

"Why would anyone want to kill me?"

"I've said my piece, Sullivan. The rest is up to you."

I watched them drive away. When the car turned onto Second Avenue I returned to the studio. My anger turned inward. I had been a fool.

While I waited for the operator to place the call, I fought the urge to blame Mary. Why had she not warned me? Why had she told them where I was staying? Her sweet voice crossed the ocean. Though it calmed me, I poured out my regret that my dying father had confessed his crime in an affidavit without telling me, without giving me a chance to make amends.

"You didn't know about the affidavit?" Mary said.

"No."

"If you hadn't cut him off, you would have known." Her sharp words stung me.

"You spoke to him and he did not tell you," I said, hating how I sounded.

"You are his blood, Connie. Don't blame me. Call him, why don't you?"

"What would I say?"

"Ask for his forgiveness."

"Even if he forgave me, what good could come of it? He is dying."

"All the more reason you should call."

"I am afraid."

"*They told me you were there when the shooting happened. Why didn't you call me? How could you not call me?*"

"*I was in the courthouse,*" *I said, finding it easy to lie.* "*I was in no danger.*"

"*Was Mr. Brandt there as well?*"

"*Why are you interested in Brandt?*"

"*Not I. You. Should I remind you that you were curious about him?*"

"*Brandt is dead.*"

"*Dead?*"

"*He committed suicide.*"

"*Oh my God. This explains why the man telephoned.*"

"*Peter Varick?*"

"*No, someone else . . . wait, I wrote down the name.*" *The sound of rustling papers or static on the line, I could not tell which. The noise grated like a teacher's finger scratching on a blackboard in the drab classroom of the church school, where I was expected to believe. But in what?*

"*Connie? Here it is. His name is Fischel Schaechter.*"

If Fischel Schaechter had been in the studio, I would have gripped his throat with all my might. How dare he?

"*Connie, are you there?*" *Mary sounded frightened.*

"*I am here, my love,*" *I said.*

"*He said he was Mr. Brandt's friend and was helping on the case.*"

"*What did he want from you?*"

"*I don't know. He told me about the case in Boston. He said Mr. Brandt was supposed to give evidence against some terrible people . . . he called me to say you were all right. It was such a shock . . . I had no idea . . . oh, Connie, what are you up to? Do you know this man?*"

No, I wanted to say, I do not know him. "*Yes, I know him,*" *I said.*

"*He said you could help Tommy Glynn.*"

"*Me?*" *I laughed. This was insane, I thought.*

"*I wondered the same thing. But he said you would know. I don't understand. I feel so alone. Why did he call me, Connie?*"

How could I answer her questions when I could not answer my own? "*Mary, I wish I knew why he telephoned you, but I do not.*"

"*You must know.*"

The phone had become heavy in my hand. What a cruel joke for Mary to think I could tell her anything.

"Connie, are you there?"

"Yes."

"Is there something you're not telling me?"

The fire in my brain was forging a memory. "I remember now. That day . . . at the car shop . . . "

I heard Lucy in the background clamoring for the telephone. Mary put her on, and I tried to pay attention to her chatter. Mary reclaimed the telephone. I could not speak.

"You should come home," she said.

"Not yet."

"Why?"

"Because of what happened."

"What happened? When?"

"The day of the bombing, when the boy was killed."

"What could you remember? You had nothing to do with it."

"I know, but there's—"

"What could you learn in New York? Besides, you know what happened. You said so yourself. Your father was arrested and he blamed Tommy. Now, on his deathbed, he owns up to it. What else could there be?"

"There is something else. By Jesus, there is more to this than I thought."

"Connie, you're frightening me."

"No, forgive me. But . . . "

"Please, come home."

"I have a new friend."

"Who?"

"A cat. I named him Cuchulainn."

"Why would you buy a cat?"

"He came to me. He needed a home."

"Have you lost your mind, Cornelius Michael Sullivan? For all you know, he is carrying a disease."

Oh, the common everyday fears that keep us from remembering the truth.

Cuchulainn was on my lap, luxuriating in the rhythmic movement of my fingernails on his back. What was I remembering? Morning, a crisp day in May. I had gotten to work earlier than usual to repair a car with a defective muffler. As I lay on my back under the chassis I heard voices. One was my father, the other, high-pitched, vaguely familiar, someone younger. I started to crawl out and stopped. My father had said something that froze me.

Cuchulainn squealed from his perch on my lap. I had scratched him too hard. He jumped away. And with his leap my mind went dark.

I walked to Marinelli's. In other circumstances I would have enjoyed retracing my steps. I paid little attention to the sights or sounds of the city, trudging along and looking, I am sure, like a man with no destination.

I was surprised by how narrow the alley was, barely three paces across. The opening to the pipe was so small I was astonished that I had been able to scrunch up enough to fit into it. I hesitantly put my hand inside, worried I might be intruding upon the rodent's hone. Jimmy Crosetti had called it a rat, but I could not bring myself to view the creature that way. Rats were traitors and this rodent was a survivor, living in its own kind of war zone. My fingers touched soft leather and I pulled out my wallet. I was relieved to see that no money was missing. Encouraged, I put my hand back inside, but as far as I could reach I touched only cold metal. I got on my hands and knees and pushed off the ground, contorting my body as I had the night before. The effort was unavailing; I came out the other side with two quarters, a rotten apple, and an empty beer can.

I searched the alley for the next twenty minutes without success. I sat on the pipe to rest. As unlikely as it seemed, my passport might have fallen out of my jacket when Jimmy dropped me off, or on my walk around the block and through the causeway leading to the alley. But a half-hour walk with my eyes fixed to the ground produced nothing other than an occasional sighting of dog droppings, crumpled cigarette packs, and old newspapers.

I was in front of Marinelli's. Perhaps I had left the passport inside.

"Good afternoon, Mr. Sullivan," Salvatore said. "It is so good to see you. But we do not begin serving for another hour."

"Thank you. I came to see if I left my passport here last night."

He tilted his head in apparent surprise that I would leave such an important document in a restaurant. "Let us take a look," he said. He led me to the booth where Fischel and I had dined.

While I looked on the floor and between the cushions he went into the kitchen. In a few moments he returned, shaking his head. "I am very sorry, but no one has seen it. Perhaps you dropped it on the street or in Jimmy's car. Jimmy will be here in an hour."

"Will you ask him for me?"

"Certainly. Or you may wait and I will serve you tonight's special pasta. It is oh so spectacular, from my grandmother's recipe."

"I've heard about her secret recipes."

He looked at me blankly and then laughed, his deep guttural laugh. "Oh, yes, the pizza man in Chicago who had the recipe stolen by the McDonald's entrepreneur."

"Is Danny Marinelli still in business?"

"I admit not to know. His side of the family and mine . . . shall we say we do not see eye to eye." He laughed again. "No, I should say an eye for an eye."

A terrifying aspect was hiding behind his play on words. I would not wait for Crosetti to return. "If your driver has my passport, please ask him to drop it off at Murphy's."

"Murphy's?"

"A tavern on Second Avenue, between fifty-first and fifty-second. He knows the place."

"Ah, yes, he picked you up there last night."

"Yes, with Fischel."

"Fischel," he said softly, as if it were a holy name.

I shook his hand and said I would call in an hour. He led me to the door. "I hope you will return for another dinner."

"I would like that."

"You should not be concerned. Of course, I tell everyone that."

"Thank you," I said, not knowing whether he was joking again. "If your driver does not have my passport, I will obtain a replacement tomorrow."

"I was not referring to your passport."

"What then?"

"You are in good hands. He will make sure no harm comes to you."

Connie, I've got a present for you. Close your eyes. OK, now you can look. You left it in Jimmy's car. You walked to Marinelli's? What's wrong with a cab? You also lost your wallet? On the street? If you drop money in New York, it's gone before it hits the ground. You found it? You're a lucky Irishman, I guess.

How do you like my new clothes? It's been a long time since I wore jeans. What am I going to do with my suits? The Armanis, Zegnas, Ferragamos, and all the rest. For twenty-eight years I've worn suits. I've been reborn. I've given up the practice of law for good—breathtaking, like giving up life. When you practice law as long as I did, it consumes you until the only way to save yourself is to die and be reborn, even if your journey from being to nothingness and back to being is a fantasy.

Why do you look so out of sorts? Didn't you sleep well? I know I kept you awake, but I didn't tell you to walk home. Dishonesty? Evasiveness? Sorry, Connie, I can tell you the truth about the past, but don't expect the truth about the present.

I lied about the past? What was it? You are truly silly, Connie. I called him Peter Varick because I couldn't remember the name of the fellow who ran the strike force. I bet you don't remember every name from thirty years ago. What's in a name?

What am I supposed to say? It's like your walk home. You can't blame me for your jaunt to Boston, your penchant for standing in the line of fire, which I am sure is not the first time you've been in harm's way. No, I'm not getting at anything. You grew up in a war zone, didn't you? You're free to do as you please, just don't blame someone else if things don't go as you like. Peevish, you say. Look in a mirror. You're petulant ninety percent of the time. There, drink your Guinness and calm down. Please, let's talk law. If you get bored, interrupt and harangue me some more, if it makes you feel better.

Harm's way? When had I been in harm's way? In truth, despite having grown up in the middle of armed conflict, I had a normal childhood. The Troubles did not start until I was eight. And thereafter, violence engaged my senses only from a distance, when I heard the faint echoes of gunfire in the night.

I remembered one incident in particular, though it represented only an intimation of violence. It was 1974 and we had just gotten settled in our new home. I shared a bedroom on the second floor with my two younger brothers. My parents' bedroom was across the landing. For my sisters' bedroom we had converted a small room off the kitchen. We all shared the bathroom next to the living room that overlooked our narrow street. One evening, as I was coming down the stairs to dinner, my father stopped me and took me into his bedroom. He said it was time I learned about our troubled world; I would accompany him to a meeting of the Provos that evening. At dinner my mother said nothing, though from her disapproving look it was apparent she knew what my father intended. Later, as my father and I were leaving, she kissed me on the cheek, a kiss that had the tenderness of a mother's prayer for a safe return.

The meeting took place in the back room of the Kashmir Pub, a neighborhood drinking spot. My father told me to stand off to the side and say nothing; I should listen and learn. I leaned against a wall next to a dozen buckets stacked in the shape of a pyramid and watched the proceedings, more a disorganized screaming match than a formal meeting. The dozen or so participants talked over one another, yelling and cursing, but not cursing the British as much as the "Stickies," the Officials of the IRA, given the name because during parades they used tape to wear the paper Easter Lily. The Provisionals, known to the neighborhood as the "Pinheads"—they used pins—considered the Stickies to be sell-outs, because they had agreed to pursue independence by political rather than violent action. Toward the end of the meeting, everyone, including my father, grabbed a bucket. The bulging veins in their forearms caused me to take a closer look. The buckets were filled with red paint.

We got in a car with another man. I sat in the back seat and stared out the window while we drove, headlights off, through Fruithill Park, a neighborhood of well-to-do Catholics. We stopped in front of a large house and they got out of the car, taking the buckets with them. They traversed the yard to the porch of the house and splattered paint across the front door. When they returned to the car my father said, "Red paint for the blood spilled because of their inaction." At the time I was not quite sure what he meant, but that night, as I lay in bed, I heard my mother demand that he swear to never again involve me in his nefarious escapades. She said he was the devil to be in league with a gang of murderers. She was right. Paint sprayed on a door was the antithesis of the biblical protection given the Jews when the angel of death came to take the first-born male sons of the Egyptians. Here, the paint marked the house as a target for the Pinhead death squad who went about their work of punishing Catholics who did not support the cause.

Snap out of it, Connie, and pay attention. I've got stories to tell you.

Jersey Reynolds, Gordon's secretary, was an overweight woman nearing thirty, blessed with a smile that forced others to smile with her. A more giving person you would never meet. She devoted most of her free time to helping others: volunteer work at a hospital near where she lived, one evening a week acting the big sister to a motherless child, on Saturday and Sunday typing letters at a legal aid clinic in a crime-infested part of town. Her life, though, suffered from a glitch, a tear in the fabric of her existence that exposed a tragic vulnerability. Late at night, she cruised the dozen or so bars on Division Street, the street not of dreams but of nightmares, the sort of nightmares lonely people have, though they often come when they're awake, nightmares from which you can never escape.

She had been Gordon's secretary for ten years, hired at his previous firm when she was eighteen, a high school dropout just recovering from an abortion. When Gordon and I formed our partnership he brought Jersey with him. This is commonplace in the world of law where legal secretaries often see themselves as surrogate wives, providing their bosses with the benefits of the marriage contract: servitude, understanding, tolerance of extreme mood swings, companionship, sounding board, and sometimes sex. They follow their bosses from job to job, like gypsy wives follow their husbands from town to town. Jersey and Gordon, however, weren't having an affair; he was involved with a married real estate broker whose husband was serving time for fraud.

Jersey avoided getting drunk on the job until Gordon decided to maintain a stock of liquor in the office so we could have after-work cocktails at five without leaving the office. We kept a bottle of scotch for him and a bottle of vodka for me. Soon, he was complaining that he had to replace the vodka twice as often as the scotch, implying that I was sneaking a swig or two during the day. But it was Jersey doing the extra drinking. On slow afternoons she would sneak into the file room and drink away whatever was left of the day.

The Christmas holidays were a bad time for Jersey. Her family lived in a retirement community in Key Largo, Florida. Though always welcome, she had visited them only once during the previous five years. She didn't see how anyone could spend the holidays in warm weather. So, during the week between Christmas and New Years Jersey cruised the single bars, with drinks simultaneously sitting on the bar at two or more places. She flitted from one to the other, surveyed the landscape, flirted with a few lonely guys who looked like they would be cheered by her smile and then moved on. Her next day hangovers lasted into the afternoon, but Gordon wasn't around to deal with them; he and Jackie took the kids every year to his parents' house in Boca Raton.

Jersey's luck ran out on the firm's third New Year's Eve. She got dressed in her favorite outfit: a too tight lavender pants suit that displayed more than a hint of her ample breasts. Knowing she was in for a night of drinking, she called Lincoln Cab, a small company she had used on other barhopping jaunts. She knew most of the drivers, but this time a new one picked her up. He said he had just moved to Chicago from Moline, a farm town a hundred miles or so away.

Mother's on Division was the quintessential Chicago singles bar. During the week, it attracted the new professional middle class, the so-called Yuppies: single lawyers, married lawyers who told their wives they were working late, stock brokers, investment bankers, anyone who wore a tie and jacket to work. New Year's Eve brought out a special kind of clientele, men and women of all ages with one thing in common: no family, spouse, or friends to keep them company.

When the driver pulled up in front of Mother's he handed Jersey a card with a telephone number on it and said he would be happy to take her home when she was ready. She noticed that the number was different from Lincoln Cab's, but didn't care; she was happy to have a ride. In past years, finding a cab in the early morning hours of the New Year had been difficult.

As Jersey walked into Mother's she reminded herself of her New Year's resolution. Not the hopeless resolution made year after year to stop drinking, but a new resolution, a determination to resist taking men home with her. This habit of hers—being able to call it a habit gave her hope she might someday break it—had gotten out of hand during the past year when she had gone to bed with more than one hundred men.

Jersey got drunk of course but she tried to be responsible about it. She didn't jump from one bar to the next; she even stayed on the same bar stool all night. She danced to "Auld Lang Syne" with a young stockbroker who liked her, as unattractive as she was but he said oh so nice; he had tenderly kissed her when the bartender stood on the bar with a megaphone and announced the New Year. And she had given him her telephone number and watched him put it in his wallet under the picture of his mother.

She was thinking of going home when the cab driver came in and sat next to her. She was so drunk she didn't recognize him at first, thought he was just another lonely guy. He said he was ready to take her home and she said, "I don't do that." He laughed and showed her his cab license, making her feel foolish. She didn't like feeling foolish, a shame because she was foolish and should have known it. And so she decided to leave with him. Having managed to resist the stockbroker, she was actually looking forward to spending the rest of the night alone. They walked out to the bartender saying enjoy the New Year, though, pardon my language, what he actually said was "fuck out the old, fuck in the new."

As soon as she got in the back seat she passed out. The driver turned off Division Street into a dark alley. He stopped the cab and opened the back door. She was lying on her side, curled up in the fetal position. He rolled her over, split open her leather jacket, and started fondling her breasts, which were half out of her bra. She regained consciousness, felt the unshaven face pressed against her, and vomited. He fell back in surprise while she went after him with her fingernails, but he ducked under her hands and dragged her out of the cab. She vomited again and he slapped her back into unconsciousness.

Two cops on patrol entered the alley from the other end. The driver jumped in the cab and tried to back up, but the alley was narrow and he crashed against a building. The cops arrested him and called an ambulance to take Jersey to the hospital.

Because New Year's Eve was on a Friday night that year, I didn't find out what happened until I arrived at the office Monday morning. She was wearing sunglasses to hide her two black eyes. Gordon, back from Boca Raton, talked to her first and then came to see me. He wanted me to sue Lincoln Cab. He said he couldn't do it because he would be too emotionally involved (implying of course that I was incapable of being emotionally involved with anyone); he was already beside himself with rage that someone could do this to his secretary. Gordon's anger was an act. He was worried she would depend on him. Gordon didn't like people to depend on him.

The case should have been open and shut. The cab driver pled guilty to aggravated assault and received jail time because of a prior conviction for beating up the girlfriend he left back in Moline. But the world of civil litigation is not an open and shut world; it's a world where blame gets spread around like bird droppings, a little here and a little there, but more often than not on the head of the victim. The law is forever blaming people for what happens to them.

A practical problem was that recovery against the driver was tantamount to no recovery, since the driver lost his job and his assets consisted of an old car that cost more to maintain than it was worth. Unless I could throw a little blame on Lincoln Cab, the case wasn't worth pursuing.

Fortunately or unfortunately, depending on your point of view, the law provides two ways to recover damages from an employer whose employee commits a tort. The conventional way is through the doctrine of *respondeat superior.* With the kind of cruel wit the law is noted for, this principle is considered a form of vicarious liability, as if the party subject to the liability should experience the pain of having to pay for someone else's wrongdoing. The one exception is that employers are liable only for the torts of their employees committed within the scope of their employment. In other words, if the employee is not on the job, the employer is not liable.

Lincoln Cab claimed the driver was off duty when he attacked Jersey. Their records showed that his New Year's Eve shift ended at nine. But the company's rules required him to drop off his cab at headquarters when quitting for the night. Instead, he had driven it to a friend's house, where he partied for a few hours before returning to Mother's. Jersey thought the driver was still on duty, but what she thought wasn't the issue.

The better way to get at Lincoln was to show it was negligent in hiring the driver. In violation of its procedures, Lincoln hadn't checked his background and thus was unaware of his criminal record.

I knew Lincoln would defend the case by claiming Jersey had been negligent when she left Mother's with the driver, a variation on what I had tried to show about Linda Cox in the Leonard Stone case. Under the law, contributory negligence can bar recovery of damages.

Even if Jersey won, what amount could she expect? She spent a few hours at the hospital—cost, $200—and was released. Some would say the incident had a positive effect. She stopped cruising. She also stopped having fun. She became a social agoraphobic, quitting her bowling league and no longer dining out with her girlfriend.

At work, Jersey was sullen much of the time, rarely asking me about the lawsuit. When she did raise the subject, she always turned the conversation to how much money she could win. I told her a jury verdict was unpredictable, but she persisted in throwing out various figures, asking me to quantify her chances. Then I got a notice that the court had scheduled a settlement conference.

Our legal system has a split personality, but neither half is interested in justice. We elect representatives to pass thousands of laws except a law appropriating money to hire enough judges to hear the disputes that these laws foment. Unless ninety percent of civil cases settle before trial, the system would collapse. In some cities, civil cases may not be tried for seven or eight years. There's an old phrase: "Justice delayed is justice denied," which, if true, means there is no justice in our civil system.

A settlement is supposed to be a voluntary compromise between the parties, but the voluntary part is an illusion. The system's rules and procedures are fashioned to force litigants to relinquish their claims for less than what they might receive in a trial. The law's strongest weapon is uncertainty. Even if there is agreement on the facts, there is rarely agreement on the law. And even if there's agreement on the law, there's never agreement on what the case is worth.

To make sure that the litigants recognize how pointless it is to risk the lottery of a trial, the law invests judges with substantial power to coerce, cajole, and manipulate them into settling. And Judge Jacob Grossman, to whom Jersey's case was assigned, had nurtured a reputation for using any means at his disposal to force a settlement.

Friends and enemies alike knew Grossman as "Jake the Grape," because he looked like a grape, a purple grape, the kind with seeds in it, though the warts on his cheeks looked more like popcorn kernels than seeds. Before becoming a judge he was a lawyer for the transit authority. He never agreed to settle with an injured passenger until the day of trial when the plaintiff, exhausted by years of waiting, was usually willing to accept a modest amount rather than risk getting an unsatisfactory verdict.

In effect, Jake was a third party to the litigation, a referee who decides to play in the game. His strategy was to divide and conquer.

We gathered in the anteroom of his chambers: Jersey and I, the defense attorney and a representative of Lincoln's insurance company. The defense lawyer was an amiable sort, a man in his late forties with the kind of plastic expression you'd expect of someone who has spent his career quantifying the human condition. He was devoted to his task: assigning a dollar number to every type of injury, the names of which sounded like shorthand speech in a mannequin factory—leg off, arm off, hand off . . . He called Jersey's case a "no pen" rape—that's *pen* for penetration.

The lawyer pulled me to the side and said he was authorized to offer $600 in settlement, three times the amount of Jersey's hospital expenses, the standard formula for computing the settlement value of a case not involving permanent injury. He also said he was being generous in not discounting the offer because of Jersey's suspect moral character. I said I wanted $5,000. He chortled and said my demand was out of the question; insurance companies weren't in business to give people what they want. I told him I could be flexible, but I wasn't going to bargain against myself. "Let's see what Jake the Grape suggests," he said. When I told Jersey what he had said, she cried, huge drops rolling over her fat cheeks. "Don't worry," I said. "I'll get you $2,000."

"How?" she asked.

"That's my problem, but you have to promise me you'll take it." She agreed, though I felt like a chump having to tell her that lawyers were determining the price of her dignity.

Jake asked to see me first. Alone. This was standard operating procedure in his settlement conferences. He wanted the chance to persuade me that Jersey's claim was weak. Then he could give her his spiel without worrying that I would interfere.

I sat in the chair across from his desk and waited for him to speak. He held an envelope in his hand, raising it to the corner of his forehead like Johnny Carson playing the clairvoyant Carnac the Magnificent. "In this envelope I've written what I think would be a fair settlement of this case. Would you care to guess the amount?"

"Not really," I said.

He lowered the envelope and took a pack of cigarettes from his shirt pocket. He offered me one. Though it wasn't my brand, I accepted. I didn't want to insult him again.

"You're not a personal injury lawyer, are you?" he said.

"No."

"Why are you handling this case?"

"She's my partner's secretary."

"So?"

"So we wanted to help her."

"You can help her by agreeing to settle for the amount in the envelope."

"I don't know what the amount is."

"And you won't know until I convince your opponent to agree."

"No disrespect, your Honor, but if I am to do my job, I should know what I am recommending to my client."

"It's a good thing you're a personal injury virgin," he said, blowing a perfectly formed smoke ring and admiring its flight over my head. "Otherwise, I could become very angry, and you wouldn't enjoy it if I did."

"I'm sure I wouldn't."

Let me explain the facts of life as they pertain to this case or any other case you may someday have before me. The driver pled guilty to attacking your client. At that point, society's interest was served. And since I am society's servant, my job is to make sure your client doesn't cost society more than the minimum. You see, counselor, I don't give a shit about Ms. Reynolds and neither should you."

"You are so right, your Honor. I don't care about my client. Why should I? But society isn't the defendant. Lincoln Cab is the defendant and I give a lesser shit about it."

"Every dollar Lincoln's insurance company pays out increases the cost of insurance. Every dollar in premiums gets reflected in the cab fares. Society pays."

"The cab rates are regulated by law, and it's also the law that gives my client the right to sue."

"You can't win a debate with me, young man."

"I'm not trying to."

"You think I'm out to screw your client, don't you."

I wanted to say that's exactly what I thought, but I knew better.

"I'm not, you know. I know she has to walk out of here with a check and you have to earn a fee."

I wasn't going to tell him I hadn't planned to charge her a fee. "Thank you for looking after my interests, your Honor."

For a moment, I thought I might have been a smart aleck once too often. His popcorn warts had gotten red. He pointed the envelope at me like a dagger and said, "I'm doing you a favor. Not telling you what I've written inside this envelope is what allows me to obtain the defendant's agreement. If defense counsel thought you knew the number, he'd want to pay less."

"Makes sense, your Honor, only if I don't know the number in the envelope. Problem is I do know the number."

He pulled back the envelope. "You're bluffing."

"Thanks to your lamp I could see through the envelope when you held it to your forehead."

He held the envelope in front of the lamp. "Shit!"

"Your Honor, my client was assaulted by someone who never should have been hired to drive a cab. She wants $5,000."

"I can't get you $5,000."

"We'll go to trial."

"Sure you will. Four years from now."

"She's willing to wait."

"We'll see about that. Bring her in here."

"No."

Purple veins sprouted from his neck to his jowls. "I order you to bring her in here."

"I'll make a deal with you."

"I don't make deals. I make others make deals."

"Call in the defense lawyer and the flunky from the insurance company. Tell them that despite your best efforts you couldn't get me to agree to the number in the envelope. Then say if they have an offer to make, whatever it is, they should give you the number and you'll promise to get me to take it."

"How do I know you'll take it?"

"I'm telling you I will."

"How do you know I won't tell them to offer $600?"

What a nitwit. He had just told me the amount in the envelope. "You're a judge and judges are honorable," I said.

"You're one cocky son of a bitch."

"Do we have a deal?"

"Why the fuck not? Who gives a shit?"

"Connie, I'm going to the bathroom and when I return I want you to tell me how much I got for Jersey. Here's a clue. My conversation with the defense lawyer before going in to see Jake."

With that, he got off the stool and left.

Patrick brought me another Guinness.

"He's got you thinking, has he?"

"The damn stories he tells me. They are as much a mystery as he is."

"You would think he was Irish, wouldn't you."

Here was my chance, I thought. "You've known him a while."

"Since he's been coming around."

"How long has that been?"

"I don't suppose I know exactly. A month, maybe more, maybe less."

"Then, when I met him was not his first night here."

"I wouldn't know."

"Did he ever talk to someone like he talks to me?"

"Can't say I ever noticed."

"He selected me for a reason."

"I'm not sure I know what you're getting at."

"The first night, a week ago, he was waiting for me."

"If he was, he never said."

Fischel was beside me. "Connie, you're not working on your problem."

"You were waiting for me."

"Tonight. Sure, but I didn't wait long. You were on time."

"You were waiting for me the first night."

Fischel smiled at Patrick. "Was I waiting for Connie?"

Patrick nervously took a cloth and started rubbing the bar with a circular motion, as if he were trying to eradicate a stubborn stain.

"Yes, Connie, I was waiting for you," Fischel said.

"Why?"

"To talk to you."

"How did you know I would come to this pub?"

"Enough with the questions. You've got a problem to solve. And I have to make a call. Get the right answer by the time I return and I'll tell you why I was waiting for you."

"If I get it wrong?"

"You'll get it right. I know you will."

He left to make his call, left me confused as usual. But I could not think about the Jersey Reynolds case. I stared at a bar napkin and it became a picture frame. I saw myself as a young man. I was lying beneath a car in my father's repair shop. I could hear voices and see a face, the face of a boy, the face of a dead boy blown to bits near Oxford Street bus station. "I park the car," he said. "And I walk to the corner and take the bus." "Go home," my father said. "Like nothing happened." The image faded and in its place was a number that I had unconsciously written on the napkin.

Time's up, Connie. What are you mumbling about? And what's the napkin . . . hey, what do you know! Four thousand bucks. That's right! Fantastic! Tell me how you did it. What do you mean, you don't know how you did it? Your father's auto repair shop? Forget writing history, Connie, you could be a great novelist, making connections no one else makes. Shit! Patrick! Connie needs a glass of water.

OK, so Tommy Glynn is in jail for a crime he didn't commit. Your father rigged a car with a bomb, it went off prematurely, and the kid driver was killed, along with some innocent bystanders. Go on. Your father got out of prison by blaming Tommy. But your father waited until five years ago to tell you what he had done and lied when he said the name of the scapegoat would mean nothing to you. Wait. You told me this stuff at dinner. Let me get this straight. You're saying it dawned on you at dinner that Tommy Glynn was the innocent man arrested because of your father. Oh, I see. While I was in the bathroom you learned the truth from the napkin, how you've known all along your father was responsible for the bombing. Let me see your magic napkin. Did the napkin tell you whether you realized Tommy Glynn was the one your father fingered? Of course it matters. If you knew at the time that your father had wrongly accused him, you could have gone to the police. You could have turned in your father. Be real, Connie! You would never have gone to the police. Who could betray his father, for God's sake? And did the police really believe that Tommy Glynn planted the bomb? What if the police were out to make a case against Tommy, any case at all, and used your father to do it? True, he still made the car bomb, I can't deny it.

I have to say, Connie: Your mind is a mess. I wish I had repressed memory. I remember everything, though lately I seem to be losing the knack for names, dates, and places. I don't sound like I'm having a problem? Good. I'd hate to get Alzheimer's at such an early age.

Let's begin with what I knew when I met with Jake the Grape. The defense lawyer had offered $600. Since Jake was a defense lawyer before he became a judge and was a cheapskate, I assumed his number would also be $600 or an amount close to it. As I had expected with my little ploy, the jerk gave me the number, but knowing the number wasn't the key to outwitting him. In order to move the settlement in my direction, I had to make him *think* I knew his number. My lie was a hook on which I could hang him; it enabled me to take control. Once I had his number, he realized he could settle the case only by convincing the defendant to pay *my* number. He didn't need to know my number; he simply needed to act in a way that would coax my opponent into naming my number without recognizing he was agreeing to what I wanted. In other words, Jake would be my shill.

Picture this. Here's a fresh napkin if you need help. I leave Jake's office and he summons the defense lawyer and the insurance company rep. He doesn't let on what happened in our meeting. Instead, he tells them I agreed to his secret number and now they must agree. They want to know the number. No, Jake says, they have to trust him, they have to agree to the number before knowing it—the game he tried to play with me. The defense attorney tells Jake—he's thinking out loud—that I demanded $5,000, which he rejected, so the amount must be smaller. Jake tells them he is on their side; the number is less than $5,000. The lawyer and the insurance rep look at each other, uncertain what to say, like two guys at a party who want to hit on the same pretty girl; they want to believe that if Jake got me to agree to his number, sight unseen, it must be a good number for them. They say OK, what's the number? Now Jake is the uncertain one. He remembers that I would agree to the number the defense lawyer mentioned. He asks them to guess the number, laughing like he's only fooling around. The lawyer is happy to go along because he believes he has a settlement and it doesn't matter what number he chooses. If he guesses wrong, what's the harm? This is his chance to make Jake feel good, to show Jake he appreciates what he's done. Then the next time he has a case before him things will go well again. So the lawyer picks $4,000, more than what he is convinced Jake secured for the settlement. Jake can't believe it; he wants to tell the lawyer he's the biggest idiot who ever came into his office. He laughs uncontrollably, flush with understanding how I snookered him, how I manipulated him. One thing about Jake, he understands manipulation, appreciates it even he's the one being manipulated. The lawyer—what a sap—is grinning; he thinks that Jake laughing is a sign the figure is much lower. The insurance company rep, not as stupid as the lawyer, speaks in a faint voice, as he will when he explains to the claims adjuster what happened. "The settlement is $4,000, isn't it?"

I ran into Jake a year later at a restaurant. He came over to my table and without saying hello went into a rant. He wanted to embarrass me in front of my guest, the chairman of the bar association litigation committee. He wanted him to hear how I had played fast and loose with the system, as if I were a traitor. I said I did the best I could for the client, which is what

I thought a lawyer was supposed to do. He said I had tried to corrupt the system.

Corrupt. What a laugh. You can't corrupt what's already corrupt. Two years later, he was caught accepting a bribe from a lawyer in the secret employ of the Feds. The lawyer represented a company that the residents of DuPage County sued for polluting the Des Plaines River. The lawyer paid Jake $10,000 to write his number in the envelope. He was arrested before he got to play his silly Carnac the Magnificent game.

Connie, why did you say $4,000? You don't know? The key is in the clue I gave you. When the defense lawyer offered $600 and I failed to lower my $5,000 demand, it meant I wouldn't take less than $4,000. Otherwise, I would have lowered the demand, thereby encouraging the defense lawyer to believe I was interested in splitting the difference and settling for between $2,000 and $2500. The art of negotiation: cut the baby in half. See, your intuition is better than you thought.

Ready for your reward? You wanted to know why I was waiting for you on that first night. You were Tommy Glynn's last hope. Sam was desperate. He knew the judge wouldn't consider your father's affidavit. He needed corroboration and you were the corroboration. What your father told you five years ago wasn't corroboration—no more competent evidence than his affidavit. We were counting on you to give us direct evidence, but when Sam talked to your father, he said you were still in the throes of long-term denial. You couldn't acknowledge what you knew. Your father's an interesting fellow, Connie. I don't know if you realize how perceptive he is. Sam told me he asked him, "How do we get your son to find his memory?" and your father answered, "You have to get him to find his heart."

He knew you were under the car. Remember the mirror in the shop, over the tool desk. A toggle bolt had fallen out of the wall, and the mirror was hanging at an angle. While he was giving instructions to the kid, he saw you in the mirror holding the wrench like you were trying to strangle it.

He said you were planning a trip to New York. You weren't sure you should go. He agreed to speak with your wife, tell her to encourage you to make the trip. No, he didn't tell her about his conversation with Sam or, for that matter, the affidavit. It wasn't necessary. How could I be straight with you? If I had told you the truth in the beginning, you might never have talked to me. You wouldn't have given yourself a chance to remember.

I volunteered to contact you. Sam was spending day and night on research, trying to develop more arguments to fight the extradition. And my ego told me I could be clever enough to get under your skin and force the memory out of you. Sad to say, it's too little too late. Your testimony won't help. It's evidence of your father's guilt, but it doesn't exonerate Tommy. Though your father has agreed to testify in Belfast, there's no guarantee it will do any good. Tommy's escape from Long Kesh was a separate crime. He's a bit like Jean Valjean. Only problem is, there's no Javier. Only the faceless law.

You're not satisfied, I see. I shouldn't be surprised. I've created a lifetime of mysteries for you to solve. What else can I tell you? Sam left Philadelphia a year ago. He sold his practice to his partners. He was getting tired of playing the law game every day, and he could represent Tommy from anywhere. Molly was from Boston; it was the logical place to relocate. They rented a house in Newton, near the Brookline line, not far from the cemetery where they had the funeral service. Why hadn't the clerk at the Philadelphia Inquirer heard of him? How should I know? Call the University of Pennsylvania Law School if you don't believe me. Last semester he was a guest lecturer in criminal law and procedure. Ask for Professor Tony Klein; he'll confirm what I'm telling you.

Interested in anyone else? Peter Marinelli? Sad, sad, sad . . . he'll spend the rest of his life in jail because the Feds are convinced he's the way to get at Salvatore. As you know, Sam was representing Peter . . . oh, you didn't know. He was, and . . . I don't want to talk about it. Too depressing.

One more question. I'm exhausted. You won't mind if we skip dinner, will you? Smith Corcoran? Yes, he's the man in the suit who's been following us. Sorry. Frankly, he has nothing better to do. He's assigned to the Domestic Terrorism Unit of the FBI. He's paranoid, even more paranoid than you are. He was worried Sam would change his mind, not testify at the hearing in Boston, and pester me to give him daily reports on Sam's moods. Then he overheard me telling you the Eudie Lufman story and . . . it made him crazier, like the story was code for something or other and you're a secret agent out to ruin him.

OK, I'm done for the night. Regardless of what you may believe, Connie, there is no plot, no conspiracy, and no sinister vortex sucking you in against your will. I know you've been following me here and then there, hiding behind statues and trees, sneaking through alleys, calling newspapers, hotels, and law offices. Sam was my friend. He was trying to do what was best for Tommy Glynn and Peter Marinelli. He relied on my help from time to time. And I offered to speak to you.

With this last comment, he stopped talking. Patrick put another drink in front of him. He pushed it away.

"Now I have a question for you," he said.

"Yes."

"Why do you suppose they let your father go?"

"He betrayed Tommy."

He smiled and patted me on the back. "Oh, Connie, wouldn't it be nice if life were so simple?"

Before I could say anything he was gone. I reached in my pocket for money, but Patrick shook his head. "Drinks are on me," he said.

CHAPTER NINE

May 18, 1998

IN THE MORNING, *I called the University of Pennsylvania Law School and asked for Professor Tony Klein. His administrative assistant, Bertha (the same Bertha who had worked in the placement office thirty years earlier?), said he was away on sabbatical. I asked her if she knew Brandt. I heard her stifling a sob as she said it was a terrible tragedy, he had everything to live for, a beautiful wife and daughter, and so on. I said a quick goodbye and ended the call.*

I tried Mary, but there was no answer. I took out my notebook and began to draw another chart, though it was an obvious excuse to avoid facing the truth. I was responsible for Tommy Glynn's incarceration, as responsible as my father was, if not more so. Whatever his reason for naming Tommy Glynn, it could not excuse me. I had been a coward, for years hiding from the awful truth.

I put away my notebook and got the recorder from my jacket. I sat at the desk and replayed the previous night's tape. Moving the tape forward and backward, I listened for an hour, searching for what I did not know. Had he answered all my questions? I thought not.

As the tape spun to an end, I looked up from the desk to see Cuchulainn leap onto the front windowsill. Jimmy and Fischel were walking to the front door. The day's adventure was to get an early start.

This was a good idea, don't you think. You'll talk to someone else for a change. Maybe he'll answer the rest of your questions.

Traffic is bad. How long do you think, Jimmy? An hour? Oh well. What should we talk about? Who? Sure, I can tell you about Gordon, my not so beloved law partner.

I first met Gordon while I was at the Litowitz firm. The firm represented a real estate developer who treated the law like a parlor game, but he always wanted to make the first move. The developer hired the firm to negotiate a land deal. The price was right because the county, represented by Gordon, had designated part of the land as wetlands; the flora, fauna, and resident insect population were entitled to government protection, raising the cost of development—the client wanted to build a townhouse development. Shortly after the closing, the client showed up at the firm's office with a spreadsheet. He wanted to know the penalty for violating the conservation laws. We told him $50,000 per violation; he penciled in the amount under the column for miscellaneous costs.

The bulldozers were at work the next morning. On his way home a county selectman saw the trees coming down and called Gordon. By the time Gordon got to court with an injunction motion, the bulldozers were gone and the wetlands were dry. I told the judge my client understood the consequences of his conduct and was prepared to immediately write a check for the statutory fine.

I rode down the elevator with Gordon. He was seething as if *his* backyard had been bulldozed. "How can you represent scum like that?" he asked me. I considered the various possible answers: it's my job, everyone is entitled to representation, the client paid the statutory penalty so what's the big deal, and so on, but I knew any answer would just make him angrier. I've never believed in rubbing opponents' noses in their Pyrrhic victories.

Later that day, Gordon called to apologize for his surliness and complimented me for conceding that my client had violated the law—talk about damning me with faint praise! He invited me for lunch at the Empire Room. In years past it had operated as a supper club—as had its art deco twin at the Waldorf Astoria in New York—featuring the top acts on the nightclub circuit. As the late 1960s rolled into the 1970s, the nightclubs and their middle class patrons migrated to the suburbs. In Chicago, gone were Mr. Kelly's and the London House, both converted into restaurants, followed by the Empire Room, dark at night but still open for lunch. Its clientele, semi-retired lawyers and bankers, liked the floral arrangements on the tables, the piped-in music, the slow service from waiters even older than the diners, and the dessert cart filled with stale cakes, wrinkled fruit, and melted ice cream.

Gordon was on the make. He had worked for Rosen & Schine, a mid-size corporate firm, since graduating from Northwestern Law School in 1970. He had been planning his departure from Rosen & Schine for a year. The Federal Trade Commission was investigating one of the firm's clients, a steel company, for conspiring to fix the price of scrap metal. Gordon suggested to its general counsel that he would give the company a break on his hourly rate if he got the company's litigation business. The general counsel said he would consider the proposal, provided that Gordon had a partner who could handle matters when he was unavailable.

Gordon ordered lunch for me like I was his ingénue, to be catered, seduced, and then—to give a hint of what was to come—discarded. He ordered truffles, chateaubriand steak for two, baked potatoes, and a Spanish wine I had never heard of.

Gordon was an expert in using self-deprecation to boast, a kind of *one-downmansship.* He said he was smarter than his law aptitude test results showed, he was better looking than Jackie's brother—who was homely—he was a better golfer than his eighteen handicap, and he would have won more cases if his firm had hired better associates to help him. I tried to massage his ego, saying I wasn't as smart as my law aptitude test results indicated, I was not as handsome as my brother-in-law, I was a worse golfer than my twenty handicap, and if I had delegated more work to associates I would have won more cases. His face lit up like Paul Revere's lantern, though Gordon's light was its own warning. He ordered champagne and asked me if I'd like to start a firm with him. I accepted before the cork was out of the bottle. I also agreed the name should be Lazarus & Schaechter. He said Standard English required that the name with the fewest syllables come first. In my drunken dizziness I did say Schaechter had fewer syllables than Lazarus, but Gordon claimed he meant to say letters rather than syllables.

Why did I accept? Who knows, really. Maybe because I thought I needed a change and was too cowardly to divorce my wife. Maybe I saw myself as the senior partner of a law firm and was too impatient to wait my turn at Litowitz. Maybe the law business had gone to my head.

What have I forgotten? You want to know what he looked like? A minor oversight because he never looked the same from hour to hour. I called him plastic man—not to his face, of course. He manufactured his expressions and was able to do funny things with his nose and mouth to make them seem smaller or larger. Each smile, frown, arched eyebrow, and squint was calculated to achieve a certain effect.

Jimmy, where are we? God, I don't remember the last time I was so anxious to get to a prison.

Indeed, where were we? We could have been anywhere, even Belfast, seemingly endless blocks of row houses, front yards with tiny gardens of tulips, daffodils, and begonias. Evidence of children was about: bicycles, tricycles, toy shovels and small pails, an occasional swing or stroller. On each corner was a grocery store, tavern, or dry cleaner, older men and women walking in and out.

Jimmy stopped the limousine in front of one such grocery store. "I'll be back in a minute," he said.

He paused at a table with assorted fruits and flowers wrapped in plastic bags. He took an apple and went inside; there, he tossed a bill on the counter. The proprietor, a slight Asian man, reached above his head and removed a pack of cigarettes from a rack. He took the bill and kneeled out of sight, then to rise a few seconds later with a package wrapped in brown paper. He handed it and the cigarettes to Jimmy, who left without waiting for change.

"Don't ask, Connie," Fischel said, as Jimmy got in the car. "Never question a limo driver about pick-ups or deliveries."

Gordon and I were partners for five years, hard for me to believe when I remember what happened on our first anniversary. It was a Thursday evening, a week before my thirty-fifth birthday, when he came into my office and said he wanted to buy me a drink. I knew something was up; the last time he bought me anything was the courtship lunch at the Empire Room. Was there something special he wanted to discuss? I asked, and he gave me that universal smile of his, the one he used for every occasion other than a funeral.

He pushed the martini in front of me and raised his glass of draft beer. "A toast," he said.

"What are we toasting?"

"To making twice as much money next year."

"I'll drink to that."

"Commitment," he said. He took a healthy sip and swirled the beer around his teeth like mouthwash.

"I'll also drink to that."

"For example, the Russian Jews."

"What about them?"

"I have a commitment to them."

"That's nice."

"I've been appointed President of the Chicago chapter of 'Save the Russian Jews.'"

"Congratulations."

"You should get involved."

"You know me, Gordon, I'm not into joining organizations."

He put his glass on the bar. "That's the trouble with you. You lack commitment."

"I'm committed to our law practice."

"Jackie has been a real pain of late."

"How so?"

"She wants this, she wants that, she wants everything. I got her a mink for Christmas; now she wants a sable. I say, I thought you wanted a new diamond ring and she says why can't I have both."

"Can't blame her for asking."

"She thinks our split should be sixty-forty," he said, replacing his smile with his professional look—pressed lips, grim.

"An extra ten percent won't be enough to buy her the ring and the sable, at least not the ring or the sable I suspect she wants."

"She loves me."

"My wife loves me and doesn't think I should make more than you. She's also happy with her one carat ring and wool coat."

"So what do you say?" He asked the question as if he were offering me another martini.

I thought of what I would do if I were representing someone other than myself in the negotiation. "I already talked it over with him and he won't agree. Sorry."

Who is he?" He asked, bewildered.

"Me."

"You're not taking me seriously."

"You're right, Gordon."

"You never take me seriously." He was now working on a cross between a pout and a smirk.

"It's hard to take you seriously when your wife puts you up to changing our deal."

"Deals change."

"Not this one."

"What am I going to tell her?" Just like that, he was in his forlorn mode.

"Tell her your partner is an asshole."

Gordon laughed. "She already knows you're an asshole."

"Then tell her what she doesn't know."

"What's that?"

"That you're an asshole."

Jimmy drove the car off the two-lane road into a large parking lot. At the entrance was a sign: Visitor's Parking-Riker's Island. Beyond it, the road crossed a bridge over a quarter-mile neck of water to the island. Across the bay to the east I could see airplanes landing and taking off.

"LaGuardia Airport," Fischel said. "It must drive the prisoners crazy to see the planes. All those people free to go anywhere they please."

We left Jimmy in the car and walked onto the bridge. At the other end, electronic gates blocked the entrance to the complex. Guards were stationed in two booths on either side. Behind the gates were a series of mid-rise brick buildings and a patchwork of streets. On our side of the gates a road branched off to the right and passed two one-story gray-stone buildings that faced the airport. A city bus stopped in front of one and passengers alighted to join a long line leading to a locked metal door. The front door to the other building was open, but only a few people were going in and out.

In the middle of the bridge Fischel stopped and leaned against the railing. "I love watching planes. When I was a kid, I used to pester Albert to take me to the airport."

"I first saw an airplane when I was eighteen," I said. "It was shortly after my father was arrested. I had saved a little money from my earnings at his shop. One morning I packed a small bag, a few clothes, and a couple of books and took a taxi—"

"Where were you headed?"

"Nowhere special. I was not sure I wanted to leave. I was testing myself."

"What was passing the test? Staying or leaving?"

"Staying. It would have been wrong to abandon my family."

"What about now? Do you pass the test by staying or leaving?"

"I have not decided."

We continued our walk across the bridge. Between the bus stop and the first building was a bench. Fischel told me to wait while he went inside the open building to get a visitor's pass.

Rules, they can drive you crazy. Because I'm a lawyer, I don't have to wait in line. I could go right through the back door of the other building and take the "3" bus to Tommy's cellblock. But you're a mere relative—I told them you were his brother-in-law—and we can't go inside until one o'clock when regular visitor hours begin.

Excuse me for a moment. I see someone I know.

In the middle of the visitor line that now stretched for more than fifty yards, Fischel tapped an old black man on the shoulder. The man turned and they embraced, slapping each other on the back, laughing and shaking hands. Fischel pointed at me, and the black man waved. They talked for a bit and then Fischel came back to the bench.

"That was McKinley Washington," Fischel said.

"The man you taught to read?"

"Yes."

"He is quite old."

"As well he should be. It's been thirty-eight years since that summer."

"What is he doing here?"

"His grand-nephew from his sister's side is here on a minor drug charge. McKinley says he's about to get out. The police, no surprise, arrested the wrong guy."

"Fischel, please answer a question for me."

"Here we go again."

"I am growing used to the coincidences. But did you know this man was in New York before you told me his story?"

"Yes."

"Why not tell me? I would have appreciated the coda."

"If what you want is a coda, stick around until the end of the week."

Don't worry. We've got time. McKinley will save us a spot in line. Is your recorder still on? Good. I'm ready to focus on the cases that became my life's work as a lawyer. The death of me would be more accurate. Investment litigation. Probably sounds dull to you, but it was anything but dull.

I got my first such case from Gordon. He asked me to meet with Dr. Mort Harris, his neighbor and golfing buddy. Gordon said Mort needed a lawyer to represent him on a contingency, a fee arrangement Gordon hated. He believed lawyers should be paid for their time, win or lose. His real reason, I suspected, was that if I lost Mort's case, he would have another excuse to change our profit split. And if I won or settled the case, he'd take credit for having brought the client to the firm.

Mort's story began a couple of years earlier. His wife had been hounding him to buy a new and bigger house in a better area of Highland Park. But his dental practice, operating out of a cubbyhole of an office in a rundown office building, produced barely enough money to pay the mortgage on their existing home. Mort started looking for investments that could produce large returns.

One Saturday, a year before we started the firm, Gordon's golfing foursome had an opening and Gordon invited Lester Scheinberg to play. Lester, the president of the synagogue where Gordon belonged and who had appointed Gordon to run the Save the Russian Jews campaign, was the senior partner of a firm specializing in corporate and securities law. Of late the firm had been concentrating on tax shelters: investments structured to generate tax credits and deductions, so large that in some instances an investor could make a profit from the tax refunds even while losing what he invested.

By the end of the golf round Mort convinced Lester he needed caps on his front teeth to improve his smile, and Lester convinced Mort he could reduce his income taxes and generate enough money to make the down payment on a new house. With Gordon playing the part of matchmaker, they set a date to meet Lester's client, Joseph Korn, at Biggs.

Biggs, like many restaurants of its type, was on its way out as a place to wine and dine wives, girlfriends, and clients, as the typically out-of-shape American man could no longer tolerate French food. Korn had been a restaurateur in New York—before he realized he could make more money selling investments—and spent the first part of the dinner entertaining his company with stories of the cognoscenti who dined at his restaurant and invested in his deals.

Korn knew how to sell, knew the power of appearances even if the appearance was of someone else. He had brought with him a tall blonde, a recent arrival from Sweden, who smiled a lot as she affectionately rubbed his arm and said how much she loved his mind. A good thing, for Korn was an ugly man in his late fifties, with a freckled forehead, oversized nose, and fat lips.

Mort was hooked before Korn explained the deal. But what a deal it was. Korn had seen a way to make a quick profit. He had formed a company called Athena Art that purchased the plates from which lithographs are made. He then used the ten-percent investment tax credit to offset the purchase price. Turning ten percent into one hundred percent was a neat trick indeed.

The numbers dazzled Mort, had the appeal of alchemy, a chance to get something for nothing. Korn's company, Athena, would acquire a lithographic plate for $200,000, paying $5,000 and signing a note for $195,000. The note was to be a non-recourse obligation, paid from ninety-eight percent of sales revenue, leaving the other two percent for Athena. Athena would then assign this purchase contract to Mort; he would pay $10,000 to Athena and assume the obligation under the note for the two percent share in the revenues. Mort would end up with an investment tax credit of $20,500, giving him an immediate cash profit of $10,500.

Mort ordered five after dinner drinks and agreed to buy one plate after each drink. In total, he would pay $50,000 in cash and $975,000 in notes, yielding him $102,500 in investment tax credits and a deduction of more than $25,000 for depreciation (based on a useful life of forty years for the lithographic plates). Since Mort was in the fifty percent tax bracket, the deduction saved him an additional $12,500 in taxes, which together with the tax credit gave him a total profit in the first year of $65,000, enough to give his wife the go-ahead to buy the new house.

Mort wasn't satisfied. He said he wanted to make more money but couldn't afford to buy additional plates. Lester had an idea—what else are lawyers for? Mort could contact friends, neighbors, and fellow dentists to interest them in the investment. He, Lester, would help Mort prepare the necessary documents. Korn was happy to go along with Lester's plan—unbeknownst to Mort, he had already agreed to pay Lester a commission on Mort's investment—and said he would pay the same five percent commission he gave his salesmen in New York. Gordon was too skittish to partake of this deal, thank God.

During the next two weeks, Mort referred twenty dentists to Korn and earned $50,000 in commissions. He used the money to buy his wife a new diamond ring, which greatly annoyed Gordon's Jackie.

Korn left one important fact out of his sales pitch—he was under investigation. The IRS had organized a task force to investigate Korn and other promoters for using investment tax credits to create windfalls for greedy investors. As you might have already surmised, the structure of Korn's deal could be used in a host of other businesses. There were Korn clones selling negatives for movies, master tapes for records, machines to make stamps, windmills in the California desert, printing plates for books, and coal mining equipment. Investors were receiving notices from the IRS that their investment credits and deductions were disallowed and assessing them the saved taxes plus interest and a whopping penalty of thirty percent of the tax credits. And soon after Mort and his fellow dentists had filed their tax returns taking the credits and deductions, they received similar notices.

Mort consulted a tax lawyer. He learned to his dismay that interest would continue to run on the assessment during a court battle and the IRS might seek an additional penalty for negligence. Mort decided to pay rather than fight, though he'd have to stop construction on the backyard swimming pool, relinquish his membership in the country club, and raise his rates for filling cavities. As if that wasn't aggravation enough, the other investors also received notices from the IRS and were looking to him to get their money back. The next Saturday, on the first tee at his final round of golf at the club, he told Gordon he wanted to sue. Gordon told Mort he had just the man for the job, which of course was me.

The law says the aggrieved party in a breach of contract suit is entitled to damages equal to what would have been earned had the contract been performed—*benefit of the bargain*—whereas the victim of a fraud may recover only what he lost. If you compare the case against Korn with the typical contract case, this rule makes sense. The government, not the contract, gave Mort the tax credits and deductions. And though Korn used the sales projections to interest Mort in the investment, the contract didn't promise a particular level of sales.

Focusing on what Mort lost, I made the following calculation: $45,000 (he had received $5,000 from the sale of lithographs), $19,500 in tax penalties for the disallowed investment tax credit and $1500 in interest on the penalties for a total of $61,500. I couldn't claim damages representing the lost tax credits; but for the deal, Mort wouldn't have received the tax credits. The law doesn't allow the recovery of legal fees, so a victory at trial would be reduced by the one-third contingency fee, netting him at most $44,000, less than his loss.

Korn was not defenseless. The prospectus included a host of disclaimers, warnings, and descriptions of the risks associated with the investment: the projected sales revenues might not be achieved, the IRS might successfully challenge the legitimacy of the tax credits and deductions, the market for lithographs was highly competitive, and art galleries might decide not to carry the lithographs. It would do no good for Mort to claim he was lulled by fine wine and the seductive ambience of Biggs into not giving as much weight to these warnings as perhaps he should have, since the prospectus cautioned him not to rely on anything he was told that was inconsistent with what was contained in the document. The other plaintiffs were in worse shape. They hadn't gone to Biggs, had never met Korn, and if they were charmed by anyone it was Mort, whose credibility with the jury wasn't going to be helped when it heard about the commissions he received for putting his friends into the deal.

Mort's dual role of investor and ad hoc salesman worried me. I told Mort I had a conflict of interest. How could I represent the other investors who might have a claim against him? He understood the problem and suggested I represent only him. But the damages for his case weren't large enough to justify prosecuting just his case. I was as much a prisoner of the almighty dollar as the next lawyer; a $20,000 fee for what might turn out to be several years' work and a lengthy trial was hardly a cheery prospect.

Enterprising fellow that he was, Mort came to my office a few days later with signed letters from the other investors waiving the conflict of interest. Regardless of whether they tabbed Mort as a villain in league with Korn, they knew Mort lacked the money to pay them back. More to the point, most lawyers would insist on being paid by the hour. The one thing neither Mort nor the others wanted was an obligation for legal fees.

What a case! I was representing a bunch of adherents to the "something for nothing" religion. But Korn was no better. In promoting an investment that would reap him a financial windfall, he had exploited the all too human, all too American, character flaw: the desire to make money without working for it. This was what the law had wreaked: a lawsuit between the stupidly greedy and the cleverly immoral. In a battle between two such undeserving combatants where would justice be found?

Before filing a lawsuit, it's a good idea to know whether you can collect any money if you win. I wasn't surprised to learn that Athena was a corporate sieve and money it received never stayed in the company, but I was chagrined that Korn, despite his trappings of wealth—dinner every night at restaurants like Biggs, residence in a fifteen-bedroom apartment on Park Avenue in New York, and gross profits of thirty million dollars in the art deals sold around the country during a two year period—had no assets; he wasn't even a shareholder in Athena. A trust he had created for his children owned the stock. The trustee was his cousin, a maintenance man at the New York Athletic Club, who hired Korn—at Korn's direction, to be sure— as a consultant for a million dollars per year.

I was so discouraged I wanted to back out of the case. I told Gordon that we'd have to return the retainers we received to cover expenses, but he said, "We deserve to be paid for your work in determining that we can't bring the suit." When I said his analysis was unlikely to impress the Attorney Registration and Disciplinary Commission—the Illinois guardians of legal morals—he shrugged and said, "Then file the fucking suit and let the chips fall where they may."

In a funk, I sat in my office and tried to figure out what to do. Who could I sue that had money? Better still, who could I threaten to sue that would settle? It didn't take me long to realize who it was.

I wrote the complaint and gave it to my secretary. As Gordon was walking out to lunch, he saw the first page sitting next to her typewriter and lost his appetite. He stormed into my office, huffing, puffing, and grunting.

"What are you doing?" he asked.

"What am I doing?"

"You know what you're doing."

On the off chance he was paying me a compliment, I said, "Thank you."

"Don't play games with me. How can you sue Lester? He's a friend."

"Your friend, not mine. Besides, he was working for Korn. He introduced Korn and the investment to Mort. He's a lawyer and must have known the deal was bullshit."

"Using that logic, you could name me as a defendant."

"Even *I* draw the line somewhere."

Gordon was so flustered he rushed out of the office, cursing under his breath.

A few minutes later the telephone rang. Lester's secretary was on the phone. "Mr. Scheinberg would like to have lunch with you," she said.

"When?"

"Now," she said, as if I were an underling in his firm.

I wasn't going to stand on ceremony. "Where?"

Le Perroquet was located in the ritzy section of Chicago, off Michigan Avenue—called the Magnificent Mile, magnificent if you marvel at high-priced stores, towering condominiums, and the best hotels. Set on the second floor of a three-story Victorian townhouse—above a jewelry store and below a rare coin dealer—Le Perroquet was, to quote a local food critic, a "dining experience." That means the size of the plate is inversely proportional to the size of the food portions, you can't order wine by the glass, the menu is in French, the waiters act as if they are doing you a favor, and the delay between ordering and receiving your food leaves plenty of time to get drunk.

Lester was waiting at a table when I arrived, a scarf tied around his neck like a hangman's noose, an American flag pinned to his lapel, and one of those watches where you can see the inner works—in this case, all platinum.

Lester was the kind of lawyer I hoped I wasn't and wouldn't become: self-righteous, unctuous, convinced that the world would be a lesser place without his presence. He had hired a public relations firm to promote him to the community. Every week you saw his name mentioned in the Tribune—usually, in Kup's column, Chicago's top gossip columnist. He was the president of Chicago Big Brothers, a board member of several charities, and attorney for the Highland Park School Board, the Little City Foundation for retarded kids, and the American Civil Liberties Union, that is, when he wasn't representing shady tax shelter promoters. His public face was unblemished; his soul was badly scarred.

The waiter listed the appetizers and then told us which ones *he* would order for us. First up was a puddle of cold soup for Lester and a salad consisting of a single green leaf for me. In between sips, he regaled me with his struggle against adversity, including how he overcame the death of his father when he was thirteen, worked his way through night law school as a bartender, and supported his invalid mother.

"So why did you wreck it by representing a scoundrel like Joseph Korn?" I asked, thinking I could fight self-righteousness by acting self-righteously.

"We both represent scoundrels."

"Dentists drill holes in teeth; Korn drills holes in pockets."

"I wrote a full and fair prospectus," he said, staring into his soup as if he were reading tealeaves.

"There's a difference between saying an investment is risky and saying an investment is a sure loser."

Lester took his napkin and lifted it to his face. I thought he was going to dab his mouth, but he rubbed his eyes instead. "I've worked hard to get where I am," he said.

"Your eyes are red."

"I'm an emotional person."

I looked around the restaurant, worried he was making a scene. Two old ladies with faces as pink as the carnations they wore were sneaking glances at us, probably thinking we were gay lovers having a squabble.

"I owe it to my clients to sue everyone who participated in the sale," I said.

Now, he did dab his mouth. "Shall we order?"

"Let the waiter do it; he thinks it's his job."

The waiter ordered me a steak, even let me say how I wanted it cooked. For Lester, who was thin and athletic, he ordered escargot. I liked the steak all right, but there weren't enough potatoes to enable me to form an opinion: only three the size of walnuts clumped together on a saucer painted with dancing maidens. Lester saw I was still hungry when I finished and offered me his last escargot. I told him I wanted a martini—our bottle of wine was still breathing—and he clapped his hands like he was a camp director. The waiter came over, heard my order, and said something uncomplimentary about my palate. I withdrew my request and asked him to pour me a glass of wine. He gave me a dirty look and I said, "Can't you see. The wine isn't breathing. It died an hour ago."

For dessert, Lester had an ice-cream concoction that looked like an Eskimo Pie off the stick. I picked at the miniature butter cookies the waiter put on the table.

"Earlier," Lester said, "you were talking about duty to your clients."

"Was I?"

"You said you should sue everyone who participated in the sale."

"Yes."

"And who would that be, besides me?"

"Korn."

"Go on."

"His company Athena."

255

"Aren't you leaving out someone?"

"Who?"

"Your partner."

"Gordon? What did he have to do with it?"

"He introduced me to Dr. Harris."

"I wouldn't say an introduction on the golf course is participating in the sale of lithographic plates."

He chomped at the Eskimo Pie, leaving bits of chocolate on his lips.

"What would you say if he received a finder's fee?"

I pointed a finger at him, ready to go on the offensive, but he thought I was drawing his attention to the piece of chocolate that dangled from his mouth. He stuck his tongue out and sucked the chocolate in, quickly like a frog. "Thanks," he said. He looked like a clown who had unaccountably used black instead of red paint on his lips.

"How much did Gordon get?" I asked.

"What's the difference? If you name me in the suit, I'll cross-claim against him."

"So much for honor among thieves."

"I'm not a thief," he said

"Then so much for honor."

"We're talking litigation here, not honor," he said, a statement impervious to rebuttal.

⚖

I stopped at two bars on the way back to the office. I didn't want to be sober when I confronted Gordon. But when I got to the office, he was gone. Jersey told me he went to a "Save the Russian Jews" meeting. I knew better. It was his night for a romp with the mistress.

I called Mort. "I'm withdrawing from your case," I said.

"Why?"

"I can't sue Lester."

"Why not? If it wasn't for him, I'd never have met Korn."

"He says if I name him, he'll sue Gordon."

"Fine with me."

"You don't understand, Mort. Suing Lester is suing my partner."

"Is there a law against that?"

Mort wasn't so dumb. "There are unwritten laws."

"Name one."

"Suing your partner."

He was breathing heavily "Who do you think you are, fucking Sam Spade?"

"It's the way it has to be, Mort."

"I'll tell you how it has to be. You're my lawyer until I say otherwise. This is your problem, not mine. I have to hang up. Got a broken filling to repair."

"Did you crack a tooth?"

"I'll crack yours if you don't get my money back."

Mort couldn't stop me from withdrawing. No ethics board would compel me to continue the representation if it meant suing Gordon. And I doubted whether he'd find another lawyer willing to sue Lester.

I called Lester the next morning. "Meet me for breakfast."

"I already ate."

"You'll eat again."

This time I picked the restaurant, a seedy diner next to the train station. Instead of old ladies in frilly dresses, the place was crowded with men wearing tee shirts that last fit them fifty pounds ago.

I dug into my omelet, combination style like a Marinelli's pizza, stuffed with pastrami, salami, corn beef, and bacon.

"That's no good for you," Lester said. He was dressed in the same suit as the day before, but wearing a different colored scarf.

"What's the deductible on your malpractice insurance?" I asked.

"Why do you want to know?"

"I'm still planning to name you in the suit."

"I don't believe you. Partners don't screw their partners."

"You'll have to notify your insurance carrier. It will settle for the deductible."

"The same goes for you. What's your deductible?"

"$25,000."

His eyes widened. "Mine is $100,000." I felt a sudden twinge. I kicked my self under the table. This was not the time to feel sorry for him.

"That's a nice number," I said.

"We're a big firm and we do securities work. For a smaller deductible, we would have to pay a shitload in premiums."

"See, progress. You'll pay $100,000, you'll convince Korn to come up with the same amount, and I'll get Gordon to throw in $25,000."

"Why should I?"

"Because you can't be sure I won't sue. And if I do, you'll pay the deductible to your insurance company or to me. Either way your premiums will triple. If you settle now, no notice to your insurance carrier, problem disappears, and life goes on like nothing happened."

"You're a bastard."

"I could say 'takes one to know one,' but that would be so childish, don't you agree, Lester?"

He picked up his fork. For a moment, I thought he would run it through my hand. But he just wanted a piece of my omelet.

"Help yourself," I said.

"Did the dentists give you authority to settle?"

"You tell me we have a deal and I'll get the authority."

He chewed on his scarf for a moment and then said he had to call his partner. He left the diner and got into his car. I wondered whether I had outwitted myself. I couldn't be confident Mort would accept a settlement that was less than twenty-five percent of their loss. And who knew what Gordon's reaction would be?

"We have a deal," Lester said when he rejoined me. "If you get Gordon to go along."

"Relax," I said, wanting to give myself the same command. "I saved the rest of my omelet for you."

⚖

Gordon wasn't at the office. I called Mort. His nurse said he was seeing a patient and would call me back. Then Gordon walked in.

"How was your lunch with Lester?"

"We settled the case."

"Funny, he didn't tell me."

"Not at lunch. At breakfast."

"Wonderful," he said, wringing his hands. "How did you convince him that Korn should pay?"

"That was the easy part."

Gordon was trying to keep his smile in place, but he wasn't succeeding. "What was the hard part?"

"Listening to Lester cry about his career going up in smoke if I sued him."

His smile blossomed again. "Fabulous. You're not going to sue him."

"Nope."

Gordon stood behind me, kneading my shoulders like he was a masseur. "I knew I was smart to want you for a partner. How much is Korn paying?"

"$100,000."

"Seems low."

"Lester is matching it."

"What?"

"The deductible on his malpractice insurance. I could have demanded more but it wouldn't have been fair to you."

Gordon removed his hands. "I don't get it."

"If I asked him for more, it would have cost you more."

"More?"

"More than your $25,000 deductible."

"You said I would pay $25,000?"

"What's wrong? You got that much in commissions."

"He told you?"

"He told me."

He sat on the end of the desk and lit a cigar.

I had to admire his stage presence, even if he was playing the lead in a flop. "I'm glad you think it's cause for celebration," I said.

"I hope you have $12,500."

"Lester threatened to sue you, not me."

"We're partners."

"I'm not your partner in the past."

"At the rate you're going, you won't be my partner in the present."

"I saved your ass."

"Yeah, then kiss my ass."

"I don't think so, Gordon."

He slid off the desk. "What did Mort say?"

"I haven't told him yet."

"Don't. Not until I make a call."

He returned five minutes later. "You can call Mort. Korn will pay $125,000. You don't need my $25,000."

"Says who?"

"Says Lester. He got Korn on the line. It's done."

"You're reimbursing Korn for the $25,000, aren't you?"

A quick flash of his eyes said I was right. I knew he wouldn't admit it, though. "Just get the case settled," he said. "And don't go spreading your wild theories around town. I have a reputation to maintain."

When he left the office I called Mort. He wasn't happy about the proposed settlement. He refused to agree until I made him an offer he couldn't refuse. I said he didn't have to pay the contingency fee.

"What the hell did you do that for?" Gordon screamed when I told him.

"Small price to pay to get out of an impossible situation."

"What's impossible?"

"I couldn't represent Mort without suing Lester and as soon as Lester sued you, I would have had to withdraw. I couldn't represent the other investors for the same reason. So, we wouldn't have made anything on the case. All I did was give up nothing for nothing."

Gordon wasn't smoking a cigar, but it seemed as if cigar smoke was coming out of his nostrils. "You and your goddamn nothings."

As I was walking out of his office, a question occurred to me. "Gordon, do you think lawyers are honorable?"

His eyes narrowed, gauging whether I was serious. I guess he thought I was, because he said, "If you believe there's honor among thieves."

We slipped into line next to McKinley Washington.

"He sure do talk a lot, don't he," McKinley said.

"Yes he does."

"He probably told you his life story by now?"

"By now?"

"You been talking to him for more than a week."

"How did you know?"

I wanted to see Fischel's reaction, but he had wondered off toward the fence that reached from the building to the shoreline.

"He told me about you," McKinley said.

"What did he tell you?"

"That you and him see eye to eye."

Fischel was walking along the fence to the water's edge. "What is he doing?"

"I wouldn't know."

"He told me about you too."

McKinley's face brightened. "Damn!"

"What?"

"Nothing. Just damn! I'd do anything for that man."

At the security desk Fischel asked me for my passport. I gave it to him and walked through the metal detector. The alarm went off, a high-pitched siren that sounded like an ambulance. The guard asked me to step to the side, then patted my clothes and discovered the recorder.

Fischel retrieved my passport while he argued with the guard. Apparently, lawyers were permitted to tape record their conversations with prisoners, and Fischel tried to persuade the guard that the recorder belonged to him. But the guard remained unconvinced and told me I could collect my recorder upon leaving.

When we boarded the bus, Fischel said, "You should have given it to me before we went inside."

"Would you have returned it to me?" I said in jest, though I could as easily have been serious.

The bus stopped in front of a two-story concrete building. McKinley said goodbye and got off.

"Is this a cellblock?" I asked.

"The medical clinic. A guard beat the crap out of his grand-nephew."

"How terrible."

"Being in prison isn't punishment enough for some."

How many surprises does it take before one is beyond surprise? Our stop was at the Anna M. Kross Center, named after a former commissioner of the New York Department of Corrections. We entered through large steel doors to arrive in a spacious lobby enclosed by a floor to ceiling metal partition with a door at one end. A guard ushered the other passengers through the door. "They're family," Fischel said. "They sit in booths and talk to the prisoners through a window. We have to wait for another guard to take us to the lawyer's room."

"Why am I allowed to join you?"

"I told them you were my investigator."

Then the surprise. The guard who came to escort us was none other than Patrick, Murphy's bartender.

"This is my day job," he said as he led us down a long windowless corridor.

"I did not know a foreigner could work in an American prison," I said.

"He can't," Fischel said. "Patrick was born here. Went to Ireland with his family when he was three. He has dual citizenship."

We came to a door and Patrick pressed a button on a wall speaker. He said his name and a buzzer rang. He turned the knob and we walked into the next room. It was small and unfurnished. Each wall had a door with a number on it. "You'll see Tommy in number two," Patrick said and left.

Fischel and I went into the visiting room. An oval table and two chairs took up most of the room. The cork walls gave it the look of a padded cell in a mental institution. "You'll talk to Tommy and I'll wait for you," he said.

"Why?"

"You're the one with questions."

Fischel left and shut the door. I sat at the table and considered what I would say when Tommy entered. Should I apologize for my father? Should I apologize for myself? Perhaps I could then learn what was happening. The door opened and Tommy came in with outstretched hand. I took his hand and stared at his face. It was as if I were looking into a mirror. No wonder the bartender at McInaney's had teased me. Tommy had my brown hair and eyes, pasty white skin, even the same small mole on his neck.

"Well, well," he said, as he sat at the table. "We finally meet."

"I wish it were under different circumstances."

"Next time," he said with a thick accent, much like my own before I attended the university and worked so hard to change who I was.

"I was sorry to learn of the recent court decision."

"Fighting in the courts for thirteen years is too long."

"I know what my Da did."

"Do you?"

I turned away from shame. "Yes, and I did it too."

"Tell me," he said in such a gentle voice I turned back to him.

"I knew from the beginning, from the day it happened. I was at the car shop and overheard him give instructions to the young boy—"

"Seamus."

"Yes, Seamus. That was his name."

"A tragedy. A fine young man he was."

"Why did the bomb explode before he reached the bus station?"

"A loose wire, a spark, you never know with explosives."

We sat in silence for a few moments.

"Say what's on your mind," he said.

"How could my father do such a thing? How could he cause an innocent man to be imprisoned?"

"I am not innocent. Under the Emergency Provisions Act, membership in the IRA was a crime."

"You would not have been sentenced to so many years for membership."

"Maybe not. They were out to get me. Patty gave them the excuse."

"Patty. So you knew my father."

"We used to go to meetings. You rode in the car with us once."

"The painting of the houses. I didn't know it was you in the front seat."

"You didn't look so much like me then."

"Da betrayed a friend. I cannot conceive of a more awful sin."

"There is worse, believe me," he said.

"What could be worse?"

"Betraying a people." He pulled a pack of cigarettes from a pocket in his overalls.

"You can smoke in here?"

"No. But bribes go a long way in American prisons, further than at Long Kesh after they took away our Special Category status and treated us like ordinary criminals."

He offered me a cigarette. Seeing my reluctance, he said, "Don't worry. The guard is a friend."

I laughed and accepted the cigarette. "Yes, and a good bartender."

"Ah, what I would do for a Guinness."

"What does Fischel want with me?"

Now Tommy laughed, a boisterous laugh, as if I had told a grand joke. "What is funny?" I asked.

He pointed at a heating vent in the baseboard. "The walls have ears."

"Then you will not tell me what I want to know."

"What is it you want to know?"

"Why I am here?"

"Because I am here."

"I had hoped only Americans were so cryptic."

He circled the room, pausing now and then to take a drag on his cigarette.

"I enjoyed my time with Patty. We met in '72, just after the internment began. We were evicted from our homes. I used to hang out at his car shop. We talked a lot. He took me to my first meeting. I remember it like yesterday."

He stopped circling and sat again, dropping the cigarette on the floor. "A tough man, your da. He got up in front of everyone and said we had to face choices, hard choices. We had to choose."

"Yes," I said bitterly. "He chose to betray you."

"He chose to save you, Cornelius."

"Save me from what?"

"Tough and hard, like I said. Whatever they dished out he could handle. His legs split apart, pencils and sticks rammed up his ass, cigarettes scorching his skin, no sleep, threats that he'd never see his family; nothing would break him. Except . . . "

"What?"

"They told him the Provos were getting set to kneecap your brothers."

"Kneecap . . . but why?"

"*The interrogator said your brothers liked to go joyriding. He said one night they took you along and picked up a girl in Divis Flats. He said you all took her to a junkyard and raped her.*"

"*Nonsense! We never set foot in Divis Flats. A slum. Why would we go there?*"

"*No matter. Patty knew how easy it was for the Brits to pass word to the Provos. You know what kneecapping rapists got.*"

"*Shot in both legs.*"

"*Through the arteries, crushing the nerves. Crippled for life.*"

"*So that is why . . . .*"

"*Yes.*"

"*Even so, to forgive him for—*"

"*He helped me.*"

"*How?*"

He leaned across the table and took my neck, pulling me close. "*When I escaped,*" he whispered. "*Johnny Delaney.*"

"*Whitey Delaney, the gangster?*"

"*Bridget's father to me. He got a passport under an assumed name and sent it to your da. He met me at the border. It's the last time I saw him.*"

He released my neck. "*There is so much I never knew,*" I said.

"*Maybe you didn't want to know.*"

His comment wounded me, but I was determined to continue. "*Why you? Why did Da accuse you?*"

"*The RUC [the police] wanted me because of Bobby Sands. Bobby and I grew up together in Rathcoole. It was a Protestant neighborhood, a very bad place. So bad, we were scared to walk down the street. One night, potshots were fired at our houses. We couldn't take it anymore and moved into Twinbrook estate. The house was new, too new, no plumbing or electricity. In the rush to move, we left our furniture in Rathcoole. Bobby and I stole a truck and used it to haul beds we took from an abandoned house on Springfield Road. Around this time we joined the IRA. A little later, he was arrested for possession of handguns and they gave him five years at Long Kesh. He got out in '76 and I helped him organize a tenants association. Then he was arrested for bombing a furniture store in Upper Shankill. The charges were phony. Even in the Diplock court where you*" weren't given a jury and had to prove your innocence they couldn't convict him. He had an alibi. We were drinking at a pub when the furniture store was bombed. But they nabbed him anyway. He had left the pub to take a ride home. The RUC stopped the car and found a gun under the floorboard."

"He did not know it was there."

"So what. They still gave him fourteen years."

"You said they wanted you."

"They wanted me because they weren't through with Bobby. He was a leader. After the prisoners were ordered to wear the standard uniforms, he joined the blanket protest, you know, where they had nothing to wear but the blankets in their cells. He wrote articles on toilet paper for the Provo newspaper. They wanted to bring him down. They were convinced he had done the bombing and that I could give them evidence about other bombings."

"You told them nothing."

He smiled. "There was nothing to tell. Bobby was an ordinary man made extraordinary by circumstances."

"Why? Because he starved himself to death?"

"No. Because he stood up for what he believed. He was a natural leader. Don't you remember? He was elected to Parliament while he was in prison."

"It did him no good. It did no one any good. More people dying, more lives wasted."

"I joined the hunger strike too."

"But you survived."

"I was in the twelfth day of my fast when Thomas McElwee died. He was the tenth. He was a good man, an expert with explosives. He used to give me lessons every day, told me how to build powerful bombs with very little material. His death was the last gasp for us. The INLA [National Liberation Army, smaller than the IRA] had enough and withdrew their support. We would have kept going, but the families lost heart. Mum lost Da in prison and she didn't want to lose me. So I stopped. So did the others. Thatcher wasn't going to give an inch."

"Then you planned the escape."

"Yeah. Two years later. Thirty-eight of us took over H-Block 7 and hijacked the truck they used to deliver food. We made it through several checkpoints, ran into trouble at the exit. They caught a bunch of us."

"How did they finally catch you, here in New York?"

He folded his hands in front of him. They were white with pinkish knuckles, like mine. "Let's talk about your father," he said.

"What is there to talk about?"

"You tell me."

"He lied and ruined your life. What more is there to say?"

"He lied for you and your brothers."

"I should forgive him then."

"I do."

"I remember something . . . "

"Yes?"

"A man talking to my father at the shop."

"Go on."

"Nothing. A man."

"When did this happen?"

"During the hunger strike."

"When your family moved to the big house in Lenadoon."

"How did you know that?"

"People were talking."

"About what?"

"Nothing. Everything."

I was flustered. "We had nothing to hide. My father's business was grow-ing. In those days, there was no shortage of broken-down cars."

"Wrecked a few myself," he said, breaking into a broad smile. For a man who had spent so much of his life in prison, he was remarkably at ease.

"When I left to work for the newspaper he took on my two brothers and another repairman. He worked all the time."

"Think about the man at the shop."

"I do not know. I never saw him again. I never asked my father. I forgot about it until the other day."

He emptied his pack of cigarettes and asked me for a pen. He scribbled on the wrapper and handed it to me. I looked at the writing.

He placed his hand on my lips. "Shh," he whispered.

My eyes asked him the question.

"Yes," he said.

"Speak, Connie," Fischel said as we boarded the bus.

I handed him the empty cigarette pack. He crumpled it in his fist. "Go for it," he said.

"Will you come?"

"The restaurant is closed on Mondays."

"So I have been told."

His hand opened and I stared at the crimpled ball of paper as though it were a crystal ball and I could see what Salvatore Marinelli would tell me. Of course, I saw nothing.

When I got to the apartment, I called Mary and told her of my visit to Riker's Island. She was more interested in reporting on my father's condition. He was stable, she said. The news soothed my burning conscience.

I spent the rest of the afternoon writing what I could recall about my visit with Tommy. He had mentioned the house in Lenadoon. Why would he care in what house we lived? My father had enjoyed an increase in his business at the shop, and I remembered the family praising God for the miracle of so many new customers. But I also remembered what one of my brothers said. "A fucking miracle it is, his customers. All Protestants."

What a strange question to open the evening. Gordon and I were partners from 1978 until 1983, so the *Harris vs. Korn case* was in 1979 or early 1980, not too long after your father was arrested and fingered Tommy Glynn. What of it? Parallel lives? I don't think so. Parallel lines don't converge. Wait a second, maybe they do. Non-Euclidean geometry. Our convergence was a week ago Sunday. Earlier? Sam? How did his life converge with yours? Yes, Sam married Molly who is Tommy's sister. If I remember correctly, they met in 1984 and were married in 1985. And 1985 was when the FBI captured Tommy.

You're exhausting me, Connie. Why are we still talking when your testimony can't help Tommy? Why don't I let you go on with your life? Those are excellent questions and I'll give you the answers, on one condition. You ask me nothing more tonight. OK? Good. We're still talking because you want to know what happened to me and you think what happened to me would help you understand what happened to you. You think we might still help Tommy and you're hoping I will show you the way. Sorry. I have had enough trouble finding my way.

Haven't you been listening? Talk about losing one's way. How I settled the Harris case sounded the death knell of my relationship with Gordon. And my relationship with Gordon wasn't the only thing falling apart. My marriage was racing to conclusion.

You see, Connie, I had no mission. Everyone needs a mission. The guy on the assembly line needs a mission; the salesman needs a mission; the professor needs a mission. Without a mission, you can't see who you are or who you're becoming. You can't love yourself. You lack character; you're an impressionist, impersonating yourself. And it's a poor impression at that.

July 1982: My wife and I had been separated since January and our lawyers were working on a divorce agreement; Gordon was making noises again about changing our equal split.

Lester, of all people, referred the case to me. He represented the National Credit Union Administration (NCUA), drafting for it a code of conduct that specified what investments a credit union could make. On the surface, the rule looked easy enough to follow. A credit union could only invest in government guaranteed securities. This limited investments to deposits in federally insured bank accounts, purchases of government bonds, and securities issued by states and certain municipal taxing authorities.

The NCUA also acted as a clearinghouse for its members, circulating a monthly bulletin reporting on issues and problems facing the credit union industry. In February 1981, it reported that the University of New Mexico Credit Union lost $10,000,000 investing in an arcane, little understood variation of a government mortgage security called a GNMA forward contract. The credit union collapsed and the members recouped only ten percent from insurance.

The Board of Directors couldn't afford to pay a lawyer by the hour and ended up hiring Albuquerque lawyer Jack Vickers, a twenty-seven year veteran of representing insurance companies in automobile accident cases. Jack agreed to take the case because he was a friend of the board chairman. The case would also give him the chance to take his mistress to Houston, Memphis, and New York, the three offices of Jackson, Curtis & Madden, the firm that sold the forward contracts to the credit union.

Jack hadn't considered the significant cost of prosecuting the lawsuit. There would be deposition transcripts, document reproduction, and expert witness fees. So, after he filed the action in April 1981, he did nothing—did not even take the trips with his mistress. What was the point if he wasn't going to take depositions? He did serve the defendant with a document request, but when he was told the copying charges would be $5,000 he withdrew the request. He asked Wayne Luther, the defendant's lawyer, if he wanted to settle. Luther, an alcoholic on the wagon, married four times, and undefeated in his last seventy-five jury trials, said he'd be tickled to settle the case—for nothing, of course.

Nowhere was where the matter stood for more than a year. Then Luther filed a motion to dismiss the case "for want of prosecution"—substitute "lack" for "want" and you get the gist of the motion. Fortunately for Jack, Judge Jose Santiago was a fellow member in the Rio Grande Hunting Lodge. He denied Luther's motion, though to preserve the appearance of impartiality he admonished Jack to take depositions and prepare for the trial scheduled for the first Monday in October. That was it for Jack. He told Santiago he wanted to withdraw—fine with Santiago who thought Jack was no match for Luther. He had watched Luther try a case in Denver on behalf of a swindler in an oil and gas lease case and was impressed when the jury returned a not guilty verdict.

When I told Gordon I wanted to take the case, he smiled perversely and said if I lost, I would have to agree to a reduction in my share of the profits. I asked him what would happen if I won. He said he would give me a cigar.

I registered at the new Marriott hotel in Albuquerque, not far from Jack's office. Jack said he'd come over for a drink after work and brief me on the case. But I had checked him out and didn't have high hopes that he would be informative. In his twenty years in Albuquerque, he had spent all his legal time on car accidents and his personal time on collecting mistresses. He was originally from Traverse City, Michigan, where his law practice failed to bring in enough fees to pay the modest office rent of $150 a month. He decided he needed a fresh start. One day at a barbershop, he read an article that listed the best places to live. It named Albuquerque as number one for people who had failed elsewhere, perfect for anyone who wanted to be a big fish in a little barrel. That did it for Jack, who had thought about going to New York until he saw that the article listed it as last and he realized that there he would have been a very tiny fish in a very large barrel. And he wasn't bothered that Traverse City was listed number two after Albuquerque.

I spent the day reviewing the file Jack had sent me. In it was a letter from the NCUA to the president of Jackson, Curtis saying the investments it was selling to credit unions were proper investments under its rules. I was amazed. What the credit union bought were forward contracts, and though they were contracts to buy GNMAs, they involved a very different set of risks.

A forward contract delays payment for 120 days. If during this time interest rates rise, the purchaser will suffer a loss when the time comes for payment. And since the purchaser need not make a payment when signing the contract, he can buy an unlimited number of forward contracts. The risk would seem to be obvious: buy enough forward contracts and the slightest rise in interest rates translates into an enormous loss.

How could the NCUA approve this type of investment, when it was obvious that it was so fraught with risk? How could it fail to understand the critical economic difference between buying a guaranteed GNMA and signing a contract to buy a GNMA, where the risk of loss ballooned with every purchase? Did a bunch of morons run the NCUA? Did someone pay off someone? And what was manager Sylvester Hodges thinking when during a six-month period he signed billions of dollars worth of forward contracts like a madman who can't stop buying lottery tickets. There was nothing in it for him. His salary was $20,000 per year and the credit union didn't pay bonuses. Who were these board members who ignored the monthly reports detailing the ever-growing positions in forward contracts?

Albuquerque was a mish-mash of five kinds of people: descendants of Spanish aristocracy longing for the old days when they controlled the fertile lands along the Rio Grande, university types, the fast growing high-tech industry, engineers from around the country, American Indians disgusted with life on the reservations, and losers like Jack. I expected that some combination of representatives from these groups would sit on the jury.

Jack met me at the bar. He pulled a roll of bills from the pocket of his tight denim pants, decimating the roll in the process. He asked me what I wanted to drink in between expletives and reconstituting the bills into a new roll. He licked his right thumb and fanned the bills, as though he had just come from the racetrack and was proud of his take.

He had little to say about the case. His work on the file had been limited to attending the one deposition in the case: Sylvester Hodges, who had spent two hundred pages saying "I don't know," or I don't remember." He died the day after the deposition. He fell off a ladder in his back yard while picking apples from a tree, cracking his head on the concrete patio. He never regained consciousness.

Jack also showed me a notice he received from Luther, scheduling the depositions of the sixteen board members on consecutive days beginning the following week. I asked him if he knew anybody who could help me, but he just smiled and said, "This is the West. Got to learn to have that independent frontier spirit." Then he told me the bad news. The clerk from his office who filed the complaint had forgotten to pay the fee for a jury trial. I wouldn't need to worry what kind of people lived in New Mexico. The fate of the case would rest with the judge.

Jack ordered another round of drinks and I looked out the window. Beyond the parking lot I could see Interstate 40 and the Sandia Mountains. Jack had loosened his tie and switched to draft beer, which he was guzzling while trying hard not to look sheepish. He couldn't pull it off, though, too stupid or too disconnected from reality to manage more than a grimace, which he accomplished by crinkling the bridge of his nose.

He seemed distracted by a bearded man talking to an attractive young woman in the lobby. She wore a heavy turquoise necklace and beige shift that nearly reached the floor. Her skin was dark brown. Though Jack said he didn't know who she was, he had that funny embarrassed look people get when they run into someone they don't want to see. He did admit he knew the man, Marty Glickman, chairman of the credit union.

Jack said that Marty had moved to Albuquerque ten years earlier from New Jersey. He had made his mark as the only experienced orthopedic surgeon in town. He joined the credit union board at the request of the Dean of Admissions, a satisfied patient who said the board needed someone with a brain. That was two months before Sylvester started investing with Jackson, Curtis.

Suddenly, the young woman walked away. Marty stared after her for a moment and then sauntered over to us, affecting a casualness I didn't think was real. Jack introduced us and said he had to leave. He was taking his mistress for a weekend trip to the Petrified Forest, a trip he hoped would mollify her after she complained that his withdrawal from the case had scotched the jaunts to Texas, Tennessee, and New York.

The first deposition, on Monday, would be of a former board member, a retired professor of nutrition, who lived in an assisted housing complex north of the city. Marty offered to arrange a meeting, though he said it would be a waste of time. The professor was trapped in the later stages of Alzheimer's disease and no longer remembered his name or much else.

I asked Marty if the board had known and understood what Sylvester was doing. He turned away and asked the bartender for a Dewars and soda. He was upset about something and kept looking toward the lobby. I thought it might have to do with the young woman, but I didn't want to intrude. When he got his drink he relaxed, though he still didn't answer my question. I wondered whether he had forgotten or just wanted to avoid the subject.

I asked him again, and he started talking, but I knew he was measuring his words as he took long pauses between each sentence. He said he was the only board member who paid attention to Sylvester's activities, so much so that after a dinner with Jimmy Wayne Tufts, the Jackson, Curtis salesman, he bought five million dollars worth of contracts for no money down, selling them a short time later for a profit of $42,000. "I was lucky," he said. "And it was my money. Sylvester caught us by surprise when we found out he booked several hundred million dollars worth of contracts."

The young woman reappeared at the lobby entrance and Marty waved for her to join us. She glowered and went the other way, through the lobby and out the door to the parking lot.

"You win some, you lose some," he said.

"Investments or women?"

"Both."

"Who is she?"

"Judy Lightfoot."

"She's beautiful."

"Native women are beautiful. She's Sioux. I operated on her back. She had to stop teaching."

"She looked upset."

"Probably the medication."

"How so?"

When he didn't answer, I thought it might be that he didn't want to divulge a patient confidence. But then a funny look came over him, a child-like smile of someone proud of his own genius.

"Are you married?" he asked.

"Separated."

"Good enough. I'll give you her number."

He made it sound like I was part of an experiment, but I said nothing while he wrote her number on a bar napkin. As he gave it to me, he said, "I'm late for a meeting. What else can I tell you about the credit union?"

"What did the salesman say to the Board? There was nothing in the minutes."

"No one understood what he was saying, that's why."

"Did you know the contracts weren't guaranteed?"

"I took the letter from the NCUA at face value."

"Was this before or after you made the $42,000 profit?"

His eyes narrowed as if he didn't want me to see into them. "What's the difference?"

"If you made $42,000, you must have realized you could lose $42,000."

"You sound like you represent the defendant."

"What's the answer?"

"Haven't you gambled? When you're ahead you can't imagine you'll ever lose."

"Did you invest again?"

"Once. Took a small loss."

"After that?"

"I'm not a gambler."

"Sylvester was, is that it?"

He pointed at the napkin, which was still in my hand. "Call Judy. You'll have a nice time."

Suspicion travels along a telephone line as efficiently as words. She wanted to know how long I had known Marty. I said a couple of hours. There was a short gasp and then silence. I thought the phone had gone dead. Then, in a voice suddenly silky she asked me why I was calling. I didn't know what to say: a date, a drink or two, company, or just a conversation. I was so tongue-tied that the words finally came out as, "I want you."

"One-night stand, is that the idea?"

"No."

"If not that, what?"

"A date?"

"Are you Catholic, Protestant or Jewish?"

"Does it make a difference?"

"Depends on your answer."

"Agnostic." I sounded as unsure about myself as I was about the existence of God.

"Good. I prefer a man who has doubts."

I thought I might already be falling in love.

She agreed to meet me the following evening. Yes, meet me. Despite my offer to pick her up at home, she said she'd prefer to rendezvous at the hotel. She wouldn't let go of her suspicions and was careful not to tell me where she lived. I told her to choose a restaurant for dinner.

In the morning Marty took me to the retirement home to see the professor. As he warned, the interview was a waste of time. The professor remembered nothing about credit union investments, claimed he never heard of Sylvester Hodges, and thought Marty was his priest. I showed him a set of minutes from the meeting when the forward contracts were discussed. He frowned when he saw his name listed. "I should have spoken up," he said, then retreated into the fog and said he couldn't remember more. Before we left, he signed a note authorizing me to talk to his doctor. I couldn't let him testify.

Marty drove me to the warehouse where the credit union files were stored. I wanted to discuss the case, but he was more interested in my conversation with Judy.

"Did she tell you about the accident?" he asked.

"What accident?"

"Head on collision driving to Corrales. Year ago."

"Obviously, she came through it OK."

His arms were straight against the rim of the steering wheel. "Maybe I should let her tell you."

"Tell me what?"

He didn't answer and I dropped the subject. I wondered what irremediable defect my date could have.

I spent the afternoon rummaging through the documents, trying to get a picture of what had happened during those critical months between July 1980 and February 1981 when the credit union's investments in forward contracts mounted to obscene proportions. The countless charts, forward contracts, and confirmations were dizzying; I couldn't tell when the tide had turned against the credit union. There was a curious Mailgram on December 22nd from Jimmy Wayne in New York to Sylvester. It read: "Blizzard kept me out of the loop yesterday. No problem. Putting through for an extension. Everything taken care of." For the next two hours, I went through the documents looking for anything that would explain this message; I found nothing.

I went downstairs to the bar a half-hour before Judy was to arrive. Nothing depresses me more than a hotel room. But for a guide magazine with the name of the city on the cover, you wouldn't know where you are. You're in a generic place I call *Hotel City, USA*, a land of wake-up calls, Gideon bibles, and chocolates on the pillow.

The bar didn't help my mood. An older man wearing a leather vest was circling the room, acting as if he couldn't decide on which of twenty stools to sit. A middle-aged woman with a huge mound of hair resembling an ice-cream cone was licking the salt from a glass of margarita. Every so often she would look at me and smile, which I returned with a gawk, like I was a kid at the circus.

I didn't know what to expect. Judy hadn't been in a wheelchair when I saw her in the lobby talking to Marty. Brain damaged? Not judging from the way she spoke on the phone. Scarred? Perhaps. But where? Face? Arms? Body parts I might never see? Emotionally scarred? That, I didn't want to think about.

I was so lost in painting morbid mental pictures I didn't notice her standing next to me.

"You wouldn't be the big shot lawyer from Chicago," she said, climbing on the barstool next to me.

One sentence and I was already intimidated. "I'm a lawyer from Chicago; the big shot part you'll have to decide."

Beauty sends me reeling, leaves my face and mind locked like a computer with the keys stuck. When she had been standing in the lobby the night before, I couldn't see her well enough to get the sense of a face that rivaled Helen of Troy's ability to send thousands of men to their deaths . . . no, I'm not exaggerating, though maybe I am, just a little. She was pretty, what can I say, with large eyes, straight nose, and high cheekbones. No lipstick, but shining pink lips that made watching her speak as enjoyable as listening.

"Cat got your tongue," she said.

"Yes, and you're the cat."

She laughed. "And I still have my claws."

We took a tram to the restaurant at the top of Sandia Mountain. She leaned against the railing while I swayed through the car, mesmerized by the view of the valley and the city lights disappearing behind low clouds. I felt out of place in my suit—everyone in the car was wearing jeans or khakis. She was dressed in dark skirt, white blouse, and light blue cardigan sweater. A gold chain with a small diamond ring hung from her neck. "The engagement ring my ex-husband gave me," she said. "He wouldn't take it back in the divorce, I saw no reason to sell it, and it seemed a shame to leave it in a drawer." That was another feminine attribute that drives me back into myself: answering the question you've asked only in your mind.

It was the middle of dinner, at a table with a view of the tram and the valley six thousand feet below, when she described the accident.

"I was headed for Corrales to see a friend. He's a lobbyist for the tribe. He was helping me with a proposal to get funding for a special education program I wanted to set up. It was raining. I was thinking about the program when a car swerved over to my side. Suddenly, I felt as if I was being dragged, thought my arms were being pulled off. I opened my eyes and saw this guy lying on the ground by the other car. The windshield was gone. He must not have been wearing a seatbelt. It was awful. His head was covered with glass and blood was coming out of his nose and mouth."

"Was he dead?"

She silently answered yes and said, "I told the police what happened, but the D.A. wasn't satisfied. I had a little wine before leaving that night and I guess my blood alcohol level was over the legal limit."

"So what, if the other driver was at fault."

"What was I going to do? I was flat on my back in the hospital. That's how I met Marty. He was on the staff and said I needed immediate surgery. The first thing anyone told me when I came to in the recovery room was that I had been indicted for manslaughter."

"You don't have to tell me this, you know."

"Sure I do."

I didn't ask her why.

"It's a small world," she said.

"What's small about it?"

"Jack Vickers was my lawyer."

"So that's why . . . he's a personal injury lawyer."

"I didn't know what kind of lawyer he was. Marty told me to use him."

Something wasn't right, I thought. Something about what she had just said. A sneering roll of the words. But she was continuing her story and I lost the line to what was bothering me.

"I went to trial while I was recuperating from the second operation. Could hardly walk, the pain was so bad. Jack told me to plead guilty. The D.A. would recommend probation. But I was innocent."

"You refused the deal."

"Wouldn't you have if you were innocent?"

When I didn't answer, she said, "Fucked up."

"What?"

"The fucking system."

We had stopped eating. She was stabbing her steak with the knife like it was alive. My swordfish suddenly seemed to have an acrid odor and I pushed it away.

"What happened?" I asked.

"Later," she said.

I paid the check and we went outside. I could see the tram coming up the mountain, floating against the black sky. She took my hand.

She said nothing more until we got to her car at the hotel. "You can drive," she said.

She lived in a complex near the banks of the Rio Grande River. We parked in a court between several sandstone villas arranged in a quadrangle fronting a grove of willow trees. She led me on a trail through the grove to the river. She took off her sandals and sat on a rock. I sat next to her. The willows, black against the sky, looked like the bowed heads of mourners at a funeral. She dangled her feet in the brown water and we listened to soft night sounds, interrupted every few minutes by howling.

"What's that?" I asked, thinking I should keep my shoes on in case we had to make a fast getaway.

"A sad coyote."

"Do you want to tell me what happened in your case?"

"My friend, the Indian lawyer, came to see me in the hospital. He told me I should take the deal. He said the D.A. was a business partner of the dead guy's father in a land deal that was tied up in court because the Indians were claiming an interest in the property."

"So that explains—"

"Why I got indicted. I should have listened to my friend. I didn't think a trial could be fixed."

"Anything can be fixed."

"I knew the cops took pictures at the scene, which would have showed the tire marks of the other car. But when Jack asked for them, the D.A. said they hadn't come out. As soon as the trial started, I knew I'd be convicted. The look on the jurors' faces. To them I was just another drunken Indian."

The howling came again, but I didn't care. I took off my shoes and put my feet in the water.

"Big shot lawyer turns Huckleberry Finn," she said and kissed me.

I put my arm around her and she told me more. She fired Jack, had a third operation, and represented herself on appeal. She spent day and night at the library. "I was screwed," she said. "Forget about winning the appeal. I couldn't find a single case where the court threw out a jury verdict."

"What did you do?"

She kissed me again. "Close your eyes and listen," she whispered.

"Corrales is a dump," she said, "a typical southwestern town that at some point lost its identity. It can't make up its mind whether to be quaint, trendy, or just plain backward. The main street is an amalgam of overpriced Mexican restaurants, trinket shops, phony Western-styled bars decorated with tomahawks, cheap Indian rugs, and arrowheads made in Taiwan. The D.A.'s office is on the second floor of the Post Office building at one end of the street.

"I explained the plan to my friend. At first, he thought I was nuts. What you have in mind is against the law, he said. I told him forget it, I'll do it myself. He saw I wouldn't let it go and said he'd help me. I don't know why. He'd have lost his license if we were caught, maybe worse, not like me who didn't have anything to lose. I was already looking at three years at Roswell State Prison.

"Talk about a makeshift operation. I rented a van, not to carry anything but because the carriage was high and I could stand on it and reach the second floor window in back. I brought a screwdriver with me, which I used to pry open the window. My friend was nervous, though, and stayed in the truck.

"I really didn't know what I was looking for. I was hoping that a sleazy D.A. would keep some evidence of his sleaze lying around. I started with his desk. Nice desk, an upright antique with carvings of the Spanish conquistadors. Wouldn't you know it, what I was searching for was in the top drawer, underneath a picture of a girl in a bikini with "I love you" written on the back. I thought about taking the picture and blackmailing him—the girl in the bikini wasn't his wife—but what good would money do me in prison? The photograph under the photograph was the prize, the one he claimed hadn't come out— skid marks clear as can be, my innocence right there in black and white.

"I climbed out the window and got on top of the truck. I leaned over and handed the photograph to my friend. He started the truck—he wanted to get out of there fast—but I told him to wait.

"I went back inside the office. I had seen a bucket full of rags in his bathroom. There was also a small stove and refrigerator in the corner, next to a cot. He slept there, I guess, or he slept there with his girlfriend. Anyway, I took a couple of the rags to the stove and turned on a burner. The rags were dry, caught fire right away. I put one burning rag in the wooden waste-paper basket by the desk and lit the blanket on the bed with the other. I don't know if I intended to burn the whole office—I was so angry I couldn't think straight—but it didn't matter what I intended. I was lucky to get out the window before I caught fire.

"We were turning off the main street to the highway when I heard the fire trucks. I later read in the newspaper that the office was destroyed and the floor collapsed into the post office."

"Shit," I said.

"You think I'm a criminal, don't you."

I could see the moon in her eyes. "A terrorist, maybe. Not a criminal."

"I thought terrorists are criminals."

"Depends on who you're terrorizing."

"There's more," she said.

"I filed a motion to vacate the conviction because of prosecutorial misconduct—don't I have the lingo down pat? I attached the photograph as an exhibit. I also included an affidavit from my friend about the relationship between the D.A. and the driver's father. I thought for sure the photograph would win the appeal. I used the affidavit only because my friend said the law was like shit; you had to throw as much of it as possible against the wall if you wanted any of it to stick.

"He was right. The judges didn't care about the photograph. Innocence to them wasn't relevant. They said my drunkenness justified the verdict. If I'd been sober, they said, I could have avoided the other car. Yeah, right. On a rainy night in the desert, no moon, no stars, just headlights rushing toward me. But I won anyway. The judges said the D.A. should have disqualified himself because of a conflict of interest.

"I had broken into the office for nothing. And the D.A. figured I must have done it. How else did I get the photograph? He asked the Mayor to appoint a special prosecutor to investigate me. It sure was a special prosecutor, special because he was another partner in the real estate deal. But they couldn't prove I broke in the office. They indicted me for possession of stolen merchandise—the photograph. Can you believe it? And can you believe this? I was convicted and sentenced to a year.

"I thought I was finished. But my friend wrote a letter to the Governor, threatening to get the tribe to cancel a deal with the state. In exchange for some new subsidies, the tribe had agreed to let a prominent real estate developer build condominiums on Indian land. The Governor asked the Attorney General to review my case. Yesterday I got this."

She showed me a stipulation vacating her conviction. "Building those condominiums was more important than putting me in prison," she said.

"It got you justice," I said.

There, on the bank of the river, we made love. Except for the occasional howl and the sound of wind through the willows, we heard only our breathing.

We should continue over dinner, Fischel said, and we went to our usual table in the back.

"Enjoy your time with Tommy?" Patrick said as he handed us menus.

"It saddened me."

"On Friday, when they ship him out, I'm going back to Belfast."

His plans stirred my longing for home. "Perhaps I will as well. Thursday, I think."

"You're leaving?" Fischel said.

"Yes."

"Stay a bit longer."

"You said a few more days. Thursday is a few more days."

"What time is your flight?"

"I have yet to make a reservation. But I believe there is a plane leaving at five. Why?"

"No reason."

"You never ask a question without a reason."

"Maybe we'll have lunch before you leave," he said. "Jimmy will take you to the airport."

Though I preferred to take a taxi, I said, "That is very kind of you."

The menus were of no use to us. We ordered as we always did. Patrick left, but looked at Fischel in some kind of silent communication.

"Why did you tell me that story about New Mexico?"

"I'm not finished. More drama to come."

"Why tell it at all?"

"Same reason I tell you all my stories."

"Which is?"

"Changed my way of thinking."

"How?"

"This one especially. First time I didn't think it was so terrible to commit a crime."

"You approve her setting fire to the building?"

"Of course."

"I do not approve of violence."

"Destruction of property isn't violence, Connie. It's not even a crime against nature. Unless you think crummy man-made structures are part of nature."

"You are making light of a most serious subject."

"And you, Cornelius Sullivan, are far too heavy too much of the time."

"I do not believe I like your sarcasm."

"After nine days you should be used to it."

"On that I can agree. I am used to much I do not like."

"Ah, the Irish wit breaks through into the sunshine."

"There is no sunshine here in Murphy's."

We laughed. Soon I was laughing so hard my eyes began to water.

"Oh, I forgot to tell you," Fischel said.

"What?" I squeaked.

"The D.A. was indicted. An insurance company investigator found his fingerprints on the bucket. Also, he had taken out an insurance policy on

his desk for $20,000 after he had unsuccessfully tried to sell it to a gallery in town. He was indicted for what Judy had done."

The horror stopped my laughter. "He was innocent."

"He got five years."

"An innocent man in prison. How can you laugh? How can you be so callous?"

"Hey, I didn't send him to the can. The law did." He laughed harder.

"He was innocent," I said again.

"Of setting fire to his office. He was guilty of everything else."

I was livid. "Is that your idea of justice?"

He stopped laughing and looked straight into my eyes. "Pretty close," he said.

I must say you were unusually quiet during dinner. You went from endless laughter to endless silence. We were like a long-married couple who have run out of things to talk about. Empty silences, a vacuum not even outer space can match.

After Judy and I had our fill of nature and lovemaking we returned to her villa. She opened a bottle of wine and we drank and talked until morning. Romance is a funny thing. You can dress it up in sweet lovemaking, a touch of the hand, and candlelight dinners, but at the core it's about intimacy between strangers. And in those first weeks, we shared all the romance you could want without ever getting to know one another. Occasionally, she'd talk about her life, her father especially. He was a construction worker, killed in an on-site accident when she was ten, a man proud to have left the reservation as a boy to make it in a white world, even if it was just a hamlet called Mobridge, South Dakota.

She got married to a local high school teacher when she was seventeen. For six years they traveled around the world, earning their keep with English lessons to families in remote places like Nepal, Borneo, and Sumatra. She got to longing for more out of life than drifting. She wanted to return home, not Mobridge but where she thought she could do some good. But her husband liked floating, a life without direction or place. One morning, on the island of Corfu, while he was off teaching English to an old nun, she left him a note and hitched a ride on a tanker. Two months later, she alighted in San Francisco and spent a month in a seedy motel sending applications to colleges. She picked the University of New Mexico because it reminded her of home with its special blending of earth and sky. That was in 1972, when she was twenty-three. She gradually found peace in her life, took a short-term lover when she needed one, and devoted herself to teaching, until that rainy night driving to Corrales.

I had less to say about my past. I hadn't traveled, reflected on my place in the world, or thought of life as a journey to any place in particular. I stayed away from my life's subjects: Cincinnati, Sarah and Albert, law school, crazy lawyers, and crazy cases. I wanted that wall of ignorance, or whatever you want to call it when lovers share everything but the past, to keep our romance alive, in a state of suspended animation. She loved me, I think, simply for being there, a companion easy to love because he stayed out of the way, which is what she needed, I suppose, after what the law and lawyers had done to her.

She *was* interested in the credit union case. She attended every deposition and soon knew as much about the case as I did. I moved in with her. We'd sit on the couch in front of the fireplace, review the day's deposition, and discuss strategy. In the mornings, I walked her dog, a playful German shepherd with soulful eyes. It would lead me along the river and stop occasionally to pick up a broken branch, giving it to me for a toss down the trail. When we returned she'd have breakfast waiting, hearty helpings of eggs, home fries, and bacon, with coffee made in a stone pot. Then we'd climb in her Volvo and drive to the deposition. It was as if we had eloped and become law partners.

She unlocked the puzzle of the Mailgram. She prepared a chart of interest rate movements that revealed a sudden increase on December 21, 1980. She remembered seeing a curious reference in Sylvester's deposition to "buying on margin," curious because a forward contract doesn't involve a loan. Stapled to the confirmation slips were documents called "repurchase agreements," each bearing the same date as the closing date for the corresponding forward contract.

We went to the business school library, where we consulted a weighty treatise, *Risky Hedges and Arbitrages.* Several chapters were devoted to repurchase agreements and how they extended the time for payment.

As of December 21, the credit union owned 266 million dollars worth of forward contracts with due dates running into early January. The increase in interest rates, though modest, would have resulted in a $2,000,000 loss. And experts were predicting further interest rate increases over the short term. In exchange for a five percent down payment, the closing date was delayed and the credit union could hope for a decline in interest rates. In effect, the credit union was borrowing ninety-five percent of the price, the margin Sylvester had mentioned in his deposition.

Interest rates continued to rise. The day of reckoning became a day of disaster, as the loss had mounted to $10,000,000. The stunned board members couldn't believe the credit union had lost everything. I couldn't believe Marty had told me none of this.

I met Marty at Bennigan's, a hamburger restaurant near the university campus. He was at the bar having a drink with a young redhead in a miniskirt. He was describing her bone structure, touching each bone in her legs as he identified them. I sat a few stools away and ordered a martini. I was on my second drink when she left.

"Where's Judy?" he asked.

"She went to a school board meeting."

"I didn't know she was on the school board."

"Neither did I." His answer sounded like a question to himself, what someone does in a conversation when he knows more than he's letting on. It didn't seem like the right time to start an argument and so I just rambled on about the credit union's loss.

"Has anything I said jogged your memory?" I asked.

"I said everything I knew in the deposition."

"Look, I'm on your side."

"Settle the case."

"They won't pay a dime."

"I can't help you."

"I think you can."

"You saw the redhead?"

"I saw her."

"It took a while, but she gave me her number. Face it, I'm a charming guy."

"Charm won't work in the law. The law is addictive, not seductive."

"You have to be seduced before you can be addicted."

"One doesn't automatically follow the other."

"You should try it anyway. Knowledge is power."

"It can also be an abuse of power."

He was caught off guard. "You're a judgmental sort."

"I'm not trying to be."

"I'm leaving."

"Answer one question."

"One."

"On December twenty-first interest rates rose. Sylvester could have sold the forward contracts and taken his lumps. The losses would have been substantial, but not catastrophic."

"So?"

"At our first meeting, you told me you made another investment in which you took a loss."

"It sounds like you're going to ask me a second question."

"Forgive me."

"Why should I?"

"When did you make that investment?"

"In August."

"Was it August twenty-first?"

"I said one question."

He wasn't getting off the stool. He had plenty to say. "Could have been," he said. "I don't remember those kinds of dates."

"If it was, your contract would have come due on December twenty-first."

"So?"

"That's the day interest rates jumped."

"I guess that's why I took a loss."

"Why not do the repurchase agreement like the credit union did?"

"I never heard of it. Didn't know it was an option."

"I think you have heard of it. I think you know a lot more than you're willing to admit."

Marty slid off the barstool. I had lost him. "While you're finishing your martini, chew on something."

"What?"

"Don't push the limits of knowledge. They exist for a reason."

"Sylvester is dead and I need someone to testify at the trial."

He got back on the stool "Have it your way. This is the short of it. I don't like doing things I haven't checked out. After I bought the first forward contract I did a little research. It was obvious you could lose your shirt if you weren't careful. I subscribed to a newsletter that gives you the daily scoop on interest rates. On December twentieth I noticed interest rates had risen a bit, not of any consequence, but an analyst for the newsletter said: watch out, a wave of selling in the bond market will soon be upon us. I called Sylvester and told him it was time to sell. He said he'd rather not; he wanted to show a profit at year-end. The next day I called New York for an update. The gal on the switchboard said Jimmy Wayne hadn't come in."

"What was he doing in New York?"

"He used to go there every month to see the head honchos. I asked where he was and she said at the hotel. They were in the middle of a blizzard and New York was paralyzed. I asked the girl to connect me to the bond desk. A broker got on the line and said interest rates were rising as fast as the snow was falling. I told him to sell my forward contract."

"Did you call Sylvester?"

Marty took my martini and finished it. "No."

"Why not?"

"When I hung up on the broker I called Jimmy Wayne at the hotel. He sounded like he had a hangover. But it wasn't a hangover that kept him at the hotel."

"Why then?"

"I heard a broad cooing."

"That's it?"

"He had called his office. He knew what was up. Begged me not to call Sylvester."

"Why?"

"He wanted to do the repurchase agreement. What Jackson, Curtis does is lay off the agreement with another broker at a slightly higher price. They make a profit in the spread without the risk. I told him I wanted no part of his game, but he said he would call Sylvester as soon I got off the phone."

"Did he?"

"You saw the Mailgram. He waited until the next day. He knew Sylvester would do anything to avoid the loss."

"And you didn't call Sylvester."

"I thought about it."

"What stopped you?"

"You don't want to know."

"Why don't I want to know?"

"Take my word for it."

"Why should I?"

"Look, I did think about it, but I had other things on my mind. By evening, it was clear the credit union would have to take a huge loss. Interest rates were way up. What could I do?"

"You could have told him to take the two million dollar loss and be done with it."

"Nobody forced Sylvester into the repurchase agreement."

"If you had called earlier. If you had warned him..."

Marty sighed. "We wouldn't be having this conversation."

"Shit."

"Do me a favor," he said.

I didn't like how he said it, as if he wanted something personal from me. "What?"

"Don't tell Judy."

"Why?"

"She's a nice girl. Why upset her?"

"Why would it upset her?"

"Now you *have* asked one question too many."

I ate dinner alone, a king-size bacon burger and thick greasy fries that stuck in my throat the way the case was stuck in my head. Marty had lied in his deposition. If I put him on the stand at the trial and he told the truth, the judge could blame him for what happened to the credit union. Though Sylvester might not have known that interest rates were up, Marty did. Jimmy Wayne had committed fraud by failing to warn Sylvester, but the blizzard was the perfect excuse.

During my fourth Amaretto I had an epiphany, the kind you get when you're drunk, when the world and the facts and the people are turned upside down. My star witness wouldn't have been Sylvester if he were alive and it wouldn't be Marty. My star witness would be Jimmy Wayne Tufts. Not the star witness against Jackson, Curtis, but in a new case called *The University of New Mexico Credit Union vs. Marty Glickman*. I ordered a fifth drink and fantasized about the $10,000,000 insurance policy for negligence by a board member.

Judy was waiting for me with an expensive bottle of Merlot sitting on the dining room table next to a vase filled with desert flowers.

"Where have you been?" she asked.

"You know where. Dinner."

"It was a long dinner."

"You were at your meeting."

"There was no meeting. I'm not on the school board."

"Why did you—"

"I didn't want to go with you."

"Thanks a lot."

"You're drunk."

"Marty likes to drink," I said, with a silly grin on my face.

I stopped grinning when I saw the look on her face. "What did he tell you?" she asked.

"Everything."

"He promised he wouldn't."

I was confused. "You knew?"

"What are you saying? You weren't supposed to know. You never were supposed to know."

Even drunk, I saw we were moving in opposite directions. This time, however, I was the one crossing into her lane.

"Know what?" I asked foolishly, irrevocably.

"Marty and me."

If there was a statement that could sober me up fast, that was it. "Marty and you?"

"We were having an affair, if that's what you call non-stop fucking. After the second operation he said I could convalesce at home, regain my strength for the next one. I was a mess, not just from the constant pain, but emotionally. I was lost, he was so kind, empathetic, so . . . " She broke down, her shoulders heaving, but there were no tears.

"He seduced you?" As soon as the words were said, I knew they were the wrong words with the wrong punctuation, a statement turned into a question, a question that answered itself with blistering disapproval.

"I knew we would never work out."

I was angry. "We are working out. We're living together."

"I was like his concubine. He didn't let up, was at me before and after the third operation. Three times a week he'd come over and spend a few hours, most of them in bed. I was in constant pain. I was drinking day and night, out of it on pills he kept feeding me. Finally, I got hold of myself. I met him at the hotel to tell him we were through. But I didn't think he would leave me alone. So, the next day I drove to his office. Didn't go inside. Didn't want to go inside. Wrote him a note. I said, stay away from me; stop calling me. I put it under the windshield wipers on his car and spit on it to make sure it stuck."

I put my hands on her shoulders but she shook them off.

"It wasn't all I wrote. I wrote something on the outside of the note."

"What?"

"I wrote, 'Dr. Glickman seduces patients.' In big fat letters. You could see it from across the lot."

"Damn."

"You called me a few hours later."

"But my call was innocent. I didn't know—"

"I'm damaged goods."

"Don't be ridiculous."

"And now he's told you."

"I swear to you he didn't."

"What's the difference?"

"I love you."

I reached for her, but she took a step backward. She hit the table and the vase fell on the floor, breaking in tiny pieces, scattered on the floor with the flowers.

I bent down to pick them up. She remained standing, sobbing. "What you love is being on the case. Your passion rises and falls with the case. When the case is over, I'll be over. You'll be done with me."

I had pieces of the vase in my hand. Blood was trickling down my wrist, making a bracelet around it. I used the flowers to wipe it off.

"I know what you're thinking," she said. "You're thinking how you're going to get the credit union's money back. When you do, it will be like you've just come and want the girl to get the hell out."

She had me pinned—down for the count had I been counting. "What happened after you left the note?"

"Another doctor parked in the spot next to Marty's car and saw it. He sent it to the license bureau. It started an investigation. I'm supposed to testify next week before the medical ethics board."

"What are you going to say?"

"That I made the whole thing up. That I was whacked out on drugs. That I came on to him and he turned me down."

No wonder Marty had been so casual about everything. I sat on the couch and put my head in my bloody hands. She went into the bedroom and returned carrying a book with a red cover. "My diary," she said, turning the pages. "December 21, 1980. He was with me, here, in my bed, all day. In between our lovemaking, he told me the credit union was going to lose a lot of money, maybe all of it. He said he could have prevented it. I asked him why and he said he couldn't pull himself away from my hot body."

"I'm sorry," I said.

She closed the diary and put it on the table. She started picking up the rest of the flowers. "Now you know. Marty let the credit union lose millions because he didn't want to take his cock out of my cunt."

Excuse my French, Connie. Excuse hers. No, for Christ's sake, I'll say it again. These stories have nothing to do with you. Connie, I'm shocked. I've never heard you talk like this. Sarah would wash your mouth with soap, mine too. My hand has not been up your *arse* for the past week. Where are you going? You stay right here. Secrets. Life is full of secrets. They surround us, cover us when we're not looking, smother us while we try in vain to throw them off. They pile over us like an avalanche until the air is gone, until we expend out last breath.

I ran out onto the street. Damn the man, I thought. Damn his stories.

I was sitting on the curb when Jimmy drove up in his limo. He rolled down the window.

"What's with you?" he asked.

I picked a can off the ground and threw it down the street. "I wish you people would do whatever it is you intend and finish with me."

Fischel came out the door. "There you are."

I ignored him.

"Don't you want to hear what happened with Judy and me? Don't you want to hear how the case ended?"

"You will finish with me like you finished with her."

He put his arm around me. "You're talking nonsense, Connie."

"You arc using me like you used her."

"It was a long time ago."

He lit a cigarette and handed it to me. He sat on the curb by my side.

"That's better," Fischel said as I puffed on the cigarette.

"Did you file the lawsuit against Dr. Glickman?"

"Yes. I told her she would have to tell the truth at the ethics hearing. I couldn't let her deny the affair. It would have destroyed her credibility when she testified in the case against Glickman."

"She agreed?"

"Not at first. She wanted me to quit the case. She was smart. She said I had a conflict of interest and the attorney-client privilege would prevent me from using what Marty had said."

"What did you say?"

"I said there was no privilege for lovers."

"Her response?"

Fischel laughed. "She slapped me. She told me to get out."

"Did you?"

"I got my things and went to the hotel."

"Did you win the case?"

"The insurance company settled for the policy limit. The credit union got its money back."

"What happened to Dr. Glickman?"

"He lost his license."

"Did you and Judy reconcile?"

"No. It was over. Whatever we shared was gone. You might say the law came between us."

"You said you loved her."

"I did love her."

"I am sorry for you, Fischel."

"Don't be."

He was silent now, hands in his pockets, a long ash hanging on the end of his cigarette. "Goodnight, Fischel," I said and got off the curb.

"I'm taking you to see Salvatore tomorrow," Jimmy said.

I started walking.

"I'll be at your apartment at nine," he added.

"Goodnight, Connie," Fischel called out, his voice filled with longing and remorse.

At the corner, the garbage man greeted me with a smile. I returned his smile. An exchange between strangers, however momentary. The intimacy of strangers in a city of strangers. Romance.

BOOK THREE

MY FRIEND

CHAPTER TEN

May 19, 1998

A LOUD SERIES OF KNOCKS sent *Cuchulainn* darting to the front door. *Expecting to see Jimmy's limousine, I got out of bed and went to the window. Instead of the limousine, however, a familiar looking late model sedan was parked in front of the building. Another knock came, even louder, the kind of knock that used to announce the arrival of the RUC. I quickly threw on shirt and pants and opened the door. Gold and Varick stood before me, both in black suits. They looked like they had come from Mass.*

I ushered them into the studio. Cuchulainn held his tale low, ready to defend his territory.

"We apologize for not calling first," Susan said. Oddly enough, I had become so comfortable with Ms. Gold that I could only think of her as Susan.

Varick grunted. "Our investigator didn't have your telephone number."

"I believe the number is listed in the landlord's name," I said.

Varick grunted again.

"What can I do for you?" I asked.

Susan looked at the mess in the apartment: clothes strewn about, notebook open on the desk, bedcovers on the floor from my restless sleep. "Do you burn the candles at both ends, Mr. Sullivan?" In other circumstances I could have taken her for a concerned neighbor.

"I am a night person," I said.

"We'll keep this short, Mr. Sullivan," Susan said.

Varick pulled a folded paper out of his pocket and opened it. "Recognize him?"

The drawing was a reasonably good likeness of Fischel. "Why do you ask?"

"You were seen in his company."

"Do you have a photograph?"

Susan frowned. "The investigator's camera broke."

I could not resist. "They could not find an arse if you put their noses to it."

"Come again?" Varick said.

"Something my father said about the RUC."

"It's not helpful for you to be making fun of us," Varick said.

Susan pointed at the drawing. "Who is this man?"

"I have no idea," I said guardedly.

Varick refolded the drawing while Susan removed a small notebook from her pocketbook. "Since our last visit," she said, "we took the liberty of having you followed, for your protection of course."

"Why do I need protection?"

"You're a witness to a gangland slaying," Varick said.

"I saw nothing."

"They don't know that."

"They?"

"Salvatore Marinelli and his associates."

I could not help but laugh. If only they knew, I thought.

"What's so funny?" Varick asked.

"I thought America would be safer than my homeland."

Susan began reading from her notebook. "May 18. Subject seen getting in limousine in front of his apartment on Fifty-First Street. Driver of limousine is one James Crosetti, long-time bodyguard for Salvatore Marinelli and reputed hit man. Also present in vehicle is unidentified passenger—see accompanying sketch—late forties or early fifties, curly white hair. Followed limousine to Riker's Island. Crosetti stopped at Korean deli on corner of Hazen Avenue and Twentieth Avenue. Crosetti went inside and returned with package. Continued on to Riker's where Crosetti parked in visitor parking lot. He waited while subject and curly-haired man walked across bridge to prison. They returned three hours later, whereupon I followed them to subject's apartment. Subject went into building and I followed limousine to Parker Meridian Hotel. The curly-haired man went inside and returned twenty-two minutes later with garment bag and suitcase. Crosetti loaded bags into trunk and drove away with his passenger. I made decision to remain so that I could interview hotel clerk, who informed undersigned that one Fischel Schaechter of Chicago, matching above mentioned description, had just checked out, paying his bill in cash."

She stopped reading. "They took me to visit Tommy Glynn," I said, trying to sound blasé.

Varick moved closer to me, swaying in a threatening manner. "Let's have it Sullivan. The truth. You never told us you knew Crosetti."

"I did not know his name. I knew the other man . . . ."

"Schaechter," Varick said loudly.

"Yes, Schaechter. He was a friend of Mr. Brandt, or so I was led to believe."

"I'm confused, Mr. Sullivan," Susan said. "At our previous meeting you said you sought out Mr. Brandt and met him at Marinelli's."

"On the eleventh, the day the restaurant is closed," Varick added sarcastically.

"I realized after you left I had been mistaken. It was the twelfth."

"Tell us about the meeting."

"I have already told you what I remember."

"You didn't mention Schaechter."

"I thought I had."

Varick shook his head in disgust. "What can you tell us about Schaechter?"

"He was with Mr. Brandt at the restaurant. But other than saying he was a friend, I do not recall him participating in the discussion."

"Go on," Susan said gently.

"After Mr. Brandt's death I called Mrs. Brandt to offer my condolences. I gave her my telephone number in case she wanted to contact me. Then, I believe it was the day before yesterday, I received a call from Mr. Schaechter. He said he could take me to see Tommy."

"Just like that?" Varick said. "Out of the blue."

"Yes, it would seem so, though I had spoken of Tommy at my earlier meeting with Mr. Brandt."

Susan turned several more pages in her notebook and stopped. "When you were at Riker's Island did you proceed through the security check-in with Schaechter?"

"Yes, I did."

"Did you see him sign in?"

"No."

"So you didn't know he signed in as Samuel Brandt?"

There was no use trying to hide my surprise. *"Mr. Brandt is dead."*

"Brilliant, Sullivan," Varick said.

"We are trying to help you, Mr. Sullivan," Susan said.

For every off-putting remark by Varick, Susan was quick to be solicitous. If this was a deliberate strategy, it was quite effective and I reminded myself to say as little as possible.

"Schaechter's registration card at the hotel listed his office telephone number in Chicago," Varick said.

"He said he was from Chicago."

"The number is disconnected."

"A mistake, no doubt."

"No mistake. The number was listed in his name."

"I see," I said, but I was as blind to the truth as I had ever been.

"It wasn't a number to an office, but a voice mail."

"I do not understand."

"Schaechter, or whoever he is, got the number from the phone company two days before he cancelled it."

"What could that mean?"

"You tell us, Sullivan."

"I cannot."

"Maybe you would also like to tell us why there is no such person as Fischel Schaechter in Chicago or anywhere else."

What could I say to such shocking news, and so I said nothing.

"Look, Mr. Sullivan," Susan said. *"We don't know who this man is or what he is up to. We don't know where he went after he checked out of the Parker Meridian. We don't know the extent of his association with Marinelli and we don't know why he is interested in you. We need your help."*

"What kind of help?"

Susan handed me a card from her pocketbook. *"This is my home number. If he contacts you again, call me."*

"I shall."

"I'm not finished, Susan," Varick said.

"Very sorry, Peter," Susan said.

I felt as if I was in the middle of lovers' quarrel, and then in looking at them both I realized that they had been lovers. "What is it?" I asked.

Susan stepped closer to me. I thought she might ask me to leave with her, help her get away from Varick. It was a bizarre fantasy to have at that moment and she must have seen my quizzical look, because she quickly returned to her former position.

"The prison records indicate Schaechter saw Peter Marinelli when you were with Glynn," she said. "Do you know why?"

"No."

"You don't know much, do you, Sullivan," Varick said.

Susan's face turned red. "That is totally uncalled for, Peter."

Varick ignored her. "What was in the package, Sullivan?"

"What package?"

"The one Crosetti picked up at the Korean deli."

"A bag of groceries, I imagine."

"I said package, Sullivan. Customers don't get their groceries in packages."

"I was not paying attention."

"Susan, what do we know about the proprietor?"

"He's under indictment for smuggling."

"What did he smuggle?" I asked.

"All kinds of things," Varick said. "Squibs, powder, caps, safety fuses, delay connectors . . . "

"I do not understand."

"The stuff of bombs, Sullivan."

"The strike force lawyers just left," I said to Jimmy as I got in the limousine.

"What did you tell them?"

"They did the talking."

Jimmy pulled away from the curb. "Let's have it."

"I am being followed."

"Not this morning,"

"But they said—"

"He's resting quietly on a stoop down the street."

"What?"

"He'll be on his feet in an hour or so. With a headache. No matter how hard they try, a Fed never looks like John Q. American."

"They told me something else."

"Yeah?"

"There is no Fischel Schaechter."

"That's funny, 'cause he looks real enough for me."

"What is his name?"

"You'll have to ask . . . Fischel." He stared at me in the rear view mirror, stone-faced, then letting his mouth open into a toothy grin.

Jimmy told me to take the chair across from the desk where Salvatore was sitting, while he leaned against the wall a few feet from the shuttered window. Needles of light were streaming through the holes in the wood, illuminating particles of dust floating in the air like bubbles in water.

"A pleasure to see you, Mr. Sullivan," Salvatore said warmly. On the desk was a figurine, six inches tall, of a man with a mask over his face. "Darth Vader," he said. "In need of repair. See, his light saber is falling off."

"Who is Darth Vader?"

"You are not familiar with Star Wars?"

"I am afraid not."

"A pity," Salvatore said. He opened the top drawer. "Look. I have all the characters. My grandson gave them to me."

"The one you are holding. What is his story?"

"In his youth Darth Vader was a great warrior, a Jedi. But he went over to the dark side. His son Luke does not know Darth Vader is his father. He knows only that Darth Vader is a defender of the empire. In the last of the films, 'The Return of the Jedi,' Darth Vader must either defend the empire or save his son. He chooses his son and helps him destroy the empire. He also removes the mask, revealing himself to Luke."

"A happy ending."

"No."

"What happened?"

"The mask gave Darth Vader life. Removing the mask took his life."

"Then, he deliberately chose death in order to reveal himself to his son."

"Yes."

I had the feeling that Darth Vader's broken light saber was no coincidence and that Salvatore told me the story of the film and the conflict between father and son to convey a message.

"What do you know of my father?" I asked.

He opened the desk drawer and removed a photograph. "Not a very good picture, I'm afraid," he said. "Your mother was not good with a camera."

I recognized the Divismore tenement where I lived as a boy. Da was standing behind me, his arms slung over my shoulders. Flanking him were Salvatore, a stocky man with bushy white hair, and a younger man in a business suit.

"Who is the man with the white hair?"

"Whitey Delaney."

"And the other man?"

"The owner of the car repair place where your father worked."

"Why were you in Belfast?"

"To conclude an arrangement with your father and Delaney."

"What sort of arrangement?"

"Delaney had come to me with a proposal. As you know, his partners were my cousin Vincente and Carlito Gavencci. They were interested in moving into Connecticut. They wanted me to help them."

"What did my father have to do with that?"

"Nothing. It was, how should I say it, an omnibus ... that is the right word, I believe ... proposal." He stopped for a moment and smiled. This rough man had an air of Continental sophistication that I found irresistible. "Well," he continued, "our dear friend Mr. Delaney had come into cash, cash that friends of the IRA raised, which he proposed to use for the purchase of arms, at a handsome profit of course. He also said that your father was disturbed at the IRA's lack of action and was working with others to form a new organization."

"The Provisionals?"

"Yes. But that was of no interest to me. I am a businessman. I was acquainted with a man in Milan who knew the weapons trade and worked

303

with a merchant from Hamburg. So, Delaney and I negotiated a mutually profitable agreement. He supplied the cash and I provided the contacts. I helped him in Connecticut and received my fair share of the take."

"My father was a gun runner?"

"I prefer to call him a purchasing agent."

"How long did this arrangement last?"

"Many years. Then, certain difficulties arose."

"What difficulties?"

"You must understand that my participation was limited. I only facilitated contacts with my European connections. But then Milan called to say payment had not been forthcoming for certain shipments. The FBI had intercepted the wire transfers. The Provisionals made other arrangements, with Libyan suppliers, I believe."

"Did you keep in touch with my father?"

"From time to time. But until a month ago I had not spoken to him in many years."

How little I knew, I thought. "You talked to him a month ago?"

"Yes, it was very kind of him to call. He wanted to express his concern for my son's plight."

"How did he know about that?"

"Forgive me, Mr. Sullivan. I am getting senile. I leave out many facts. Mr. Brandt had told him that Peter was in prison. You know that they were in touch, I assume."

"I knew that Brandt was interested in testimony I might supply to support my father's confession."

"Yes. Such a curse. Two innocent men in prison."

"I visited Tommy Glynn yesterday."

He put the figurine on the desk. "A fine young man. And such a tragedy, one for which I feel responsible. He was in my care, you know. Delaney sought my assistance after Tommy escaped from that prison in Ireland. Normally, I would have not concerned myself with such a matter, but your father called me and . . . well, I agreed. Tommy came to live here." He pointed to the ceiling. "I converted the upstairs space into an apartment, hardly what one would call a home, but sufficient for his needs."

"How did the FBI find him?"

"Tommy was a good boy. He wanted to earn his keep. He offered to assist me in my operations. I saw no need to involve him in the questionable aspects of my business. I gave him simple jobs: delivery, watchman, carpentry work on my home. And then I sent him to paint my building on Thirteenth Street."

"Where he was arrested?"

"Yes."

"Who betrayed him?"

"You know the answer, Mr. Sullivan."

I was shaking. "It cannot be," I cried. "It cannot be Da."

He reached over and clutched my hand. "No, Mr. Sullivan, it was not your father. It was Delaney."

I took my hand away and sighed with relief. "Thank the Lord."

Salvatore shifted sideways and looked at Jimmy, who had been standing still, arms folded, throughout the conversation. "Tell him," Jimmy said. "He deserves to know."

"Know what?" I asked, alarmed. "What else is there to know?"

Salvatore turned back to me, his face suddenly soft with sadness. His elbow hit the figurine and it toppled off the desk. As I snatched it out of the air, I was vaguely aware of a shadow crossing my hand, the needles of light from the shutters disappearing. Salvatore grabbed my hand as if to thank me for catching the figurine, but then his other hand shot upward. From the corner of my eye I saw Jimmy broad-step to the window. Using my grip on Salvatore's hand, I forced him down and toward me. It was too late. With a pop, like a balloon bursting, his head snapped back and blood sprayed against my chin. We collapsed on the floor, Salvatore on top of me.

Another pop and a piece of wood from the edge of the desk shot up to the ceiling, piercing the drywall. Jimmy crashed his shoulder against the shuttered window. Planks flew outward. Jimmy stuck his gun through the window. Still another pop, this time from Jimmy's gun, then silence.

Jimmy was at my side, shaking his head. "Shit, shit, shit," he wailed, his chest expanding and contracting. He pushed me away and put his head to Salvatore's chest. I stumbled to the window. A man, middle-aged, thin and wiry like Salvatore, lay on his back against the pipe, the pipe that had served as my hiding place three nights before. His leather jacket was soaked with blood and a revolver lay on the ground next to his hand.

Jimmy was crying, rocking back and forth, cradling Salvatore's head in his lap. I staggered to the desk and picked up the telephone.

"No," Jimmy said.

"We must call the police."

Jimmy lowered Salvatore's head to the floor and stood. He rubbed his eyes and said, "No police."

"What are you going to do?" I asked.

He hoisted his bulky frame through the window. I knelt on the floor next to Salvatore. His head was lying in a pool of blood; his white hair was matted and stained red. I whimpered, "I'm sorry," the very words I would have said had I been standing next to my dying father.

I remained there until Jimmy crawled back inside. He then turned around and reached through the opening. The muscles in his back rippled against his shirt as he strained in a lifting motion. In a moment, the dead man's face appeared.

"What are you doing?" I cried.

He continued lifting until he had the body halfway through the window. He moved to the side and put both hands on the legs. With a shove, the body fell inside the office.

"Wait here," Jimmy said, as he kicked the dead man in the face and left the office. I sat cross-legged on the floor, in shock.

He returned with two large black bags. "We've got to get rid of the bodies," he said. "You have to help."

"No," I screamed, and lunged at him.

He took my arms in his powerful grasp and threw me to the floor.

"What's gotten into you, Sullivan?"

I was unafraid, almost emboldened. "I want no more to do with any of this."

"You don't have a choice. You're going to help me clean this place. Then we're going to load the bodies in the trunk of my limo."

"Why not call the police? You shot the man in self defense."

"Christ, Sullivan, be real. Besides, the plan . . . "

"What plan?"

He did not answer, going to the other man and rolling him over to search inside his jacket. I stood behind him as he removed a wallet. Inside was a photograph underneath clear plastic, showing a smiling man with a woman and three small children. Wedged behind the photograph was an Illinois driver's license.

"Can you fucking believe it?" he said. "The one person I didn't figure on."

I looked at the name on the license. "Oh, my God."

"Fucking pizza man."

"Danny Marinelli," I said.

"Yeah, Vincente's son."

Yet again, a character from Fischel's past had penetrated the present. "Is that what you people do?" I said, nearly babbling. "Kill each other until no one is left? Is this your idea of justice?"

"Shut up, Sullivan. You don't know what you're talking about."

He began to search the rest of Danny Marinelli's clothes. But as he turned him on his side to get at a pants pocket, the other arm twitched and moved in the opposite direction. I heard a soft groan.

"He is alive," I said.

"You're crazy."

The arm moved again, though the groaning had stopped. I knelt over the body. I could see his eyes moving under the eyelids, as if he was dreaming. "Look, Jimmy. I tell you he is still alive."

Danny's lips parted to emit a gurgling sound. Blood filled his mouth. His tongue was moving.

"What's he saying?" Jimmy asked.

"Shh," I said.

More gurgling and then a cough, as blood splattered against my cheek. I put my ear to his mouth.

"KE, KE, KE . . . " Danny mumbled.

"Shit, Sullivan, what is it?"

There was another gurgling sound, as more blood dribbled out of his mouth down his chin. I put my hand on his neck and searched for a pulse.

"He is dead," I said.

"It's about time," Jimmy said and opened the bags.

"He was trying to say a word, something beginning with K or C."

"I don't give a shit. Come on, let's get moving."

For the next few minutes we performed our bloody task in silence. With rags Jimmy brought from the kitchen, we wiped the floor and walls. We nailed the broken shutters over the window. Then we carried the bodies through the restaurant to the front door.

The street was crowded with traffic and pedestrians. "This isn't going to work," Jimmy said, looking through the window. "We'll have to take them upstairs. Give me time to figure out what to do."

"To the apartment?"

"Come on."

We carried the bodies up the stairs. The apartment consisted of one room and a bathroom. We put the bodies in the bathroom and shut the door. Jimmy sat on the bed.

I could not believe what I had just done, as I stood in the middle of the room staring at my bloody hands.

"We've got to get the blood off us," Jimmy said, pointing at the bathroom. "You first."

"No."

I heard street sounds suddenly grow louder.

"Shit," Jimmy said. "Someone's downstairs. Stay where you are and keep quiet." He rushed out of the apartment.

I found the strength to move and went to the bed. There was a telephone on the floor and I considered calling the police. But I knew this would accomplish nothing. I closed my eyes and pretended I was home, sitting with Mary and Lucy in our gazebo. I put my face into the pillow.

I stayed there until Jimmy returned. "Just the chef," he said, pulling my head off the pillow. "Get your shit together, Sullivan."

He coaxed me into the bathroom and turned on the water. I avoided looking at the bags resting against the bathtub. "Wash your hands," he said. "Then get the hell out of here." He reached in his pocket and pulled out a twenty-dollar bill. "This time, take a goddamn cab," he said, handing the money to me.

"But the chef?"

"He's in the kitchen."

I put my hands under the cold water. The blood was stuck to my skin like dried paint. "How do you know I will not call the police?"

He rubbed my hands together. "Call the police and you'll never know the truth about your father."

He rubbed harder. "I want to know," I said.

We heard another noise from downstairs. He ran to the door and looked down the stairway. "Just a waiter. Let's go."

"Not until you tell me."

"This is no time to play games."

He pushed me to the stairs. I stumbled down the steps and through the front door into the sunlight. I walked a few blocks before hailing a taxi.

The telephone was ringing as I entered the studio. But when I picked up the receiver, I heard only a click and then a dial tone. I called the long distance operator, and she connected me to my home. The phone rang a dozen times with no answer. I hung up and called the operator again, giving her the number of my father's house. No answer there either.

There was one decision to make and I made it. The time had come. I went to the closet.

When I finished packing, I filled Cuchulainn's dish with food and poured fresh water into his bowl. I would call the landlord from the airport and hope that he would find him a new home. But Cuchulainn knew my plan and did not come to eat. He purred loudly and arched his back, imploring me to take him. I scooped him in my arms and went out the door.

I asked the taxi driver to stop at the pet store, where I purchased a carrying case. From a nearby payphone, I again tried to call Mary and my father; the result was the same. I thought of calling the Boston Strike Force and decided against it. I just wanted to go home.

At the airport, I asked a porter to check my suitcase. He refused, saying that security rules required me to first exchange my ticket. I went inside and stood at the end of the ticket queue. I touched the outside of my jacket and felt the comforting bulge of my ticket and passport.

In twenty minutes, I neared the front of the queue. A man of advanced age was having difficulty getting the agent to understand him. Although he was speaking slowly, his heavy brogue laced with Irish had the agent shaking his head in exasperation. I started fidgeting, anxious to be on the plane home. Finally, the agent gave the old man a boarding pass and I moved forward.

I told the agent I wanted a seat on the next flight. He took my ticket and punched several keys on his computer terminal. "Very good, Mr. Sullivan," he said with a smile. "We are able to give you a seat, 22J, for no additional charge. Passport please."

I handed him my passport and raised the carrying case to wish Cuchulainn a safe trip before I put it on the luggage scale with my suitcase. The agent's smile turned into a frown.

"What is wrong?" I asked.

"Are you traveling alone?"

"Yes. Why?"

He handed me the passport. "You have someone else's passport," he said.

I opened the passport folder and saw the name and accompanying photograph. It was all I could do not to laugh at the hideous absurdity of it all. What I was holding was a cruel variation of telling a joke and having the listener respond that, "The joke's on you, fellow."

While the agent waited for an explanation, I emptied my wallet and showed him other identification. He said he could not issue a boarding pass without my passport.

A supervisor in a suit with the close-cropped hair of a bureaucrat approached us. The ticket agent handed him the passport.

The supervisor pointed at the picture. "Do you know this man?"

I was unsure whether to answer yes or no. And what would I say when he asked how I had come into possession of the passport?

"Yes," I said, desperately trying to think of a satisfactory explanation. "He is a colleague of mine. We met for breakfast together this morning at the hotel. There must have been a mix-up when we checked out."

He looked incredulous and said he would retain the passport. I would also have to wait while he investigated the matter further. He told me to come around the corner, where a doorway in the back wall led to a small room.

"I will miss the flight." I said.

"We must follow procedures."

He was closing the door behind me when I heard a voice, "Cornelius, Cornelius Sullivan, wait."

The supervisor and I turned at the same time to see an out-of-breath Patrick running toward us. "Thank God you're here," he said. "You must have my passport."

"Are you Patrick Casey?" the supervisor asked.

Patrick nodded and handed his wallet to him. "Here, look at my driver's license."

The supervisor opened the wallet and pulled out the license. After comparing it with the passport, he handed them to Patrick. "Do you have Mr. Sullivan's passport?" he asked.

"Yes," Patrick said. "In my car." Then, looking at me, "Come, Connie. I'm double parked."

I started to follow Patrick, but the supervisor stopped me. "You will have to take your baggage," he said.

"May I not leave it here? I will return, I assure you."

"I'm afraid not," he said. "As I said—procedures."

Patrick took my suitcase and the cat carrier, and we headed for the exit. "What are you doing here?" I asked.

"Good thing this is my day off."

Jimmy was waiting outside, standing in front of his limousine talking to a police officer. "I told you they would be here in a minute," he said to the officer as we approached.

Jimmy took a firm hold on my elbow and nudged me into the back seat. Patrick got in the other side.

"Where are you taking me?"

"Where you should have stayed," Jimmy said.

Before you complain about Patrick keeping you captive this afternoon . . . try to think of someone else for once in your life . . . that's right, don't be so self-involved. You're damn right I should talk. In your mad dash for the airport, in your desperation to return home, you were running away. Connie, please, this is not the time for psychoanalysis. I have to tell you something. Are you listening? For God's sake, pay attention. Your father is dead. Yes, he is dead. He died an hour ago. Stay right where you are. There's no reason to call. Everyone is at the hospital. Your wife tried to reach you this morning, but you had already left to meet Salvatore. She called me. Yes, me. I had given her my number. Who am I? I'm me, that's who. Slow down, you're speaking too fast. Patrick! Get Connie a glass of water. Here, hold on to me. It's all right. Let it out.

That's better. Take a drink. Slowly, Connie. No, you can't go. In the first place, there are no flights to Belfast at night. Second, you don't have a passport. I have it. Since the day you fainted over on Lexington. Well, not fainted, I admit. Smitty knocked you on the head, which, I must say, upset me. It wasn't necessary. I can't tell you that right now. We need your passport. More important, we can't let you leave, not yet anyway. Sure, you can go to the Irish office tomorrow and get another passport. But I wanted to see you today before you made a decision, one you might later regret. You see, you should know about your father—

For God's sake, Connie. Jimmy told me you have a violent streak, but you'll learn nothing by strangling me. And look around, these nice people want to enjoy themselves. They don't need to witness a crazy Irishman murdering a crazy Jew.

KE, KE, KE. Beats the hell out of me. Was he trying to say a name? I don't know anyone whose name begins with K . . . or do I. Maybe he was asking for his wife. Damnit. I can't remember her name. Oh well, it's probably nothing. What? Rosalie. That's right. God, Connie, you have a marvelous memory. It makes me wonder why . . . no, I'm not being fair. I know you would remember if you could—whatever it is you think you've forgotten.

I'm so sorry about your father. I know he would have wanted to tell you himself when this business was finished and you were back home. But he knew yesterday that the end was near. He asked your mother to call Salvatore and give him permission to tell you. Frankly, I was a little worried that once you knew, you'd get the hell out of here and return to Belfast, but it was his call. I must say he took a fatherly interest in you. So, Salvatore is gone . . . excuse me, now I need another drink. I loved that old man. He lived in a strange and violent world, but he was gentler than the rest of us.

No, I won't tell you what he was going to say. This last secret is my trump card, the reason you'll stay. And believe me when I tell you that your father wanted you to stay in New York. To finish what we started. OK, to finish what *I* started. I know I said the original purpose was to see if you could help with Tommy's appeal. As you might have suspected, it was a half-truth, less than a half-truth, a one-quarter truth at most.

Do you want another drink? Patrick, another drink. Aren't those strike force lawyers smart? So much for Fischel Schaechter. Gold and Varick were wrong in one respect. Fischel Schaechter does exist; or rather, he did exist. He was Sarah's brother; he died of a brain tumor when I was a boy. Who I am? I am everything I have told you except a name. How important can a name be at this moment? Your poor father has passed, Salvatore was shot dead, and mayhem surrounds us. I don't know what will happen next? We should be thankful for this temporary sanctuary called Murphy's. And you're not the only one who will be leaving the country in a couple of days. I need a vacation.

I had to sign in as Sam when we went to Riker's Island. This is his bar registration card. Molly gave it to me. Since I'm not related to either Tommy or Peter, they wouldn't have let us in. I visited with Peter to see how he was doing. Why sit around while you were talking to Tommy.

What's that? Susan Gold's number. Sure, you can call her. What are you going to say? The truth? You don't know the truth. You have your lies and you have my lies. If you call her, I'll perform my disappearing act and then where will you be? You won't be allowed to return home; they'll keep you here until they find out what's going on, which may be a very long time. Is that what you want? Put her card away, don't call her, stick it out, and in due course you'll know more.

What can I say? How would I know what Danny was capable of? How could I know that he would fly to New York to avenge his father's death? I'll tell you one thing, though. We should be on the lookout for anyone I name in one of my stories. You're right. I'm not being very clever or funny.

One last question? A package. What package? I don't know. I thought he stopped for cigarettes. I wasn't watching. Did you ask him? Maybe you should. You don't say. Maybe Jimmy is going to blow up the headquarters of the Savin Hill gang. I wouldn't put it past him. Of course, since the leaders are dead . . . no, I'm assuming Delaney is dead. He disappeared, which is the functional equivalent of being dead. If the package contained explosives, I'm glad we didn't know it. If I remember correctly, it was a bumpy ride to Riker's. We would have been terrified the whole way.

Stop shaking. Tell you what; let's return to the past, my past. It may not be comforting, but it's diverting and it will take your mind off the here and now. The funeral? When will it be? Friday or Saturday. We'll see, Connie. We'll just have to see.

I know how you feel. I lost Sarah and Albert. Death isn't as tough on the living as life is.

When I got back to Chicago, Gordon said he wanted a divorce. Not from his wife, Connie. From me! I hadn't charged a third for the case against Marty, just the regular hourly rate because there was no risk to the case. It was obvious the insurance company would pay. Gordon was pissed, accused me of not caring enough about money. Disingenuous on his part, considering he would never handle a contingency fee case anyway.

He handed me an agreement dissolving our partnership. "Wonderful," I said. "I might as well get both divorces over at once." That night I told my wife reconciliation wouldn't be possible.

Though I could sit here and give you lots of reasons to justify why I divorced my wife, I will resist the temptation. Divorce is so catholic—pardon the reference—yet so pedestrian. Anyway, I would end up blaming her rather than looking inside myself to see what was really at work. Why would you, a happily married man, want to hear about a divorce? You learn nothing from divorce. I don't think I learned anything from my divorce except that pain hurts, which I already knew.

So there I was, without wife or law partner trying to make ends meet in a new firm with one secretary and one associate when into my life and practice walked Garth James. He was not someone I wanted to see. The deal with Gordon left me with a dozen contingent fee cases and my share of our profit sharing account—$40,000— which I used to pay my divorce lawyer a $10,000 retainer, first month rent and security deposit on new office space, and as collateral for a bank loan to purchase office furniture. I needed more clients who paid by the hour, not a destitute interior designer intent on suing his former lover.

But when you're down, even if not out, you take what comes, and I was cynical enough to think Garth might have a case that could produce a quick settlement and fee. He had gotten my name from Chad Billings, a partner at the Washington firm of Williams & Connelly who I knew from my strike force days—Chad had worked for the Justice Department in Washington. Garth had gone to Chad because he had seen him on television representing one of the Watergate burglars before Congress and thought he would be perfect to handle his planned suit against Charles Roberts III. I asked Chad why he called me, a Chicago lawyer, to represent Garth. He said no one in Washington would touch the case; he had also contacted lawyers in New York, Philadelphia, and Boston, working card by card through his Rolodex, moving west, when he came across my name.

I wasn't sure I should even bother meeting with Garth and sought an opinion from the one person whose judgment I respected, my associate Kathy Shawn. She hadn't been a lawyer long enough to be cynical, but she wasn't an idealist either. The youngest of six children from a Polish-American family and the only one who had graduated from college, she worked at night as a bartender right through law school. She had wanted to become a lawyer, she said, because she believed that the legal profession held opportunities for women, though she learned during her interviews that the doors of opportunity opened only to the ground floor. She then decided to look for work at a small litigation firm where she'd have a chance to prove her worth.

Gordon, who insisted on doing our hiring—he claimed to have superior judgment about people—offered her a job halfway through the interview because he liked her legs and thought she might be a desirable love option if he grew bored with his current lover. But shortly after she started, she told him she preferred to work on my contingency fee cases because I had agreed to let her argue motions and take depositions. Gordon said he wanted to discuss her request over dinner. She said she never mixed business with pleasure. He assured her that the dinner would be all business, but she was too clever for Gordon, saying, "Food is pleasure."

Kathy had been my sounding board, lending me moral support in my manipulations in the Athena Art case and telling me I was doing the smart, if not the right thing, when I sued Marty Glickman in those dark days following my falling out with Judy.

Kathy and I had gone office hunting together, like lovers looking for their first home. I would see space and immediately want to sign a lease for some cockamamie reason—nice view, oversized office for me—while she paid attention to what counted: the amount of rent, hidden charges, elevator presence, the things that could determine whether we would be in business for six months or six years. I let her negotiate the lease because the building manager would give us an additional concession for every inch she let her skirt ride up above her knees. She used her brains to decide what she wanted, and then used whatever else necessary to accomplish it.

Despite her dictum prohibiting mixing business with pleasure, she spent every work evening drinking with me at Yvette, which catered to young professionals like Kathy and lonely estranged guys like me. I liked the bar for the little things: the clocks on the wall that showed the time in different cities around the world, the two gay pianists who played show tunes on back-to-back Steinway grand pianos, the bartender who served straight-up martinis with a bucket of ice and a free refill, and the men's room attendant who announced the sports scores when he handed me a towel.

Kathy said our drinking together didn't fit her definition of pleasure. She said alcohol made me talk about the law more, not less—as I am sure you know, Connie, from these many nights here at Murphy's. With her glass of Budweiser Light next to my martini, a metaphor in my mind for two suitors feeling each other out, I told her I did not want to meet Garth James.

"It's just a meeting," she said.

"I have a bad feeling about it. A breach of promise cases is a glorified form of blackmail."

"That's a man going through a divorce talking."

"How do you talk?"

She put the bottle of beer to her lips, oblivious to the fat businessman next to her, who appeared to have lost his capacity to breathe while looking at her. "Like a lawyer," she said.

"Go on," the fat man said. "You're not a lawyer."

"And you're not a gentleman," she said.

Garth was not what I expected. I thought he would be short with a pretty-boy face, southern accent—don't ask me why—maybe an albino who never left the veranda for a walk in the sun on sticky summer days, drinking mint juleps with the "girls," trading catty comments about the old geezers in town, gesturing with an arm stretched out, palm up, like a waiter carrying a tray. Or maybe I expected someone tall, with a soft belly and thinning hair, but possessing a flair for the devilish insight, tinged with good-humored bitchiness, dressed in white suit with carnation pinned to the lapel. Well, he was tall and he was bitchy, but his flair resided exclusively in his looks. Actually, he was taller than tall, closer to seven feet than six, so thin he seemed to be walking on stilts hidden beneath trousers at least two sizes too big, lending his gait the fluidity of a ghost gliding on air. His face was even more striking: classic features like what you would expect to see on an ancient Roman bust, aquiline nose, sensuous mouth, golden brown skin, a model's face—no visible wear in this thirty-two-year-old visage of lust.

As Garth sat across from us, his grace and mesmerism faded as he attended to his overlong beige colored fingernails, using the index fingers to work under each nail, scraping away microscopic, if not imaginary, particles of dust. The air was redolent with the smell of grape from cologne he must have applied before coming to the office. And when he spoke— say to ask for a glass of water to help him swallow five pills, in different colors and sizes—his voice rose toward the end of each sentence, like a tenor singing an arpeggio. "It's a wonder I am still alive," was his favorite refrain.

His story, a "tale told by an idiot, full of sound and fury, signifying nothing," drove Kathy to put down her notepad after a few sentences. He first met Charles eight years earlier in the steam room of an Alexandria, Virginia health club. "I was allowing my pores to be cleansed," he said, "when Charles entered, towel covering his manhood. It was passion at first sight." Kathy put a hand to her mouth, trying to stifle a chuckle. Garth turned to her with the haughty look of a head butler in an English manor. "Passion, my dear, is ever more rare than love."

Some time thereafter, while still in the steam room, Garth became "tumescent,"—provoking another laugh, this time from me—and Charles, seeing through the droplets of water in the air, reciprocated with his own "flagpole," an "irresistible temptation," but one Garth resisted despite his urgent need to "wrap" his lips on a "living member of the kingdom of Eros." No wonder Kathy stopped taking notes!

Charles thought he was as straight as they come, married for twenty years to his college sweetheart, proud father of two teenage daughters, and a hard-working man to the core, toiling as regional sales manager for Northern Virginia Cable. He had learned in the steam room, however, that a little push would bend what had always been straight. Before he left, he gave Garth his telephone number at the office and said he'd be happy to meet him for lunch later in the week.

Garth wanted more than just another date—he was a notorious cruiser of the gay scene. His self-proclaimed expertise in designing palaces for foreign potentates failed to produce the large volume of clients he had hoped for—his only assignment had been the design of a new kitchen in one of Gaddafi palaces—and he desperately needed financial support. Banks had grown tired of his defaults; so, becoming a "kept" man seemed like a reasonable option. He thought, wrongly as it turned out, that Charles was awash in cash because he had worn a gold Rolex into the steam room. (Charles's grandfather had given him the watch for his forty-fifth birthday.)

They had a whirlwind courtship, starting with lunch at the Georgetown Four Seasons Hotel. By dessert they were holding hands under the table. Charles confessed he was a virgin, insofar as same-sex sex was concerned, but the experienced Garth said it made his desire even more intense. They retired to a room—which Charles paid for—and Garth initiated Charles into the pleasures of homosexual love. Three days later, Charles told his wife he wanted a divorce.

Garth's hopes for the good life waned when Charles moved into a studio apartment at Buckingham Court, a low rent subdivision in Arlington for bottom-rung government workers, furniture rented from Swingles. But Garth figured he might as well play the hand the gods had dealt him, which included two eviction notices, one for his apartment in Capital Hill's newest high rise, the other for his office, overpriced but with a view of the White House. And the bank had repossessed his car the day after he met Charles at the health club. Of course, he still had his oozing sexuality.

Then something happened, so wonderful it brought Garth to tears as he sat in my office, tears he wiped from his cheeks with a silk handkerchief. Charles's boss at Northern Virginia Cable formed a group to buy out ownership and wanted Charles to run the company for a salary of $200,000 per year plus a signing bonus of $50,000. Garth and Charles celebrated at the Four Seasons, where Charles wrote Garth a check for $25,000. Garth paid his past due bulls, leased a new Jaguar, and traveled to North Africa in search of palaces to furnish.

Charles's corporate career took off. Northern Virginia Cable's revenues increased and incentives in his employment contract kicked in. He organized a team to take over the company and resold it three months later for $1,500,000. He settled with his wife and bought a penthouse condominium overlooking the Potomac, designed and furnished by Garth, with his and "her" bedrooms, the larger one for Garth.

Around this time, Garth introduced Charles to *The Course in Miracles,* a book written by a married couple of no special distinction, but who had tapped into what the emotionally dispossessed need by way of "new age" sustenance. It became a best seller, helping to give birth to a new religion—or cult, depending on you point of view. They organized workshops around the country, though most of them were in places where lost people liked to go to find themselves: Taos, Carmel, Lenox, New Hope, Moab, Elko, Missoula, Provincetown, Uvalde—yes, Uvalde, the birthplace of John Nance Garner. Read the book, if you can get through it. A Russian novel is light reading compared to that compendium of New Age doggerel. Imagine wading through several hundred pages of exercises, admonitions, and rules of living. You feel like you've tied your shoes a hundred times. And guess what? Instead of researching the law of palimony, breach of promise, and alienation of affection, I would study *The Course in Miracles,* for both Garth and Charles were to claim the book was, as legalese would have it, incorporated by reference in their love agreement.

Garth took the book from his briefcase and presented it to me like it was a wedding present, saying if I read it we could dispense with further discussion. I assured him I would read it, but said it would be useful if he told me what to look for. The importance of love and commitment, he answered, as if no other work in the history of humankind contained this piece of wisdom. While he droned on about his years with Charles, how he cooked and cleaned while Charles added to his millions, lifted his spirits when he was down, and shared his joy when he closed a deal, I absentmindedly turned the pages, stopping at the section on the most important rules of life. "I don't think we'll want to use this book," I said. "Why?" Garth asked, as if I was heartless to reject what he thought was the equal of God's word. I said, "It says here to accept what life dishes out." He stretched his long arm across the table and snatched the book from me. "It doesn't say I can't sue," he said obstinately. I shrugged and said, "Like the Bible, it's a matter of interpretation."

In the seventh year of their relationship Charles sold his cable holdings for 200 million dollars. He established a fifty-million-dollar trust fund for his children and purchased 1,000 acres in the Shenandoah Valley where he wanted to build a mansion, golf resort, and vacation home community. Charles had also invested the modest additional sum of $200,000 in Garth's company, none of which Garth repaid. Charles soon got tired of Garth's trips to North Africa, his thrice weekly tours of the D.C. gay bars, and his monthly demands for money.

Garth said he'd be pleased to work on the Shenandoah project—calling it "Garthro"—but he wanted a $50,000 retainer. When Charles reminded him that he hadn't received a return on his investment, Garth said, "How can you expect anything if I don't charge for my work." I asked Garth to show me in *The Course in Miracles* where it said it was OK to charge your lover for the design of his home when you owe him so much money. He said, "Why do attorneys insist on being so literal?"

The heart of Garth's case lay in various letters Charles wrote while away on business. Viewed as a whole, you could get the impression that Charles had promised Garth everlasting love and—here's the operative phrase from one of his letters— "everything I have, including all the clouds in the sky." I was fortunate Garth didn't demand that we sue for half the firmament.

Even if Kathy and I agreed that Charles's epistolary covenant was legally binding, he had written the letters before he closed his first deal, before his everything became valuable. Moreover, he was in the middle of divorce proceedings, and it remained to be seen what he would own after his wife's lawyer got through with him. His later letters never talked about sharing clouds or money. Absent were further protestations of love, leaving the letters burdened with lengthy and turgid discourses on economic theory and the virtues of capitalism.

"What do you think of my case?" Garth asked.

Kathy placed her hand on mine, her usual means of telling me to keep my mouth shut. "Have you told us everything?" she asked.

"When it comes to love, words are inadequate."

"I saw you taking various pills. What are they for?"

"My health."

"You said, 'It's a wonder I am still alive.' What did you mean?"

"I am HIV positive," he said, as if it was a badge of pride.

"Since when?"

"I don't know. But it showed up in a test I took three years ago."

"Did Charles know?"

"Yes. But so what. He was so strict. He refused to make love without a condom anyway." He sighed. "He could be so stubborn."

"Engaging in safe sex is not being stubborn."

"But then he said not even condoms are adequate protection. It was so unfair for him to blame me . . . "

"For contracting HIV?"

"No, for seeking other lovers. I do have my needs, you know."

I couldn't keep quiet any longer. "You want us to sue Charles for breach of contract, even though you spent the better part of your relationship cheating on him."

Garth reached in his pocket and took another pill. "You're not being very supportive."

"We have to know the facts," Kathy said.

"I just want what is coming to me," he said. "I am sure Charles will want to settle as soon as you file the complaint."

"Is that right," I said.

"The world still believes he's straight. He'll pay to keep it that way."

Though Garth sounded like a blackmailer, we agreed to take the case. If Charles offered an immediate settlement, it would be easy enough to withdraw the complaint before the press got wind of it. And if he decided to litigate, the early letters and length of their relationship would be sufficient to survive a motion to dismiss and send the case to a jury.

You might say Garth's case was the inevitable result of the law of contracts, which champions the idea that parties to a contract are entitled to the "benefit of the bargain." But what had Charles gotten out of the bargain? "Sex," Garth said—that is, until he contracted HIV. We explained that sex for money is not an enforceable contract except in marriage. Garth, not one to stubbornly stick to a losing argument, changed his answer and said he had given Charles the benefit of his love and companionship. But hadn't Charles reciprocated in kind? Why should Garth be entitled to half of Charles's money? It wasn't as if Garth could say he was forced to give up his career to be a homemaker or raise their children. That's the law of contracts for you. It sanctifies written deals, oral deals, deals made in a fit of passion, deals made out of anger, good deals, bad deals, and crazy deals. It will even manufacture a deal where none exists, calling it "quantum meruit"—the value of services rendered.

Garth underestimated Charles, who had made his fortune and was no longer worried that his sexual orientation would be made public. He also wasn't about to give in to blackmail, whatever the law said. He hired A. Collins Wickersham, Washington's preeminent civil litigation lawyer, senior partner in a law firm of thirty-five lawyers molded in his image: crafty, aggressive, and uncompromising. Wickersham threatened to file a motion for sanctions, claiming the suit was frivolous, unless I withdrew the complaint. When that stratagem failed—such a motion can only be lodged after you win the case—he filed a counterclaim accusing Garth of misappropriating Charles's investment in the interior design business. Although Charles hadn't restricted the use of the money, he was miffed that Garth spent more than $50,000 on clothes and cosmetics. The counterclaim was a paper tiger. A signal benefit of poverty is the inability to pay a judgment.

As soon as we sued, Wickersham requested Garth's deposition and the production of his documents, including letters he received from Charles, the books and records of the interior design business, and diaries.

Kathy and I spent two evenings at Yvette reading the diaries. They consisted of twelve spiral notebooks, numbered one through twelve in various shades of red and pink. I took the even numbered notebooks and gave Kathy the rest. Even with the fortification of alcohol and background music of show tunes, the reading was tough going, not unlike wading through *The Course in Miracles.* The diaries portrayed a man who loved only himself. Tidbits like "What a genius I was to seduce Charles," "He finds my beauty irresistible," and "It is a miracle that someone will finally support me," sounded like the reflections of the evil queen in Snow White. Kathy came across the most damning entry, dated one day after Charles sold his cable interests: "Will tell Charles I'll sue him if he tries to break up with me." Kathy was not discouraged. She reminded me that threats were an integral part of divorce, and *Garth vs. Roberts* was just another kind of divorce suit.

I took Kathy to Washington for the deposition. We stayed at the Georgetown Four Seasons—how appropriate—where I treated us to a two-bedroom suite that cost more per night than Judy's rent for a month on the banks of the Rio Grande. We told Garth we wouldn't be arriving until the following day; we wanted to review our game plan in peace.

After unpacking, we went downstairs for drinks. I could see why Garth liked the hotel. The spacious lobby and the adjoining bar reeked of the traveler's good life: expensive floral decorations, finely carved wood molding, thick carpeting, gold fixtures, and the highest priced drinks I'd seen anywhere. We took a seat in a deep-cushioned leather couch with a view of the outside garden. A comely young waitress in an open-necked blouse and shoe-length wraparound skirt took our order. As she left who should appear but Garth and a blonde-haired man with bright blue eyes, wearing a brown bomber jacket. Garth introduced him as Dolph Jurgens, from Bremerhaven, on assignment for Exxon to design the kitchen and employee cafeteria in its new Silver Spring office building. To me, however, he looked like he'd been sent from the casting office to audition for the part of a Luftwaffe airman in a World War II film.

Dolph bowed and kissed the back of Kathy's hand while Garth summoned the waitress.

"What a pleasant surprise," I said.

"This is my favorite place in the whole world," Garth said, as he and Dolph, holding hands, sat on the couch to my right. "Dolph and I met at this very spot. It was a miracle."

"From the course in miracles," I said.

"Oh, you're such a facetious man," he said.

"I took the course in facetiousness."

Garth was too happy squeezing Dolph's hand to be upset. "Dolph helped me design the kitchen for Garthro."

"You don't say."

"And he had dinner with Charles and me one night."

"You don't say again."

"He will corroborate my testimony."

"How convenient."

Garth said that following Charles's purchase of land in the Shenandoah Valley they went for a weekend to the Homestead, a posh hotel and golf resort in the mountains of Western Virginia. Garth asked Charles if he could invite Dolph, who he proposed would be the ideal choice for supervising the design of the clubhouse kitchen and dining room.

"What happened?" I asked, when our drinks arrived.

"Before I tell you," Garth said, "let me propose a toast."

"How sweet," Kathy said, oozing with gushiness.

"'After all, my erstwhile dear, my no longer cherished, need we say it was no love, just because it perished.'"

"Very nice, Garth. Here's my toast: 'We always deceive ourselves twice about the people we love—first to their advantage, then to their disadvantage.'"

Garth turned to Dolph. "Lawyers always insist on the last word."

Kathy lifted her glass of wine, but instead of making a toast, she took a sip. "I love Edna St. Vincent Millay and Albert Camus, but what I want to hear is what happened at the Homestead."

"Oh, Kathy," Garth said. "I wish you were a man."

"I don't," Kathy said.

"Thank goodness," I said. "OK, Garth, let's hear it."

Garth patted Dolph on the knee and smoothed his hair. "Tell them," he said.

"It was like so," Dolph said in a crushing German accent, "we had sat down for dinner—"

"The three of you?" I interrupted.

"*Nein*, we were *vier*."

"Who else?"

"My wife."

"You're married?" Kathy said, stealing my shock.

"*Jawohl*, but no longer."

"Dolph is AC-DC," Garth said.

"Bisexual is the term, is it not," Dolph said, glaring at Garth.

"Keep going," I said.

"Charles offered a toast."

"What did he say?"

Garth tickled Dolph's knee, as if to say don't blow it. Moving away his leg in what I interpreted as a gesture of independence, Dolph said, " 'To our future life together, sharing everything I have and will ever have,' " and then relaxed with a wide grin of a job well done.

"Are you sure?"

He laughed, no doubt relieved to have survived the most arduous part of his performance. *"Enschuldigen sie,* I do not wish to make light of the matter, but I am quite sure. I remember my wife saying that she wished I would make her the same promise."

"Did you?" Kathy asked, looking like she was enjoying the show.

"On the spot."

"We would like to interview her," I said.

"I'm afraid that is not possible."

"Why not?"

"Six months ago she died climbing the Matterhorn."

Kathy was quicker than I was. "I am so sorry, Mr. Jurgens."

"As was her new husband. They were on their honeymoon. He was drinking at the hotel when he got the news."

"What a shame," I mumbled and looked at Kathy, then back at Garth and Dolph. *"Enschuldigen* us," I said, picking up our drinks.

"Where are you going?" Garth asked.

"To a meeting of the Reichstag."

Kathy followed me across the bar, through glass doors, into the garden. We sat on a swing in the shape of a bench next to a hibiscus tree lit like a Christmas tree, though it was the middle of August. "What a toilet full of crap," I said.

"How do you know he's lying?"

"Charles makes a shitload of money and promises to give Garth everything? Sorry, but my romantic nature can only handle a small dose of nonsense."

"It's not for us to judge."

"Right. It's our job to advocate, but do we have to believe his tripe?"

"We can't know for sure they're lying."

"Even if what they say is true, it shouldn't be."

"You're not making sense."

"What kind of law is it that says a promise of love is a promise of money?"

"We don't make the law."

I looked through the window. Garth had his arm around Dolph and was whispering in his ear. "We're the executioners, is that it?" I said.

Kathy took my hand and kissed me, a playful peck that ended with a sharp bite on the lips, breaking the skin. "You're mixing business with pleasure," I said.

"Don't tell anyone."

We kissed again and she threw a leg over mine. She put my hand to her breast. "Let's negotiate our own love contract," she said.

"I gave my wife what little money I have."

"You give Garth the benefit of the doubt and I'll do the same for you."

"What's there to doubt about me?"

"Everything."

What could I say? She was sexy, smart, and had me pegged. I didn't have her pegged, though. No idea what she saw in me or wanted with me. Just one of those things, I guess. Ironic. A suit between two gay lovers inspires romance between two straight lawyers. Go figure.

"Do we have a deal?" she said.

"Let's tell Garth and Dolph we have to prepare for the deposition."

"Shit, what's he doing here," he said, as I followed his line of sight through the mass of people to the front door. Smith Corcoran had entered and was pushing people aside as he walked toward us.

"Hello, Sullivan," he said, as if I were a fellow agent.

"Hello," I said.

"We've been looking for Salvatore. Checked at the restaurant, but they said he took the night off."

"He's entitled," Fischel said. But he was not Fischel, I thought. What was left for me to call him? My friend? My enemy? My friend, I decided.

"Crosetti is outside," Corcoran said. "He wouldn't talk to us."

"Want a drink? Connie, you don't mind if Smitty joins us for a drink."

"I do not mind," I said, moving to the next barstool so he could sit between us.

"How much does he know?" Corcoran asked as if I were not present.

"About what?" Fischel said.

"Don't be coy," Corcoran said.

"He doesn't know a thing." My friend glanced at me over Corcoran's shoulder.

"Danny Marinelli is in town," Corcoran said.

"God, I haven't seen him in a couple of years," my friend said.

"He's pretty upset about his father."

"Can't blame him."

Corcoran moved closer to my friend and hunched his back so I would not hear what he said. As he spoke, my friend's face lost some of its usual luster.

"What is it?" I asked.

"Stay out of this, Sullivan," Corcoran said.

"I wish I could."

Corcoran fingered his tie and said to my friend, "I hope you understand."

"Even when you were incomprehensible I've never had trouble understanding you, Smitty."

"He nodded and turned to me. " So long, Sullivan." He walked away.

"Interesting," my friend said.

"What?"

"KE, KE, KE. Corcoran, maybe. What do you think?"

At that instant, I was more afraid than I had ever been. "What did he say to you?"

"He said Danny was looking for Salvatore."

"Yes, and he found him," I said bitterly.

"Yes, Connie, but how did Smitty know it? He said he got a call yesterday from one of his old Chicago informants who said Danny was coming to New York to get Salvatore."

"Then he wanted to warn Salvatore, but—"

"Right, Connie, why wait until today?"

"Tell me."

"He had no intention of warning him."

"He wanted Salvatore dead?"

"Let's say he doesn't mind."

"Why?"

"One less witness."

"Witness to . . . I see. The hearing in Boston, Corcoran's complicity with the Savin Hill gang."

"Yes."

"Danny must have been referring to Corcoran."

"I wonder."

"But do you think Danny was talking about Corcoran? K sounds the same as a C."

"Yes, but Smitty is not a killer."

"If not Corcoran, then who? Was Danny acting alone? No, wait, why would he say . . . it is too confusing . . . I do not know what to think. But I am afraid. Very afraid."

He lifted his drink. "Don't be," he said, though when I looked into his dark eyes I saw there was little reason to believe him.

Where was I when we were interrupted? Of course, we should continue. What else is there to do? I'm not being disrespectful. Death comes with the territory. I quit worrying about the inevitable when Sam jumped off the bridge. It's not dying that matters, but what goes on while you are alive. I know your father and Salvatore would agree with me.

Garth's deposition lasted for nine days. On day three Kathy and I checked into the Willard Hotel: classy, old, and cheap, much cheaper than the Four Seasons. And we no longer needed a suite with separate bedrooms. We fell into the routine new lovers enjoy: drinks after work at quiet lounges, romantic dinners in corner booths, more drinks at a jazz club to cap the evening, and making love night and morning. Our one concession to business was an hour or two before lights out when we'd read the day's transcript.

You're right, Connie. Nine days for a deposition in a case like this was excessive. Wickersham was intent on probing every aspect of Garth's life, from childhood to the present: his domineering mother and passive father; his years at three different private schools in North Carolina, from each of which he was expelled for trying to seduce classmates; his first love affair with a classmate at Carnegie Tech in Pittsburgh; his apprenticeship and sexual relationship with a Pittsburgh interior designer who dumped him for a woman; his relocation to Washington where he worked for two years in a furniture store; a love affair with an artist from Paris, until the artist died of cancer and left him $10,000, which he used to start his design business; his fateful meeting with Charles two years later at the health club. He then guided Garth through the years with Charles, seeming to leave no hour unexamined, as if he wanted the deposition to be Garth's "remembrance of things past." He questioned Garth about the diaries, parsing each line as if they constituted an epic poem in which every word is pregnant with meaning. I could have objected or called the judge to complain that the deposition was going on too long. I did neither. In a way, I wanted time to stand still. I hated the case, but could have spent the rest of my life at the Willard Hotel with Kathy.

Each day produced at least one damaging admission from Garth: I did ask him to marry me, but he wouldn't; I don't see what the big deal is about monogamy; why is it terrible to pay for sex, do you know anything worth more; he told me I should learn to be a better businessman so I could earn money on my own; it never occurred to me that we should reduce our agreement to a formal contract, it would take the love out of our love. On the afternoon of the ninth day Wickersham turned to the last time Garth and Charles had seen each other.

"I remember it as if it were yesterday," Garth said. (When Kathy and I asked him this same question he said he recalled going to Charles's office but suffered a blackout and couldn't remember what happened.) "We weren't living together, but it was temporary. Poor man, he was working around the clock and needed some time alone. So, I was shocked, I was mortified—"

"Excuse me, Mr. James, but isn't it a fact that you weren't living together because he had told you the relationship was over?"

"He never said it was over. He said it was on sabbatical."

"What happened at this last meeting?"

"I was starting to tell you before you cut me off."

"Since this is the ninth day of your deposition, I thought you might want to move it along."

"No, Mr. Wickersham. I adore my time with you."

"Answer my question, Mr. James."

Garth pouted. "You're so domineering, Mr. Wickersham."

I sighed. "Answer the question, Garth."

"You want to get this over with so you and Kathy can roll around in bed naked."

For the first time in nine days Wickersham smiled, but I was fighting the urge to punch my client. Kathy, however, who was sitting on the other side of Garth, wasn't one to resist a natural impulse. She leaned over and grabbed his testicles, digging a long fingernail through his pants. He gripped the sides of his chair and pushed as if he were exercising his triceps, his mouth open in a silent screech. Kathy withdrew her hand and said to Wickersham, "Our client is ready to proceed."

"What was the question?" Garth asked in falsetto.

Garth answered the question as if he were giving a closing argument to a jury, complete with extraneous asides devoted to his feelings. He sounded like the hero of a Danielle Steele novel. "I threw myself on the floor of his office, crawled under his desk, and kissed the toes of his shoes. I loved him with all my heart. I would kill myself for him. I did everything for him. And then he got out of his leather chair, the one I had selected for him, the grace and power of his movements a bacchanal to my eyes . . . he helped me to my feet and kissed me on the lips, causing my knees to buckle." Garth touched his mouth, running a finger across his lips. "You cannot comprehend; no one could who has not experienced those soft lips that taste like sweet nectar, their texture as soft as velvet. And then he said in words I will carry to my grave, 'Love me Garth through this troubled time and all will be well. Our future together is assured.'"

During Garth's ode to passion Wickersham had been opening his briefcase. "What happened next?" He was holding a tape recorder.

"I left his aura," Garth said, his eyes closed. "I was happy in the knowledge that soon we would again be together."

"But you never saw him again, isn't that correct?"

With eyes still closed Garth started weeping. "Cruel, cruel, cruel. I wanted to do away with myself, end my suffering. He wouldn't see me. He wouldn't return my calls. I couldn't get out of bed. Life was over for me. Then, an intruder came, a nasty man, dastardly and uncouth. He flashed a paper in front of me and said I had to leave."

"The Sheriff with an eviction notice, is that correct?"

"He was a brute. He bruised my arm; I should sue him." He opened his eyes and saw the recorder. If he was concerned, he didn't show it.

Wickersham opened the recorder and removed the tape. He asked the court reporter to mark it as an exhibit. I put my hands over my eyes and shook my head.

Garth popped three lifesavers into his mouth. "Why have you waited all this time to record my testimony?" he asked.

"This tape is much more interesting than your testimony, Mr. James," Wickersham replied.

I don't have to tell you that Charles's secret recording contradicted Garth's rendition of what had occurred at the meeting. Garth was on the floor in both versions, though in the recorded version he was there for a different reason. He was trying to fend off the company security officer who was forcibly removing him from the office. Amidst the sound of kicking, Garth, hissing like a snake, said to Charles, "You listen to me, you pompous money bag, who I nurtured through every deal, to whom I gave my manhood whenever you wanted, you leave me and you will pay."

"This is a good time to conclude the deposition," Wickersham said.

I dashed out of the conference room. I told the receptionist that I'd be outside smoking the rest of the cigarettes in my pack. "I wish I could join you," she said.

Kathy and Garth spun out of the revolving doors before I finished the first cigarette. I walked to the corner and thought about disappearing down a flight of steps into the subway. Kathy left Garth standing by the door and ran up to me like she was about to save someone from jumping off a high ledge. "You didn't look good storming out," she said.

"I didn't look good," I shouted. "The son-of-a-bitch is a loser." Garth folded his arms and looked toward the sky.

"What's happened to your knack for splitting hairs?" she asked, as though I ever actually had that talent.

"I'd like to split our client is what I'd like to do."

"So he tried to hold up Charles. It was his way of making a settlement demand."

"Some people call that extortion."

"Have another cigarette and calm down. I'll be right back."

She returned to Garth and said something to him. He smiled and kissed her on the cheek. Then he turned and walked the other way, prancing like a stallion in heat.

"What did you say to him?" I asked Kathy, while I put a cigarette in my mouth to keep the first one company.

"I told him he did a good job."

"That's a laugh."

"He needs us."

"Wonderful."

"We're in good shape."

"That's why I love you. You're an optimist."

"Remember what you once told me."

Kathy knew me better than I knew myself. "Look at me. I didn't remember having a cigarette in my mouth."

"You said it never matters what you think of a case. It only matters what your opponent thinks."

"What are you getting at?" I had difficulty talking between the two cigarettes.

"Wickersham wants to buy us a drink," she said.

"He can't wait to drink to his victory."

She touched a fingernail to my pants just below the belt. "Do I have to do to you what I did to Garth?"

"No."

"He's going to make a settlement offer," she said.

"How do you know?"

"Lawyer's intuition."

"I've lost mine, haven't I."

She dug her fingernail into my belly. "You'll get it back." She took one of the cigarettes from my lips and stuck it in her mouth. When the smoke came out of her nostrils and formed a cumulous cloud, I calmed down.

Wickersham wanted to have drinks at the Metropolitan Club, but this artifact of a bygone age didn't allow women in the bar. We decided on the Shoreham hotel, where he said they served an excellent whiskey sour. "No one drinks whiskey sours anymore," I said. Wickersham laughed and said, "I'm sure Miss Shawn does," a comment that reflected his solid good-old-boy credentials. Kathy came right back at him: "I prefer Chivas Regal on the rocks."

We sat at a table at the far end of the lobby bar, next to a radio announcer who was hosting his talk show from the hotel. Wickersham said he'd been a guest on the show the previous week, topic "Strange cases." He asked me if I'd like to join him for a reprise of the show when *Garth vs. Roberts* was over, in which case he'd introduce me to the host. He was setting the stage for our chat, implying that he expected the case to be over very soon. I suggested we first order drinks and see what we could accomplish before launching my radio career.

While we waited for the drinks he engaged Kathy in small talk, asking her where she was from, how she liked litigation, what she wanted to do with her career, the kinds of questions you ask a stranger in a bar as you work up the nerve to ask for a date. I have to say he was a smooth talker, in and out of depositions. His sonorous voice matched his full-bodied physique; he was a man as at home listening to himself as he was looking in the mirror. He dressed conservatively and impeccably—a perfectly folded white handkerchief tucked neatly in the chest pocket of his light gray suit—and his hands, chubby with two black hairs on each knuckle, he used to good effect, punctuating every sentence with an elegantly timed twirl, as adept with gestures as a band leader with a baton. He looked like a man who knew how to throw his weight around and often did.

When the drinks arrived, Wickersham turned to business. "Your client doesn't have a case," he said.

I wanted to show Kathy I could keep my cool. "I'll drink to that," I said.

"Then you'll stipulate to a dismissal. To be fair, I'll dismiss the counterclaim."

"This is your idea of a settlement offer?"

"Don't look a gift horse in the mouth."

"My mother used to say that when I complained about my allowance."

"She was right."

"Maybe, but she always gave me more."

"I'm not your mother."

"No, and I'm not your son."

"Be smart."

"It doesn't come as easy for me as it does for you."

"You've spent a lot of time on the case. You've done well enough."

"We're on a contingency."

He put down his drink and looked at Kathy. She crossed her legs and smiled.

"That's insane," Wickersham said. "I checked you out. I was told you know what you're doing. How could you take such a piece-of-shit case on a contingency?"

"Garth has no money," Kathy said.

"For good reason."

"He gave eight years of his life to your client," I said.

"Emphasis on the word 'give.' There was no quid pro quo."

"The jury will decide."

"You can't win."

"One of the nice things about the law is there is no such thing as a case that can't be won."

Kathy slid forward. May I ask you a question, Mr.—"

"Call me Harold."

"Harold," Kathy repeated seductively.

"My real name," he said, unable to conceal his pleasure at her attention.

"What does the A stand for?"

"Nothing. I prefer it to H." He straightened his tie and rubbed his cheek. "May I get you another drink, my dear," he said, trying to make a love connection with his eyes.

"Yes, you may," she said in a tone of voice I thought was reserved for me. "You know I agree with you, Harold."

"I am so pleased. You shouldn't fret, however. I'm sure you will enjoy many victories in your career."

"You are very kind," Kathy said. "But I was referring to your name. A sounds so much more distinguished than H."

Wickersham fell back in his seat, confused and in despair. I don't think he was used to rejection.

"Here's the way I see it," I said. "We have nothing to lose and everything to gain; you have nothing to gain and everything to lose."

The waiter approached. "Another round," Wickersham said, having recovered his mask if not himself. "And a couple of cigars."

"You mean three," Kathy said.

He smiled, the uncomfortable smile of a man being measured for a suit and finding he had gained a lot of weight. "Yes, three," he said.

"No matter what you do," I said, "you can't prove a negative. You can't prove Charles never promised to share his wealth with Garth."

"You have the burden of proof."

"We have enough to get the case to a jury."

"Your client is a liar."

"We have a corroborating witness."

Wickersham stayed rock steady, like a boxer who has taken his opponent's best punch without flinching. "Who?" he asked with impressive aplomb.

"Adolph Jurgens."

"A million and a half," he said, as if he had planned to make the offer all along. "Take it or leave it."

"I'll speak to my client."

"We have plenty of time. Call him now. Miss Shawn and I will get to know each other, that is, if you will indulge me, my dear." He didn't give up easily.

"It will be a pleasure to indulge you," Kathy said, a little too lustily, I thought.

"I'll take my time," I said and left to find a phone.

Garth was more interested in apologizing than discussing the offer. "Please don't be cross with me. That Wickersham man is a beast. He irritates me immensely."

"Listen to me, Garth. Take the offer."

"I don't know how long I have to live." He might as well have said, *boohoohoo* or *woe is me*.

"You'll probably live forever."

'The money is not important."

"Yes it is."

I heard what sounded like a foghorn. He was blowing his nose. "What's your answer?" I asked impatiently.

"No."

"Garth, I'm your lawyer and I'm telling you to take it."

"You just want to make a fee. All lawyers care about is money."

"Your case is about money."

"It's about love."

"Even love has a price, Garth."

"Ten million." He said the number so quickly I almost missed it.

We went back and forth for another five minutes, but he wouldn't budge. What infuriated me was his unassailable logic. If he and Charles were married—at the time, no state sanctioned same sex marriages—and they lived in a community property state, Garth would have been entitled to $100,000,000, one-half of Charles's net worth. There would be no need to argue about promises, love contracts, infidelity, or absconding with a few bucks from the business. Who was I to say a jury wouldn't see it Garth's way or half his way or a quarter his way, and award him far more than what Wickersham had offered.

Kathy and Wickersham were smoking cigars when I stepped back into the lobby. He had moved so close to her that he had to twist his head whenever he took a puff. I wondered what his wife would think if she saw him sitting there. I wondered what *my* wife would think if she saw me with Kathy. (I was still married, though the divorce was supposed to become final in a few weeks.)

"No deal," I said, taking the third cigar off the table and handing it to Wickersham.

He took the cigar and put it in his breast pocket. He squeezed Kathy's hand and rose. "I'm not surprised at your client, but I am surprised at you."

"Don't be."

"Good lawyers control their clients."

"He'll take ten million."

He dropped a hundred-dollar bill on the table. "We'll have to do this again. When the case is over."

"Next time the drinks will be on me."

"I doubt you'll be able to afford it," he said, chomping on his cigar like a bookie after he's won a large bet.

"He didn't kiss you goodbye," I said to Kathy after he left.

"He expects to see me again." She opened the palm of her hand to reveal a business card with a number written on it. "He gave me his private-line number at the office. He also offered me a job."

"Maybe you should take it."

She took my hand and dragged me down for a kiss. "Maybe I will."

Waiting at the front desk the next morning was an envelope with a copy of a subpoena. Wickersham had scheduled Dolph's deposition for the following morning at ten. "This is bullshit," I said to Kathy. "We'll let him wait a while." But Kathy thought the deposition should go ahead. She said it was in our interest for Dolph to testify as soon as possible. "You never can tell, he might change his mind," she said.

While Kathy arranged to extend our stay, I called Garth. "Let me speak to Dolph," I said.

"He's not here."

"What's his telephone number?"

"I'll have to get it for you."

"Don't you know? Aren't you two still dating?"

"Don't harass me," he said and hung up.

When I called back, the line was busy and stayed busy for the rest of the day. At five, intending to object to the deposition, I called Wickersham, but he had left the office. And then no one answered at Garth's apartment. "Not a good sign," I said to Kathy.

That evening Kathy and I drank and chattered for an hour, ate and chattered for another two hours, and made love without chatter for an hour. Then we lay in bed together, awake, but alone with our thoughts. Before we fell asleep, I asked her what she was thinking and she replied, "What you're thinking," which was nothing. Also not a good sign.

In the morning, I asked Kathy to marry me. I had to yell out my proposal, because she was in the shower and I was standing by the bed, ironing my suit pants. I wasn't sure she had heard me until she came out of the bathroom, tying the knot on a Willard Hotel white terrycloth bathrobe with such force that it might as well have been a noose around my neck when the trapdoor opened. "You're nuts," she said.

We got to Wickersham's office building at nine. Hoping to speak with Dolph, we stopped at the McDonalds off the lobby where we had an unobstructed view of the entrance. At 9:45 Dolph came through the revolving doors. In his brown linen suit and silk shirt he looked like a European on holiday. We caught up to him at the elevators.

"Good morning, Dolph," I said.

"*Guten morgen.*"

"May we buy you a cup of coffee?"

"*Danke, nein.*"

"We want to give you an idea what Wickersham will ask at the deposition."

An elevator door behind him opened. I tried to take him aside but he backed up and slid into the elevator. "*Bitte,*" I said, using one of the few German words I knew. He ignored my plea as the doors closed.

Before going upstairs we tried calling Garth. I was worried Dolph wouldn't testify as expected unless Garth was there to encourage him. We got Garth's recorded voice at its most dulcet, reciting lines from an Emily Dickinson poem: "'I'm nobody, who are you? Are you nobody too?' "

I was surprised to see Garth in the conference room sitting across from Dolph. They weren't looking at each other and Garth was popping one lifesaver after another into his mouth. "We tried to call you," I said to Garth, but he ignored us, chewing noisily like a chipmunk.

Wickersham started the deposition with questions about Dolph's peripatetic life. He had lived in more places and held more jobs than I thought possible for one person. He aborted numerous careers: dancer (six months for the Bremerhaven Ballet when he was sixteen), professional golfer, tennis instructor, personal trainer, and schoolteacher, to name a few. He had the educational pedigree of an Oxford don: two college degrees, a year at Cambridge studying medieval poetry, and another year at the Sorbonne reading philosophy. I was beginning to think he had been joking about the kitchens when he said his hobby was cooking. He had taught himself everything there was to know about appliances, venting, plumbing, and insulation. One of his golf students was an executive at Exxon who gave him his first design job: renovating the employee cafeteria in Bonn.

Even Wickersham seemed to get tired of Dolph's self-congratulatory curriculum vitae and directed his attention to more recent events.

"You spent time in Scottsdale, Arizona," Wickersham said. Kathy and I looked at each other, both of us in the dark. Garth was plucking a hair from the back of his hand with tweezers.

"Six months ago," Dolph said.

"What took you to Scottsdale?"

"I was designing a kitchen for the Scottsdale Institute of Life. It's a retreat for people interested in self-help."

"Were you living alone in Scottsdale?"

"I was with my wife."

"Your second wife," Wickersham said. I was worried. Wickersham must have spoken with Dolph ahead of time. He knew too much.

"Yes," Dolph said softly. "My second wife. Eva, my first wife, died in a tragic accident."

"Yes, I know," Wickersham said lugubriously. "Did you hear from Garth?"

"He called me. I had not spoken to him in a while, since shortly after a dinner at the Homestead. Mr. Roberts had not hired me to design the dining room facilities at the resort he was building, and I took the job in Arizona. I needed the money—"

"Excuse me. Do you know why Mr. Roberts did not hire you?"

"I know what Garth told me."

"Which was?"

"He said Charles was upset he hadn't gotten his money back. Apparently, he had invested a considerable sum in Garth's business. Garth told me he would have to work on Charles. I could not wait. As I say, I needed the money."

"Tell us what Mr. James said when he telephoned you in Scottsdale."

"He said Mr. Roberts had ended their relationship and threw him out of the apartment. He was so overcome I invited him to Scottsdale. I also purchased the plane ticket. He said he was without funds."

"What happened in Scottsdale?"

"Nothing of importance. He stayed only a few days. He and my wife did not get along."

"Why?"

Dolph hesitated. It was obvious he preferred not to answer.

"Were you having a relationship with Mr. James?" Wickersham asked.

"We did have a brief . . . fling, I suppose is how I would characterize it. My wife disapproved. When we went to Scottsdale I told her it was over."

"Was it?"

"Garth was in a weakened state emotionally. I felt sorry for him."

"When Mr. James was in Scottsdale, did you discuss his relationship with Mr. Roberts?"

"Objection," I said.

"On what grounds," Wickersham said.

No grounds at all, I could have said, just a desire to interrupt. Wickersham and Dolph were too cozy. "On the grounds of boredom," I said flippantly.

Wickersham said to Dolph, "You may answer."

"He said many things, but in particular I remember the last night of his visit. I told him that he must return to Washington and repair his life. He said there was nothing to repair because his dreams of financial security were kaput. I asked him what he intended to do, and he said he would sue Mr. Roberts. He said: 'No one breaks up with me and gets away with it.'"

"Give me a fucking break," I said, loud enough for them to hear.

The court reporter's face turned bright red. "Do you wish me to transcribe your comment?" she asked.

"It's up to you."

Kathy put her hand on my arm.

340

Wickersham was smiling. "I'm sure counsel would prefer to withdraw his remark."

"No, keep it. I want whoever reads this deposition to know what I think of it."

"This is so exciting," Garth said, putting down the tweezers and taking a new pack of lifesavers from the pocket of his pink cardigan sweater.

Wickersham shook his head in exasperation and resumed his questioning. "After Scottsdale, did you return to Washington?"

"Yes."

"With your wife?"

"No."

Garth was busily stacking lifesavers on the table.

"What was the reason?" Wickersham asked.

"Eva and I agreed to separate."

"Was your relationship with Mr. James a factor?"

"Yes."

"In Washington, where did you stay?"

"With Garth at his office. It was furnished like an apartment."

"Did you find that peculiar?"

"What do you mean?"

"Mr. James had been living in my client's condominium. Why would he convert his office into an apartment?"

"For his liaisons," Dolph said disdainfully.

"Oh, Dolph, must you be such a tattletale," Garth said, flicking a lifesaver across the table.

"*Danke schoen*," Dolph said and put the lifesaver in his mouth.

"Are you still living with Mr. James?"

"No."

"When did you stop living with him?"

"Two weeks ago."

"Why?"

As I was calculating whether the date was before or after we met Garth and Dolph at the Four Seasons, Dolph gave me the answer. "I moved out the day after I met Garth's attorney at the Four Seasons Hotel."

"Why do you connect your meeting at the Four Seasons with your moving out?"

"I was feeling bad."

"What happened?"

"I told the lawyer about a conversation that never took place."

Why had I not known that Garth and Dolph conspired to invent the corroborating evidence? What a lesson in the danger of not leaving well enough alone. With no Dolph and no made-up dinner promise, the case would have remained a swearing match between Garth and Charles and a fight over what the letters meant. Garth had outwitted himself. But I was the real sap. Because I believed Dolph, I thought there was no harm mentioning his name to Wickersham at the Shoreham.

"You never overheard a conversation between Mr. James and Mr. Roberts at the Homestead in which Mr. Roberts made promises to Mr. James?"

"You are correct."

"And you moved out the day after your meeting at the Four Seasons because..."

"I could not in good conscience stay with a man who would use me to achieve his selfish financial goals." Dolph's voice cracked, and I thought he was about to cry. "My *liebchen* Eva would no longer have me. I helped Garth in his time of need and this is how he repaid me. He had no interest in me. He cared only for money."

"Mr. Jurgens, do you need a recess?"

"*Nein,*" he said, sniffling.

"After you moved out of Mr. James's office did you speak with him again?"

"Yes."

"When?"

"Last night. On the telephone."

"Who made the call?"

"He did. He wanted to be sure I would testify the way he wanted. I told him I intended to tell the truth. You see, I believe that taking an oath before God is a solemn deed."

"Give me another fucking break," I said.

This time Wickersham ignored me.

342

"What did Mr. James say?" Wickersham asked, knowing the answer would put an exclamation point on his destruction of Garth's case.

"He pleaded with me to help him. He said he would share his recovery in the lawsuit and I should name the price."

"What did you say?"

"I said I would not."

After the deposition Kathy went shopping—despite or because of her inexperience she was less chagrined than I was at Dolph's about face. Garth and I sat at a table in a noisy steakhouse across the street from Wickersham's office. While Garth complained that the restaurant didn't offer vegetable entrees I drank martinis, getting angrier with each gulp.

"I'm resigning," I said after my third drink.

"You can't abandon me," he said.

"Says who?"

"Says *The Course in Miracles.* Commitments should be faithfully kept."

"The Canons of Ethics says a lawyer doesn't have to represent a client whose goal is to subvert our system of justice."

"Silly man. I bet it doesn't say that."

He was right, of course, but the Canons permit a lawyer to resign if he no longer believes he can effectively represent his client. "Think what you like," I said. "I quit."

He took a pill and cracked it open, pouring the powder in a glass of water. "Besides," I added, "after today's debacle, there's no way you can win the case."

"You haven't taken Charles's deposition."

"What good would that do?"

"You would see the kind of man he is, how he took my love and devotion when he needed it and then abandoned me when he got his millions."

"It's a free country."

"You don't care about anything, do you?"

I met Kathy at our hotel room. She was packing. I told her my decision. To my dismay she was outraged, castigating me for sending her away.

"You wanted to go shopping."

"Correction," she said. "You sent me shopping."

"Whatever." I had had enough of arguing.

"What makes you so sure Dolph told the truth at the deposition?" she said, throwing my clothes on the floor.

"We might as well stay another night. The room is paid for."

She looked at me wearily, like I was the villain of a cheap melodrama. A half-hour later we left for the airport. She wouldn't even hold my hand.

The next day, I submitted a motion to withdraw and sent a copy to Garth. He called several times, asking me to reconsider. He filed bankruptcy the day before the hearing. The only assets he listed were his cosmetics.

I filed a claim in the bankruptcy court for $8250, my unreimbursed expenses for the deposition transcripts and the stay in Washington. I couldn't file a claim for our time because we had had represented him on a contingency. A month later the trustee called to tell me he was negotiating a settlement with Wickersham. (The case was an asset of his estate and thus under the control of the trustee.) Charles had agreed to pay $100,000, and the trustee wanted me to abandon my claim to reimbursement so he would have more money to pay Garth's other creditors. Disgusted and wanting to be finished with the mess, I haggled with the trustee for a while and then agreed to reduce my claim to $4,000.

Kathy continued to keep me at a distance. She would no longer mix business with pleasure and wouldn't have drinks with me at Yvette or any-where else. Then, one day a few weeks later I decided to confront her. "We can't go on like this," I said.

"You're right," she said.

"Good. We'll have drinks tonight at Yvette."

"I can't."

"Why not?"

She gave me the news. She had met a man, a young physicist at Fermi-lab where they shoot microscopic particles around a gigantic bowl, looking for the secrets of the universe. It was a whirlwind courtship and they were ready to set a wedding date. He had taken a position at Johns Hopkins in Baltimore and they would be relocating there after the wedding.

"You never responded to my proposal," I said.

"Yes, I did. I said you were crazy."

"I didn't understand why you wanted me and I don't understand now why you don't want me."

"Some things are better left not understood."

Several months later, I went to Washington on another case and checked in at the Four Seasons. I called Kathy at work, a satellite office of Wickersham's firm, of all places. She took my call and we had a pleasant conversation. She said she was three months pregnant. "Now that I have a tummy Wickersham won't even say hello to me," she added.

"I'll drive up to Baltimore. Meet me for a drink."

"Not a good idea."

"Why not?"

Never ask why you're being rejected. You just get rejected again. "There's no such thing as meeting for *a* drink," she said.

Though the bar at the Four Seasons was deserted and I had my pick of seats, I went straight to the spot where we had met Garth and Dolph. I ordered a martini and stared out toward the garden where Kathy and I had sat on the swing.

Perhaps ten minutes later, perhaps an hour—time means nothing in a lounge—Dolph appeared in front of me, arm in arm with a tall blonde woman.

"Why, what a coincidence," he said.

"Hello there," I said.

"This is my wife Olga."

"Number three."

It was the kind of remark that should have gotten me a fist in the mouth, but Dolph grinned and sent Olga to the ladies room. "I was planning to call you," he said.

"Why, do you need a lawyer?"

"No, the passage of time gives one *Weltanschauung*."

"I doubt whether we share the same view of the world."

"I lied," he said.

"You're entitled. I should have known you weren't telling the truth about the conversation in Virginia. It was too pat."

"No, I lied at the deposition. I wanted to get back at Garth. He cost me my marriage and welshed on his debt to me. Charles did make those promises at the Homestead."

"It doesn't matter now," I said, though I knew it did.

"You're right, I suppose it doesn't."

"Do you ever talk to Garth?"

"You don't know?"

"Know what?"

Olga was back. "Come," she said. "We are late for dinner."

"What don't I know?" I asked.

"Garth died a month ago. When the AIDS took hold he went *mach schnell.* I visited him at the hospital, hoping I could make things right between us. He was kind, bore me no ill will; he was kinder than when we were seeing each other. He said he only regretted one thing."

"What?"

"He couldn't make you believe in his case."

At this moment, my friend—for truly he was my friend, whatever his name— seemed overwhelmed with sadness.

"You should not blame yourself," I said. "It was so long ago."

"Contrary to the saying, time does not heal all wounds."

He was right. Some memories fade, some harden, but time does not heal, often does not even relieve the pain.

"Should we have dinner?" he asked.

"I am tired."

"Jimmy will take you home."

"Am I actually in danger?"

"Better to be safe than sorry."

Before retiring, I telephoned Mary. She did not fault me for being absent when my father died. She said she was to blame for encouraging me to make the trip. I did not tell her of my purloined passport or the killings I witnessed and handled the issue of my return by saying that I was having difficulty

making reservations but would know more in a day or two. As always, she sensed my evasiveness.

"Connie, what are you hiding?"

When I did not respond she said, "Your father wrote a letter."

"What does it say?"

"I would not open it, Connie."

"I have no secrets from you."

"I'm sure it can wait until you come home."

"Perhaps it tells more of what I want to know."

"About what?"

"The identity of the lawyer, for one thing."

"Mr. Brandt's law partner?"

"His name is not Schaechter."

"It isn't? But he said—"

"For some reason he is intent on keeping his identity a secret."

"But why? He has been so kind. I spoke to him today, when your da passed, and he reassured me that you were safe."

"He is planning something that involves Tommy."

"What?"

"I wish I knew. I want you to contact Bridget, Tommy's wife. She lives in Crossmaglen."

"What do I say to her?"

"Tell her what you know. I will call you tomorrow.

Mary laughed. "It is already tomorrow, dearest."

Belfast, my home, a world apart. I gave her my love and said goodbye.

Cuchulainn was sitting on the front windowsill staring into the night. As I went to him I saw Jimmy standing by his limousine smoking a cigarette. Though I knew he was there to protect me, Cuchulainn was not so sure. His tail flopped warily back and forth like a metronome. I scratched his head and his tail stopped moving. He continued looking straight ahead. Sentinels, he and Jimmy, exchanging "secret whispers of each other's watch."

Chapter Eleven

May 20, 1998

I SPENT THE DAY IN THE APARTMENT, *confined to quarters, as it were. It was not Jimmy who restrained me, however, but my own sense that if I stayed put, I would enjoy some well-deserved tranquility. This was an illusion and not a very effective one at that, for what peace could I find away from my family and homeland, mourning my father from afar.*

I was in a philosophical mood and spent the morning reading portions of "The History of Ideas," paying special attention to the entries on Law and Justice. But the abstractions of philosophers appeared inconsequential in the face of my friend's detailed and all too real accounts of actual cases, in which the law and human weaknesses coalesced to produce unexpected outcomes.

I called Mary and asked what she had learned from Tommy Glynn's wife. She had not been able to reach her. Bridget was visiting relatives in Dublin and had not left a forwarding number.

Periodically, I would rest for a few minutes, lying on the bed with Cuchulainn and searching my memory for events that might give further meaning to the last few days. In particular, I thought again of the man I had seen at my father's car shop and puzzled over why such a mundane occurrence would stick in my mind. "Mundane," I said aloud, sitting up on the bed with a start, as Cuchulainn scurried to the end of the bed to await my next move. That was it! There was nothing mundane about it. He was not a customer; he had not dropped off a car or come to pick up one. And he was dressed in a business suit. A business suit! My God, I said to myself, he was the man from the photograph Salvatore had shown me. The man standing next to Delaney. Why had he come to the car shop? What did he want from my father? My father had bought the car shop two years before.

I went to the window and called out to Jimmy who was sitting in his limousine reading the newspaper. He jerked open the door and scampered up the walk, probably assuming I was in some kind of danger. Once inside, his eyes picked apart the small room before he relaxed.

"What is it?" he asked.

"The man in the photograph."

Jimmy smiled wryly, as if he were a teacher amazed at the slow progress of his pupil. "The one Salvatore showed you. What about it?"

"He owned the car shop?"

"So?"

"I saw him at the car shop."

"Well, he owned it, so what's the big—"

"Da bought the shop in 1979, two years before the man came to see him. There was no reason to meet unless . . . "

"Unless what?"

"He gave the man a paper," I cried. "It had names, places . . . you know what Salvatore was going to tell me about Da."

"Did you ever wonder where your father got the money to buy the shop?"

"Why should I? He worked there for many years. He was a frugal man and he saved—"

Jimmy was laughing. "Oh, Sullivan, you are too much."

"I have had enough," I said, frothing at the mouth. "Tell me what I want to know."

"Your father got the shop in exchange for certain services."

"What services?"

Jimmy shook his head. "Come on, Sullivan. It's not for me to say. Let's take a walk to the corner and pick up some sandwiches. I'm starved."

"But you said yourself I deserved to know, and Salvatore was ready to tell me when . . . "

"You do deserve to know, but I'm not the one to tell you."

He started for the front door and I followed. I knew the truth, of course. How could I not know? My father had worked for the British. He was a traitor.

Now you know. You figured it out on your own, as I knew you would. A traitor? It depends on what side you're on. The British were in charge, de facto in charge, anyway. Treason may be the most unjust law on the books of any country. The very concept of treason is antithetical to justice. You can't betray a thing, and a government is a thing. An organization is a thing. Oh, Connie, spare me the indignation, will you. You can't generalize. "The general case, the one to which all legal forms and rules are suited," doesn't exist. The only kind of treason I'd consider reprehensible would be an individual's betrayal of the people he loves. And where do fanatics, the bane of humanity, come from? From among those who devote their passion to political and religious institutions. I've never heard anyone call the love of family and friends fanatical. My verdict in the case of *History vs. Noel Sullivan* is not guilty. He was innocent of the only treason that matters. That he took money from the British doesn't change my verdict. What was he going to do? Refuse the money? It would have made the British suspicious. He gave up his beliefs for you and your family to keep you safe. That makes him a patriot.

The people of your country are too hung up on national, ethnic, and religious allegiance, none of which has one whit to do with what gives life meaning. However you want to define the contours of the centuries-old struggle, Catholics against Protestants, Church versus State, the struggle against imperialism, the individual suffers. And each side to the conflict wants to use the law as a weapon. Whether it's the law of the State or the Church, the result is tyranny. Your father—don't be offended—was a fool. He got himself caught in a mess by subscribing to the idea that the struggle for freedom is a we-against-them enterprise, in his case, Catholics against Protestants. In this country, we like to prattle on about the "rule of law," but in your country, you might as well call it the "rule of religion." Either way, individual justice loses. I think your father came to this conclusion. He saw that he could have avoided being put to a terrible choice. Had he paid attention to his family from the beginning, he would never have been in a position to finger Tommy Glynn. Had Tommy Glynn paid attention to his family and not gotten involved with Bobby Sands and the Provos, he never would have been in the position to be fingered. Such a waste, man's allegiance to the ghosts of the past, the Christian idea of a reward waiting in the afterlife for choosing sides in the struggle for earthly power. Take the crazy saint, Thomas Moore, a lawyer no less, who forsook his family for adherence to his religion, no not even his religion, the Pope, for God's sake, the supremacy of man over God, ironic, when you try to imagine why the omniscient power of the universe would leave it to a bunch of political hacks, excuse me Cardinals, to appoint God's emissary on earth. He was also crazy to rely on the law to save him from his refusal to sign an oath of allegiance to the King—"silence," as he put it—claiming his non-act could not be considered treasonous. (His particular spin on what he was doing was that under the law silence is consent and therefore his refusal to sign the oath was legally the same as consenting to the terms of the oath!) He got convicted anyway—made easier by the perjurious testimony of a friend—and his head was chopped off. He was a martyr to his own self-righteousness. And the law and religion survived quite well without him, thank you very much. A few years later, the Pope's legions were beheading the Protestants until Elizabeth came along and stoked the nationalistic fires. She put religious conflict in a back row and set England on its way to imperialism and its true place in the sun. From this came our glorious country and its laws that are supposed to preserve our individuality but order our lives like we're animals in a circus.

See the look on your face. You're finally coming around. You're beginning to understand: what counts is the plight of those close to us—be it our family, those we love, others who circumstances have brought close to us—where we might be able to do some good.

What else can I tell you? Not much. Your father's service ended with the collapse of the gun running business in 1985. He had served their purpose and they were content to leave him alone. He spent the last thirteen years doing quiet penance, which we all have to do at some point in our lives when we seek forgiveness for the mistakes we made. But we cover our mistakes like we cover our garbage: tons of dirt overlaid with grass and a few trees. Our lives end up looking like just another landfill.

I empathized with your father's ordeal. Like me, he spent a good number of years in the service of a cause in which he didn't believe. And, like me, he eventually saw a way to serve a different cause. He wanted to die on the right side. He helped put our plan into motion. In April, we gathered at Marinelli's to finalize everything. I talked to your father on the telephone before the meeting began. That's when we decided you and I should meet. What other way was there to obtain your passport? Soon, Connie, soon. But I think you know why we need your passport.

Did I know? Was the plan to free Tommy Glynn and spirit him out of the country using my passport as his identification? I wanted him to stop talking so I could think some more, but he was full of words and energy.

You're right, Connie. But don't misjudge me. My heart aches for the loss of life, Salvatore and your father in particular. Still, the closer I come to my moment of reckoning, the better . . . well, what can I say?

We'll have a couple of drinks, talk awhile, and go out for a good dinner. Since I mentioned the Four Seasons Hotel last night, I thought we might try the Four Seasons restaurant—no connection with the hotel. I haven't been to the restaurant in years, not since I was at the pinnacle of my legal career when everything seemed to have fallen in place, when I was enjoying a modicum of success and a few notable victories on behalf of people taken advantage of in one way or the other.

The cumulative effect of my stories may be misleading. It seems I have focused on those cases in which I was guilty of some rank miscalculation or excessively manipulated the situation. These cases suggest I was running neck and neck with the law's absurdities, making the wrong choice at every opportunity. Mind you, I often chose wrong, at least according to my present sensibilities, but just as often I got my client what he wanted, which after all is what a lawyer is supposed to do. More than anything, however, I wanted to be on the side of what was right and manage it without being so goddamn calculating. Given the law's penchant for convolution it was a foolhardy idea, but I was still young and thought there was time. As was inevitable, my noble intentions couldn't compete with the law's power to bring justice to its knees. Let me give you an example.

During the years following Kathy's departure the firm grew to a dozen lawyers. I opened an office in New York not far from here, corner of 59th and Lexington, on the top floor, the whole floor, with a view in every direction. On a clear day I could see to the north end of Central Park, across the Hudson River to New Jersey, Kennedy Airport in Long Island, and the towers of Lower Manhattan. Kathy had called me a "big shot" when I wasn't a big shot, but I had become a big shot with a reputation for handling difficult cases on behalf of investors ripped off in investments.

He wanted us to walk to the Four Seasons, not far, on 52ndStreet between Park and Lexington Avenues. But Jimmy would not hear of it, and we got in the limousine.

Jimmy was looking in the rear view mirror. "We're being followed," he said.

My friend turned around. "The Toyota?"

"Yes," Jimmy said.

"Not to worry. He can't afford the Four Seasons."

Isn't this place wonderful, one of New York's finest temples for the *I have too much money and don't know what to do with it* gang. It's designed to delight the senses: the finest woods carved to perfection for the bar; stools cushioned in expensive Italian leather; crystal lights set at a dim enough level so everyone looks better than they really do. My favorite accoutremenst in this room are the shimmering window blinds, a wave moving through them, set in motion by air blowing from the floor vents. And wait until you see the main dining room. If we're lucky, we'll be seated next to the pool. I didn't tell you? This restaurant is famous for its pool. It makes me think of decadent Romans sitting in their spa eating fruit and fondling the maidens.

Jimmy was leapfrogging up the stairs. He spotted us and came over.

"Do you want to know who's following us?" he asked.

"I could guess," my friend said.

"Corcoran."

"Where is he now?"

"Parked a block from here."

"Go talk to him."

"And say what?"

"I don't know. See what he wants."

"You know what he wants."

"How long can we keep it quiet?"

I presumed they were speaking of the deaths of Salvatore and Danny Marinelli, but they were being careful with their words.

"Not much longer," Jimmy said. "The guys at the restaurant are getting concerned. I told them Salvatore went out of town on business, but I don't think they believed me. And Danny's wife called the restaurant. Danny must have told her he was going to pay Salvatore a visit."

"We only have another thirty-six hours to go."

"A lot can happen in thirty-six hours."

"A lot has already happened."

Jimmy patted me on the shoulder. "Enjoy your dinner."

"Would you care to join us?" I asked.

Jimmy looked around the room and then at the lights. "No thanks. Places like this make me nervous."

When he left I said, "Your plan will be executed in thirty-six hours?"

"More or less."

I looked at my watch. "Eight o'clock the day after tomorrow."

"A little earlier, I hope."

"How do you intend to free Tommy Glynn?"

"Excellent guess, Connie."

"How?"

"Let me put it this way. I'm glad he's not at Alcatraz."

"What is—"

"A prison, now closed, on an island in San Francisco bay. During the several decades it was operating no one ever escaped and, as they say in melodrama, lived to tell about it."

"Why?"

"The waters are treacherous. A few tried unsuccessfully to swim to shore."

"Tommy is going to swim?" I said in disbelief.

He laughed. "I hope not."

Is this table OK? Like the pool? Look here, a wall socket for a telephone. You can call Mary if you like. Yes, it is late there. Some other time then.

I'm a little tired of talking about the law. Let's go back to my youth. Where did I stop? Oh, right. After high school.

I hadn't been a good student. For a while, it looked as if I would stay home and attend the University of Cincinnati. But Sarah, a wonderfully enterprising woman, called Robert Paul, the husband of one of her customers, who was on the Board of Trustees of Brandeis. Its admission policy was as restrictive as most Ivy League schools, though one phone call from Paul could get me through the front door. I just needed to impress him at the talk Sarah arranged.

Paul's living room looked like a museum gallery: slate floors, plush drapes, onyx bric-a-brac. I sat on a hard chair and watched him expend great effort to take a puff from his cigar. Though he was just eighty-four, he looked like one of those hundred-year old men whose pictures you see in National Geographic. The skin on his face had so many lines it could have been a Jackson Pollack painting.

"What do you want to do with your life?" he asked.

"I don't know."

"Neither do I," he said, although he couldn't have been telling the truth. He looked quite satisfied with what he had done with his life and uninterested in what his future held, such as it was.

"What is your favorite movie?" he asked, posing the question in a way that made it sound as weighty as his previous one.

"Picking the first title that popped into my head, I answered, *"High Noon."*

"Why?"

"Have you seen the movie?"

"I don't go to the movies." He saw my bewilderment. "I'm sure I will understand your answer," he said, in a fatherly way.

"Garry Cooper is the town sheriff. Frank James, who he sent to prison, is returning on the noon train, bent on revenge. Cooper has just gotten married and his wife and the townspeople want him to leave before James arrives. They don't want trouble, and Cooper's wife, a Quaker, doesn't believe in violence. Cooper stays and tries to get the townspeople to help him. They refuse and he's stuck with fighting James and his gang alone. His wife, despite her pacifism and in the nick of time, comes to help and shoots a gang member as he is about to . . . I'm sorry, Mr. Paul. I haven't done a good job of telling the story."

"Why is it your favorite movie?"

Would my college career depend on my answer? "At the end, as Cooper is getting in the buggy with his wife, the townspeople gather around and wish him a good life. He takes off his badge and throws it in the dust."

"What did that mean to you?"

"Nothing, really. I just like a guy who tells the world to take a hike."

Paul laughed and stubbed out his cigar in a gold ashtray. "Sounds like the Sheriff was fed up with the law."

"I think he was fed up with the townspeople for not supporting the law."

"What do you think about that?"

Somehow, I thought everything depended on my answer. "I don't know why the Sheriff was surprised. The law doesn't solve problems, just creates more of them."

"You'll go far, young man. Though I don't think you will become a lawyer."

The menus arrived. I stared at the array of expensive dishes. My friend said, "What's the matter? Don't you see anything you like?" I replied that the expense was dismaying, but he had a distracted look. His eyes were closed and he was humming. And then I heard words.

You know the song, Connie, *Mr. Tambourine Man*. It plays in my head whenever I remember my college years. Just like the opening lines of the song, you know, about going no place. Exactly how I felt when I got off the train at South Station in Boston, a suitcase in each hand, like an itinerant salesman lugging his samples from town to town. I was a stranger in a strange land.

It was the fall of 1962, the middle of the Kennedy era. Though Brandeis was known as a hotbed of radicalism, a kind of miniature Berkeley, my friends and acquaintances were either conservative or preferred a world in which politics and ideals took a back seat to the parochial concerns of young adulthood; in other words, keeping their own lives in balance was difficult enough without having to worry about war with Russia, segregation in the south, or deepening involvement in Vietnam. I was vaguely aware of SNCC (Student Non-Violent Coordinating Committee), but I watched them from a distance, as they occupied their own table in the corner of the coffee shop, dressed in black with kinky beards and hair billowing up like dark thunderclouds.

I hung out with a coterie of lost souls whose connection with the real world was tenuous, at best. Jeff Schmuckler, my roommate, was a solid member of the resistance, fighting a losing battle against the student radicals, referring to them as "soft": soft in the head, soft on Communism, soft on their male sexuality, and soft on traditional values. But he was an agreeable living companion and kept to himself, listening to Edith Piaf records while writing poetry that he refused to read to me or anyone else.

The others on the floor were Dennis Boros and Bernie Nussbaum on one side, Malcolm Goldstein and Art Zelman on the other, and across the hall, Buddy Kornbusch. From the start, we were inseparable, a gang of seven. Not much of a gang, however—we didn't have a leader, bylaws, a mission, or girlfriends. Dennis claimed to have left a sweetheart back home in Valley Stream, but we thought she was a figment of his imagination or, if real, nothing like he described her. His looks and personality were too vacuous to attract anyone of beauty or character. He was short and skinny, had the receding hairline of someone much older, and was always smiling dumbly, as if he was hiding something. He was a compulsive gambler, monopolized the hall payphone for calls to bookies, and was constantly borrowing money to either place a bet or pay off a losing one. He never studied—not necessarily a black mark—but he didn't do much else, except sit on his bed and study racing results.

His roommate, Bernie Nussbaum, was everything he was not, and then some. He was gangly and uncoordinated, and chronic acne had scarred his face with deep craters. He loved fires and kept lit candles on his desk, striking matches every few seconds and watching them burn down to his fingers. During the winter, when there's at least one fire a day in Boston, he'd hitchhike to a poor neighborhood and walk around in the cold hoping to see a blaze. He tried to get a job as a part-time fireman, but was turned down because he was so nearsighted the examiner classified him as "legally blind." He was the tallest in our group and played center on our basketball team. We never passed him the ball; he couldn't see it coming.

Goldstein and Zelman could have been twins with their identical personalities and baby fat faces. They also shared a dream of the future: they would become rich lawyers in New York representing Fortune 500 companies, join the most exclusive clubs, marry gorgeous wives, and keep even more gorgeous mistresses. They took the same courses, studied together, and ate meals together. They weren't gay; they were celibate. Neither had a single date in four years of college. Only Goldstein's love of pipe smoking enabled one to tell them apart. Goldstein was never without his pipe and smoked a foul smelling tobacco that made the hall reek like the back of a garbage truck. He thought nothing of dropping pipe cleaners wherever he went, which Buddy Kornbusch used to make fantastic wall decorations in his room.

Buddy's pipe-cleaner art took the shape of vicious animals, unicorns, and himself, complete with a slew of pipe cleaners to represent his bushy hair and angular face, as the terrifying figure stood ready to attack a pipe-cleaner woman with breasts represented by dried grapes he got from the student union kitchen. The first and last time he brought a coed to his room she took one look at the artwork and ran out screaming.

Buddy had good cause to be "screwy in the head." When not in school he lived with his mother and his younger brother Abraham in a tiny one-bedroom apartment in Mt. Vernon, New York. His father died when he was seven and Abraham two, and thereafter Abraham called Buddy "brother," saying it the way a child would say father. His mother liked to kiss Buddy on the lips and invite him, but not Abraham, into her bed. I found out about this when I visited their home one weekend when we were freshmen. I slept on the couch in the living room. Abraham, then thirteen, slept on a torn love seat, and Buddy slept with his mother. As you might suspect, Buddy needed a bit of watching. He threatened to commit suicide once a month, got drunk every weekend, and spent his meager bank account on street prostitutes he picked up in downtown Boston.

So, this was my crowd, not a crowd you would associate with the sixties, not a freedom marcher among them, not a visionary in the group, not a nascent revolutionary to be found, just a bunch of maladjusted kids whose private demons were even more threatening than the public ones.

For my first two years at Brandeis I was satisfied to hang out with the gang. Women made me nervous. One had to be literally thrown in my lap for me to make a move, which is what happened when one day in the Commons when a police horse kicked Tiffany Malkovitch, a student at Boston University, and she fell into my arms while I was trying to get my kite to soar. She was the only woman to survive an attack by the Boston Strangler. The Strangler had a thing for nurses and snuck up on her when she was taking a shortcut through the alley on her way to the hospital where she worked. She bit the Strangler's hand and told him he had made a big mistake, she was a waitress at the Peter Pan on Commonwealth Avenue. Our relationship only lasted for two months. She broke it off because *I* insisted on using a condom.

The start of junior year found me at my usual study spot on the second floor of the library, in the Anne Frank reading room, surrounded by shelves stuffed with books on the Nazis. One night a coed I didn't recognize threw her load of books on the table and asked whether I would mind if she sat across from me. Mind? She was a stunner: wavy, dirty-blonde hair, luminous eyes, a pixyish face, and a small, slightly upturned nose, which gave her an expression somewhere between quizzical and skeptical. She was short, but curvy, and liked to show off her figure eight with tight skirts and sweaters. From the books she carried I figured she had a full-service brain; some of her more frequent companions were a volume of William Blake's poetry, a textbook on quantum mechanics, a collection of Kant's philosophical essays, and James Joyce's *Ulysses*.

I was too shy to talk to her and had to be satisfied with peeking over the top of *Oriental Despotism*, sniffing the air for signs of her sweet fragrance. Just before closing, Jack Carter came into the room. She leaped from her chair like a pet overcome with joy at her master's return. My heart sank; Jack was her boyfriend.

The next day, I cut my first class to visit the registrar's office where I scanned all the student photos until I found hers. Her name was Natalie Richman, a transfer student from Lawrence College. She lived off campus in a two-flat, the same house where Jack Carter lived. She was a National Merit Scholar and a member of Mensa.

She returned to the library that evening and every other evening. We engaged in bits and pieces of conversation, more than enough for me to realize it would be pointless to ask her out. She was in love with Jack. But he would graduate in the spring and attend medical school in Philadelphia. Then, maybe I'd have my chance.

As it happened, my chance came sooner. On a night in early December she arrived at the library minus her glittering smile, wearing a loose shift that robbed me of the pleasure of gazing at her soft breasts and round butt. She said she had broken up with Jack and had to get away for a couple of days. To New York for the weekend, she said, where her grandmother lived. I said I was going to New York to see my brother Jonathan who lived in the northernmost section of the Bronx. "Maybe we could get together," I said. She looked at me suspiciously and said the Bronx was quite a way from her grandmother's apartment on Central Park West. No problem, I said. I would borrow Jonathan's car and drive into the city. I was afraid I was too obvious, but she was so distraught she didn't realize I had something other than a friendly get together in mind.

We went to the coffee shop after the library closed. As we entered she waved at the students gathered at the SNCC table and said we should join them. She said she was a member of SNCC, a fact I didn't know how to factor into my love-addled thinking.

The head of the Brandeis chapter was Israel, "Izzy" Altman, whom I knew from Oriental history class. Izzy was the only child of a wealthy Boston neurosurgeon and had never wanted for anything. He graduated with honors from Choate, drove a new Porcche, and spent summers at his parent's villa in the hills above Marbella, Spain. He was a scratch golfer, accomplished jazz pianist, and, at fifteen, had won first prize at a national science fair with an experiment in Brownian motion. You would think he'd be the last person to rail against the establishment, but you can't gainsay the many ways the revolutionary mind can come into being.

Izzy was in the middle of urging his fellow members to organize a demonstration protesting Brandeis's failure to admit more blacks. Trying to act smart, I said I didn't think many blacks bothered to apply. He said prejudice was a vicious circle, a malevolent variation of the chicken and egg argument. I knew I shouldn't have opened my mouth. He invited me to become a member.

This was a *moment*, maybe the first moment I had had in my life. To say I was apolitical is an understatement. Not only did I avoid forming opinions on world and national affairs, I avoided collecting enough information to be tempted. I watched movies and sports on TV, listened to all-music stations on the radio, and never read the paper except for the sports section. On the day Kennedy was shot Tiffany wanted to cancel our date out of respect, but I said our lives shouldn't be disrupted because the leader of the free world was assassinated. On condition that I would keep our show of disrespect a secret, she agreed not to cancel. She insisted we take the trolley to a dilapidated theater in Revere, because no one would know us there. The theater was deserted. Even the candy counter clerk was mourning at home. Tiffany cried throughout the movie while I laughed—it was a comedy—and refused to make love afterwards, saying she owed at least that much to the dead President. As oversexed as she was, I couldn't argue with her. She was making a genuine sacrifice.

I was about to politely decline Izzy's invitation when I noticed Natalie staring at me expectantly. My romantic designs might be compromised unless I joined SNCC. Natalie rewarded me with a wet kiss on the lips, a copy of SNCC's mission statement, and excerpts from the songs, *Go Tell It on the Mountain, Blowing in the Wind, and This is Your Land, This is My Land.* The mission statement included pronouncements like "love transcends hate," "acceptance dissipates prejudice," and "justice for all overthrows injustice." Its capstone was the high-minded, though verbose, exhortation: "By appealing to the conscience and standing on the moral nature of human existence, nonviolence nurtures the atmosphere in which reconciliation and justice become actual possibilities."

Everyone in the gang but Schmuckler congratulated me for my good sense. He accused me of being a hypocrite, but he was just jealous. He wouldn't find a girlfriend at Brandeis. The coeds, political theorists all, selected lovers from among their political allies.

But I guess my political conversion wasn't convincing. The next evening at the library, she came to see me. "I don't think it's a good idea to meet in New York," she said.

"Why not?"

"It's too soon."

"Do you want to switch it to another weekend?"

"It's too soon for a relationship."

I said I understood, but I didn't.

I knew then that when you sacrifice your principles, even if it's the principle of believing in nothing, you lose your dignity. I still belonged to SNCC, though I avoided the coffee shop and the meetings, hoping Izzy would revoke my membership. It didn't work. A week later, I found my mailbox stuffed with flyers promoting a sit-down demonstration in front of the Administration building and a note from Izzy asking me to distribute them to the students in my dorm. I threw the flyers away.

My plan for senior year was to spend as much time as far away as possible from campus. I rented a one-bedroom apartment off Kenmore Square. I bought a 1952 Nash Rambler for $150 from the landlord and enrolled in the easiest courses, *gut* courses we called them: Astronomy, The Actor's Art, Introduction to Economics, The Literature of Discontent, and Primitive American Art. I spent most of my spare time at The Huddle, a bar next door to the apartment that was a gathering place for Boston Patriot football players, unemployed alcoholics, and street philosophers.

Through October and into November I lived and enjoyed a relatively reclusive life. I hardly saw the gang; when I did, I told them I had a girlfriend in Boston and a part-time job. Occasionally, one of the guys would call me and ask if I'd like to come back to campus for dinner or a game of cards, but I always made some excuse. On weekday nights I either went to the Boston Public Library to study or stayed in the apartment where I'd fall asleep watching the Johnny Carson show. Weekends, I drank myself into a stupor at the Huddle, arguing with a broken-down drunk about metaphysics or talking football with the third string quarterback for the Patriots.

I got a call from Natalie in November. She said she had been thinking of me and got my number from Bernie Nussbaum who was in her class in "Advanced Motivational Psychology." I asked her about Jack and she said they were still dating but had agreed to an "open" relationship. "It's too hard to be monogamous over long distances," she said. I said something stupid like "I've never tried it." She didn't laugh and said in quiet reprimand that I should be open to new experiences. Then she asked me if I would escort her to a SNCC party on Saturday night at Costello's, a Waltham bar. Almost immediately after we ended the conversation the phone rang again. It was Izzy. He said he wanted to meet with me an hour before the party. I asked why, and he said, "You don't have allegiances to anyone or anything." I didn't know what he meant. The point in being disconnected is that you never get asked to do anything. But I was curious. I agreed to meet him at his apartment, which I was surprised to learn was Jack's old place.

The students called Waltham "the armpit of the nation," but they were giving the town more credit than it deserved. At least armpits can be made tolerable with a little talcum powder. Fumigating Waltham would only make the ugliness more noticeable. The main street featured a row of taverns, barbershops, gas stations, car repair shops, and supermarkets with a lot of empty shelves. The residential streets, like the one where Natalie lived, were ghettoes for factory workers, plumbers, electricians, and retired railroad workers, living in two and three-flat wood houses, a stone cottage here and there to relieve the monotony. Walthamites were the "still discordant wavering multitude" of capitalism, sitting in their decrepit houses watching TV and believing, despite all evidence to the contrary, that America belonged to them, not to those crazy college kids down the street railing against injustice and plotting mini-revolts.

The house where Natalie lived had a small porch and two front doors, one to her apartment and the other to a stairwell. I wanted to knock on Natalie's door and tell her how much I looked forward to having a drink with her at Costello's, but decided against it. I didn't want to seem too eager.

I rang the bell to the second floor apartment. A buzzer sounded and I walked inside. Izzy and Natalie were standing at the top of the stairs. She skipped past him down the stairs and threw her arms around my neck, kissing me on the lips. She led me up to the apartment like a dog on a leash.

The apartment consisted of two small rooms, no door in between. The front room was unfurnished except for two mattresses on the floor, a beat-up roll desk with piano chair in a corner, and a television on a Formica table. The second room had a cot set flush against a wall, across from a cabinet kitchen. A student I recognized from the SNCC table was drinking a glass of milk and a man I didn't recognize was leaning against the refrigerator. He was older, in his mid-thirties at least. On his forearm was a black tattoo in the shape of the infinity symbol.

Everyone but Natalie was smoking and the air was full of haze, so thick it stung my eyes. Black sheets covered the windows and a single bulb in the ceiling lit the front room with a yellowish glow that gave everyone a jaundiced cast. Otherwise, the room looked like a set from one of those espionage movies made during the communist scare. The walls were covered with posters of famous revolutionaries and radicals: Lenin, Mao, Bukharin, Ho Chi Min, Castro, Chè Guevara, and Malcolm X. I didn't recognize the man in the photograph above the television. Dressed in black pants and vest with a gold chain across his stomach, he was standing in front of what looked like a rail yard. "That's Pretty Boy Floyd," Izzy said. "I cut it out of a book." "Was he a revolutionary?" I asked. The older man pushed himself off the refrigerator door and said, "Haven't you read *The Grapes of Wrath?* Pretty Boy was the Robin Hood of the Cookson Hills." He twisted his mouth and continued in hillbilly twang: "When Floyd was loose and goin" wild, law said we got to give him up—an' nobody give him up. Sometimes a fella got to sift the law." I said "Right," as if I knew what he was talking about.

Natalie and I sat on one of the mattresses. She wrapped one leg over me and played with my hair. "Now that I'm with you, I can't believe I didn't call you sooner," she said. Izzy was sitting on the piano chair. "How would you like a beer" he asked. He didn't wait for an answer and gestured imperiously at the older man. "Get our friend a beer."

"What's going on?" I felt like I had stumbled into the lair of a guerilla army and was sitting next to the leader's *woman.*

"Take off your coat and stay a while," Izzy said.

"It's cold in here," I said, wondering why they didn't turn on the heat. Despite the sheets on the windows, a frigid draft coursed through the room.

"We need a favor," Izzy said.

"What kind of favor?"

Natalie snuggled against my shoulder and threw her other leg over me. Her skirt slid up her thighs, exposing pink panties. "We're planning a demonstration for graduation," she said, as if she were announcing a church social.

"What kind of demonstration?"

"Arthur Goldberg, the United Nations Ambassador."

"I know who he is."

Natalie put her hands on my cheeks and shook my head. "Sorry, honey."

"Forget it," I said. "Tell me the rest."

"Goldberg is giving the commencement address. It will be the perfect time to show our opposition to the war in Vietnam.

"What's happening in Vietnam?"

"You're so ivory tower."

Izzy slid his chair closer and nervously scratched his beard. "My sources tell me Johnson is getting ready to order more buildups. We have to stop them. We have to make a statement."

"Buy a commercial spot on the campus radio station." I said.

The older man came over and handed me a bottle of beer. "I told you this was a stupid idea," he said to Izzy.

"Who are you and what is the idea?"

"Chris Daniels," Natalie said. "Class of sixty-one."

"I didn't graduate," Chris said, as if dropping out were a badge of honor.

"He just got out," Izzy said.

"Got out of where?" I asked.

"Leavenworth."

"He was framed," Natalie said.

"For what?"

"Rape."

I pushed Natalie's legs off my lap and stood. "I'll see you at Costello's."

"Hear us out," Izzy said.

"What's there to hear? It's a dumb idea. No one goes to graduation except students and parents. Why not do something where you'll get more publicity?"

"Like what?"

"How should I know? I don't believe in demonstrations. They're like a two-year-old having a temper tantrum because his mother won't give him a pacifier."

"He's right," the student with the milk said. "We should do something more dramatic."

"Drama belongs in the theater," I said, walking to the door.

Natalie rushed after me as I ran down the steps. She grabbed my arm as I opened the outside door.

"What's going on?" I said. "What are you doing hanging around with a rapist? Why are you setting me up?"

Her mouth turned upside down in a pout. "I called you because I wanted to see you."

"Sure you did."

"I told you, I've been thinking of you."

I took out a cigarette and lit it. In those days, I smoked Newport Menthol. I thought it made my breath smell good. "Are you still in love with Jack?" I asked.

"No," she said and kissed me.

Everyone was at the party, and I mean everyone: more than a hundred students; two dozen faculty members, including historian and New York Post columnist Max Lerner, who was famous at Brandeis for other things, like attacking coeds in the basement of the library—next to the Botany books—and maintaining a sperm bank so his chromosomes would be available for future generations; the novelist Mark Harris; Scopes Monkey Trial expert Ray Ginger; conservative political scientist John P. Roche. The gang was also there, even Schmuckler, if only to check out what leftists did for fun. SNCC was the "hot" group on campus and even the "noncombatants" like my friends didn't want to be left out, especially if there was a party involved.

Buddy had missed me the most. He said things had gotten bad at home. His mother was dating a pencil salesman from Schenectady she met at the Holiday Inn where her book club gathered on Thursday nights. The salesman had seen her sitting in the lobby waiting for friends, trying to write in her notebook with a ballpoint pen that had run out of ink. He offered her a pencil, and their romance began. He was coming in every weekend, Buddy said, and they were sleeping together, "confusing the hell out of Abraham," as if he wasn't already confused. "Are they getting married?" I asked. Buddy shrugged forlornly. "Look at the bright side," I said. "Abraham will have someone he can call father, and he'll start calling you Buddy." "Stepfather, you mean," Buddy said, in a funk.

Izzy was the life of the party. He spent two hours arguing with Roche about our involvement in Vietnam, a half-hour complaining to Ginger that too many southern schools still refused to teach the theory of evolution, and ninety minutes explaining to Lerner why the Beatles were making as significant a contribution to music as Beethoven had. Izzy and Lerner were drunk, spewing out their points with stutters and gurgles, pausing when fellow student and future Black Panther Angela Davis came into the bar wearing a tight purple dress that made her look like one of the Supremes. She only stayed a couple of minutes, enough time to heatedly exchange words with Izzy and Lerner about a guy named Eldridge Cleaver who she said was going to make SNCC look like the boy scouts. When Izzy tried to defend SNCC and Lerner began praising American liberalism, she screamed, "You're both full of shit," and left.

That did it for fun and good cheer. Izzy retreated to a corner table with Goldstein and Zelman, where they huddled in what looked like a group communion. "What do you think they're discussing?" I asked Natalie.

"Legal strategy, I imagine."

"For what?"

"If we get arrested."

"Why would you get arrested?"

Her dewy-eyed look disappeared. "God, you can be dense sometimes."

"Goldstein and Zelman aren't lawyers," I said.

"They're planning to go to law school, aren't they?"

"So are a lot of people, including me, but I don't confuse that with a license to give legal advice." I playfully nudged her. The soft spaces in between her ribs were especially inviting.

She started to slap away my hand, changed her mind, and ran a fingernail up my arm. "You're sexy," she said with deep-throated sultriness.

It was after midnight and I was tipsy. I could have left my car in Waltham and taken the bus, but it was raining and I didn't want to ruin the leather jacket my parents had given me for my twenty-first birthday. When I told Natalie I was leaving, she said, "I'm coming too."

"To my apartment?"

"No, to my apartment."

So, I had a girlfriend, even if I didn't have her to myself. In the morning, weakened from lovemaking, I accepted her terms and conditions. In exchange for as much sex as I could handle, I agreed to never tell her what to do, not see her on the third weekend of every month when she would travel to Philadelphia, accept that our relationship would end with graduation, and support her activities in SNCC. I asked her to list the activities. She said she had nothing specific in mind, but that it was time for me to "cultivate a social conscience."

We luxuriated in the stuff of companionship, though some of her tastes bordered on the bizarre. After every snowstorm she dragged me on long walks through the woods in Westin, a heavily forested area west of Waltham. One day we got lost and built a snow hut, a kind of igloo that caved in an hour later. I thought we would freeze to death. She gathered some pinecones and a few sticks of wood and started a fire with my Zippo lighter. She made me take down my pants and warm my ass over the fire. When I asked her to do the same, she said, "I never undress in public." I turned around to see an old man and woman on skis, our rescuers.

The only movies she liked were foreign language films. Once a week we'd see Italian and French films that I couldn't follow even with the help of subtitles, such inaccessible works as Antonioni's *La Ventura* about a woman who disappears from a party and is forgotten by the guests *and* the screenwriter, and the torturous *The World of Apu,* the story of a family in India who spend their time starving and praying. She said she loved music, but would only go to concerts of Baroque music. She refused to read a book written by a man and would make me sit still while she read from *Silas Marner.*

She never mentioned SNCC, never insisted I attend meetings, and never asked me to act in the name of freedom, justice, or equality. She said it was funny that I was planning to attend law school, commenting on more than one occasion that I was a slave to order instead of a master of chaos. She said she might join the Peace Corps. "If you do," I said, "can I have your car?" She wouldn't have sex with me for a week.

She invited me to her home in Westport Connecticut for Thanksgiving, a nine-bedroom ranch that she shared with her parents and her younger sister, a junior in high school and a cabbage-patch kind of girl. Her father owned a box company in Bridgeport and her mother taught English at the high school. Natalie called her family "decadent," to their faces no less. I had a good time, even got to have sex with Natalie, on the couch in her father's library the day after Thanksgiving when her parents and Sophie went roller-skating. The one uncomfortable moment came at Thanksgiving dinner when Natalie refused to give thanks; she said Thanksgiving was invented to make Protestants look "holier than thou" and to conceal that they had stolen the Indians' turkeys.

In January, I invited the gang to dinner at my apartment. It was the third Friday of the month and Natalie was visiting Jack in Philadelphia. I went to Star Market and loaded up with supplies. I had been practicing my cooking and was looking forward to making meat loaf with my own special sauce—canned tomatoes, bay leaf, tons of garlic, and a dash of sugar—and apple pie. I dumped the grocery bags in the kitchen and turned on the TV. Mike Douglas was interviewing Bob Hope.

I was putting away the food when a news bulletin interrupted the show. Three men, dressed in work clothes, had entered the Shawmut Bank in Brighton shortly before closing. One robber approached a teller's window and the other two stood in the middle pretending to fill out deposit slips. The suspicious guard, hand on his gun, stepped forward. They panicked and jumped him. He was shot in the ensuing struggle. The robbers fled the bank and escaped in a van. The guard died before help arrived.

I stepped into the living room. On the screen was a picture of the guard with his wife and seven children. Then Mike Douglas returned. Bob Hope was gone; in his place, Tony Bennett was singing *I Left My Heart in San Francisco*. Then the outside buzzer rang. Thinking it was the gang I pushed the button to open the door to the vestibule. My apartment was on the second floor, at the top of the stairs, and I heard the clumps of several pairs of feet. "Fucking shit," I muttered, "Why do they have to be early?"

The door was slightly ajar when they shoved it open, knocking me backwards. Chris the ex-con was in the lead, followed by Izzy and Natalie. They were dressed in overalls, like housepainters, and their faces were black from some kind of greasy substance. Chris scurried to the window and yanked it open. He stuck his head out and looked down to the alley. "Come on up here, Katz," he yelled.

"Sorry about this," Izzy said.

"What's going on?" I asked, as if I hadn't already figured it out.

Natalie kissed me. I was thinking she was supposed to be in Philadelphia. "Izzy wanted to see your apartment," she said brightly.

"I know I'm a sucker for tourists," I said. "But if you're here to look around, I should charge admission."

Katz, the guy from the alley, came through the door. I recognized him as the SNCC student from the meeting in Waltham. He was wearing a vinyl jacket over his overalls and I could see a bulge in its left pocket.

"You can't stay here," I said, thinking he looked a lot more dangerous than he had when he was drinking the milk.

"Shut up," Chris said. "We'll decide what we can or can't do."

"Nobody tells me to shut up," I said, imagining I was Bogart.

"We do," Katz said, reaching for his gun.

"Did you fill that with water?" I asked, proud to be meeting Bogart's challenge.

He tapped his pocket. "Do you want to find out?"

"Stop this," Natalie cried.

"I thought you were in Philadelphia visiting Jack," I said.

"I put it off until tomorrow."

"I'd rather be here than in Philadelphia, is that it?"

"What do you mean?"

"W.C. Fields's epitath."

"Who is he?"

I thought about folk hero Pretty Boy Floyd. I liked W.C. Fields better. "Never give a sucker an even break," I said.

"Are you calling me a sucker?" Katz said.

"Stop this," Natalie cried again, a broken record.

I pointed to the TV. "You're all over the news," I said, though the news wasn't on. A bedraggled Senòr Wences was opening and closing the box that housed his dummy, saying, "It's all right?" and the dummy replying, "It's all right."

Katz was waving his gun at the TV. "That guy's a riot."

"Why don't you put the gun away?" I suggested.

"Where is the fucking news?" Chris said.

"Not on yet," I said. "But there was a bulletin."

"What kind of bulletin?"

"You know, the kind that says, 'We interrupt this broadcast for an important—'"

"What did it say?"

"A guard was killed."

Natalie put her hands to her face in horror, spinning around to face Chris. He backed away from the window and eyed me with a combination of disdain and wariness. "You said you just fired a shot in the air," she said.

"Yeah, well, somebody got in the way," Chris said.

"Oh my God," Natalie screamed.

Izzy was pacing the floor, rubbing his stubbly beard. "Shit, fuck, cocksucker, asshole."

"I have to think," Chris said, as if thinking had become a chore.

"Am I a hostage?" I asked.

"We haven't decided," Chris said.

Izzy and Katz sat on the couch while Chris assumed control of the TV. He turned the channels, cursing when he found nothing but soap operas, old movies, and talk shows. He slammed his fist against the knob, which fell to the floor and started spinning like a top.

"Hey, watch what you're doing," I said, replacing the knob on the TV. "That's an RCA."

"A capitalist good," Katz said.

"Don't knock it. It will be around longer than you."

We heard sirens in the distance. "Shit," Chris said.

I looked out the window. A green van was parked in the alley next to my car. "Were you followed?"

Natalie's face had turned white, the color bordering on that of an albino. "Natalie, snap out of it," I said, shaking her.

"I can't," she whimpered.

"Who were you in this escapade?"

"I drove the van to the bank and waited outside. I heard a shot, but they told me no one was hurt."

"Shut the fuck up," Chris said.

"Don't tell me to shut up, you fucking rapist," Natalie said.

The buzzer rang. "Who the fuck is that?" Izzy said as Chris ran out the open front door and looked down the stairs.

"Probably my buddies," I said. I pointed to the groceries on the kitchen counter. "I was planning a quiet dinner."

Chris was returning to the apartment as the buzzer rang again. "OK, we'll have a party, like nothing happened."

"If nothing happened, we could invite the guard you shot."

"You got a better idea?"

"You could leave. Or, if you were really divine, as apparently you think you are, you could start the day over and think of something better to do than play bank robbers."

Chris looked at Natalie. "Where did you find this asshole?"

"In the library."

"The Anne Frank Reading Room," I said. "A place where it's hard to pretend nothing happened."

The buzzer rang again. "Let them in," Chris said.

"What do I tell them?"

"Tell them what Natalie said. We stopped by to see your apartment."

"Then you'll leave?"

"Maybe."

Katz had meandered into the kitchen and was rummaging through my groceries. "We should stay for dinner," he said.

"Shut your mouth, Katz," Chris said.

I wish I had had a movie camera. What a scene! Cramped into the small living room were my six buddies and four bank robbers. My buddies didn't suspect a thing, even when Buddy started out of the apartment to buy more beer and Chris grabbed his collar. "We're not thirsty," he said.

During all this time, Schmuckler was in some kind of reverie, humming his Gregorian chants sotto voce. Suddenly, he stopped and said that wearing overalls on a Friday afternoon was "low class." Then he said they reminded him of the gangsters in the movie, *The Desperate Hours*, though not as sympathetic. Goldstein and Zelman were happy to see Izzy and asked him why he had never called to continue their legal discussion. "I never got arrested," Izzy said, a temporary state the way things were going. Bernie scoured the apartment collecting matchbooks. He sat at the kitchen table and lit them one at a time. The apartment soon smelled of sulfur.

Ignoring everyone, Dennis picked up the phone and called his bookie. He screamed at him for not extending more credit. Next, he called the collector, a guy named Serge who was a grad student at MIT, and begged for time to pay the $1,000 he had lost on the NFL championship.

The news came on and the lead story was the failed bank robbery. Everyone gathered in front of the TV. I dragged Natalie into the bathroom and shut the door.

"This is my fault, isn't it?" I said.

She was crying. "What do you mean?"

"Saturday, the day of the party, at your house, I suggested you do something dramatic."

She was hysterical, sobbing and sniffling, tears streaking her cheeks. I wiped her face with a towel. "I didn't know anyone would get hurt," she said.

"For God's sake, banks have guards. With guns."

"We needed the money for the revolution," she said softly, like a little girl.

"A revolution costs more than what you can get out of a bank in Brighton."

"We had six more robberies planned, including the main one downtown."

"What are you going to do?"

"Go underground."

"There hasn't been an underground since the Civil War."

"There will be now."

"Why did you come here?"

"You heard the sirens. We never would have made it back to Waltham."

"Did anyone see you?"

"Chris said they got us on the TV cameras in the bank."

"But you said you waited outside."

"I did, but when I heard the shot I stepped inside the front door for a couple seconds."

"Did you see the guard?"

"No, just the customers and employees. They looked so scared."

She stopped crying and looked at me straight on, like she did when we made love. "I have a confession to make," she said.

"I'm not the cops."

"I've been with Chris."

"You slept with a rapist?"

"I haven't been going to Philadelphia. I broke up with Jack for good over the summer. I met Chris at a SNCC meeting and couldn't resist him."

"So what did you need me for?"

"I couldn't resist you either."

"Hey, you two, open up," Chris yelled. I pressed my back against the door.

"Do you want me to bust this fucking thing down?"

I opened the door. He looked at Natalie who was wiping her nose on the towel. "We're leaving," he said.

"Hey," Zelman yelled, eyes fixed on the TV. "It's Izzy." Natalie and I pushed Chris aside and raced to the TV. On the screen was a fuzzy tape of a man in overalls, walking stiff-legged to a teller's window.

"It's not Izzy," I said.

"I say it is," Zelman said.

Katz came out of the kitchen, a hand on his gun, half out of the pocket. Chris stepped in front of him and laughed. "You guys are too much."

Zelman moved away from the TV and walked over to Izzy, Goldstein trailing behind. "You guys robbed the bank," Zelman said, for the first time in his college career not trying to sound like a lawyer.

"Oh, my God, you're criminals," Goldstein shouted.

Katz moved between them and Zelman grabbed him in a bear hug. Katz started swinging his body, but Zelman just held on tighter as Goldstein ran behind them and jumped on his back like a little kid playing horse with his father. Katz disappeared from view, his head caught between two crotches. Chris crashed into the standing pile and they went reeling across the room, falling against the radiator. The steam cap flew into the kitchen and hit Bernie in the head, knocking a lit match out of his hand. The match landed in the garbage basket and set the plastic ground beef package on fire. While the apartment filled with smoke, a hot mist spouted upward from the radiator, accompanied by an insanely loud whistle. Katz recovered and stood pointing the gun at the prone Zelman and Goldstein. "Please, don't kill us," they said, looking like two deserters facing a firing squad.

"It's a good thing you're Jewish," Katz said.

"I'm not," Goldstein said. "I'm adopted. My real father is German."

"Shut up, Goldstein," Zelman said.

"I should do you right here, you fucking Nazi."

"He was just kidding," Zelman said.

"Nazis don't kid."

Katz was squinting in the smoke and tears were incongruously streaming down his cheeks. If you didn't know what was going on, you'd think his feelings were really hurt.

"Nazis do kid," I yelled, jumping him from behind, "Didn't you ever see *Stalag 17*?" I managed to get the gun out of his hand as we toppled backwards. We fell on the couch next to Schmuckler. We were too out of breath and blinded by smoke to keep fighting.

The apartment and its inhabitants looked like a freeze frame. Natalie was staring at the TV, which was tuned to a soap opera. Dennis was on the phone, mouth open, no words coming out. Bernie held a bucket of water over the wastebasket, no doubt regretting he would have to put out the fire. Buddy was in the bedroom, lying on the bed like a corpse, drunk and unconscious. Schmuckler was curled into a ball on the couch next to Katz and me, the book *God and Man at Yale* open on his lap. Izzy, Chris, and Katz were standing in a row, their kinky hair more disheveled than ever, as if they were ready to audition for a slapstick comedy about crazed house painters who wreck every house they paint. I felt like the curator at a wax museum. I could have arranged them any way I wanted, who knows, started them like wind-up dolls and sent them backward in time, changing history.

The moment ended. Goldstein climbed to his feet and fell against the radiator. "Shit! I'm burned."

You're lucky they're not powder burns, "Katz said, squirming off my lap.

"Give me the gun," Chris said.

I fiddled with the gun, trying to picture Tom Tully in *The Lineup*. "I have a question," I said, as five bullets fell between the cracks of the cushions.

"We have more in the van."

"Better the van than here."

"What's your question?"

"What does a bank robbery have to do with civil rights and the war in Vietnam?"

"You don't know?"

"No."

"Well, you better find out before this fucking decade is over."

They were at the door when I said, "What happens if I don't figure it out?"

Again, I had opened my big mouth. "I need to see you outside," he said.

"I like it here."

"If you don't come, I'll be back with the bullets."

"I'm coming," I said.

We went downstairs to the back door. "What do you want?" I asked Chris.

"Give me your car keys."

"What for?"

"We can't go in the van. We'll be spotted. We've got another car back at the house. We'll leave your car there. You can get it later."

"I don't know."

"Please," Natalie said.

"SNCC will never call on your services again," Izzy said.

I handed my keys to Chris. "You have to floor the pedal before you start the car."

Chris gave me the keys to the van. They went into the alley while Natalie stayed behind. "Don't think poorly of us," she said. "We did it for the revolution."

"Natalie, there is no revolution."

She started crying again. "We wanted there to be one," she said.

On the front page of Monday morning's Boston Globe were pictures of Izzy, Chris, Katz, and Natalie. I don't know how they got them, but the pictures of Izzy, Katz, and Natalie were the ones taken for graduation. They had the happy countenance of kids with their lives ahead of them. Chris's photo was his Leavenworth mug shot, in striped shirt with the numbers across his chest.

At dusk, I met with the gang on the snow-covered outfield of the baseball park. I could see the dorm where I lived as a freshman, the building we called the Castle, which looked like a castle, used by the medical school that predated the university; the contemporary glass and steel twin towers of the science center where some of the world's greatest physicists sought the secrets of the universe; on the other side, the Spingold Theater Arts Center where I took an acting class, pretending I was an ant, or a monkey, or a horse, depending on my mood; the music pavilion where Schmuckler used to drag me to hear chamber music; the bio-research lab, where rumor had it that faculty members were conducting secret experiments in germ warfare; the reservoir by the library where, on what they thought would be a fun-filled afternoon buzzing the campus and their fellow students, three graduate students died after their light plane hit the top of a tree and plunged into the muck and two feet of rainwater; the library where I read history, philosophy, literature, and psychology, studied chemistry, math, and physics, researched term papers, and dreamed of romance. Quiet, with enough of a breeze to still the sound of cars speeding along the street between the field and the circular drive to the entrance, passing in front of the hundred-foot brick cylinder the students had named the "Eichmann Memorial Smokestack." We must have looked small standing there, shivering in the cold, bewildered that our innocence should be unceremoniously stripped from us.

While our fingers and toes got numb from the cold, we argued what to do. It started to snow. Bernie took out a box of wooden matches. We held hands, thumbs locked with baby fingers over the transitory flames.

I said we should keep quiet. We had no good explanation for not calling the police on Friday. I played on Zelman and Goldstein's fear that we'd be tagged as after-the-fact accomplices. I told Dennis the cops would find out about his gambling. Bernie was running out of matches and said he'd go along with what I wanted. Only Schmuckler held out. SNCC members everywhere were guilty, he said, and they should be prosecuted, "to the full extent of the law," quoting the public address announcers at baseball stadiums when they would warn fans not to interfere with the ballplayers on the field. I was too cold to reason with him and threatened to break his Edith Piaf records. I called him a coward. What was he doing at Brandeis, I said, a bastion of liberalism? Did it make it easy for him to sit on his beliefs and hum dead melodies from the middle ages?

A month later, the cops stopped me for speeding on the way to a Celtics game. When I opened the glove compartment to get the registration, a piece of paper fell out. It was a note from Natalie. After the cop gave me the ticket and left, I drove into a construction site and parked behind a mountain of steel girders. I opened the note and read it a dozen times, though it consisted of just one line: "Thinkers prepare the revolution; bandits carry it out."

Four or five years ago Natalie was in the news. She was living in Eugene Oregon, a housewife with three kids, when she got in her car, drove to Portland, and surrendered. She said she couldn't live any longer with the guilt. They shipped her back to Boston and she was sentenced to fifteen years in prison. She came up for parole last year, but withdrew her application at the hearing. She looked at the guard's widow and her seven kids and said she would prefer to serve out her sentence. She said, "We were drenched with dangerous romanticism and saw ourselves as noble warriors for a great cause. We thought there was glamour in gun-toting violence."

I was at the hearing. I sat in the last row where she couldn't see me. I would never have recognized her. She had put on quite a lot of weight—haven't we all?—and the fire in her eyes was gone, long gone, the suffering on her face stark and permanent. Her blonde hair had turned gray and purple bags had reduced her eyes to pinholes. She looked like she was eighty years old. Her husband and children were sitting in the front row. They burst into tears when she said she was withdrawing her application. Obviously, she hadn't told them. I don't think she realized she was going to drop her request for parole until right before she did.

I went down to the lockup and asked to see her. I thought about what she had said. I remembered the look on her face when she and the others came to my apartment, before she knew the guard had been shot. She was flush with the sense of having done something, right or wrong, participated in an act of defiance that took her out of the ordinary. Sure, it was madness—wrong, immoral, and illegal—but she thought she was giving her life to a cause instead of just throwing it away on hot dogs and mustard, polka dots and moonbeams, and the rest of the twentieth century's idea of a good life. And then, in the apartment, when she heard the guard had been killed, her world came crashing down on her. She wasn't a gangster or gun moll. She wanted to make love, not war. She said she wanted to be in the Peace Corps.

A marshal came out and said she didn't want to see me. I said there must be some mistake. No mistake, he said. "Did she say why?" I asked, feeling empty inside. "No," he said, and that was that.

The others? No one surrendered and no one was caught. Natalie could have stayed in Eugene, Oregon forever. If she knows where the others are, she's not saying.

Izzy's father gave up his practice to look for his son. He hired lawyers, investigators, search firms; nothing worked. He traveled around the country, staying in cheap hotels in neighborhoods thought to be enclaves for the disaffected; let his hair grow and posed as a radical from San Francisco; showed Izzy's picture to thousands of people on hundreds of street corners. His wife left him. Last year he was found dead of a heart attack in a seedy hotel in Oakland. On the night table was a notebook filled with his jottings of past leads that had led nowhere: people to see, new ideas to check out, beginnings without endings. No one came forward with the money to ship his body back to Boston. His body was laid to rest on a surgical table at the University of California, where medical students dismembered it and studied his organs before tossing the remains in the incinerator.

The gang? Buddy wanted to be a doctor and got into Columbia Medical School. He had a nervous breakdown the day after graduation, disappeared for two years, and reemerged delivering mail to the people of Modesto, California. Dennis married and divorced his sweetheart, has a daughter who became a newscaster, and still bets all his money and more with bookies. In 1985, a collector smashed his fingers when he welshed on his gambling debts. Jeff never became the true conservative he wanted to be; he joined the Marines right after law school and was killed in Vietnam. Goldstein and Zelman formed a law firm in New York. Last I noticed, they employ over two hundred lawyers and represent several Fortune 500 companies. Goldstein gave up pipes for cigars and then gave up cigars when he got throat cancer and his larynx was removed. Bernie works for a large insurance company. He specializes in fraudulent claims and loves it when a policyholder torches his own business to collect on the insurance. He's married and has two sons. They're both firemen.

Then there's me. I went to law school, worked for Judge Gunderson, strike force for three years, Litowitz firm, partnership with Gordon, then on my own. I was making six figures by 1974 and broke the seven-figure barrier in 1987. I can go and eat where I please. I've owned big houses, summer houses, and nice cars. I've laughed a lot. Then there's me, the least important character of all, the apolitical, detached observer who for a time got attached. I went to law school, worked for a judge, was a prosecutor for three years, joined a law firm and became a partner five years later. I was making six figures by 1974, and I broke the seven-figure barrier in 1987. I have a lovely wife. When we argue, it's about nothing: where to take our next vacation, whether we want to delete a certain couple from our social list, if and when to visit our respective in-laws. If I get the urge to see a ball game, want box seats at the opera, or orchestra tickets at a sold-out Broadway show, there are plenty of people I can call. My friends, even my enemies, say my life is wonderful.

I still believe in as little as possible. I am still uninvolved.

Sometimes, I think I'm better off this way; sometimes, I don't.

I survived the sixties. A lot of people didn't.

Was he really uninvolved. I wondered.

After dinner, my friend suggested returning to Murphy's for a nightcap. He wanted to walk, which did not please Jimmy. Corcoran, however, had apparently given up for the night, as he was nowhere to be seen. But when I started to ask why Corcoran had been following us, both my friend and Jimmy dodged my questions.

We walked the eight blocks in silence, Jimmy driving slowly alongside us. I spent the time thinking about his last story and how what had happened to Natalie might somehow be connected to his view of the world. Though he had portrayed himself in the story as cynical and apolitical, there was nevertheless a sense of regret that I felt most deeply, as if he had been commenting on my own detachment from the world in which I lived.

Jimmy parked in front of Murphy's. Patrick had already poured an Amaretto for my friend and a Guinness for me. The tavern was as quiet as on that first night. The only other people present were a young man and woman, holding hands, faces close together as they whispered what I imagined were sweet words of love. My friend swirled his drink and the ice cubes seemed to sing.

The telephone rang. Patrick picked up the receiver and immediately began to fidget. He shook his head several times. Then he cupped a hand over the mouthpiece and looked at my friend. As if carrying a great weight on his shoulders, he slowly got off the stool and went to the phone. Patrick whispered a word or two and handed him the phone. My friend turned his back to me and cradled the phone on his shoulder. He reached across his body and snapped his fingers, which brought Patrick scurrying to him with a pen and paper.

"Who was it?" I asked when he finished the call.

"Gene Lufman. He wants me to meet him for a drink."

"At this hour?"

He shrugged. "He said it was urgent."

"What is it?"

"I'm not sure."

We walked out onto Second Avenue where Jimmy was waiting. As Jimmy was opening the car door, my friend said to me, "Let's meet for lunch tomorrow."

"If you wish."

"At noon. There's a bookstand on the west side of Second Avenue between Fifty-ninth and Sixtieth, near stairs to the Roosevelt Island tram."

"Why there?"

"It's easy to find."

He started to get in the car. "I was thinking about your story," *I said.*

"What about it?"

"Surely, what Natalie and the others did was wrong."

"Yes, it was wrong."

"Yet, the way you told it . . . I am not certain, but I thought you were defending them."

"No, not defend, but to look for innocence in others so that we may recognize it in ourselves."

I knew something was amiss as soon as I entered the studio. Cuchulainn's eyes were glowing, but they were not only disembodied in the dark but too high off the floor. I turned on the lights to see Cuchulainn sitting on my suitcase. Instantly, I remembered that I had left the suitcase in the closet after my abortive attempt to leave for Belfast.

"Oh, no," I said out loud. The suitcase was open and a side pocked unzipped. The tapes were gone.

CHAPTER TWELVE

May 21, 1998

I SLEPT FITFULLY. *I thought the cause must be the despair that accompanies the death of a loved one, the stab of mortality prickling my heart and reminding me that there are only so many beats in a lifetime. My poor father was gone, and I had witnessed the violent deaths of four others, holding one in my arms as he expired.*

I wondered whether my anxiety was related to the immersion in my friend's life: his stories, his legal career, hour after hour inside his head and heart. Despite the deep differences in our backgrounds, I identified with him more than I wanted to acknowledge. He had spent his life believing in nothing, enduring life's skirmishes as if they were odd twists and turns on a deserted mountain road, where to either side are precipitous drop-offs. If one were to fall asleep at the wheel, the car would speed straight ahead at the next bend and fly off the edge. He seemed to have avoided such a calamity, but I was not sure of my destiny. Was I now asleep at the wheel?

Here in New York, life had kept me awake by showing me death, challenging me to believe in something, to be genuinely afraid for the first time in my life. The future, always unknown, had taken on the quality of unexpectedness. It is one thing to not know the future, but to be deprived of the anticipation of it, the expectation that it will be as one wishes, that is quite another matter. How does one embrace the unexpected?

I telephoned Mary and learned that funeral preparations were proceeding apace. My parents' home was a way station for mourners who passed through with stories of my father's good humor and impassioned opinions. He was to be buried the following morning at Milltown cemetery, in a grave less than a hundred yards from where Bobby Sands was interred. I still did not tell her of my purloined passport. Instead, I said I would not take a flight until Monday, so I would have the opportunity to interview Irish Americans, which, after all, was the purpose of my trip. I had become rather adept at lying. For that, I suppose, I could thank my friend.

Like old friends, Gold and Varick made their third appearance at the studio. They brought with them a surprise: Smith Corcoran. I introduced myself to him, hoping he would go along with my pretense. Ignoring my outstretched hand, he dipped his head once, as if I were a combatant with whom he was about to do battle.

"Our investigation has taken a new turn," Susan said.

Corcoran was circling the room like a predator on the prowl. "We believe an act of terrorism is imminent," he said, pausing at the desk to finger my notebook.

"Special Agent Corcoran is with the domestic anti-terrorism unit," Varick said.

"Certainly, you do not think I am involved in terrorism."

"You're Catholic and you're from Belfast," he said, as if no more was needed to brand me.

"Let me tell you what we've learned since we were last here, Mr. Sullivan," Susan said. "We obtained a search warrant for the Korean's premises. We found this." She opened her briefcase and took out a sheet of paper enclosed in a plastic sleeve. On it was an array of lines forming a grid. One line started at the bottom and ended at the top. It was labeled "Queens Blvd." At the right edge was a mark in the shape of an "X."

"It looks like a map," I said.

"Turn it over," Varick said.

A number was scrawled at an angle. "A telephone number," I said.

"Very good, Sullivan. Whose number is it?"

Corcoran was now leaning against the desk, studying me.

"I have not committed American telephone numbers to memory."

Varick took the sleeve. "It's Samuel Brandt's home number, presumably the one you called when you arranged to meet him?"

"What is the connection between the Korean and Mr. Brandt?"

"That was my next question."

Susan glared at Varick. Their relationship had not improved since the last visit. *"Let's return to the map, shall we?"* she said. *"The X mark seems to correspond to a cluster of abandoned warehouses in Long Island City. They're scheduled for demolition next month."*

"Why bomb buildings that are going to be destroyed anyway?" I asked.

"We don't know," Susan said.

"When is the last time you spoke with your father?" Varick asked.

"My father died the day before yesterday."

Varick looked at me with a combination of surprise and disappointment. *"We were planning to speak to him,"* he said.

"Concerning . . . ?"

"Concerning his dealings with Marinelli."

"How do you know about that?"

"No, Sullivan. How do you know about that?"

"He was my father," I said.

Varick snapped his fingers like a head butler summoning his lackeys, and Susan took a tape recorder out of her pocketbook. She turned it on. In a faint wheezing voice, I heard my father say, *"Are you sure it will work?"* There followed Salvatore's familiar cough and *"One can never be certain of anything in life. But it is worth the effort, no?"* I struggled to hold back tears as I heard my father's labored breathing and heartfelt words: *"It would do me good if Tommy could sit in the sun with his family."*

Corcoran stepped away from the desk. *"Come on, Sullivan, tell us what you know."* His eyes flashed with a bit of tomfoolery.

"What do you say now, Sullivan?" Varick asked.

"Many of my countrymen wish Tommy Glynn were free."

Varick kicked my suitcase. *"Were you planning a trip?"*

"I am returning home."

"When?"

"Soon. I have not yet made a reservation."

Corcoran removed a notepad from his suit jacket. *"Flight number, please."*

"We want you to stay until Monday," Varick said.

"Why Monday?"

"In case we have more questions."

"I see," I said. We stood silently for a few moments. Varick seemed to be thinking whether he should say more.

"Is that all?" I asked.

"We had assigned an agent to follow you. Unfortunately, he's in the hospital."

"Is he ill?"

"After we left the other day, someone put a dent in his head with the butt of a gun."

"He was careless," Corcoran said.

"Do you know who the assailant is?"

"No, but we had an idea we wanted to check out," Varick said.

"What?"

"We went to Marinelli's restaurant," Corcoran said.

"Yes?"

"Marinelli has disappeared," Varick said.

"Oh."

"Our Chicago office received a call from Daniel Marinelli's wife."

"I am sorry. I do not know a Daniel—"

"His wife said he went to New York to visit Salvatore. Arrived here on the night of the eighteenth and called her from the Marriott Hotel. She hasn't heard from him since. The concierge identified him from a photograph and said he asked directions to Marinelli's restaurant on the morning of the nineteenth. He never returned and he never checked out of the hotel."

"Have you found him?"

"No."

"I know nothing—"

"Mr. Sullivan," Susan said, "isn't it a coincidence that we saw you on the nineteenth, and it was the day someone decided to put our agent in the hospital?"

"Your insinuations are insulting!" I sounded ridiculous, even to myself.

"What if we were to arrest you?" Varick said almost jauntily, as if he were offering me a present.

"On what charge?"

"Obstruction of justice."

"I have been arrested before," I said. "I am not afraid." Indignation followed by stoic courage. I liked that.

Varick and I stared at each other in a battle of piercing gazes. Corcoran whispered to Susan. She nodded and put her hand on Varick's elbow. "Will you excuse us a moment," she said to me.

I stepped out the front door into the hall. Through the glass panel on the outside door I could see Jimmy's limousine parked at the corner of Second Avenue.

Varick came up behind me. "We're finished with you for now," he said.

"Well then, no arrest," I said. "So the law does have some meaning in this country."

"Don't be smart with me, Sullivan. If you're hiding something and ... well, let me put it this way. It won't be just the law that holds you responsible. I will hold you responsible."

Susan pushed Varick out the front door. Corcoran trailed behind and paused at my side. "Not bad, Sullivan. Not bad at all."

After Varick and Susan drove away, Corcoran walked to the building next door and sat on the stoop. He lit a cigarette and leaned back on his elbows, looking as if he did not have a care in the world. I wanted to approach him and learn more if I could, but Jimmy had driven up. Corcoran tossed away the cigarette and went over to the limousine. I could not hear what they were saying, but they appeared to be having a disagreement. Then, abruptly, Corcoran walked away.

As I watched Corcoran walk toward Second Avenue, I joined Jimmy at the car. "What is the matter?" I asked.

"Smitty thinks they suspect a prison break. He's running a little scared. Anyway, they can suspect what they want. It won't do any good."

"They found a map, a map ... " I gasped and fell to my knees.

Jimmy knelt beside me. "Are you OK?"

I tried to slow my breathing. I did not know what was happening to me. "Please, I beg you. Tell me what is going to happen."

Jimmy helped me to my feet. My legs were unsteady. "I never told you anything," he said. "Do you understand?"

"Yes," I whispered.

"I mean, nothing."

"I understand. I swear."

"Tomorrow morning, at six a.m. your friend and my friend will be free."

"What friend?"

"You know who."

"Tommy Glynn?"

"Not so loud."

"He is your friend?"

"No."

Jimmy would say no more. And when I returned to my apartment to rest, I realized I had not asked him about the missing tapes or who his friend was.

When I arrived at the stairs to the Roosevelt Island tram my friend was not there. I waited until 12:30. Jimmy came across the street and told me to take the tram. He was certain my friend would meet me at the other station. He said I must have misunderstood the instructions.

The tram was a scary looking behemoth. Its rusted girders, chains, and pulleys creaked and strained as it moved into the station. The cabin's outside coat of red and black paint was chipped; inside, colored plates rattled against brackets that were missing so many screws I was surprised the plates did not fall off. It was hard for me to believe that anyone would voluntarily board this creature—yes, creature, for I thought of it as a dying and desperate animal struggling to free itself.

I followed a horde of people into the car and was barely seated when it bolted out of the station and then rose high above the 59th Street Bridge. To the south I could see down First Avenue past the Manhattan and Brooklyn bridges; to the north I could follow the East River Drive as far as the Harlem River, which zigzagged north and west on its way to the Hudson River.

The Roosevelt Island station was drab and uninviting: graffiti covered walls, litter and paper bags scattered about, broken metal fittings stuffed in one corner. It was situated some seventy-five yards from the river, along which was a walkway and narrow strip of parkland.

I did not see my friend and considered returning to Manhattan. But the tram had left the station and I decided to walk along the river path. It had been designed with some care: benches and elm trees every twenty or thirty feet, closely cut well-tended grass on either side. Oddly, the path was being used not by pedestrians but by people in wheelchairs, including several amputees with awkwardly bent necks that flopped to the side like Raggedy Ann dolls. Others were paralyzed from the waist down. One poor soul could only move his head. Still others appeared mentally deranged. One gentleman, wearing a torn New York University sweatshirt, wheeled past me, laughing and mumbling unintelligibly.

After about a hundred yards, the row of trees ended at a bend in the path. Across the way was a large u-shaped building, black with soot. I sat on a bench and gazed at the skyline on the other side of the river. It looked like a picture postcard. The tall buildings seemed close enough to touch. I could hear the steady low hum of the cars moving along East River Drive, an occasional honk or siren, and the dull roar of an airplane flying overhead. The air smelled fresher than in Manhattan. A sea gull swooped to the ground near my feet. I sat quietly, hoping it would make a sound, perhaps a chirp or two.

My friend quietly slipped beside me. "I thought you'd never come," he said. He was wearing a white turtleneck and jeans and looked very much at ease.

"Where were you?" I asked.

"What do you mean?"

"You told me to meet you on the other side, at the entrance to the tram." He rubbed his forehead and eyes. "I did?" he asked.

"You forgot. It is all right."

He rose and walked to the railing. With his back to me he said, "It's not all right."

"What?"

"Something like this happened a couple of weeks ago. I was in Cambridge, you know, in Boston . . . "

"What were you doing there?"

He wheeled around and looked distracted. "What?"

"What were you doing in Boston?"

"Right, Boston . . . shit!"

"What is it?"

He rubbed his eyes again. They were clouded, the whites milky and opaque. "Forget it, Connie," he said.

"No, tell me."

"I came out of a bookstore in Harvard Square and had absolutely no clue where I was."

"What did you do?"

"I went to the nearest payphone and called my wife. She asked me where I was. I opened the door to the booth and asked a passerby. God, that was embarrassing. She came and got me. But I was better by then."

"Did you go to a doctor?"

"No, it was just a migraine."

"You must have it looked into."

"Aren't you sweet?"

We returned to the bench. "Why were you in Boston?" I asked.

"To see Sam. I've already told you." He appeared distracted again and stared across the river.

"Yes, you did tell me," I said.

His mood lightened and he slapped me on the back. "You probably want to know what happened to your tapes," he said.

"It would be appropriate, I believe, to explain why you instructed Jimmy to break into my apartment."

"How else would I have gotten them?"

"You could have asked."

"Jimmy didn't want to take any chances."

"I would have given them to you."

He looked into my eyes. "Yes, I suppose you would have."

He was playing with me. "This is outrageous," I said angrily.

"Don't worry. You'll get them back."

"What if I no longer want them?"

"Be real. That's my life you're talking about."

"Nothing but words."

"Words are what make us human."

We sat quietly for a while. He slouched against the back of the bench, moaning contentedly in the soft breeze, his eyes closed.

"The strike force lawyers came again this morning," I said. "With Corcoran. He's been assigned to them because they think a terrorist act is in the offing."

"I love it."

"They played a tape of a telephone conversation between Salvatore and my father."

"What was on it?"

"Nothing much, though they seem to suspect an attempt to free Tommy."

"After what happened to Gotti, Salvatore should have known better."

"Who is Gotti?"

"One of Salvatore's rivals. They recorded his schemes on tape. He's in prison for life."

"They showed me a map they found in the Korean's store."

"A map of what?"

"Streets in Queens, abandoned warehouses."

He sighed. "Whew. For a second I thought . . . "

"What?"

"Nothing."

I was tired. "I would like to return to the apartment."

"Don't you want to know why I suggested we meet here?"

"At this point, I do not care."

"Don't be such a sourpuss."

He draped an arm over the back of the bench and pointed at the building. A large sign in a wood frame stood on the inside of a circular driveway that passed in front of the entrance.

"Goldwater Memorial Hospital," I said. "The one who ran for President."

He laughed. "Something in New York named after him? You must be kidding."

"Who, then?"

"A hospital commissioner of New York. He had the crazy idea that even the poor deserved medical care."

"It looks like a prison."

"For some, it might as well be. There's a whole wing for patients who are ventilator dependent. They can't breathe on their own. Their bodies are like the walls of a jail cell, two eyes for small windows and a mouth for a vent to let in fresh air, otherwise an escape proof cage. A life sentence with no parole, not even time off for good behavior. The body is the door to your inner

self. For these people someone slammed the door shut. And for most of them, the doors will stay shut." He took my arm. "Let's take a closer look, shall we?"

We walked across the grass past the sign and through the front door into a spacious lobby. On the far wall was a plaque with the hospital's mission statement, promising care for the disabled, regardless of cost.

"Fine words," he said, "But look at this place. Nothing to write home about. The public doesn't like to spend money on the people who need it."

We continued on to the elevator and rode it to the second floor. A nurse's station stood between the elevator bank and the hall beyond.

"Who are we here to see?" I asked.

"George Glynn," he said. "Tommy's brother."

Afterwards we returned to the bench.

"What happened to him?" I asked.

"George was a fireman. Saved lives while risking his own, never violated the law. But the law deals in guilt by association. When Tommy escaped, Immigration thought he might know Tommy's whereabouts. One evening, some cops and agents stopped by his house in Astoria. His wife and two kids were visiting her sister in Great Neck."

"Did he tell them anything?"

"He didn't know where Tommy was."

"But—"

"They didn't believe him."

"You do not mean . . . ?"

"All anybody knows for sure is that George's wife discovered him on the living room floor with his head bashed in. Later, the agents said that when they left he was fine. Of course, the cops stayed around and—"

"Mother of God!"

"She got in touch with Molly and told her what happened. Sam sued the Feds. Uphill battle. No, let me correct that. A war he couldn't win. George was the only witness and . . . well, you saw George."

"He lost the suit?"

"Settled it. Fifty grand for the wife, free care here. No big deal, considering the place is free."

A sea gull—could it have been the same one that kept me company when I arrived?—whizzed by my head and landed on his lap.

"Let's play a game," he said, scratching the bird's neck.

"What kind of game?"

"A mind game. We'll each play a character. I'll be justice and you'll be law."

"Should it not be the other way around? You know the law."

"I get it. You're an expert on justice."

"That is not what I meant," I said, insulted.

"I'll start. Even though I asked Jimmy to unlawfully enter your apartment—that's burglary—to take the tapes—that's theft—justice entitled me to reclaim my words."

"You consented to the taping. Therefore, you relinquished your right to possession. What is the phrase? Possession is nine-tenths of the law."

"Actually, the correct statement of the principle, though it isn't much of a principle, is 'Possession is eleven points in the law.'"

"Who said that?"

"An obscure Elizabethan playwright."

"Shakespeare?"

"I said obscure."

"In any case, I am correct, am I not? Your words belong to me."

"Not so fast, lawyer Sullivan. Justice does not give up easily."

"Continue."

"Let's assume you still have the tapes. On them is evidence, no not evidence, a hint, the suggestion that I will soon commit a crime. What is your obligation?"

"To give the tapes to the authorities."

"What law requires you to disclose evidence of a mere intent to commit a crime, a mental state, as it were?"

"You have gone beyond intent."

He raised his eyebrows. "Oh, really."

"The map Varick and Gold showed me."

"You have no evidence I drew the map."

"You are part of a conspiracy."

Laughing, he said, "Did I teach you the law of conspiracy?"

395

"I do not remember. Am I wrong?"

"You are right."

"Then, by not surrendering the tapes to the authorities, I become a conspirator?"

"Yes."

"Even though I am unaware of the conspiracy's purpose."

"Isn't the law marvelous," he said, reveling in the irony. "It loves to cast as big a net as possible. If fishermen used nets that large, there would be no fish left in the ocean. That is why I am happy to be justice."

"I am innocent."

"Not under the law. And you have furthered the aims of the conspiracy in other ways."

"How?"

"Your passport for one."

"You took the passport without my permission."

"You didn't report your missing passport. Again, the evidence suggests you are conspiring with me and unnamed others."

"I am sick of your game."

"You want to see Tommy Glynn freed as much as I do."

"No!" I shouted and was surprised in my anger that the bird did not stir from his lap. "You go too far. He escaped from prison once. Escape is a crime. Now, with your help, he intends to escape again."

"True enough. The law does not sanction self-help. But justice does."

"Wait," I said, now thoroughly involved in the game. "You tip the scales too much in your favor. Even though Tommy was innocent, his conviction was rendered according to law."

"Wrongly convicted under an unjust law."

"The law against terrorism is not unjust. You are pushing your notions of justice at the cost of innocent lives."

"How can there be innocence in an unjust world?"

"You assume too much. It is not the world that is unjust, but individuals."

"Ah, yes, Mr. Sullivan, you make a valid point. And it is individuals forming governments who make law."

"Then no law can be just in and of itself."

"You see my point, then."

"You have a morbid view of the world."

"There are only two possible ways to view the world. We can see it as absurd or we can see it as part of us."

"I do not understand."

"If we see the world as part of us, we want to integrate it as part of us. We want to accommodate ourselves to the world, as Heidegger suggested. He was true to his philosophy. He accommodated himself to Hitler and became a Nazi. Or we can take the existential approach and fight for our individuality, resist the absurdity of the world."

"Believing that we belong to the world does not mean we must accept injustice."

"Wait a second, Connie. You are the law. If you belong to the world, you must accept the law. You no longer need be concerned with justice."

"As part of the world I have the right to seek the repeal of laws that are unjust."

"What if you fail? What if you are unable to change the law?"

"Then I must accept it. Otherwise, there would be anarchy."

"Utopia, you mean."

"You are a dreamer."

"Nothing happens unless it's first a dream."

I got off the bench and walked a few steps away. Though my shouting had not disturbed the sea gull, it now left his lap and flew to the railing a few feet in front of me. It flapped its wings, mocking me.

"What if I were to go to the authorities now? What if I were to tell them everything I know?"

"You would be playing your part perfectly. You would be upholding the law."

"Perhaps that should be my course."

"Your father told the British everything he knew to protect his family. Who would you be protecting?"

"Myself."

"You would be protecting the law."

He put two fingers in his mouth and whistled. The sea gull flew off the railing and glided back to his lap. "Do you want to continue?" he said, smiling at the sea gull.

"No."

"Why not?"

"I am weary."

My friend lifted the sea gull in the air and gently tossed it upwards. It spread its wings and floated for an instant before flying out over the river. "Already tired, Connie?" he said, watching the sea gull's graceful flight. "How do you think I feel?"

"I would not know," I said bitterly.

"I'll tell you. I feel like Eugene O'Neill's father must have felt after playing the same meaningless role in the same romantic comedy for decades. Except I hope I haven't ended up like him."

"What do you mean?"

"If we're to believe 'Long Day's Journey Into Night,' he spent his last days rationalizing everything he had done, every misstep, every neglectful act, every materialistic choice, every compromise. I am prepared to plead guilty to many things, but I insist on asserting my innocence to the charge of rationalization. I refuse to become absurd like the world."

I could not plead innocent to such a charge.

When I got back to Manhattan, Jimmy was gone. As I walked south along Second Avenue on the way to the apartment I thought about what my friend had said. He had manipulated the facts to reduce my choices to two: I could either report everything I knew to the authorities or do nothing and let him and his colleagues carry out their plan to free Tommy. But there was a third choice, one he had conveniently failed to mention in his game of law and justice. I could report my lost passport and obtain a new one. And then I could fly home, grieve for my father, and resume my life.

I turned right on 54th Street, intending to walk to the Northern Ireland tourist office. When I reached Lexington Avenue my walking became labored. And then the strangest, most terrifying thing occurred. I came to a stop in the middle of the street. Paralyzed, I could not move forward or backward, though my sudden halt had caused two pedestrians to crash into my back. I focused on the street light on the far side and saw it change from green to red. But I still could not move. Angry drivers were honking horns and cursing in the foulest language imaginable. A taxi driver threw open his door and threatened to run me over. Then all became quiet. I saw hands pressed on horns, lips of drivers moving, but I heard nothing. Suddenly, I was moving forward, my feet dragging on the pavement, a hand insistently pressing against the small of my back.

Safely on the sidewalk, I turned to see my benefactor. He was a tall, well-groomed older man, perhaps nearing sixty, with a rolled up newspaper under his arm. He wore stylish wire-rimmed glasses. "You could have gotten killed," he said.

My limbs tingled. "I was not able to move."

"Catalepsy."

"Excuse me?"

"You had a catatonic fit. Ever had one before?"

"Why, no . . . I mean . . . my body stopped working."

"Stress related, I would think." He reached in the back pocket of his slacks and took out his wallet. With long delicate fingers that stretched from his palm like the arms of an octopus, he extracted a card. "This is my office number at Mt. Sinai Hospital. Give me a call. We'll set up an appointment."

"Thank you." I took the card and put it in my pocket without looking at it.

Thus, life's decisions are made. I looked west in the direction of my intended destination and east in the direction of my apartment. I took a deep breath. When the light turned green, I made it across Lexington and continued on the way to the apartment. Inside, as I undressed, the card fell out of my pocket and I saw the name of the person who had helped me.

You definitely should tape our conversation. When we're done for the night, you'll give it to me. At the appropriate time you'll get it back with the rest of the tapes. Why let my wonderful oral history get carried away on the wind? I'd hate to see you rely on your memory when you write my story. Sure you will. You won't be able to resist. You're an historian.

It serves you right. Thinking you were going to leave on the eve of the main event. I tell Jimmy it's safe to leave you alone for the afternoon and look what you do. Yes, *that* Stephen Bamberger, one of the psychiatrists in the Leonard Stone case. He moved to New York a few years after the trial. Be paranoid if you want. Assume I asked him to follow you. It seems you need following, don't you think? I hadn't seen him for years, you know, until he called me for representation. He was teaching at Einstein Medical School. Of all my cases, his got the most publicity. Maybe I'll tell you about it later.

I think we're both falling apart. I black out and can't remember where I am, and you're like a car with a broken transmission. What a pair we are!

Last night? Oh, right. Nothing special. Gene Lufman panicked a little. Gold and Varick went to see him. Then he came here to New York. It appears Gene is not quite the harmless son of a harmless father. He makes a double agent's life look simple. Until last night I didn't realize he spied on everyone, betrayed everyone, lived in a universe of so may dimensions that saying he plays both ends against the middle is too linear a way to describe what he is up to. He's the lawyer/gangster version of parallel universes. In no particular order, he reported to Gavencci, Delaney, and Vincente on what businesses Salvatore controlled and how much he made, blackmailed Smitty into forking over a portion of his take for protection, and was an FBI informant.

All right, I'll tell you. Lufman knows the plan. Smitty told him. Last night. Before he called. I don't know why Smitty . . . I do know why. Gene's a smart guy. He was putting the pieces together and he...Smitty made a judgment call. While we were at the Four Seasons Varick called Smitty and told him to hop on the shuttle to Boston. They wanted him present when they questioned Gene. Smitty got nervous and called Gene, told him more than he should have . . . he knows and I have to deal with it. What? I told you we met for a drink. It was nothing special . . . except . . . wait a second . . . wait just a goddamn second! He asked me when I had last seen Salvatore . . . be quiet . . . let me think. Christ! Stay put. I'll be right back.

He rushed out of the tavern. Through the front window, I could see him speaking to Jimmy who was preternaturally calm, given my friend's jittery hand movements. I had never seen him so agitated. Whenever Jimmy spoke, my friend interrupted him with a wave of the hand. Then Corcoran came into view. My friend said something to him and he nodded, smiling and patting his suit jacket where he kept his gun.

Sorry. I'm losing it. No, we're OK. Yes, I mean we. And no, I'm not going to go into it right now. If you want to know the truth, it's too damn complicated. I'm not sure I even have it straight.

At this rate we'll never get back to my life story. Time is running out, Connie. When I came in here the night we met, I said to myself I'll never think of enough things to say to you. Look what's happened.

Money, Connie. I want to tell you how I made my first million, then my second million, and then millions more. I want to tell you how I discovered I could use the law of money to make some for myself. I even thought that the law of money could be used to obtain justice for those who lost it, as if justice can be measured in currency. I told myself I would find justice in the redistribution of wealth business.

You're not familiar with the laws of money. There are thousands of them, though they're not called laws of money. They go by other names: contract law, securities law, common law, partnership law, fiduciary law, negligence law, tax law, and all those other laws I've talked about. But it was the day after my wife and I returned from our honeymoon that I got introduced—I mean, really introduced—to the laws of money. The introduction came from an unlikely source: Stu Gittner, a Midas muffler franchisee who thought he had a case despite having been turned away by twenty-two law firms.

Money was on my mind at the time. My secretary was threatening to quit for a higher paying job and I was struggling to scrape up enough for alimony and child support. I lived in a factory that was converted to loft apartments. Everything in my apartment was brick except for the metal spiral staircase that looked like part of a Jungle Jim. The walls were brick; the ceiling was brick; the bookshelves sat on bricks I swiped from a brickyard. Even the floor was brick. But the rent was the right price and the apartment came with a free outdoor parking space, though I had to shovel the spot myself when it snowed, and it snowed a lot during that winter of 1985.

Did I tell you that Sam's wife, Molly, introduced me to my wife Beth? They were neighbors in Boston. It was love at first sight. Don't look at me like that. She was different from the others. Her brains and beauty captivated me; she had a special way of looking at me, challenging me to be sincere, knowing the game I played by hiding inside myself. It's a *gotcha* way of looking at someone, enthrallingly enchanting and disarming.

The day my life as a lawyer moved in a different direction started out normally enough: wrote a brief in the morning, lunched with a sole practitioner with a few small cases to refer, attended a settlement conference in the afternoon. When I returned to the office my secretary Charlene greeted me in her trademark manner: blowing an enormous bubble of gum until it popped and covered her nose and mouth in pink goo. I had hired her six months before Gordon and I split up. She was one of twelve children, the daughter of an evangelical preacher who spoke in tongues every night and molested her once a week beginning when she was seven and ending when her parents went to prison for bank robbery. She was married and divorced before she was eighteen, gave up her baby daughter for adoption, and gained seventy-five pounds during the two years she worked for me, still persisting, however, in wearing her old size eight dresses, let out so much the seams were splitting. Nearly every week she asked for a raise. She showed me a book on profit sharing plans and suggested I establish one. What's the point, I said. You need profits to start a profit sharing plan.

Beth was sitting in a vacant office, dutifully recording the entries from my time sheets and talking on the phone. "Oh, here he is," she said. "Just a second."

"Who is it?" I asked in a whisper.

"Stu Gittner. He stopped in while you were in court."

"Never heard of him. Did he have an appointment?"

"No. He picked your name out of the legal directory."

"There are thousands of lawyers in the legal directory."

"Then it's your lucky day."

"Maybe it will be my lucky day," Gene Lufman said from behind me.

"What are you doing here?" my friend asked.

Lufman looked around the bar. "Doesn't look like a private club to me."

"What do you want?"

Lufman looked at me. "Been to any funerals lately?"

His comment drove me into a fury. I got off the stool and shoved him. He took a step backward. "Hey, what's the big idea?"

"His father just died," my friend said.

"How was I supposed to know—"

"He didn't know, Connie."

I could not believe what I had done. I had never laid a hand on any-one. "I apologize," I said and returned to the stool.

"We're a little on edge," my friend said.

Lufman straightened his herringbone jacket and stepped between us. "Makes sense, with your big day tomorrow."

"Not so loud," my friend said.

Lufman looked at me again.

"Say what you came to say," my friend said. "He's fine."

"About our conversation last night," Lufman said.

"What about it?"

"It will take more than I said."

"How much more?"

"A hundred grand."

"Total?"

"A hundred grand more."

"I don't have that kind of money."

"Sure you do. You made more money in one year than I've made in ten."

"As a lawyer maybe."

Lufman grinned. "Breaking the law is not as profitable as most people think."

Jimmy entered and stood by the front door.

"I'm waiting," Lufman said.

"I'm thinking," my friend said.

Lufman turned to me. "Did you enjoy dinner at Marinelli's?"

"You know Mr. Marinelli?"

"I knew him," he said grimly.

My friend touched Lufman's back and he spun around. "Yeah, that's right," Lufman said in a harsh whisper. "I got it figured out. Salvatore is too old to disappear, and Danny is too much a family man not to call his wife."

"I'll send you the money on Monday."

"Not good enough. I want it tomorrow."

"That's impossible."

Lufman took a piece of paper from the inside pocket of his jacket. "Wire instructions. You can do a transfer until three o'clock. You've got plenty of time."

Lufman stepped away from the bar. "Sorry about your father," he said and left, brushing Jimmy as he exited the door, on purpose, it seemed.

"His old man was a much nicer guy," my friend said.

See, Connie, everything is about money. Perfect for what I was telling you.

Stu came to the office the next morning and told me his story. I never stop being surprised by the naivete of people. Here was a man of reasonable intelligence (college degree and MBA), the owner of a business for fifteen years, presumably knew the value of hard work, yet clung to the idea that there was a deal out there that would make him rich.

His story sounded strikingly similar to Mort Harris's experience with Athena Art. In each of four years from 1980 until 1983, Stu had invested $50,000 in books, but they weren't limited editions like the lithographs. They were ordinary hardcover books: thrillers, romances, spy novels, cookbooks, self-help books, children's books, science books, pseudo-science books. As in the Athena Art investment, the money was used to buy the plates from which the books were printed, thus supposedly allowing the investment tax credit and a quick profit. The deal also made it easy for an investor to invest more than he could afford. On a $50,000 unit, the investor could put up one-half and sign a note for the balance, due three years later. According to the projections, there would be ample funds from book sales to pay the balance on the note and return a profit.

You're right, Connie, the revenues never materialized. Stu hadn't paid the notes for the first three partnerships and said he would not pay the last note when it came due. He showed me demand letters from the Grosse

Deutsche Bank, a Munich bank with a branch in New York, to whom the notes were pledged as collateral for loans to the partnerships.

The promoter was Nate Goldblatt, a former high school English teacher with a yen for making money. In 1975, when he was twenty-eight, he earned an extra $100,000 for designing a business plan that resuscitated his father-in-law's failing heating and air-conditioning company. He quit his teaching job and went into the coal mining business, making enough money within two years to buy his wife a new house with a view of the Long Island Sound and a coop on Park Avenue to keep his mistress comfortable. Then Congress took away tax incentives for coal mining, and he started looking for new business opportunities.

Though Nate had given up teaching, he hadn't lost his love for books. On a visit to his favorite bookstore, he engaged the owner in a discussion about the mechanics of bookbinding. The owner explained how a fifteen-dollar hardcover book began life as a set of one-dollar plates. But Nate wasn't interested in making books and he wasn't interested in selling them. He had heard about Korn's investment tax idea for lithographs and thought it would work for books.

He started small in 1979, striking a deal with Exotica Books, a fly-by-night publisher of romance novels and soft-core porn. Adopting Korn's modus operandi, he agreed to purchase the plates from Exotica for $50,000 per book, which he would pay with a cash deposit of $2500 and a non-recourse note for $47,500. He would assign the contract to the investor with no increase in the total price, but a down payment of $5,000, equal to the investment tax credit. As Korn had needed an art gallery to sell the lithographs, Nate needed a book distributor. He contacted Richard Mavens, a Yale Law School graduate and former assistant general counsel for Random House, who had recently formed Mavens Distribution, a book wholesaler. Mavens had an ongoing arrangement with Exotica to sell its leftover books at a discount to newsstands. Mavens then agreed to sign distribution agreements with Nate's investors in exchange for twenty-five percent of the down payment and two percent of the net proceeds from the sale of books.

Besides the dubious legality of using the investment tax credit for the plates, Nate's scheme funded the printing of books that would not otherwise have been published. In the year before Nate and Exotica came to terms, Exotica published twenty-three books. The next year it published seventy-seven books, the additional forty-four published because of the cash infusion from Nate and the investors. The first printings were small, averaging a hundred copies per title. An investor could not recoup his investment unless sales justified additional printings— unlikely, given the competition in mass-market books.

Nate's first investors were friends and acquaintances, but he soon broadened his investor base by talking to accountants. They told him that if he acquired more books, they could solicit their clients to invest. So he spent the latter part of 1979 seeking small or undercapitalized publishing houses to either sell him the books they planned to publish or publish additional books with the cash he was offering. Mavens acted as a middleman, obtaining authorization from the publishers to negotiate with Nate on their behalf. By the beginning of 1980 Nate had secured commitments from twenty-three publishers to publish 1600 hundred books. To accommodate this ballooning inventory he formed partnerships; each had thirty-five investors who owned interests in forty sets of plates. Stu bought his first unit in one of those partnerships, named Ulysses Associates. (The partnerships were named after classic books, none of which were included in the partnerships; Lady Chatterley's Lover Associates, Catch 22 Associates, and Gone with the Wind Associates were among the more memorable partnership names.)

Nate's business continued to grow. Over four years he organized five hundred partnerships with 20,000 books; 10,000 people invested more than a billion dollars. Nate made $200 million and Mavens made $40 million. Nate leased offices in Lake Success and rented a penthouse apartment at the Regency Hotel. He divorced his wife and married his mistress, bought homes in East Hampton and Palm Beach, rode around New York in a Mercedes limo, got a nose job, hair transplant, and tummy tuck, and deposited his profits in secret bank accounts on the Grand Cayman Islands. He fathered three kids to go with the three from his first marriage and established a generously funded trust for each. He was on top of the world until late 1983 when Congress eliminated the investment tax credit.

The reports Stu received made clear that at least twenty percent of the books would have to be runaway bestsellers for him to make a profit. To make matters worse, the IRS notified him that it was investigating the legitimacy of his tax deductions in the partnerships, *ala* what happened to Mort in the Athena Art deals. A disallowance of his tax credits would bankrupt him. His claim wasn't large enough, however, to warrant suing Nate and the law firm that wrote the prospectuses— Finley Kumble, then the largest law firm in the United States with over 1,000 lawyers in a dozen offices around the country. Thinking I might be able to put together a group as I had in the case against Korn, I asked him if he knew other investors. Though he said he didn't, his files contained the certificates for Ulysses Associates and the other partnerships. They listed the names and addresses of his fellow limited partners.

That was all I needed to hear. I sent a letter to the investors explaining what claims we could file. The letter said the limited partner could hire me, do nothing, or write or call with questions. As in the Athena Art case, I asked for a retainer— two percent of the amount invested—nonrefundable but to be credited against a one-third contingent fee. I called the Secretary of State for New York and requested the limited partnership certificates for all the other partnerships. When I received them I was disappointed to find that they did not include addresses. (Stu then told me he had gotten the lists by calling Nate's office, something he could no longer do because word was out about my letter.)

The letter produced a surprisingly positive response, surprising because I was skeptical that anyone would send money to a stranger. Fifteen partners returned the fee agreements with checks totaling $30,000. They were not only miffed by the lack of sales, but they too hadn't paid the notes they signed and were receiving threatening letters from the bank. I told them not to pay until I researched the issue.

I filed the complaint ten days later in New York federal court. The defendants were Nate Goldblatt, Richard Mavens, and Finley Kumble. As is the practice in New York, a magistrate, Tina Petrovich, would supervise pretrial matters.

Though I was entitled to apply to the New York federal court for permission to appear on behalf of the investors, the rules required me to retain what's called local counsel, a lawyer licensed to practice law in New York. I picked Larry Sands, a sole practitioner with an extra office I could use when in New York.

I had met Larry at a breakfast hosted by a mutual acquaintance. I looked him up in Martindale Hubbell, a directory that lists every lawyer in the United States. His credentials seemed impeccable: Phi Beta Kappa at Brown, Order of the Coif at Columbia Law School, several years working at a prestigious New York firm before starting his own practice. He was Jewish, but wouldn't admit it. He was afraid he'd be thrown out of the WASP country club where he belonged. I found out he was Jewish when he invited me for cocktails to his apartment on Park Avenue and I saw a *Jahrzeit* candle on the Steinway grand piano. He said it was the tenth anniversary of his father's death. His father was a professional boxer and psychiatrist, murdered by a patient who lost a big bet when he took a dive at the Garden.

Larry said he was an expert litigator and would act as my local counsel for one-third of the contingent fee. A steep price to pay, but I wanted to avoid traveling to New York for every status conference and routine depositions.

The defendants demanded production of my clients' documents, not just the documents concerning their investments in the book partnerships, but also documents relating to every investment they had ever made. I moved to strike the interrogatories and document request. No matter how sophisticated an investor might be, I argued, he was entitled to receive accurate and complete information in the prospectus. Other investments were therefore irrelevant; so were the interrogatories, since the prospectus said the investors should only rely on written information provided by Nate. Magistrate Petrovich set the motion for a hearing. Larry wanted me to appear at the hearing. He said he shouldn't have to deal with matters of substance.

Larry met me at the airport, and we rode together to court. On the way, he showed me a Wall Street Journal article about the case. He said twenty-seven investors had already called, asking to join the litigation.

Magistrates are second-class citizens in the judicial world. Petrovich's courtroom was stuck at the end of the corridor, a long narrow room with two tables for the lawyers, one in front of the other. By tradition, the plaintiff's lawyer sits at the front table. When the defense attorney speaks, you're forced to withstand the hail of words pummeling you from behind.

Four lawyers were there for the defendants. I introduced myself to Nate's defense team, Arnold Conklin and Maria Lopez. Arnold, bald, dressed in gray suit, white shirt, and bow tie, refused to shake my hand and said, "Your case is frivolous." Maria, not yet thirty, with smooth dark skin and big black eyes, seemed embarrassed at Conklin's comment and gave me a firm handshake. "I've heard so much about you," she said. I didn't believe her.

Larry was chatting with Mavens' lawyer, Robbie Rothstein, also wearing a gray suit, white shirt, and bow tie, which made me think that this was the New York fashion for lawyers. A few feet away flipping through a yellow pad was a nondescript fellow of average height and build: Bertram Flomenhoft, the lawyer hired by Home Insurance to represent Finley Kumble.

The clerk and court reporter entered the courtroom and took their seats. A few seconds later the door behind the bench opened and Petrovich appeared, or, I should say, flew into the room in a blur. I never saw anyone move from one spot to another so quickly. Her robes fluttered behind her, looking like the wings of an angel—or maybe the devil, since they were black. She waved her arms like a mad conductor, simultaneously whipping her head from side to side. "Sit down," she said, saying the words as one—"siddown."

Though Larry knew he wouldn't have to say a word, he looked tormented, as if he were in the dock on trial. Droplets of sweat were beading on his forehead like raindrops on a waterproofed coat. His lips were purple and quivering.

"Everyone, please introduce yourselves," Petrovich said, like she had gathered us there for a coming out party.

You would have thought she had asked Larry to jump out the window. The beads of sweat coagulated into what looked like small balls of ice, and the purple color of death spread from his lips to his cheeks. He was having trouble breathing. I could hear the tiny bursts of breath of someone struggling for oxygen.

To save Larry's sanity, if not his life, I stood. "Did you prepare this motion?" she asked, shaking it like a political manifesto.

"Yes."

"Were you trying to insult the court?"

"No, your Honor."

"Well, it is an insult."

"The document request and interrogatories are—"

"I know what they are, counsel," she said. Her arms were gyrating at incredible speed, like an airplane propeller does right before taxiing and you can no longer see the blades. I heard defense counsel giggling behind me.

"It's called discovery," she said. Her arms were now raised, palms up, as if she were summoning the gods. "Discovery is what defendants like to do when they're accused of fraud."

"Yes, your Honor," I said.

"And another thing, counsel. You are not going to win this case in the Wall Street Journal."

"If it please the Court, I had nothing—"

"Don't compound your crime by pretending to please me."

"I haven't committed a crime, your Honor."

"This isn't a joking matter."

I stepped to one side so she could see defense counsel. "They're laughing, your Honor, not me."

My little move had exposed their show of disrespect. Maria wasn't laughing, however; her black eyes were propped wide open in amazement at the spectacle. Petrovich fumbled for her gavel, which she knocked on the floor as her arms continued to draw circles in the air. The clerk retrieved the gavel and gave it to Petrovich, scurrying away as she hammered the desk like she was beating a side of beef. "We will proceed with this case in an orderly manner," she said. "Plaintiffs' motion to strike the interrogatories and document request is denied."

"What about Rule 1?" I said.

"What are you talking about, Counsel?"

"Rule 1 of the Federal Rules of Civil Procedure."

Petrovich looked at the clerk and banged the gavel. "The Court will take a brief recess. Stay right where you are."

Larry took his handkerchief from his breast pocket and wiped his brow. "I hope you know what you're doing," he said.

"Does it make a difference?"

"What's Rule 1?"

In my sixteen years of practice, I couldn't recall any lawyer citing Rule 1. And I hadn't mentioned the rule in my motion, remembering it only as Petrovich was ruling against me. Funny, how in defeat you can have the most startling epiphany.

Petrovich was back on the bench, her arms at rest. "You're a very clever lawyer," she said.

"Thank you, your Honor."

"It wasn't a compliment."

"Should I apologize?"

"Only if you're into that sort of thing. Are you, counsel? Do you enjoy asking for forgiveness?"

I looked around the courtroom as if I expected someone to give me the answer to the question. Everyone stared at me as if I were a customer at a dungeon for masochists.

Petrovich didn't wait for my answer and said, "Having failed to cite the rule in your motion," she said, "you are deemed to have waived its applicability."

I didn't want to give up. "The Court should apply the rule on its own motion. Its provisions are central to our system of justice."

"System of law, you mean."

"Whatever."

She leaned back and folded her arms. She started to rock like a grandma sitting on a glider. Then she stood and put her hands on the bench, leaning forward like a football coach getting ready to exhort the team, but encouragement was not what she had in mind. "I don't like your style, counsel. No, style is not the right word. I don't like your manner. This Court, however, is above personal feelings. The law knows no prejudice and your point is well taken. The document request is stricken as contrary to the spirit of Rule 1. Court is adjourned. I need a cup of coffee."

It was a warm spring day and I decided to relax on the steps of the courthouse. Larry had stopped in the bathroom to wash his face and put the brakes on his racing heart. The defense contingent walked by and I wished them a good day. They didn't reciprocate. Two limos were parked along the curb. Flomenhoft and Rothstein got in one, and Arnold opened the door of the other.

Maria suddenly turned and shimmied up the steps. "What's Rule One?" she asked.

"You don't know?"

She shook her head like a little girl chastised by her teacher. At the limo, Conklin had hands on hips, scowling like a jilted lover.

"Rule 1," I said, "says that the rules should be 'construed and administered to secure the just, speedy, and inexpensive determination of every action.'"

"Neat," she said. "I didn't want to ask Arnold."

"What makes you think he knows?"

She looked at the now fuming Conklin. "You know something? I don't think he does."

She skipped back down the steps and jumped in the limo, still the schoolgirl but now on her way to the prom. Arnold didn't move, staring at me with that haughty air that announces, "OK, so that's how you want to play this game." I acknowledged the challenge with a smile. He got in the limo and rolled down the window so he could continue to stare.

Larry came out of the courthouse, squinting like he hadn't seen the sun for weeks. "Do you want to know what Rule One says?" I asked him.

He quoted the rule. "Larry," I said. "I *am* impressed."

He looked like I had accused him of a crime. "I stopped in the library and looked it up."

At the far end of the bar, Patrick was pointing a remote control at the television, pushing buttons to move through the channels. He appeared to be looking for something in particular. He passed a news station, stopped, and returned to it. A newswoman was interviewing a New York policeman. My friend moved closer to the television for a better view and Patrick turned up the volume.

The officer was explaining that the captain of a tugboat had found the bodies of Danny and Salvatore Marinelli in the East River near the

Manhattan Bridge. Both had been shot, but the ballistic report said the bullets had come from two different guns. "Although no suspects have been identified," the newswoman said, "informed sources have told us that the killings may be connected to last week's gangland slaying on the steps of Boston's federal courthouse."

"Brilliant deduction," my friend said to Patrick and returned to my side.

"Are you worried?" I asked.

"Their sources are uninformed. By the time they figure out what's going on, it will be over."

"What about me?"

"What about you? On Monday, you'll pay a visit to the Irish office, get a new passport, and be on your way home."

"Leaving nothing but a memory," I said sourly.

"Memory is all the past leaves us, Connie," he said.

The law gets you coming or going. If you're an idealist, it sets you up for disappointment. If you're a cynic, it gives you success and then beats you over the head with it. And if, God forbid, you're an idealist and a cynic—a freak of nature, to be sure, but I don't know how else to describe myself—the law slaps you around like you're a double-jointed ragamuffin.

My idealistic side believed that the investors had gotten a bad deal from Nate and deserved to be vindicated, even if vindication was nothing more than taking money from his pocket and putting it into the pockets of my clients. The cynical side said it was time I did something for myself, and the only thing to do was to make as much money as possible.

I returned the telephone calls from investors. Each one led to another dozen investors, either directly or through their accountants. Within a month I had garnered another hundred clients, and the deluge continued unabated. I became a traveling medicine man, though my briefcase carried fee agreements instead of elixirs. During the next six months I visited every major city and a dozen hamlets that to me had previously been nothing more than dots on maps: Wichita Falls, Helena, Bowling Green, Greenville, Grand Junction, and my favorite, Big Stone Gap, Virginia.

To get to Big Stone Gap, you change planes in Atlanta and board a "puddle jumper" to the Tri-State Airport, located in a Tennessee valley near the borders of Kentucky and Virginia. I rented the last car on the lot, a Lincoln Continental the size of a pickup truck, with synthetic leather bucket seats. The driver's side seat had been pressed into the shape of a toilet bowel, as if the car had been the exclusive property of overweight renters. The rental agent gave me an old telephone book to sit on so I could see over the steering wheel.

My contact in Big Stone Gap was Jeremiah Cohan, a lawyer who had put $200,000 of his own money into the partnerships after a meeting for his clients and friends at the country club to hear about the deal. Nate had done his usual sterling sales job. The two-dozen clients invested more than four million in the partnerships. They included six members of the Monaghan family, from the family patriarch, ninety-five year old Ryan Monaghan, to his great-grandson Jimmy, a multi-millionaire the day he was born. Ryan's father had emigrated from Ireland during Reconstruction, worked in the coal mines for three generations, and then convinced a German Jewish banker in New York to finance him in his own mining venture. Thereafter, the family invested wisely, taking the investment banker's advice to buy into Federated Department Stores. They sold the stock in 1980 and were harvesting a crop of cash when Cohan introduced them to Nate. They trusted Nate because he was Jewish. They thought he knew how to make money.

Cohan told me he was Irish, name spelled like the songwriter, he emphasized, as if he was worried I would think he was Jewish. He said he was descended from Thomas Meagher, the Civil War hero and leader of the failed movement for Irish independence at the time of the potato famine. Cohan had led a simple but profitable life, during which he earned ever-larger fees representing the coalmine owners in the area. He lived like the English aristocrats his ancestors hated: he owned a sprawling mansion on three hundred acres a few miles from town and two Rolls Royces; his wife, the great-great grand daughter of Jefferson Davis, hosted lavish parties on Saturday nights. Everyone who was anyone in the surrounding counties lusted for invitations. He was the president of the Friars Club, the American Legion, and his country club, where he told me to meet him for lunch.

The clubhouse was situated on a hill overlooking the town. Imported luxury cars crammed the long oval driveway that led to the entrance. Double oak doors opened to an airy vestibule with a skylight through which you could see the twin turrets that bounded the entrance. An older black gentleman with a weather-beaten face took my coat and said I should proceed to the reading room.

Cohan was sitting at a table with a view of the putting green. He was smoking a cigar and reading the business section of the Atlanta Constitution. In his late fifties, he was a stout ruddy-faced man with a full head of white hair rising to a pompadour. He looked relaxed and at ease with himself, a wry smile crossing his face as he turned the pages.

"This country is in service to the almighty dollar," he said, not looking up from the newspaper.

I sat across from him. "Yes, sir," I said.

"Bankers run this country."

"Yes, sir."

"And not even American bankers, but a bunch of Krauts."

"Where does it say that?"

Cohan tossed the newspaper on the knotty pine table in front of him. His bushy eyebrows made me think of a dangerous bear. "I'm the one saying it."

"Yes, sir."

"You're not German, are you?"

I laughed nervously. "I'm Jewish," I said.

He chewed on the cigar like a cow chews its cud. "You could still be German," he said.

"Austrian. My parents are from Vienna."

"They weren't bankers, were they?"

"My father manages a paint store; my mother is a seamstress."

"A lost art."

"Retail?"

"Sewing." He held his steely gaze on me for a moment and then laughed, a thunderous cackle that threatened to dislodge the dust covered paintings on the walls. A dozen heads appeared from around the sides of high-backed leather chairs that I thought were unoccupied.

A waiter, another black gentleman also with weather-beaten face, handed us menus. "We order here," Cohan said.

The menu was a single typewritten page bound in a thick leather cover. "What do you recommend?" I asked.

"The rabbit," he said without hesitation. "Killed it myself." He cackled again.

"May I order a drink?" I asked.

"I got gin and Scotch."

"I'd like a Vodka martini."

"No can do," he said.

"I'm sorry, I don't—"

He took the cigar. "We're dry in these parts," he whispered conspiratorially. "I got a stash in my locker. A bottle inside each golf shoe." He raised his eyebrows. "The law is a bitch. Always telling us we can't do what we want to do. But we lawyers know better, don't we."

"I suppose we do."

He got out of his chair. "Order rabbit. I'll be right back with your drink." His cackling followed him out of the cavernous room.

It wasn't long before I understood the significance of his comments about Germans and bankers. In the dining room, while the waiter was presenting us our rabbits from under a metal cover, Cohan told me he had no particular quarrel with Nate Goldblatt; if he was going to be bested in a deal, it might as well be by a scoundrel. He was furious, however, that he might have to write a check to the Grosse Deutsche Bank. As he kept his cigar in one hand while eating with the other, taking a puff after every bite of rabbit, he shook his head in dismay that a Jew was associated with a "Kraut" organization.

I concentrated on beating the leathery meat into submission. Then he handed me an envelope. "Got this in the morning mail."

In it was a notice of bankruptcy with a letter from Nate. He wrote that his company had guaranteed the notes signed by investors, and an unscrupulous lawyer—yours truly—had sent letters to investors telling them to withhold payment. The bank exercised its rights under the guarantee and sued the company, forcing Nate to put it into bankruptcy. He ended the letter with a reminder that it was the investors' solemn obligation to pay the notes, failing which the company would not be able to reorganize and all would be lost.

"What say you?" Cohan asked.

I wasn't sure what to say. In telling the investors not to pay their notes, I was involving them in an elaborate bluff that a judge would likely call when the bank sued. It was just as Cohan had said in the reading room. Bankers ran the country.

"It will be tough," I said. "Although the banks must have seen the prospectus and been aware of the deal's economic vacuum, I doubt that a court will be sympathetic to the investors."

"You doubt?" he said, snarling. There would be no more good-natured cackling.

"The bank will claim it's a holder in due course and therefore took the notes free of defenses the investors would otherwise have against the promoter."

"Spare me the law school claptrap."

"The law protects the bank unless I can prove they were involved in the fraud."

"Goldblatt says here you told your clients not to pay."

"I did."

"The son-of-a-bitch is right. You're an unscrupulous lawyer."

"I'm not unscrupulous. The law is. It protects the financiers, in this case the banks. If necessary, I'll negotiate a discount."

"On what basis, if we would lose in court?"

"You're a lawyer, Mr. Cohan. You know that avoiding the cost of litigation is always worth a few bucks."

"Big fucking deal. I'm supposed to give you a retainer, and you'll save me a couple of bucks on the hundred grand I owe."

"My primary goal is to recover damages from Goldblatt and the other defendants."

"Goldblatt is too smart a Jew to leave his money lying around."

"Maybe. But we're also suing Mavens and Finley Kumble. Mavens has money and the law firm has insurance. They'll fold under the pressure. The fear of a judgment is more important than the actuality."

He took the last piece of his rabbit and swallowed it whole. "You *are* an unscrupulous lawyer," he said.

I could see the outline of the meat in his throat, which expanded like a snake's gullet. "Is there any other kind," I said.

That evening, after the meeting, I checked into the Inn of the Coal Miner's Daughter. The woman behind the desk, chewing gum and hair in curlers, said she would give me the room Loretta Lynn stayed in fifteen years before. It could have been any motel room in a small town: sagging bed with a blanket that felt like burlap; two towels with frayed ends, neither of which were big enough to dry more than ten percent of my body after a shower from the nozzle permanently set to "mist"; Magic Fingers over the bed—for a quarter the bed would vibrate for forty-five seconds; a sign warning me not to leave valuables in the room. I turned on the TV and switched to the only channel without snow: a religious station out of Richmond. Jerry Falwell was fulminating about Larry Flynt and Hustler magazine.

I sat on the bed and opened my briefcase. It took me a while to record the $127,000 in retainer checks I had received from the investors at the meeting. Of the total, $70,000 was from the Monaghan family, two percent of the $1,400,000 they invested in the partnerships. This included young Jimmy. Though a vice president of the family corporation, he reported every day for work in the mines. He said he liked being around miners. He said you had to trust them with your life and they had to trust you. He said he didn't understand the world of money and was shocked that a man would make his living using and losing other people's money. When he wrote out his retainer check for $10,000 he asked me if the law would get him his money back. I said he couldn't count on it. "Why not?" he asked. I said, "The law prefers that parties settle their differences before trial." He rubbed his chin, leaving a fingerprint of coal dust from his day's work in the mine. "Well," he said, elongating the word like he needed time to get his thoughts together, "the other day a miner, my age or thereabouts, first day on the job, came up to me and said, Jimmy, I'm kinda scared. I ask him, what are you scared of, we're just going into the ground. It's dark, he says. It's damp, it's cold, and the coal dust is so thick you're amazed you don't choke on it. But, I say, there ain't nothin' to be scared of. As long as there ain't no explosion, we'll be OK. He does some ponderin' for a while, kinda scrunchin' his nose so he looks like a turnip, and says, yeah, I get you, Jimmy, but that ain't making me feel no better. I can't keep from laughing no how and he laughs right along with me, 'cause he knows facin' death is kind of funny when you think about it."

As I took the check I asked him what his story had to do with investing in the book partnerships.

"Not the book stuff, but investin' with you. Investin' money to get money you already lost is a heck of a lot more scarifyin' than crawlin' through a dark mine."

As I recorded his check in my notebook, I noticed that he had signed it with an X. Jimmy Monaghan may have been a youthful millionaire, but he couldn't read or write.

Six months later Arnold Conklin came up with a new offensive. By then, I had amassed more than 1,000 clients and $2,000,000 in retainers. The 1,000 clients referred me to a host of other cases involving scam investments. I hired several lawyers to investigate and sue. Because some of these promoters were based in New York, I rented offices on Third Avenue and at Larry's insistence hired Manny Golan. Larry and Manny met at Studio 54 when they both tried to pick up the same woman.

I called Arnold after I got his motion. He wasn't in and Maria Lopez took my call. She said she was on her way to meet a girlfriend at Ernie's Pub, a restaurant and jazz club that happened to be in the same building as my office. She invited me to stop by for a drink.

Maria was sitting with her girlfriend in a corner booth. The room was what I would call "neo-English stuffiness," all heavy oak tables set with dark print tablecloths and Victorian china. The waiters were older men, well past retirement age, shuffling like residents of a nursing home pacing the halls out of boredom. Woody Allen was sitting alone at the bar, reading a biography of Scott Joplin. Every Monday night Woody performed in a combo at Ernie's. I had seen his name on a list of investors in a bogus real estate deal involving the purchase of post office buildings. I wondered if I might talk to him about it, but Maria was waving at me like I was her boyfriend.

Lawyers always have ulterior motives for their actions, and Maria was no exception. For now, however, she introduced me to her friend Victoria, an associate from her firm's wills and estates department. Maria offered to buy me a drink, but I declined, saying I was late for a meeting.

"With more investors?" She said with a glint in her eye.

"I don't need any more investors."

"With the last complaint you filed, how many investors do you represent? A thousand?"

"Something like that."

Daintily sipping white wine like two dowagers out on the town, they inspected me as if I were on display at Ripley's Believe It Or Not museum. "You called me," Maria finally said.

"I called Arnold," I said.

She had the glass to her mouth and was widening those big black eyes in disappointment. She put the glass on the table. "You can tell me," she said.

"I got the motion today."

"Sorry, but we have to represent our client."

"I wasn't looking for an apology. Anyway, the motion is bullshit."

"Not according to the bankruptcy code." She gave me her best infectious smile. "I did the research and drafted the motion. Arnold only changed a couple of words."

"He put *his* name on the motion."

They chuckled at the same time, like two little old ladies sharing a naughty secret.

"Will you hire a lawyer?" Maria asked.

"I haven't decided." I thought about whether I should say to her what I was intending to say to Arnold. The motion was beside the point. It sought an injunction to prevent me from further advising clients or other investors not to pay the balance due on the notes, citing a provision of the bankruptcy code that empowered the judge to act in whatever way he thought necessary to promote a plan of reorganization. Arnold had filed such a plan for Nate, providing for a deferral of the bank's lawsuit until litigation against the investors could be brought and resolved. I wanted to tell him his scheme wouldn't work. Existing clients had already received my advice and other investors could obtain the same information in any number of ways. But I was also prepared to recommend that my clients pay eighty percent of the balance due in exchange for a release from the bank, with Nate paying the remaining twenty percent. I could then continue the litigation against Mavens and Finley Kumble.

I told Maria none of this and said instead: "So, really, tell me, why did you invite me for a drink?"

"I want you to hire me."

And then she let it out in a cauldron of words boiling over with disillusionment. Her shiny black hair fell across her black eyes as she said she hated Arnold, hated Nate, hated what she feared she had become.

"You hate being a lawyer?" I asked, sounding more surprised than I was.

Her passion was depressing, a scattergun that deadened everything in its path. There's nothing worse than idealism gone to rot—I should talk. She said she became a lawyer to help people, and she had learned how to use the law to help people, but they were the wrong people, the Nate Goldblatts who achieve their success by hurting others. She said that after she started at the firm she asked Arnold if she could do volunteer work for the Hispanic Legal Aid clinic in Harlem, but he said she couldn't afford to take time from the law firm to engage in "monkey business." If she was intent on helping the poor Hispanics of New York, she should teach them English. She said her work consisted of nothing more than helping clients in their endless quest to screw the "little people." She rattled off a list of her cases: defending a suit the city filed against a slum landlord who refused to abate toxic levels of lead paint in his Bronx tenements; defending a man accused of being a guard at Treblinka; a suit on behalf of a large corporation to enforce a non-competition agreement against a middle manager forced to move to California to have his wife treated for a rare disease and could only get a job with a competitor; representing a military academy in its continuing effort to exclude women students; defending box companies that were fixing prices and squeezing out the small independent manufacturer; suing for a neo-Nazi group that wanted the right to march through a neighborhood of Holocaust survivors. Taking up the mantle of the law, I said everyone is entitled to representation. She looked at me bug-eyed and her eyelashes stiffened. "Not everyone is entitled to representation by me," she said.

"If not you, who?'

"At least you try to help people who have lost money."

I thought of the $2,000,000 I had collected, the three-bedroom condo in Chicago, and the Park Avenue coop Beth wanted to show me the following morning. "You can't work for me," I said.

"Why not?"

"Conflict of interest. I'll be disqualified."

"Not if I don't work on the case. What do they call that?"

"A Chinese wall."

"Right. Build a Chinese wall around me."

"I can't take the chance. Anyway, I don't have the time or inclination to fight disqualification."

She looked into her empty glass. She was close to tears. Victoria touched her shoulder. "Transfer over to wills and estates," Victoria said. "We're harmless. We make sure wealth stays in the family and heirs don't have to pay estate taxes."

"I'll ask Mr. Goldblatt to waive the conflict," Maria said, with that determined look some of us practice before the mirror every morning.

"Why would he do that?"

"To be a nice guy."

"He's not the type, Maria."

"If he agrees, will you hire me?"

If Beth had been there she would have kicked me in the shin, and I would have said to Maria no thanks, love to help you, but can't. She wasn't there, and so I said, "You get his agreement and I'll take you on." Maria gave me a juicy kiss on the cheek. I smiled meekly and left the table.

At the bar, Woody was facing away from me, face buried in his book, holding a cup of coffee. I wrote on the back of a business card: "If you need help with your post office investment, give me a call." I put it on the bar next to his elbow. He didn't move a muscle. A month later, we filed suit against the general partner and Drexel Burnham, the Michael Milken investment banking house that was to collapse in scandal a couple of years later. We recovered $30,000,000 for the investors, but I never got a call from Woody.

Success has its dark side. People think that success robs one of humanity, but it does more harm to the unsuccessful. Like a swarm of bees, the losers

422

surround the winners with hate and jealousy. You better wear a mask or you will be stung to death.

The Wall Street Journal reporter turned against me. She wrote a follow-up piece to her original story, quoting eminent lawyers who found my "wholesale nationwide solicitation distasteful" and opining that I had nothing more in mind than "fattening my bank account with the hard-earned money of hapless investors." Magistrate Petrovich got after me, asking at a status conference how many people invested in the partnerships. When I told her I estimated the number to be more than 10,000, she said, "In another six months do you think you'll have the other 9,000 under contract so we can move forward with the case?" When I told her I hadn't solicited anyone, just returned calls from investors, she flapped her arms like that sea gull on Roosevelt Island. And she looked like she was about to swoop off the bench and poke my eyes out. "Don't play this court for one of your naive clients," she said. If I brought claims for additional investors, she would hold them in abeyance. I suggested that the law gave her no right to issue that order. "I make the law in this courtroom," she said.

You see, Connie, trouble follows success the way a shadow follows you down the street. As the day grows late, the shadow grows longer. Only when the sun sets does the shadow disappear.

"Should we have dinner?" he asked.

It was after eleven. "Are they still serving?"

He smiled as if to say I should know better than to ask such a silly question. He got off the stool and walked outside. He returned with Jimmy. "If you don't mind," he said, "Jimmy will join us."

When we sat at our table in the back, however, my friend said he had to run an errand and would return in thirty minutes. He left without ordering.

"Where did he go?" I asked Jimmy.

"Like he said, an errand."

"Did he ask you to join us for dinner so I would not be alone?"

He looked offended. "I'll leave if you want."

"I am sorry. Please stay. I am very nervous."

He laughed. "Can't say I blame you."

I ordered a bowl of boiled potatoes. Jimmy ordered a plate of spaghetti.

"They don't make pasta here like at home," he said.

"Where is home?"

"Not my home, home of my mother and father, where they were born. South of Italy, outside Naples, on a farm near the ruins of Pompeii, a farm they lost because it couldn't grow anything but weeds and brush. They came here right after the war. Papa got a job cleaning the subways. He spent the morning at the Union Square station and the afternoon at the Rockefeller Center station. Said he liked the Union Square station better. No tourists, real people, a guy in a suit was unusual. I grew up in Forest Hills, lots of different people, but Papa didn't care. He liked that America had all types."

"Where are your mother and father now?"

"Papa passed away. Long time ago. Bad heart."

"He must have been a young man."

"Forty-two."

"A shame. How did you meet Mr. Marinelli?"

Jimmy laughed. "Which one?"

"I know how you met Danny," I said.

"That still leaves Vincente and Salvatore."

"Both."

"Salvatore, I met after Papa died. Mama had a stroke right afterwards. I was going to Hunter College. She needed taking care of, we were running out of the insurance money . . . Papa worked for Salvatore, you know."

"I did not know."

"A waiter. He didn't start that way. A subway worker introduced him to Salvatore. Said he could make some extra dough. Papa was a big man, like me. He did odd jobs for Salvatore. He never talked about it, but one day he came home and said he was quitting the City to work full time for Salvatore. He figured anything was better than working underground and keeping the rats company. It wasn't long before Salvatore made him a waiter. He was able to change his life. I wish I could do that."

"If only we could," I said. "What was he doing for Salvatore before he became a waiter?"

"Rough stuff. Stuff you don't talk about. You understand?"

"I believe I do."

"Anyway, like I said, when Ma had the stroke I called Mr. Marinelli. He said he needed a driver. I said, sure, I'm your man. Once he got to know me, I did other things."

"Such as?"

"I keep my mouth shut like Papa."

"And Vincente Marinelli?"

"Met him a few times, never talked to him much, sat in on a couple of meetings . . . Salvatore said it was better I don't know too much, in case . . . "

"You would have to testify?"

"Yeah," he said. "But I know what I know. I was supposed to testify in the Boston deal."

"The strike force lawyers told me."

"Bail out Corcoran. Say he was never on the take."

"Was he?"

"Sullivan, you've been here awhile, you got an education, what do you think?"

"Why would you lie to protect him?"

"Same reason anybody lies."

"To get something in return."

"I knew you were quick on the uptake."

"What did you receive in return?"

My friend was back. I would not get the answer to my question.

"Sorry," Jimmy said to my friend. "Sullivan knows how to keep a guy talking."

"He should," my friend said. "I've been talking non-stop for eleven days."

"Twelve," I said.

"Tomorrow will be thirteen, then. My lucky number."

"Thirteen is an unlucky number," I said.

He smiled. "Now, why would you want to ruin my fantasy?"

To save you the trouble of asking, I'll tell you where I went. Then we can eat dinner in peace. Afterwards? Let's not get too far ahead of ourselves. It's a long night.

I may be a brilliant lawyer, but I'm a forgetful son of a bitch. I left my wallet at the hotel. I feel naked without my wallet. See, I'll show you. You remember. There's my Dad. I also stopped at the corner and bought some aspirin. I've got a wicked headache. Whoops, I'm sounding like Boston again.

We did enjoy our meal in peace, in silence almost, except for some talk about sports, about which I know little. I was surprised, even shocked, that after what had happened, they could speak seriously about such a trivial subject. Yet, I must say I was a willing audience to their passionate musings. I listened and laughed when they laughed, nodded my head in agreement when they criticized this or that team or athlete, and shook my head in disappointment when they bemoaned the year-in-year-out failure of the local professional basketball team.

When the meal was over Jimmy resumed his post outside. My friend and I returned to the bar.

He asked Patrick for a glass of water. He was holding the bottle of aspirin. "You took two at dinner," I said.

"I did? Are you sure?"

"Yes."

He put two in his mouth. "Two more won't kill me. But this headache will if I don't get rid of it."

Judge Vernon Blackthorn was ill suited for the bench. Any slight, however unintended, would send him into a rage. He was a lover of power and unafraid to use his position as a bully pulpit. He didn't give a damn about anyone, least of all the bankrupt souls who appeared before him, and reveled in making life miserable for whoever had the misfortune to enter his courtroom. Most of all, he hated anyone who challenged his authority.

He had been a bankruptcy judge for ten years. Before that, he was a homicide detective on the New York police force. He went to law school at night and graduated at the top of his class. The law degree was his ticket out of the police force and into the legal department for the City, where he worked on municipal bond financing.

Everyone was there for the motion. I was sitting at one table alone, having decided I would perform as capably as any lawyer I could have hired. My opponents were sitting around the other table: Arnold, Maria,

Nate, Mavens and his lawyer Robbie Rothstein, and Finley Kumble's lawyer, Bertram Flomenhoft. Except for Maria, they were hunched over, conferring as if they were arguing for the right to destroy me: "Let me take him," or "I want the son of a bitch" were just two of the entreaties I imagined them saying. Maria obviously wanted no part of it, at one point pushing her chair away from the table in disgust. I hadn't heard back from her after Ernie's and didn't know whether she had given up the idea to work for me. Beth was in the first row of the gallery ready to root for me, though I was afraid she might change her mind. I could see that she didn't care for the way Maria was looking at me.

The side door opened and the court reporter entered with Blackthorn trailing behind. The reporter was in her early twenties; she wore a short skirt and a blouse that was little more than a tank top. Though it was only a few steps to her desk, she used it to shake her bottom, much to the delight of Blackthorn, whose eyes were moving back and forth in time with her hips.

Everyone had risen and, as protocol required, was waiting for Blackthorn to sit. But Blackthorn didn't sit. He stretched his bulky frame and looked around the courtroom like a king surveying his dominion. He even smiled at me, but it was not the smile of friendship or professional courtesy. It was a malevolent smile, the smile of a killer at the point of murder, the helpless victim before him. Then he said, "I have been invited to give a speech to the New York Bar Association over the lunch hour. The press of work from my overflowing docket has prevented me from adequately preparing the speech. This court is in recess until two o'clock." He turned sideways and leaned over the bench. In a stage whisper he said to the reporter, "I'll see you in my chambers, Miss Hazeltine." She nodded and grinned. Her body was vibrating like a reggae dancer.

"Excuse me your Honor," I said.

Blackthorn looked up from Miss Hazeltine and stared at me, his face square and hard, a slab of granite. "What is it, counsel?"

"I have a flight to Chicago at three."

"You'll have to cancel it."

"I have an important meeting—"

"With more investors, I'm sure," Arnold piped up.

"Your Honor, I don't see how the purpose of my trip is any business—"

"You may have the right to argue your position in the case before me, counsel, but you don't have the right to manage my schedule."

"I understand, your Honor."

"I will see you at two o'clock. That is, unless you wish me to decide Mr. Conklin's motion without you."

Miss Hazeltine suppressed a giggle and picked up the steno machine. Her breasts nearly fell out of her blouse. As she walked to the side door Blackthorn's malevolent smile turned to mush. He followed her, a dutiful slave to the law of sex.

In the park across the street from the courthouse Beth and I relaxed under a tree, holding hands like youthful lovers.

"I don't like what's going on," she said, as I watched two men playing chess at a nearby table.

"What's going on?"

"The judge. The motion."

"He can't order me not to communicate with investors. It's absurd."

"I've been married to you long enough to know that nothing is too absurd for the law."

"We've only been married for two years."

"Long enough."

"Don't worry," I said. One of the chess players raised his hand in triumph; his opponent flicked over the king and walked away from the table.

"What will you do if I'm right?" she said. "What if he does order you to stop advising investors to stiff the bank?"

"I'll appeal."

"And in the meantime, while the appeal is pending?"

"I'll disobey the order."

"What will the judge do?"

"What's the old saying? Throw the book at me."

She put her head on my shoulder. "Law books are heavy," she said.

We lay on the grass and dozed. When I opened my eyes I saw Arnold standing over me. "May I have a word with you," he said in about as friendly a way as he could manage, which wasn't that friendly.

I gently nudged Beth awake. She murmured and rolled over on top of me. I looked through her hair at Arnold.

"I'm listening, Arnold," I said.

Beth rolled off me. "Can't you see we're busy?"

Arnold was out of his element. His sweat formed a ring around his shirt collar. "The offer you called me about," he said.

"Which you rejected." I said.

"Not rejected. I said I would not recommend it to my client."

"A distinction with very little difference."

"My client would like to discuss it in more detail."

"When?"

Arnold looked at his watch. "Now would be convenient."

He said Nate was waiting for us at a Chinese restaurant six blocks away. We took a cab out of deference to what Arnold said was his bum knee. Beth refused to sit next to him, forcing me to sit between them. I slinked toward the floor to get away from his arm, which was resting on my shoulders as if I were his date. Only one statement was made during the ride. Arnold said, "I know about your unethical attempt to steal Ms. Lopez."

At the restaurant we joined Nate in a booth next to the kitchen. The smell of egg rolls and fried rice clogged the air. Nate was slurping hot soup from an enormous bowl. "I know about your unethical attempt to steal Ms. Lopez," he said.

"Did you guys rehearse or what?"

"Attorney and client should be on the same page," Nate said.

"I didn't ride six blocks in a cab to hear a lecture on ethics."

"How much do you want?"

"Twenty percent of $100 million is twenty million."

"I don't have twenty million."

"My rough calculations say you've made more than three hundred million."

"Expenses have been running neck and neck with revenues."

A short Asian man in white shirt and pants approached. I thought he was a waiter, but he was Nate's accountant, there to explain his boss's finances. I wasn't interested.

"You invited me to lunch," I said to Nate when menus weren't forthcoming.

"Who said anything about lunch?"

"I thought—"

"You thought wrong."

He was right. Arnold hadn't mentioned lunch.

"Here's my offer," he said. "I've spoken with Grosse Deutsche Bank. They're willing to give a five-percent discount. I'll match it."

"Another five percent? What about my clients who have paid for their investment?"

"You aren't listening. What I mean by matching the five percent discount is I'll give those clients, the ones who paid in full, five percent of their investment."

"My clients will lynch me if I recommend your offer."

Nate smiled. "Come now, we know your clients have no say in this."

"Of course they do."

"You represent them on contingency. Their investment in you is negligible compared to your investment in them. If you hadn't made it financially easy for them to sue, they wouldn't have bothered."

"They—"

"I'm making a substantial offer. You'll walk away with a nice little fee of three million plus, and your clients will have made a nice return on their retainers."

"You're making the lawsuit sound like one of your investments."

He had reached the bottom of the soup bowl. He lifted it and used his mouth to drain the last bit. "What else would you call it? The investor paid a retainer. He invested in a lawsuit and expects a return. My settlement offer more than doubles his investment. Not bad, I'd say, for a few months of litigation."

I pushed back my chair. "Let's go, Beth," I said.

Nate lurched forward and took Beth's hand. "Talk some sense into your husband." She grimaced and removed her hand.

On the way out, another Asian man, this one a waiter, bowed his head, as if I were a dignitary of some sort.

"I still don't like what's going on," Beth said when we got outside.

"I should have taken the offer?"

"You could have stayed and negotiated."

"They think they have me at a disadvantage. After Blackthorn rules for me, Goldblatt will raise his offer."

"And if Blackthorn goes their way?"

"I prefer to be optimistic."

Blackthorn made his appearance an hour late, looking refreshed. Another court reporter had replaced Miss Hazeltine: a dowdy woman who neither smiled flirtatiously nor swiveled her hips. Blackthorn must have given Miss Hazeltine the rest of the day off in exchange for services rendered.

The clerk called the case and Arnold stood to make his presentation. "I don't need oral argument," Blackthorn said dismissively. "I've studied your motion and the opposition brief. I am prepared to rule."

I turned and smiled at Beth. If Blackthorn intended to rule against me, he would have allowed me to argue. It's another way for judges to show that their sadism is in good working order. Even when they've already made up their minds, they allow the victim to plead for mercy. Due process the defenders of the Constitution proclaim, but it's like the innocent man who's been framed and asks the prosecutor if he's going to get a fair trial.

Blackthorn opened a notebook and began reading. With each sentence my heart beat a little faster. He began with a review of the legislative history, saying Congress had intended the statute to reflect its desire to ensure that businesses in financial difficulty have the unfettered freedom to reconstitute their debts. "Nothing must stand in the way of the legislative purpose," Blackthorn said in a monotone, but his words were pregnant with doom. I glanced across the room and saw a thin smile forming on Arnold's lips. Nate was sitting next to him, arms folded across his chest, the picture of smugness. Then came Blackthorn's final words: "In view of the foregoing, I grant the motion. Respondent will cease and desist, by written communication or otherwise, advising, suggesting, or implying to limited partners that they should refuse making payments to the Grosse Deutsche Bank."

Blackthorn nodded at the clerk. "Call the next case."

"Your Honor," I said.

"What is it now?"

"I would like clarification of your ruling."

He looked at me with amazement. "What could possibly need clarification?"

"If a client calls me and asks my advice, what am I supposed to say? I have a duty as a lawyer—"

"Your duty is to comply with the order of this court."

"With respect, your Honor, I don't agree."

"This isn't a debating society, counselor."

"I don't mean to debate, but your order makes no sense. Investors have legitimate defenses to payment and the right to advance them with advice of counsel. And other investors would be prejudiced if I am not permitted to communicate my views."

"This court is not interested in your views. The court has made its ruling. Do you intend to comply?"

"No," I said softly. Then, "No," in as strong a voice as I could muster.

"No?" Blackthorn said disbelievingly.

"No!"

The lawyers in the courtroom were abuzz like movie extras responding to the director's cue. With his eyes inviting Arnold, Blackthorn said, "This court will entertain a motion to hold respondent's counsel in contempt."

I wasn't supposed to go to Riker's Island, but the federal lockup was full. My parting words to Beth as the marshal led me away were "call Larry and tell him to get a mandamus petition on file." Her blinking eyes disappeared behind the throng as I worried whether Larry knew what a mandamus petition was: a special kind of appeal where you seek an order commanding the lower court judge to act in a particular way, in this case, letting me out of jail. I rode the elevator reserved for judges and stood next to another bankruptcy judge. He acted like I was a contagion as he squeezed into a corner, terrorized.

I rode to Riker's in an Oldsmobile with broken air conditioning. My sweaty pants glued me to the vinyl seat. The marshal, a rough looking man with an angular jaw and a barrel chest, said nothing while we crawled through the city streets on the way to the 59th Street Bridge. I had never been to Riker's, knew it was an island but that was it. I pictured some sea swept fortress like Alcatraz, where with one misstep a sadistic guard would feed me to the sharks. What I couldn't picture was the reality, a perverted kind of public housing project, a metropolis populated by the law's victims, America's version of Devil's Island.

As we approached the bridge I took out a cigarette. The marshal saw me in the rear view mirror. "No smoking," he said.

"What if I opened the back door and jumped out?"

"The childproof lock is on and you need the code to open the door."

"I've got a few bucks on me. What's the code?"

"Do you want to add attempted bribery to your rap sheet?"

"Civil contempt doesn't go on a rap sheet."

"I can understand why Blackthorn held you in contempt."

"Is that so?"

"You're a contemptuous man."

I couldn't have wished for more: a marshal who knew how to use the English language. "You don't even know why I was held in contempt," I said.

"What's the difference? You're a lawyer. You'll figure out how to get yourself out in no time."

"Thanks for the vote of confidence."

I tried the door. Not that I was intending to escape. Believe me, I'm no Tommy Glynn, then or now. But who knows what I would have done had the door opened? My hand fell on a strip of numbered keys by the window switch and I absentmindedly pressed them like I was playing piano. The lock popped up. The marshal swung around, his gun drawn and pointed at me. He was driving with one hand, swerving from lane to lane.

"Hey, put that away," I said.

"Just what do you think you're doing?"

"I was playing with the buttons."

"This isn't a game."

"I was nervous."

"Do you want me to pull over and put the cuffs on you?"

"If it will make you put the gun away."

He lowered the gun and pulled into the right hand lane. "You are a real son-of-a-bitch. Typical lawyer."

Ahead of us a bus stopped for passengers, several of whom were carrying Barnes & Noble shopping bags. "Let me out here for a minute."

"Why?"

"I need a book to read."

"Man, you're unreal."

I felt unreal. I'd never seen a gun, let alone had one drawn on me. And I couldn't imagine myself in prison. Prison was something you read about or see in a movie. When I was a child, my parents never spanked me, never sent me to bed without supper, or denied me dessert. Sarah's idea of punishment was sending me to my room where I couldn't watch TV.

The marshal said he'd give me five minutes in the store before coming after me. "Maybe you should buy two books," he said. "In case the judge doesn't let you out for a while." A frail older woman, exiting the bookstore with a bag full of books, overheard him and took an extra step or two away from my path. I was beginning to understand how lepers feel when society abandons them.

A crowd had formed a long line at the checkout counter. I decided to buy the first book that looked interesting. The table nearest the front door had a sign on it, "Reissued Classics." I went straight to it and took the first book I saw: *Discipline and Punishment,* by Michel Foucault.

The marshal was waiting for me when I came out the door. "The line was long," I said.

He took the book from me as we walked to the car. "I read this," he said.

I must have looked surprised, for he added quickly: "Because I'm in law enforcement doesn't mean I'm stupid."

"I guess you're an exception," I said, taking the book back.

The rest of the ride was uneventful. He told me about his family: a brother and a sister, both lawyers.

"What happened to you?" I asked, my nose pressed against the window, watching the people; none showed the slightest bit of awareness that they were free and I was not.

"I was a philosophy major in college."

"That's when you read Foucault?"

"My philosophy professor at Queens College was a commie."

"Foucault may have been a Marxist, but he wasn't a communist."

"What's the difference?"

"Big difference. One is a philosopher, the other is a revolutionary. Besides, Foucault was more of an anarchist."

"What are you?"

We were on the bridge and I could see the hospital on Roosevelt Island. "I don't know."

"Also typical of lawyers. They don't believe in anything."

At the Riker's check-in station for new inmates the inventory clerk, a fat Hispanic woman who couldn't stop smiling—or wouldn't stop smiling—confiscated my wallet, watch, and seventy-five bucks and gave me a receipt, illegible like a doctor's prescription. She said I could wear my own clothes, though she should have seen that I hadn't packed for the trip. I got to make two telephone calls, which I used to reach Beth and Larry. I was right about Larry. He said he couldn't find a form for a mandamus petition. I told him to forget the form and file a motion with the chief judge of the district court, which hears appeals from orders of bankruptcy judges. He offered to post bail, but the judge hadn't set bail. When you defy a judge's order, you aren't given a get-out-of jail card.

I wasn't taken to a cell. I had been assigned to the Anna Kross Center, but it was full: nearly 2800 inmates and a waiting list, for God's sake! In fact, the only facility with vacancies was a newly constructed one for gay prisoners, and I was given the option of going there or waiting in the recreation room at Anna Kross. I chose the recreation room.

The recreation room didn't offer much in the way of recreation. There were a few wobbly wooden tables and fifty or so prisoners milling around. A couple of card games were in progress, but most of the prisoners were talking or sitting quietly staring at the windowless walls. Drowning in a sea of bemused eyes, I sat at a table in the corner and opened the Foucault book. I knew little more about Foucault than what I had told the marshal. I was aware he was embittered by society's treatment of the marginalized, nonconformists in general, among whom he counted the insane and the criminal. He was a moral relativist in the extreme; he believed that political movements were disguised grabs for power. He hated the professions. He had nothing good to say about lawyers.

Two inmates came over to my table. I said hello, but they didn't answer. One was tall and heavyset, the other short and skinny. The heavyset man was grinning. I tried to act cool and continue reading, but I kept watching them from the tops of my eyes.

"You a lawyer man?" the heavyset man said.

"Yes," I said.

"You here to see a prisoner or are you the prisoner?" He laughed heartily, as if he knew the answer to his question and thought it a joke to pretend he didn't know.

"I'm a prisoner."

The short man said, "You stole some dough from one of your clients?"

"No."

"Selling powder, maybe," the heavyset man said.

"No."

"Then you is a secret man that's keeping his thing secret."

"I won't be here long," I said. "I told a judge I wouldn't comply with his order and he held me in contempt."

The heavyset man turned and faced the room. "Hey, dudes, this lawyer man was sent here 'cause he told some judge to fuck hisself."

The room got quiet. "Show this lawyer man how you feel," he said.

There was murmuring in the room and then one prisoner started to clap. Others soon did the same. Cheers and shouts of "the lawyer man is the man" and other similar expressions of honor echoed around the room. The two men slapped me on the back. They sat at the table and took out cigarettes, already half-smoked, with the ends curled up. They offered me one and I put the book aside. Like it or not, you make fast friends or enemies in prison. I was happy to have made friends.

Beth and I caught the last flight to Chicago. On the plane she fed me one chocolate chip cookie after another, asking me if I was OK after my four-hour stay at Riker's. She wanted to know if I had been raped or beaten. On the contrary, I said, I enjoyed the company of two fine individuals. I said I wished other people were as nice.

Jimmy walked into the bar. "We should go," he said.

My friend looked at his watch. "We have another hour until closing."

"It's better we leave. Just in case."

"In a few minutes."

"I'll wait outside."

Jimmy left and my friend leaned over the bar.

"What are you doing?" I asked.

He pulled out a cardboard cylinder from a shelf underneath the counter.

"What is that?"

He unscrewed the cover and turned the tube over. Two dozen long colored sticks fell on the bar. They were equally divided between red, green, and yellow except for a single white and a single blue stick.

"Did you ever play pick-up-sticks?" he asked.

"No."

"I'll show you."

He set the white stick to the side and bunched the other sticks in the closed palm of his hand. He stood them on their ends until they were straight and then opened his palm, letting them fall to the counter. They came to rest in a pile, arranged like firewood.

He picked up the white stick. "The idea is to either use your fingers or the white stick to remove the colored sticks one at a time without moving the others. Each color is worth a certain number of points. You keep your turn for as long as you successfully remove sticks. The blue stick is the most valuable."

He carefully placed the white stick under the blue stick that was sandwiched between a green and yellow stick. It seemed impossible for him to extract it without causing the others to move. But instead of touching the blue stick, he flipped the green stick off the pile.

"There," he said. "I've exposed the blue stick for you. You try."

"It is still your turn."

"Don't worry about it."

I took the white stick in my hand. Though I considered the game an exercise in silliness, I could not stop my hand from shaking.

"No reason to be nervous, Connie. If you fail, you place the stick back in the pile and it will be my turn."

I placed the white stick under the blue stick and with a rapid motion flicked upward. The blue stick flew across the bar, nearly hitting Patrick in the face.

"Hey, watch that," Patrick said.

"This man has real potential," my friend said.

I removed several more sticks before erring. I gave the white stick to my friend, and he proceeded to remove the rest without incident.

"You are a superior player," I said.

He gathered the sticks and let them fall again. "This reminds me of the game of life. The idea is to get what we want without disturbing anyone. Not an easy task. We reach for the blue stick and, more often than not, we move the others. Once, I accidentally broke a yellow stick when trying to flip a blue one. That's no reason to quit, however. Once you start the game, you're duty bound to finish.

"It is what you said many nights ago. About the end justifying the means."

"You're learning, Connie. The end also explains the means."

"Explain what? That in your effort to achieve your goal, what happens to others is of no moment?"

"Remember the game. You're not entitled to the blue stick if you disturb another one. In fact, sometimes getting the blue stick is impossible. On occasion, the sticks fall in such a way that the blue one is so buried and connected with the others that you can never reach it. The way the sticks fall can doom you to failure."

"Then what?"

"You pick them up and drop them again. You hope they'll fall in an arrangement you can manage."

"People are not sticks."

"Society treats people as if they are sticks, all but the blue one anyway. For society, the blue stick is the law. Society protects the blue stick at all costs. Even the most ardent proponents of the law, the ones who have the nerve to call our legal system a system of justice, concede that on occasion an innocent defendant is convicted. The wrongly convicted are the green and yellow sticks. They must yield to the blue stick, like Tommy Glynn and many others had to yield, different colored sticks that get knocked about. The

nonconformist, the rebel who refuses to go along to get along, has his freedom taken from him."

"You sound like Michel Foucault."

"I'd rather sound like Foucault than Holmes."

"You are cynical and bitter."

"You're not?"

"You intend to pursue your goal no matter who is hurt. Your philosophical discourse is just a criminal's rationalization."

"Listen to you, Connie. Does a butterfly stop flapping its wings in Brazil because it might cause a tornado in Alabama?"

"The Lord programmed butterflies to flap its wings. They possess no will to do otherwise."

"You know what they say about butterflies, Connie."

"What?"

"Butterflies are free."

I took a yellow stick and stuck it under a green one. With a flick of my wrist I sent the green one flying in the air. "Beautiful," he said as I removed the blue stick. The other sticks remained in place.

"Lucky," I said.

He laughed and said, "Ready?"

"For what?"

"A new experience."

I must have shown some apprehension, for he said, "Nothing you can't handle. We'll go to this neat little drinking spot I know. It stays open until four, even five or six if you give the manager a big enough tip."

"Are we to stay up all night?"

"It's our last night together . . . ."

His words had trailed off, leaving unspoken that final irrevocable word: forever.

BOOK FOUR

SUPERHEROES

CHAPTER THIRTEEN

May 22, 1998

W E DROVE A FEW BLOCKS TO 61st and Park and stopped in front of a five-story brownstone. Narrowly spaced black bars protected the windows, two to a floor. Through laced white drapes on the third floor I could see a glittering candle and the figure of a woman playing the piano. The faintest sound of a haunting Chopin sonata drifted through the air.

A short set of stairs led down from the front gate to a paneled door. Engraved on the top panel was an art deco carving of a martini glass and a man and woman in evening dress, smoking cigars.

"A quiet place to continue our conversation," my friend said.

Couches instead of bar stools, martinis in martini glasses, and beautiful people to look at if we get tired of talking. Look at her, over by the front door, in the red dress, beautiful, elegant woman, don't you agree. Wonder who she is. Oh well, the city holds secrets close to the heart.

I won the appeal from Blackthorn's order and returned to my humdrum lawyer life. The book case settled into a marathon of discovery disputes, depositions, and endless arguments before Petrovich on how a case with more than 1,000 plaintiffs could be tried. I suggested a bellwether trial, one where a few plaintiffs serve as a kind of laboratory test for all the claims. The defendants objected. Arnold said a bellwether trial would effectively convert the case into a class action, improper because I hadn't filed the case that way. Having chosen to organize a group of individual plaintiffs, he argued I was duty bound to present their cases to the court.

Arnold wasn't objecting just to be ornery. He was terrified that the doctrine of collateral estoppel would apply. A jury's decision in the bellwether trial that the prospectuses contained false statements would also determine the issue in later trials. And the doctrine was a one way street. He would not be able to argue that a victory for Nate would be binding on the other hundreds of plaintiffs. In a class action, however, an adverse judgment against the named plaintiffs would be binding against the rest of the class. Through such arcane distinctions the law dispenses its particular brand of justice.

The case had sapped her vitality. There is nothing worse for a judge than loss of control. It's the judicial version of incontinence. Instead of ruling on motions she babbled incessantly about her inability to manage the lawsuit. Her brunette hair became spotted with wisps of gray and her judicial robes turned wrinkled. She bit her nails down below the fingertips. I pictured her sitting in chambers, pouring over Arnold's briefs and my lengthy dissertations on how the case should be tried, chewing on one nail at a time as she turned the pages, tear drops forming eddies over the paragraphs.

When at the final argument on my motion to schedule a bellwether trial I rose to give my presentation, she said, "Whatever you were going to say, please don't."

"You don't want me to respond to Mr. Conklin's arguments? They have no merit."

"Of course they don't. And neither do yours. You and your prattle about the cost of litigation, your invocations of justice and fairness, your cloying self-righteousness, your penchant for citing arcane rules just to embarrass this court, your . . . your."

"I'm trying to vindicate my clients' rights, your Honor."

"Vindicate? You're trying to bury this court!"

"A bellwether trial will solve everything."

She put her hands on her cheeks, pressing so hard her lips doubled in size. "I'm a lowly magistrate, a carbuncle on the judicial system. I can't solve anything."

She refused to decide the motion and sent it to the trial judge. He didn't decide it either. Discovery continued for five years: 200 depositions, 150 by the defendants (plaintiffs and their accountants in alphabetical order) and 50 by me (the defendants and the publishers). The clients stopped inquiring about the status of the case. Some clients forgot they were plaintiffs. At least two dozen clients called after receiving my reports on the progress—I mean lack of progress—in the case and said there must be some mistake, they had never heard of me or the case. I sent them copies of their signed retainer agreements. Six clients wrote back saying I forged their signatures.

The legal system is like a broken time machine. It goes nowhere. It sits moribund, stuck in the present. No longer able to bend time, it just takes up space.

Even the bankruptcy case stagnated in limbo. The Grosse Deutsche Bank decided it didn't want to spend money suing investors all over the country. Until the litigation was concluded and Nate's liability was determined, it refused to take a position on the plan of reorganization. Blackthorn didn't care. He spent his days haranguing lawyers in new cases and attending to Miss Hazeltine.

After these many nights of drinking martinis, Amaretto, and beer, isn't it nice to enjoy a good bottle of wine? I once handled a case dealing with wine. A company called the Wine Depot sold bottles of supposedly high quality vintage wines to gullible investors. We filed the case in California. Haven't I told you I opened an office in Los Angeles? Sorry to say I did. And I have only myself to blame. I staffed it with a group of nitwits: three lawyers culled from more than a hundred resumes and thirty interviews, presumably the best of the best until I realized that in Los Angeles the most you can hope for is the best of the worst. Dave Lapidus, the partner I dispatched from Chicago to forestall disaster, was competent enough . . . no, he was more than competent; he was bright and hardworking. But, alas, California deleteriously affects people on the make; it can even unmake someone who has it made. Dave earned $750,000 a year, bought a three-bedroom ranch with lap pool in Beverly Hills, and could fly anywhere in the world for nothing, compliments of an air-pass card I bought for him. But with my focus eastward, to New York, and dealing with . . . give me a minute, I want to organize my thoughts.

Nothing captures the essence of law practice better than incompetence. It's as if lawyers possess an algorithm for error. The mass of laws, rules, and procedures encourages mistakes. A lawyer is like a drunk driver who never sees the oncoming car until it's too late. The adage, ignorance of the law is no defense, is more of a cruel joke than a warning. Despite their training, lawyers know little more law than laypersons. This kind of ignorance in other walks of life would be calamitous: there would be hundreds of plane crashes every day; hospitals would be morgues; buildings would be deathtraps; the underground would be a junk heap of subway cars mangled from head-on collisions; salmonella would be an unwanted guest in every foodstuff.

Sometimes I think I had a special knack for attracting incompetents, as if my goal was to test the limits of ineptitude. The lawyers I hired provided enough material to compile a dictionary of tics and aberrant behavior in the practice of law. Tony Galvin was convinced his weak heart couldn't tolerate speaking louder than a whisper. At his first trial, he said he needed a microphone for his argument to the jury, then fearfully yelled into it, causing the painting of Felix Frankfurter to fall off the wall and knock three jurors unconscious. Walter Sullivan never wrote a brief less than fifty pages even when the court rule limited the length to fifteen pages. Bob Hatfield, an Oklahoma Indian and graduate from Harvard Law School, missed court appearances for clients so he could attend hearings to determine whether he should be cited for the slum apartment buildings he owned. Gerry Schine supplemented her pay by table dancing at a topless bar three afternoons a week when she was supposed to be at the library doing research. Connie Gerstein had sneezing fits in court. Phil Moran's imperious manner with witnesses invariably caused them to give testimony helpful to the opponent. Yehuda Rabinowitz thought a brief was a feat of architecture, cutting and pasting sections of other briefs, often forgetting to change the names, and more often including arguments on both sides of an issue. Seymour Schatz refused to work on more than one case at a time; he said a client had the right to demand the full-time attention of his lawyer. Ralph Baum tried to turn incompetence into an advantage by beginning every argument with a confession of his inadequacy, thinking it would gain him a sympathy victory with judge or jury. John James couldn't get through the day without masturbating while playing Pac-Man on his computer. And Larry Sands, besides having the most active sweat glands I'd ever seen, once filed a brief on behalf of his opponent's client because he got confused as to who he was representing.

Manny Golan treated bungling as an art form. It was as if he organized his life to make sure it would be filled with errors, miscalculations, and poor judgment. In his first two years at the firm he lost his wallet twenty-seven times, broke his right ankle four times tripping over the jagged concrete steps to his apartment building, and lost $8,000 when he let a woman he dated only once use his credit card. Once, on the way to see his grandmother in Philadelphia, he fell asleep on the Metroliner and didn't wake up until it was in Washington.

Manny was a pathological liar. He lied about everything. The more inconsequential the subject, the bigger the lie. He even lied about where he went on vacation. He said he had scaled mountains, run rapids, gone scuba diving off the coast of Cozumel, and hunted big game in Africa. He fictionalized history: he insisted John Adams was John Quincy Adams's son, Bismarck's first name was Carl, Thomas Edison invented the telephone and Marconi invented the telegraph. He railed against Indians because he said they got the better of the deal when they sold Manhattan and vilified Albert Einstein for making the first Atomic bomb.

Manny lied to compensate for his lack of memory. He invented the past because it otherwise would not exist for him. He had neither short nor long-term memory. He lived so entirely in the present that within a minute into a phone call he forgot who was on the other end of the line. He couldn't tell you the name of a single case he was working on or what any of them were about.

Maria Lopez had also joined the firm, having gotten Nate's approval shortly after I was released from Riker's. She and Manny quickly became friends. In addition to working on her own cases, she helped Manny in every way possible: organizing his files, updating his lists of cases, and keeping track of court dates. She was like a secretary with a legal degree. Most nights you could find them at Maxwell's Plum, a bar on the Upper East Side, where they would drink B&B and Maria would tell him what he should do with his cases. They weren't lovers. Though Manny was forty-two, he still preferred older women and was dating a fifty-two-year-old Norwegian domestic who he met through the cleaning service he hired to take care of his apartment.

It was hard not to like Manny. He was a high-spirited, jolly fellow, arriving at work every day with a smile on his face and a kind word for the employees. He wasn't handsome, but had a kind face and bright eyes, with wavy brown hair that flopped around as he walked like a bushy haired-kid who helped at the firm after school. His office was no more organized than a typical teenager's room. Loose papers and ragged redwelds littered the floor and snapshots of beautiful women he said were girlfriends—actually cutouts from old magazines—covered the walls. On the floorboard heater were piles of telephone message slips. Every message he ever received was in those piles. And the messages represented every call he had ever received because he had given the receptionist a standing order to say he was on trial.

Why didn't I fire him as soon as I knew what he was like? I guess I didn't want to believe he was unsalvageable. I thought I could use my special brand of alchemy—which had made money on lousy cases—to human effect. The letters to investors not only generated interest in the limited partnership cases but also inquiries about handling claims against stockbrokers. Since Manny had once worked at Sample & Company, a brokerage firm where he lost every case, I figured he'd be an expert on what a claimant's lawyer needed to do to win. I told him he would be in charge of our new arbitration department. I gave him a raise.

The first client I assigned to Manny was Dr. Michael Gusto, an urologist from Ft. Wayne, Indiana. Gusto had invested $3,000,000 in limited partnerships sold by Prudential Securities. Prudential's advertising touted the company's trustworthiness—you're familiar with the nonsense about the rock—but during the 1980s its brokers sold more bad deals sponsored by more crooked general partners than any other major securities firm. With the left hand the brokers distributed prospectuses containing dire warnings of economic risk and with the right hand distributed flyers and glossy colored brochures extolling the safety and profit-making potential of the partnerships. Gusto had received my letters and sent in retainers to join the lawsuits. Then, on the advice of his personal lawyer, he called and asked if we would bring a separate suit against Prudential and the broker.

Arbitration was the ideal way to prosecute Gusto's claims. Unlike court litigation, the procedures are streamlined and cost-effective. A trial usually occurs within a year and the judgment is final. Though the inability of the loser to appeal may invite an arbitrator to be arbitrary, even ignore the law to decide the dispute by whim, there's a certain purity in knowing that you need only tap into the arbitrator's psyche to prevail. Appealing to a person's individual sense of justice is so much easier than manipulating abstruse and often contradictory legal principles to support your position.

Manny could bring Dr. Gusto's claim before the National Association for Securities Dealers (NASD) or the American Arbitration Association (Triple A). The conventional wisdom favored the NASD. Its panels of industry members were thought to favor claimants, as if their mission was to always rule for the customer in order to deliver a message that the industry was capable of effective self-regulation. On the other hand, Triple A panels were stocked with lawyers. And most lawyers mimic the conservatism of judges. But Manny's decision to file before the NASD wasn't based on conventional wisdom. The customers who sued Sample & Company always filed before the NASD. Manny never thought of the Triple A.

Maria had thought of the Triple A. When she reviewed Dr. Gusto's documents, she noticed that he had invested more than six years earlier. The NASD rules included an eligibility rule that barred claims more than six years old regardless of when the investor discovered the fraud. Filing Gusto's claims before the NASD would spell immediate dismissal. No such requirement applied to Triple A arbitrations. The arbitrators would act as a court, applying the applicable state statute of limitations, in this case that of Indiana where the period for suing didn't begin until the investor realized he'd been defrauded.

Manny wouldn't listen to Maria, not even when she hoisted her briefcase onto the bar at Maxwell's Plum and pulled out copies of Indiana court decisions that could be used to promote Gusto's claims in a Triple A arbitration. "My friends at Sample & Co. gave me the inside scoop on what's going on at the NASD," Manny said. "The NASD is about to void the six-year rule." What could she say? She didn't know it was just another invention of Manny's arid, but strangely fertile mind. If he had friends at Sample & Co. and if he'd spoken with them, he wouldn't have remembered what they said. Maria was so devoted to Manny she didn't suspect he was incapable of telling the truth. Nevertheless, she told him to consult with me before filing Gusto's claim. He nodded in apparent agreement and they drank a toast to victory. (For obvious reasons, Manny always toasted his victories ahead of time.)

Manny never consulted with me and Maria didn't mention their conversation at Maxwell's. She assumed Manny had discussed the matter with me as he had promised.

He left for the bathroom. As he walked away I reached in my pocket to stop the recorder. The tape was almost finished, and I wondered whether I should hide it and the other one from earlier in the evening. Would he not insist I give them to him? And would he return the others, as he had promised?

When in doubt, proceed as before. I put a new tape in the recorder and put the used tape in my shirt pocket. I glanced toward the front of the room. The woman in red was still there, her face in shadow. I thought she was looking at me.

A number of minutes passed. Perhaps he was on the telephone. Who could he be calling at such a late hour? I rose from the couch and walked to the front, half-wanting to have a closer look at the woman. But she had turned around toward the window.

A long staircase led to the basement. At the bottom was a pay telephone. No one was using it. The men's room door was next to it. I went down the steps.

When I opened the door to the bathroom I was surprised to see Jimmy standing at the basin. He was drying his face with a towel. I was even more surprised to see McKinley Washington. He was sitting on a chair, a pile of towels in his lap. To his side was a table and radio. On the radio was a book. Its plain yellow cover had faded with age, and the binding was broken.

I did not know what question to ask first.

"Nice place," Jimmy said, looking at me in the mirror above the sink.

"What are you doing here?" I asked, staring at Jimmy, but thinking about McKinley, whose Cheshire grin was threatening to push his nose between his eyes.

"Can't sit in the car all night," Jimmy said.

I pointed to McKinley. "No, I mean Mr. Washington."

"Not too many jobs for an old man like me," he said.

"He did not tell me," I said, referring to my friend. "Where is he?"

"Went for a walk," Jimmy said.

He continued to stare at my reflection in the mirror, as if he was trying to judge my state of mind. I saw only my tired and drawn face, eyes red and puffy.

Jimmy finally moved away and I took his place at the sink. I splashed cold water on my face. McKinley brought me a towel. "You need some sleep," he said.

"Our friend has not seen fit to include sleep on his agenda."

"Soon enough," Jimmy said.

"What is soon enough?"

"When you will be able to sleep."

"When will that be?"

McKinley reached in his pants pocket and took out a gold watch. He flipped open the cover. "Two more hours until closing."

"Then what?"

He closed the watch and wiped the cover with a hand towel. "I go home, sit by the window, and wait for the sun to come up."

"That is a beautiful watch," I said.

He flashed his Cheshire grin. "Best present I ever been given."

"Who gave it to you?"

McKinley looked at the ceiling. "He gave it to you?" I said.

"He surely did. Said it was his grandpa's. See, look here." On the cover was an inscription, faded from age, but I could make out the year: Eighteen-ninety-six.

"How long have you worked here?"

"Since the place opened, maybe two years now, give or take. I lose track down here in the cellar. Reminds me of that place Riker's. Small, no windows. Course I get to leave every morning."

"McKinley is going to lend us a hand after he gets off work," Jimmy said, playfully hitting him in the shoulder.

"How?" I asked.

Jimmy was looking at the bulge in my pants pocket. I took the recorder out of my pocket and showed it to him. "It's off," I said.

But Jimmy would say no more. On the radio a newsman was talking about the referendum, saying the ballots would not be counted until the day after the vote. He reviewed the accord, including the amnesty provision that would allow political prisoners to obtain their freedom during the ensuing two years. Hearing the news made me wish I were home to cast by ballot for peace.

"See there," I said, pointing at the radio. "Tommy will gain his freedom without your intervention."

"Not the way I hear," Jimmy said. "Bombers, proven or not, don't get a pass."

"Who told you that?"

"Who else?"

I was overcome with frustration. "Why are you doing this? Why do you care? A Jew, an Italian, a black . . . none of you has reason to be interested in Tommy Glynn. It makes no sense."

"What's right always makes sense," Jimmy said. He leaned under the faucet and took a drink of water. "Have to get back to my car. I'm double parked."

"You sure don't want no ticket tonight," McKinley said, laughing.

I started to follow Jimmy out the door when McKinley, his ear pressed to the radio, said, "Shit to fuck."

"What is it?" I asked.

"Goddamn Reds."

"Communists?" I said.

Jimmy shook his head and left. McKinley was slapping his knees as if they were bongo drums. "Damn, you is a funny man."

"You must forgive me," I said. "The hour is late, and I thought—"

"No, my man, not them kind of Reds!" He opened the cabinet doors under the sink and pulled out a cap with a bright letter "C" embroidered on the front. "I been a Reds fan since I moved to Cincinnati. Damn fine ball-players in those days."

"I see."

"My favorite was Frank Robinson. Robbie, they used to call him. Number twenty. That goddamn Negro was the best. They was always tryin' to tear him down. The law I mean. The law don't like the black folk. It especially *don't like uppity black folk, or somebody with extra special in him. One time a cop caught Frank carrying a gun. Shit, he always carried a gun. For protection. Frank was buying a cup of coffee at the White Castle when this cop came in. He saw the gun stickin' out of Frank's jacket. Wanted to cause him trouble, so he arrested him. Shit, arrested him for nothin'. He had a license."*

"That sounds familiar."

"Yeah? You know the story."

It was my turn to laugh. "No, I was referring to home, in Belfast, where the RUC would make arrests without cause."

"Yeah, like that fellow who was in jail with Tommy Glynn, back your way, what's his name?"

"You know about Bobby Sands? Unbelievable."

"I should say I knows plenty of unbelievable things."

"Arrested because the RUC found a gun under the floorboard of a car in which he was a passenger."

"Same all over. Alls I know, I got no use for the law. And it sure in hell never had no use for me. Never did me no good, like that time the law gives me a raise and Steiner, the old fool, except he weren't not fool, he knew how to get around the law . . . shit, maybe he probably a lawyer hisself."

I wanted to take advantage of his loquaciousness. "Tell me, McKinley, how are they going to do it?" I moved closer to him and whispered, "The escape, that is."

He put the cap on his head and fingers to his mouth. "Shh, you don't want to be talkin' about that."

"Then you know."

He folded a towel and put it on the sink. "I don't know nothin'."

I would not learn from McKinley what I wanted to know. As I went to the door, he said, "Hey wait a second, Mr. Sullivan. Don't you want to hear more about Frank?"

I was anxious to return upstairs, but it was clear he would be disappointed if I did not hear him out. "If you wish," I said.

"A couple of weeks after the damn arrest—the papers really got on Frank, no black folk were newspaper men back in those days—my buddies and me were havin' a couple of beers and shooting' a few games of pool at our tavern when guess who walks in, but the man himself. Couldn't believe *it. Hell, that ole place was good for beggars and vagrants, not bona fide athletes like Frank. Course, everybody in the place recognized him and we got real quiet, like we was in church or somethin'. If there'd been a mosquito flying around you could have heard its wings buzzing. The place was pretty crowded and there weren't no seats at the bar, so Frank, he jest comes over to the booth my friend and I was sittin' at—only one booth in the joint, you see—and says he'd like to sit and order a beer if it was OK by me. I slide over and he sets next to me. My friend, he runs to the bar to order Frank a beer. I say, 'Mr. Robinson, it sure is an honor to meet you,' and you know what he says, he says, 'The honor's mine, pops.' Well, I needs to tell you I's jest about to shit a brick. No, it was more like a slab of concrete. My friend returns with the beer and we sits there talkin' to Frank for two hours. Said he stopped in our joint 'cause he figured no one would look for him there. He was fed up with the papers, the cops, fans, goddamn everybody. Anyways, it gets to be kinda late and he says he got to go, get his beauty rest he says before the doubleheader against the Pirates the next day. I get myself on my feet—I mean you got to stand when Frank Robinson stands— and I says once more what an honor to meet you Mr. Robinson. And he jest smiles at me and pulls out of his pocket two box seats for the doubleheader. Hands 'em right over to me. Doesn't that tickle your fanny? It sure tickled mine. Then he tells me I don't need to call him no Mr. Robinson. I can jest call him Frank."*

"A nice story," I said, hoping I could now leave.

"Now, jest you hold on, Mr. Sullivan. I ain't finished. See, you probably don't know this, 'cause I know our friend wouldn't mention it, but I had a son. Lived with his mother in Louisiana. Never did see him after I moved to Cincinnati. He was damn angry with me for walkin' out on his mother. Didn't want to hear no excuses from me. Can't blame him. I was a kinda unreliable type. He got killed in Vietnam, by the Vietcong the Colonel said, but I heard from another father it was by our own, what do they call it, friendly fire, somethin' like that. Shit, can you believe them guys the way they use words. Nothin' friendly about getting' killed. I went to Louisiana for the funeral ... turned out to be two funerals, 'cause his mother ... shit, she was a damn fine .... The day before the funeral, she got caught by a stray bullet from some damn sucker cop who was shootin' off his gun, like a nervous *dude shootin' off his mouth, tried to nail the tire of some black ass sucker's car makin' his get-a-way . . . the bullet hit off the fender . . . she was on her way home from St. Francis Hospital . . . a nurse's aid . . . the patients loved that woman . . . goddamn, it was a long time ago . . . more friendly fire everywhere, over there, over here. Seems like friends are a shitload more dangerous than enemies. Hell, they're not friends, leastwise not the way I see it. Like the goddamn law, I say. No friend of mine. No sir."*

McKinley had slouched against the back of the chair. His eyes were closed. I quietly opened the door to the stairwell.

"Hold on there, Mr. Sullivan, don't go yet. I ain't finished."

"I really should."

"You must be speculatin' what my dead boy has got to do with Frank Robinson."

"I suppose—"

"See, my buddy and I, we went to the doubleheader, seats right in back of the Reds dugout, and Frank, he came over and talked to us while he and the other guys were playin' pepper. He remembered everythin' we done talk about at the bar, not jest about baseball, but other things to, important things like civil rights, the big bad bomb, books I was readin', and my son. He remembered me braggin' about my son. Course I never told him I hadn't seen my son . . . .

"I see you want to go back upstairs. I'll make it short. Frank got my boy's address from me and sent him an autographed baseball with a note sayin' I was a good friend of his, which made me, you know, proud and got my son to start callin' me once in a while, jest to say hello, nothin' special, but shit, I don't know, a father needs to have a son talk to him . . . . Frank sent him a baseball every year. Even after he was traded to Baltimore, goddamn shame, shippin' him to another city, like he were a damn slave or somethin' . . . ."

As he was speaking, he turned slowly to the side. I believe he did not want me to see that he was crying. Tears were trickling into the wrinkles on his cheeks, making them sparkle like crystal. Thinking I would console him, I put my hand on his back. He reached over his shoulder and lay his hand on mine, pressing on it.

"Sorry to hear about your father," he said. I was not consoling him, I realized. He was consoling me.

After a few moments, he removed his hand and picked up the yellow book. He opened it to reveal pages of handwritten notes and photographs of Frank Robinson. One in particular made me swallow in sadness. The baseball player was handing the boy a glove. They were standing on bright green grass, the ball field, I supposed. Stately palm trees were in the background beyond a metal fence and the sky was a crisp blue.

"That there was in Clearwater," he said. "Spring training. See, I wrote it right here, so's I wouldn't forget, so's if I weren't here no more, you'd know where it was. Course I wrote it much later, after I learned to read and write."

"Will you be all right?" I asked.

"Surely will," he said, the Cheshire grin returning.

As I was leaving, a question occurred to me. "Why are you interested in Tommy Glynn?"

"He's somebody's son, ain't he."

When I got upstairs I looked around the room. My friend was not there. I went through the front door and up the steps to the sidewalk. Jimmy was sitting in his car reading a newspaper. My friend was walking toward me from the direction of Park Avenue. Behind him and through the nighttime shadows I saw a flash of red.

"The woman from the club," I said.

He looked in her direction. "I hope she'll be all right," he said.

Manny filed Dr. Gusto's action before the NASD, and Prudential promptly moved to dismiss. Manny couldn't foist his fiction on the NASD. He couldn't tell the arbitrators that the NASD was about to abrogate the six-year rule, when no such change was in the offing. Manny cried on Maria's shoulder. How could he be so stupid, he asked her. Rather than answer the question, she gave Manny his only hope: an argument that the six years didn't start to run until Dr. Gusto lost the money he had invested. Though this approach found no support in the NASD rules, it was sufficiently creative to tantalize one arbitrator, a vice-president from Merrill Lynch and a graduate of Yale Law School who had never practiced law.

With Maria's help, Manny found some early NASD memos that noted the difference between a rule of eligibility and a law of limitation. In other words, although a statute of limitations reflects a public policy to preclude lawsuits arising from wrongs committed outside a specified time frame, limiting eligibility is an administrative convenience that could be abrogated when justice required. Because Dr. Gusto's partnerships collapsed financially within a year of filing his claim, it wasn't fair to prevent him from proceeding. Or so the argument went.

The NASD arbitrators took two years to decide Prudential's motion. The decision was by two of the three arbitrators. The Merrill Lynch guy—who might have favored our position—died of a heart attack six months earlier. He was dictating his views of the case the night before he collapsed. Manny agreed not to ask for a replacement. Don't ask me why. He courted disaster like a bug flying into the fire. Had Manny thought about it, he would have realized he'd lost his only supporter on the panel.

As the NASD was issuing its decision to dismiss the case, I was looking through a fog of steam rising from a broken radiator in a dusty conference room at the Supreme Court. Sitting with me was Dr. Bamberger.

Why am I now telling you his story? When I was taking a walk, I happened to pass the building on Park where Bamberger lives. He's a night person like me, and I saw him through the window of his study. He was sitting in a comfortable, deep leather chair, next to a bookcase, listening to Beethoven, I'm sure, and reading. Probably a history book, Elizabethan era I would guess. Stephen loves English history and like me takes comfort in the past.

Anyway, Judge Margaret Wilson sat at one end of a long table and at the opposite end sat opposing counsel Ralph Golden and his client, the distraught Patricia Garrett, though not so distraught to forego a chance to use the law to turn vengeance into cash. Bamberger, Chief of Psychiatry at Mt. Sinai Hospital, had been treating Patricia's ex-husband for depression, including two extended hospital stays when he was unable to get up in the morning to make the rounds of the three apartment buildings he owned in Chelsea.

The problem began when Patricia and their two sons, ages six and seven, went to live at her mother's house in Astoria. She said she couldn't deal with her husband's sullenness. Seeking to deny her husband access to the kids, she filed a lawsuit alleging that his emotional difficulties were detrimental to their welfare. He got the summons on a Friday morning, the day he was supposed to pick up his children for the weekend. He showed the complaint to Bamberger and said he would kill himself if the court granted his wife's motion to prevent him from seeing the kids. Bamberger urged Garrett to commit himself, but he refused. Garrett said he was afraid commitment would guarantee his defeat in court.

Bamberger couldn't see a satisfactory solution to the dilemma. If he persuaded Garrett to commit himself, Garrett would, as he said, risk losing the right to see his sons. However, if he told Garrett to go home, take his Lithium, and enjoy the weekend, he'd be neglecting his responsibility to his patient. He knew Garrett needed more help than a drug could provide. He proposed a compromise: home for the weekend, the court hearing on Monday, and then hospitalization. But Garrett couldn't look past the weekend. He wanted Bamberger to explain how the law could take his kids from him just because he was sick. "I'm not a lawyer," Bamberger said, but he knew that wasn't much of an answer.

Maybe Bamberger should have been more prescient and called Mrs. Garrett or given his patient more hope about the hearing, even if it was false hope. I don't know. I don't think anyone does. But the law knows. It knows everything. Failure to predict what a person might do is the fodder of litigation, the stuff that the law likes to use to fatten you for the kill.

After Garrett left Bamberger's office, he picked up his sons in Astoria and took the subway to 23rd and Park. Inside the station, he bought a box of Milk Duds for the seven-year-old and a bag of licorice for the six-year old. They sat on a bench. The kids ate their candy. A woman stopped to compliment him on his handsome sons. When they finished eating he made sure they threw the boxes in the garbage. Taking their hands, he led them to the far end of the platform. As they neared the stairway a whoosh of air filled the station. The woman remembered hearing giggling. She remembered thinking that the boys sounded like kids at an amusement park. A train was approaching. The kids tugged at their father's hands. They wanted him to hold on to them tightly as they leaned a little over the edge to see the car rumble around the bend. Garrett smiled as they looked into the darkness. He held their hands for a bit and then let go. When the light appeared from the train he put his hands to their backs and nudged them off the edge. If the boys screamed, the whining and screeching of wheels on rusted tracks forced the cries back into their heads.

Garrett calmly left the station. He strolled west on 23rd Street, stopped at a Dunkin Donuts and bought a coffee, drinking it as he continued his walk. Five minutes later, he reached the apartment building. He said hello to Mrs. Roth, his long-time tenant on the first floor. He continued through the hallway and down the stairs to the basement. Next to the furnace was a desk. In the top drawer he kept a ledger of tenant complaints and requests for repairs. In the drawer below he had put a small photo album with pictures from the previous Easter's family trip to Disney World. This was the only drawer he cared about. He thumbed through the album and set it on the desk, open to his favorite picture, the one Patricia took of him and the boys standing on the dock, ready to board the fake submarine that would take them on a fake undersea adventure. He reached to the back of the drawer and removed a gun. He checked the chamber and crawled under the desk where there was a blanket, which he put over his head. He wanted to muffle the sound when he squeezed the trigger.

Mrs. Roth never missed keeping track of who passed through the building. When she realized he hadn't come back upstairs, she went looking for him. She saw the photo album first, then his legs sticking out from under the desk.

I tried in vain to convince Judge Wilson to dismiss the case. Bamberger hadn't the power to commit Garrett and couldn't have predicted that he would murder his children. For negligence to exist, I said, the consequences of an act must be foreseeable. Perhaps Bamberger had exercised poor judgment, but only because his patient appeared to be suicidal. "Counsel," Judge Wilson said, "someone has to take responsibility for the death of those children and my job is to make sure that happens."

"When you have a spare moment, perhaps you'll show me your job description."

"Sarcasm won't help your client," she said, with the look of a poker player holding a pat hand.

She scheduled the case for trial. Bamberger was facing a possible judgment of millions, far more than his insurance coverage.

The air was thick with steam as Stephen and I listened to Patricia's demands. She would accept $10,000,000, the policy amount. She also wanted more than money, something in exchange for not pursuing the case to judgment. She wanted him to resign his post at Mt. Sinai.

"That's an unconscionable demand," I said to Golden when he finished his presentation. "The board of Mt. Sinai cleared Dr. Bamberger of wrongdoing. If they say he may continue in his post, who are you to insist otherwise?"

Golden didn't have to respond. Wilson, acting more like an advocate than a judge, gave the answer for him. "I think Mr. Golden has made an eminently fair settlement offer."

"But my client wasn't negligent."

"I think he was," she said. "Indeed, I am convinced he was."

"You haven't heard any evidence. How can you say that?"

"If the plaintiff were to file a motion for summary judgment, I will rule—"

I pushed my chair away from the table. "Damnit, Judge, now you're prejudging the case, which is worse than—"

"Watch your language or I'll hold you in contempt."

"You'd have to get back on the bench to hold me in contempt, and I don't think you'd like me to repeat on the record that you made up your mind before you heard all the facts."

She was a large woman with a neck like a football player. But the mounds of fat couldn't restrain her jugular, and the folds in her skin turned bright red. "Are you threatening this court?" she said with contrived chagrin.

"I'm not threatening you. I'm warning you."

She would have climbed on the table to strangle me, but her bulk wouldn't allow it. And I wasn't about to give her the last word. I took Stephen's arm and we left.

What a waste. I was a blowhard, wallowing in rage to no effect. I knew we should settle; so did Stephen. He resigned his position and gave up teaching. He kept his office at Mt. Sinai, though he doesn't see patients. Yes, he did offer to see you. Must be your round face: pink, boyish, irresistible.

His case didn't sour me on the law, no more so than every other case I've told you about. Each one has its place in my natural museum of dishonor. What the law and its servant Wilson did to Bamberger isn't worse than what the law does everyday in less important matters, like who should recover what amount of money under what circumstances against whom. Which is why I should return to Manny, Dr. Gusto, and something else that happened. Something from that garden spot called California.

More than on the other nights, my head was reeling from his patter. I said I needed some fresh air and wished to take a walk. He apologized and offered to walk with me. I said I wanted to be alone.

The sky had begun to lighten and a mist of dew freshened the air. I started walking toward Park Avenue. Near the end of the block, I passed Jimmy's limousine. His head was against the headrest and his eyes were closed. If he was relaxed enough to sleep, I should be able to take a walk without worrying.

A truck driver was dropping off bound stacks of newspapers at the corner newsstand. On the front page of the New York Daily News was a picture of Salvatore. His eyes were fixed—no doubt it was a police photograph—as they had been when they saw their last light.

The inside page story added nothing to the television report. Another story on the same page said pollsters were predicting a substantial margin in favor of the Northern Ireland referendum, and President Clinton was already boasting about his role in the peace process. A new era of peace and harmony was at hand, he and Prime Minister Tony Blair had declared. But I knew that political and personal peace were altogether different states; for me, personal peace would forever remain beyond the horizon.

Thinking I might get a glimpse of Bamberger, I walked along Park Avenue. But I did not know which building was his. And what difference would it make if I did see him? Would I try to gain his attention? Visit with him and verify what my friend had reported? To what end? My friend could have invented the tragic case of Garrett the landlord. He could have invented everything. Like Manny Golan, he could have created an imaginary past to give himself a life. I wondered if I would ever know the truth.

As I returned to 61st Street, I saw McKinley and my friend standing next to Jimmy's limousine, whispering to each other and looking through the window. Their positions blocked my view and I could not see if Jimmy was participating in the discussion.

My friend moved away from McKinley, who had taken a place with his back to the driver's side window. I peeked around McKinley, and he shifted his body to further prevent me from looking into the car.

"What is it?" I asked.

My friend's face was pale and drawn. He looked as if he was about to faint. McKinley stepped away from the car. "Might as well see for yourself," he said.

Between red streaks I saw Jimmy's head against the headrest. His mouth was open. Blood coated the steering wheel and dashboard. Soft instrumental music was coming from the dashboard speakers. He must have been asleep when the bullet struck.

"He wanted to change his life," my friend said, echoing Jimmy's words at Murphy's.

"Who did it?"

"Whoever it was didn't kill him for this." He was holding a brown envelope. It looked like the one Jimmy had gotten from the Korean storeowner. "It was on the front seat," he said.

"We must call the police," I said.

"No police," my friend said, echoing what Jimmy had said when Salvatore was murdered.

"There has been too much killing."

"Any killing is too much."

McKinley stepped between us. "This ain't no time for a debate," he said.

"Get in the car," my friend said.

"You are insane," I said.

McKinley gently pushed me to the rear door. "We is all crazy."

"Where are we going?"

"To do what we got to do."

They pushed Jimmy's body into the middle of the front seat while I got in the back. My friend drove and McKinley sat on the other side of Jimmy. I paid no attention to where we were driving. Jimmy's head was lolling back and forth with the movement of the car, splattering the blood from a hole in his neck down the back of the seat onto my shoes.

The limousine skidded to a stop. We were beneath a highway, in a dark place between huge concrete posts. Predawn light slithered through crevices in the roadway above us.

"I don't see nobody," McKinley said.

"Good a place as any," my friend said.

McKinley got out of the car and reached back inside to Jimmy's body. With my friend pushing and McKinley pulling, they managed to drag him out the door. "Want to give us a hand?" my friend said.

His eyes were ablaze with fear or fury. "Connie, this is not the time to go into one of your catatonic states."

In his maddened look, with curly white hair sticking up as if shocked to attention by a burst of electricity, I tried to see some semblance of a man who had lived his life in the law. I saw only desperation.

"Fine," he said. "Stay where you are. This is not your problem."

I realized it was my problem. How could it be otherwise? And so I forced my limbs to move. I helped them drag Jimmy's body along the stone-strewn ground to a concrete pillar. We propped his body against the side facing away from the street. No one would see him unless almost upon him.

We rode out from under the highway down a narrow street to a ramp. We sped north on East River Drive. I lowered my head in despair. My bloody shoes transfixed me. I could not look away from them and repeatedly mumbled, "Where are you taking me?" I sounded like I was singing the refrain from a well-worn tune, my voice elevated like a half-drunk Irish tenor singing in a beer hall. I rubbed the shoes with the palms of my hands, a man obsessed.

He was driving fast, narrowly missing cars. Then he shifted to the right-hand lane and off an exit. A sign said 116th Street.

He stopped the car on the ramp. "This is where you get out, Connie."

I raised my bloody hands.

"Christ, Connie."

I pointed at my shoes. He leaned over the seat and looked at them. "Get them off."

McKinley climbed into the back seat and took my shoes. My friend took off his shoes and passed them over the seat. I put them on and began to laugh.

"What's so goddamn funny?"

I had never seen my friend so exasperated. "They fit," I said. "Your shoes fit."

My inane comment broke the tension and he laughed. "Jesus, Connie," he said.

My laughter turned to sobs. "Maybe we should take him to my place," McKinley said.

"No," my friend said. "We don't have the time. Point him in the direction of Second Avenue."

"Take me with you," I said.

"No."

"You have kept me prisoner this past week. You must take me with you."

"You haven't been a prisoner, Connie."

I had gone from abject misery to hot anger. "What would you call it? You have talked and talked, but told me nothing. You have pretended to lay your life before me, but your stories are a ruse to hide the truth. You send me here and you send me there, but the journey always leads to death. Now you discard me in the middle of nowhere, in this God forsaken place, worse than where I came from . . . "

"Get a hold of yourself, Connie. It's finished."

"What is finished?"

"What I started. I am releasing you. You need do no more. Go home and forget you ever met me."

I put my hand on the door handle, but leaving was too easy. "What is your name?"

"My name wasn't important before and it's not important now."

I reached in my pocket and took out the tapes.

"Here," I said, "these belong to you."

He smiled. "Keep them."

"You never finished the story."

"Which one?"

"Dr. Gusto. The malpractice case. California."

McKinley had gotten out of the car and was opening my door. "We's got to go," he said.

As I slid across the seat, my friend's hand brushed my shoulder, a touch of caring and concern, a touch of sadness. I did not pause. Outside, McKinley shook my hand and flashed his Cheshire grin.

As they drove away, my friend yelled out the window. "Take the bus. Those shoes aren't made for walking." The sound of his laughter lingered in the air after the car was out of sight.

Chapter Fourteen

May 22, 1998

I
N MY YOUTH, we never took the bus. Everything we needed was a short walk from the house, including the offices of the Sinn Fein for those who wanted information on the conflict. For trips to the city center or the university we rode in the black cabs, the semi-private livery for Catholics.

I rode the bus once. It was the night I brought Mary home to meet my parents. Da spent the dinner hour giving his usual lecture about politics and religion. Then he got on the subject of Bobby Sands and the hunger strike. He said he had been reading an account in the newspaper of what befell the families since then, five years past. It was not a happy report. Mothers who losc their sons never stop grieving and no longer look to the future.

We retired to the living room after dinner. Da called the family around him and told Mum to open the bottle of champagne he had bought for the occasion. He wanted to propose a toast to Mary and me. It was a strange toast, an Irish proverb, which he recited with a sneer. "What is the world to a man when his wife is a widow."

As we left Mary said she wanted to see where Bobby Sands was buried. Though she lived near the cemetery, her home might as well have been located in a distant land. For the most part, middle-class Catholics had avoided the conflict, even to the extent of pretending that the symbols of the struggle did not exist. It was as if her comfortable Andersontown home was a stately tree in the jungle. Though able to see the world from its highest branch, she was blind to the roots directly below.

Night had fallen and I suggested we should visit the cemetery another time. Just then, a bus arrived and she insisted we board. It was empty. Few of my neighbors had reason to travel from our section of Falls Road to Andersontown.

I could not remember the location of the grave. It had rained through-out the day, and the sky was black with overcast. Along the paved roadway that cut through the center of the cemetery we paused to kneel before various headstones. We must have looked like grave robbers looking for a suitable candidate to unearth.

The road ended in a parking court. A dirt trail led off to the right, and Mary took my hand to continue our walk. I knew Mary to be a determined woman, but her dedication to the search mystified me.

Slopping through mud and tripping on stones, we inspected hundreds of graves, old and new, most clustered in family groups. Then we came to an area near a work shed, where the graves were adorned with plastic flowers. She crouched before the first marker: Francis Hughes, 25, May 12, 1981. Then the others: Raymond McCreesh, 24; Patsy O'Hara, 23; Joe McDonnell, 30; Martin Hurson, 27; Kevin Lynch, 25; Kieran Doherty, 25; Thomas McElwee, 23; Michael Devine, 23; and Bobby Sands, 27. Upon reaching the Sands marker, Mary solemnly shook her head.

"They could have given them a more decent spot, you know," she said.

"The earth is cold everywhere."

She rubbed the petals of a plastic tulip. "You think to God their families would come every day with fresh flowers," she said.

"The dead live in one's memories, not in the ground."

She leaped to her feet and hugged me. "You're a regular philosopher."

I was not a philosopher. I was a bitter young man who wanted to write history so I could forget the present. "May we go now?" I asked.

"They gave their lives for us," she said. "We should show our respect. Say a prayer."

"I do not know what prayer to say."

"A silent one then."

She sat on the concrete slab and closed her eyes. Her lips moved ever so slightly. I did not have it in me to join her. They had not died for me. They had not died for anyone. Their suffering had not changed the world.

"You don't get along with your da," she said.

"We have our disagreements."

"Like what?"

"He is a firebrand. He believes violent change is the only kind of change."

"What do you believe, my husband to be?"

"I do not believe in change. Things appear to change, but they never do. Nothing ever makes a real difference."

She pointed at the Sands marker. "He died for what he believed in."

I bent over to brush the dirt from my shoes, not in some mad, panic-stricken way as in Jimmy's limousine, but like a man nervously wiping imaginary lint from his clothes.

"I'll shine your shoes when we get home," she said. "My da has the best shoe polish."

We walked the three miles to her home on the far side of Andersontown, holding hands and enjoying the crisp night air. When we got to her house she said, "Would you sacrifice anything?"

"You mean die, like Sands and the others?"

"Not necessarily die. Give up whatever has meaning for you."

"There is nothing that means so much to me that I would not readily relinquish the privilege of keeping it."

"Then you would sacrifice me?"

"I would never give you up, but I would give myself up for you."

"Ah," she said merrily. "Then I suppose I will go ahead and marry you, Cornelius Michael Sullivan."

"You will, will you?"

"What's a life for, but to give it to someone else."

"What's a life for?" I thought as I walked home. Mary had made it sound like life was a gift one gives to another. And was that not a worthless sacrifice, if one had not lived to the fullest? Assuredly, my life was not a life that had been lived. I was a visitor to life who like a weary traveler spent too much time in his hotel room and missed most of the interesting sights. My friend, on the other hand, had toured the entire land of his life in the law and had exposed himself to the stuff of human drama.

At the entrance to the 59th Street Bridge, I headed east. For some reason, I wanted to avoid walking by Murphy's. I wanted to pass buildings I had never seen, stores I had never visited, people I had never encountered. I wanted something new and fresh. I wanted the morning to cleanse me, to give me a reason to go on. Without conscious deliberation I was on my way to the

East River, where if I gave in to cowardice I might leap into the water, like Sam Brandt, and hope to be carried out to sea. If there had been no Mary and Lucy, perhaps that is what I would have done.

From the corner of 56th Street and Sutton Place I could see to the dead end that overlooked the East River. A row of handsome stone buildings ended at a concrete ledge where a crowd had gathered. Their arms were raised to the sky as if to praise the heavens, but they were pointing to large tufts of black smoke drifting upwards in the calm morning air.

By the time I reached the onlookers the smoke had darkened the eastern sky. From where I stood, it was difficult to determine the exact site of what must have been a sizeable explosion, but it appeared to be centered in a complex of several old buildings on the other side of the river. Bright red flames shot into the smoke, and a dull roar accompanied the collapse of the largest structure, a several story warehouse.

A man next to me pointed to a spot in the sky north of the fire. A white cloud had appeared from nowhere, followed by three booming sounds that reminded me of the bombs that often shattered the peace of Belfast. "Are we under attack?" a woman behind me asked. "By whom?" asked another. "Terrorists," the man next to me said. "That's dumb," a teenage boy said. "Why would terrorists bomb Queens?" I smirked with the memory of saying something similar to Gold and Varick.

After a few moments, I negotiated my way out of the crowd. Near First Avenue I came upon a parked taxi. "Of all places," the driver said in a loud voice. As I drew closer, I heard his car radio: "We're receiving fragmented reports that the damage to the Riker's Island facility may be considerable. The other explosion has destroyed an abandoned warehouse in Long Island City. As yet we have no reports on the number of casualties."

I continued walking. Traffic was everywhere snarled. It was as if fear and uncertainty had paralyzed the city. Americans had been secure for so long, they could not tolerate the slightest instability.

When I got to the apartment I lay on the bed. Cuchulainn jumped on my chest and curled his face against my neck. While I scratched him, I took the tape recorder from my pocket and rewound the tape. I fell asleep to my friend's voice.

I had a strange dream. An old woman was walking along a West Belfast street. Blood was pouring from her eyes. Behind her bombs were exploding and fire was consuming one building after another. I ran to her with a cloth and tried to wipe the blood from her face. She took the cloth and covered her eyes. Then she asked me to tie a knot at the back of her head. As I was tying the knot, she raised her hands. An old-fashioned scale, the kind assayers traditionally used to weigh precious metals, fell into her grasp. In one bowl was my tape recorder, in the other the pistol from the wall at Marinelli's. She faded away and my friend appeared, holding the scale. He handed it to me. "I have no more use for this scale," he said. "It's out of balance."

I awoke with a start. My friend's voice still filled the studio, but what he was saying was unfamiliar. I examined the recorder; the tape was moving in reverse. The side on which I recorded our last conversation had finished while I slept, and now the second side was playing. But I had recorded nothing on that side. I pressed the rewind button.

I have no more use for this scale. It's out of balance.

I had walked past the pawnshop for years without stopping. On the day I cleaned out my office, however, I decided to have a look at the place. I wanted to be surrounded by the discarded goods of strangers, to see if I could somehow get inside their lives.

I was surprised when the pawnbroker offered me the scale. He didn't ask me what I wanted to pawn. Anything to get it off his shelf, he said, where it had gathered dust for two years. The pawnbroker was a tiny wisp of a man, not even five feet tall; he had a flinty look, his face chalky and ghostly.

Years of negotiating with the downtrodden had sapped him of empathy. While I looked around the store, he unceremoniously relieved a matron of her diamond engagement ring, giving her not much more than the price of a gold wedding band.

The scale wasn't a work of art: no elaborate carving on the stand, dull brass unevenly polished and rough to the touch. In its best days it was merely functional and the out-of-kilter bowls confirmed that it had long ago lost its ability to accurately weigh anything.

I thought of the Erte sculpture on the dressing table in Beth's bathroom. I never cared for Erte's art and harbored a special dislike for this particular piece. The bronze woman with a white metallic gown was cold to the touch and the tiny face had the look of an avenging angel. When I got home I took the sculpture into my study and placed it on the stand of the scale. There was her proper place in the world. Lady Justice. But I didn't bother putting a blindfold across those unfeeling eyes. Let her see the justice she dispensed with those out of kilter scales.

By the way, I'm sitting on Sam's bench in Central Park. Remember? The Hans Christian Anderson statue. What a gorgeous day. There's a strong breeze. Can you hear it? Probably sounds like tape hiss to you.

He stopped talking and there was a clicking sound. Hissing and scratching followed, interspersed with his cursing.

Damnit, I stand to stretch and get dizzy. Dropped the damn thing. Hope I didn't break it. OK, here we go. It's ... it's ... oh yes, it's May 20, 1998, two days before the big event. I won't have enough time to finish my story in person and decided to make this tape. Jimmy will find a way to slip it in with your other tapes. I've noticed you only use Side A of your tapes. How wasteful. But then you might not play this side and thus never hear about my last days as a lawyer. Listen to me, I think my brain is fried. I shouldn't worry about posterity. It will prosper without me.

Since I can't predict how far along in my story I'll be when we part, you'll forgive me if I repeat something I told you or have skipped too far ahead. If it's the latter, don't fret. You didn't miss much.

The book partnership case came to a decidedly anti-climactic conclusion: a settlement with Mavens and the insurance company; a discount on the notes from the Grosse Deutsche Bank; a bellwether trial against Nate, in which he represented himself after Arnold resigned. (Judge Blackthorn tired of Nate's unworkable reorganization plans and dismissed the bankruptcy.) The jury awarded the plaintiffs a judgment for their losses and punitive damages. They never collected a penny. Nate claimed to be broke, though he was living with his mistress in a million-dollar condo on Third Avenue. I hired a private investigator to look for assets. His twenty-page report was as useless as it was detailed: Nate's cousin, a boxing promoter, owned the condo; Nate went to the Grand Cayman Islands twice a month but never left the beach; former business colleagues recounted Nate's exploits with women but said nothing about assets or bank accounts. The report's conclusion was short and bitter. "The subject owns nothing, earns nothing, and otherwise has no visible means of support."

Sure, my clients were angry. The settlements netted them about ten percent of their losses, a lousy result though enough to give me a million-dollar fee in addition to the retainers. They weren't the only disappointed clients. In other investment cases, the collapse of the real estate market plunged partnerships and promoters into insolvency. The courts threw out several cases, ruling that the complaints didn't allege "fraud with specificity" or the statute of limitations had run. I usually eked out a settlement—the defendants worried what might happen on appeal—but investors rarely got back more than a modest fraction of what they lost. Like a mercenary, I was the only one to profit from an otherwise financially ruinous war.

Dr. Gusto's litigation, however, wouldn't die a natural death. Though I was upset when I heard about the NASD's decision to dismiss the case, I had been a lawyer long enough to know that a case can live on like a patient in a coma. The patient can suddenly emerge from his slumber. Miracles do happen.

Ian Duddy, Prudential's General Counsel, laughed when I suggested he should make a settlement offer. "What's there to settle?" he said. "Your case is over." I told him cases don't die, they hibernate; I would refile the case in an Indiana court and take advantage of its more liberal statute of limitations. He said he wasn't worried. The pincers of res judicata and collateral estoppel would squeeze the life out of a new lawsuit. I reminded him that the NASD rule was one of eligibility not limitations and therefore the dismissal didn't preclude trying again.

Ian invited me for a drink to discuss the case. He said he wanted to see my face when I repeated my argument. I love Irish lawyers. They always combine business with pleasure. (I wish Kathy were still around; I could tell her how the Irish practice law.)

I bet you can guess where we met. Murphy's, naturally. In fact, I had never heard of the place until Ian told me to meet him there. Snob that I was, I had never gone to an Irish pub anywhere. I did my drinking at upscale establishments: luxury hotel bars, cigar bars, wine cafes, and the like. It never occurred to me to hang out with ordinary folk. And despite his lofty position in the world of commerce, Ian was ordinary folk. He looked more like a barkeeper than the senior lawyer for one of the world's largest financial conglomerates. With a face that rivaled pink desert sandstone in graininess, a nose flatter than a punch-drunk fighter, and a jaw as powerful as a battering ram, Ian could afford to act like just another guy.

"That lad of yours, Manny, did your case in," he said, inspecting his finished glass of Guinness like it was Steuben crystal. He drank his Guinness like a man dying of thirst. He could outdrink as well as outtalk anyone. But foolish me had been matching him glass for glass.

"We need a couple of bucks to make Dr. Gusto happy," I said.

"Prudential isn't in the business of making people happy."

"That's not what the TV ads say."

He ordered another pint, and drank down half of it in one huge swig. He wiped his lips with the back of a red-knuckled hand. "You have a bit of the Irish in you, you certainly do," he said.

"My wife is Irish."

"My wife is Jewish."

"How ecumenical."

"I'll give your lad $300,000 for the doctor, but he's got to take it by pub time tomorrow."

"What time is pub time?"

"When it's time to be locked in the dark snug of a public house."

I didn't know what time that was or who said it first, but it wasn't Ian Duddy. I staggered to the payphone and called Manny. Too drunk to think clearly, I told him he should call Gusto.

Back at the bar, Ian was on his next Guinness and there was another one for me. "Really," I said, "I'm past my limit."

"You push the limits of the law, you did, with your grand theories of litigating, so you might as well push the limit of your gullet."

We stayed until closing. When I got home I found Beth asleep and a note on my desk that said Manny had called with the good news. Gusto had accepted the offer. I lay on the floor. Dean Martin said you're not drunk when you can lie on the floor without holding on. I was drunk. I clawed at the floor before I passed out.

Lawyers are a devious lot, but Ian was more devious than most. He knew not to tell you what you most needed to know. Two weeks after the settlement, I opened the morning paper to read that Prudential had signed an agreement ending the long-standing, hitherto secret government investigation of its sales practices. The deal would allow investors to sue Prudential regardless of statutes of limitations. For the investors who had sued and lost, the claims could be reinstated before a reparation commission.

Oh, the law and its cursed affection for irony. One class of potential claimants would be excluded from this new process. If you lost your case, you could seek compensation from the commission. But if you settled because you were afraid you might lose, you were done. The agreement rewarded the stupid or stubborn plaintiff with another chance for recovery and excluded the reasonable plaintiff who settled.

Manny was waiting for me in my office. He had taken to wearing steel-framed reading glasses; he had the lenses tinted to achieve what he called "coolness." He was reading a letter, mouthing the words as he moved down the page. "Stabbed in the back," he mumbled. He tossed the letter on the floor, as if he were entitled to litter my office with the refuse of his failures.

"What's in the letter?" I asked.

"Gusto heard about the Prudential deal with the government. He wants me to call Prudential and undo the settlement."

"Do it," I said.

"Why?"

"Duddy knew about the Government deal. That's why he offered to settle even after the NASD dismissed the case."

Manny's arms were tightly folded against his chest, as if he were preparing to be wrapped in a straitjacket. "I won't do it," he said like a child refusing to eat dinner. "The doctor agreed to the settlement."

"So?"

"So, he should live by the agreement he signed."

"Then I'll call Duddy."

I went behind the desk and accessed the speed-dial directory on the phone. Lawyers always want the latest in office technology. "Please, don't," Manny said.

"Why not?"

"I got the check from Prudential last week, deposited it in the client funds account, and transferred our fee to the firm checking account."

"We'll transfer the money back and send a check to Prudential."

Duddy came on the line. "Always nice to hear from former enemies," he said.

"Ian, we have a problem," I said.

"You sound like an astronaut."

"You snookered us into the Gusto settlement."

"Pub agreements are inviolate."

"Manny is sitting across the desk from me. He wants to sue Prudential for fraud."

"A lot of people want to sue us for fraud."

"I'll return the money and go before the new reparation commission."

"Don't bother. We'll just send it right back to you."

When I hung up I said to Manny, "Tell Gusto we'll give it a shot. Prepare the complaint."

Manny never called Gusto and he didn't prepare the complaint. Gusto's messages formed their own stack in Manny's office and continued to grow like a skyscraper under construction. By the time I realized Manny hadn't gone forward with the case, it was too late. Gusto had sued us.

Our failure to vitiate the settlement, however, was only one of the malpractice claims. Gusto's new lawyer seized upon Manny's original decision to file the case before the NASD. He said Manny should have gone to the Triple A, where eligibility wouldn't be an obstacle. He also alleged that the Triple A could have invoked a statute that would have resulted in an award three times Gusto's actual losses, or $9,000,000. (The NASD limited damages to the amount lost plus interest.)

Duddy decided Prudential would be better off buying peace with Gusto. It agreed to pay Gusto $1,000,000 to waive his claim to cancel the settlement. He had done me the dubious favor of reducing my exposure in the malpractice case to $8,000,000 —the difference between a triple damage award and the new settlement.

Our malpractice insurance wouldn't protect me. The maximum coverage was $1,000,000. Even if I thought I could win at trial, I couldn't take the chance. I had to persuade Gusto to settle for the insurance.

The world of the law is a small world. The insurance company appointed A. Collins Wickersham to represent us. (Charles Roberts' lawyer in the gay palimony case.) It didn't bother me that my former opponent was now my champion. Nothing is ever personal in the law, which I suppose is one of the few things favorable I can say about the profession. Besides, A.— he got mad when I called him Harold—was smart, savvy, and cold, the kind of lawyer I needed to clean up the mess Manny had made.

A. wanted to meet in New York. I took him to a Knicks game because he said he liked basketball and we could talk during timeouts. But he got so into the game he put me off. He wouldn't even talk at halftime, saying he never mixed business with pleasure. "What about the time you flirted with my associate, Kathy Shawn?" I asked. "That was business," he said.

After the game, I called Beth to see how she was doing. She said she had gotten a call from Jared, a lawyer in my Los Angeles office. He wanted to speak to me as soon as possible. I called Jared . . . no, wait . . . I'm confused . . . that was another basketball game, an Indiana Pacers game at Market Square Arena, the night before the settlement conference. You'll have to forgive me. I can't seem to keep dates and places straight. Too many late nights, I guess. I'll get a hot dog and collect my thoughts.

There was a click, then silence. I pressed the fast forward button, waited a few seconds, and pressed the play button again. I could hear the wind and the muffled sound of children in the background, but nothing from my friend, that is, until near the end of the tape.

I ate the hot dog, fell asleep on the bench, and woke to see the tape running. I could rewind it and continue the story, but it's too late now. Anyway, why give you a detailed account of what happened during the case or even at the settlement conference the morning following the basketball game? Why obsess over such an absurd calamity.

Oh, well, since you are probably dying of curiosity I'll give you the highlights. Manny flew in for the conference but his flight was late. He showed up as Gusto and I were getting on the elevator after the conference. (A. stayed behind to talk to the judge.) The first thing Manny said was, "I'm late." Not a smart thing to say, and Gusto said, "I'm not surprised, seeing as how careless you are." There's no more provocative an insult than a truthful one. Manny shoved Gusto, causing his glasses to slide off his nose and onto the floor. With considerable glee Manny stepped on the glasses and crushed them, grinding the frame and the glass like he was stamping out a cigarette. Gusto pressed the emergency button and the elevator suddenly jolted to a stop. It threw Manny and me against him. I heard a snap. It sounded like a toothpick breaking in half, but it was Gusto's collarbone that had cracked.

Manny and I shared a cell for three hours while Wickersham and Gusto's lawyer debated our fate before the judge. The lawyer said Manny and I were thugs, bent on using whatever means necessary to bludgeon poor Gusto into a settlement. Gusto sat in the first row where the judge could see him squinting through two black eyes, a rotund blubbery man who looked like he deserved to be beat up. The lawyer pointed at him and said, "I haven't seen a crime this horrendous since what Mike Tyson did to that poor teenager," a bit of hyperbole that caused the judge to laugh and say, "Knocking a man's glasses off isn't the same as rape."

The judge told the marshal to bring us in the courtroom. We were in handcuffs. The judge asked us to give our version of what happened. I tried to stop Manny from speaking, but his mouth was like a leaky faucet. He couldn't keep quiet. He did convince the judge that the collision was an accident, but he admitted that he had pushed Gusto. The judge let us out of jail, though Manny still had to defend a criminal complaint for assault and battery. He pled guilty and paid a $500 fine.

I should have been mad at Manny. Not because he pushed Gusto—I would have liked to push him—but because the incident destroyed the possibility that Gusto would take the insurance proceeds in settlement. He also refused to make a counter-offer.

The tape had run out. I got off the bed and turned on the television. Every station had interrupted programming to cover the bombings. CNN was broadcasting live from the rubble at Riker's Island when it cut to a video-tape of the visiting area where I had waited to see Tommy. A photographic insert of Patrick appeared on screen. An announcer said that Patrick was dead. The police had found his body floating in the water a few yards off the island. Speculation was that a brick from a collapsing wall had knocked him into the water. What the announcer did not say, however, was why Patrick was outside or what he was doing when the bomb exploded.

The scene shifted to a large room where the warden was holding a press conference. Standing with him were Mayor Rudolph Giuliani and Smith Corcoran. A reporter asked whether the FBI had identified any suspects. Corcoran refused to comment. Another reporter wanted to know whether prisoners escaped in the confusion following the explosion. Again, Corcoran would not answer. The Mayor said it would be some time before local authorities would be able to account for the inmates.

In the television studio the anchorman was interviewing the Deputy Mayor. The Deputy Mayor urged the public to remain calm. He said that no one had come forward to claim credit for the incident, and it was therefore premature to conclude that a foreign terrorist was responsible for the bombings.

I switched off the television and returned to bed. I rewound the tape and replayed my friend's story about the scales of justice. His past was more comfortable than my present. I closed my eyes and saw myself riding through the air on an invisible carpet, setting down in a world of tranquility where no harm ever came to anyone.

I encountered difficulty persuading the agent to sell me a ticket to Boston. I had no photographic identification and I could tell that she didn't believe me when I said I had lost my passport. She demanded proof of my identity. I replied that I needed no proof who I was and that should be good enough for her. Although she did not share my by now twisted sense of humor, she relented and sold me a ticket when I told her my sister in Boston was ill. My friend would be proud of me. I had successfully skirted the rules by appealing to the heart.

In the waiting area next to the departure gate, I found a bank of phone books for the New England area. The Boston suburban directory listed Sam Brandt. His home was in Newton.

At Logan airport, I asked the manager of the taxi queue to tell me the price of a trip to Newton. When he said thirty dollars, I realized I had insufficient funds to take me there and back. The manager said I could use public transportation, though it would require both a subway and bus ride.

The trip took more than an hour, longer than required to drive from Belfast into the country and even out of Northern Ireland. In America, geography is more than a state of mind.

I was tired from the journey and lack of sleep. When I got off the bus, I sat on a bench and looked at the map I had purchased. The Brandt home was two blocks away, across from the Boston College campus.

I took out my recorder and turned it on. My friend's voice had become a tranquilizer. It was as if what he said was not as important as how he said it, the mixture of pathos and cynicism that had mesmerized me for so many days. As I listened to his description of Manny Golan, laughing several times at the absurdity of it all, my eyes started to close.

"It makes me want to cry."

I opened my eyes to see a beautiful young woman with flowing blonde hair. Of course, I said to myself. She was the woman in red. "Hello, Erin," I said.

Smiling warmly, she said, "My name is Rachel."

"Rachel? But Rachel is . . . "

"Yes, I am his daughter."

"My friend said . . . "

She laughed. "How sweet that you call him your friend."

"What else should I call him? My enemy."

"Names are not important," she said, still smiling, unaffected by the hostility in my voice.

"So he liked to say." I said.

"My father can be very playful."

"Perhaps. But there has been nothing playful about what has happened."

"If he were here, I am sure he would explain everything."

"No, he would torture me with some Byzantine fiction."

She took my hand. "Come, you did not fly to Boston to argue with me."

The Brandt home was a large three-story colonial at the end of a heavily wooded street. A path along the side of the house cut through tall, well-groomed hedges. As we walked, I could see through the windows into the house. We passed the living room, then the dining room and kitchen. A library with floor to ceiling bookcases took up the rear of the house. A large desk stood in the center of the room. Only a framed photograph was on the desk, but its subject was hidden in the dark room.

"He enjoyed reading," I said, admiring the hundreds of neatly shelved books.

"Mr. Brandt loved books. He said a good book was a companion who never disappointed."

"What will Mrs. Brandt do with them?"

"Keep them, of course."

We continued to the back yard. A raised granite patio afforded a view of the grounds, considerable in depth and breadth. Closely cut grass extended at least a hundred yards before ending at a strand of oak trees. Molly Brandt sat alone at a white table. Her red hair hung loosely below the turned up collar of her simple blue dress. She sat regally like a queen on her throne, just as she had sat at the funeral. And there was that physical resemblance to me, the resemblance of a sister, but with a beauty and dignity that I knew I would never see in my face.

Though she must have heard us approaching, she seemed content to look toward the oak trees.

"I have brought Mr. Sullivan, Mrs. Brandt," Rachel said. She made it sound as if they had known I would be coming.

Molly stirred and looked at me. "It's a pleasure to meet you, Mr. Sullivan," she said with a trace of brogue. "Please sit."

I sat next her. Rachel remained standing.

"Remarkable," Molly said.

"What is remarkable?"

"If I were to trust my eyes, I would think you were Tommy."

"Yes, I know."

"We knew you would come."

"I see that. But how?"

"He told us you would not stay put. Who else could you seek out?"

"No one is left," I said. "Patrick, the bartender at Murphy's, died in the explosion.

Neither Molly nor Rachel reacted, as if they expected the news.

"You look afraid, Mr. Sullivan," Molly said.

"I have good reason to be afraid."

"Tell me what you want to know."

My questions came in a rush. What did she know of the bombings? What had become of Tommy Glynn? Why would my friend risk everything? What would happen now? On and On. She listened patiently. When I finished she said, "Your friend is a good man. He was Sam's friend. He was my friend. He wanted Sam's dream to come true."

"What dream?"

"To help those he loved."

"Did Tommy escape?"

"If God has answered my prayers."

"You know about the others, I assume."

"What others?"

"Salvatore and Danny Marinelli, both dead. Jimmy Crosetti, shot to death last night as he sat in his car when . . . " I paused and looked at Rachel. " . . . after you left the club. Why were you there? Why did you not come over to us?" I wanted to be calm and dispassionate, but could not control myself.

"Excuse me for a minute, Mr. Sullivan," Molly said. She rose and walked though a double set of darkly tinted glass doors into the house.

Rachel took Molly's seat. "My father said I should meet him at the club," But when he arrived with you he looked like he didn't want to be disturbed. I waited for a while but he was so occupied with talking to you." She smiled. "He's like that, you know. It got late and so I left. There was nothing more to it, Mr. Sullivan. If I had known . . . " Her voice faltered and she started to cry. "I loved Jimmy. He was a wonderful man."

I could call on nothing to comfort her. "Why did your father tell me you were Erin Brandt? And why did you register at the Park Lane Hotel in the name of Erin Glynn?"

"He wanted to protect me. And to protect you, Mr. Sullivan. He thought it better that you not know the truth."

I was tired of hearing that my ignorance was a state I should covet. "At least tell me your father's name. Sooner or later—"

"Not now," she said.

"Why did Brandt commit suicide?"

"I don't know," she said in the fractured tone of someone who is uncomfortable at hiding the truth.

"I know," Molly said. She was standing by the door.

"I am sorry, Mrs. Brandt. I did not mean to intrude. I was only—"

"No, it's all right. I don't like the word suicide. Sam was not an easy man to understand. He always did what he wanted when he wanted, but would never explain his reasons. He took life seriously, much more seriously than he let on. The most trivial case was important to him. The most obnoxious client he treated with respect. And he was a bitterly disappointed man, Mr. Sullivan."

"Disappointed in what?"

"The law. Those years in the law. Wasted, he said. It's a terrible thing, Mr. Sullivan, to believe you have wasted your life."

"One can always start over."

"You can start anew, but you can't start over."

"An attitude he shared with Rachel's father."

"Two peas in a pod. They could have been brothers."

"And your brother, Tommy. What of him?"

"What happened to my brother . . . I'm to blame, I suppose. I wanted Sam to get Tommy out of prison. The case was his biggest disappointment."

"I must tell you, Mrs. Brandt, it was my father who—"

"Please, Mr. Sullivan, let's leave the past in the past."

"As I have discovered, the past stays with us forever."

"Your father protected his family. He did the right thing."

"He was cooperating in the plan to free Tommy, and I was a pawn . . . ." My words sounded empty, a lame attempt to excuse what my father had done.

"I'm sorry for your inconvenience." At first, I thought she was being sarcastic, but her eyes glowed with sincerity.

"Was your husband part of the plan?" I asked.

She did not answer. A small knot appeared above the bridge of her nose.

"Forgive me," I said, worried that I had ventured where I was not wel-come. *"I am trying to determine if there is a connection . . . "* My thinking sur-prised me. I had wondered about the relationship, if any, between Brandt's suicide and the plan to free Tommy Glynn. But how could Brandt's suicide have facilitated the escape?

"What kind of connection, Mr. Sullivan?"

"I am sorry, Mrs. Brandt. I cannot understand why your husband would commit suicide. Surely, disappointment in the law is no reason to . . . and . . . why would he take his life a few days before . . . "

She opened the palm of her hand to reveal a tape, a cassette like the ones I used. *"From your friend,"* she said and handed it to me. *"Perhaps you will hear the answers to some of your questions."*

"You saw him?"

"No," she said abruptly. Then with deliberation, *"I have only spoken to him on the telephone. He made the tape several months ago. Made it for me, actually. But he said I should give it to you."*

"What is on it?"

"The story of a legal case."

"What legal case?"

"The United States vs. Peter Marinelli," Molly said. She clasped my wrist. *"I'm glad you came, Mr. Sullivan."*

She turned away to look toward the house. As quickly as it had begun, the interview was over.

On the way to the street, I stopped to look into the library. The sun, low in the sky, bathed the room in pink light. The photograph seemed to jump in the air. It was a black and white portrait of an older man. As I was shifting my line of sight to obtain a better view, Rachel came up behind me. *"Have you lost your way?"*

"The photograph on the desk. Who is it?"

"Sam's father. He died a few years ago."

I looked again but the photograph had fallen into shadow. Behind the desk, on a credenza, were a penholder, legal pad, three books whose titles I could not make out, and a portable computer with the top open. And at the far corner stood a pedestal, a sculpture of some sort. It was six or seven inches tall, cylindrical, molded out of platinum. Like the photograph, the *sculpture struck me as somehow significant, though I could not fathom the reason. I also could not shake the feeling that Rachel and Molly had been no more truthful than my friend had been.*

"Someone still uses the library," I said.

"Is that a question, Mr. Sullivan?"

"A meaningless observation," I said with as little rancor as I could manage.

She left me at the bus stop. I sat on the bench and tried to organize my thoughts. But then the bus arrived and I realized there was nothing to do but return to New York.

As I took my seat and stared out the window, the most obvious question occurred to me, one I should have asked but had not: Where was Erin Brandt?

Molly and Erin, you know I hate to write. The only way to preserve the story of the trial was to put it on tape. By the way, I should apologize for refusing to let you and Erin come to court, especially Erin. [*Why should they be interested in Peter Marinelli's trial?*] I don't know. I was too nervous. With the years I've spent in the courtroom, I should have been able to banish nerves to a place from which it could never return. But you know me, high-strung as always. I hadn't tried a criminal case since God knows when . . . Leonard Stone . . . whatever . . . I still should have let you watch. Sorry. [*What about his wife, Beth?*]

Since you know the end, I want to tell you how I got there. The law did me in. Rather, it did Peter in. [*Even more strange. My friend said Sam represented Peter Marinelli in the government's case.*]

Before I get into the case I want to tell you a story, a story more revealing than I like to admit. No one ever knows another, even when they're close. [*Were my friend and Molly romantically attached? Was that why he made the tape for her? A husband betrayed by his dearest friend?*] We never do reveal ourselves. How could we when few of us know who we are?

When I was a kid my parents protected me from the world. I never even had to worry about getting along with babysitters. Sarah and Albert never went out. Occasionally, though, Sarah would leave the house for an hour or two. One of her customers, old and infirm, was a homebody. She considered herself a fashion plate and insisted that Sarah come once a week to hem her dresses.

I was ten, a month shy of my eleventh birthday. I liked to sit on the porch waiting for Sarah to come home from her weekly excursion. As long as I could spread my comic books before me, I was happy. I was crazy for comic books, especially the ones with superheroes, the defenders of truth, justice, and "the American way." I liked the way the hero invented a second identity to conceal his heroic self, as if a defender of justice must always wear a mask, protection against not just the bad guys but also the law. Superheroes operate outside the law, sometimes above it like Superman, flying around the world swooping down here and there to dispense justice. My favorite hero was the Count of Monte Christo. He was an ordinary guy dealt an extraordinary injustice, then got his revenge and his treasure.

On one of Sarah's absences Mike Zermansky, a brawny thirteen-year-old from the neighborhood, stopped by the house. He said he was thirsty and I invited him inside. He followed me into the kitchen, chattering on about Annabelle Laughlin, the twelve-year-old girl next door with the budding breasts we all wanted to get our hands on.

Once inside, he told me not to bother with getting him a drink. He wanted to see the house. No one had ever asked me for a tour of our home, and I thought maybe it would be fun to pretend I was an official tour guide, like the friendly old man at the wax museum.

When we got to my room he plopped on the bed, testing the mattress like it was a trampoline. I asked him if he wanted to see my games, but he said games were for little kids and he wasn't a kid anymore.

He got off the bed and stood in front of the full-length mirror on the door. He lowered his pants. He wasn't wearing underwear. I was standing behind and to one side of him and could see his gargantuan *thing* from two different angles. Next, I remember lying next to him on the bed, remember him touching me, remember seeing my *thing* grow big, though not as big as his got. Nothing else happened. I felt a little something, but not enough to mean anything. Out of boredom or disappointment, he slid off the bed and left. I stayed and straightened the sheets and blanket and waited for Sarah to come home. When she did, I told her nothing.

Every week, Mike came over when Sarah went to see the customer. And each time he was a little more determined. He used petroleum jelly, baby oil, his own spit, and finally his mouth. I lay there and stared at the ceiling, counting the lines where the paint had cracked. When I got tired of counting, I thought about superheroes.

When Sarah returned home after Mike's fifth visit, she said she wanted to have a talk with me. I said I didn't feel like talking. I knew she was suspicious. Mothers have a way of knowing. Maybe I wanted her to figure out what was going on. She later found a semen-stained piece of toilet paper behind the clock radio in the shelf of the headboard. I guess Mike had put it there while I was staring at the ceiling.

Sarah gave me permission to skip dinner that night. I heard her and Albert arguing in Yiddish. Jonathan, who understood some German, came up to the room and said in the serious patronizing way older brothers talk to younger brothers, "You should know better than to jack off and not throw away the evidence." I smiled and agreed to be more careful.

When Mike came over the next time he never made it inside the house. As he turned off the sidewalk to approach the porch I told him to stop. He laughed and continued walking. I took the rock I had gotten from the tulip bed and threw it as hard as I could. It struck him in the forehead and he did a three-sixty, falling to the ground like a dying top. I thought he was dead. I hoped he was dead.

I sat on the steps and stared at him. His face was tilted to one side, flush against the pavement, blood flowing from the gash in his forehead and dripping from his nose. Then I heard a groan and knew he was alive. I was disappointed. I wanted him to lie on the ground until the ants crawled through his eyes and used his brain cells to build a colony, or if the ants didn't find his skull appealing lie there until Sarah and Albert came home or a neighbor arrived on the battlefield and praised my courage and marksmanship.

Mike struggled to his feet. Tears and snot mixed with the blood running down his face. His shirt and pants were torn. He stumbled toward his house, looking like one of those wounded soldiers in the old wartime newsreels, shell shocked into numbness, eyes rolled up into his head, leaving behind him a spotted trail of blood. I retrieved the rock and returned to the porch and my comic books. I was reading Captain Marvel when Sarah and Albert drove up.

I didn't tell them about the sexual assignations, but I confessed to what I had done to Mike. I even described the path of the rock, saying it flew through the air like out of a slingshot. They didn't have time to interrogate me further. A blue and white Chevrolet, red light flashing, screeched to a stop in front of the house. I recognized Officers Bundy and Morrissey as they got out of the car. A year earlier they had found my cat, Wyatt Earp, sleeping in a garbage can and returned him to me. Jonathan, already anxious to display the political talents that would later win him the presidency of the American Psychiatric Association, raced in front of Sarah and Albert and told the officers I was in no condition to speak, so shaken was I from Mike's unprovoked attack. He had the facts reversed and the cops knew it, having come from Mike's house where they had calmed the overwrought Mrs. Zermansky, back from the local church's assembly to discuss what to do about comic books, which according to Dr. Frederic Wertham, were twisting the moral fiber of America's youth.

Officer Bundy, a middle-aged woman with a scar across her right cheek, explained to Sarah why she had to take me downtown to Juvenile Court. Officer Morrissey, younger than Bundy, ran his hand through my hair. This was my first experience with the law or its agents, but I wasn't scared. In fact, I was kind of excited. I wanted to enjoy the legal process like I enjoyed a cops and robbers show. I thought of Bundy and Morrissey as real life detectives from *Dragnet* or *Highway Patrol*.

Jonathan stayed home while Sarah, Albert, and I rode in the backseat of the squad car. Sarah clutched my hand and held back tears while Albert plowed through his catalogue of German obscenities. Then he said, "I remember when the Nazis took away the children." I had seen Nazis in the movies and on television. I wasn't worried; Nazis had blonde hair. Bundy's hair was brown and Morrissey's was black.

When we got to the courthouse, Officers Bundy and Morrissey took us to the courtroom. Except for the lobby of the Union Terminal, it was the biggest room I had ever seen. As we waited for the judge, Albert studied a painting on the wall. He said it was a portrait of Lucius Quinctius Cincinnatus, a Fifth Century BC Roman general and statesman. I was amazed that someone would name the city after an ancient Roman.

I even had a lawyer representing me. I felt honored, felt I had *arrived*, was now a true citizen. Like my other ideas, my notion of lawyers came

from comic books and television. Lawyers belonged to one of two catego-
ries: sleazy, greasy-haired men in pinstripe suits who were mouthpieces for
gangsters or old men with receding hairlines who sat behind gigantic desks
in musty offices and asked out wealthy widows. My lawyer, though, worked
for the public defender's office and didn't fit into either category. For one
thing, he wasn't even wearing a suit; he wore khaki pants and a plaid sport
jacket with a ripped lining. His black shoes were scuffed and spotted with
some kind of white goo. He was fat and the back of his shirt hung out of
his pants, the shirt slapping at his ass like a waiter's apron. He had difficulty
breathing and couldn't complete a sentence without swallowing his words.

Sarah and Albert told the lawyer that Mike had attacked me. They
couldn't come up with a credible motive, however, except to say that
Mrs. Zermansky had set Mike against us because Sarah had accidentally
ripped one of her dresses. The lawyer belched and looked at me for confirmation, but I lowered my head like I was ashamed I had wet my pants. I
knew from shows on television that I had a right not to incriminate myself
and, besides, I didn't think that Mike introducing me to sex was a defense to
attempted murder.

The judge continued the case for a week so my lawyer could prepare my defense. When we got home Albert lectured me about the evils
of violence and Sarah said she'd never leave me alone again. Afterwards,
I dragged Jonathan upstairs and made him join me in a fast-draw contest
with my imitation Roy Rogers six-shooters. I figured I'd better get in my
practice before Albert confiscated them.

For the hearing, Sarah made me wear Jonathan's bar mitzvah suit and
one of Albert's ties. Sarah wore one of her customer's dresses. Albert put
on the suit he used when he became a citizen. He called a taxi. I had never
been in a taxi.

The driver cruised along Mitchell Avenue to Reading Road, tracing my
bicycle route to Schlancer's drug store, where I regularly used my allowance to buy comic books, Chuckles candy, and Double Bubble gum. Then
down Reading Road past the corner where Sarah had left me stranded when
she went to the Laundromat, the synagogue where two years later I would
celebrate my Bar Mitzvah, over a hill past the Pontiac dealer where Albert
bought his car—I asked him why we were taking a taxi when he could have

driven, but he wouldn't say—and into downtown, a place of foreboding tall buildings, dark movie theaters where strangers lurked, a place that I knew must be the center of the universe, a dark and dangerous place like the moon, cold and airless, where the next breath would be your last.

My lawyer met us on the courthouse steps. With his tousled brown hair he would have looked like just another fat kid but for his ability to use big words that terrified me. He said that unless I confessed to being "incorrigible, in need of therapeutic counseling," I would be sent away—he didn't say where. Sarah grabbed my hand and took me down the steps, out of hearing of Albert and the lawyer. "Now, *meine schoenum punim,*" she said, kissing my face like I was a newborn, "this is what you must do. You must confess that you are bad. It is our only hope." I looked at her eyes; I'll never forget the sadness in them. "Tell him I'm bad," I said. "Yes, *meine schoenum punim.*" Defeat, capitulation, surrender, Molly. That's what I learned that day, the size and shape of law's heavy footsteps.

I stood before the judge and tried to look guilty. The judge, a hulking giant whose smallish face seemed to be hiding between his square shoulders, grabbed one end of his robes and swung it over his back like he was a Roman emperor and wanted to impress Cincinnatus. But he didn't impress Sarah, that's for sure. Before he could open his mouth, Sarah was on her toes, wagging a finger at him. "I want to give you a piece of my mind," she said, exaggerating her accent so much she sounded like a German general. "I know people like you, plenty of people like you. We came here to escape from people like you. You are a judge, but you have no right to judge my son. He had good reason to throw the rock."

I was surprised by Sarah's violation of her own advice. There I was with an expression that said how bad I was, and she was attacking the judge.

"You should ask permission before you address the court," the judge said.

"The last person I asked for permission was a guard at the Austrian border. No more; I ask permission never again."

The judge jerked his head like a spasmodic crane. A man in a uniform started across the courtroom toward us. I thought we were going to jail, not just me, Sarah too. Albert was sitting in the first row, looking as if he wished he were somewhere else. But as the uniformed man approached us Albert stood and said "Your Honor," nothing more. He delivered those two words with such respect coloring his rich baritone that the judge nodded and the uniformed man stopped as if someone had yelled *halt.*

The judge reminded Sarah that it was fortunate I hadn't killed Mike, but his sudden monotone told me that he was fed up with the case. He looked away from Sarah's combative eyes and said to me, "Whatever provoked you to throw the rock, you must learn that violence is never a solution to a problem." I didn't mind what he said. It's what Albert had said. But his next remark was uncalled for, at least by the light that I used to see the world. "You must never break the law." I wanted to show him my comic books, point to those drawings of my heroes breaking the law whenever necessary to save the world. But I knew he wouldn't understand. He was wearing a robe, not a cape. He wasn't a superhero.

On the way out we ran into Mrs. Zermansky. She was wearing one of those veils, the kind Marlene Dietrich wore when she wanted to be an over-the-top *femme fatale*, fool you into thinking her face was more mysterious than it really was. She stuck a sculpted pink fingernail into Sarah's arm and said, "They should put your child in jail, where he'll have to behave himself."

Sarah took Mrs. Zermansky's hand and squeezed it so hard her rouge-covered cheeks got redder. "Listen to me," Sarah said, using the tone of voice that would send me scurrying to my room in fear, "you tell your perverted son to keep his hands to himself."

I was mortified. I knew mothers always know everything, but did she know what Mike had done? How could she know it was his semen on the toilet paper?

While Sarah and Albert stood in the street trying to hail a cab, I sat on the front steps to the courthouse. Officer Bundy came over and asked how my cat was doing. I said, "Fine," the typical one-word answer from a kid who trusts no one. Then she asked me what happened between Mike and me. I responded with the other useful one-word response: "Nothing." She said, "You should remember that we have laws against that sort of thing." That sort of thing? Did she know what Sarah knew?

In the taxi going home, Albert said to Sarah, "A good thing the judge didn't know about his comic book collection. He would have sent him away. *Gott in Himmel*! What would he do without his comic books?"

On my birthday, Albert came home from work with a huge carton. He said my present was inside. He helped me open it with a butcher knife while Sarah complained we were ruining her cutlery. Inside the box were several leather-bound notebooks, like the kind in which you keep family snapshots. "What are these for?" I asked, disappointed that my birthday present was so useless.

"Bring me a comic book," Albert said.

I ran upstairs and got my favorite comic book, the one that tells the story of Superman's childhood on the planet Krypton.

Albert took the comic book and slid it into one of the books, carefully fastening it under the cellophane binder. He smiled and kissed my forehead. "You won't have to worry now. These books will keep your comics forever."

OK, so much for allegory. On to Peter. I knew we were in trouble after Judge Beauregard denied my request for a continuance—

Pardon the interruption, Connie. If I placed this message at the end, you might not have heard it. You could have stopped listening in disgust. You'll either have gotten this tape from Rachel and Molly (I bet Rachel that you'll fly to Boston) or Rachel will find another way to deliver the message to you. It's the last request I'll make of you. Go to the club at eleven tonight, see McKinley in the bathroom, and then go on to Murphy's.

More intrigue, as if I needed more. How odd that a tape made for Sam Brandt, filled with asides to Molly, would contain a direct address to me.

I stopped the tape and reached for the telephone. As I waited for the connection to be made, I mulled over what I should tell her: Jimmy's death, my trip to Boston, what might happen next. Nothing, I decided. I would simply talk with her about my father's funeral.

Milltown cemetery. Again. He was buried in a plot not far from Bobby Sands and his fellow hunger strikers. Meaningless irony or punishment, perhaps both. My mother, brothers, and sisters were there, as were Mary and

Lucy. They had not bothered to vote on the referendum. Mary said everyone went out of their way not to mention my absence, as if they had written me off as a chronic truant.

She asked me when I would be coming home, and I said, "When God chooses," as if God would be interested in where I was and where I was going.

Yes, the love was there. How could I ever stop loving Mary? But I was changing. The Cornelius Michael Sullivan I had known was dying.

"You knew," I said to Mary.

"Knew what?"

"What would happen to me in New York?"

"No, Connie. I know only what I told you."

"They bombed Riker's Island today. Tommy Glynn is either dead or—"

"What are you saying? Who are they?"

"Even if you thought you do not know, you do know."

"Connie, stop! You're not making sense."

Even Cuchulainn was disturbed. He jumped on the desk and was pawing at the telephone. "Mary, I know what is troubling me. Open the letter."

"What letter?"

"The letter from my father."

"You said you would read it when you came home."

"Read it now. You must read it now."

I can still feel the words scraping my mind, a dictionary of regrets.

My dear son, Cornelius Michael,

> May this letter find you safe and in good health. Thank almighty God for relieving me of pain. It is hard to tell a son what he needs to know when he doesn't want to know it, or worse, knows it but won't admit it. Maybe you're lucky to have already discovered that I was a traitor to everyone but you and your brothers and sisters. It doesn't matter. What matters is that you know what my old broken-down Celtic heart could never say in life. We are not innocent in life or in death. I sent that poor lad to his maker in front of the Oxford Street bus station, and others before and after me did the same. So, when it comes to redeeming, I'm not the only one in need of redeeming. And either are you. I sent you

*on your way to New York to free the Irish, and by God, I know
that's what you will do. For in helping to get Tommy out of prison,
you have forever freed me from my prison. My own da used to
tell me how St. Patrick banished all snakes from the land, except
one. He promised that last snake a drink, but instead he put it
in a box. The snake begged to be freed. St. Patrick promised to
grant the snake's request the following day. Instead, he threw it
in the lake. To this day, you can hear the snake asking, "Is this the
"morrow?" My dear son, I am a snake, and for eternity I will ask
the snake's question. May the Lord have mercy on my soul.*

Da

*P.S. The Brits figured they had me, but the Brits could never have
an Irishman.*

When Mary finished the letter, I put down the telephone and wept.

Beauregard was one of those judges who liked to kill you with compliments. While denying my request for more time, he said I was a fine trial lawyer who would have no difficulty presenting a strong defense. Then he added that no one had forced Peter to change lawyers two weeks before the trial.

Did someone once say the gods visit the sins of the fathers upon their children? Whatever your opinion of Salvatore, he made sure to keep the Mafia and his children as far apart as possible. But that makes no difference to the Government; it believes that crime runs in the family and I don't mean the Mafia family. From the time Peter was a teenager he lived with the law's agents watching his every move. The FBI interviewed his high school teachers every six months, put a bug in his beat-up Oldsmobile, and harassed his girlfriend so much that her parents made her end the relationship. They did the same with his older brothers, but stopped when they realized there was little to gain from writing reports about a doctor, engineer, and high-school teacher. It was different with Peter. He wasn't interested in medicine, science, or education. He wanted to be a businessman. For the FBI, the son of a Mafioso who goes into business, any business, is in the Mafia business.

Peter worked at Salvatore's restaurant through high school. He developed a cash management system for the restaurant, ensured that taxes were paid on time, and protected Salvatore from falling prey to the kinds of sneak attacks prosecutors launch when they can't get a Mafioso for murder, bribery, or extortion. Peter even learned how to massage the numbers to avoid IRS detection for the twenty-percent skim Salvatore took on liquor sales.

Understandably, Salvatore was disappointed when Peter said he wanted to go to Oklahoma State University. Peter was a star on the high school wrestling team and his coach told him he could obtain a full athletic scholarship.

Peter didn't complete his freshman year. During an exhibition match in November he broke three ribs and spent two weeks in the hospital. On the day he was discharged he got a call from Salvatore. Salvatore said the family home was destroyed by a fire that started with an errant spark from a frayed wire. Peter didn't believe the fire was an accident and decided to return home.

Whether the fire was an accident was never determined. But Peter had made up his mind. He wanted to be part of the world. He told Salvatore he was through with college, said he never should have gone in the first place. Salvatore said he'd look around for a suitable opportunity, but Peter was impatient. He called Carlito Gavencci. Carlito used to charm Peter with stories of business—legitimate business, I should say—as Carlito was forever presenting himself as a dapper investor rather than a cold-blooded killer. Carlito and Peter arranged to meet at a steakhouse in Hartford. Carlito also said he'd bring along his partner, Whitey Delaney.

At dinner, Gavenchi talked about a group of hotels in the South Beach area of Miami. The hotels were classics of the art deco era but had fallen into disrepair. The business was in bankruptcy. The court had scheduled an auction and the First Security Bank—the holder of the mortgage—was willing to finance a responsible bidder. "A sure moneymaker," Carlito said. "But with my record I couldn't get a home mortgage." Carlito then offered to lend Peter the money for the bid.

Salvatore wasn't pleased when Peter told him of the deal he had made with Gavencci and Delaney. In fact, Salvatore had been thinking of severing his relationship with the Savin Hill gang. And he was tired of the mobster's

life. He intended to anoint Jimmy Crosetti as his successor, though he knew
it would be a hard sale among the older capos who resented newcomers,
particularly non-Sicilian newcomers. Peter insisted the hotel deal was legitimate and then further lightened his father's heart when he said he had fallen
in love with Joanie Klayman, a ravishing Jewish doctor from Philadelphia.

The wedding was a cornucopia of good food, strong drink, energetic music,
and promises for a wonderful future. Even the bride's parents were in high
spirits, having convinced themselves that their daughter was marrying into
a typical European-American family of strong and lofty values. The reception took place in the ballroom of the Bellevue Stratford Hotel. More than
400 guests attended the wedding, including former Philadelphia mayor
Frank Rizzo who minded not at all cavorting with the New York and Boston Mafia. Gavencci, Delaney, Vincente Marinelli, Jimmy Crosetti, and Gene
Lufman were there, even Smitty who had finagled an invitation by telling Salvatore he would otherwise station a dozen agents in the hotel lobby. I was
there too. Did I ever tell you? Can't remember. It was before we met, Molly.

*When had he met Molly? I could not remember. I wished I had the tapes. I
wished I had taken notes. And what of his first wife and Rachel? She would
have been too young, perhaps, but . . . I buried my head in my hands. I could
do nothing but listen.*

Guess who else was there? Your brother Tommy. It was a great joke on
Smitty, who for all his dash, cleverness, and duplicity had never seen Tommy's photograph and didn't know what he looked like. Salvatore took a picture of Tommy and sent it to Bridget. She still has it, your handsome brother
dressed in a white tuxedo; he looks nothing like a terrorist in hiding.

I danced with the bride, never . . . sorry, I shouldn't . . . it's been a tough
time, I'm sure you can understand . . . shit, this is supposed to be about
Peter, straight from the legal pad, not my lament . . .

You know what happened soon after. While Joanie and Peter were
on their honeymoon, staying where else but at the Carlisle—one of the
three South Beach hotels Peter purchased at the auction—Tommy was

arrested. Neither Peter nor Salvatore knew who betrayed him, but we found out, didn't we.

The First Security Bank gave Peter the mortgage he needed and added another $5,000,000 to complete the renovations. He was on his way to becoming the uncrowned king of South Beach, the new kid on the block, the young real estate entrepreneur who would single-handedly turn the area into an American Riviera.

Gavencci and Delaney called Peter when he got back from his honeymoon. They weren't satisfied that their investment was adequately protected. They wanted Peter to have day-to-day assistance now that he was a big-time real estate maven. They met at the Diplomat Hotel where Peter had set up his offices. Corcoran was in the next booth, listening to the conversation through a hole he dug out of the cushion with a government-issued Parker ballpoint pen.

Gavencci told Peter he should hire cousin Kurt Hauer. Peter had the same reaction as everyone else. How did a German become Gavencci's cousin? "He isn't my cousin," Gavencci said, laughing. It was the kind of inside joke only an irredeemable Mafioso could make, self-deprecatingly poking fun of the idea that a gang of criminals can constitute a "family."

Gavencci called Kurt "Cousin" because Kurt's father, a part owner with Gavencci of the Revere dog track, was known as "Uncle"—no one knew how he got that nickname because he wasn't the friendliest of fellows. He did say he liked to perform a few acts of kindness every day, minor though they were: he passed out cigars to strangers at restaurants, delivered bags of fruit to the homeless who lived under Interstate 93, and stationed Gamblers Anonymous volunteers near the betting windows to counsel the big losers.

Kurt's ambition was boundless. He would do what was necessary to get ahead. He was also smart. He graduated at the top of his class at Wharton, where he managed an investment club that consistently produced profits for the members.

Uncle was a Nazi. Born in Munich, at age thirteen he became a happy and willing member of the Hitler Youth. I hate to say I have anything in common with Kurt, but we both carry pictures of our fathers in our wallets, though Uncle is hardly the professorial type. Uncle is staring at the camera like it's an adoring *Fraülein* impressed with his uniform, a shiny black swastika on his arm, blonde hair and blue eyes, all somehow magically coming across in the black and white photograph, a future leader of the Third Reich had there been a Third Reich to lead.

I suppose Peter had no choice but to hire Kurt, though he couldn't have been comfortable doing it. Whereas even the most ruthless Mafia killer retains a kindly sparkle in his eyes when he's off duty, Kurt's eyes were empty, the look of a heartless fiend. His skin was almost Albino white. From a distance, he looked like a body without a head, Washington Irving's headless horseman on foot. Scary, though scarier to look into his blue eyes and see nothing there.

Even before the hotel renovations were completed, Gavencci passed the word through Kurt that he wanted his loan repaid. The request caught Peter by surprise. He had used the $100,000 from Gavencci to secure the winning bid, the money transferred to First Security bank as pre-paid interest on the mortgage and construction loan. There were cost overruns on the rehab work, and Peter had his hands full keeping the laborers on the job.

Kurt handled all of the business dealings with the First Security Bank. He prepared the draw requests and accompanying affidavits necessary for the release of funds, money that was supposed to be used to pay the subcontractors. When Gavencci said he wanted the $100,000 Kurt knew what to do. He drafted a loan request and attached phony payroll records. Trusting Peter signed the affidavit without reviewing the attachments.

The $100,000 never passed through Gavencci's hands. On Gavencci's instructions, Kurt sent $50,000 to Uncle to cover his losses at the dog track and kept $50,000 as his compensation for services to be rendered—what services, Gavencci neglected to specify. Peter never knew what happened. The renovations were completed three years later, funded by First Security Bank when it enlarged the loan by $2,000,000 to cover cost overruns. Immediately, Peter was in financial trouble. Revenues from hotel operations weren't high enough to service the debt, and Peter put his company into bankruptcy.

While compiling the records for submission to the court, Kurt remembered the false affidavit. He mentioned it to Gavencci and Delaney and they called Smitty. Smitty relayed the information to the Philadelphia Strike Force. Soon thereafter, Peter was indicted for fraud and racketeering.

When Salvatore found out what happened he wanted to kill Gavencci, Delaney, and Hauer. But Jimmy talked him out of the idea, saying a gangland war would start. So, Salvatore hired Gene Lufman to represent Peter, not realizing that at trial Gene would be wary of aggressively cross-examining Kurt Hauer and Gavencci. Gene had had been playing both ends against the middle for so long no one could be certain where his loyalties lay.

Salvatore came to the trial every day, taking the same seat in the last row, barely able to see over whatever head was in front of him, a broken-hearted man fast growing old as he watched his youngest son twist in law's wind and then succumb to a sentence of eighteen years for a crime he hadn't committed. Salvatore wanted to kill his enemies, use the pistol and knife from the wall of his restaurant, like in the old days, a child of violence in Sicily. This time Peter was the one who talked him out of it. "I want no part of murder, Papa," Peter said to him during their visit in the lockup. "I'll win on appeal. You'll see. The law will protect me."

Peter wasn't mad at Gene. In fact, he wanted to use him again in the Jones Printing case. But Salvatore intervened because . . . Molly, you know what happened there. I don't even know why I started to go into it. I guess I can't stop thinking . . . I didn't want to be responsible for . . . forget it. I'm supposed to tell you about the trial I wouldn't let you see.

Nightfall. Only Cuchulainn's bright eyes shed light on the rotating tape, shadows floating across the desk like a murky stream. I heard footsteps and the sound of a key turning in a lock. On the tape or somewhere else? Somewhere else. The sound came from the vestibule.

I stopped the tape and listened. Again, a key turning. Silence, then the turning, then a pushing against the door, the wood straining at the frame. Cuchulainn and I stared through the dark at the door. The footsteps sounded again and a door opened—the outside door. I went to the window and saw a man hurriedly walking across the street. I did not recognize him. He took one quick look toward my window before getting in a car and driving away.

*I took the recorder and sat on top of the radiator by the window. Cuch-
ulainn jumped on the sill. He would be my nighttime eyes while I listened to
the tape.*

When the Feds indicted Peter for embezzlement and money laundering
in the Jones Printing matter, he was serving his Philadelphia sentence at a
prison farm outside of Scranton. And you know that Joanie filed for divorce
on the same day Lufman filed the appeal.

What you don't know is that Salvatore never found out about Smitty's
double-cross. He knew Smitty was getting paid to let the Savin Hill gang do
their thing, but he never suspected that Smitty was behind Gavencci and
Delaney's decision to drum up the Philadelphia fraud case. He also didn't
know Smitty told Gavencci and Delaney to shovel some more dirt over
Peter, just in case the appellate court reversed the conviction. And Peter
never told his father that Smitty came to see him at the prison farm, where
he said that unless Peter delivered the goods on Salvatore, he'd make sure
the government prosecuted Peter until . . . he never said until when, but it
was out there, in a future beyond the future we can see.

If Salvatore had found out what Smitty had done, Smitty would be
dead. I couldn't allow that. I needed Smitty's cooperation to make my plan
work. It never occurred to Salvatore that Smitty was going along with us for
more than Jimmy's favorable testimony in Boston. Smitty knew he couldn't
double-cross me.

God, it's hard to stay focused. I'm talking about everything except
Jones Printing. Give me a second.

Charlie Jones, the founder of Jones Printing, had died of throat cancer. But
the prosecutor was better off calling the comptroller, Beatrice Guggen-
heim. I could have dirtied Charlie on cross, shown how he nearly bank-
rupted the pension plan before Peter bought the company. I had to be careful with Beatrice. I wouldn't score any points by attacking someone who
looked like everyone's grandmother.

Beatrice had been with the company since it opened for business in
1960. For a time she watched the company prosper. It employed 150 men

and women and was one of Livingston, New Jersey's largest employers. Then business began to decline. Computer technology allowed for entire textbooks to be encoded on compact discs and the demand for printed books evaporated. Jones couldn't bring himself to lay off workers and let the business fall into debt. He reached the limit of his credit line in 1995. The bank told him he should find an investment partner or sell the business.

Jones's younger brother was a stockbroker at Merrill Lynch in Boston. He knew about the company's financial woes and mentioned it Uncle, his best customer. Uncle in turn mentioned it to Kurt. Kurt told Peter he'd like to look into the company and Peter agreed it was a good idea.

As I said, Kurt was a smart guy. In an hour, he convinced Charlie Jones that his company needed experienced financial management. A new holding company would purchase the stock of Jones Printing for one dollar and agree to assume its liabilities, including the bank debt. Most important to Charlie, however, was that Kurt told him he would continue to manage the company's day to day operations and act as co-trustee of the pension and profit sharing plan. Kurt never mentioned Peter, the failed hotel business, or the Philadelphia indictment. Beatrice testified that Kurt presented himself as an independent entrepreneur with financial backing from his father. And Kurt charmed Charlie with stories of his success running the investment club at Wharton. Beatrice said Charlie was much taken with Kurt, though she turned to the jury with an *I-knew-better* look. "He didn't fool me," she said before I could object. The judge instructed the jury to disregard her comment, but that was like asking someone you insulted to forget rather than forgive—just another example of the law demanding the impossible.

I had slid my chair away from the table and was sitting with one leg over the other, affecting casual indifference so the jury wouldn't think Beatrice's testimony was important. But then the prosecutor asked her to describe a meeting at Marinelli's restaurant. "What's going on?" I whispered to Peter. "I'll explain later," he said.

The prosecutor showed Beatrice a set of handwritten notes, which she said she had written during the meeting. In attendance were Kurt, Uncle, and two other men, Joe Girardi and Jack Burke. As soon as she described them, I knew their real names: Gavencci and Delaney. She then testified that about fifteen minutes into the meeting a man and a young woman joined them, introducing themselves as Ed and Jennifer Talman. "Do you see Mr. Talman in the courtroom?" the prosecutor asked Beatrice. "Yes," she said and pointed at Peter. The prosecutor didn't ask her to look around the courtroom for Jennifer Talman. You know why, Molly, and I was to know a few minutes later. I wish she would have told me that she was at the meeting, but I guess it wouldn't have made a difference. Oh, and a lawyer showed up as well. Guess who. No, don't guess. You'd never think . . . it was Arnold Conklin. Can you stand it! I don't know how he got involved—just another one of those crazy coincidences. Anyway, Arnold said he was representing Uncle.

I should tell you about the prosecutor. What an asshole. He was the head of the Boston Strike Force, a fellow named Peter Varick.

If my friend had been present, I would have wrung his neck. For all he had told me, there was so much information he had withheld.

The chief of the Organized Crime Section didn't want to leave the case to some inexperienced assistant United States Attorney in the Newark office, and Varick had asked to try the case. You see, Varick wanted Peter in the worst way, was looking to use Gavencci and Delaney to get him, then turn on his own witnesses and put the Savin Hill gang out of business. I have to tell you, Molly, no one can outdo our government when it comes to back stabbing and treachery, two sins God should have included in the Ten Commandments instead of those trivial vices like fucking your neighbor's wife and . . . sorry, there I go again.

I had never met Varick. He'd been with the Justice Department for only a year. He had struck out in private practice—no surprise, he's a dope—and what better place is there for a lousy lawyer than the government. You're laughing, I can hear you. You're saying I should remember my own house of lousy lawyers. But I would never have hired Varick. His cloying self-righteousness could make you puke.

I liked his assistant, Susan Gold. She was a straight-up person, careful to say what she meant, too young to be jaded and smart enough to know that our way of life wouldn't be destroyed if Peter enjoyed the same freedom as the rest of us. She even tried to talk Varick into agreeing to the deal I proposed. Peter would plead guilty to one count of embezzlement; the other embezzlement counts and money-laundering charges would be dismissed. I also suggested that Varick agree to a five-year sentence to run concurrently with the Philadelphia sentence. If the Court of Appeals vacated the Philadelphia conviction, Peter would be out of jail in a few years. I knew he'd be pleading guilty to what he didn't do, but after what happened in the Philadelphia case . . . it didn't matter. Varick said no way. He hadn't come to Newark to be a nice guy.

You know what else pisses me off. Susan was probably having an affair with Varick. Ugh! She looked at him like she knew he was an asshole. I don't know, Molly. Why are some women attracted to . . . no, I shouldn't say that, because you'll think I'm referring to . . . and I'm really not.

I shut off the recorder and reached for my wallet. I wanted to call Susan Gold at home. She would tell me the name of my friend. Finally, I would know. I took her card and sat at the desk. My finger shook as I punched the keys. After two rings, Susan came on the line. She sounded tired. I could hear the echo of my breathing in the mouthpiece. I could not speak. If I asked Susan his name, I would be telling her with whom I spent those nights at Murphy's. I could not betray my friend.

Her insistent hellos faded into nothingness as I hung up the phone.

Beatrice testified that Kurt introduced Talman as another Conklin client who knew of a shrimp importing business for sale at a bargain price. (Peter later told me it was Uncle who found the shrimp business and talked Peter into agreeing to manage it if Jones went along with using the pension money to fund the acquisition.) Arnold pointed out that the deal required $2,000,000 to lock up, though the money would be returned to the pension fund within thirty days after the closing, together with a $100,000 fee. Varick asked Beatrice what she thought of the deal. I objected. It wasn't relevant what Beatrice thought. Varick asked her if she ever told Charlie what she thought, and I objected again. Her opinion, even if expressed, wasn't relevant. But Beauregard said she could answer the question, and I had to sit there listening to Beatrice smugly calling everyone a crook.

Varick said he had no further questions. Beauregard looked at me, expecting I'd cross-examine. But I'd been a lawyer for too long to step on an obvious landmine. Varick had deliberately avoided asking the most obvious question: what had Talman/Peter said during the meeting. I asked to see her notes. They only said he was present with his wife. (They do make an attractive couple.) I knew she'd testify she hadn't made a note of everything said and would volunteer some inculpatory comment Peter had supposedly made. Varick wanted me to bring out the statement. He knew if he did it, I'd get her to admit it wasn't in her notes. Besides, he would be calling Gavencci, Delaney—maybe also Arnold—for corroboration. And because I couldn't call Peter to the stand—Varick would bring out his Philadelphia conviction—I'd have to call Mrs. Talman, and you know what that would have meant. Varick was a goddamn snake; he knew who Mrs. Talman was and knew I knew.

I told Beauregard he could excuse Beatrice. He raised his eyebrows to let the jury know he was surprised. A trick of the trade. On appeal, the judges receive only the transcript. They can't see the trial judge's expressions that said more than words.

I visited Peter that evening at the Union County jail. It was a twenty-minute drive from my hotel. Remember? The fancy hotel across from the Short Hills Mall where every night I ate alone in the candle-lit restaurant, obsessing over what game to order from the menu and what game to play in court, where you came to see me that one time, that wonderful Indian summer evening, when we sat on the terrace, the mellow Merlot, caviar, the piano player singing show tunes . . .

He and Molly were having an affair. I could not believe it. Yet, it would explain his snide joke about coveting thy neighbor's wife.

Peter had been moved to Union County, because it was the closest prison to Newark. It is one-thousandth the size of Riker's. I doubt if it houses more than thirty prisoners, squashed together in two rooms they call dorms. The guards lounge around with feet propped up on desks, smoking Pall Malls and watching TV.

The visiting rooms are on the eighth floor. I rode an elevator with a Seeing Eye on the ceiling. When the doors opened a voice from a speaker told me to turn left and continue to the waiting room. There was no place to sit in the waiting room: two desks where the guards sat, a table and water cooler, and a boom box playing country and western music. In a corner were two TVs, one tuned to a soap opera, the other offering a split-screen view of the hall and elevator. The guard at the first desk told me to wait in the conference room.

The conference room was a squalid dustbin six feet square. A red no smoking sign in curlicue letters was taped to the wall above the table. The window was open, exposing rusted bars, two of which were bent as if someone had tried to climb out. Cigarette butts were wedged in the metal track. The room was stuffy and had the feel of a closet full of old clothes. I lit a cigarette and stuck my face in the opening between the twisted bars, thinking this must be how the resident of a tenement feels when trying to cool off on a hot summer day. A policewoman was putting a ticket on the windshield of my car. I hadn't put any coins in the meter. I guess I had wanted to break the law before visiting Peter.

Peter came in carrying an armload of documents. He looked like he had just gotten out of bed. He was wearing standard jail issue: a gray crepe pajama suit with drawstring in the back and brown shoes that looked like moccasins. His face was sallow and his eyes were bloodshot. But I could still see the toughness in him, a hardness both emotional and physical, that strength that would keep him from giving up or giving in. This quality seemed to complement the wiry, tightly muscled body he inherited from his father along with the sloping shoulders of a man who stayed in shape, and a prominent Adam's apple framed by two folds of muscle on the sides of his neck. He looked like the younger Salvatore in the photographs at the restaurant.

"Put out the cigarette," he said, dumping the documents on the table.

"What will they do?"

"Make you move in with me. Suspend your visiting privileges. Put me in the hole for encouraging you. Take your pick."

I squeezed the butt in among the others in the windowsill.

"You looked fine in court," I said. "Now you don't look good."

"I got some bad news when I returned from court. Joanie died this afternoon."

"How?"

"She was riddled with cancer. They found it three days ago. She was too interested in divorcing me to notice that her body had turned against her. The surgeon opened her, took a quick look, closed her right back up. That's what they do when they don't like what they see."

"That's what we all do."

"So much for her divorce action."

"You weren't contesting it."

"Right. I pled guilty to being a lousy husband a long time ago."

"Have you called . . . "

"No. You tell her."

"If you want." I needed another cigarette. I looked out the window. The ticket on my car was hanging by a corner under the windshield wiper. A gust sent it soaring like a paper airplane.

I thought about what I'd say and her reaction. Under different circumstances, they'd wait an appropriate amount of time and then announce a wedding date. I wondered how I would feel. What was the use? If I was going to worry, I would worry whether she'd still want to marry Peter, be the jailhouse wife that longs for the diluted pleasure of seeing her husband in a prison that allows conjugal visits.

"Give me one of those," he said.

I handed him a cigarette and lit it. "What happened to worrying about getting caught?"

"I'll blame it on you."

I sat at the table and stared at the pile of documents. The case wouldn't come down to pieces of paper, exhibits, and company memos. Testimony would be the key. "You never told me about the dinner at Marinelli's."

He shrugged. "I didn't want to."

"Why not?"

"You'd be pissed. You know, bringing her along, using the fake name."

"I'm pissed anyway."

"Hey, I'm not going to apologize when things happen beyond my control."

"You could have controlled your hormones."

"Yeah, and what about her hormones?"

Molly, this is no time to lie. I confess. I lost control. I lunged at him. Me, of all people. The last time I was that angry I stoned Mike Zermansky. Peter fell back and the chair slid out from under him. Then I was on top of him with my hands around his neck. I would have crushed his Adam's apple, but stopped when I heard footsteps. We had just returned to our chairs when the guard entered.

"I smell smoke," he said, looking at the papers scattered around the floor, one smoldering from a burning cigarette that had rolled under the table.

"The wind is blowing this way from the factories east of town," Peter said.

"Ain't no factories east or west of town. None north or south either." He looked out the window. "That your Benz down there?"

"Yes."

"You're getting a ticket."

I looked out the window. A different policewoman was writing out a ticket. "I got one already. It blew away."

"You want to go tell her?"

Peter was grinning like a kid who just had a good time in a scuffle with a buddy. "I'll stay with my client," I said.

The guard nodded and backed away from the window. As he was walking out, he said, "Keep the racket down the next time you have a disagreement on a legal point."

"It wasn't a legal point," Peter said.

The guard wasn't sure how to take this, so he just shrugged and walked out.

Peter said, "Is it too late to say I'm sorry for what happened?"

"Yes."

"Too bad, because I am sorry."

"It's always too late to be sorry. If it weren't, there'd be nothing to be sorry for."

"Get me out of here and I'll make it up to you."

I switched off the recorder. Although it was only half-past nine, I decided to go to the club. Maybe McKinley would be there. Listening to the tape saddened me, but I was not sure why. What had Peter done to my friend? Who had accompanied him to Marinelli's? Not his wife. Someone else.

I turned on the television. Not a single channel was broadcasting reports of the bombings. I laughed. I had assumed I was surrounded by a city in fear. Now it seemed that only I was afraid.

The manager, a placid looking fellow smaller than even Salvatore, said McKinley would not arrive for work until eleven. I sat on the same couch as the previous night. The recorder was in my shirt pocket and I set the volume so only I could hear. I put my head back, closed my eyes, and listened.

Peter had gone to the window and was squeezing his shoulders between the bars. Then, in a Houdini-like move, he twisted around and faced me. He held the bars the way you hold the chains when you're sitting on a swing "A fly on the wall was more involved in the conversation than I was," he said. "I was there to talk to my father."

"What do you mean?"

"He never wanted me involved with them. I wanted him to know that the deal was legit."

"What did he say?"

"He said nothing they do is legitimate."

"I don't get it. Didn't he know . . . didn't you know they were setting you up?"

"I didn't know Hauer submitted phony draw requests to First Security Bank. I didn't know they were going to testify against me. I was concerned that the indictment was getting in the way of business. I saw nothing wrong with what I was doing."

"And the phony name?"

"The smart thing to do. Charlie Jones was a strait-laced guy. I could see his reaction if he thought he was doing business with the Mafia."

"He was eating at a Mafia restaurant."

Peter laughed. "Maybe he likes Mafia cooking. For all I know, he hates Jews but loves their blintzes."

"Tell me everything you remember."

"What's there to remember? Arnold did most of the talking. Made the shrimp business sound like the greatest opportunity since . . . " He stopped.

I spoke without rising. "Your Honor, I would like to postpone the hearing until this afternoon."

"Would you also like to stand when addressing the court?"

I stood. "I need time to speak with my client."

"He's sitting next to you. We'll wait."

I looked at Peter. He was shaking his head. He scribbled a note on the yellow pad. His long, bony fingers reminded me of Leonard Stone. The note said, "Withdraw the request."

"Well, counselor," Beauregard said. "Do you wish to speak to your client?"

Susan and Varick were staring at me. Smitty was smiling. "We're waiting," Beauregard said.

"I withdraw the motion, your Honor." Smitty's smile expanded across his face.

Varick didn't waste a moment. "Your Honor, when a cat climbs out of the bag, it doesn't want to be put back in. During the recess, I learned from Agent Corcoran that there is a tape, and it may be pertinent to the case. We are prepared to tender a copy to defense counsel."

"I object," I said.

"Object to what?" Beauregard said.

"Your pretrial order requires exhibits to have been marked prior to trial."

"Yes, it does, but I don't believe in running from the truth. If the tape contains relevant evidence, it ought to be admitted." He looked at Varick. "Mr. Varick, listen to the tape during recess. We'll decide tomorrow if it should be admitted. Is your next witness ready?"

Varick looked around the empty courtroom. "He must be delayed."

"Who is your next witness?"

"Arnold Conklin."

Beauregard snickered. "It figures. Lawyers are always delayed."

"I want you to make a deal with Varick," Peter said. We were in the lockup. I could barely see Peter's face through the tinted double-paned window that separated us.

"What's going on?"

"I can't win this case. I can't testify because they'll introduce the Philadelphia conviction to impeach me. Delaney, Gavencci, and Kurt are lined up to say I was behind taking the pension fund's insurance money to buy the magazine business. Even Conklin, the snake, is going to say I was involved, say I was using a fake name at the dinner to conceal my role."

"He's right about that, isn't he?" As cynical as I was, I hated being sarcastic, especially when so much was at stake.

"You see what I mean? It's hopeless."

"That's not the reason you want to deal. It's the tape, isn't it?"

"Make the deal now," he said insistently, as if he were pleading for his life.

"I don't get it. You were the one who mentioned the conversation in the bathroom and said it would help you."

"There's something else."

"What?"

"Jesus," he said. "Is it so hard to do what I want?"

"We've got no leverage. Varick will hold out for heavy prison time."

"I don't care about that. I want you to get something else from him."

"What else could there be?"

"An agreement not to prosecute."

"Who? You? What else is there to prosecute you for?"

"Not me."

His face moved a little to the left, where I could see his eyes. They told me who he wanted to protect.

We met at a gyros joint. It was in a two-story building, the one building left in the block on which the city had planned to build apartment buildings before it ran out of money. The kitchen was set off from the small dining room by a counter with an old cash register sitting on one side and a coffee burner on the other. The place reeked with the smell of grease.

I drank a Coke and watched Varick and Smitty eat their sandwiches like they were drinking milkshakes. Susan was blowing on a bowl of hot vegetable soup. Two partially submerged pieces of green beans floated in the slop. Arnold was sitting next to her. I hadn't seen him since he represented Nate in the book partnership case. He looked the same, though he had abandoned his nondescript business suits for the slick outfit of the Mafia mouthpiece he had become: shiny black pinstripe suit, red tie with diamond tie tack, a leather belt that probably cost more than the three suits hanging in the closet of my hotel room. He was picking at a Greek salad, looking for the black olives that were buried under the dried-up lettuce.

"You wanted to talk to me," Varick said, his mouth full, a sticky white sauce sticking to his chin like plaster. Susan grabbed a napkin and dabbed the flow before it reached his tie. He accepted her ministrations like he was a baby in a high chair.

"I prefer we speak privately," I said.

"You're among friends," Varick said.

"Yours or mine?"

"We're your friend," Smitty said.

"Speak for yourself for a change, Smitty," I said.

"The fight's gone out of your guy, is that it?" Varick said, as if Peter were a defeated bull and he was the toreador.

"He'll plead to embezzlement. Drop the money laundering."

"I already rejected that proposal."

"The money was used to buy the magazine business. That's not money laundering."

"The statute says it is."

"Even if the jury convicted him of money laundering I'd win on appeal. The statute requires either concealment or financial transactions that further the commission of a crime. The embezzlement was completed when the proceeds from the insurance policy were taken."

"You're wasting your time arguing the law with me. You should be offering."

"Offering what?"

"The old man."

"Peter can't give you Salvatore."

"You mean he won't."

"Can't or won't, it adds up to the same thing. He's not going to betray his father."

I could see that Smitty didn't like the way the conversation was going, but he knew better than to open his mouth.

"Let the rats give you the cheese," I said.

Arnold stopped picking at his salad and laughed. "Rats giving the cheese. I'll have to use that line sometime, either for or against the rats I deal with these days."

"Have you listened to the tape?" I asked Varick.

"Not yet."

Smitty had finished his sandwich. A piece of lamb was stuck to his tie, hanging by one end like a worm. "We told him what's on the tape," he said, flicking the lamb off his tie.

"Then you know it was Delaney and Gavencci who came up with the idea to use the insurance money."

"Doesn't mean your guy wasn't involved," Varick said.

"He was set up," I said.

"You're wasting my time."

He was right, but I had to try. It ran counter to my lawyer's mentality to plead Peter guilty for no reduction in sentence. And I didn't know how to ask for her protection.

"Your guys won't testify the way you expect," I said. "Maybe Kurt will, but not Delaney and Gavencci."

"What makes you say that?" Varick asked. He was interested.

"The old man is watching the trial. They know what will happen if he finds out what they did."

"Are you threatening me, because if you are—"

"Get off your donkey, Varick. I'm not threatening you. I was in the strike force. A prosecutor, like you. I know the rules of the Mafia game and I know the rules of the prosecution game. Their rules may stink, but yours stink worse. You go after people because of who they are not what they've done. You decide whom you want to nail. And you've got hundreds of nails in your toolbox. Where do you come off being so high and mighty? Someone might upset your little game, might take the law, not in their hands, but out of yours. Face reality, Varick. They don't live by your rules. Salvatore isn't going to like it when he realizes your rats served Peter to the rodent patrol. Maybe he already knows. Maybe that's why he sits in the courtroom. It won't be the first time an informant got on the stand and—"

"He's got a point, Varick," Smitty said, taking a bone from his plate and chewing on it.

"I can't give you what you want," Varick said. He sounded almost apologetic, like he was actually embarrassed that he was a prosecutor. And Susan was looking at him like she had just seen him for the first time.

"What can you give me?" I asked.

"He pleads to one count of embezzlement and one count of money laundering. I make no recommendation. The Judge sentences him to whatever."

"Beauregard will follow the sentencing guidelines."

"So?"

"It could mean ten years."

"What of it? He's stuck with more in Philadelphia."

"That conviction will be reversed."

"You're an optimist."

"Better than being a pessimist." I was running out of time. "I need something else."

"What?"

"Immunity."

Smitty stuck a finger in Varick's plate and removed a piece of feta cheese. He licked it while his eyes remained fixed on me.

"I don't get it," Varick said. "Immunity for whom? Peter—"

"Not Peter," Smitty said. "There's another part of the tape we haven't told you about. He plunked the cheese in his mouth, took a single bite, and said, "Our buddy here wants immunity for the beautiful Mrs. Talman—Erin Brandt."

Peter pled guilty. As you know, Molly, Beauregard gave him the ten years. I was disgusted. The Sam Brandt we knew would never have gone along with what Peter wanted. He would have resigned from the case rather than cave in like that. Even if it meant putting his daughter at risk. For him, doing what was right for the client, regardless of what the client wanted and regardless of his daughter . . . he would have done what the law said he had to do, just like I did in New Mexico, threw my love for Judy out the window so the room would be empty except for my legal toys . . .

After court that day, Varick played the tape for me. Erin was stupid, what can I say? A week before the trial, yet. Meeting Whitey at Jimmy's. Watching him slobber over lobster, slobber over her. Letting him paw her . . . you should listen to it, Molly. No, you shouldn't listen to it. It would make you angry, too angry. Then, when he's got a hand on her . . . she begs him to testify Peter had nothing to do with the embezzlement, that it was Kurt's idea from the start, which, of course, it was. Delaney is eating it up, and I'm not talking about the lobster. In between chirps that sound like an out of tune bugle—his idea of a love call—he's saying "obstruction of justice." Must have said it a half-dozen times. What a half-ass-backward world. She's asking Delaney to tell the truth, and he's acting as if she wants him to lie.

Varick listening to the tape and smiling. Made me want to push his nose through his head. Smitty wasn't smiling. Maybe he was worried. He knew Varick's next order of business would be to go after the Savin Hill crew. And when that happened, they'd stick it to Smitty, though God knows he would deserve whatever they did to him.

Molly . . . I'm standing here counting the number of people dead, dead because of what I started. The first one I can deal with. Never thought I'd be happy about someone's death, but there's a lot I never thought. One dead, two alive, and the two worth more than twice the one. But I was stupid. I didn't count on . . . well, I just assumed Salvatore . . . and I should have known that Salvatore never breaks a promise and he said he wasn't interested in taking out Gavencci and Vincente, at least not right away. No great loss, of course, but Danny . . . I assumed it was Smitty who got Danny to take out Salvatore. But I know better; Smitty isn't like that. Still, according to Connie, Danny was trying to say Corcoran's name when he died. But . . . something's wrong there. If it isn't Smitty . . . couldn't be Lufman. Talks tough, but he's not a killer. He knows he's getting money out of me . . . he couldn't have hit Jimmy. It had to be somebody who knew how to . . . Jimmy . . . I can't believe it. I loved that guy . . . his father worked in the subway, can you imagine . . .

Clearly, he had not made this tape several months ago as Molly had said. I was beginning to think that despite addressing "Molly", he had made this tape for me, or at least for Molly and me.

I filed a motion to transfer Peter to New York, said it was for my convenience so I wouldn't have to go to New Jersey to work with him on the appeal. Bullshit. There was nothing from which to appeal. He pled guilty. But I said we would appeal and claim Beauregard violated the guidelines when he used the Philadelphia conviction to increase the sentence. Beauregard granted my motion and Peter was sent to Riker's. I knew that's where they'd send him. The federal lockup in Manhattan was full. It's always full.

I had dinner at the restaurant and, afterwards, cognac with Salvatore. I told him what I had in mind. He hugged me like a son and told me a story. He would tell it often. The story when he was a boy and went to the volcano with his father . . .

Scratching drowned out his voice and then several seconds elapsed. The familiar click and . . .

Hear that. Sounds like rain. Feels like rain, but it's the spray off the bow. This is no place for a lawyer, believe me. You should see us. I don't look like a yachtsman, feel like a wanderlust who hitched a ride on the Kon-tiki, or that shipwrecked explorer, what was his name, oh yeah, DeVaca with the black slave Esteban, the hulking Moor, the guy the Indians believed was a god—until they killed him, which makes sense, the faithful always kill their gods—only here McKinley is the master and I'm the slave. I hope he knows what he's doing. I tried to drive the goddamn thing, but it's not like steering my model boat by remote control.

The Korean chickened out. Worried he would be caught and deported. You should have been there. McKinley may be old, but he gave the Korean such a whack on the back of his head it knocked him out cold. We left him at the dock, put him in a garbage can, actually; he's covered with leftover Chinese food.

It's going to happen any second. Hope the blasting cap works. And the timer over in Long Island City . . . shit, it's loud.

I only got a minute. I never told you when I got the idea, the exact instant it came to me. It was after the sentencing. I was on the plane ... through the window, I could see Elizabeth, could even see the Union County Jail. The plane took a left turn, flew over the coastline of Jersey— Statue of Liberty on one side, lower Manhattan on the other. The water, the sky, blue, blue like the hull of my model boat. Flying gracefully over the East River. Queens. LaGuardia and Riker's. Recalled my time there, brief as it was. The idea hit me like a lightening bolt, jagged, sharp like the drawings in my favorite comic books, when the hero has the idea that will save civilization. I'm no hero, can't save civilization, but maybe I can—

This is it, Molly. Listen. Holy shit! A wall ... oh, jeez, watch it, McKinley ... goddamn, it's like those shoeboxes falling at Steiner's when I was a kid ... I wish the crickets were cheering me on ... Molly, Molly ... say a prayer.

CHAPTER FIFTEEN

May 23–24, 1998

A FEW MINUTES PAST MIDNIGHT. *Waiting for Gene Lufman. Pint of Guinness in front of me. Reluctant to drink and lose my senses. Afraid not to drink and lose my courage. One hand on the glass, the other inside my jacket, feeling the envelope, its thickness, remembering how McKinley's knurly fingers flipped through them while he counted and called out the new total after each bill.*

The television screen was blank. Would I ask the bartender to turn it on? Would I ask him if he knew Patrick? He could have been Patrick, with his young face and easy manner. He was chatting with two young men at the other end of the bar. I lifted my glass and drank, drank until it was empty, until I could see the bottom of the glass, a reflection, a familiar face, not the face of Gene Lufman.

"We specialize in doing other people's dirty work."

He sounded different, resigned, tired. Smith Corcoran's brashness was gone.

I pantomimed a drink from the empty class. "You have come for Lufman?" I asked.

"Lufman is a chickenshit. He tells us if we want our share, we have to get it."

"We?"

"Me."

"Very Irish."

"What is?"

"Doing the dirty work of others."

"We wouldn't know. We're not Irish."

"No? I thought you were."

"German, so our mother claims. Personally, we figure it was a Jap. I mean, look at our nose. It's a Jap nose. What the fuck. Corcoran was the jerk she married when we were five. Paddy O'Corcoran. But we got rid of the goddamn "O." Like somebody probably did with you, Mr. Cornelius O'Sullivan. O'Corcoran. What a lush. A crazy, drunken Irish lawyer. Wrote wills, needed people to die to make a buck. Got disbarred when they caught him stealing money from an estate. Went back to Ireland. Owns a potato farm and some fucking sheep. Never heard from the bastard."

"Your mother?"

"What's with the small talk, Sullivan? You got the money?"

"Yes."

"The hundred-fifty grand?"

"Fifty."

"It was supposed to be a hundred-fifty."

"McKinley gave me fifty."

"Fuck. He's not going to like this."

"Who?"

"Lufman. Who else? We don't do what he says, he blows us out of the water. Hah, that's a good one. Like our fucking friend thinking he can blow Riker's into the water and get away with it. Shit, he was an idealist when we met him twenty-six odd years ago. He was such a goddamn ninny, talk about wet behind the ears, a hick, if you ask us, full of all those bullshit ideals that might work on Pluto, but don't work on this fucking piece of real estate. And he's still an idealist. Fuck it, we need a drink."

He snapped his fingers and the bartender left the two men. Corcoran ordered a glass of draft beer.

"What happened?"

"What happened where?"

"Today. The bombings."

"You don't know. The nigger didn't tell you?"

I cringed.

"Come off it, Sullivan, how many black folks in Belfast? Not too many, huh. You fucking Irishmen are just as bigoted as us good fucking American white men."

"I heard that Patrick died."

"He's not the only one."

The bartender placed the beer in front of him. Corcoran reached in his pocket. "Shit, left our goddamn wallet in the car. Give us the money."

"Who else died?"

"The man wants to be paid for the beer. Give us the money."

I took out the thick envelope and handed it to him. He removed a hundred-dollar bill. "Now, the asshole will feel shorted. Fuck if we care." He put the bill under a plastic ashtray.

"Who else died?"

"Your buddy."

He saw the look of horror on my face. It was not possible. The tape was in my pocket. He must have survived.

"Fucking shit. You look like you're having a goddamn heart attack. Not that buddy. Your fucking twin, Tommy Glynn. He got in a fight with a guard, knifed him in the leg. Didn't kill him, though. Should have. The guard pulled his gun. One shot. No more Tommy Glynn. So much for the best laid plans . . . "

Tommy had joined my father. It had come to naught, everything, every day, every minute, every walk on the street, every glance at the city, every sentence at Murphy's, every Guinness, every memory, every death . . . "Did anyone escape?"

"Like who?"

"Peter Marinelli?"

"Missing."

He finished his drink and got off the stool. "It's late Sullivan. Better get some sleep. Big day tomorrow."

"Tomorrow?"

"You're a key witness. At least Gold and Varick think you are."

"Witness to what?"

"They're not sure. The agent tailing you finally managed to keep up. Last night he saw you leave here, but he lost you when you got in the limo. And what's really a hoot is he didn't recognize our friend. The fucking nitwit wouldn't recognize Paul Newman if he saw him."

"Who is Paul Newman?"

"Sullivan, don't split our gut."

"Please, I do not know—"

"Only the greatest fucking actor of all time. The best, positively the best, was when he played Harper. Shit, wish we were a private dick instead of an asshole . . . "

Somehow, the worst of times have a way of being the silliest of times. *"What is his name?"* I asked.

"Who?"

"My friend."

"Jesus, fucking Christ on a stick, you don't know, do you."

"No."

"Ho, ho, ho. If you knew, you'd have to lie to Varick. Wouldn't want you to lie to Varick. He doesn't like liars."

"What should I say?"

"As little as possible."

He was halfway to the door when he stopped and returned. *"By the way, where's Crosetti?"*

He saw the answer on my face. He also saw a question. *"When? Where?"*

"Last night."

He seemed scared. *"Who?"*

"I thought it might be you."

He walked to the other end of the bar and looked out the window, checking in both directions before returning.

"Who were you looking for?" I asked.

"Nobody."

"Is the other agent still following me?"

"We called him off. Told him we'd take over. But we're fucking tired. So, do us a favor and go home. But to be safe . . . "

He looked at his watch again. *"There's got to be a back door to this joint."*

He moved along the bar and spoke to the bartender. He came back and stood behind me. I watched him in the mirror. *"Don't look so down, Sullivan,"* he whispered. *"It was a bullshit idea from the start. Clever guy, to be honest with you, even if he was a bumpkin. We knew he was smart from the start, maybe too smart for his own good. He was an idealist, though. No question. Did he tell you about the case against old man Lufman? Still have a good laugh when we remember it. The old man was a trooper. Never could get the goods on him, never could get him worried, he did his thing, all the time, anytime. Once, at this beer joint, Berghof's, after he was acquitted . . . we were having a couple of beers, so our buddy, big shot young prosecutor, but with his fucking head in the clouds, he walks by, sees us, can't resist, comes inside, we offer him a beer and he looks like he's gonna pee, that's how worried he was about being seen with the mob . . . Christ, we have to hand it to him . . . he came a long way, we came a long way baby.*

"Look at yourself, Sullivan. You should be fucking ashamed. You're fucking ready to cry. The plan blew up in his face. Don't be so damn depressed. The fucking grand scheme, a scheme only a lawyer could think up. No, not just any lawyer. A fucking fed up lawyer. Blew up bigger than the bombs the dumb ass Korean made for him from a bullshit recipe Glynn got from some fucking bomber over at that prison in Northern Ireland, Long Kesh, something like that. Fucking crazy. He could have built a better bomb from a recipe on the Internet. Can't blame us. Did our part. Fucking Boston cops, rest of the Bureau, still think . . . listen to us . . . we talk too goddamn much . . . fucking problem our whole life."

I looked away and stared at his reflection in the glass. I felt him moving away. He was walking through a door next to the far end of the bar. I called the bartender over and pointed at the door. "Where does that lead?"

"The alley."

I got off the stool. I would follow him, make him tell me my friend's name. Out the door and into the alley, an alley like the one I had stumbled through that night at Marinelli's. The alley was empty.

I walked to the left, toward Second Avenue. Jutting out from the opposite wall was a step that led to a recessed metal door. Something was set against it. But then I heard the sound of air, and before I could react a great weight fell on me—dead weight. A sticky substance covered my face. I pushed against the weight and an envelope fell into my hand, the envelope I had just given Corcoran.

I lowered the body to the ground. My back was to the end of the alley that opened onto Second Avenue. What little light there was allowed me to see as far as the door to Murphy's. I thought I saw a shadow in the shape of a man. I scrambled to my feet and ran to Second Avenue.

I double-locked the door and shoved the desk against it. Next, I removed my bloody clothes and washed the blood off my face. After I put on a clean pair of slacks and shirt, I went to the desk and found Susan's card. I started to dial her number and then stopped. Seeing the tapes lying on the floor next to my old shirt changed my mind. I hung up the telephone and went to the back window. I opened it and crawled out. In a rear corner of the yard, I found a stone planter filled to the rim with caked dirt. I dug a hole and buried the tapes and the money. It took all my strength to lift the planter and push it through the window into the apartment.

Exhausted, I lay on the bed. As I started to doze, I heard a noise. How foolish and unthinking I had been to leave the window open. I turned and saw a man. He was holding a gun. I could not see his face, just his hair, blonde and straight. A tube was attached to the barrel. I heard what sounded like a kernel of corn popping and felt a sharp pain in my neck that pushed into my shoulder. It was as if a heavy object had suddenly fallen on me. I rolled off the bed. In rapid succession I heard footsteps, a screech so high pitched it stung my ears, another click, a thud, and the same rush of air I had heard in the alley behind Murphy's. Something rough, like flypaper, but familiar, rubbed against my face and my eyes until I saw another set of eyes, green and bright, peering into mine, wide open as my own eyes closed and blackness darkened my mind.

I could not understand how black could have turned to white. Then I saw a planter and was relieved. It must be day. Sleep had erased the night. But the planter was not made of stone. I twisted my head. That pain again, shooting into my shoulder then down my side. A clock on the wall. I realized I was not in my studio. I lost consciousness.

Three people stood around the bed. One, a man dressed in white, a doctor perhaps. Gold and Varick were on the other side. Susan was smiling; Varick was frowning. A hand, not from them, touched my head. Mary.

Mary had gone to the cafeteria. Gold and Varick were standing by the bed. Another man entered. In his dark suit, he looked like Smith Corcoran. But he was not Smith Corcoran. Then I remembered. The alley. The stickiness. The blood.

"My name is Special Agent Jones. You have the right—"

"What happened?" I asked.

"We'll ask the questions for now," Varick said. He nodded at Jones to continue.

Susan raised her hand like a schoolgirl seeking attention. Varick frowned but she ignored him. "Mr. Sullivan, you were shot in the neck. The bullet missed your jugular by a fraction of a centimeter. When Agent Jones found you, you had lost a lot of blood. You were lucky."

"Where is Agent Corcoran?"

"Dead. Shot in the face. Behind Murphy's. What can you tell us about that?"

"Nothing."

Jones shuffled his feet. "Excuse me, sir, the reading of the rights."

"Screw the rights," Varick said. "We're just trying to get information."

"Tell us what you know, Mr. Sullivan." Susan said.

"Nothing. I . . . I . . . a man came through the window . . . I do not know . . . "

"Mr. Sullivan, would you prefer—"

"No! Who shot me?"

Varick and Susan looked at one another. It seemed that they did not want to tell me.

"After he shot you," Varick said, "you must have managed to get the gun from him and—"

Suddenly, there was something more important than the identity of my assailant. "No, I did not . . . Bright, green eyes . . . My cat, Cuchulainn, where is he?"

"This is not the time for cats," Varick said.

"Your cat is fine, Mr. Sullivan," Susan said. "Your wife is taking care of him."

"I know what happened. He tripped over Cuchulainn and the gun went off."

Susan smiled. "As I said, Mr. Sullivan, you were lucky."

"Cuchulainn's namesake was a great Irish hero."

Varick forced a smile. "Was he also a cat?"

"Tell me now. Who shot me?"

"Kurt Hauer," he said.

My shock was overcome by a memory. "K, K, K . . . "

"What's that, Sullivan?"

"Nothing."

"You were mumbling something."

"No, I was remembering."

"Remembering?"

"When you came to see me at my studio, you mentioned another Marinelli, a Daniel or Danny, I believe."

"What about it?"

"Did Mr. Hauer have anything to do with Salvatore Marinelli's death?"

"What makes me think you know more than you are letting on?"

"I could not tell you."

He twisted his nose and sniffed, like a weasel testing the air. "You went to Boston yesterday?"

"How do you know?"

"Delta Airlines told us. As soon as there's an act of terrorism, the airlines send us their passenger manifests. Why did you go?"

"I was interested in Tommy Glynn. When I heard about the bombing on the news, knowing, of course, Tommy was to be transported to Belfast, I decided to speak to his sister."

"Did you call first? Make an appointment?"

"No."

"What made you think Mrs. Brandt would see you? Varick was eyeing Susan as he questioned me. It was evident lying would not be as easy as before.

"We talked to Mrs. Brandt," Susan said. "She said you had called."

"I must have forgotten."

"Where were you when the bombing occurred?"

"In my studio."

Jones pulled a small tablet from his suit jacket pocket. "My notes say that ten minutes after the first explosion you were walking west on 51st Street."

"I took a morning stroll. I like the mornings."

"My notes do not show you leaving the apartment. In fact, they reflect that you didn't return to the apartment after you left the night before."

My father used to tell me it is best to show anger when lying. Anger, he said, makes one sound truthful and indignation makes one sound righteous. I said with all the anger and indignation I could summon: "Your notes are incorrect!" But my words sounded so stiff I wanted to laugh.

"Can you account for your whereabouts from Midnight until six-thirty?" Varick asked.

Mary entered the room, dressed in a long white dress, my angel. "Cornelius telephoned me from the studio," she said. Her face seemed thinner than the morning at the Belfast airport when we said our farewells.

"What time was the call, Mrs. Sullivan?" Susan asked.

"Half past seven in the morning. I was waiting for the polling place to open."

"Two-thirty, New York time," Varick said. "How do you know he was calling from the studio?"

"He said he was tired and retiring for the night."

Varick rubbed his nose. It was obvious he did not believe her.

He turned to me. "How well did you know James Crosetti?"

"I told you. Not well at all. He drove us to Riker's Island to see Tommy."

"Oh, come on Sullivan. We found him, you know. Dead."

"I do not know anything." I sounded like a child whose parents had scolded him for some rebellious act.

"I think you do, Sullivan."

Mary pushed Varick and took my hand. "Can't this wait until he feels better?"

Varick looked at Susan and she nodded. "We'll come back tomorrow," he said. "One more question. Maybe one you will answer."

"Yes."

"Where is your passport?"

"I do not understand."

"It wasn't on you when Jones found you and it wasn't in your apartment."

I thought of the tapes. "You searched my studio?"

"It wasn't there. Where is it?"

"I do not know."

"The more I ask you, the less you seem to know." He walked to the door.

"Mr. Varick," I said. "In the explosion, did anyone die? Did anyone escape?"

"No one escaped. Two dead that we know for sure."

"Who?"

"Patrick Casey, a guard, and Tommy Glynn."

"Yes, Patrick Casey. I saw the announcement on television."

"He was a bartender at Murphy's."

"Are you sure about Tommy Glynn?"

"Very sure. Corcoran was on the scene within an hour of the bombing. He identified Casey and Glynn."

"You said two that you know for sure. There are others?"

Three prisoners we haven't been able to account for, probably drowned, but one in particular you might be interested in."

"Who?"

"Peter Marinelli."

"I tried to pretend I did not already know about Peter's disappearance. "Oh," I said. "The son of the restaurant owner."

"You wouldn't be able to help us on that one, would you?"

"No, I would not be able to help."

"We'll see you tomorrow, Mr. Sullivan," Susan said.

"Maybe his memory will improve," Varick said to Susan, as if he blamed her for my intransigence.

When Mary came the next morning she told me she had retrieved the tapes and the money from the planter. Though she had spent the night listening to the tapes, she wanted to know about the money. I told her what had happened.

Gold and Varick entered. Agent Jones was not with them. Varick removed papers from his briefcase and spread them on the bed.

"What are they?"

"A copy of the motion and brief we filed in court this morning," Varick said.

"I do not understand."

"Immunity, Sullivan. We're giving you immunity."

"I still do not understand."

"It means we can't prosecute you for your role in the bombings."

"I was not involved in the bombings."

"You have no reason to lie now. In fact, perjury is the one crime for which you could still be prosecuted. We suggest you tell us everything. The truth this time, please."

"I have discussed the matter with my wife. I will say nothing more."

Varick looked at Mary. "Understand this, Mr. Sullivan. You have no choice. Under the law, if you do not testify you can be jailed for contempt."

"Please look at me when you are speaking," I said.

"How long will he be in jail?" Mary asked.

"Until he testifies."

"The term of the grand jury," Susan said. "Six months."

"And we can extend the grand jury for another six months, Sullivan," Varick said. He seemed to be relishing the prospect. "And six months more, and still more until you cooperate."

"This is outrageous," Mary said. "My husband has committed no crime."

"It's the law, Mrs. Sullivan," Varick said.

"What kind of law? It is worse than the British laws. You have no right—"

"Mary, please," I said.

"What'll it be, Sullivan?" Varick said.

"I have nothing to say."

CHAPTER SIXTEEN

November 18–19, 1998

I SIT IN MY CELL *writing these words. Has it been that long? One-hundred-seventy-eight days. My cell is a spacious room above the infirmary. I believe it was previously used as an office for a staff doctor. I am the only prisoner here and eat my meals alone in the room. Each day a guard escorts me to the Anna Kross building—where Tommy had been housed—for exercise and an hour in the recreation hall. One end of the building is walled off and under construction, as it was badly damaged in the bombing.*

I have met a few inmates. Carlos Montez, a Cuban with a red pock-marked face, is awaiting sentence for the murder of an eighty-year-old woman he robbed of twenty-five dollars. He pled guilty to avoid the death penalty and will likely receive life in prison without parole. Oddly enough, Carlos is my best friend here. On the surface he is a gentle, soft-spoken man, which I suppose conceals the evil that is inside him. He tells wonderful stories of the Cuban Revolution. Fidel Castro is his hero. After his sentencing he expects to be transferred to Attica, which he says is a hellhole, far worse than Long Kesh. (Carlos is an expert on prisons; his cell is crammed with books on the subject, including a volume on famous prison escapes.)

Willy Martin and Max Stofer are always looking for a game of cards. Willy is a car thief, a profession he says he got into because he has loved cars since he was a child. When I asked him why he does not do honest work with cars, as Da had, he laughs and says the difference between kids and adults is that adults love money more than anything else. Max is a burglar and has been shuttling in and out of jail for years. He likes to read comic books, although he calls them graphic novels and says they are the best examples of post-modern art.

Occasionally, we are joined by Abdullah, a newsstand operator whose real profession is bookmaking, and Michael, the thirty-year old brother of a famous movie star, who while under the influence of cocaine drove his car through a Newark clothing store window, crushing a clerk against the sales counter.

These prisoners regard me as some kind of hero. My protestations notwithstanding, they believe I masterminded the bombing. Carlos says he used to play cards with Peter Marinelli. He claims Peter once mentioned my name, but I do not know whether to believe him. In prison, fiction is a more valuable currency than truth.

None of them has a formal education past high school but they play with ideas as much as they play with cards. They believe that despite their crimes they are political prisoners. They see their anti-social conduct as protests against an unjust society. When I suggest there is a difference between stealing and civil disobedience, they laugh as if I am a simpleton. Carlos will shed his placid exterior when challenged, one time nearly bludgeoning to death a fellow prisoner who imprudently observed that the robbery and murder of a helpless old woman was not a political act. Yesterday, Max challenged him. He said no matter in what kind of society he lived, he would be trying to steal other people's money. Political and cultural norms, he says, are irrelevant. I thought Carlos might hit him, but he was satisfied to say that in a perfect world there would be no room for capitalists.

I organize my life around visits from Mary and Susan Gold. Mary has just left. She is doing as well as can be expected, since we have agreed not to spend my friend's money. Today, I told her to return home; a daughter needs a mother more than a husband needs a wife. She said she will not leave until I am free. She has been working as a sales clerk at Macy's department store and living at the studio. She cares for Cuchulainn. She says he is growing fat and lazy.

Mary has gradually withdrawn her support for my decision. Each day she asks me why I will not tell them everything they want to know. I always answer the same way. I do not know why I remain silent, but I fear speaking more. I fear living the remainder of my life as my father did, with the knowledge I betrayed those who trusted me. Mary says I owe nothing to my friend.

I no longer care to know my friend's name. It would serve no purpose now; whatever reason he kept it to himself is reason enough for me. I have chosen to be silent and what I know or do not know is of no moment.

The appeals court has thrown out Peter's conviction in the Philadelphia case and Judge Beauregard has done the same in Newark. The disclosure that Kurt Hauer was a "hit man" while serving as a star prosecution witness offended even Beauregard's sensibilities. Moreover, if Peter is alive and apprehended, he will face charges only for the escape.

If my friend had aborted his plan, Peter Marinelli would have been free by now. And further initiatives in the Irish court might well have resulted in Tommy's release. With Da's affidavit and my newfound recollection of what happened, the evidence of his innocence was at hand. The bombing, the attempted escape, the loss of life, all unnecessary.

Why had I not voiced strong objections to my friend's plan? Why had I been so passive? At every juncture I had done as he asked. Yes, on occasion I had voiced faint-hearted protests, but I knew they would accomplish nothing. Perhaps I did not want to dissuade him. As he had mentioned that afternoon on Roosevelt Island, I behaved as a co-conspirator, however differently I viewed myself.

I think of the bond Susan and I have forged during the months of incarceration. She has acted almost as an ally, trying, for my own good she says, new ways to coax me into telling all. Her current approach is to suggest that my information will only confirm what she already knows or at least suspects. For instance, she has guessed that I was with Smith Corcoran when he was shot and that Kurt Hauer followed me to the studio. Though I generally do not respond to these bursts of intuition—if that is what they are—I did reveal to her that a man resembling Kurt Hauer had tried to enter the studio during the night of the twenty-second. Perhaps I wanted her to know the fear that was stalking me, gain her empathy, or just create an illusion of candor.

Included in what she has told me are facts not reported in the newspapers. When the Korean regained consciousness he called the police. He claimed he had done nothing more than provide blasting caps to Jimmy. He said Jimmy had told him that the plan was to blow up the warehouse in Long Island City and file an insurance claim. He said Jimmy never mentioned Riker's Island.

He became worried when instead of Jimmy an old black man (McKinley) and a middle-aged white man (my friend) arrived at the dock. He told them he was backing out and they could not take his boat. The next thing he remembered was waking up in a sea of rotten Chinese food.

Gene Lufman and Uncle Hauer have been indicted. Susan said that tapes Delaney made and gave to Smith Corcoran reveal Gene's role in the scheme to rape the pension fund, his activities as an intermediary between Salvatore and the Savin Hill gang, and his association with Uncle and Kurt Hauer. Susan said she believes Kurt had been working for Lufman since at least the acquisition of Jones Printing.

Most surprising to me is Susan's theory that it was Kurt, not Jimmy, who assassinated Gavencci and Vincente Marinelli. She believes that Kurt and Uncle were embarked on an elaborate scheme to eliminate anyone who might stand in their way.

None of this information means much to her. What she really wants to know is my friend's name. She is certain that he is the man who accompanied McKinley to meet the Korean.

Susan will soon arrive. It will be her last visit. She has tendered her resignation and will be joining a law firm in Boston. She does not know who will replace her. Not Varick. He resigned shortly after I came here. Varick left in disgust, if not in disgrace. Susan said he has rented a small office in downtown Boston, but has encountered difficulty obtaining clients.

"I have good news and I have bad news," Susan says. We are sitting at a table in the radiology room. On a screen behind her head are photographs of some poor inmate's lungs, taken from every conceivable angle. They show scarring from years of smoking. And so the urge strikes me.

"May I have a cigarette?"

She reaches in her pocketbook. "Why, Cornelius, I didn't know you smoke."

"No, but . . . "

"Can we smoke in here?"

"You represent the law."

She laughed. "Not for much longer."

I am not certain I want to hear any news, good or bad. "I never under-stood the murder of Salvatore Marinelli."

"Lufman and the Hauers wanted to continue the Savin Hill opera-tions. They needed Salvatore out of the way. Danny was a convenience. We found Kurt Hauer's address book in his Revere loft. Danny Marinelli's phone number was written on the inside cover. Poor Danny was a sucker."

"And was himself killed."

"You were there, weren't you."

"Does it matter now?"

She looks wistful, soft, vulnerable. "Only to me."

I know I must face what she has come to tell me. "Is the good news that I am to be freed? Or is the good news that I am not to be freed? Or is that the bad news? Perhaps the good and bad news are the same."

"Cornelius, I love your Irish humor."

"Morbid and fatalistic, as much a reason to cry as to laugh."

"It makes me laugh."

"Tell me the good news first."

"You have the keys to your freedom."

"How is this different from before? I have been hearing this news for six months. The keys might unlock the doors to the world but they would imprison my conscience forever."

"If you will admit you knew what was planned, but in fear for your life were afraid to speak up, I could get you out of here."

"Ah, I see. You would have me lie. Interesting. And you still want to know his name."

"If you say you don't know, I won't press you. You don't even have to tell me anything he said that might lead us to him."

"Are you not betraying your mission?"

"That's my business, Cornelius."

"But you're leaving the government. Your replacement will not be so generous."

"If you tell me now that you'll cooperate, I'll stay until you're out of here, until you're back home."

"What is the bad news?"

"We're in court tomorrow. I have to ask the judge to extend the grand jury for another six months."

"You mean ask him to keep me here for another six months."

"Yes."

"Who will represent me?"

"I don't know. You've refused to talk to the lawyer the court appointed for you."

"I am sick of talking to lawyers."

"Lawyers? More than one?"

I smile at my gaffe. "It popped into my head. You are the only lawyer I know and I love to speak to you."

"Then listen carefully. I haven't told you everything. I'm not supposed to, but . . . "

"What things?"

"Peter Marinelli must be dead. We didn't find his body, but we found his shoes. They floated ashore, not far from here. He almost certainly drowned."

"What else?"

"McKinley Washington."

"Excuse me."

"You know him, don't you?"

"Two Presidents of the United States."

"Cornelius!"

"Who is he?"

"We believe he is the black man described by the Korean. He worked at an after-hours club on 61st Street. In Crosetti's jacket there was a matchbook with the club's number scribbled on it. We interviewed the employees, showed them your picture. A waitress identified you."

"She is mistaken."

"We arrested Washington at his apartment in Harlem. His prints match those we found on Crosetti and on his limousine, which, by the way, was left parked in a lot at Kennedy Airport."

"This . . . this McKinley Washington. You think he killed—"

"No, I think Kurt Hauer killed Crosetti. But Washington was on the boat. He's old and he's scared. He'll talk and we'll know who your companion was. So it doesn't matter what you tell us. Give it up and go home."

She sees me staring at her pocketbook. "Do you want another cigarette?"
she asks.

"Yes, thank you."

It would be so easy to believe her, so easy to return home with Mary. But
I know that McKinley will not talk.

"Please, Cornelius, tell me. Let me leave this godforsaken job knowing
you will be reunited with your wife and child."

Something in her voice says she wants more than my freedom.

"I am not your concern," I say.

She wiggles her head ever so slightly. A lock of brunette hair falls over
one eye. She brushes it aside with the tip of a peach-colored fingernail. "I
might be concerned if you weren't married," she says. She is flirting with me. I
am speechless.

"I am married," I say. What a weak riposte! The truth is I am attracted
to her. Damn this prison and what it does to one's mind and heart. "I love my
wife," I say, my voice stronger now.

"Forgive me, Cornelius. I'm depressed. Fucking depressed."

"I am so sorry," I say. Here I am, facing another six months or more in
prison, and I want to comfort her. "What is the matter?"

"I thought it was my job. I thought I would feel better when I decided to
resign and work for a law firm. I'm fooling myself. It's not the job. I hate the
law. I don't know why I became a lawyer."

"You sound just like . . . "

She quickly transforms herself from the forlorn young woman into the
mature interrogator. "Who do I sound like?"

"Never mind. Why do you hate the law?"

She takes two quick puffs of her cigarette and mashes it under the heel
of her shoe. "I'm from a family of doctors. My mom and dad are doctors. So
is my brother. I didn't want to be a doctor. They never talk about patients,
only diseases. The patient is the enemy. Then I find out it's no different with
lawyers."

"If you dislike the law, why not find another profession?"

"I'm afraid I wouldn't be good at anything else."

"Do you have someone, a special someone?"

"No. I meet only lawyers and criminals. Assholes all." She puts a hand to her mouth and giggles. "But you are neither lawyer nor criminal. Listen to me. Am I daffy or what?"

My cigarette has burned down almost to the filter. She takes it and lets her fingers linger on mine. She puffs once and inhales deeply.

"I do wish you would testify, Cornelius. Otherwise, the law will never leave you alone."

"I am sorry, I cannot."

She nods and goes to the door. "Please, Cornelius. I'm sorry for the way I behaved. It was out of line. Unprofessional."

"I am not sorry," I say.

"Thank you," she says.

"Susan, I am curious about something."

"What?"

"You and Varick prosecuted Peter Marinelli."

"Yes. How did you know?"

"I read it somewhere."

If she is suspicious she does not show it. "What do you want to know?"

"I hope you will not be offended, but did you not ask yourself whether he was guilty, whether you should be relying on the testimony of admitted gangsters who protect themselves by informing, and by a young man—"

"We didn't know Kurt Hauer was a killer." She takes a step back toward me. The softness in her face is gone, her chin tightened to expose a dimple. "You get so damn wrapped up in the law you forget about the people it affects. You don't think of the defendant as a person. It reminds me of when I was in this play in college, and the director rewrote the third act. He changed the characters' lives with his pen. We do the same thing."

She looks at her watch. Her dimple disappears and the softness returns. "I'm sorry, I have to go." She knocks on the door. A guard opens the door.

"Someone else asked the same question," she says.

"Who?"

"Peter's lawyer. I gave him the same answer. He said: 'How can you live in a world where half the people are fools, and the other half hypocrites?' "

"Thomas Jefferson."

"*Thomas Jefferson said that?*"

"*Yes, in Notes on the State of Virginia.*"

"*Wow, Cornelius.*"

"*I am a historian, you know. Jefferson also said, 'Ignorance is preferable to error, and he is less remote from the truth who believes nothing, than he who believes what is wrong.' *"

She is on the verge of tears. "*See you in court, Cornelius. Thanks.*"

She is out in the hall. The door slams before I can ask her the name of Peter Marinelli's lawyer, the name I thought I no longer needed to know.

Susan Gold, disillusioned at a young age. I, Cornelius Sullivan, disillusioned at a somewhat older age. And my friend, disillusioned . . . what is the point of such thoughts, I say to myself as I sit in the recreation hall. My fellow inmates are playing poker. Cigarettes are the chips. A filter is worth two dollars, a smoked cigarette is worth five dollars, a half-smoked cigarette worth ten dollars, and a pristine, ready to be savored, never before lit cigarette is worth twenty-five.

"*What's the matter with you?*" *Carlos asks.* "*You haven't opened your mouth.*" *He has just won a pot heavy with unsmoked, cigarettes. His round stomach moves in and out, like an oxygen bag connected to a patient under anesthesia.*

"*I did not want to disturb your game.*"

Max throws down his cards and takes a comic book out of his overalls. There is a drawing of a card game on the cover. "*At least these guys in here can win hands.*"

"*You can't win shit in the can,*" *Abdullah says.*

Max laughs. "*That ain't a pot I'm interested in.*"

"*It's the only pot you'll ever sit on.*"

"*Listen to that third world bull,*" *Willy says.*

"*You lose me,*" *Abdullah says.*

Michael puts down his cards. "*This sounds like dialogue in a bad movie.*"

"*Your brother tell you that, pretty boy.*" *Carlos says.*

"*My brother doesn't tell me shit. Hasn't come to see me once.*"

"You're a criminal now," Max says. "You don't exist anymore."

"It was an accident. I was high. I didn't know what the hell I was doing."

"No such thing as accidents, my man," Carlos says. "Marx teaches us—"

"Shut up and deal," Willy says.

"I was in a movie," Max says. "I played a burglar. One line. One fucking line they gave me."

"What was it?" Willy asks.

"Finger me and I'll stick a finger up your ass."

"What kind of line is that?" Max says.

"How should I know? I ain't a screenwriter."

"What they call that?" Abdullah says.

"Typecasting," Michael says.

"I was an actor before I was a thief," Max says. "I went to the Stella Adler acting school, you know, the broad who taught Marlon Brando how to act."

The group laughs as one. "We are not interested in your fucking life," Willy says. "Let's play."

"Fuck the game," Carlos says. "We need to take care of our friend here. He looks like he's got that homesick virus, same bug that follows me around wherever I go."

"No," I say. "I am thinking about tomorrow."

I explain that I face at least another six months in jail.

"Wait a minute, man," Carlos says. "You mean to say they're not charging you with a crime?"

"Contempt. I am in contempt of the grand jury."

"I have contempt for those motherfucker capitalists."

"Hey, now," Max says. "Wait just a goddamn second. Capitalism pays the rent."

"Man, you don't know what you're saying."

"Yeah, well check this out," Max says. I steal a TV, VCR, stereo—Bose speakers are the best, they're small and I get a good price for them. Capitalism is the best economic system. The people can't do without the garbage. They work, make the bucks, then buy the garbage. I steal it, they're happy, collect the fucking insurance, they sue the fucking landlord for bad security and collect from him. I sell the garbage to a fence, maybe I get five

cents on the dollar of what it originally cost, and somebody buys the garbage for half of retail. Everybody makes out, even the insurance company because it rakes in the bucks from the suckers who are afraid of getting burgled and losing more bucks in increased premiums than they would from losing their garbage.

"I burgled this guy's house in Great Neck two times, a year apart. I liked the garbage he had the first time I was there and knew he'd replace it with garbage just as good or better. What do I find the second time? A barometer, fourteen-carat gold. The same barometer I swiped from his house the first time. I know, 'cause the glass has his initials engraved on the bottom. See what I'm saying about capitalism. People got to own things. They go crazy if they can't."

Willy's bulbous nose turns red like a light bulb. "That story—and I'm not even saying I believe it—isn't about capitalism."

"So, smart guy, what's it about?"

"A slob who is in love with a fucking barometer."

Max stands and pushes the table into Willy's chest. "Are you ragging me?"

Carlos shoves the table away and inserts himself between Max and Willy. "Are you assholes looking for some action? If you are, I'm your man."

Michael is shuffling the cards like nothing has happened. "Can't we all just get along?" he says.

The tension is broken and everyone laughs. "Funny," Carlos says. "You the wrong color to be Rodney King."

Max's body falls limp; he shakes his arms and legs, effecting the jittery movements of a man in the throes of a convulsion. More laughter as the others break into the same motion. They look like folk dancers high on drugs.

Carlos stops dancing and faces me. "What you going to do, man? You going to tell them what they want to know so you can get out of here?"

"No."

"Why not?"

"I am not sure."

The others have stopped and are looking at me.

"Man," Carlos says, "if you're going to fight the Feds, you got to have a philosophy."

"Why is that?"

"They got their philosophy and you got to have yours."

"The Feds don't have a philosophy," Michael says.

"Yeah, they do," Willy says. "If you break their rules, you're fucked."

"That's not a philosophy," Carlos says.

"This isn't helping Sullivan," Max says.

I smile at their childlike concern. "Thank you, but I do not need help."

Willy slams his fist on the table. "Damn it," he shouts.

"What's your problem now?" Carlos asks.

"No problem. I remember this guy who was in here a while back. A lawyer man. He told a judge to get lost. The judge fucked him, held him in contempt."

"I remember him," Max says. "How long ago was that? Shit, I've been in here forever. Fucking jail. Fucking island. They got plenty of clocks here, but try to find a fucking calendar."

"Time flies when you're having fun," Michael says, holding an Ace in front of his face.

"What's your point, Willy?" Carlos asks.

"I don't got to have no point," Willy says. "I'm making an observation. If a lawyer can be put in the can for telling off a judge, what chance does Sullivan got? What chance do any of us got?"

"No chance, unless we overthrow the government," Carlos says. "Eliminate the regime, that's what we got to do. Like the man Marx said, we're alienated. We have to act on our alienation. Maybe I can't start a revolution, but I can revolt. That lawyer you're remarking on. He proves what I'm saying. If he told a judge to fuck off, he was alienated. He revolted."

Willy is laughing.

"What's so goddamn funny?" Carlos says.

"One time I try to get a job at the post office. They give me a form to fill out, some goddamn security questionnaire. There's this question: 'Do you advocate the overthrow of the government by force or violence?' So I write force; I mean they were asking for one or the other."

"You didn't get the job, did you?" Michael says.

"Shit, yeah, I got the job. They even changed the question on my account."

"This is all crap, if you ask me," Max says. "That lawyer wasn't in here long enough to be alienated."

I had fallen into a kind of hypnotic haze. I slowly realized that they were referring to my friend.

"I know the lawyer," I say.

"You're shitting me," Willy says.

"I spent several evenings with him. He is the reason I am here."

"Is he your lawyer? Did he fuck you over?"

All the while Abdullah has been sitting quietly, chain smoking cigarettes from his pot. "Lawyers don't fuck, they suck."

"No," I say, "he was a fine lawyer, he . . . " I am ready to tell them what I have only told Mary. "He is the one I will not talk about. He planned the bombings."

The men look at each other to make sure they have heard correctly. "Fucking shit, Sullivan," Willy says.

"He didn't look like a revolutionary to me," Max says.

Carlos grunts. "The mind is revolutionary, asshole. Don't matter what you look like."

"Cut the crap," Willy says. "Fuck it, I can't remember the lawyer's name. Sullivan, what was the lawyer's name?"

"I do not know."

"You don't know? How can you know the sucker and not know his name? Jesus, this is fucking out of Kafka."

"Who is Kafka?" Abdullah asks.

"He used various names," I say.

"Kafka?" Abdullah says.

Willy is rubbing his chin "Not Kafka, asshole. The lawyer. Sullivan, come clean. What's the fucker's name?"

Michael is now examining a King. "Hey, we could go to the Feds, tell them what Sullivan said. They'd figure out who the lawyer is from their records. Could be our ticket out of here."

"We're not telling anybody anything," Carlos says.

"Why not?" Willy says. "For once, the kid has a good idea."

"We start snitching, we got nothing left," Max says.

"It's Sullivan's call," Carlos says.

I look at each one in turn. A murderer, a drug addict, two thieves, a bookmaker—riffraff, discontents, malcontents, society's dregs debating what they should do. I remember something I had read as a child: "He noblest lives and noblest dies who makes and keeps his self-made laws."

"What's it gonna be?" Willy asks. "Do we turn the lawyer-man in?"

"No, we do not," I say. One by one each nods his head in agreement.

Mary comes this morning with an unexpected visitor. I remember his face and see the pain that I had missed on our first meeting.

"Nice to see you, Mr. Sullivan."

"Good to see you, Dr. Bamberger."

"Even considering the circumstances, you look better than you did that day, frozen in the middle of Park Avenue."

"Much has happened."

"So I gather."

Bamberger is wearing a jacket and vest. He sweeps the flap of the jacket to one side and I see a gold chain hanging from the vest pocket. He takes out a watch and opens the cover.

I am amazed. "It looks like the watch he gave to McKinley Washington."

"It is the watch, but it doesn't keep the time anymore." He shows it to me. The second hand is not moving.

"Is it broken?"

"Press the button on the side."

I press the button and hear a voice: "How are you, Connie?" Startled, I nearly drop the watch. It is my friend's voice.

"You have seen him," I say.

"No. He sent the watch with a note."

Mary opens her pocketbook and takes out the note. She says, "He wants you to tell what you know. He says it's all right. Oh, Connie, you'll be able to get out of here."

I take the note from her and read: "Dear Connie. You didn't warn me that you had a noble streak. I needed a couple of days, not six months. The world is a big place, much bigger than their little world of law. They won't find me."

"I do not understand," I say.

"There's nothing to understand," Mary says. "It's over, thank God."

"Where is he?"

"Doctor-patient privilege," Bamberger says.

"I will not speak."

"Why, Connie? He says you should."

"I cannot."

Mary is crying. "Cornelius Michael Sullivan! What are you saying?"

"I will not be responsible for his apprehension."

"But he says they won't find him!"

I put my arms around Mary, but she pushes me away. She buries her face in Bamberger's jacket.

"I know him," Bamberger says. "He does want you to stop."

"Night after night," I say, "hour after hour, he bombarded me with his tales. I do not know if they were real or imagined. What I do know is this: he taught me that to believe in something, you must first believe in nothing."

"You're not making sense," Mary says. She lifts her head and looks at me with red eyes.

"I believed my father was an evil man. I was wrong. I will not betray my friend."

Connie, I trust you can hear this well enough. I hope my grandfather, wherever he is, isn't annoyed. It's not as if the jewels in this watch were real jewels. When you get out of there, you can take it to be repaired.

I sent you this tape because you should know the ending of both stories, the one from the past and the one in the present. But I'd rather talk about the story from the past, for our present story has ended poorly. People I loved are dead: Salvatore, Jimmy, Smitty, Patrick, Tommy. And Peter . . . I couldn't save Peter. But you're alive, Connie. Thank God. Stupid me knew Smitty was the bad guy—he was a bad guy, but he wasn't a killer—and I should have done something about the Nazi kid, Hauer.

I put the firm into bankruptcy. It was the only way to stop the Gusto suit. The rolling stone that gathers no moss gathered shit instead. Before I filed bankruptcy, I went to see my banker, William Willis III. William—he wouldn't lend you a dime if you called him Bill or Will—came from a long line of bankers. Though he was only thirty-one, he was the senior lending officer. He got to be senior—although he was just a junior—because he had never made a bad loan. He told every applicant that he was determined to keep his record unblemished, a kind of veiled threat that a borrower had better not default. Naturally, like any threat from a banker, the borrower had nothing to fear. William was ready and willing to lend additional money to cover payments in arrears. A Ponzi scheme is what we call it out here in the real world.

I told William about the proposed bankruptcy and asked him to assure me that he wouldn't declare a default. (Bankruptcy constituted a default under the loan agreement even if payments were current.) Instead of reassuring me, however, he said, "You have a problem,"—banker-speak for saying *he* had a problem.

"What's the matter?"

"Your partner, what's his name, who runs your Los Angeles office."

"Dave Lapidus."

"He owes the bank $250,000."

"I didn't know he had a loan."

William's chronic post-nasal drip was acting up. He coughed in short, discrete bursts. He sounded like a creaky door opening one inch at a time.

He smoothed his already smooth black hair and coughed again. "He said you knew."

"Why did he need a loan? He's single, his ex-wife is rich so he doesn't pay alimony, and his salary is $750,000 per year."

"We only make loans to high wage earners," he said, an illustration of an important banking principle: lend money only to those who don't need a loan.

"What I mean, William, is that with his income how could he be in default?"

"He told me he's broke."

"Impossible."

"He says he is also planning to file bankruptcy. Very unfortunate."

"You still haven't told me why he borrowed the money."

"I can't tell you. Confidential."

I called Dave from my office. The receptionist said he hadn't come in and he hadn't called for messages. I asked to speak to Jared, the next senior lawyer in the office. He said he hadn't seen Dave for three days, though he had received a strange call from a man named Applegate. Applegate said he was a client and wanted to send Dave a gift.

"What's strange about that? No, you're right. It is strange. I've never had a client who's given me anything but a pain in the ass."

"Did you ever hear of Applegate?"

"No," I said. "But so what? I don't know the names of all our clients."

"I couldn't find a file on him."

"Did you get his number?"

Jared hadn't, but I wasn't surprised. Lawyers are so busy with complexity they ignore simplicity.

"Dave is throwing a party tonight," he said. "Got the invitation a week ago."

I hadn't gotten one. "What kind of party?"

"For a movie he produced."

This was news to me. "I didn't know Dave was in the movie business."

There was silence on the other end of the line. If Jared knew what Dave had been up to, he wasn't saying.

"I'm taking a plane this afternoon," I said. "Pick me up at the American terminal at five."

I hung up and went to see Rosie, the bookkeeper.

"I know who Applegate is," Rosie said. Rosie was a jolly, chubby woman who cherished her role as financial mother hen for the firm.

"Don't keep me in suspense," I said.

"The firm's only pro bono client."

She opened a file drawer and retrieved a thin manila folder. Inside was a new client form that had been filled out six months earlier. There was a note in the section for describing the fee arrangement. It read: "No fee, pro bono." I recognized Dave's handwriting.

"Why didn't I know about this?" I asked.

"When I got the form I called Dave. He said a charity had hired him to file an investment fraud case and that it would be good public relations for the firm to handle it for nothing. He said you were all for it."

I took another look at the form. Under Applegate's name was a phone number. I thanked her and went home to pack.

On the way to the airport I called the number from the limo. Applegate's secretary said he was out. She agreed to schedule an appointment for the next morning. As soon as the call ended the phone rang. It was William.

"Good news," he said. "We got the $250,000. Came in from Wells Fargo Bank a few minutes ago."

"Good. Dave came through."

"It is good, but the money didn't come from Dave."

"Then who?"

"Just a second. Let me look at the wire advice. Lila Montenegro."

"Never heard of her."

William laughed, more of a squeak than a laugh, but then he didn't have a sense of humor. "Probably a rich widow," he said.

"I doubt it."

"A starlet with a movie contract."

"Could be. It's LA."

He squeaked again and then coughed. I wondered what William's wife was like. Then I realized I didn't know whether he was married. For all I knew he was gay, in the closet, or maybe in the vault where he had secret liaisons among the safe deposit boxes.

I thought to ask him, but you don't ask your banker a question like that.

On certain days, from a distance, Beverly Hills looks like it's floating on a cloud. The cloud is a bank of smog.

Jared picked me up in his new blood red Porsche convertible. He was independently wealthy, practiced law for the fun of it—can you imagine!—and was married to an ex-cover girl who had been operated on more times than Elizabeth Taylor. We were suing her plastic surgeon for botching the operation to take the droop out of her droopy eyes. After the operation she could no longer blink, couldn't even get her lids to close when she wanted to sleep. A hypnotist moved into their guesthouse; every night he put Jared's wife to sleep with her eyes open.

As we were driving north on the San Diego freeway I asked Jared to tell me what he knew of Dave's movie business. He said that six months before, Dave introduced him to Rodney Bates, a film producer. Bates had a deal with the Playboy channel to produce videos and was looking for a composer. Jared represented several bands and gave Bates some names. When he didn't hear back from Bates he forgot about it.

About a month later he saw a young woman come out of Dave's office. She was pulling at her sweater and tugging at her skirt, and her hair looked like it had been in front of a wind machine. Then Dave came out with a dumb grin on his face and said she was starring in a film Rodney was producing. Her name was Lila Montenegro.

Dave's house was located on one of those hills from which you can see as far as downtown LA when the smog isn't in the way. He paid a million dollars for the house. Elsewhere, it wouldn't have commanded more than $200,000. It could have been a ranch, in the mission style, but for a cathedral roof over the center, looking as though a tornado from Kansas had dumped it there, like the missing piece of an erector set. There was a garden and patio in front next to a vine covered walkway, brown from lack of water. The stucco walls were cracked in several places, and tiles were missing from the roof. The wooden eaves over the patio were splitting.

Dave's Fiat was parked next to a van in the driveway. Stenciled on the side of the van was a sign: "Bates Productions, Inc." The cul-de-sac was full of cars and we had to park a few houses away. A woman in a bikini was sitting on the second floor porch smoking a cigar and holding a miniature poodle. A man in a terry cloth robe joined her. The woman put down the poodle and bent toward his crotch. We could only see the top of her head, hair so blonde it looked white. Her head was moving in circles like a flying saucer. "LA," Jared said. It occurred to me that all you needed to say was "LA" and you had conveyed all anyone would want to know about the place.

The door to the house was unlocked. We entered a foyer bathed in bright light coming through the large windows in the cathedral ceiling. A spiral staircase in the middle led to a balcony that ran the length of the house, with glass windows facing the rear. I smelled marijuana.

The living room was off to the left. Several people were milling around, drinking from paper cups, not talking to each other, like travelers waiting in a crowded terminal. There was no furniture, except for a beanbag in one corner with a small telephone table next to it. A petite woman in her twenties was bouncing on the beanbag. I didn't see Dave.

"Aren't the other lawyers coming?" I asked Jared.

"They weren't invited."

I left Jared and walked across the living room into an open archway that led to the country-style kitchen. The counter faced another room, the family room, though I'm guessing, because it had no furniture. Through the sliding glass doors I could see a lap pool, a narrow strip of patchy brown grass, and beyond the grass a thicket of elm trees. The trees were leaning away from the house, as if they were being blown by an invisible hurricane.

Dave was sitting next to a man and woman on the far side of the pool. Their feet were hanging over the side, swishing the air. (There was no water in the pool.) Dave was wearing a white tee shirt and Bermuda shorts and talking to the woman. She was dark, exotic looking, and wore a man's white button-down shirt that reached the edge of her bikini bottoms. The man was shirtless; his chest and arms weren't more substantial than a skeleton on display in the lecture hall of a medical school. His face was scarred from acne and his neck was covered with red bumps. His eye sockets were dark and deep, shaped like shot glasses.

I stepped into the dusk light. The sky was aglow with LA's typical pollution sunset, a palette of color only sun in partnership with smog can paint. Dave introduced me to Lila and Rodney. Lila continued swinging her feet while she hummed atonally. Her body may have been there—and it was quite a body—but her mind was somewhere else, or maybe nowhere. Rodney acknowledged me with a limp handshake.

Dave was swaying. I thought he might be on something. "Out here for a surprise inspection?" he asked.

"Is there something I should inspect?"

He smiled dumbly and swayed a little faster, like to the quickened beat of a song only he could hear. He certainly wasn't the Dave I knew back in Chicago, where he had been a scratch golfer and a better than average tennis player. Before he moved to LA he went to the gym twice a day, once in the morning before coming to work and again in the evening. But you wouldn't know any of this from the way he looked that evening. His eyes were bloodshot and mucous was dripping from his nose. His lips were cracked, as if he had been in the sun for a long time without a drink, and his fingers were swollen.

"Sorry about the interior design," he said.

"What interior design?"

"The interior design that used to be here."

"What happened?"

Rodney, as if responding to a command, walked to the other end of the pool, where he leaned on the diving board. "A minor dispute with the leasing company," Dave said.

"They took the furniture?"

"No *problemo*. I like the *Last Tango in Paris* look."

Lila was now crouched on all fours. She was staring over the edge.

"Is she all right?" I asked.

"She's got a hangover."

"From last night?"

"This morning."

"She wired $250,000 to our bank in Chicago."

"You know about the loan?"

"Why did you need a loan?"

"Post production on our movie."

"What kind of movie?"

"Adult film." He put his mouth to my ear. "Very adult." He knelt by Lila and kissed her neck while he rubbed her butt. "Lila was the star, weren't you honey."

Lila kept looking into the pool.

"It was your money, wasn't it," I said.

"I had a nice turn of luck in Vegas yesterday."

I didn't know that Dave was a high stakes gambler, but that wasn't what I was thinking. "Why did you put the money in her account?"

He used Lila's butt to push himself to his feet. "I don't see how that's any of your business."

I was getting nowhere. "Tell me about the Applegate case," I said.

I heard a noise coming from the house. I turned to see a man pressing a woman against the kitchen counter. She was the woman who had been bouncing on the beanbag. Her legs were raised and his pants were wrapped around his ankles.

"Nice to see my guests having fun," Dave said.

"We need to talk," I said.

"We're talking. You want to know about Applegate. Not much to know. He had a case. I gave him a freebie. Good for our reputation to help the little guy."

"Rosie said he runs a charitable organization. That doesn't sound like a little guy."

"The beneficiaries of the charity are the little guys."

"Why would we handle an investment fraud case for nothing? Why not on a contingency?"

Dave sniffled and more mucous dribbled out of his nose. His eyes had turned cloudy.

"Are you OK?" I asked.

"Allergies."

"So what's the answer? Why didn't we take the case on a contingency? And why did you tell Rosie you talked to me when you hadn't?"

"The foundation's bylaws prohibit it."

"Talking to me?"

"Hiring lawyers on a contingency."

"I don't believe it."

The couple in the kitchen was taking turns moaning, louder on each go around, as if they were in a competition. Lila looked up from her imaginary search of the empty pool. "See ya," she said.

She walked around the pool into the kitchen. She wiggled out of her bikini bottoms and climbed on the counter. The man stopped moaning to kiss her. The woman couldn't moan, because Lila was sitting on her face.

"Can't we talk about this tomorrow?" Dave asked.

"No."

Rodney was on his way back from the diving board. "I'd rather not discuss this in front of my partner," Dave said.

"I'm your partner, Dave."

The threesome in the kitchen had rearranged themselves. The man was on top of Lila and the woman was squatting on the floor behind the man. She was looking in our direction.

"She wants you next," Dave said to me.

"She's hot," Rodney said. "She was nominated for an award."

"What kind of award?" I muttered.

"Best supporting actress in a gonzo video."

"What's a gonzo video?"

"A film without a plot, a series of scenes, she's in every—"

"Never mind," I said. "You win for now, Dave. I'm going back to the hotel. We'll talk tomorrow."

As we drove down the hill Jared took several deep breaths like someone who is preparing to stay under water for a while. "There's something I haven't told you," he said.

"Good. My day has room for one more surprise."

"We were sued today."

"For what?"

"Fraud."

"What kind of fraud?"

"Securities fraud."

"We don't sell securities."

"I should have told you, but ... Dave came to me, said he had investors for his film, said he needed a private placement memorandum ... so ... well ... "

I didn't want to hear any more. I told him to drop me off at the hotel and come back with a copy of the complaint. I needed a drink.

We pulled into the driveway of the Beverly Wilshire Hotel. A white Rolls Royce was parked in front of us. The valet opened the door and Ronald Reagan stepped out.

"Look!" Jared said. "I've got to get his autograph." He jumped out of the car and ran up to Reagan. A hotel security officer grabbed Jared from behind, locked his wrists with one hand and put them in handcuffs with the other.

Jared called me an hour later from the police station and said he would be over with a copy of the complaint. I told him it could wait.

The tape stops. I shake the watch. No sound. I look at the clock on the wall. They will be coming in twenty minutes. I am beside myself. As I am rolling the watch in my hand I hear a whirring and then my friend's voice. But it is what I have already heard. I push the button on the side of the watch. More whirring.

I ate dinner alone. I sat by the window and looked out onto Rodeo Drive, a street where the beautiful people shop for beautiful things. Above me, on the eighth floor, was my room: a spacious suite with fax machine, fully stocked bar, and combination TV-VCR. Fifty lawyers were working for me in three cities. I was leading the good life.

Had I practiced law for twenty-five years to see it end in wackiness? Dr. Gusto had sued me for what Manny had done. Investors in Dave's porno film were suing me for what no doubt was a litany of misrepresentations in the prospectus Jared had written. Yet to come was whatever I would learn about the Applegate case. I couldn't blame the law for my troubles. Maybe the cliché applied. My legal career was just another sword, and I was dying by it.

I thought back to those days on the Chicago Strike Force. I remembered a trip I had taken with Pete Varick—I still can't remember his real name. There was nothing special about the trip, but for some reason an inconsequential episode had taken on a strange kind of significance, like a dream that only makes sense years later.

We were in San Francisco interviewing witnesses for a union corruption case. An old army buddy of Pete invited us for an afternoon of sailing. We met him at the boat, which was docked in Tiburon. It's across the bay and you can see the city and its hills on a clear day. He was a partner in a law firm. Every Wednesday he took the day off to sail. He said if doctors can take a day off to play golf, lawyers can take a day off to sail. We were sitting outside, next to the pier. The gusty wind had stirred up whitecaps on the water that looked like a blue dress studded with diamonds. San Francisco was shrouded in fog, but the Golden Gate Bridge sparkled in the sunlight.

The lawyer said we would try for Alcatraz. "What's there to see on Alcatraz?" I asked. "The prison has been closed for years."

"Nothing," the lawyer said. "It's a target." He explained that the currents moved away from the island. Approaching from the Tiburon side was a challenge. In five years and fifty attempts he had never made it to the island.

I sat at the bow, holding on to the side as the lawyer tacked this way and that. He looked like he was trying to shake off a rabid dog. We were being so buffeted by the high winds I felt like I was on top of a rickety roller coaster. Water was coming at us from everywhere. I remembered the stories about the prisoners who tried to escape from Alcatraz. Most were shot or captured. Some drowned in the cold choppy waters. There were rumors, like campfire stories, that a few prisoners had made it across the bay. I couldn't see how. It was all I could do to stay on the boat.

Over the next couple of hours it became apparent that we wouldn't make it to the island. In fact, we were farther away than when we started, closer to the Golden Gate Bridge than either Tiburon or Alcatraz. I asked the lawyer whether there was a chance we could be swept out to sea. He thought I was joking.

We made it back to shore as the sun was setting. We got an outside table at a bay-front cafe and ordered a round of lemonades. The lawyer was tight-lipped, angry like a marathon runner who falls twenty yards from the finish line. When the drinks arrived, he drank his lemonade like it was mouthwash, swishing it around his mouth and then gurgling. He finally swallowed, whereupon he began a long-winded explanation of what had gone wrong, an incomprehensible soliloquy sprinkled with nautical terms.

I wanted to cheer him up. "Hey, I had a great time. Got a terrific tan. Or is it a windburn? No matter. It looks good."

He sent me that look I'm sure he reserved for ignorant landlubbers. "You must be crazy. Don't you get it?"

"Get what? That we didn't make it to Alcatraz. So what. The ride was great."

"Are you one of those *it's the ride that counts* people?" He made it sound like a murderous religious cult.

Pete hadn't been paying attention. He was too busy using his fingernails to clean salt out of his pores. But he knew his old Army buddy. "Hey, let's stop this before it gets out of hand."

"Out of hand?" I said.

"Army habits die hard," Pete said.

As we were leaving the café the lawyer grabbed my arm and said, "Isn't there any place you'd like to get to, a place that's hard to get to, a place you can say you got to, say you did it?"

"Not particularly," I said.

I remember being scared. I thought he would push me over the side of the dock or stab me with the penknife he carried on his belt. Instead, he smiled and shook my hand. He said, "I hope I never get to the point where I'm not reaching for something."

I wanted to say that Alcatraz was not much of a goal, but I thought I should give him an upbeat answer. "Next time we can give Alcatraz another go."

I've been to San Francisco quite a few times over the years. But I never called him. I wonder if he ever made it, to Alcatraz, that is.

Applegate's office was in a high-rise across from Universal Studios. You could see the whole complex from his conference room, and if you concentrated, you could hear the happy screams of children. He was an older man, nearing or past seventy. You could tell by the way he smiled, soft and sweet, that he was the kind of man that enjoyed helping others.

"It was a nightmare," he said. "Thank God I found Dave."

"He did a good job on your case?"

"Couldn't have done better. Where did you find him? He's a real gem."

Dave had found me. He was living in Detroit, working at a large law firm when his wife said she wanted a divorce. He decided to return to Chicago where he'd gone to college and law school. He saw the article in the

Wall Street Journal about the book partnership case and came in for an interview. We talked for fifteen minutes, and I offered him a job. As bad as I was at being interviewed, I was worse at interviewing. I never thought I could judge the worth of an individual in a few minutes. If I needed help and the applicant wanted to work for the firm, I hired him.

Dave worked all the time. He ate lunch and dinner at his desk. After he moved to LA the profits there exploded. But I should have seen the warning signs, odd bits of behavior like footprints muddy shoes make on a polished floor. He never dated a woman more than once; he'd get tipsy after one drink and break into a sweat. Despite his devotion to exercise and fitness, he was always fighting a cold. He would disappear for a couple of days at a time and when he'd call the office he was evasive about where he was calling from. His best friend was a professional gambler who ran the biggest sports book on the south side of Chicago.

Warning signs notwithstanding, Dave was a good lawyer and Applegate was anxious to tell me how Dave saved him. "When I came to the foundation, the investments were at an all time low. That was in early 1988. They had been hit hard in the '87 crash. I got out of equities and went into bonds. We did well. By '91, I had brought the fund back to where it was before the crash. I started investing in covered options, did passably there, dabbled in a few real estate partnerships, no complaints. Everything was dandy. The portfolio value was rising fifteen to twenty percent a year. I met the bastard who ran the Wine Depot and he convinced me it was a sure thing. Invest in vintage wines at a discount, hold the stock for a year, and sell at a big profit. He didn't tell me the vintage wines were overstocks and couldn't be sold at any price.

"How did you meet Dave?" I asked.

"In Vegas. At the craps table. The Mirage Hotel. I'd fly up to Vegas once a month and gamble for two days. Some people do Yoga, some people lift weights, I go to Vegas. I never bet much, don't think I ever lost more than a couple grand on a trip. Dave was a high roller. He'd come to the table, plunk down bills with pictures of Presidents I didn't recognize, and in fifteen or twenty minutes he was either up or down ten grand. On the first trip after I learned of the losses in the wine investment I was sitting at the table, depressed and betting unconsciously—suicidal, if you must know—at a loss what I was going to tell the board. The funny thing is I was winning; I was on an incredible hot streak. Dave made a comment, don't remember exactly what he said, something witty, how could I look so down when I'm so up, along those lines. He was laughing. Why, I don't know. He had dropped a bundle. He invited me for a drink in Steve Wynn's private club . . . you know Wynn owns the place, along with half of Las Vegas. Dave was a happy-go-lucky guy, even when he was losing."

"So you hired him."

"Right. A godsend. Of course, we couldn't get all our money back. That would have been too much to ask. He told me even if we went to trial and won, we couldn't recoup our legal fees."

I had been listening to him ramble, though my mind was drifting. But when he mentioned the legal fees it was like someone had taken a nail and driven it into my head.

"Excuse me, Mr. Applegate," I said. "Run that by me again."

"As I said, I was grateful to Dave that he, and of course you . . . he spoke highly of you, said he would be forever indebted to you for giving him a job after his divorce . . . oh, yes, the legal fees. He said he wouldn't charge us for the work unless . . . What's the matter? Is there something wrong?"

"No. *Unless he got a recovery.* That was what you were going to say, isn't it, Mr. Applegate?"

"Yes, contingency fee is what I think he called it. And I'm happy to say we recovered two-thirds of the foundation's money. I intend to work hard at making good investments to make up the difference . . . and I certainly am thrilled your firm was rewarded . . . $800,000 is a princely sum, don't you agree?"

"Kingly, I think."

I won't say I staggered out of his office. That would be an overstatement. I did feel like I was dragging my feet as he escorted me to the elevator. I didn't tell him Dave had listed the case as pro bono or I suspected that Dave had deposited the fee at Wells Fargo—in the name of Lila Montenegro, no less. I thought only of finding Dave and . . . well, I wasn't sure what I was thinking.

I told the cab driver to wait. He wanted to know how long I would be. I said what's the difference, he could let the meter run. He said he couldn't make a living on waiting time. Fine, I said, leave. Who cares. I was not in a good mood.

The cab was gone when I noticed there were no cars in the driveway. I had been too angry to check if Dave was home. Since he wasn't at the office when I called I had assumed he would be at the house. I walked up the path and knocked on the door. No response. As it had been the night before, the door was unlocked.

The remains of the party were on display. On the living room floor were crushed plastic cups, empty liquor bottles, and several used wads of cotton. A syringe was nestled in a fold of the beanbag.

I stepped into the middle of the room and looked through the kitchen into the back yard. Lila was lying on her back by the pool. She was wearing sunglasses that were configured in the shape of Donald Duck. Otherwise, she was naked.

I slid open the patio doors and coughed. She propped herself on one elbow and removed the sunglasses. "Do me a favor and bring me a towel," she said. No hello, no surprise; she acted as if I belonged there.

"Where does he keep the towels?"

"Oh, never mind. I don't care."

"I do."

A hall on the other side of the kitchen led to the master bedroom. A king-size mattress on the floor was the centerpiece, the only piece. I could see Lila through another set of sliding doors. She had turned over on her stomach. The bathroom was through a doorway on the other side of the bedroom. I found a soggy towel hanging from the shower.

When I got outside Lila had moved to the diving board. She was dangling her feet and looking down, a reprise of her search the previous evening. I wondered what she expected to see in the concrete. I said, "Where's Dave?"

She opened her arms and pushed out her ample breasts. I handed her the soggy towel. Instead of covering herself, she wrapped it around her head like a turban.

"I wouldn't stay here too long if I were you," she said.

"Why not?"

"Daddy will be here any minute."

I heard screeching tires and wood splintering. I thought it must be Daddy crashing into the garage door. I left Lila and walked quickly to the house. As I stepped inside, Dave came rushing through the living room holding a thick letter-size envelope. "I've been looking for you," I said.

"I was taking care of business."

I pointed at the envelope. "That looks like money."

"I said I was taking care of business, my business."

"I met with Applegate. I know about the $800,000."

He handed me the envelope. "Take it. It's all there. What's left, anyway."

I opened the envelope and counted the money. "Five hundred bucks."

"They would have killed me if I hadn't paid them."

"Who are they?"

"Nobody you'd want to know. People I wish I didn't know."

"How could you possibly owe anyone that much money?"

The syringe was still on the beanbag. He saw me looking at it. "I needed $250,000 to pay the bank. I owed $300,000 to the casinos—"

"More than one?"

"Six. Besides the Mirage, there's Bally's, Caesar's Palace, MGM—"

"I don't need the list, Dave."

"The rest of the money went to some people—"

Again, screeching tires—no wood splintering, just a car door slamming. Three things happened at once. Dave grabbed the syringe, Lila came running into the living room, and a man barged through the front door. After a moment of everyone looking at everyone else, Dave grabbed the envelope from my hand and raced out of the house.

"Identify yourself," the man said, as if I were a foreign agent or, even more to the point, a visitor from another planet. He was looking at Lila's naked body—and it wasn't a Daddy look.

"I'm a lawyer," I said, quite possibly the dumbest statement I have ever made.

Lila saved me. "Daddy, the other guy's Dave."

Daddy was a sturdily built man, my age, maybe a little older. His thick eyebrows were black, but his hair was as white as mine. We stood there, both red-faced with rage, though the object of our rage had fled. I don't know who relaxed first, but he opened his arms and Lila fell into them. She was crying. Pathetic. She no longer looked like a porno star.

"Wait in the car, baby." he said.

Daddy called the police. (Turns out, he really was her father.) They arrested Dave two hours later at the airport. He was boarding a plane for Mexico City. Five hundred bucks doesn't get you as far as it used to.

If you asked me then, I'd say good riddance to Dave. If you ask me now, I say I should have known better. I paid him too much for being a good lawyer, and I paid him too little attention. I can say he was an adult and should have known how to deal with success. That's not entirely fair. No one knows how to deal with success. We could all use a little help, and I didn't give it to him. Working at the law turns one inside out. We can analyze the facts, massage the clients, play games with opposing counsel, and butter up the judges. But we're no good at dealing with each other.

In no particular order of time or importance, here's the epilogue to this sorry affair. The Feds indicted Dave for dealing in cocaine and heroin; California indicted him for whatever they call these days contributing to the delinquency of a minor (Lila was fifteen). The investors in the porno film turned out to be the *they*. Salvatore's financial assistance and his special brand of argument persuaded them to drop the suit. But the damage had been done. Because the $250,000 came from the fees earned in the Applegate case, the court ordered the bank to pay the money to the bankruptcy trustee. The trustee then used the money to pay himself and his lawyer. Understandably annoyed, Willis forced the firm into liquidation. I resigned—a funny feeling to resign from your own business, a little like moving out of your house.

I had had it with the law. Don't get me wrong. I'm not blaming the law for the ignominious end to the law firm. Wait . . . of course I am. I'm blaming everyone who is involved with the law because *they* are the laws. Manny Golan is the law. Dave Lapidus is the law. Every lawyer is the law: the mercenary, Arnold Conklin; the odious yet somehow likeable A. Collins Wickersham; my self-involved ex-partner Gordon Litowitz; the romantically inclined—for a time anyway—Kathy Shawn. The clients are the laws, the sympathetic ones like Jersey Reynolds, the trapped ones like Peter Marinelli, the conniving ones like Uncle Lowell, the spurned lovers like Garth James. The innocent bystanders are the laws, like Judy Lightfoot and Stephen Bamberger. The crooks are the laws: from sleazy tax shelter promoter Nate Goldblatt to the corrupt Smith Corcoran. Prosecutors are the laws: the sniveling Peter Varick, the wholesome Susan Gold, the realist Gil Rose. Judges are the laws: the honorable Judge Gunderson, the clown Julius the Just, the manipulative Nate the Grape, the savvy Judge Stinson, the excitable Magistrate Petrovich. The nameless millions controlled by the laws are the laws. You, Connie, and your father, and Tommy Glynn are the laws. Everyone is a conspirator, working to elevate the law to the crowded summit of its own Mount Olympus. And, yes, Connie, I too . . . but no more. I'm not the law anymore.

Does justice need a defense? You bet it does. Did I provide justice with an adequate defense? I gave it my best shot during my time with you. I tried to heed Elie Wiesel's admonition: "Not to transmit an experience is to betray it."

It is noon and time to leave for court. Distant chimes sound a revel to his tale.

I have passed through a magic gateway to another universe. Before me, a windmill of arms like the many limbs of the Medusa, is Judge Tina Petrovich, new on the bench, promoted from Magistrate while I passed the days and nights at Riker's Island. Sitting with me is A. Collins Wickersham. He is my new lawyer. He replaced the public advocate with whom I steadfastly refused to consult. Wickersham is neither fearsome nor loathsome. His carriage is that of a patrician, as comfortable in a courtroom as in a smoker, a gentleman barrister, different from the person my friend described as the fierce and ruthless competitor who cunningly orchestrated Garth James's defeat. I ask him who enlisted his participation. He points to Dr. Bamberger who is sitting in the first row with Mary, Molly, and Rachel.

Sitting at the table to my right is Susan Gold, my prosecutor, persecutor, and friend, a mélange of incongruities that I have come to realize only the law can conjure up.

The clerk is calling the courtroom to order. Petrovich's arms come to rest in front of her. "I have read your motion, Ms. Gold. Do you have anything to add?"

"No, your Honor."

Wickersham stands. He is holding a legal pad with words scribbled close together, some scratched out, interlinear notes on every line, my hope for freedom illegible except to him.

"Before you begin, Mr. Wickersham, I want to ask your client a question."

Wickersham helps me rise as he would help a paraplegic. "Mr. Sullivan," she says, "this court does not enjoy the prospect of extending your incarceration."

"Then release him," Wickersham says, his forceful baritone descending to bass, a Roman senator pleading for justice. "The government is using the law of immunity to punish my client. No evidence exists that my client directly or indirectly participated in the bombings of May 22, 1998."

Petrovich's arms retract to the classic pose of modesty, demurely covering her breasts as if she were wearing no clothes. "Please, Mr. Wickersham. Passion will accomplish nothing. This is a court of law. I'm not the Queen from whom you must seek a dispensation. How can I sanction Mr. Sullivan's refusal to answer questions when he has been granted immunity? The law is not to be trifled with. Now, Mr. Wickersham, will you permit me to ask your client a question?"

"Yes," Wickersham says, his face drawn. He is already bloodied and bowed.

"Mr. Sullivan. Do you intend to persist in your silence?"

I see Da sitting in an empty room, his eyes focused on a blank wall; the interrogators wait for his answer. He meets their gaze and the blank wall reveals the faces of his family. He breaks his silence and speaks. He gains his freedom, and I am enslaved.

"Mr. Sullivan," Petrovich says. "Are you with us? May I have your response?"

I am on Roosevelt Island. The sea gull's wings flutter with power and grace. "There would be no fish left in the ocean," I say to Judge Petrovich.

Petrovich frowns. "Excuse me, Mr. Sullivan?"

"Such a large net would catch all the fish in the ocean."

"*I am not sure I understand . . .*"

I hear a rhythmic sound, like a swing cutting through the air. Petrovich is looking past me. A voice fills the room: "He's talking about the law, your Honor."

"*Is it you?*" *Petrovich says.*

I feel as if the room is turning. I see the benches of the gallery, the backs of heads, one head that still faces forward, Molly's eyes closed, her quiet sobs of endless grief sounding like leaves rustling in an autumn's breeze.

He is wearing a multi-colored turtleneck sweater and his face is tanned. "How are you, Judge?" my friend says.

"*Always the same, of course. But I thought you had gone to a better place.*"

"*I decided to return.*"

"*Welcome back . . .*"

Judge Petrovich says the two words I must have known had always belonged to my friend: "*. . . Samuel Brandt.*"

CHAPTER SEVENTEEN

May 22, 1999

T HE MORNING IS BRIGHT AND CRISP. *I arrange tables and chairs in front of our new pub: Sullivan's on Falls Road, one door away from the old Sinn Fein offices. It is one year to the day since I saw the black smoke above the East River. Mary is inside brewing a pot of tea. We will have our cups outside; a friend or two will stop by and chat with us. It will be an altogether pleasant morning.*

I go to the shop next door and purchase the Irish Times and International Tribune. Every week brings more news. A judge in Tucson ordered the exhumation of the body. It was buried in a plot next to Sarah, Albert, and Jonathan who had died of a brain tumor in 1996. Naturally, it was a foregone conclusion that the body was John "Whitey" Delaney.

The debate continues as to who murdered Delaney. Some say Jimmy Crosetti; others believe it was Kurt Hauer. I suppose no one will ever know, though if it was Hauer then Jimmy must have found the body and deposited it in the water under the Mystic River Bridge.

Gene Lufman is awaiting trial; Arnold Conklin says he expects that his client will be vindicated.

Sam and McKinley pled guilty to all charges and were sentenced to life in prison without the possibility of parole. Sam is incarcerated at the same prison farm that had been Peter Marinelli's home. Molly visits him once a week. Shortly after I arrived in Belfast, she wrote me a letter, saying that Sam wanted us to keep the money. Compensation for my months at Riker's, he said. She said it would do no good to protest, and so I used the money to open our pub. She also said that Sam would not be writing, that he wants me to go on with my life, free from the past. I have written him to say that I no longer believe the past is to be ignored or forgotten, but I have not received a response. McKinley is at a prison near Amarillo, Texas. He works in the library. He writes me twice a month. He says he has never been happier and that only in his dreams would it ever have been possible to be surrounded by so many books.

Marinelli's is no more. The new owner converted the space into an office supply store and cyber café. He also purchased the photographs of Salvatore and his guests, which still adorn the walls. He even bought at auction the case with pistol and knife. It is a conversation piece for the young people who gather there to "chat" with friends on the Internet.

Molly continues to live in their Newton home. Her daughter Erin has apparently left the United States. Despite the efforts of journalism's best sleuths, she has not been found.

I lean against the wall of the shop and flip through the newspapers. The peace agreement is in danger; the IRA refuses to give up its arms until the Northern Ireland government fulfills its obligations. The government, of course, takes the opposite view. President Clinton will attempt to break the impasse, but he is caught in the miasma of his impeachment. The more important news to me is that Tommy Glynn has been exonerated, though if he were alive he no doubt would be charged for the escape from Riker's and perhaps for the bombings.

The most striking news, however, is that Sam and the government lawyers are negotiating an agreement and Sam will tell what he knows. The article does not say what he will receive in return, though the authorities emphasize that his sentence will neither be commuted nor reduced.

As I am puzzling why Sam would now tell all and what he could hope to gain, Mary comes outside with the tea. We sit at a table and I show her the article. She is as perplexed as I am.

I lift the cup to my lips and look back through the window into our pub. Cuchulainn is resting on the bar. A reflected shadow passes over him like an eclipse, and his eyes open wide. Mary grabs my shoulder and turns me around. Strong arms are holding a box, the arms of Tommy Glynn. Standing next to him is Patrick Casey.

I told you I would get you the tapes. So it's taken a while. Big deal. And speaking of deals, I'm about to make *the* deal. In exchange for what I know, they've agreed no one else will be prosecuted. Hah! They think they are giving me nothing. But as you can see before you, they have given me everything. I couldn't do anything for McKinley, though.

Where to start? Where I left off, I guess. You heard it on the tape. The wind and the water—in their own way, as bad as the aborted trip to Alcatraz. And the map we had was no good. Smitty drew it in front of a mirror, I think. It was upside down and backwards. We ended up on the wrong side of the island and had to back track. Thank God for the thick fog. Otherwise, in the morning light someone would have seen us. I have to hand it to McKinley. He not only knew how to steer the boat; he also knew how to handle the bomb. The Solidex and Potassium chloride were so volatile I was afraid to light a cigarette.

Even though the Long Island City bomb exploded first and I realized how powerful the bombs were—neat diversion don't you agree—I was unprepared for the force of the explosion at Riker's. It blew out the windows in Tommy's building and one entire wall collapsed. Patrick got Tommy out of there, though. I just don't know what happened with Peter. He was in the exercise yard . . .

I was seasick. I threw up on the deck and on myself. I'm such a wimp. But I got it together when Tommy and Patrick appeared out of the fog. They looked like they were running on air. There were others racing around, a few security personnel and lots of inmates.

A gust of wind pushed the boat backwards. I was standing on the bow with my hand outstretched for Tommy, but I lost my balance and fell. The wheel slipped out of McKinley's hands. The boat was listing; it kept scraping against a concrete breaker. A few yards behind Tommy and Patrick inmates had pinned a guard to the ground. They were hitting him. I shouted for Tommy and Patrick to jump on the boat, but they turned and ran towards the melee. They were too late. One prisoner had stabbed the guard. Tommy grabbed him from behind while Patrick took the knife. The wounded guard staggered to his feet and fell against Patrick.

In the meantime, McKinley regained the wheel and steadied the boat. I got into the shallow water and waded to shore. The wounded guard was on the ground. Blood was oozing from his thigh. I didn't know what to do. Tommy ripped off his shirt to make a tourniquet. The prisoner who stabbed the guard was lying a few feet away with the knife sticking out of his chest. I think that when the guard fell he shoved Patrick onto the handle of the knife, and the blade plunged into the prisoner's chest.

To add to the developing tragedy the wounded guard managed to draw his gun and fire a shot before Tommy took it away. The bullet struck a prisoner who was trying to find shelter. I ran over to him but he was already dead. There was nothing to do but return to the boat and get the hell out of there, though we waited a bit for Peter. The boat was rocking like a broken wooden horse on a carousel. I wanted to look for Peter. Tommy and Patrick stopped me, sat on me, in fact, pinned me to the deck while McKinley maneuvered the boat into the bay. I sat alone in the back of the boat until we got to the dock. The Korean was still in the garbage, wallowing in the rotten Chinese food. It sure did stink. We drove the limo to McKinley's place, got cleaned up, and then headed for the airport. I couldn't stop thinking about Peter. And then the next day, I heard about Smitty. Damn!

Smitty . . . . God, I knew that man longer than I knew almost anyone outside my family. Not a single moral fiber in him, but he was a man of his word. He did better than keep his word. The Feds were as stupid about what happened at Riker's as the Boston cops were about my fake suicide. The reports made it seem that Tommy and Patrick had died rather than the two prisoners. The medical examiner was in Tarrytown with his mistress, and Smitty knew someone who knew someone—what's the difference. Smitty got it done. It helped that the dead prisoners had no family, no friends, no one who would miss them. They were dead before the law sent them to Riker's. Riker's was their tomb. Buried alive the day they got there.

Still, Smitty couldn't change what happened. He couldn't save Peter. I didn't save Peter.

Tommy stops the recorder. "You know about Erin and Peter?" he asks.

"Yes," I say. "Is that why Sam agreed to represent Peter in the Newark case?"

"It was a shocker when Sam learned that Erin was involved with Peter. Think on it. Salvatore and your father in business together, Salvatore hides me, Salvatore introduces my sister to Sam, Salvatore—"

"How did he find out?"

"Salvatore told him. The old man didn't know where to turn. He couldn't trust Lufman and he didn't want another Mafia lawyer representing Peter. Erin begged Salvatore not to tell Sam. She said she would tell him. But she couldn't do it. Then, Sam asked Salvatore for a favor. He needed help with some problem he had in California, something to do with one of his partners."

"Dave Lapidus." I reach in my pocket and pull out the watch. "It no longer tells time, but it tells an interesting story."

Tommy laughs. "That Sam Brandt; he sure is a pisser."

"So Salvatore gave Sam the money to repay the investors."

"Yeah, and Salvatore assumed Sam would return the favor and represent Peter. He read Sam wrong. No surprise. No one could ever read Sam right. When Sam said he was done with the law, he meant it. Nothing would change his mind, except . . . . And Salvatore knew what it was. He told Sam about Erin and Peter."

"He must have been quite angry."

"Not like you think. Sam was not the kind of man who got angry when things weren't to his liking. He'd get a bit sad, that's all, blamed himself most likely. He once said to me: 'When you don't see it's because you got your eyes closed.'"

I lowered my head and said, "I lived my life with my eyes closed."

Tommy restarted the recorder.

You'll never guess who came to see me the other day. Dave Lapidus. How do you like that? He got off with two concurrent sentences, light sentences, and was out in a year. He's working in a community health program in Chicago. He counsels recovering drug addicts. He said he's turned his life around, hopes someday to practice law again. (I'll have to talk him out of that.) He wanted to know what he could do for me. I liked him better when he was a sniveling, drug-crazed, porn filmmaker. But I gave him my blessing anyway, told him I forgave him, as I'm sure God has. (God, are you listening? Don't forgive him.)

In case you're wondering, I came back for me, not for you. It might seem to you that I started on the run after the bombings, but the truth is that I had been running for most of my life. I got tired of the race.

I remember the first time I ran away from something. I was nine or ten, before they built the Interstate. An unused rail bed sliced through the woods along the Mill Creek. From those woods came endless sounds from birds I couldn't name even if I saw them, furry creatures I had seen only at the zoo, maybe even a coyote, according to Jonathan, who refused to go there with me.

At least I could count on Jonathan to keep my secret. He didn't tell Sarah and Albert I was skipping Hebrew School to ride the Number 52 bus along Mitchell Avenue, past the Sunoco station, to the far end of the high school football stadium.

It was a cold and damp November day. Old man Bernstein, my teacher, had become suspicious of my absences. In the hall I had heard him whispering to the principal that he should call Sarah and Albert. My array of excuses was wearing thin: staying late at soccer practice, researching a geography paper, two thugs accosting me on my way to the synagogue. For that last excuse, I had crushed my face against the hood of a rusted Chevrolet in the parking lot of the school, so it would still be black and blue for the next time I showed up at Hebrew School. I hadn't considered the fuss Sarah would make, however. She called the principal to complain about the lack of security.

Getting to the Mill Creek required a climb over the garbage dump across from the football stadium. Albert said that calling it a garbage dump was a cover. He said it was a missile silo controlled by a general in Washington, his finger poised over a button, ready to defend America if the Russians started World War III. I would press my ear to the ground, thinking I might hear the rumble of rocket engines or the hiss of steam rising from their snouts. I never heard anything. I did smell garbage, though it didn't make me disbelieve Albert. I never knew Albert to tell a lie.

On the other side of the dump was a clearing, approximately the distance from home plate to the left-field wall at Crosley Field. I always jogged across the clearing. I held my left hand a little above my belt, pretending I was Wally Post running out to his position right after he had hit a home run, fans cheering his return to those left field pastures, so green, so peaceful. And when I was ready to dash through the woods to the rail bed, faster than any coyote, I'd wheel around and raise my glove hand to snag an imaginary liner.

I had only a little time for my walk that day. There had been an accident on Mitchell Avenue and the driver waited until the policemen cleared the wreck with their brand new tow truck. I figured I had forty-five minutes before darkness swept over me, time enough to enjoy the familiar trail, to walk in my footprints from earlier hikes. Time enough to listen for those strange sounds. Time enough to make it to the rise from where I could see the bend in the Ohio River and the hills of Kentucky.

I hadn't counted on a bank of fog drifting over the landscape, bringing darkness before its time. The wind came up. I heard a sound. A sad sound. I hoped it wasn't a coyote.

To my left was a familiar sight: the old and half-dead giant oak tree with a cavernous hole straight through the trunk. On other walks I would rest by the tree; sometimes I would take a nap in the hole. I had grand plans for that tree, if it lived long enough, didn't fall over from the rot. I would get some wood and make a kind of mausoleum, modeled after a drawing I'd seen in the World Book Encyclopedia. I'd gather some fossils, arrowheads, and whatever else I could think of and put them in the hole so it would look like the burial site of an ancient people—the kind of people who must have lived along the Mill Creek, before there were garbage dumps that were really missile silos, thousands, maybe tens of thousands of years before the interstate. From where I stood, I couldn't see the hole. The sky was dark gray and the wind was gusting. As I approached the tree, the sound of sadness grew louder. Suddenly, a light shined through the blackness and blinded me, like the time I tried to look at the sun during an eclipse.

As I got closer the sound grew softer. The wind stopped. The light disappeared and was replaced by stars, thousands of them, stars like the kind I'd see if I took off my glasses and looked at distant city lights. I heard a voice and the stars disappeared. Everything was black. I felt like I was falling. The voice was louder, insistent; it was beckoning me, calling me into the void. I was afraid, afraid of what I would find in the black hole. I turned and ran as fast as I could.

The next day, Jonathan told me never to return to the Mill Creek. He read in the newspaper that a man was found in those woods, scrunched up inside a hole of a tree. He was a drifter, Jonathan said, and had died of some kind of fever.

I went to my room and lay on the bed. I remember how wet the pillow became with my tears. The drifter had been alive when I ran away from the sounds and the darkness. I didn't realize it then, but I was to keep on running, and I did run, for all those years, until I stopped running when I walked into the courtroom and saw you standing at the dock.

Patrick reaches inside his jacket and pulls out a package, long and round. "Here," he says. "Sam wanted you to have this."

I unwrap the package and smile.

"What is that, I wonder?" Mary asks. "A sculpture of some kind? One of those modern types, I bet."

I remember the platinum cylinder on Sam's desk. "Not a sculpture," I say. I unscrew the cap. I flip over the cylinder and colored sticks fall to the table.

This afternoon, we hang a new sign above the front door of our pub: THE PICK-UP STICK. Along the top of the sign is a thin fluorescent bulb, blue of course.

EPILOGUE

O N MY LAP IS A LETTER *from Sam. He recounts a meeting at Marinelli's before I came to the United States, a prologue, he says, should I wish to write a book. But he writes nothing of another day, the day he learned that God was writing his final chapter. I put the letter into my briefcase and look out the window. We are descending below the clouds, gliding between craggy mountaintops over a barren sun-drenched landscape.*

I knew it would be hot, though I am unprepared for heat that renders the world a mirage. The airport is south of the city in a swath of irrigated land surrounded by straight roads that cut through arid wasteland. I drive north past a museum of old aircraft. It looks like an excavated dinosaur bed. Military aircraft of all types and sizes are scattered haphazardly across hundreds of acres. Though I had experienced too much death in this country, the sight of those planes, like dead warriors on an ancient battlefield, fill me with the kind of hopelessness and sense of loss that philosophers like to call intimations of mortality. Mary was right. I should not have come. The dead are gone and I should not deign to visit them.

But I am here, and the town is spread out before me: watered lawns so green it seems the grass was painted; shiny new office buildings sandwiched between stores in old wooden buildings; restaurants, motels, petrol stations, and used automobile lots. I am on a road called Speedway, but I will not speed. I stay in the right-hand lane, driving slowly, delaying, dreading my arrival.

The entrance faces me. A grove of spruce trees with arching branches forms a leafy gateway to a narrow, winding paved road. At the end of the road is a rectangular brick building with a single stained glass window. I park in the adjacent lot.

A man approaches. He looks cool and relaxed in a cotton shirt bisected by a string tie with a piece of turquoise hanging on the end.

"What can I do for you?" he asks.

"I am looking for the Brandt family plot."

"I need a religion."

"Jewish."

"On the other side of the chapel. Follow the path and you'll come to the Jewish section."

The path crosses an undeveloped section of dirt and scrub vegetation. In the distance I see a few scrawny saplings amidst mounds of bulldozed earth. The heat-thickened air sends the scrawny trees dancing.

The Jewish section is quite large. For at least fifty yards in every direction markers and headstones are close together, making for a crowded city of the dead. Some are decorated with clumps of fresh flowers, others with a variety of green plants. I walk past the headstones. Names and years rush by me.

And then I am there. I kneel in front of a row of plates, each the same size, four–inch square: Sarah Schaechter Brandt, October 29 1910—August 24 1992; Albert Brandt, October 24, 1909—April 15, 1991; Jonathan Brandt, April 4, 1940—June 22 1996; Samuel Brandt, May 10 1944—August 10, 1999. No flowers or plants here, just dirt blown across the plates. Red ants are my only companions.

I sit on the ground beside the plates. It is still hard to believe. He died of the same kind of brain tumor that took the life of his brother Jonathan. Sweat burns my eyes.

Time passes, I do not know how much. The sun is lower in the sky and the dirt has turned from brown to rust.

"Would you care for a cold drink?"

She hands me a can. The metal is cold. My throat is too dry to speak.

A man's face blocks the sun. "The caretaker said you've been out here for three hours." He is shorter than the woman by a head: lanky, dark-skinned, with the same eyes as his father.

I wet my lips and mouth. "You are alive," I say.

He smiles, as his father had smiled when I caught the figurine of Darth Vader before it hit the floor. "I am alive," he says.

"Where have you been?"

We are sitting in a small café in the old section of Tucson. A scruffy young man is sitting on a stool at the back of the room, playing Malaguena on the violin.

"Taos," Erin says.

"Time to rejoin the world," Peter says. "I got word yesterday. Clinton promises not to renege on Sam's deal."

"Word from whom?"

"Susan Gold," Erin says.

I nearly choke on my Margarita. "But how—"

"I called her," Erin says. "Nice lady. She even mentioned you."

"She was a friend," I say softly.

"What goes around comes around," Peter says.

I laugh and look at Erin. "Something your father would have said."

Her eyes water. "Yes."

"Tell me," I say. "Who was Sam Brandt?"

Though the café is not air-conditioned I feel a chill.

"You know who he was," Erin says.

"I wonder."

"Dad had a favorite story. He said it wasn't much of a story, but he would tell it anyway, said he couldn't help it. He was like that. He'd tell you the same story over and over, like he was worried you wouldn't get it. And he'd change something every time he told it. I asked him whether the stories were true. He had a habit of answering a question with a question. He asked me whether his stories sounded like they could be true. He made everything sound real, you know. In his mind there was no difference between what could be true and what was true. Anyhow, do you know the story? When he met Potter Stewart, a Supreme Court Justice?"

"No," I say with a smile, though I am hurt that my friend, teller of tales, had never told me his favorite story.

"He said that his most exciting time ever was the day he picked up Justice Stewart at the airport. Dad was in law school. He was in charge of the moot court. Justice Stewart had agreed to judge the competition. Dad said it was a great honor to meet Stewart. He thought a Justice of the Supreme Court was justice personified. He said he was terribly nervous as they were driving from the airport to the hotel. He had dozens of questions to ask but was afraid to ask them. He thought he would get in an accident and be known as the man who killed a Supreme Court Justice. I don't know what he told you, but he never wanted to be anything but a lawyer."

"Tell me the rest," I say.

She continues the story and her voice becomes Sam's voice. Her lips are his lips; her eyes are his eyes. We are sitting at Murphy's.

I'm going crazy, Connie. Absolutely crazy. And it is crazy. After all, he's just another guy. Like Bamberger used to tell me, the easiest person to convince may be yourself but he's also the one person you never believe. I want to ask him *the* question. I can't get the words out of my mouth. I take a quick look at him and see that he's reading my mind.

"Justice is no mystery," he says. Just because we know what justice is doesn't mean we do justice. Our mission is to tread lightly, make sure we don't step on what came before us. I thought it would be different. I thought I would spend the rest of my life doing justice. Was I ever wrong! We decide 250 cases in a year. Out of how many? Tens of thousands. We sit on top of a mountain that grows higher every year, a mountain formed by disputes, most of them petty, and crimes against society, most of them ignoble. It's a mountain most people have no hope of climbing. We reject ninety-nine percent of the cases that come to us. We're supposed to select the ones we deem the most important, the ones where our decision will clarify some point of Constitutional law. What kind of choice can you make when you've got the law looking over your shoulder, the law judges before me fashioned from what judges before them had decided? I know what you're thinking, young man. The Supreme Court has shown courage. It has turned its back on an unjust past when warranted. *Brown vs. Board of Education*, you'll say. No more separate but equal, because separate is unequal. Or after thirty odd years, we finally awarded compensation to the Japanese Americans whose property and livelihood we confiscated. So, you say, we did justice. Did we? Or did we only engage in the law's special brand of tokenism. Parcel out a little justice over the land, but never, oh never, make too much of it. Always bow to precedent even if you modify it a bit. Keep on worshiping the past."

His eyes dart across the windshield and he slides closer to me, touching my elbow. "Now, don't you go telling your classmates what I just said. I am a middle of the road kind of guy and I don't want to be the fellow that steers you young people off the road. The law is a wonderful vehicle, though it does tend to hog the road."

I can't believe it. This guy is talking to me like I'm his buddy. What's going on here? He a Supreme Court Justice! He laughs. He's reading my mind again. "Let me tell you," he says, "there is no comfort in who the world says you are. There is only comfort in who you know you are."

I nearly sideswipe a pedestrian in a crosswalk, the fool. Doesn't he know who is sitting next to me?

Justice Stewart is oblivious to the close call with the pedestrian. His eyes are unfocused, or are they focused on a spot in the past?

"It was the day I took the oath," he says. "Reporters surrounded us, clamoring to ask the same tired questions: What does this appointment mean to you? Where do you see the law taking us in the next thirty years? In your opinion, what is the most important question facing our nation? Do you have ambitions to be the Chief Justice? Who is your idol? Nonsense questions, questions that I never ask myself, so why answer them. But one reporter, a pleasant young man from a local radio station, no one important, walks up to my wife. That was nice. No one was paying attention to her. He says to her, 'Mrs. Stewart, what do you think of your husband now that he's on the Supreme Court, a position many would say is as important as the President of the United States?'"

"My wife doesn't hesitate. 'He'll always be Potsy to me.'"

Erin touches my hand and brings me back from Murphy's. "He'll always be my Dad to me."

"A brother to me," Peter says.

Now, everything is clear. I say, "A friend to me."

I am at my desk, writing in my notebook. In front of me are the assayer's scale and the Erte sculpture, a gift from Molly. I put down my pen and take a handkerchief from my pocket. I tie the handkerchief around her eyes and lean a letter opener against her right arm. I adjust the bowls. Satisfied that the scale is balanced, I resume writing.

THE END

ABOUT THE AUTHOR

HERBERT BEIGEL is a graduate of Brandeis University and the University of Pennsylvania Law School. He also holds an MFA in Fiction from the University of Arizona.

As a young lawyer, he was a Special Attorney for the Organized Crime Section of the United States Department of Justice, leading the largest investigation of police corruption in American history. Since then, he has been a trial lawyer in private practice for forty-six years, trying major cases throughout the United States on behalf of victims of fraud and the those wrongly taken to task by the judicial system.

Mr. Beigel also has enjoyed a varied career as an actor, writer, and theater and motion picture director and producer. Among his productions are the movies, *Heavy* (1996) and *First Love Last Rites* (1998) and off Broadway revivals of *A Soldier's Story* and *Rhinoceros*. He wrote and directed the film *Camp Stories* (1997), starring, Elliott Gould, Jerry Stiller, and Jason Biggs. He is also the author of *Beneath the Badge*, a true story of police corruption (Harper and Row, 1976) and numerous short stories, including his collection, *Empire of the Self* (Lightsway Publishing, 2012).

He lives in Tucson, Arizona with his wife, the artist Kim Marie Webb, and three dogs. He and Kim have four children and five grandchildren, all devoted to the arts.

The Justice Tapes is set in 10.5/15 Warnock Pro by Dovetail
Publishing Services using Adobe InDesign. The decorative intial
caps are set in ITC Mona Lisa Recut. It is printed on 60# Accent
Opaque by Edwards Brothers Malloy.

John Warnock is the American computer scientist best known as the
co-founder of Adobe Systems Inc., the graphics and publishing software
company. Adobe revolutionized methods of graphics production.

In early 1997, John Warnock's son, Chris, approached Adobe type
designer Robert Slimbach with a request to design a typeface for his
father's personal use. Warnock Pro is the result of those efforts.